SONG OF SONGS

All day I waited apprehensively – surely something would be done, somebody would act? But it was too late; by the afternoon the newsboys were shouting in the streets: 'British Ultimatum to Germany – War at Midnight!'

I went to bed early that night, and hid my head under the covers. First thing next morning I sent Liliane down for the paper. I opened it with shaking hands and read the stark black capitals:

WAR DECLARED

I handed the paper back to Liliane and went over to the little heap of elegant embroidered monogram patterns on my bureau. I carefully wrapped them in tissue paper before I put them in the back of the drawer and pushed it shut. It closed with a soft decisive click.

SONG OF SONGS

Beverley Hughesdon

ARROW BOOKS

To Adrian

Arrow Books Limited
62–65 Chandos Place, London WC2N 4NW

An imprint of Century Hutchinson Limited

London Melbourne Sydney Auckland Johannesburg
and agencies throughout the world

First published in Great Britain by Century 1988

Reprinted 1989

Phototypeset by Input Typesetting Ltd, London
Printed and bound in Great Britain by
Anchor Press Ltd, Tiptree, Essex

ISBN 0 09 953820 2

PART I

OCTOBER 1895
to
AUGUST 1909

CHAPTER ONE

I was very small and the steps were very steep, but Ena clasped my hand firmly and steadied me as I climbed laboriously up them. At last we reached the top and I stood, panting, surveying the challenge of the long shadowy passageway. When the shadows shifted, and grew taller and more menacing, I shrank back against the warmth of Ena's skirts. Her voice was comforting.

'Nearly there now, Miss Helena.' She tugged my hand. So I squeezed my eyelids tightly together and stepped forward. When I opened them again the shadows had backed away a little, and we ploughed steadily on until we reached the door of the nursery.

Ena turned the knob and I came out of the icy corridor into my warm safe haven, running eagerly around the screen towards the figure sitting beside the flickering firelight – anxious for the reassurance of Nanny's enveloping lap. But I stopped, suddenly, confused – there was no lap, only a large white bundle in Nanny's arms, in my place. My lip trembled. Then warm and welcoming came the loved voice:

'Have you had a nice walk, Miss Helena? And, do you know, a present came for you, just while you were out – fancy that, a present for Miss Helena! Come and look at it now, dear.'

As she spoke the white bundle was transformed; magically it became exciting, intriguing, special. Ena picked up Nanny's footstool.

'Up you get, Miss Helena.'

She swung me on to it, and kept a steadying hand at my waist. I gazed intently at the white mass on Nanny's lap. Nanny raised her plump hand and very gently lifted one corner of the shawl, and as I watched a soft black down appeared, then two perfect half-moon fringes of lashes, a small nose, a tiny curved pink mouth. I gasped and leant forward, but Ena pulled me gently back, and I saw that Nanny's hand was moving again, and to my astonishment she unveiled another black fuzz of hair, another pair of crescent lashes, a second nose, a second mouth! I reached out a tentative hand, feeling that I would burst with pride.

'Kiss your little brothers, Miss Helena – but gently, now.'

Ena held me as I leant over and pressed my lips against one soft warm cheek, and then the other. And as I raised my head the dark lashes fluttered, first one pair, then the other, and I stood gazing down into four bright eyes, which all seemed to be looking straight back into mine. Joy and pride surged through me. I tore myself free from Ena's restraining hand and flung myself forward, arms reaching out, to burrow into the soft breathing, living whiteness, determined to grasp them, to hold them to me for ever – and all the time I cried:

'Hellie's! Hellie's!'

CHAPTER TWO

'Out you get, Miss Helena.'

The warm towel enveloped me as Ena's strong hands swung me over the rim of the bath. Behind the criss-cross mesh the flames leapt and spurted, but I stood obediently still as Ena briskly rubbed me dry. There was the familiar moment of panic as the heavy flannel engulfed me, then my head broke safely through and I could see again, and Ena's sure hands were tying tapes and fastening buttons.

'Now, hold still while I brush your hair.'

The brush caught and tugged, but I stood bravely still, basking in the warmth of Ena's 'There's a good girl now.'

At last the brush stopped.

'Miss Helena's ready for her bread and milk, Rose.'

I clutched the warm cup to my chest and dug my spoon into its white depths, savouring each sweet, satisfying mouthful as I watched Rose lift the brown-lidded can and pour more hot into the bath water. Ena's elbow dipped in, and Rose tipped the can again before calling,

'Ready, Mrs Whitmore.'

I turned my head to watch Nanny lead my brothers round the screen. They tumbled on to the rug, giggling and pushing at each other. Robbie rolled over and bumped into the leg of my chair. For a moment his soft dark hair tickled my bare toes, then I felt the tug at my nightdress as he hauled himself up and hugged my knees. Eddie pushed his way in, trying to climb on to my lap, and my bread and milk tilted dangerously as he grabbed at my spoon.

'Now now, Master Eddie, where are your manners? There'll be none for you if you can't behave.'

Eddie slid reluctantly down, and I carefully inserted my spoon once into each waiting mouth, as four hands clung to my knees.

Nanny briskly wiped the milk from Robbie's chin and swooped down; Ena was only seconds behind. I watched as each wriggling body was swiftly unwrapped and swung into the round bath, leaning forward for my nightly glimpse of the fascinating extra between their legs, that Ena said made them boys. It was still there; I leant back, satisfied. My brothers, mine.

As soon as they were being buttoned into their night-dresses I slid down and ran across to Nanny's big chair, climbed up on to the seat and waited. First one warm body and then the other was tucked in beside me, and

9

each round mouth fed with bread and milk. I watched anxiously as the bowls emptied, but Nanny and Ena always remembered. I held the last spoonful in my mouth, unwilling to let it go.

'Come along, Miss Helena, you can't sing with your mouth full.'

I swallowed quickly as strong arms bore my brothers away and left me bereft. But Ena soon came back for me, and took me into the shadowy night nursery to kneel beside Nanny's bed.

'God bless Eddie and Robbie, and Nanny and Ena and Rose – and Guy and Alice and Miss Walker' – I thought again – 'and Mama and Papa – and Jem!' I finished triumphantly.

Ena laughed. 'I'll tell Jem you remembered him, when he comes up with the coals. Up you get now, Miss Helena, and we'll sing the boys to sleep.'

Nanny bent over the cot and tucked the blankets tightly round the twins. Ena swung me up on to the low stool. I clasped the wooden bars and looked down into the two pairs of dark eyes, gazing straight up into mine. I swelled with love and importance.

'Ready now?'

'Now the day is over,
Night is drawing nigh,
Shadows of the evening
Steal across the sky.

Now the darkness gathers,
Stars begin to peep,
Birds, and beasts, and flowers
Soon will be asleep.'

As I sang with Ena I thought of the bright shining stars glinting in the dark velvet sky outside the nursery window, and of the horses in their warm stables, heads drooping sleepily over their mangers. I sang on, picturing the jolly sailors we had pasted on the nursery screen now tossing on the deep blue sea, and the angels in our prayerbook spreading their wide white wings over my brothers, keeping them safe.

When at last we came to the final, unimaginable:

> 'And to Thee, Blest Spirit,
> Whilst all ages run'

my brothers' eyes were closed.

Ena held my hand as I tiptoed across to my bed in the soft glow from the night light. She tucked me in and I felt her warm kiss and Nanny's quick hug, and then I lay still, listening to the murmur of their soft voices next door, and the even breathing of my sleeping brothers. I knew I was safe.

CHAPTER THREE

Robbie's fingers under mine clung to Dapple's grey mane as I hung below the flaring nostrils and round, rolling eyes. Then, far above me, Eddie jerked at the long tail and I pressed my chest against Dapple's hard wooden head as I soared up and up until Eddie's dark hair dipped to the floor far below me. We hung poised for one dizzying moment, then I was plunging down again in silent ecstasy, while my brothers squealed with excitement above me.

All at once Nanny was beside us; Dapple juddered to a halt. She lifted a protesting Robbie from his perch while Eddie and I stumbled off the rockers.

'Quickly Ena, Miss Helena's hair.'

I stood mute while Ena knelt to pull up my socks and tug my sash straight, then gasped as the heavy bristles came down on my scalp.

11

'Sit down now, and don't move a finger – there's a good girl.' Ena's starched skirts bustled away and I sat still, watching as my wriggling brothers were tidied in their turn.

We sat in a row, waiting. Then the door clicked softly and the lady called Mama glided across the nursery linoleum in a whisper of silk. Nanny prodded us to our feet and I clutched my brothers' hands as cool lips brushed my cheek. I gazed in fascination at the slim bronze feet, so different from Nanny's big black boots.

'Don't stare at the floor, Helena – it's time you learnt to stand up straight.'

Slowly I raised my head. Mama's dark eyes appraised me.

'I hope she doesn't pick at her food, Mrs Whitmore.'

'Certainly not, my lady.' Nanny's voice was ruffled. 'There's no daintiness in my nursery. What's not eaten at dinner comes back at teatime.'

Horrible, horrible sago; my stomach lurched.

'Look *up*, child.'

My head jerked up again. Mama's glance flicked to my brothers, her face softening.

'The twins look sturdy enough.'

'We've had a little trouble with Master Robbie's chest, my lady, but a good rub with wintergreen and a cotton-wool jacket soon put him to rights.'

'I'm sure I can rely on you to take care of him, Mrs Whitmore.'

Nanny's broad bosom swelled. Mama's dark eyes were on me again.

'Such very *straight* hair – perhaps you could do some-thing about that, at least, Mrs Whitmore.'

'Yes, my lady.'

'Lord and Lady Pickering will wish to see their grand-children while they are here – have them ready to come down to the drawing room after tea tomorrow.'

The tiny bronze heels tapped away in a parting rustle of silk.

That night Ena and Rose bathed the twins. Puzzled, I watched Nanny tear an old strip of sheet into neat lengths.

'Hold your head still now, Miss Helena, there's a good girl.'

My hair was twisted and tugged as she wound it up round the white strips until my face was stretched tight. The twins were round-eyed as I ate my bread and milk.

'Knobs,' Eddie demanded. 'Knobs for Eddie and Robbie.'

Nanny smiled. 'No, Master Eddie, only girls have their hair curled. We want Miss Helena to look pretty tomorrow, don't we?'

I glowed.

My pillow was full of wooden bricks: their sharp edges dug into my head. But as I woke and dozed and woke again I thought of my beautiful curls and was content.

Ena threaded pink ribbon through my Sunday-best frills. Layer after stiffly starched layer crackled scratchily over my head, to be held in place by my beautiful pink sash.

'Now, don't lean back, Miss Helena, else you'll squash your lovely bow.'

I perched on the edge of the chair, gazing down at my feet, so closely enfolded in the soft sheen of my best 'glassy kid' shoes, fastened, oh joy, with a narrow elegant strap.

I heard Jem come in with the coals as I sat waiting. I raised my eyes from my toes and looked up at him, expectantly. He put the hod down beside the hearth and stood inspecting me, mouth pursed in concentration. I held out my feet and he gave a long 'ah' of admiration.

'Fancy that, strapped shoes and all! Well, don't you look smart, Miss Helena, with your hair all in curls too. My, ain't you a pretty girl today.'

I gazed up at him adoringly.

Jem bent down confidentially. 'You and Ena must be the prettiest girls in the whole wide world!'

Ena glanced up from Eddie's buttons, her face flushed. 'Go away with you, Jem Barnett – you've been at the honey pot again.' But she laughed as she spoke.

Jem grinned. 'It's Miss Helena who's got the sweet voice – have you got a song for me today, then?'

I slid off my chair and stood up straight with my hands behind my back. Could I remember 'All Things Bright and Beautiful'? I bit my lip, not quite certain, then Jem winked at me and I knew I could. I began to sing.

Jem's 'There's a clever girl now' rang warmly in my ears as I climbed back on to my chair. Today was a special day.

Their hair brushed and shining, the twins climbed up beside me. Not daring to move we sat in a row in front of the fire.

I whispered, 'When are we going, Nanny?'

Nanny creaked over to the mantelpiece. 'When the hands stand quite straight, Miss Helena, that's when Jem'll come for you. Now, sit still and see if you can see it move.'

I glued my eyes on the clock. At last it was one long line. I held my breath. But the door did not open, and the top of the line began to bend – it moved on. I turned and looked at Nanny, aghast.

'Well, now, maybe her ladyship's busy for the moment.' I breathed out, slowly.

The hand moved inexorably on, and now there was a thin black corner etched on the clock's face, and a tiny frown on Nanny's. Ena began to tell us about Tommie, the Boots, how he had kicked a ball right over the kitchen garden wall into Mr Parton's best cabbages, and how Mr Parton had been so angry he had chased Tommie, so Tommie had climbed a tree and put out his tongue at Mr Parton. 'Just fancy that, put his tongue right out – wasn't that naughty!' The twins giggled; Ena was smiling. I tried to smile back, but the two hands had met now, and one had disappeared.

14

Then, at last, the door clicked and Jem came in in his best striped waistcoat and green jacket. I jumped down off my chair, but he did not look at me.

'Mrs Whitmore, her ladyship says to tell you she forgot about the nursery and it's too late now. Get the children ready tomorrow, maybe then, she says.'

I could not believe it.

Nanny said calmly, 'Thank you, Jem.' Her stays creaked as she bent over me. 'We'd best get you undressed, then, Miss Helena – it's nearly bedtime now.'

I hid behind my beautiful useless curls as my shiny shoes disappeared in a blur of tears.

That night I twisted and turned my bumpy head, vainly searching for a smooth place on the pillow. Dreams and memories became confused in my aching mind: huge hands picked me up and tossed me into the air, laughing as I screamed. I woke panting, and fixed my eyes on the faint glimmer of the night light and the shadowy mound that was Nanny's body. But when I fell asleep again I still dreamt. I had shrunk down on to the floor, surrounded by endless black legs and looming muffling skirts. Great staring faces swooped down on me, cold mouths sucked at my cheeks while long hard fingers stroked my hair and became entangled with it and tugged and tugged – until I woke again, shaking and frightened. I did not want to go down to the drawing room now.

At last Rose padded in and I slipped out of bed and ran to lean against Nanny's white counterpane, beside the shiny black tray. Nanny, little finger crooked, held her cup to my lips so that I could sip a little of the sweet brown liquid. My dreams faded in the light of the new day.

Ena unravelled the tormenting rags and delicately combed and brushed, but the curls fell limp and sad on my neck. My throat closed against the porridge, but I knew I had to swallow it, all of it.

Outside the sky was grey. Nanny called the twins from

the wet grass. They ran ahead, then the two dark heads dropped suddenly down. Eddie poked with his stick at a small brown bundle on the ground.

'Look, Hellie, bird!'

I looked down. A wing fanned over the gravel, two fragile feet stiff below it. The tiny black bead eyes were dulled and empty. I clutched Nanny's skirt, shivering.

'It won't hurt you, Miss Helena, it's only a poor little bird.'

Eddie pushed his stick beneath the bird, but the small brown bundle fell back stiff and still.

'Why doesn't it fly?' I whispered.

'Because it's dead, Miss Helena – its little soul's flown straight away up to heaven. Come along now, if you walk very fast we just might have time to visit the stables. Won't that be nice?'

Eddie dropped his stick and two pairs of boots pounded off. Nanny tugged me forward, but I craned back at the limp mound of feathers – if the bird's soul had flown all the way to heaven, why were its wings still here?

'Hurry up, Miss Helena – don't dawdle.'

Indoors my hair clung clammily to my neck, and misery closed my throat as Nanny said, 'What a shame, all your lovely curls have dropped out – nasty damp day.'

The tears spilled over and dripped down my face. Nanny's voice was heavy with disapproval. 'Handsome is as handsome does. I don't want vain little girls in *my* nursery.'

I ate all my slimy tapioca, so Nanny let me read my book to her but I stumbled over: 'I met ten pigs in a gig', and stared dumbly at the next line as it danced before my eyes until Nanny lifted me firmly off her knee with 'Time for afternoon naps – and if you've not picked up by teatime it's a nice spoonful of Gregory Powder for you.'

I crept quickly away to my bed.

Ena tickled Eddie and he squealed as she dressed him in his Sunday best. I sat, poker-stiff, mourning my lost curls. I was not pretty tonight. I watched the hands of the clock, frightened that Jem would come, fearful that he would not. But tonight he came.

The stairs seemed steeper, the hall wide and cold. A big door swung smoothly open and the sound of voices swelled up and died away. I stood fixed on the threshold, terrified, until Nanny gave me a push. 'Take your brothers in, Miss Helena – you're a big girl now.'

I stepped on to the endless carpet.

Mama's tall figure was above us. 'Come along children, your grandpapa is waiting for you.'

She propelled us forward until we stopped before a heavy gold chain curving over a rounded grey waistcoat. A large head like an old grey lion's bent over the twins. I stood behind, waiting. Eddie laughed, the lion rumbled, then suddenly the twins were gone and I was alone in front of him.

'Kiss your grandpapa, Helena.' Mama's voice was high above me.

I looked desperately at the hairy face in front of me, then, eyes tightly shut, I launched myself forward. Large hands gripped my arms, there was a smell of cigars and smoke as bristles scratched my lips, then I was released and set back on my feet again. I swayed slightly.

'How d'ye do, young Helena?'

I guessed from the tone of the rumble it was a question, but whatever was the answer? I could only stare, dumb, at the small dark eyes amidst the whiskers. He rumbled the query again, more loudly.

Mama's hand hurt my shoulder. 'Helena, wherever are your manners? Answer your grandfather – have you completely lost your voice?'

I tore my eyes away from the grey lion and looked desperately around for my brothers, but the only familiar sight was Jem's green shoulders straightening up from the fire. He turned, and as he saw me his face broke into a smile and he dropped one eyelid in a wink. Relief flooded through me; of course I had a voice – a sweet voice, Jem had told me so. I knew what to do now.

I planted both feet more firmly on the carpet and raised my chin. My voice quavered as I began: 'All things bright and beautiful', but the soothing rhythm caught hold of me, and now I saw the birds and the flowers and old Mr Jeffson in his little house at the gate. The clear bright pictures rippled through my head and out of my mouth.

When I had finished the lion clapped. 'So, you've bred a little songbird, Ria. Bravo, Helena.'

I trembled with relief at his approval. He fumbled below the chain and a shining gold coin appeared between his broad finger and thumb. 'For you, my dear.' My 'Thank you' was a whisper as I took the hard, warm coin. 'Now go to your grandmama, little one.'

He pushed me gently away. I followed Mama's trailing skirt across the carpet.

Grandmama's cheek was like fine tissue paper under my lips, her hair very white above her dark eyes. She spoke softly. 'You sang very nicely, my dear – do you like to sing?' I nodded. 'Who taught you?'

I whispered, 'Ena'.

'And who is Ena?'

I looked at her blankly. How could I explain Ena? Ena was just – Ena.

Mama broke in, 'The nursemaid, I believe.'

Grandmama turned her head. 'When you come to engage a governess for this child, Ria, you must ensure that she is well grounded in music. Little Helena has a good ear – it will repay training.'

Mama's voice was impatient. 'Obviously she must be able to play, but she isn't a grocer's daughter, singing for her supper in the parlour every evening.'

Grandmama's lips tightened. 'I sang to entertain our guests when I was a girl.'

'Times have changed, Lady Pickering. If my guests

18

wish to hear music, then they expect to hear it from professionals.'

Grandmama's voice was low but imperious. 'Muirkirk – please come here a moment.' Papa, tall in black and white, appeared above me. 'I've just been telling Ria that this little one will need a musical governess.'

Papa's dark head bent in acknowledgement. 'Of course, Mama. Ria will see to it.'

Grandmama smiled. 'Send the dear little boys to me now, Ria.'

Mama and I were dismissed. I almost ran to keep up with her skirts as they swished angrily over the carpet.

A hand reached out and barred my way. The long fingers sparkled. 'So this is your other daughter, Ria. Let's have a look at her.' I was pulled round to face glittering greenish eyes set above high red cheekbones. The mass of brilliant hair above was the exact colour of the ginger cat that patrolled the kitchens. I gaped at her in amazement. Two rows of large white teeth smiled at me. 'She's all neck and eyes – like some wretched fledgeling that's fallen out of its nest. Don't you feed her, Ria?'

'I suppose Nanny does.' Mama shrugged and dropped into a chair. 'God, what wouldn't I give for a cigarette.'

The lady laughed loudly. 'Ah, one of the joys of matrimony – mothers-in-law!' She turned her attention back to me. 'So what's your name, little fledgeling?'

I took a deep breath, but I was too slow. Mama's voice broke in sharply, 'Answer Lady Maud, Helena.' But now I could not. Mama gave an impatient sigh.

'Don't waste your time trying to talk to Helena, Maud – she has no more conversation than a deaf mute. God knows how I'm ever going to bring her out.'

Lady Maud's laugh rang out again. 'That's years ahead, Ria – you can soon get her trained up to say yes and no and to simper in the right places, that's all these young girls do today, and most of them capture husbands. Besides, how can you expect the child to learn how to talk in the drawing room when you never have these youngsters down?'

Mama said defensively, 'Alice comes down, and Guy when he's on holiday – I can't be bothered with the other three as well. I'm not turning my drawing room into a nursery.'

Lady Maud gave an emphatic shake of her ginger head. 'I've always had Juno and Julia down when I'm at home. They can speak up for themselves now: it's the only way. Ah, Muirkirk.' Papa was beside her chair. 'I've just been telling Ria she must get the youngsters down more often, teach 'em some manners – you don't want them talking like nursemaids, now do you?'

Papa's mouth smiled at Mama. 'Lady Maud's talking good sense, Ria – as always.' He bowed towards the ginger hair. 'Perhaps you should see more of the younger children.'

There were two red spots on Mama's cheekbones. 'Mrs Whitmore is totally competent.'

'But still – ' Papa shrugged.

Lady Maud interrupted. 'Why not ask the child, since she's here? You, Helena, how would you like to come down to the drawing room every day?'

Mama and Papa both turned their eyes on me, but I didn't know how to answer.

Papa said coaxingly, 'Now, wouldn't that be nice, Helena – to dress up and come downstairs every evening? You'd like that wouldn't you?'

Uncertain, I glanced down at my beautiful shoes.

Mama's voice was persuasive. 'But you much prefer staying upstairs with Nanny in the nursery, don't you?'

I looked from Papa's dark shining moustaches to Mama's arched eyebrows, and with a sinking heart knew then that whichever answer I gave one face would turn in anger from me. My tongue stuck to the roof of my mouth.

'Now, Helena – downstairs, eh?'

'Of course you don't want to – answer me, Helena.'

The voices were sharper now. Tears welled up; I tried to blink them away, but it was no use. I gulped and began to sob. For a moment silence fell in the room; my cheeks burnt as my shame was exposed to all – my sobbing was louder now.

'I told you she doesn't know how to behave downstairs!' Humiliation washed over me at Mama's words. I began to shake.

'Guy, Alice – take your sister away.' Papa sounded angry.

I was propelled across the floor so quickly that my feet barely touched the carpet. The door slammed shut behind us.

'Well, what a cry-baby! You can see to her, Guy – I was talking to Juno.' Alice was gone.

I dared not look at Guy; instead I stumbled away from the door – then stopped and gazed desperately about me. I did not recognize the wide staircase – but it must surely lead to safety. I ran towards it, but the step was too high and I collapsed, still sobbing, at the bottom. I felt Guy pat me awkwardly on the shoulder before he pushed his handkerchief into my hand. I buried my face in it.

'It's all right, Master Guy – I'll carry her upstairs for you.' It was Jem's voice. 'Up you come, littl'un.'

I clutched his lapels and pressed my face into his warm, tobacco-smelling neck as he carried me back to Nanny and Ena.

CHAPTER FOUR

Another red-jacketed Guardsman pitched forward and fell, to lie stiff and lifeless at my feet. Quickly I loaded my cannon and fired: Eddie's crow of pleasure became a howl of dismay as the dried pea demolished three kilted Highlanders with one lucky shot. Robbie and I took heart and the tin cannons jumped and recoiled as we fired round after round, until only one prancing Hussar was left of Eddie's once-mighty army, while behind our lone crouching Rifleman a column of Life Guards still stood firm.

But at Nanny's 'Just five minutes more, then it's teatime' Robbie grew reckless: his missiles flew wide while Eddie, chin jutting and lips set, trained his cannon mercilessly on our men. One by one our cavalry fell, until only Hussar and Rifleman faced each other across the carnage, locked in a last deadly duel.

'Up you get now, Jem's here with the tea tray.' Robbie gave a last desperate tug at the string – and watched disbelieving as the Hussar shivered, toppled, and slowly fell to the rug.

'We've won, Hellie, we've won!'

'Who's won then?' Jem dropped down beside us. 'Why, if it isn't a rifle-and-pack man, just like me!'

I reached for the green-tuniced Rifleman. 'Did you look like him, Jem, when you were a soldier?'

'Just like him, Miss Helena.'

I felt a rush of pleasure, and gently stroked my little lead Rifleman – he was real now, he was Jem. Jem had often told us how he had run away to take the Queen's Shilling – 'When I was no older than Master Guy is now – silly young blockhead I were then.'

Eddie butted his way in between us. 'Tell us about the Fuzzy Wuzzies, Jem.'

Jem shook his head, 'It's your teatime – Ena'd give me what for if I started yarning on when yer tea's on the table.'

Eddie, lower lip thrust forward, reached out a sulky foot to my Rifleman – I snatched him up and clutched his small hard body next to my chest.

'*All* away in their boxes, at once.' Nanny's voice was inflexible. Reluctantly I opened my fingers and slowly reached out to the box. But I saw now a tiny grey patch where the green paint had flaked off his shoulder, and even as I restored him to his comrades I knew I would be able to recognize him again, *my* Rifleman. Satisfied, I jumped up and headed for the table.

When Robbie and Eddie were splashing in their bath Mrs Hill came to the nursery. Her hand smoothed the black silk of her dress as she spoke softly to Nanny. Nanny frowned and nodded and I wondered whyever Mrs Hill had come all the way up the back stairs herself instead of sending one of the maids.

After we were in bed we heard footsteps and voices next door, and something heavy being dragged across the nursery floor. Next morning three large boxes stood beside the screen. Eddie ran to them and tugged at the heavy leather straps.

'Leave those alone, Master Eddie.' Nanny's voice was sharp; Eddie turned reluctantly away.

We looked at each other as we drank our milk – what did it mean?

As soon as we had finished Nanny said, 'Now you've to be good children today, and behave yourselves.' She looked round at each of us in turn; we nodded. 'Your grandpapa is poorly and wants to see you, so we're all going to Cheshire.'

Cheshire! I slid the name over and under my tongue. Cheshire – it sounded smooth and silky, not like our hard blunt Yorkshire. I felt a thrill of pleasure.

It seemed a very long time before we were all buttoned into our boots and gloves with our hat ribbons tied. Hands tightly held, we set out behind the oddman, our trunk balanced on his shoulder.

The engine came thundering into the platform, with its exciting, heart-stopping clamour. As the brakes squealed I glimpsed high above us the dark, godlike figure who ruled all this noise and power.

Robbie clung to my hand and whispered, "gine driver, Hellie – Robbie be 'gine driver when he's big.'

Mr Lewis, glossy top hat in his hand, stepped forward to find our compartment for us. He swung the door open and we clambered in.

Eddie began to bounce on the seat, but Nanny was in no mood for play today. 'Stop that at once Master Eddie – and no taking gloves off until I say.'

We waited obediently while Nanny produced a cloth from her large handbag and dusted the compartment.

Jem jumped in seconds before the whistle blew. 'Trunks in safe and sound, Mrs Whitmore.' And as we watched, the platform slid slowly away from us, then faster and faster, until it disappeared. I gasped with excitement and pressed my nose against the windows to stare at the toy houses and tiny white sheep and rushing green fields.

Eddie began to jiggle on his seat, 'Wee wee, Nanny, wee wee!' Robbie's voice joined in. Nanny reached into her bag and produced the squashed india-rubber cocked hat. Ena unbuttoned Eddie and held him still, then Nanny tipped the hat out of the window with a quick flick of the wrist and it was Robbie's turn. I watched him longingly – my own discomfort was increasing, but Jem sat solidly in the corner, reading his newspaper. I pressed my legs together and sighed as Nanny stowed the hat away. Ena patted my hand.

As we drew into the next station Nanny said firmly, 'I'm sure you'll want to go back for a smoke, Jem lad.'

Jem looked up, surprised. 'No, no, that's all right, thanks Mrs Whitmore.'

There was a pain in my belly now. I looked up pleadingly at Ena. She jumped to her feet, opened the door and said firmly, 'Out you get, Jem Barnett, we'll see you at York.' She snorted 'Men!' as his bewildered face disappeared.

I hung on grimly, but Nanny did not fail me. The black hat reappeared in a trice and Ena was unbuttoning

24

the flap of my drawers even as the train began to move. I sank down on to the squashy rubber in an ecstasy of relief.

Eddie said loudly, 'Why Hellie sit down, Nanny?'

'Because little girls are made differently from little boys, Master Eddie, and I'll thank you not to comment on it.'

We left our beautiful green engine at York. Jem strode ahead, elbowing his way through the bustling crowd. We fixed our eyes on his broad shoulders and followed anxiously, clinging to Nanny and Ena, while Rose pressed close and the porters rattled their trolleys behind us. At last we were safe in our new compartment, watching Nanny's duster carry out its familiar ritual.

Manchester was a vast gloomy cavern – hissing, clanking, clattering. As we drew level with the shining black monster which had pulled us so far, so fast, I hung back and gazed up in awe at the red-faced driver leaning over the side of the cab. He looked down, saw me and touched his cap. 'Good afternoon, Missie.'

The engine driver had spoken to me! I drew a deep proud breath as Ena tugged me on.

We had pea soup at Manchester. As she placed my bowl in front of me the waitress said: 'My, are these young men your brothers?' I nodded proudly. 'Well aren't they alike. Do you know which is which?'

I ducked my head in turn and whispered, 'Robbie, Eddie.'

'Aren't you a clever girl – but don't you get them mixed up sometimes?'

I shook my head indignantly. Mama and Alice could not tell them apart, and even Ena and Guy got them muddled sometimes, but Nanny and I – never. Eddie was Eddie, and Robbie was Robbie.

Jem found us a cab and we sat mute while traffic rattled and thundered past. Dark high walls hemmed us in, and we could not see the sky. We climbed out, dazed, and stumbled along another platform and on to another train.

Robbie's soft hair lay against my cheek; Eddie sprawled on the seat beside him, fast asleep with his head in Nanny's lap. I struggled to keep my eyes open.

Ena whispered, 'Wake up, Miss Helena, we've arrived.'

The porter called: 'Hareford, Hareford,' as a strange stationmaster swung the door open. We tumbled out and stood shivering in the cold air, then we were hustled through the barrier and into the waiting carriage. Nanny bundled us up in our rugs again as with a 'Gee up' we jolted forward and bounced out on to the cobbled street. It was dusk now but I could see pale faces peering out of shop doorways. Hands were raised to foreheads and women's white aprons bobbed in clumsy curtseys as we rattled past. Then we were through the street and slowing down for the park gates. A plump woman swung them open and I glimpsed a row of noses pressed flat against the lodge window, round heads outlined in the lamplight.

The steady clip-clop and the familiar jingle of the harness closed my lids; I could scarcely prise them open when at last Nanny lifted us down. We staggered after her and stopped, blinking, in the bright light of a strange hallway. A butler with a long, sad face murmured to Nanny, and I caught the words: 'He's sinking fast.' Who was sinking? Where? And why didn't someone pull him out? But Nanny was chivvying us on, up the wide staircase, along a corridor, up again, and into a dimly lit passageway – until, finally, we came into a strange, shadowy nursery.

But our tired legs were not allowed to rest. With hands and faces quickly scrubbed, we were out and down again. A wide door opened; we walked into warm air and Papa came forward. He led us to a high bed, and then I was swinging up and up, and there, sunk into the pillow, was the grey-maned lion – Grandpapa. He was a very tired old lion now, his yellow skin stretched tight across his face, his beard straggling over the counter-pane. His weary eyes gazed up into mine, his lips moved and I just caught the muttered: 'God bless you, my child.' Papa swung me down and the twins were lifted up in turn. Then we were all hustled out again.

When I woke next morning I clambered out of the unfamiliar bed and ran through the open door into the day nursery, then stopped, bewildered: Ena sat by the fire threading shiny ribbon through the skirt of my petti-coat, just as she did every morning – but today the ribbon was black.

Nanny told us our Grandpapa had died in the night: 'Gone straight to heaven my dears.' Her tone forbade questions – but I wondered how he could have gone to heaven when he had no wings? The dead bird had had wings, but Grandpapa was a dead lion – how did dead lions fly to heaven?

We all wore black sashes on our frocks now. Then one afternoon Nanny made us sit down in a row with our backs straight while she read to us from the Bible – but it was Thursday, not Sunday. Faintly in the distance we heard the dismal toll of a church bell – on Thursday?

Nanny was reading the story of the Good Samaritan when Jem came in; she closed her Bible with a snap and took me by the hand. I walked beside her along the passageway and down the endless flights of stairs until we stood outside a high panelled door. The sad-faced butler swung it slowly open and his heavy voice announced: 'The Lady Helena.' I stood in the doorway looking for this strange lady with my name, until Nanny tugged me in. Papa led me over to Grandmama; she bent over me – her face a carved ivory mask – and murmured my name, then dismissed me. So I found myself on a window seat, my back against the black menacing glass, with Alice beside me. She flicked back her glossy dark curls. 'How dull. I wish Juno were here – but Lady Maud came without her.'

I reached out and touched Alice's sleeve. 'Alice, which one is 'Lady Helena'?

She brushed my hand away and began to laugh, then hastily converted it to a cough. 'Really, Hellie, you are so silly – *you* are Lady Helena.' I stared at her. 'You're Lady Helena, I'm Lady Alice.' It was clear from her tone that Lady Alice was far superior to Lady Helena. I was still bewildered. Alice went on: 'Grandpapa's died, and now he's buried we're Ladies – so much nicer than plain *Miss* Alice, don't you think? There must be lots of *Miss* Alices, but I bet there's only one *Lady* Alice.' She looked at me condescendingly. 'I daresay there's lots of Lady Helenas though – still, it's better than *Miss* Helena, don't you think?'

I did not know what to think, but I nodded: I knew Alice liked to be agreed with.

She turned and exclaimed, 'Why, there's Muirkirk, talking to Great-Uncle John – I didn't see him come in.'

I followed her gaze. 'Papa?' I could not see him, only Guy looking very stiff and strange with his dark hair slicked down either side of his white parting.

Alice shrugged her shoulders exaggeratedly. 'Oh Hellie, Papa isn't Lord Muirkirk any longer – don't you know anything?' She sounded impatient, but Alice always did sound impatient. She went on, 'You must call Guy "Muirkirk" now – *he's* Lord Muirkirk.'

This was too much: my whole world was crumbling. Lady Alice, yes, this seemed only right and proper; Lady Helena – well, I didn't believe that, I knew I had not changed – but Guy, turning into Papa, that was too much! My lip began to quiver. And suddenly I thought – what of my twins, Eddie and Robbie – my brothers – surely they were not changed? I turned to Alice and whispered, 'Eddie? Robbie?' I gazed despairingly up at her.

'Oh, they're still just Eddie and Robbie,' she said impatiently. A wave of relief swept through me. 'Except on envelopes,' she added, 'they'll be 'Honourables' on envelopes.'

Whatever were 'Honourables'? A sudden picture came before my eyes: Eddie and Robbie, pinned to two enormous white envelopes, transfixed like the butterflies in the glass case in the library at home. At home, when were we going home? Guy was beside us now – I opened my mouth to ask him, but Guy was now Muirkirk – I did not know who he was anymore. I looked up helplessly.

'What's the matter, Hellie?' And it was Guy's concerned eyes which looked down into mine.

At last I whispered, 'When are we going home?'

Alice broke in, 'You are a baby, Helena – we're not going home, this is our home now.'

I looked round at the sombre black-filled room and the tears began to trickle down my cheeks.

Guy – or Muirkirk – took my hand, led me out of the room and hauled me up the steep stairs, along the gloomy passageways, back to Nanny. I ran across the nursery floor and threw my arms round her and clung as though I would never let go. She dried my tears and told me firmly that we were *all* going to stay at Hatton: Jem was already here, and Jem's friends Albert and Frederick would soon be coming with Mr Cooper; Mrs Hill and Cook and the maids would arrive as soon as they had packed; and Mr Jenkins would be bringing all the horses, and especially Bessy, my grey pony. I looked at her, and then away at the strange bare nursery, and asked, 'Dapple?'

'Yes, we've sent for Dapple.' I breathed a long sigh of relief. Nanny hugged me. 'Now see how silly you were to get upset, Lady Helena.' I jumped, but then I lay back again on Nanny's large warm bosom. If Nanny said I was Lady Helena, then I was Lady Helena – but it would be all right. As long as Nanny was with us nothing could go wrong.

CHAPTER FIVE

But one evening, Nanny left us.

Dapple had arrived, and our lead soldiers with the fort; the dolls' house came, and we arranged its furniture; then we lined up all the animals two by two ready to take refuge with Mr and Mrs Noah in the Ark. Outside, a new young gardener with a friendly brown face took us into the maze, and we raced between the high green hedges with beating hearts, until we reached the little house in the very centre.

One morning Miss Walker came to the nursery and took me to the schoolroom. I read to her as Alice sat painting, and then she taught me to copy long rows of curving pothooks and beautiful, looping hangers. Every day after that, Ena took me along to the schoolroom. Then Alice announced that she was going all the way to Germany, to Dresden, and she would be taking Miss Walker with her; I was sorry, because I had enjoyed copying pothooks and hangers. But before she left, Miss Walker told me that Mama would find a new governess for me and the twins, and then we would all go along to the schoolroom together, to copy pothooks and hangers.

But then Nanny left us. She told us we must be good children and do everything Ena and the new governess said until she came back, but her Mama was very poorly and so she must leave us for a while. We nodded, stunned, and did not really believe it until we saw her come out of the night nursery in strange clothes, jamming a long hat pin through a battered brown hat. And then she had gone.

We were very quiet at first, but Ena let us stay longer in our baths, and tickled the twins until they splashed her apron, and she was not cross like Nanny would have been.

Jem spent longer in the nursery now, and told us wonderful stories of Fuzzy Wuzzies and assagais; Ena laughed more than ever. One teatime, Jem was crouched by the fire, helping us toast our bread – Nanny only let us toast on Sundays but Ena let us toast every day – when the door opened and there was Mama, and a strange lady. Jem jumped up very quickly and dropped his piece of bread inside the fender; he backed away from Mama's angry frown and disappeared out of the door. Ena, very red, stood waiting for Mama to speak.

'Children, this is Mam'selle Vigot.' Mamselle's hat was low on her forehead, her face quite square beneath it; I stared in fascination at the wiry black hairs which sprouted from her chin. Beside me Eddie quivered with excitement:

'Lady with 'tache, Hellie, *lady* with 'tache!' Mamselle's lips tightened and a pair of black eyes bored into mine so that I dropped my gaze in confusion to the round dusty toes of her boots.

Mama ignored us. 'Mam'selle Vigot will take complete charge of the nursery in Mrs Whitmore's absence.' Ena ducked her head. 'You will sleep with the children, of course, Mam'selle.'

'Of course, my lady.' Her voice seemed to twist and slither in the air before it reached my ears.

'Now, Mam'selle, I trust that's all you need to know.' Mama frowned. 'I must leave at once – I've already had to delay my departure – it's been most inconvenient.' She spoke directly to the subdued Ena: 'Mam'selle is in complete charge, please remember that.' She left the nursery with a flick of her skirts.

Mamselle advanced; her voice barked above my head. I stared up at her, the bark came again, more sharply, and at last I realized that she wanted my name. I was slow to obey, too slow. The boots clumped further forward; now she loomed over me and the strange distorted words attacked my ears, 'You do not *sulk*, leetle girl – I do not like children who sulk.'

Ena was quickly by my side. 'Tell Mamselle your name, Lady Helena. I expect she didn't understand you, Mamselle, you're the first French lady we've seen in the nursery.'

'She will have to *learn* to understand me, quickly.'

I blurted out: 'Helena, I'm Helena.'

'Then you will be Helène.'

I wanted to protest. I was Helena, not this strange, ugly Helène; but Ena's hand on my shoulder kept me quiet.

Mamselle bent over the twins; Eddie planted his feet squarely apart. 'I'm Eddie, he's Robbie.'

'Edd*ie*, Robb*ie*, what sort of names are these, for boys?' Her voice sneered.

Ena said quickly, 'Master Edwin and Master Robert, Miss, but we've always called them by . . .' Her voice trailed away in the face of Mamselle's frown.

'I do not agree with *pet* names.' She spat the 'pet'. 'It must be Helène, Edwin, Robert – so.' Her fierce glare crushed us. A finger stabbed out: 'Which one are you?'

'Robbie.'

'Rob*ert*!' The tip of the finger dug hard into my brother's shoulder.

'Robert.' Robbie's voice was a frightened whisper.

'Lady Helena can tell you which is which, Miss – Mamselle.' Ena was flustered now.

Mamselle ignored her. 'I will have labels – two pins, paper, pencil – at once.' She stabbed a pin into each starched frock, and my twins stood labelled, like two small bewildered parcels.

The nursery was safe no longer – it had been invaded by a stranger. A stranger who banished me from the twins' bath, a stranger who put out the night light and forbade me to sing 'Goodnight' to my brothers – 'I will not leesten to a child caterwauling' – and then, I could not believe it, as I bent to kiss them a hand pulled me roughly back! As I lay in bed, the tears wet on my cheeks, Nanny's voice echoed through my head: 'Now kiss your little brothers goodnight, Lady Helena', 'Kiss and make up, Master Eddie, there's a good boy' – but Mamselle said kissing was unhygienic!

Our porridge grew cold in the morning as we became clumsier and clumsier.

'Lift your mug with *one* hand, Helène.'

'Elbows into your side, Edwin.'

'Spoon in your *right* hand, Robert, must I tell you again?' Robbie dropped his spoon with a splash and milk spotted the tablecloth. 'Clumsy boy, clumsy, clumsy boy – stand over there in the corner, you are not fit even to eat with the pigs!'

I hated her.

The schoolroom was bleak and unwelcoming; the newly lit fire crackled and spat. We stood in a huddle by the door, but with brisk tugs Mamselle separated us and chivvied us forward until we sat, feet dangling, round the high battered table.

My eyes brimmed as *Reading Without Tears* was thrust in front of me; I longed for Nanny's comforting lap and slow, patient voice. This voice snapped; it hurt my ears and confused me, but somehow I stumbled through the first pages until the book was snatched from me and thrust under Eddie's nose.

Eddie pointed to a word here and another there; I knew he was guessing, but Mamselle was appeased. Now it was Robbie's turn. His eyes flickered desperately across the page. The fat finger stabbed down. Robbie's lips moved, but no words came.

'Read, silly leetle boy, read!'

'Robbie can't read.' Eddie's voice was belligerent, but he backed away from the black glare.

'Four years and one half, and you cannot read – not one single word?'

Robbie shook his head: I saw the glint of tears. Eddie and I sat frozen. Her face came very close over the table.

'Then you will learn, now. If you do not learn five words by the time for tea there will be no jam and no cake.'

There was no jam and no cake for Robbie. And no jam and no cake for Eddie, because he had tried to whisper the words to Robbie. My jam tasted sour on my tongue and I shook my head at the plate of currant cake, but Mamselle hissed, 'Eat it Helène, eat your cake,' and her black eyes bored into mine as I chewed and chewed and tried to swallow over the lump in my throat. I could not meet my brothers' eyes.

Next day her fat fingers swiftly traced a line of pothooks, then thrust the pencil at Eddie. He took it and slowly began to copy. Another line of pothooks for Robbie, then the pencil was thrown down in front of him.

'Pick it up, Robert.'

Slowly he reached out, with his left hand. We jumped as the pencil was knocked from his grasp.

'*Right* hand, Robert, *right* hand.' Robbie cowered back. The pencil was thrust at him again. '*Right* hand.' The hiss came a third time, but I knew he could not tell his right from his left. Eddie and I held our breaths, but it was the shaking left hand which came forward again. Robbie yelped as the ruler sliced down. Mamselle's eyes bulged. 'Every time you use the wrong hand I will *hit* you.' Robbie began to cry. 'You are a leetle coward, do you know that, a *coward*.' Robbie's tears were flowing faster now.

It was too much for Eddie. As the ruler was raised before his frightened brother he suddenly flung himself forwards, wrenched it from Mamselle's grip and threw it across the table. Her face flamed red and all at once we were very frightened. She moved slowly towards Eddie; his cheeks whitened. Her voice was flat and harsh. 'You will regret that.'

We were mesmerized by the round bulging eyes. I breathed fear. Her hand flashed out once, twice. Two red weals stood out on Eddie's cheeks, but he did not move. Then she tossed her head. 'Back to your work.' There was a small smile on her face. We bent our heads, and knew we were defeated.

At last Robbie did hold the pencil with his right hand, but his pothooks wavered and shuddered across the sodden page.

'Again, Robert, again.' She bent over him. 'I go to my room now, if you have not done better by the time I come back you will stay here all day – and all night, on your own – and the goblins will come for you.' She swung through the door.

Robbie began to sob – huge, gulping sobs. We both ran to him, but he sobbed on. We looked at each other helplessly, then I picked up the pencil and began carefully copying the hated pothooks.

When Mamselle came back she studied them with narrowed eyes. 'Helène, did Robert copy these himself?' Her eyes swivelled – now they bored into mine – but the ruler hung poised over Robbie's hand.

I cried out desperately, 'yes – he did, he did!'

'Then I think you are a liar, Helène, a liar.' I crumpled before her. 'Do you know what happens to leetle girls who tell lies?'

I stared back dumbly. At last I whispered. 'They go to hell.'

She laughed. Her large yellow teeth were inches from my face. 'Yes, they do, leetle girl, they do – but first *you* must be punished on earth.'

I braced myself for the stinging slap, but instead a large sheet of white card was thrust in front of me, and I watched, horrified, as she swiftly traced in high, wide capitals the legend:

I AM A

LIAR

'Just this once, Helène, I will allow you to use your paints; a nice bright green, I think.'

I felt sick; but I was a liar. I dipped my brush into the pot of water, licked the tip into a fine point, and began to paint. A second piece of card was produced, a second legend traced – and put before my brothers.

'You will paint a placard too, like good, loving brothers – in red, I think, scarlet.'

HELÈNE
TELLS LIES

She was smiling now. Eddie had opened his mouth to protest, but at her smile he closed it again. His eyes met mine, then slid away. He reached for his brush and began to paint. For a moment I hated him.

At eleven o'clock we went back to the nursery to dress for our walk. As soon as Ena had buttoned my coat Mamselle beckoned me to her. 'Come here, Helène.'

I stood mute before her as the green legend was tied to my chest, and the red to my back. 'There, now the whole world will know you are a liar.'

Ena spoke angrily. 'Lady Helena does *not* tell lies'.

'But she did, Ena, she will tell you.'

Ena looked beseechingly at me. 'You didn't, Lady Helena, did you?'

The hot shame dyed my face. I muttered, 'Yes, I did,' and walked stiff-legged out of the nursery.

I wore my badge of shame all week, until it was time to visit Grandmama; then she took it off. I sang to Grandmama that afternoon, but my voice felt rusty and strange.

Robbie hardly ever spoke now, and when he did he stammered. Mamselle mimicked him, and laughed in his face until he cried, then she would proclaim triumphantly: 'Robert is a coward, a coward. Helène is a liar, Robert is a coward – and what are you, Edwin?' Eddie looked back at her with hatred in his eyes, but he dared not speak. 'I think you are a coward also, Edwin, are you not?' And she laughed.

One morning Robbie had wet his bed. 'Dirty boy, dirty, dirty boy! You smell, how you smell!' His eyes were wide and frightened -- and despairing. At the break-fast table he put forward one small, trembling hand,

36

then withdrew it. He had forgotten which was his right and his left again. He did not dare pick up his mug or his spoon; he stared helplessly at his milk and his porridge, unable to touch them. And she laughed. I lowered my eyes and gripped my own spoon until it hurt.

We were set to our endless copying. Robbie seized the pencil – he did not dare do otherwise – and the ruler descended. She laughed as he fumbled desperately for the pencil, and knocked it so that it rolled off the table on to the floor. She did not seem to care about me and Eddie now: it was Robbie she watched, like a fat dark bird, ready to swoop and peck and destroy . . . And as I watched the ruler hang poised to slash down again. I was off my chair and running round the table, and I caught the hand with the ruler and held it back with all my strength. And she laughed her ugly screeching laugh and with her other hand she seized the fold of Robbie's soft neck and began to pinch and twist until his breath came in short hunted gasps – and all the while her bulging black eyes jeered at me. So I bent my head and sank my teeth deep into her mottled brown hand until I hit bone, and hung on.

She prised my jaws apart at last. My hot anger had fled now, I was cold and shaking, I knew I had done a terrible thing. She wrenched me forward by the arm and dragged me out of the room.

I stumbled on the stairs, and began to fall, but she hauled me up. She pulled me on, opening doors, looking in, then slamming them shut again – until she came to Mama's bedroom. Then it was the big wooden cupboards she was opening, one after the other, until I heard her grunt of triumph – she had found what she was looking for. It was Mama's furs which filled the cupboard; her fat hand began to rifle through them. Then she pulled one out; I cringed back from the sharp pointed teeth, bared in a snarl. Hard shiny eyes winked evilly at me.

'You bit me, Helène, you dared to use your teeth on

me, like a leetle animal. Now here is a leetle animal which will bite *you*.' She thrust the head suddenly forward; I cowered back, eyes fixed on the wicked little snout.

'I will put you in the cupboard, Helène, and I will place my leetle animal over your head – oh so gently will I hang him over you, ready to pounce. And if you move, if you make one tiny, tiny little move – then he will *bite* you!'

I tried to pull back, but she was too strong for me: she thrust me contemptuously forward into the soft menacing darkness. I tumbled on to the wooden floor.

'He is there above you, Helène, waiting for you.' The door shut with a click and I heard the key turn as I crouched in rigid terror.

Time passed, but I dared not move: fear held me fixed and still. My knees began to hurt, my legs throbbed, but I dared not move. I must not move. My eyelids drooped in the darkness – I felt my body about to jerk forward – I panicked as I fought to control it. Something shifted above me, I froze – and crouched grimly on. I had forgotten everything now, my brothers, the schoolroom, even Mamselle had receded and left me – alone in the darkness with the terror above my head. I had to stay still, I must stay still. But the insistent pressure in my belly was growing: it mounted and mounted, it was a pain now. I knew, dully, that further disgrace was about to befall me. I must not – but I could hold out no longer; the warm liquid began to run down my legs as the tears of shame trickled down my cheeks. Motionless, I began to sob.

There was a loud bang outside, I jumped – I had moved! The furs above me slithered; I waited in terror for the sharp teeth to meet in my helpless neck.

Then I heard the voice, a high-pitched: 'It's a mouse, I swear it's a mouse – I'm feared o' mices.'

There was a low reply – and the key began to turn. I

screwed my eyes up in pain and fear as light flooded in, but I did not move.

'Whatever – it's Lady Helena!'

Dimly I recognized Jem's voice – but I was beyond reason now: terror held me fixed. I felt a hand on my shoulder, but as it touched me the furs shifted and I opened my eyes wide and saw the evil pointed teeth swooping down on me and now I screamed and screamed and threw myself back into the corner of the cupboard. I could not look away from the sharp animal teeth and the vicious blinking eyes.

Then a large hand reached out and covered the face and snatched it away from me. It was thrown down outside and and Jem cried out: 'Look, Lady Helena!' And I saw his large boot come down hard on to the evil little head and grind it into the carpet. My rigid legs gave way, I fell in a heap on the cupboard floor, and feeling the damp wood was engulfed in shame.

'You'll catch it when her ladyship gets back and sees what you done to her necktie, Jem Barnett.' The maid's voice was shrill. 'And look what she's been up to in there – all among my lady's furs!'

My cheeks burned. I turned my face away.

'Sod 'er necktie, and sod 'er furs! It'll serve 'er right for engaging a bitch like that "Mamselle"!' He spat the word. 'Ena's been worried sick these past weeks, the way she's always going for the littl'uns.'

The maid said, 'Well, she'll go for 'em even more now, her wetting 'er drawers like that.'

I began to shake.

Jem was shouting. 'I'll be damned if she gets 'er 'ands on 'er again!' Then his voice came very close to my ear. 'Come along sweetheart, come to old Jem, then.' But I was too ashamed to move. I hid my face. 'Now, now, anyone'd 'ave a little accident, shut up all this time, 'tis only natural. Come along then.'

His warm, sweaty, comforting body came closer and closer, and at last I turned and flung my arms round his neck. My head buried itself under his chin as I clung desperately to him. I was safe now, I would never let go.

I felt his body jolting as he carried me downstairs, and I clung even tighter. Dimly I heard Mrs Hill's voice; she tried to coax me from Jem's arms, but I would not let go. At last we set off again: limpet-like I clung to my rock. There was the jingle of harness and I knew Jem and I were in the governess cart; I could hear Mrs Hill's voice, giving orders to the groom. I heard the 'Whoa' as the cart pulled up, then Jem was carrying me carefully down the steps and crunching across gravel.

Doors opened and closed; we were inside again, but still I hung on Jem's neck. It was Grandmama who was speaking now; Jem's replies resounded angrily in my ear, but the anger was not for me.

'Helena, Helena.' My arms tightened as Grandmama addressed me. I kept my face hidden. 'Put her down.' Jem tried to ease my arms apart, but I would not let go. Then Grandmama spoke to me again, slowly and sternly, 'Helena, unclasp your hands, I *order* you.'

Slowly my aching fingers disentangled themselves, and Jem put me gently down on the carpet. I swayed against him, and gripped the thick cloth of his trouser leg. I felt his reassuring hand touch my shoulder, and at last I raised my eyes to Grandmama's ivory face.

'Helena, why did Mademoiselle shut you in the cupboard?'

At last I whispered, 'Because – because I bit her.'

'I see. And why did you bite her, Helena?'

Tears filled my eyes. 'Robbie, she hurt Robbie. She hit Eddie and she hurt Robbie.' Grandmama's face was impassive. Desperately I said again, 'She *hurt* him, she *hurt* him.'

It was Jem who spoke for me. 'My lady, Ena, the nursemaid, said as how she seemed to turn against Master Robbie – she wouldn't leave 'im alone. 'E's left-handed, you see, and a bit slower, so she tormented 'im.'

I trembled in gratitude against Jem's warm leg, and nodded speechlessly.

Grandmama murmured to Mrs Hill; Mrs Hill rustled to the door and left us.

Then Grandmama turned back to me. She spoke slowly and clearly, 'Helena, young ladies do not bite.' I stared dumbly back at her. 'I have sent for Mademoiselle, when she comes you must apologize to her, do you understand?'

I sagged helplessly against Jem's leg. Grandmama told him to fetch me a footstool; I sat crouched on it, staring at the fat red rose on the carpet, the smell of my soiled drawers filling my nostrils. I was beyond tears now.

At last Mrs Hill came back – with Mamselle. Her cheekbones were an angry red, but she bobbed politely to Grandmama.

'Lady Helena wishes to apologize to you, Mademoiselle Vigot.'

My eyes fixed on the swollen red rose, I managed to whisper, 'I'm sorry, I – I bit you, Mamselle.' And waited, hopelessly. I could feel her sneer of triumph.

But Grandmama spoke again: 'We will not require your services any longer, Mademoiselle. My butler will give you a month's salary in lieu of notice. That will be all.'

I could not believe it. Mamselle spoke angrily. 'It was Lady Pickering who engaged me – if she is satisfied . . .'

Grandmama raised her hand. Mamselle's voice stopped, abruptly. 'My daughter-in-law may be satisfied, but I am not. I will inform my son of your departure. Mrs Hill, please see that Mademoiselle's belongings are packed and sent down. She will be spending tonight at the Dower House. Tell the nursemaid to sleep with the children.'

As soon as we were in the governess cart again I climbed on to Jem's lap and he rocked me to sleep against his chest.

Ena's gentle hands undressed me, and as she took off

my smelly drawers she gave me a warm hug of forgiveness. Washed and clean again, I was led through to the
night nursery and tucked up in bed with a whispered:
'Don't wake your brothers, now.' But I knew they were
not asleep.

As soon as the door closed Eddie whispered, 'Hellie?'
I pushed back the bedclothes and crept over between
their beds. 'She's gone, she's gone – Grandmama sent
her away.'

Robbie began to whimper.

'Don't cry, Robbie. She won't come back ever again.'
I pulled back the sheet and climbed into his bed. Putting
my arms round his small, shaking body I held him tight.
After a moment Eddie's feet pattered over the floor, his
arms came round my neck and his warm damp cheek
pressed against my back. And so we fell asleep, together.

CHAPTER SIX

Mamselle had gone, but still Robbie did not speak, and
every time the nursery door opened his body froze. All
day he sat crouched, waiting, like a small frightened
animal. Eddie fetched box after box of gaily painted
soldiers and tipped them out at his feet: 'All Robbie's,
all Robbie's.' Robbie tentatively put out one hand, then
the other; both began to shake and he pulled them
quickly back as though he had been stung. Ena picked
him up and sat him on her lap; his head lolled against
her shoulder, his face set and still.

At teatime Ena held the cup to Robbie's lips, but he
turned his head away. Ena's face was pale and anxious;
Eddie and I watched dumbly, frightened. When the door
clicked behind me I thought it was Rose; I did not even
glance up until Robbie began to cry great, heaving sobs.

I looked up, startled – and there was Nanny. Still in her coat and hat she limped painfully over to Robbie and held out her arms to him; he flung himself into them, and clung to her, sobbing, sobbing. Eddie and I scrambled down and threw ourselves against her safe, camphor-scented body, and wept with Robbie.

Robbie would not let her go. He screamed when she tried to put him in the bath that evening, so she washed him on her lap like a baby. That night, when the small snarling animal came to bite me again and I screamed, it was Nanny's calm voice which woke me. 'There, there, Lady Helena – you must be a good brave girl now, so as not to wake your brother.' And in the glimmer of the night light I saw Robbie, still fastened to her neck as she lay in bed. I dropped back on my pillow, shaking a little; but I would be a brave girl – now Nanny was back.

For days Robbie clung to her, while Eddie and I played at her feet, or squabbled over the small piece of her lap left over from our brother. Jem brought a strange little bowl with a spout, and while we sat at the table and ate our bread and jam, Robbie slowly sucked from the spout, his head pressed into Nanny's swelling bosom. As he slept, Nanny spoke quietly: 'Remember that, Ena, when you've a place of your own – a child who won't eat'll often take nourishment at the breast – 'tis only natural. A nice fresh egg beaten in milk, with a touch of brandy and sugar, that's the thing.' She sighed, and gently stroked Robbie's dark head as he snuffled in his sleep and pressed closer. 'But oh, Ena, I never thought the day would come when I'd have to let my own flesh and blood go into the workhouse infirmary – it fair broke my heart, it did – but when I got her ladyship's letter, what could I do?'

I looked up, to see two large tears trickle slowly down Nanny's red-veined cheeks. Nanny crying! The world would never be the same again.

Robbie was still clinging to Nanny when Grandmama

came up to the nursery. Her breath came in short harsh gasps, and she leant heavily on her stick and on Mrs Hill's arm. Ena rushed forward with a chair, and Grandmama dropped stiffly down on to it.

'Sit down, Mrs Whitmore, I'm sure the child is heavy.' She spoke slowly: 'Children, a new governess will be coming next week.' Eddie and I reached for each other's hands. 'She is a very kind lady.' She emphasized each word. Robbie's face was white and Eddie looked as doubtful as I felt.

He said suspiciously, 'Nanny go?'

'Certainly not, Mrs Whitmore will not be leaving you again. Nanny will stay in the nursery; Miss Ling will take you up to the schoolroom for a few hours each day.' We stood mute and apprehensive. Grandmama said with a note of finality, 'Miss Ling is an *English* lady.' She took hold of the silver knob of her stick, levered herself slowly upright, and limped out.

When I sang to my brothers that night Robbie's dark eyes gazed up at me from Nanny's arms, and as I finished and bent down to kiss him goodnight he gave me a small, sad smile. I felt ten feet tall as Ena lifted me down and led me off to my bed.

Next morning he slid off Nanny's lap and walked unsteadily over to where we were playing. We made room for him between us, and Eddie handed him his favourite giraffe. With a shaking left hand Robbie put it carefully inside the Ark.

One afternoon the new governess arrived. Miss Ling was very tall and broad; the light glinted on her small round spectacles as she bent down to ask us our names. Robbie did not answer, but she seemed not to mind when Eddie spoke for him. She said she would come to fetch us in the morning. Nanny looked after her, frowning.

We hung back at the schoolroom door, but Miss Ling ushered us firmly in. We sat very still at the hated table while she read us a story about a little girl called Lucy.

I did not listen, because my eyes were on the pencils and rulers by her hand.

She set me to copy, then Eddie; then she held out a pencil to Robbie: he cringed away from it, staring glassy-eyed as if at a snake.

'Robbie don't want to write.' Eddie was belligerent.

Miss Ling looked at Eddie silently for a moment, then said, her voice very calm, 'Perhaps you would like to watch your sister, then, Robbie.' We breathed out again.

I had moved on to the hangers when we heard a creaking sound outside the door. Miss Ling looked puzzled. After a few more minutes there was a shuffling noise; she got up, went swiftly to the door and pulled it open. Outside in the corridor bent nearly double, was Nanny! Nanny began to slowly creak upright, her face very red.

Miss Ling spoke quickly. 'Why, how nice of you to come along to see us, Mrs Whitmore, the children will be delighted – do come in. Helena, show Mrs Whitmore how neat your copying is.' Nanny shuffled over to the table, her cheeks still very pink. Miss Ling reached for the bell. 'There, I've rung for our milk and biscuits, you must join us, Mrs Whitmore. Eddie, be a little gentleman and pull up another chair.'

That afternoon Nanny and Miss Ling took us for a walk. Nanny spoke urgently; Miss Ling nodded as she listened. After we got back in, only Eddie and I returned to the schoolroom; Robbie stayed down in the nursery with Nanny.

Next day Nanny brought her mending up to the schoolroom and sat by the fire while we did our lessons. Miss Ling said perhaps Robbie would like to help me to write, and his small hot hands clung to mine while I carefully traced pothooks and hangers. That evening I heard Nanny tell Ena that Miss Ling was a lady, 'Not like most governesses I could mention – I never had any time for that Miss Walker – but Miss Ling is a lady, a real lady.'

By the time Mama and Papa came back Robbie had learnt to read. And I, I had learnt to play the piano. Miss Ling sat down in front of it one day: her fingers moved quickly over the black and white keys and I heard 'All Things Bright and Beautiful' – just as Ena and I sang it! It was a miracle. Miss Ling smiled at my amazement and said that I could learn to do the same as her if I were a good girl and worked hard. And just as letters in books made words, so did the little black notes make tunes – and I began to learn their language.

Now I watched the schoolroom clock every day as I copied, longing for my piano lesson; letters only made words, but notes made tunes. I began to learn the names of the sounds; Miss Ling made me stand with my back to the piano while she pressed a key, and soon I felt the bliss of triumph as I learnt to name each one correctly.

The leaves were turning golden and swirling in the wind when Mama and Papa came back. Mama came up to the nursery after tea with a tall thin gentleman with fair hair and a drooping moustache. She smiled and said, 'Children, this is Mr Barbour.'

The gentleman held out his hand to me, and I shook it, feeling very grown up. He said, 'We've met before, Helena, when you were in your perambulator – I remember that you pulled my moustache until I begged for mercy.' I blushed.

Mama said, 'Say, "How do you do?" to Mr Barbour, Helena.'

I stumbled over the words, but she did not seen annoyed today.

The gentleman smiled again and said, 'Do you know, I haven't any nieces of my own – just big strapping nephews, not one pretty little niece – so perhaps you would adopt me, Helena, and call me Uncle Arnold.' I smiled up at him: he had called me pretty!

Eddie butted in, 'Me too, me and Robbie too.' I felt quite angry with my brother – he was *my* Uncle Arnold.

Uncle Arnold came up with Mama again the next day; he knelt down on the floor in his beautiful grey trousers and mended our engine for us. I did not mind going down to the drawing room so much when he was there; he always spoke to us politely, and one day he gave me a golden sovereign for singing to him. But Nanny made me put it away in my money box; I wanted to cry when I saw its shining beauty slip through the slot and disappear.

Another day when we went down to the drawing room Lady Maud called us over. Her eyes snapped and flashed as she said, 'You must get out your toy soldiers, boys.' Then she broke off as Uncle Arnold came up to her, and turned to him. She talked very quickly and excitedly, he answered her more slowly, his face serious. I listened to the unfamiliar names – 'When Milner met Kruger . . . in the Orange Free State' – and I pictured two men solemnly shaking hands in our light airy orangery – but it soon became clear that they had not shaken hands; they had argued with each other, so my picture changed to two angry men plucking oranges off the trees and pelting each other with them – as Eddie and I had done one glorious day until Nanny had arrived, panting, and very, very angry.

But later Miss Ling said the Orange Free State was in South Africa; she looked very solemn as she pointed to it on the globe. Eddie studied the pink mass and said firmly, 'Ours.'

Miss Ling nodded. 'Yes, Eddie, but we may have to fight Mr Kruger to keep it.'

We all looked at each other wide-eyed. Fight! That evening we played with our fort.

We were playing with our fort again the next afternoon when the door flew open and Jem burst in. Nanny's protesting 'Really, Jem' died on her lips as she saw the piece of paper he waved in his hand. She sat down suddenly. Ena came running from the night nursery,

Jem thrust the paper at her, and her face went white as she read it. 'Oh, Jem,' she whispered.

Jem laughed. 'Don't worry, my girl, I'll soon be back – we'll give those Boers such a trouncing – and still be home for Christmas. They'll not stand up to the British Army.'

'Oh, Jem, I knew you were still on the Reserve, but I never thought . . .' Ena's mouth quivered.

Jem turned to us, his face excited. 'I'm going to South Africa, to fight the nasty old Boers – I'll be a soldier again!' The twins jumped up and down in excitement; Ena began to cry.

Now we played soldiers every day. But I would not let my brothers touch the little green Rifleman with the missing flake of paint. Ena found me a box and I wrapped him in a scrap of red flannel and hid him in the back of the nursery cupboard. I would keep Jem safe from the Boers.

Ena cheered up when she got her first letter from Jem. She read us part of it and then carried it with her in her apron pocket. Now we sang: 'Goodbye, Dolly, I Must Leave You' and 'Soldiers of the Queen Are We' while Eddie and Robbie beat the toy drums Lady Maud had given them.

Miss Ling drew a large map, and we painted it very carefully. She wrote on it in neat letters, strange foreign names like 'Johannesburg' and 'Bloemfontein'. I asked her if I could write a letter to Jem, in ink, and she ruled the lines and gave me a new nib. Very carefully, in my best hand, I wrote:

Dear Jem,
I hope you have had a good journey and are in good health. Bessy has had a foal with a white patch on her nose and the tabby and white stable cat has had six kittens. Two are black all over.

I stopped and sucked my pen. Then I added:

I hope you are having a nice time.
Believe me,

Very sincerely yours,
Helena Alexandra Feodorovna Girvan

I folded it carefully and Miss Ling put it in the envelope she had addressed, and let me go all the way downstairs by myself, to post it in the box in the hall.

But when we went down to the drawing room soon after, the grown-ups looked very grave. They spoke in low voices of Colenso, Magersfontein, Stormberg – and a lady called Smith. Miss Ling said we must pray every night for our brave soldiers.

Alice and Miss Walker came home for Christmas, and Miss Ling took us to the station to meet Guy. Then Mama came up to the nursery and said it was time the twins were breeched. That evening Nanny cut off their long hair, and next morning they looked very grown up and rather strange in their navy serge knickers and with their dark heads cropped.

After Christmas a letter arrived for me – from Jem, all for myself. He wrote that it was very hot, but one day hailstones had fallen, as big as eggs! And on the journey his ship had called at an island with very high mountains named after me! I rushed to the globe and searched for the island. I felt very proud when I found it, and very proud too of Jem's letter rustling in my pinafore pocket.

I wrote: 'January 1st, 1900' in my schoolbook, and sat back, admiring. It looked very exciting – a whole new century.

But downstairs in the drawing room the grown-ups were not excited. They still talked of Ladysmith – I knew now it was a town, and not a real lady, and Miss Ling had told us that some of our brave soldiers were trapped there.

Eddie said firmly, 'Jem will get them out.' Remembering Jem's strong arms as he had lifted me out of the hated cupboard, I nodded in agreement. I imagined Jem stamping on small ugly men with sharp teeth, grinding them into the ground and killing them, just as he had killed the vicious little furry animal in Mama's bedroom. I went to the cupboard and checked my box. The green Rifleman still crouched on his stand, safe in the soft flannel. Satisfied, I put him back.

At the end of January Miss Ling dabbed at her eyes with her lace-edged handkerchief as she wrote: 'Spion Kop' on our large map in her small neat hand. But late in February she told us that our brave Lord Roberts had captured a Boer general called Cronje – and that he was being sent as a prisoner to my island, that Jem had seen. I put my finger on the small pink dot on the globe and smiled with pride.

It was March when Miss Ling opened the nursery door and called, 'Children, Ladysmith has been relieved!'

We jumped up and down in excitement, but Ena cried. Nanny patted her shoulder: 'Don't fret, dearie, Jem'll soon be home now.'

Guy came back from Eton at Easter, and we showed him our map. Afterwards he came to the nursery and sat on the floor and generously agreed to be the Boers, so that we could defeat him.

It was a Saturday afternoon. We were in the nursery with Nanny and Ena and Rose – Miss Ling had walked down to Hareford for her afternoon off.

Nanny bustled through from the night nursery with our coats and hats. 'Put those soldiers away now, it's time for our walk.' We were reaching for the boxes when the door opened, and we stopped in astonishment, staring at Mr Cooper. He never ever came up to the nursery. His face was very solemn. Nanny looked up, but it was Ena he spoke to.

'Ena my dear, Mrs Barnett is downstairs. She wishes to see you.'

Ena looked at his face, and her eyes went round and

frightened. She dropped my boots with a clatter and ran to the door.

Nanny said quietly, 'Put those soldiers away now.' Subdued, we fitted them carefully into their boxes.

Ena came back, but it was a very strange Ena. Her cap was askew and she stared at us as if she did not know who we were. Then she ran to the grate and fell to her knees beside the coal bucket and threw her apron up over her face; we heard the terrible racking sound of her sobs muffled in the white folds. Rose stood gaping at her.

Nanny spoke sharply. 'Rose, get those children dressed – you'll have to take them out by yourself today.' She limped over to Ena and put her hand on her shoulder. The fearful sobs continued as Rose began to tug on our boots.

The door opened and Guy came in. 'Nanny, Albert says . . .' He looked at Ena's shuddering body and went white. Nanny nodded. Guy's front teeth bit hard into his lower lip, as if he had a pain.

Nanny spoke quickly. 'Master Muirkirk – would you be a good boy and take Lady Helena for her walk – Rose should be able to manage the twins on her own then. Put her bonnet on Rose, quickly now.'

Guy held out his hand, but he did not look as if he wanted me. We walked down the back stairs in silence. Two of the maids were by the pantry, whispering excitedly together. They broke off when they saw us, bobbed to Guy and slipped quickly away.

As soon as we got outside Guy dropped my hand and strode off across the lawn; I had to run to keep up with him. He pushed open the gate of the walled garden, and went in; I followed him, breathless. Guy threw himself down on a seat and sat staring straight ahead; I climbed up beside him.

At last I ventured, 'Guy, why is Ena crying?'

He turned a bleak face towards me and said flatly, 'Because Jem's dead.'

51

I stared at him. 'He can't be — I've kept him safe in the nursery cupboard!'

Guy looked at me blankly. I tried to explain about the lead Rifleman and the box in the back of the cupboard. At last he said, 'Hellie, that's a *toy* — Jem went to South Africa with the soldiers, and a lot of soldiers have been killed in the battles with the Boers — you must know that.'

'The *Boers* killed Jem?' I was still disbelieving.

'No, Hellie, Jem died of a fever, Mr Cooper told Albert — enteric he called it.'

I thought of the dead bird, and Grandpapa, the old dead lion, and at last I whispered, 'Has he flown to heaven, then?'

Guy said angrily, 'Hellie, Jem's *dead* — he died in South Africa, and he's buried there, in a hole in the ground.' I began to tremble. But Guy was not looking at me; he stared straight ahead. 'I never told anyone, but when I first went away to school a group of older boys set on me — they wouldn't leave me alone, they bullied me and I was terrified of them. When Jem came to fetch me at the end of term I cried in the train. So he said: 'Don't worry, I'll sort 'em out for you, Master Guy." I was still frightened, but when he took me back he made me take him up to the dorm, and asked me to point them out. They were waiting for me — they'd opened my box and thrown everything on the floor and trodden in Mrs Hill's cake. Jem took off his belt and he thrashed them, just like that. Then he said very loudly: "Any more trouble with this lot, you send for me, Master Guy, and I'll come right away and do it again, harder." Then he put his belt back on and went home. They never touched me again. I realized afterwards he could have got the sack for what he'd done — he must have known, but he went ahead and did it all the same. I never told anyone.'

Guy's voice broke, and I saw there were tears on his cheeks — Guy, a big boy like Guy, crying. Then I remembered Jem lifting me out of the cupboard out of that menacing darkness, and I began to cry too. Guy pulled me on to his lap and I put my arms round his neck and buried my face in his collar. He hugged me very tightly as we wept together.

CHAPTER SEVEN

I cried when Miss Ling took us to see Guy off to school again. He hugged me and kissed my wet cheek, saying, 'Be a good girl, Hellie, and I'll write to you.' I waved to the train until it was a little black dot in the distance, then Robbie tugged me over to see the station cat, and I went home with the twins.

In the summer Ena left us. Nanny said she was going to look after a new baby, up in London, with a nurse-maid of her own to order around. Before she went Nanny gave her lots of advice as they sat at the table after tea together. Ena listened and nodded, 'I'll remember that, Mrs Whitmore.' Then she would get up and undress us for our baths, and tickle Robbie and Eddie until they squealed with laughter. She would smile as she looked down at them, but Ena never laughed now.

After she left, Rose became nursemaid. Nanny was not very pleased, but I heard her mutter, 'Better the devil you know than the one you don't.' Then Miss Ling told me that I would soon have a bedroom of my own, next door to hers. I felt very grown up.

Early in June Mama came to stay, and Miss Ling took us down to the drawing room. Mama sat with her feet up on the sofa; her ankles were swollen and puffy, and when she leant over to smack Eddie she moved slowly and clumsily. She soon told Miss Ling to take us away again.

A few days later Miss Ling said, 'I've a surprise for you, Helena – the twins must stay up with Nanny – I'll show them later.'

I walked downstairs beside her feeling very important. She took me into Mama's bedroom. Mama was lying in bed, looking pale and bored. She called me over and pointed to a cradle beside her. 'You've a new sister, Helena.'

I stared in astonishment at the round red face. I was not at all sure I wanted a new sister – Alice was enough – I only liked brothers. Miss Ling said, 'Isn't she beautiful, Helena?' I looked more closely. The baby glared at me with bright blue eyes, fringed with lashes so pale I could hardly see them; there was a wisp of flaxen hair on her bald head.

Mama said, 'Well, what do you think of her, Helena?'

I thought she was very ugly, but it did not seem polite to say so; Mama looked quite satisfied with her. I remembered my beautiful twin babies, and at last I said, 'She's very nice – but I like dark babies better.'

Mama's face went very red, and suddenly she was angry; Miss Ling took me quickly away. I knew I had said something wrong, but I did not know what it was – Mama and Papa were both so dark, surely they liked dark babies better too?

Papa did not come home at all that summer. I heard two of the housemaids talking in their pantry as I went to the water closet one day. One of them said that Papa had gone big-game hunting, in Africa, and the other one replied that Mama had hunted *her* big game last October – then they both began to titter, until they came out and saw me and went very red and rushed off down the corridor. I knew they must be wrong, because Mama had been at home last October: it was when Uncle Arnold had come to stay, and Jem had gone away to the war.

Later the new baby came up to the nursery. Nanny fussed over it and kept sending us away to Miss Ling. I felt hurt at first, but then I decided I did not mind because the baby just slept and slept, and when it woke it screamed and had to be taken down to Mama. Its name was Violet, but everyone called it Letty. Nanny let me watch its bath one day, but it was quite round and smooth; I decided I would only have boy babies in my nursery when I grew up.

Papa came back in the autumn. We were coming round from the stables when we saw him drive up with Lady Maud. He handed her down from the carriage and she saw us and came striding over, tanned and smiling. 'How do ye do? Bin ridin'? Enjoy it, do you? That's the spirit, I can hardly wait to get back on a good British horse again – those foreign nags are all crocks.' Papa strolled over, his hands in his pockets. We stared in amazement: the lower half of his bronzed face was covered in a thick bushy beard! Lady Maud burst out laughing. 'Didn't recognize him, did you? Don't worry, your Mama'll soon have that face fungus off him – looks a fright, don't he? But Victor, it's time you mounted young Helena here for hunting.' I gasped with excitement.

But I was not so grateful to Lady Maud the next day, when she looked me up and down in the drawing room and said loudly, 'Ria, this child is beginning to stoop.'

Mama strolled over and scanned me critically. 'You're quite right, Maud. I'll tell Miss Ling to get the back harness out for her.' Mama continued her survey as I stood stiffly before her. At last she shrugged, 'There's not much else we can do – Nanny's given up on the curling rags, though she does look like a plucked chicken with her hair scraped back in those plaits.'

Lady Maud said, 'What a pity she's got the Girvan nose – yours and Alice's are so beautifully straight.'

Mama smiled. 'Perhaps we should put a little nose harness on her and straighten that ridiculous tilt.'

They both burst out laughing before they strolled off,

arm in arm. I slunk back to the schoolroom and consoled myself with the piano.

I waited apprehensively for my two sets of harness. The back harness was a collection of braces and straps; if I bent too low over the piano it jerked me upright, cutting into my arms and shoulders. I asked Miss Ling about the nose harness, but when I had explained she said Mama and Lady Maud had been having a joke. I gazed disconsolately into the mirror: Alice had curly hair and a straight nose, while I – I had straight hair and a nose which curled.

Lady Maud must have reminded Papa, because I was taken to the next meet. I had to stay with Jenkins, but when he beckoned me on and we galloped over the first field to the thunder of hooves and the baying of the hounds my excitement rose to the point where it hurt. After that I begged Papa to let me go out whenever the Hunt met anywhere near Hatton; he generally said yes.

Cousin Conan came over from Ireland before Christmas. Jenkins swore at him and said he was a silly young fool and deserved to break his neck. I watched his black cap bobbing far in front and was breathless with envy. But I was a little frightened of Conan: he swaggered round the schoolroom and broke our fort and told my brothers only sissies played with dolls' houses. Eddie and Robbie followed him everywhere, and I seethed with jealousy.

Alice was home from Dresden now; she was to be presented at Court in April – but then Grandmama died the day after Christmas. Alice came up to the schoolroom and said Papa wanted to delay her presentation, but Mama said she was old enough already. 'I am, I am,' Alice cried as she tossed her dark curls angrily.

But then the Queen died. We could not believe it, the Queen and Grandmama. I thought I should wear two black sashes, not just one. I swirled my skirts so that the black ribbons in my petticoats danced – but Miss Ling rebuked me and I was overcome with guilt. Alice was angrier than ever: Papa had won now the Queen had died. But the next day she was smiling and laughing. Mama had decided to take her to Paris; she could go to dances there and then come out properly in London the year after. Papa went off to hunt in the Shires and it was very quiet again downstairs.

Alice came back from Paris with trunk loads of new dresses – she paraded them in front of me, but would not let me touch. I knew my sister was beautiful, and that evening as Rose brushed out my plaits in front of the dressing table I stared at my straight dark hair, and thin pale face and long narrow neck and thought despairingly of how the new King would despise me when it was my turn to curtsey to him.

Mama was angry with Alice when they came back from her first Season – her anger simmered in the drawing room when we went down after tea. Alice tossed her head and hung on Papa's arm, and soon she was triumphant, and Mama's anger had transferred to Papa.

A week later we were coming in from our walk with Miss Ling when Alice ran quickly down the steps of the terrace, a strange young man behind her. 'Miss Ling, this is Hugh Knowles: Mr Knowles and I are going to be married.' We stared up at Mr Knowles: he was tall with very broad shoulders and a nice square face under thick brown hair.

He smiled at us shyly and pulled at his moustache. 'Steady on Al – Lady Alice, Lord Pickering hasn't consented yet.'

Alice ignored him. 'Helena, you may be my brides-maid.' I gazed up at her, thrilled. 'Come along Hugh, I'll show you the fern house.' The young man followed her, his face bemused.

My bridesmaid's frock was beautiful; as Rose unwrapped it, it fell in endless shining pink folds. I could not sleep the night before the wedding, from excitement and the curling rags. Nanny dressed us herself, and I scarcely dared move in my lovely pink frock, for fear of catching my foot in the flounce and tearing it. Best of all were the white glacé kid shoes, which fitted my feet like gloves, and were just as soft and supple. Eddie looked sulky in his velvet trousers; he tugged at Robbie's sash and Robbie pulled back until they both fell on the floor and rolled fighting into the grate. Nanny hauled them up and smacked them hard on their blue velvet bottoms. They stumped down the stairs behind me, pushing each other and giggling. I ignored them and stepped carefully over the carpet to Alice's room.

Alice was glowing. Her dress clung to her and shimmered as she moved to the dressing table. She bent forward for her maid to put the veil on her head and her round, swelling breasts brushed the shining mahogany top. I squinted down at my own flat chest and sighed with envy.

Her bosom was fuller than ever when she and Hugh came to visit Hatton in November, but Alice was not glowing any more. She sat on the sofa with her feet up and snapped at Hugh as he patiently fetched and carried for her. I liked Hugh; he was kind and never teased me, and he took us all riding and talked to us as if we were grown up. Mama sat with Alice and smiled when poor Hugh blundered against the sofa and Alice's tongue lashed out at him.

In the new year Miss Ling told us that God had brought Alice a new baby, a dear little boy named Hugo, so now I was an aunt, and the twins were uncles. I preened myself – 'Aunt Helena' – I was glad it was a boy baby. Eddie, very interested, asked Miss Ling: 'Does God bring foals as well?'

Miss Ling said quickly, 'Of course he does, Eddie.'

'Then why does he put them into the mare's belly first?' Eddie leant forward and added earnestly, 'Because Flirt had to squeeze and squeeze before she could get her foal out – didn't she?' Robbie and I nodded, but I wished Eddie had not said anything – Jenkins had told us not to tell Miss Ling, he said governesses were easily shocked – and now it was obvious she was shocked. She gave a funny choking noise, then said very quickly, 'Get out your arithmetic books.'

We struggled through our sums. I hated arithmetic, and I don't think Miss Ling liked it either; she got flustered and kept peeping at the answers in the back of her book.

When Mama said it was time for the twins to go away to school I felt as though the world had ended. I cried and cried all through the night before, and I cried all the way to the station. My eyes were so red and swollen I could not see out of them, and I bruised my hip when I blundered into the ticket barrier on the way out. I was grateful for the pain: I wanted to suffer.

Miss Ling held my hand in the dog cart all the way back. Then she sent me off to bathe my eyes and said that if I was a good girl and stopped crying I might go and play the big piano in the music room. Even that promise did not make me feel any better, but I had no more tears to cry now. But when I placed my hands on the ivory keys of the grand piano it spoke in a voice of velvet; I could scarcely believe such lovely sounds had come from my fingers. Miss Ling sat beside me and I played and sang until lunchtime.

But I could not eat, and after lunch my misery returned. I walked in a daze; the park seemed empty and bleak without my constant companions. Miss Ling spoke to me, but I scarcely heard her words. And when I sat upstairs again the letters on the page of my history book jumped and shifted before my eyes.

After tea I slipped up to the nursery; Letty had been sent to bed early so I sat on the rug at Nanny's feet and watched her needle flash backwards and forwards as she darned one of the twins' socks. At last I asked, 'Please, Nanny, teach me to darn. I want to darn their socks for them.'

Nanny pursed her lips. 'They've grown out of these, they're being sent to Rose's nephew.' But I felt that even if my brothers never wore these socks again still, it was some comfort to hold them.

So Nanny taught me to darn, and all week I went up to the nursery in the evening and sat on the rug at her feet and darned my brothers' old socks. Nanny said I was a neat little darner, and could be trusted with my own cotton stockings, so I mended them as well. I liked darning: I liked the precise, regular movements, and the sense of satisfaction when the hole had been completely filled in.

When my brothers came back in the summer they had changed. They talked casually about boys I did not know and a life I could never share; I cried into my pillow for my lost twins. But after a few days it was as though they had never been away; we roamed the park together and I learnt to swim at last. As we lay drying in the hot sun beside the lake we talked of how we would skate again next winter.

But then Conan arrived for his summer visit and the boys talked together in the mysterious language of school. Conan said girls were sissies, and one day they would not wait for me to finish my practising, and I shed bitter tears because they had gone off with a picnic and left me behind. Mama made me sit down to luncheon in the dining room because the numbers were uneven, and I sat dumb and miserable, while she glared at me from the head of the table. Afterwards she called me back and told me I was a little pudding, and a bad-mannered pudding at that. 'Goodness, Helena, you'll be eleven in September, it's time you learnt at least to exchange a few platitudes with your neighbour at the table.'

I muttered, 'I'm sorry, Mama.'

She snapped back, 'You're too old to call me by that childish name any longer, address me as "Mother" in future – that is, if you can ever think of anything to say.'

I sat miserably in the drawing room, not daring to leave, until Guy told me to put my hat on; he was taking me for a drive. When I went round to the stableyard the groom was harnessing up the gig. Guy strode forward, his sleek dark head gleaming in the sunlight, the soft down of his new moustache showing proudly above his smiling mouth. I gazed up at him adoringly: he was so tall and handsome.

'I thought you'd like a change from the dog cart today, Hellie – up you get.' He handed me up as though I were a grown-up lady, then sprang lightly up beside me. 'Gee up.'

The gig was light and bouncy and Guy drove at a spanking pace through the park. Bowling along in the sparkling sunlight, I began to feel happier. We drove down the narrow main street of Hareford and out into the surrounding lanes. Guy said little, but then Guy never chattered. As we swung round to the next village he looked sideways at me and smiled. 'Better now, Hellie?'

'Yes Guy, thank you.'

He put his gloved hand lightly over mine for a moment, then he touched the reins and we bounded forward under the flickering leaves.

Guy went up to Cambridge that autumn, and the next year the twins reached double figures. Great-Uncle John, their godfather, gave them identical gold hunters on their birthday. Mother said they were far too young for gold watches, but Uncle John told her he was sure they would look after them. My brothers' faces glowed with pleasure as they cupped their gifts in their hands.

Letty was coming up to the schoolroom now and she was a great nuisance. She hated copying pothooks and hangers; she kept asking what they meant. In the end Miss Ling let her start writing words instead, although she was not nearly neat enough. It did not keep her quiet, though, she never stopped asking questions. She even argued about our Bible stories: 'If *I*'d been the elder son and that stupid young one came back and got all the best food *I* should have been annoyed too – it wasn't fair.' When we sang 'All Things Bright and Beautiful', and Miss Ling explained that God had arranged that some people should live in castles, or big houses like Hatton, and be very rich while others should live in small houses and be poor, Letty said, 'Well, I don't think that's very fair of God, is it?'

Miss Ling looked horrified, so I said quickly, 'But wouldn't you rather live at Hatton than in one of those dirty little houses outside the gate?'

Letty said sturdily, 'Of course I would – but that doesn't make it *fair*, does it?'

Miss Ling and I looked at each other. Then Miss Ling said firmly, 'Letty, God doesn't have to be fair.'

'Then why do *I* have to be fair, if God doesn't?' It was very difficult to answer Letty sometimes.

The following summer the preparations began for Guy's coming of age in August. An enormous striped marquee was set up on the lawn the day before, and we were not allowed to go near the kitchens, everyone was so busy. Guests arrived all through the day. There was a big dinner party in the evening, and the twins and I crept out on to the stairs and peered through the balustrade at the glittering procession below. Robbie whispered, 'It's like the Ark – the animals going in two by two!' We stifled our giggles as each shimmering figure passed through the dining-room door on the arm of her black-coated partner. Albert saw us, and winked, and after he had served the dessert he ran up with a tray, just for us. We gorged ourselves on tiny little pancakes stuffed with truffles and lobster in a melting creamy sauce, which exploded in your mouth out of a casing of light flaking pastry. There were oysters in little cones of puff pastry – we pretended we liked them as we chewed and swallowed, then reached for the tiny stuffed birds and bit into them. We scarcely had room for the sweets, but we ate them all the same. Soft, light meringue left a delicious sweetness in the mouth; the trifle had a strange, warm biting tang to it; the tarts tasted of almond, and of other flavours we could not name. And then Albert came up again – with the ices: vanilla, chocolate, and strawberry. We licked every wonderful smear off our spoons, then crept away to bed, replete.

I woke early the next morning; it was a lovely day, warm and clear. After luncheon the tenant farmers and estate workers began to arrive, scrubbed and in their Sunday best. There were games for the children on the lawns, and then everyone trooped into the big marquee and tucked into an enormous meal. Mr Anderson from the Home Farm made a speech and presented Guy with an inscribed silver tray and tea service. Very red in the face, Guy made his speech in reply; when he had finished the canvas walls resounded to the claps and cheers.

By the evening I felt very tired and rather sick, so I sat in the window seat above the stairs and watched the brightly-coloured ladies and more sober-suited gentlemen parade on the terrace. At last all the lemonade I had drunk drove me to the water closet. Inside I looked disbelievingly at the blood on my drawers. I could not remember hurting myself, and yet I was bleeding! I leant against the wall for a moment, trembling, then I buttoned my drawers up again and went rushing up the stairs to Nanny.

She was quite calm. 'Are you, my chick? Well, you'll be thirteen next month, it's only to be expected. I'll fetch you a napkin for now, but my lady will want to send for one of the special belts, like Alice had. Wasteful I call it, throwing cotton pads away every month when there are plenty of good linen rags to be had – still, that's her way.'

I stared at Nanny, and squeaked, 'Every *month?*'

'Yes, Lady Helena, you're a woman now.'

But to Mother I was still a child. She was annoyed when Papa suggested that I go with them to London for the Season the following year. Mother said extra piano lessons were completely unnecessary; Miss Ling was perfectly competent. In the end it was Uncle Arnold who persuaded her to let me go. I was thrilled, but when we got there I wished he had not bothered.

I hated London. It was smelly and noisy and dirty. Miss Ling was always harassed, and blushed in shame as I stumbled and faltered in the weekly French and German lessons. I shrank with embarrassment from the other girls who rattled off their verbs as if they had been born knowing them.

Each afternoon we set out grimly for the Park. The only excitement was when we met a column of soldiers on the way: a company of infantry in scarlet tunics marching in the tune of the band, or a troop of Life Guards in their gleaming breastplates and be-furred saddles. Best of all I liked to see the Grenadiers, because as soon as he came down from Cambridge Guy was going to be a Grenadier, just as Papa had been when he was Guy's age.

Letty liked London. While Miss Ling escorted me to my lessons Rose would take her into the private garden of Cadogan Place. At lunchtime she had to be dragged out, face and hands smeared with soot, pinafore dirty and torn, knees scraped and bleeding. Nanny would mutter darkly about Rose under her breath as she dug gravel out of Letty's knees and poured on the stinging brown iodine, and the next day Nanny herself would sally out to the garden, with a sulky Letty firmly clasped in one hand. Letty would come back cleaner, but both of them looked so bored that I knew the unfortunate Rose would be sent the next time. Nanny did not like Cadogan Place; she waged an endless, useless war on the smuts that settled on every surface in the nursery, and harried Rose mercilessly.

Three mornings a week Miss Ling and I set out for the Park as usual, but instead of sauntering aimlessly along beside Rotten Row we would stride purposefully through the Albert Gate, cut directly across to the Grosvenor Gate and then head for Hanover Square. Just the other side of it, in Tenterden Street, was the Royal Academy of Music, where I could forget I was in London and focus all my attention on the piano as I played and transposed. The thin, bearded tutor rarely smiled and spoke of nothing but music. I practised diligently every day and glowed when I earned one of his rare words of praise. He told Miss Ling she had taught me well, and we both went home to Cadogan Place with a lighter heart.

Next year I went to London again. One day Miss Ling took me round to Eaton Terrace, to see Alice. Alice lay in bed, looking pale and beautiful. She waved a languid hand at the cradle beside her, and I realized I was an aunt once more: Alice had had a second son. As we left my sister said, 'Tell Nanny the nursery's all ready for her, as soon as the monthly nurse leaves.'

I stared at her. 'Nanny?'

'Didn't Mother tell you? Nanny's coming to me, now, to look after William.'

I was still stunned. I could not imagine Hatton without Nanny. 'What about Letty?'

Alice said grimly, 'Letty doesn't need a nurse, she needs a jailer. No, Helena, it'll work out very well, you'll see. I don't intend to have any more after this one – I've done my duty by Hugh – it's time I had some fun. By the time William's out of the nursery you'll be married, and then Nanny can come to you.'

Miss Ling called, 'Come along, Helena, you'll be tiring Lady Alice.' She looked rather pink as she spoke, and rushed me out of the room.

On the walk home I thought about what Alice had said. I hoped my husband would be as nice as Hugh, but I decided I would like more than two boy babies. I told Miss Ling this, but she said I was only fifteen and far too young to be thinking about getting married. She seemed almost annoyed with Alice for speaking of it; I would not even be out for years. So I thought instead about the new song we had bought that morning; I would practise it after tea.

The next time we went to see Alice, Nanny was already installed in the nursery at Eaton Terrace, with the new baby on her lap. And then we were not allowed to go again because Letty had caught scarlet fever, and so we were in quarantine. Mother was furious; she and Papa had to move out to stay with Lady Maud because we were infectious.

Letty had to have a real nurse, from a hospital, to look after her. One day she was so ill that straw was put down in the street outside to muffle the noise of the traffic. But then she began to get better, though she still looked an odd colour. The doctor told Mother she needed sea air to recuperate, so it was decided that Miss Ling would take her to Cromer for the summer, while I went back in the train to Hatton with Mrs Hill and the staff.

The housemaid who had looked after me since Rose and Nanny had left would still maid me, Mother said, but otherwise I would have to take care of myself – after all, I would be sixteen in September. I felt guilty when Miss Ling kissed me goodbye and said how much she would miss me, because I was pleased at the idea of a whole summer on my own with my brothers – except for Conan, of course.

CHAPTER EIGHT

Mother already had a houseful of guests when Conan arrived, so he bunked in with the twins. He was seventeen now, taller and stronger and more reckless than my brothers; they were ready to follow him anywhere. We went down to the larger lake on the evening he came;

Conan dared Robbie to climb out over the water on the old willow. Mouth set, Robbie inched his way further and further out, the branch dipped dangerously and I called to him to come back, but he ignored me; seconds later there was an ominous creaking, Robbie scrabbled desperately, then toppled helplessly into the dark water in his best suit. I screamed, Conan laughed, – and Eddie jumped in after his brother, fully clothed.

Mother came forward angrily from the terrace as the twins dripped their way up the lawn. 'Really, Helena! Why ever didn't you have the sense to stop them?'

As I stared at her, dumbfounded, Conan pushed past me. 'My fault, I'm afraid, Aunt Ria – I dared Robbie.'

My mother's face softened. 'You're our guest Conan – besides, Helena should have stopped you.' As I stalked off I heard her saying to Lady Maud, 'Boys will be boys – high spirits are only natural at their age.'

There was a painful tug at my plait; I turned, hand raised to Conan, but he danced out of range, cried, 'Boys will be boys', and ran off, laughing. I trudged up to my bedroom, seething.

But at least with Conan there we had an excuse for leaving the house at breakfast and roaming over the park and into the woods as we pleased – until we would hear the distant stable clock strike, and race back, dishevelled and hot, with barely time to wash our hands before luncheon. I did not enjoy luncheon. New guests would turn to me, expecting Mother's daughter to be quick-witted and lively. They always seemed to speak just as I had filled my mouth with roast meat – I would chew desperately, racking my brains for a reply while Conan laughed at me from the other side of the table. When at last I had managed to swallow my half-masticated food and whisper an answer, it would sound weak and silly even as I uttered it. The guest's eyes would glaze as he listened, before turning away from me with a politely dismissive smile, and I burned with shame as Mother glared at me from the foot of the table. Once I heard her say loudly to Sir Ernest Webern on her right that she dreaded, simply dreaded, the thought of having to bring Helena out. I cringed as Sir Ernest smiled his wolfish grin and whispered his reply in her small shapely ear.

When Conan had been at Hatton for almost three weeks a letter arrived from the twins' godfather, inviting them to join his fishing party in Scotland. They were wild with excitement at the idea. 'Say we can go, Mother, please say we can go.'

Mother frowned. 'It's not very convenient, with Conan here,' but Papa broke in curtly.

'John's been very good to them – of course they must go.'

Mother tossed the letter angrily down on the table. 'You answer it, then.' She turned back to the rest of her correspondence.

After breakfast we wanted to go out to the head game-keeper's cottage. Papa had taken the dog cart so we had to cram into the governess cart behind the lawn-mower pony. The boys thought this quite beneath their dignity and made me drive. Then they taunted me because the lawn-mower pony was so slow. As we came back to the house I gave him a last desperate flick with my whip and he turned and looked at me reproachfully, then suddenly broke into a trot. The cart lurched forward and there was a shout from behind as the gate flew open and Robbie fell headlong out, to land sprawling on the gravel at Sir Ernest's feet. Mother came quickly down the steps as he picked himself up. 'Really, Helena, your driving is atrocious – you wouldn't be safe with the garden roller!'

I smouldered; it was Conan who had vaulted in over the side and not bothered to latch the gate, but I knew better than to say so.

The next day it poured with rain, so we played billi-ards. Conan produced some cigarettes; the boys all puffed on them until Mother walked in and told them only cads and women smoked cigarettes. She tossed them a box of Papa's cigars and then sat down to watch. The twins inhaled manfully until they both went green and had to leave the room hurriedly, but Conan smoked his cigar with a swagger, right down to the butt. When he had finished Mother laughed, and smoothed his lapel before she rustled out.

She was always nicer to Conan than she was to us. Alice said it was because Aunt Alice had been Mother's twin, and they had done everything together until she had died having Conan's baby sister, and Conan's sister had died as well. Alice said Mama had come to the schoolroom and told her, and had cried and cried while Miss Walker patted her shoulder and then sent Alice away to the nursery. I did not know whether to believe Alice or not – I just could not imagine Mother ever crying.

Next day it was fine again so we bicycled over to the Home Farm in the morning. As soon as we had started Conan challenged us to race him and my brothers pedalled furiously ahead. My serge skirt clung damply to my black-stockinged legs as I pedalled and my face was wet with sweat, but I could not catch them up. My front wheel veered into a pile of chippings, I bounced madly and then felt the ominous bumping. I slid forward out of the saddle and began to push my useless bike towards the red-brick cluster of farm buildings.

Forlorn and miserable I trudged up the short hill. There was a derisive shout from the top window of the mill. Conan's laughing face yelled, 'Slow coach – old Hellie's a slow coach!' Bitterly I pushed on.

I left my bicycle outside the farm workshop; one of the men would mend the puncture and ride it back for me later. I went into the sties, but the piglets seemed to have lost their appeal today so I wandered disconsolately out again. The goose hissed warningly at me, protecting her goslings, so I stood still, and stared glumly at the red-combed rooster. He strutted superciliously among his flock, carelessly elbowing one of his wives out of the way, so he could peck at a particularly luscious beetle, then, casually bestriding her and tugging sharply at her neck feathers with his beak, he trod her. Arrogant, thoughtless males.

Suddenly there was a whirr of panic-stricken wings as Conan appeared round the corner of the cowshed, flapping his arms and emitting hideous crowing noises. The cowardly cockerel leapt off his hen and led the squawking retreat. I called, 'Oh, the goslings – mind the little goslings, Conan!' But the heavy grey goose was already running forward, wings spread, neck arched, hissing her defiance. Conan shot out his hand to catch her below the beak, but she was too quick for him – he gave a sharp yelp of pain and backed away, nursing his injured hand. I started to laugh at his astonished face.

'Serves you right, young Master Conan – playing the fool like that.' It was Mary, the cowman's wife, stout and red-faced as she came waddling out of her kitchen in her sacking apron. 'Come on then, I'll put it under 'pump.'

The twins and I stood watching ghoulishly as Mary sluiced the blood from between Conan's finger and thumb, and inspected the damage. I said reprovingly, 'The mother goose was only protecting her young, Conan. She was very brave, you're much bigger than she is.'

'All right, Goody Two-Shoes, spare us the lecture.' But his bright blue eyes flashed a grin in my direction as he spoke. Mary was smiling at him as she wrapped a rag round his hand.

Eddie offered to take me back on his crossbar, but Conan insisted I ride on his. I clung to the handlebars as his strong legs thrust the pedals round, and felt the heat of his panting breaths on my neck. We left word at the stables for our horses to be ready saddled after lunch, then rushed into the house.

The afternoon was hot so we kept to the shade of the

trees as we roamed over the park, until Eddie called,
'Race you to the oaks – ready, steady, go!' We galloped
off, hooves pounding on the springy turf.

Conan won, but I was close behind. We reined in,
laughing and panting. I patted Flirt's sweaty neck, then
we began to walk the horses on. The sun beat down on
our backs, my head felt damp under my boater so I
pulled it off and swung my plaits free. Ahead of us the
lake shone in the sunlight. It was Eddie's idea. 'Let's
bathe. The horses have cooled off now, but I'm hotter
than ever.' The water shimmered invitingly before us.

I protested, 'But we haven't got our things with us.'

Robbie said quickly, 'There's no one about, we don't
need our suits. And Mrs Rendell will lend us something
to dry off with – I'll go and ask her now.' He cantered
off towards the gamekeeper's cottage.

I still protested. 'But what about me? I can't go all
the way back to the house for my bathing dress.'

Conan drew level and grinned at me. 'So poor little
Hellie will just have to sit on the bank like a good little
girl – and not get her feet wet.' His eyes taunted me.

'I shall bathe if I want.'

He laughed, and cantered ahead.

Eddie and Conan were already ducking each other in
the water by the time Robbie got back with a bundle of
towels. He sprang off his horse, dumped the towels on
the ground and headed for the shore, undressing as he
ran. Boots and socks, jacket and shirt, trousers and pants
were scattered each side of him. He leapt up on to the
diving rock and stood poised for a moment with arms
outstretched, then his slim young body flashed through
the air and sliced the shining surface.

I led my horse and Robbie's into the shade and teth-
ered them. In the shelter of their bodies I began to
unbutton my habit. Eventually I was down to my camisole and knickers; bending down I untied the ribbon
below my knees so that the frills hung loose, then ran
towards the lake.

71

The sudden cold shock of the water took my breath away and before I had a chance to get it back, Eddie's arms came round my waist in a bear hug and my feet shot from under me. I gasped and choked and fought until he slipped away like an eel; I followed in my slow, serious back stroke.

The boys were racing each other across the lake, but I did not like to go so far out of my depth, so I floated in the shallows for a few minutes then swam slowly back along the shore. The thin nainsook of my underwear clung to my body as I clambered out by the diving rock. The rock itself was too hot to lie on until I fetched one of Mrs Rendell's threadbare towels and stretched out on it. When the sun had dried me I turned over to lie on my front, but this year my chest hurt on the hard surface. Raising myself on my elbows I gazed down proudly at the small curved swellings of my new breasts as they hung forward inside my camisole. I slid my fingertip inside the lace frill and gently stroked their soft fullness, dreaming in the hot sun.

'Helena.'

I jerked my head up quickly, and looked straight into Conan's bright blue eyes. He was crouched beside the rock, his head on a level with mine. We gazed at each other for a moment, then he lowered his eyes, and I lay very still while he stared at my breasts. I watched the pink flush run up his cheek until it met the dark curve of his lashes, then slowly he raised his head, and the familiar teasing smile was on his face again. He sprang up on to the rock beside me and commanded, 'Dry me, Helena.' But as he squatted down in front of me the towel round his waist slipped, and in the moment before he caught it I saw his maleness, larger and fuller than my brothers'. His face reddened as he tied the towel tightly round himself again, then he suddenly threw back his head and laughed. 'So we're quits now, Helena!'

My own face flamed as I picked up the old towel and began to scrub his back.

Next day I woke with the familiar sense of misery as I remembered that my brothers were leaving me. They were laughing and joking at the breakfast table, while I pulled a piece of toast to pieces and tried to force it down my throat. I would miss them – how I would miss them.

'You'll drive us to the station, Hellie.' It was a statement: they did not wait for my nod of acquiescence.

Conan's long lithe body uncurled itself as they jumped up. 'I'll come too.'

I looked up in protest. I did not want to share my brothers' last hour with anyone else, least of all Conan, who always teased me when I cried. But it was too late, he had already left the morning room. Drooping, I followed. By the time the twins and I were outside Conan was perched up in the driving seat. Eddie jumped up beside him, and I climbed resentfully into the back of the dog cart with Robbie.

Tears filled my eyes as I desperately hugged my brothers goodbye. Then the train was in, they were on it, and only two waving hands in the distance were left to me before they too disappeared. I turned and walked back to the barrier, swallowing the lump in my throat, trying not to disgrace myself in the face of Conan's mocking grin. But at least he did not say anything as the tears began to trickle down my cheeks.

I hardly noticed that we had turned off the main drive, and were following a rutted track. As we bumped along I raised my swollen eyes to Conan. He said, 'It'll be boring back at the house – all those smart friends of Aunt Ria's waiting for me to make some witty Irish quip.'

He sounded almost resentful, and I felt a flash of sympathy between us. I gulped down my tears. 'I hate house parties – I don't know how to converse, and Mother always looks at me so scathingly, as if she knows I'll never say anything clever in my whole life.'

'Poor old Hellie.' Conan's voice was quite friendly. I liked him better on his own. He pulled Daisy up as we curved past the copse. 'Let's go for a walk – it'll be cooler in here. Will the mare be all right?'

'Oh yes, Daisy's very placid.'

Conan looped the reins over the railings and knotted them; Daisy lowered her head and began to graze. He vaulted lightly over the top rail. 'Come on then.'

As soon as I had climbed over he seized my hand and pulled it through his arm, and for a moment it was as if I were walking with my brothers – but only for a moment. The muscles of Conan's arms tensed as I held him, and he pressed my hand too tightly against his chest. But I did not mind; I was grateful for his company.

We walked for a while, then he stopped. 'Are you sad, Hellie – because the twins have gone?'

'Yes, yes I am – and Guy won't be home for weeks.' My voice trembled.

'Then why don't we pretend *I'm* Guy, come early – that would cheer you up, wouldn't it?'

I opened my mouth to say that he was not really like Guy at all, but there was a look of excitement in his eyes, and I found myself infected by it. 'Yes,' I said recklessly, 'Let's pretend.'

Conan walked away and jumped up on to a log. 'There, the train's just come into the station. Now, Hellie, I'm Guy.'

And for a moment, by a trick of the light, he *was* Guy. I ran forward, arms outstretched, and he threw himself into them and we hugged each other and I felt suddenly happy again. I raised my head and put my lips to his cheek – but it was smoother than Guy's. I moved, uncertain, but Conan's grip tightened and now I wanted to kiss him, so I did. But he turned his face until our lips met. His mouth was soft and warm under mine and I clung to him for a moment, then I broke away and whispered breathlessly, 'But I don't kiss Guy like that.'

Conan grinned his wicked grin. 'Well, I think old

Guy's served his purpose – stand still, Hellie, I'm going to kiss you again.'

I stood quite still while his lips roamed over my neck and cheeks, and circled my mouth and then came to rest on it again. His lips were soft but insistent and gradually I opened my mouth under his, until the tips of our tongues met and danced together in the warm moistness. I clung and clung until he suddenly lifted his mouth and pulled me down hard on to the springy pine-smelling turf. I tripped and fell sprawling on top of him and began to giggle, and he laughed with me as we lay in a tumbled heap.

In the still air we heard the chime of the stable clock and I jumped up and began to brush down my skirt. 'We must get back – Papa will be wanting the dog cart.' I felt very shy now, and I ran ahead through the trees – then stopped, confused. Sir Ernest was sitting in the back seat of the cart, legs stretched out, puffing on a large cigar.

'Ah, good. I was waiting for you youngsters to reappear. I came out for a stroll after breakfast, but it's too hot for walking now, you shall drive me back.' He was smiling, but I saw his eyes flicker over my crumpled frock, where stray pine needles still clung. He looked over my shoulder at Conan; his eyes narrowed a little then he guffawed and leant down to give him a buffet between the shoulder blades. Conan laughed as he sprang into the driving seat with the reins in his hands, but I felt hot and embarrassed as I climbed in beside him.

We played croquet in the afternoon. I was very conscious of Conan as his strong arm swung the mallet, and once he brushed past me and my heart beat faster and his bare hand touched mine.

Mother sent Miss Fisher to tell me I must come down to dinner tonight: a guest had had to leave early, so she was a lady short. Normally I would have been apprehensive, but tonight I felt a little thrill of excitement at the idea of dining downstairs.

Conan sat opposite me at dinner. He laughed and joked with Juno while I sat dumb. But as Juno turned to her neighbour he raised his wineglass and, in an almost imperceptible gesture, tilted it in my direction before he drank. The colour rose in my cheeks as I looked down at my own childish lemonade.

The gentlemen came into the drawing room almost at once after dinner. Conan strolled over to me. 'It's too fine a night to stay indoors – come out on to the terrace.' I looked up at his face; the blue eyes staring down at me were quite serious now. My heart beat faster as I stood up and followed him.

But we did not stay on the terrace. As soon as we were out of the pool of light cast by the window, Conan reached for my hand and pulled me down the steps and on to the lawn. I glanced back a moment, and saw Sir Ernest's broad shoulders outlined against the open window – then I was running hand in hand with my cousin across the springy turf. The moon was full and the night was silver and I laughed aloud as we leapt down the last flight of steps. Conan pulled me to a halt; I swayed towards the black shape of his body outlined against the moonlight and felt his warm lips come down on mine. Excitement coursed through me. Then he pulled free and caught my hand again, tugging me on. 'Where are we going?'

'To the maze – to see the maze by moonlight.' His strong fingers hurt my hand as he pulled me on, but I did not care.

The moon cast strange eerie shadows in the maze. They confused me, and once I went wrong, but then we were in the well of light in the centre. Conan's face was black and white as he turned towards the small pavilion in the clearing and hauled me after him. Inside he suddenly dropped my hand and began to rush from seat to seat. I stood in the doorway, bewildered, as he seized cushion after cushion and threw them in a pile on the wooden floor. Then he swung round, caught me by the arms, and pushed me down in the midst of them.

'Hellie, Hellie, I've wanted to hold you again all day.' He buried his face in my neck and my hands slid round his back as I hugged him as hard as I could. I was panting with excitement, and then I held my breath as our tongues danced again.

I cried out in soft protest when he pulled away. I heard his voice, very determined. 'I want to see your breasts again, Hellie.' He sat back on his heels, his eyes pools of darkness in his pale face as he stared at me.

I raised my hands and began to undo the buttons of my bodice. In silence I started to pull my frock and my camisole down over my shoulders. When my arms were free I began to unfasten my corset. I had to struggle to tug it out from my waist; he leant forward to help me, and it was his hands which pushed down my petticoat until I sat before him, with my small round breasts swelling in the moonlight. He looked at them for a long moment, and I felt my nipples rise and tighten in his gaze. Slowly he leant forward and I sat quite still while his warm hands stroked me. Then he sat back again, pulled off his jacket, threw his tie to one side and began to unbutton his shirt. As I saw the dark downy shadow on his chest my heart leapt and I threw myself forward – so we sat, clasped breast to breast in the pale moonlight.

At last he eased me down, until we lay side by side on the cushions. It seemed only natural then that his caressing hand should slide down my back. He curled his head against my breast and stroked the length of my leg, gliding over the filmy stuff of my skirt, down, down until his warm fingers clasped my ankle. He paused, and I shifted a little, so that his questing hand could find its way under my petticoat, into the warmth below. We were breathing more quickly now. He raised his head and his eyes were dark as we stared at each other, but we both lay quite still, only his hand moved. Slowly but inevitably it slid up my calf, slipped inside my drawers and up over my knee. And as it moved I felt an exquisite sweetness in the pit of my belly, growing and swelling, to a pitch where my body seemed barely able to contain it. I waited for his hand to creep higher, my eyes fixed on his face, until with a last swift movement it slid over the top of my stocking and touched my bare flesh. And as his strong fingers probed higher the pressure in my belly mounted and became beyond bearing, so I moaned aloud until he bent his head and fastened his lips on mine, and as he thrust his tongue into my mouth the exquisite sweetness reached bursting point and exploded. I jerked and clutched at him until at last I lay limp and shaken, with a strange slippery wetness between my legs.

He slid his hand out from under my skirt, sat up and reached for his trouser buttons. I lay quiescent, waiting for him. But even as he undid the first button the stillness was shattered by a deep, rasping cough. We both froze. Then Sir Ernest's voice, very loud, rang out over the hedges. 'Now, Lady Pickering, I'm not sure that I trust your guidance in this undoubtedly puzzling maze.'

'I am going in, with or without you, Sir Ernest.' It was my mother's voice.

I jumped up, frantically holding my frock up to my breasts. Conan sprang to his feet, seized his jacket and began kicking the cushions under the seats.

'If you insist, Lady Pickering.' Sir Ernest's voice still rang out loudly.

We ran out of the pavilion and headed for the exit from the glade. A noisy burst of coughing rent the night air. 'I'm so sorry, Lady Pickering – the smoke . . .'

I collected my scattered wits and ran to the left, twisting and turning, away from the true route out, away into the shelter of the thick green walls. At last we reached a dead end. I huddled against the privet and Conan stood over me, very still.

My mother's shoes stirred the gravel of the central

clearing; Sir Ernest trod heavily behind her. We heard his exclamation, 'Ah, a deserted glade!'

'Deserted now – oh!' My mother's sharp intake of breath told me she had seen the cushions. I thought frantically, but it might have been one of the gardeners, with a maid – oh please let her think that. Then Mother's voice rang out, very loudly and distinctly, 'I am rather concerned about Helena, Sir Ernest – perhaps she is unwell. I will send Fisher to her room to inquire as soon as we get back.'

The footsteps moved off. I sagged against the hedge as Conan began to shake with laughter. 'Caught in the act – Sir Ernest is a shrewd old so-and-so – still, at least he did the decent thing and gave us time to escape.'

I whispered, 'You don't think he knew?'

'I'll bet he guessed this morning I'd be trying to get you off on your own somewhere. No doubt he's been up to the same game himself in the past.' Conan actually sounded admiring.

I felt sick. I pushed past him and began to run out of the maze.

'Hey, Hellie, I don't know this place as well as you do!' But I ignored his protest and ran on, doubling backwards and forwards until I reached the entrance. Outside I took to my heels and sped like a hare up the path, desperate fingers fumbling with my frock as I ran. I was doing up the last button as I panted across the magnolia lawn; I pushed back my plaits and circled round the orangery so as to slip in by the servants' door. They were all in Hall at this time of the evening, so I ran unseen up the back stairs. Once in the safety of my room I flung myself down on my bed, panting and trembling.

Suppose Mother and Sir Ernest had come upon us in the glade without any warning? I shuddered with relief, then went to the dressing table and began to attend to my hair. It was tidied again by the time the tap at the door came.

I called, 'Come in,' and it was Miss Fisher. But my mother's maid was carrying a brown paper parcel. She placed it carefully on the dressing table, murmured, 'With her Ladyship's compliments,' and left. I stared at it for a moment, then broke the seal with shaking hands and began to undo the string. I unfolded the paper, and looked down – at my corset.

CHAPTER NINE

I dreamt I was being chased through the maze by an enormous man who was hooded and wrapped in a long black cloak. He moved quite slowly, but my feet were leaden – I could not run – so I could never escape from him. As I reached each corner the looming dark shape appeared round the one behind, blocking the way back. I twisted and turned frantically until I reached a dead end, and swung round at bay, crouching with my hands over my eyes while his steady padding footsteps came nearer and nearer . . .

I woke up, drenched in sweat. I only slept in fits and starts for the rest of the night and was wide awake long before breakfast time – but I dreaded the thought of going downstairs. Agnes came in with my tea and drew back the curtains. 'Another lovely day, my lady.' But it was not a lovely day. I watched her come back with the can of hot water, and lay my clothes out, then I climbed reluctantly out of bed. I washed quickly; perhaps if I hurried I might be down and finished before anyone else arrived. I struggled to hook myself into my treacherous corset.

At first I thought the morning room was empty, then I saw Sir Ernest over by the sideboard, helping himself to kidneys. He replaced the silver cover with a clang and smiled at me, showing his strong yellow teeth. 'What a careless little girl you are, to be sure!' His vulpine grin widened, then he threw back his head and roared with laughter.

I turned to run away, but I cannoned into Papa in the doorway. At his look of surprise I went slowly over to the table. Papa held out his cup and I lifted the coffee pot – and splashed the tablecloth as Mother walked in. 'Helena, how very careless. Ring for someone to clean up that mess.'

I tugged at the bell and tried to slip out of the door, but she called me back and I sat with my eyes on my plate until she had finished her breakfast. She ate slowly, her face thunderous. Conan came in, but I did not look at him. At last Mother rose, and gestured to me to follow her.

I walked after her into her boudoir, my legs shaking. She sat down at her writing desk and I stood in front of her, staring at the floor.

'I want to know exactly what happened last night, Helena.' Her voice was very cold. I was dumb, what could I say? 'I've spoken to Conan already.' My head jerked up. 'He swears he never laid a finger on you below the waist.' The hot blood rose in my face. 'Mm, I assumed he was lying – men always do in these situations. Come along, Helena, I want the truth – what exactly did the two of you get up to?' I stared at her, horrified. How could I tell *anyone*, let alone Mother? 'Helena, I must know.' She was very angry now. 'Don't you realize you could be with child? – and the pair of you are far too young to marry, there's not a penny between you – but if the damage has been done . . .'

I was bewildered, 'with child'? Me? But I was still a child myself. At last I blurted out, 'But I can't be with child – I'm not out yet.'

Her cheekbones flared red. 'Helena, are you totally stupid? Don't you know what I'm talking about?' I looked back at her blankly. 'I see you don't – really, the time you spend round the stables I would have thought by now . . .' She leant forward and spoke very clearly, as though to an idiot. 'Helena, you know how your brothers are made?' I nodded. 'Tell me, truthfully, did Conan put his cock inside you?'

The astonishment on my face must have given its own answer. She sat back in the chair, her shoulders sagging. 'Thank God for that. I'd never have forgiven you if we'd had to ruin his life like that, with a marriage at seventeen – my own dear Alice's son.'

I was beyond thought now: too much had happened too quickly. It took me a moment to realize what Mother was saying next. 'I was going to send you abroad next autumn in any case – I shall send you this year, now, as soon as I've found a really trustworthy governess. I had thought of Paris, but' – she shuddered – 'and not Dresden, there are too many English, so Alice told me. Sir Ernest suggests Munich: you should be safe enough there. I shall make inquiries at once about a reliable German governess – I understand they can be positive gorgons – and I shall instruct her *never* to let you out of her sight. In the meantime Conan has promised me solemnly that he won't be alone with you again, and I want the same promise from you, Helena.'

I whispered, 'I promise.' The tears trickled down my cheeks.

'Why ever did I have daughters inflicted on me – a dozen sons would be less trouble. Go to your room and make yourself presentable.'

I crept out. My thoughts were in turmoil; when I had been with Conan everything had seemed so natural, so right – yet clearly what we had done was dreadfully wrong.

When the luncheon gong sounded I stole downstairs and slid into a seat at the bottom of the table. I looked from under my eyelashes at my fellow criminal, but he was laughing and joking with Juno as he came in. He flushed slightly when Mother beckoned him to the seat on her right hand, but she turned a smiling face in his direction and soon they were chatting easily together. Sir Ernest joined in, and their laughter seemed to mock me as I pushed my food around the plate, utterly miserable.

In the drawing room after dinner Conan sauntered over to me as I sat in the window seat. He gave a rueful grin. 'Hard luck, Hellie, but I suppose it's as well they flushed us out before any harm was done. After all, as Aunt Ria says, you're not a kitchenmaid to be tumbled and forgotten.' I stared at him blankly. He gave a slight frown. 'You should really have known better, Hellie – you are a girl, it's different for a man, he can't help it. But a girl shouldn't let him behave like that.'

Hot anger flared up, but I sat dumb until he shrugged his shoulders and walked away, whistling. I saw him join the group round my mother; her high clear laughter rang out as he spoke to her. He was base, a traitor.

Sir Ernest's dark bulk loomed over me. 'Ah, Lady Helena, it's time we had a song from you. Lady Maud tells me you have a nice little voice – come to the piano and sing to us now. I will accompany you.'

I muttered, 'I can accompany myself.'

'No, no – I insist. I enjoy tinkling the ivories. I am quite competent, I assure you.'

Ungraciously I followed him through to the piano and began to turn over the music, then stopped suddenly. 'I will sing this song, Sir Ernest – can you play it?'

'Why yes, in the key of F; you are a soprano, of course.'

He walked to the connecting door and clapped his hands. 'Ladies and gentlemen, Lady Helena and I are about to entertain you, so you must all come through, draw up a chair, sit down – and be silent!' His gaze fixed on my mother; she tossed her head, but stepped forward. Conan rushed ahead, swung a chair into position for her, then stood behind her like a young squire, his hand on

the back of her seat. I took a deep angry breath and
went to the piano.

'Ready, Lady Helena?'

I nodded to Sir Ernest and stood very straight, my
gaze fixed on Conan. I did not need the music. Sir Ernest
played the opening bars and I began to sing, in my
fullest, strongest voice:

> 'Early one morning, just as the sun was rising,
> I heard a maid sing in the valley below:
> "Oh don't deceive me, O never leave me!
> How could you use a poor maiden so?" '

The complacent smile was wiped off Conan's face as
though by a cloth. I sang on:

> 'Remember the vows that you made to your Mary,
> Remember the bow'r where you vowed to be true;'

My voice filled the room, but I sang only to Conan, until
the last plaintive:

> 'How could you use a poor maiden so?'

Sir Ernest took his hands from the keys and clapped
loudly. 'Bravo, Helena, bravo!'

Conan joined in the polite applause of the other guests,
looking rather foolish. Juno called 'Encore!' but I shook
my head decisively. The murmuring of conversation
filled the room again.

'Thank you for playing, Sir Ernest – I don't wish to
sing any more.'

He gave his reptilian smile. 'You could hardly follow
that, my dear – but one moment,' his heavy hand on my
wrist detained me. 'Lady Maud is wrong: you do not
have "a nice little voice" ' – he mimicked her hoarse
tones for a moment – 'no indeed, you have a voice, a
good voice, which with proper training could be a very

good voice indeed. You are going to Munich, your mother tells me – Elsa Gehring is the best singing teacher in Munich – I will write to her. She is much in demand but she will hear you at my recommendation, and if you sing as well for her as you have done for us tonight she will take you on.' He bared his teeth again. 'After all, if you are to be exiled, you might as well pass the time usefully.'

I shook my head. 'Mother doesn't like me to spend time on my singing.'

'I will speak to Lady Pickering – I can persuade her.' He bent over me until I could smell the brandy fumes on his breath. 'Run away now, little one – and dream of your faithless lover.' He burst out laughing and I hated him. I stalked from the room and up the stairs, then ran along the corridor and flung myself down on my bed to weep.

Several miserable days later Mother summoned me again. I stood mutely before her, waiting for sentence. 'A Fraulein Washeim has been highly recommended to me – she is luckily available now, due to the death of her previous charge – measles I believe, still, you've had that, so there shouldn't be any problem. She will arrange suitable lodgings and teach you German. As soon as Miss Ling gets back with Letty next week she will take you straight down to London.'

I cried, 'But the twins – the twins will still be in Scotland – I won't be able to say goodbye!'

Mother shrugged. 'You should have thought of that before you behaved like a scullery maid.' Her face was blurred now, as my eyes filled. 'Sir Ernest has recommended some singing teacher – I suppose that's as good a way as any of keeping you out of mischief. You can stay overnight with Alice at Eaton Terrace, then Guy will take you on to Germany.'

Back in my room I wept and wept.

The following evening the familiar cramping pains began. I slipped upstairs early and sent for a hot-water bottle. Agnes wrapped it in flannel when she brought it and I clutched it to my stomach until at last I fell asleep. But the pain woke me early in the morning; I climbed out of bed and knelt doubled up on the rug, gasping between each spasm. As my discomfort increased I knew I had to go to the water closet, so I wrapped my dressing gown round me and crept along the corridor.

As I came near my Mother's bedroom on the way back I heard the door handle creak and I slid into the dressing-room alcove: I did not want her to see me like this. But the footsteps that came out were heavier than hers, and I caught a glimpse of a garish red dressing gown. Shrinking back I watched as Sir Ernest Webern cautiously surveyed the corridor, then, treading as delicately as a large jungle cat, passed in front of me. I saw the look of smug satisfaction on his face before the creak of his own door handle was quickly muffled and he disappeared from sight. I stumbled back to my own room and knelt down by the empty grate, sick and cold.

Miss Ling brought Letty home a few days later. As my sister ran out of the drawing room on to the terrace the sun glinted on her golden plaits, and I remembered Uncle Arnold's blond head bending over her in the nursery, and felt very old and tired.

Mother spoke to Miss Ling before I was allowed to see her. Miss Ling was awkward and embarrassed with me, and I with her. We travelled down to London almost in silence. When she said goodbye in Alice's drawing room I wanted to thank her – but I could not find the words. She put out her hand to me and said quickly, 'Helena, you're a sweet loving girl – but don't let that loving nature lead you astray.' She looked at me anxiously.

But all I could blurt out was, 'I'll write, Miss Ling – I'll write,' and as she turned away I saw the disappointment in her eyes.

I ran upstairs to Nanny; she kissed me warmly but she was busy with the new baby. 'There, isn't he a little pet? A nice brown curl already, just like his Papa. Elsie, what *are* you doing with that towel? Really, Lady Helena, these London girls have *no* idea with young babies – you wouldn't believe the things they do. Lady Alice is in her sitting room – she'll be pleased to see you, she's been a bit peaky lately.'

Alice put down her magazine as I came in. 'Well, well, so here's the erring daughter banished in disgrace from the family mansion.' She laughed. 'Really, Helena – and you look such a child in your short skirts with your pigtails down your back! Come along now, you must sing for your supper – tell me exactly what you were doing with Cousin Conan in the maze that night. Mother's letter didn't go into details – though I gather the "Worst" did not happen.'

I sat mute, my face aflame.

'Come on, Hellie, don't be shy – if you don't tell me I shall ask Conan when I see him.'

At last I stammered, 'I – I can't tell you.'

'Mm – how delicious,' Alice smiled. 'Then at least tell me how Mother "Found You Out".' Her black eyes mesmerized me.

Finally I whispered, 'Sir Ernest brought her to the maze – and – they found my corset.'

'Your corset! She was with Sir Ernest and – oh, just wait till I tell Hugh!' My sister looked much more cheerful now. I longed for the floor to open and swallow me up. 'Oh, Helena' – Alice arranged her face in an expression of outraged modesty – 'what a naughty boy Conan is to be sure – removing your corset in the maze.' Her eyes narrowed. 'Or did you remove your own corset? Surely not!'

I said desperately, 'He helped me.'

Alice fell back on to the sofa and laughed at me until the tears ran down her face. I watched her, my cheeks burning, until she gave one last whoop, dabbed at her eyes with a scrap of lace, and rang for tea.

Guy arrived at six. I ran across the room to throw myself at him, and burst into tears.

He patted my shoulder. 'There, there, Hellie – don't cry.'

Alice called out, 'She's been playing with fire and now she's got burnt. Try and calm her down before Hugh comes in, I've got to go and feed the wretched brat.'

Guy exclaimed, 'I'll horsewhip young Conan when I get my hands on him – the thoughtless bounder. Never mind, Hellie, I'm sure you'll enjoy Munich when you get there: Alice had a whale of a time in Dresden, loved every minute of it.'

My sobs died down to hiccups; I was warmed by Guy's loyal support.

I woke next morning doomed but resigned. Guy had promised he would bring the twins out to Munich at Christmas, if he could get leave: 'I'll go down on my bended knees before the adjutant, Hellie – I can't say fairer than that.' So I had a little oasis of hope to cling to in the desert ahead.

Alice, coming down late for breakfast, opened another letter from Mother. 'Sir Ernest has apparently arranged a most strenuous musical programme for you, and assures Mother that Fraulein Washeim is a slave driver of the first order. Poor Hellie, no time for you to make eyes at those handsome German students.' She smiled reminiscently. 'Oh, I *did* enjoy Dresden. Still, it's true I didn't learn much there, whereas Sir Ernest seems determined that whatever the reason for your banishment, at least you're going to learn to sing.'

I said resentfully, 'I can sing already. When is Guy coming?'

We were to leave in the afternoon. Before lunch Guy took me out for a walk in the Park. As we strolled under the trees I heard the jingle of harness and saw a troop of Life Guards trotting towards us. Their white plumes were waving in the breeze, their red tunics glowed. I tugged at Guy's arm, and pulled him nearer. 'Oh, don't they look smart – though not as nice as the Grenadiers, of course.' Guy laughed and patted my hand.

The officer rode at the head. The sun glinted on his shining spurs and sparkled off his golden breastplate. His silver sword was held upright in one white-gauntleted hand; the other lightly clasped the reins. I looked up at the face under the gleaming helmet: his mouth was a steady line below his small golden moustache and proud straight nose. Then, as he drew level with us, for a moment his cool blue eyes looked straight into mine. I held my breath, until with the thud of hooves his troop rode past us.

I breathed out slowly, and gazing after the tossing white plumes I whispered to Guy, 'He looked at me, he looked straight at me.'

Guy laughed. 'I'll wager he looked at everybody along the route. You can always tell a man who's been on active service – he'll keep his eyes open, even in London.'

I breathed, 'Do you *know* him, Guy?'

'Only by sight. It was Prescott – lucky devil was just in time to see the fun in South Africa. Mentioned in dispatches, then got a gong – DSO, I think.'

The troop had swung round a corner now, but I still gazed at the point where they had disappeared from sight. My heart thumped. He was not only tall and handsome – he was a hero! Guy spoke again: 'He and his brother went out together, I believe – his brother was wounded; just getting over it when he went down with enteric and died out there.'

'Oh Guy.' I gazed up at my own brother. 'How awful to lose his brother like that – I just couldn't bear it.' Guy pressed my arm close to his chest, and I added, 'That was like Jem – do you remember Jem, Guy?'

'Yes, I remember.'

We began to walk on, but the clear blue eyes and tall, upright figure danced before me. The sweeper was clearing some horse dung further on; I gazed at it – perhaps it was from *his* horse. My hero.

The journey to Munich passed in a daze, but just before I fell asleep in the small cabin of the steamer I remembered Conan's hand sliding under my skirts, and I blushed with shame. How could I have behaved so? Mother was right to punish me. I was a little slut – I did not deserve even a glance from such a brave strong man as my cavalry officer. But from now on I would try to be worthy of him, oh, how I would try.

PART II

AUGUST 1909
to
AUGUST 1914

CHAPTER ONE

I learnt to sing in Munich.

Guy delivered me to the pension in the Schellingstrasse and a plump middle-aged woman with cheeks like wrinkled apples led me up the dark stuffy staircase to the sitting room where my new governess awaited me. Fraulein Washeim was broad with thick grey plaits wound tightly round her heavy-jowled, expressionless face; from under heavy lids pale blue eyes assessed me.

Guy had to return at once. I flung myself into his arms in a storm of frantic weeping and he patted my back helplessly until a firm hand on my shoulder prised me away; with a parting kiss my brother was gone. Fraulein led me, gulping and sobbing, into a small bedroom. 'I will be waiting when you have recovered, Grafin.' Through tear-blurred eyes I stared at the hideous brown wallpaper and the enormous white porcelain stove that dominated the room; then I flung myself on to the mound of feather eiderdowns heaped on the bed.

Everything was so strange. I had learnt a little German with Miss Ling, and when Fraulein Washeim spoke slowly and clearly, I could just follow her, but I gaped helplessly whenever Frau Reinmar, my landlady, addressed me. We ate lunch and dinner downstairs with the other guests, and she would rattle off the strange-sounding names: Kalbsbraten, Nudeln, Zwetschgentorte. But on the second day I acquired an ally. I had recognized pea soup – but there was a sausage floating in it! So I picked up my spoon very slowly, and sipped gingerly, skirting the intruder, until the young dark-haired boy opposite leant right over the table, pointed to my plate and said loudly, 'Sossidge! I am speaking

Englischer, Grafin. Now I teach German to you.' He sat back and beamed at me, showing a row of pearly white teeth under a short, childish upper lip. Then he leant forward again. 'Wurst – say wurst, Fraulein Grafin.'

Obediently I repeated the word after him, and he smiled again.

Franzl set himself up as my tutor. Slowly and patiently he told me he was nine years of age, and he had four sisters, and one brother, Kurt. His brown eyes lit up when he spoke of Kurt. Kurt was twenty-four and an officer – very, very clever, and very, very strong. He had seen the Grafin's brother – so he also was an officer? 'Gut, sehr gut.' We smiled at each other, and I felt slightly less forlorn.

The next day Fraulein took me to see Frau Elsa Gehring. Fraulein told me I was extremely honoured that Frau Gehring would even hear me sing. She had been a great singer, now she taught, but only the *best* pupils. I felt sick with nerves.

The famous Elsa Gehring was still blonde, though the blue eyes were surrounded by a mesh of fine lines. She smiled kindly, but spoke too quickly for me. I caught the name 'Ernst Webern', and her blue eyes gleamed; even Fraulein Washeim's stolid face relaxed into a near smile; the two ladies shook their heads indulgently.

Frau Gehring turned back to me, and spoke rapidly. I understood I was to sing, so I drew a breath and launched into: 'Where e'er you walk . . .' The gentle breezes of the song lulled me, and for a moment I forgot I was in exile.

Frau Gehring beckoned. She said loudly in English, 'Hilde' – as she gestured towards Fraulein Washeim – 'will teach you German.' She held up one finger. 'In one month you will return.' I nodded and began to turn away. 'Nein, you must learn the breath. Down.' She pointed to the square of threadbare carpet, so I knelt on the floor. Frau Gehring exclaimed, and gestured with her hands. 'Down, down to sleep.' Totally bewildered,

94

I stretched myself out on the dusty carpet and closed my eyes.

Corsets creaked as Elsa Gehring bent over me; I lay rigid in this madhouse. My left hand was seized and thrust down on my belly, my right placed firmly on my chest. She began to knead them up and down: 'In – out, in – out.' At last I understood that I must breathe out in such a way as to pull in the hand on my chest, whilst lifting the hand on my belly at the same time. I lay on the floor, gazing up at the ornate plaster ceiling, feeling a bitter hatred of Sir Ernest and all his ways – but I did as I was told: I dared not do otherwise.

For the next month every moment of my day was mapped out. Fraulein Washeim was a formidable organizer. At regular intervals she supervised my breathing exercises, then made me swing my arms in different ways and perform still more movements – 'to strengthen the belly'. But I must not sing: Frau Gehring had been firm on that point. Each day I was marched to the New Pinakothek or the Old Pinakothek: Fraulein headed unerringly for the most crowded canvases, and instructed me to describe them, in German. Back at the pension she sat down at the piano in my sitting room and played and told me each musical term in German. When I played, she questioned and corrected me.

At the end of the month we returned to Frau Gehring's studio.

'Ah, the little Grafin – come, I play you a tiny scale, and you will sing it for me, breathing as you have learnt.'

Obediently I began to sing – and the notes seemed almost to fly out of my mouth, so easily and fully did they come. Frau Gehring began to laugh. 'You are amazed, little Grafin. You thought: "What is that silly old woman doing, pumping me like a bellows on the floor?" But now you know. Breath, breath, it is vital, it is the power of the voice. When I have taught you, your voice will dance on your breath, like a leaf in a fountain, it will be so easy. Now do you believe in Elsa Gehring?'

'Yes, oh yes.'

'Now, little Gräfin, listen to me – so you know where we are going.' She crossed to the piano, struck a chord, then sang up the scale. As she glided from note to note her voice was a gleaming silver ribbon. She sang the same scale again, much louder, so that it swelled like a wide shining river, then a third time, very quietly, so now it was only a thin thread of gossamer. She smiled at my expression and sat down, hands folded. 'You have an ear – your pitch is good – I think you have been well trained. Also, you know where to put your voice.' I looked at her blankly. She touched her forehead, her mouth, her chest, 'Here, or here, or here. You look surprised, you think everyone knows that because to you it is natural, but not so, you are fortunate. Now sing a little more for me, I must diagnose.'

She took me up to the high C, and then down, lower than I normally ever went, so that my voice came from my chest. As she took me up again I heard the break in the sound. As soon as I had finished I said quickly, 'I would rather sing the high notes.'

Frau Gehring laughed. 'But of course – you are a young girl, so you love your top C like a sister! But you will not always be a young girl, and then you will need those lower notes. At present they are weak – we will strengthen them. You are able to sing in the chest, so it is wise to learn to do so.'

'But . . .'

'But now your voice breaks, that is why you are here, with me. Put your hand on my chest, I will show you what can be done.'

I stood with my fingertips resting lightly on the lace over her bosom, and I felt her sing the notes in her chest – then heard them rise effortlessly into her head. There was no break. She shook off my hand and said briskly, 'You will learn to do that, also. I think, when I receive Ernst's letter, this is a gräfin who comes to me, she will never go on the stage – not for her the Hof Theatre or

96

the Residenz – but she will need to fill the hall of a castle, or a church, with your English oratorio – so she must be able to sing forte, but also piano, all women must be able to sing piano – softly in a bedchamber,' she smiled reminiscently; I sensed Fraulein stiffen. Frau Gehring's mouth widened. 'Lullabies, of course.' Her eyelid trembled in the ghost of a wink in my direction. Then she added briskly, 'Besides, you must never practise full voice – it annoys the neighbours. Fraulein says you play well, you must continue to practise – a Grafin will often need to accompany herself, or even to sing without the piano; that also is necessary for you. You must be able to sing anywhere – in the tiny cell of a monk, or the great Schloss of a king. All men like to hear a woman sing – even monks!' Frau Gehring lowered her voice. 'Sir Ernst has sent a little note from your Mama.' I started guiltily, Elsa smiled conspiratorially. 'She wishes you to be occupied every minute of the day – or else you will get into mischief, she says.' She leant forward and whispered, 'I think you have tried to sing in the bedchamber too soon, little one.' I felt my face flush at her smile. 'Never mind, I will draw up a programme, and Fraulein will supervise – we will send you home from Munich a good singer – and a good girl!'

And they did fill every moment of my day. Twice a week Fraulein escorted me to an opera or a concert, and we analysed it afterwards. Every day I practised at my piano; I had learnt to transpose at sight with Miss Ling but now Fraulein insisted on both speed and precision. I was set to memorize pieces of music and poems: each must be repeated back to her correctly; and I was taken to elderly Herr Hoffmeier for elocution lessons, and learnt to roll the 'r' with the tip of my tongue until I could repeat every time perfectly: 'Roland der Ries' am Rathaus zu Bremen.'

I practised my breathing and strengthened my belly muscles, and walked out with Fraulein twice a day whether it were wet or fine, and came home with an appetite for sauerkraut and potato dumplings. I laughed with Franzl and admired the mustachioed Kurt – while sighing secretly for my own handsome cavalry officer. Some nights I would dream that he galloped past me with his sword flashing, leading his men into battle, and when I awoke I would be happy and excited, even though I was in a strange land.

But, above all, I sang. And slowly I heard my voice gain in fullness and strength as I practised the exercises from Concone and Vaccai each day. I was determined to sing as Elsa Gehring sang and now I had heard her I wished to sing not as a girl sings in idle pleasure, but as a woman in total command. But I knew now it would take time, and ceaseless, careful application before I could sound as effortless as she did. In this ambition Fraulein was my ally; nothing but the best would do.

But it was Elsa Gehring who inspired me. 'Your breath must caress the note like a mother's hand stroking her baby's head.'

'I will hold a lighted candle before your mouth – if you are wasting breath it will go out. Good, little Grafin, good, it barely flickers. Your voice is your instrument – care for it, and learn to play it perfectly.'

When she praised me for my legato I thought I would burst with pride – yet the pure exquisite joy I had felt as at last my breath carried my voice smoothly from note to note had been reward enough.

At Christmas, Guy brought the twins out to Munich; we walked and talked and enjoyed endless coffee and Kuchen in the cafés together. As I sang the Christmas hymns I gazed at my slim dark brothers and overflowed with love and pride.

Guy took us to the theatre each night, and after Christmas, Franzl escorted us down to the flooded meadows beyond the Englischer Garten, and there we skated. As darkness fell on their last afternoon they whirled me round and round on the ice until I was breathless and dizzy, then we strolled back to the pension through the bustling streets, together. I walked with each hand safely tucked into a twin's elbow while Guy ranged like a sheepdog beside us. I gloried in the warm protection of my brothers.

I wept when they went back, but Franzl brought me his New Year toys for my inspection, and then Elsa Gehring said it was time I learned the *messa di voce*, so I was happy again.

I learned to begin my note quietly, swell it up to full voice, and then slowly diminish it until it faded away. When Frau Gehring was satisfied, she set me another exercise – to repeat two neighbouring notes in rapid alternation, until at last I could trill. And all the time I felt my voice becoming more agile, more flexible, and more even throughout the scale, and I longed for the day when I would begin to learn my aria. The aria which must be perfect, Elsa Gehring said, so that years later I could return to it as a model, and know at once if my standard had slipped. By the time Papa came to Munich to bring me home for the summer, Frau Gehring had pronounced me ready to learn my aria on my return. I hugged the thought close to me like a precious gift.

Papa was to stay several days. He came to the Schellingstrasse and we spoke stiltedly together, then he picked up his hat and gloves and went back to the Regina Palace Hotel on Maximilian Platz, which had sixty bathrooms and a palm house – so Franzl told me with bated breath. The next day we had tea with him there, and I knew Franzl would question me eagerly on my return about the famous palm house, but Papa did not offer to take us in and I was too shy to ask. I sat nibbling meringue torte while Fraulein and Papa conversed politely.

That evening Fraulein and I had just come out of the theatre when I caught sight of Papa coming straight towards us on the crowded pavement of the Maximilianstrasse. A very pretty brunette, dressed in the height of fashion, hung on his arm. I slowed down and called

'Papa', but he merely raised his hat and walked on, while his companion continued to smile and chatter to him. I stopped, bewildered, 'He didn't introduce us!'

Fraulein seized my elbow in a painful grip and marched me on. 'You should not have spoken, Grafin Helena – he did not wish to acknowledge his daughter in such circumstances. Come, we will be late.'

Papa made no reference to our brief encounter on the Maximilianstrasse until we were on the train to London. Then, tugging at his moustache and looking out of the window, he muttered, 'The other evening in Munich, when you so unfortunately ran into me with – ah – a companion. You ah – won't mention it – will you?'

I stared down at my gloves. 'Certainly not, Papa.'

He gave a gusty sigh of relief. 'Knew I could rely on you, old girl. Maud'd give me a nasty couple of hours if she found out – women don't understand that sort of thing, y'see.' He picked up his paper.

In London I begged Guy to take me to *The Marriage of Figaro* at His Majesty's Theatre; I wore black silk gloves and a black sash on my white frock – we were in mourning for the King. I gazed around me, awestruck at the massed ranks of the stalls and circle: every woman's evening dress was black tonight. But as soon as Mozart's perfect overture began, my surroundings vanished, for this was the opera of my aria. I followed each note intently.

After a fortnight we travelled back to Cheshire. It was strange to be at Hatton without Miss Ling; she had written to tell me her mother was now bedridden, so she must go home to nurse her. I had promised to go and visit her in her West London suburb when I came home, but whenever I had asked there had been no maid available to take me – and then I forgot.

In Cheshire the peaches were ripe, so I asked the head gardener to arrange for a hamper to be packed, and sent a note with it. Miss Ling's reply, grateful and resigned, made me feel very guilty. There had been changes at

Hatton: electricity had been installed while I had been away; a smelly generator throbbed in its house behind the stables. A gleaming Delaunay-Belleville stood in the coach house; Jenkins said it was 'agin nature', and was at daggers drawn with the new chauffeur.

Sir Ernest came for a weekend, and sought me out to talk of Munich. 'Darling Elsa – she was in the full bloom of her beauty, and I was just a young student – but she was so kind and generous to me.' He smiled, a small secret smile. Then he heaved his huge bulk out of the chair and sauntered over to my mother.

The week before I was to be sent back, Conan came to stay. I was nervous and edgy and snapped at the twins as we waited on the platform at Hareford. But when Conan jumped down from the train and strolled across to greet us, he was as casual as if there had been no maze and no exile. On the way back in the dog cart he laughed with my brothers and tugged at my plaits as he teased me.

And yet there was a difference. My brothers were still boys; Conan was a man now. He spent a lot of time with Edie Cornell, who openly admitted she had only married her elderly husband because her dressmaker was dunning her. Edie was playing tennis one afternoon, dabbing ineffectually at easy shots with fluttering movements. I was sitting next to Conan beside the court, and slowly I realized that the exaggeratedly raised eyebrows and pretty, silly gestures were aimed in our direction. I glanced round at my cousin, expecting to see derision on his face, but instead it bore a look of smug satisfaction – and with a sudden shiver I remembered Sir Ernest's expression as he had stepped cautiously out of my mother's bedroom at dawn.

I stood up quickly and went over to Robbie. After a moment I asked, elaborately casual, 'Does Conan still keep the two of you up until all hours with his wild stories?'

I watched the pink flush reach the tip of my brother's

ears before he muttered, without looking at me, 'Oh, we're generally asleep early these days. How about a game of croquet, Hellie?'

I picked up the mallet and swung it with a vicious lunge at the ball.

That evening after I had gone to bed I thought of my tall fair cavalry officer. He would be strong and noble and faithful – and I would love him all the days of my life.

CHAPTER TWO

Back in Munich I began to study my aria. I had already been visiting Signor Urbini for lessons in Italian diction, so now I started to work through Susanna's song: "Deh! Vieni non tardar". Word by word and note by note I studied it. The execution of each phrase, the taking of each breath was planned like a military manoeuvre. I lived my aria, I dreamt my aria, and, at last, I sang my aria – and knew that it was good.

After Mozart, Lieder. I began with the "Wiegenlied" of Brahms – the lullaby to the beloved child – and learnt to let the notes float from my lips, delicate and ethereal. I flew on the wings of song with Mendelssohn and I sang of the comfort music brings with Schubert. 'Now you are ready for "Nachtigall". You are dreaming, begin like a sigh – the memories surge back – crescendo, warmer, warmer – end with your legato in pianissimo – let your last chord fade away.'

But at "Stille Tranen" Elsa Gehring was not satisfied. 'You can *sing* it, Grafin, but you cannot *feel* it – you are still a child, so you could not smile if your heart were breaking, you could only weep. We will put it to one side.' Instead she set me to learn the flowing rhythm of

"Die Forelle", and as I sang the trout flashed in the sparkling water before me, and Frau Gehring was pleased and praised my legato, so that after my lesson I walked through the streets of Munich as though I were ten feet tall.

Next lesson she had "Der Schmied" ready for me. I laughed at the thought of my singing a song of love for a blacksmith, and Elsa Gehring smiled slyly at me. 'Perhaps this is too difficult for the Gräfin to imagine? Her sweetheart a lowly working man hammering at his black furnace?' But I loved the strong rhythm and the emphatic consonants; I became a peasant girl in my mind and saw the rippling muscles of my work-begrimed lover and felt radiant with pride at his strength. But that night I dreamt of my brave blond cavalry officer.

At the beginning of December, Guy's letter brought bad news; he had to stay in London all through the Christmas holidays so he could not bring the twins to Munich. I gazed at the words, disbelieving – perhaps I could return to England instead? But no, Guy had already spoken to Mother about sending Fisher to fetch me, but Mother had said it was not worthwhile just for a few weeks – besides she would need her maid over the Christmas season, as she had so many engagements. So that was that.

I had already started my weekly letter to the twins. Now my tears dripped on to the paper and smeared the ink in ugly blotches as I wrote of my misery. The summer was so far away.

I went to my next singing lesson with a very long face. 'Ach! Poor little Gräfin – what sadness we feel when we are young. But take heart, Elsa will teach you to sing yourself through it.' I gazed dully at her smiling face. 'You will sing "An die Musik".' I sang, and heard the misery in my voice – but in the second verse I pictured happier times, and was comforted by the sweet harmony.

Elsa Gehring smiled. 'You see, little one? How fortunate we singers are. You must not sit and fruitlessly weep, no, you must turn your sadness into song. It will help you to bear it.' I understood, but I wept again for my brothers that evening.

Christmas was still more than a week away and I was practising at the piano in my sitting room, when the door burst open and Franzl appeared. 'Grafin Helena, Grafin Helena – come down to the dining room, quickly, there is a surprise for you.' His face was round and beaming. He turned and thundered down the stairs and I ran after him, but it was to please Franzl rather than for any hopes on my part – it would just be a package; Franzl adored packages. He flung open the door, I looked in – and there were my brothers.

I flung myself at them, laughing and crying. 'Eddie, Robbie – you've come, you've come!' I hugged them and kissed them, flying from one to the other like a dervish.

They submitted stoically to my frantic embraces. Eddie said 'Calm down, old girl,' but he grinned as he spoke, and they both looked very pleased with themselves.

I asked, 'But Guy – did Guy get leave after all?' I looked round, and it was only then that I realized there were two unfamiliar figures at the far end of the room.

But Eddie was explaining, so I turned all my attention on him. 'You see we decided we didn't need Guy to bring us – we are fifteen, after all – that's thirty if you add us together, older than Guy if you look at it the right way.' Robbie chipped in, 'When we got your letter – all blotched like that, really Hellie, and you're supposed to be our big sister! Well, I said. . . .' Eddie broke in, 'No, I thought of it first . . .'

I interrupted quickly, 'You *both* said – what?'

'Oh, that we'd come out and see you ourselves. We didn't tell anybody, of course, just made up our minds and when we got to Paddington we jumped in a cab and said, "Charing Cross", instead of "Euston" – it was as simple as that.' They smirked with satisfaction.

I gazed at them adoringly. Then a practical thought intruded. 'But Robbie, Eddie – you never have any money left by the end of term.'

'Oh we borrowed some from Staveley here – he's rolling in it.' Eddie nodded over his shoulder to a thin, fair boy half-hiding behind him.

I ran forward, hand outstretched, 'How kind of you – how very very kind!' He smiled shyly and uttered an inaudible reply.

'Then Stavey's Uncle Gerald caught up with us at Dover – well, Stavey was with him, actually – so he treated us the rest of the way.' I looked round and noticed almost for the first time the tall fair man standing in the shadows by the fireplace. I was overcome with shyness at the thought of my boisterous greetings being witnessed by a grown-up stranger; as he came forward with hand held out I dared not look at him. I touched his fingers briefly and whispered, 'Thank you so much, Mr Staveley.'

An amused voice said, 'You'd better introduce me to your sister properly, young Girvans.' Eddie stepped forward, put his hand to his waist and with an elaborate bow announced: 'Helena, may I present Captain Lord Gerald Prescott, of the First Life Guards? Lord Gerald, my sister, Lady Helena Girvan.'

At 'Prescott' my head had jerked up of its own accord. Now I stared straight into the clear blue eyes of my cavalry officer.

He said pleasantly, 'I only discovered on the boat that this precious pair were absent without leave; I suppose I should have packed them off back again on the next steamer.'

I gasped, 'Oh, I'm so glad you didn't!'

His smile was indulgent. 'After the welcome you've just given them I'm rather glad of that myself! I sent a cable from Ostend, of course, so your parents know where they are. I do hope Lady Pickering won't miss them too much over the festive season.'

'She won't,' I said firmly.

Eddie added, 'I daresay she'll be glad of our room – there's always a houseful of guests this time of year – we've done her a favour, really.'

Robbie sounded more doubtful. 'But she still won't like us disobeying her – she'll be livid.'

Eddie shrugged. 'Well, we won't be there to see it, will we? We're here now, and we're not going back.'

'No.' I clung to his arm; I could not believe they were real: my twins. And my cavalry officer. Suddenly I remembered my manners and felt the blush rise in my throat as I turned and stammered, 'L – Lord Gerald, perhaps you would care for some coffee and Kuchen?'

He smiled but reached for his hat. 'No, thanks very much, Lady Helena. Stavey and I are on our way to Carlsbad; my sister-in-law's spending the winter there. We just dropped off at Munich to deliver these two sinners – and to find out whether you really wanted them.' Wanted them! Of course I wanted them. He looked down at me. 'I can see the answer to that in your face – but hadn't you better check with your landlady – the pension might be full?'

My landlady had obviously been lurking in the hallway; she arrived at once. I said quickly, 'Please, Frau Reinmar – they can sleep on the floor of my sitting room – we could put down cushions.' She pursed her lips, so I added anxiously, 'Or they can have my bed, it's big enough for two, and I will sleep on the floor. I *like* to sleep on the floor.'

I heard a laugh from the man behind me. He broke in in slow, pedantic German: Frau Reinmar was reassured. I blushed as money discreetly changed hands – I would have to write and beg Papa to pay our debts – but the matter was soon settled, and I breathed a sigh of relief. Frau Reinmar offered refreshment, but Lord Gerald was determined to leave.

I felt terribly bereft as his tall slim figure strode out

of the room. Then Robbie's voice recalled me to the miracle of the twins' arrival.

We had a wonderful Christmas. Lord Gerald had left a fistful of notes with Eddie, and Fraulein was gracious in accompanying us to operas and plays; she even sat uncomplainingly beside me in the ornate dining room of the Café Luitpold while my brothers played billiards with Franzl in the next-door room. I sang my new Lieder, but my brothers preferred the songs we had learnt with Miss Ling – Robbie thumped them out on the piano in the salon while the old ladies smiled and clapped their hands. As casually as I could I extracted from my brothers all they knew about "Stavey's Uncle Gerald": it was not much, but at least they were sure he was not married. My heart soared.

One morning a letter lay by my plate – with a Carlsbad postmark; I opened it with shaking hands. It was a short note from Lord Gerald himself to say that, if I were agreeable, he and his nephew would wait on me on their way back to England: they would stay overnight in a hotel in Munich and then escort my brothers back home. After endless false starts and torn-up attempts I penned him a reply. His own letter I carefully wrapped up in tissue paper and locked away in my writing case: I would keep it always. I day-dreamed of his clear blue eyes and sleek blond hair. My brothers teased me mercilessly, but I knew they would not betray my secret.

The day Lord Gerald and his nephew were due to arrive I insisted on staying in the salon. The twins wanted to go out and skate on the frozen meadows, but I would not go with them. They took Franzl instead and I sat in the pension, my heart thumping, springing to my feet and rushing to the window every time I thought I heard a cab slowing down outside.

But my brothers were back again before he arrived, and when he did, all my carefully rehearsed phrases flew from my head – I stumbled over a few stupid words about the weather, agonizing over my own dullness until

Eddie butted in, 'Stavey, how about coming skating with us tonight? It's tremendous fun on the ice in the dark!'

I held my breath until Lord Gerald gave his consent and then, greatly daring, whispered, 'Perhaps you would care to come too?' He smiled down at me, and accepted.

I could not eat any dinner that evening; I kept saying silently to myself – 'I will see him tonight, I will see him tonight.' Even if I died tomorrow, life would have been worth living.

We swooped and glided over the frozen fields; I laughed with Franzl and the shy-faced Lord Staveley as my brothers cannoned into each other and skidded ridiculously past us, bottoms on the ice, feet in the air. Then Eddie found a chair on runners, carved and painted like Lohengrin's swan: 'Come on, Hellie – time to catch the next swan to Maximilian Platz!' I climbed in and the pair of them pushed off; I jerked and swayed dangerously from side to side.

Lord Gerald came skating over the ice towards us. 'Your steering's hopeless – out of the way, you two.' His strong hands gripped the back of my chariot and we skimmed over the great shining sheet of ice, away from the flares and the bustle and into the starry velvet blackness beyond. Then, without a break in the rhythm, he swung me into a great curving arc, and we sped back. My legs were trembling as he helped me out and set me on my feet. 'Come along young Stavey – it's time we were in bed, we've got to make an early start tomorrow.'

I sat in the Fiaker in a daze, and nearly forgot to murmur my thanks as we were put down in the Schellingstrasse. My brothers were to meet him at the Central Station in the morning, but I would not see him again.

Frau Gehring said I could choose which Lied I would like to study next. I searched the music shops and found the poem of Klaus Groth, which Brahms had set to music: "Dein blaues Auge". I pored over it, and sang fervently of the blue still eyes into whose depths I gazed.

Like the poet I too had been scorched by a pair of burning eyes and as I sang "Es brannt mich ein gluhend Paar", Conan's devilish face flashed before me for an instant – but now I would be healed by Lord Gerald's clear, cool blue ones.

When I had finished, Elsa Gehring laughed. I felt my face fall, but she reached out a quick hand. 'That was very good, my Grafin, you sang accurately but also with feeling. Why do I laugh? Because I think you are in love, are you not?' My cheeks glowed. 'Come, that is good – you will not sing Lieder well until you love. Now I can choose more widely for you.'

So I learnt "Im Frühling", "Der Nussbaum", and, finally, she allowed me to begin to study Schumann's romantic, beautiful *Frauen Liebe und Leben* – the story of a woman's life and love. I sang of how, since I had first seen him, his vision had blinded me to all else, nothing mattered but his image in my dreams. I sang of how wonderful and brave he was, and yet so gentle and kind. With more difficulty than the poet I accepted that only the best of women would be worthy of him, and I would bless her – but then I rejoiced when he chose me. As I sang

"Du Ring an meinem Finger,
Mein goldenes Ringelein"

I glanced down at my own left hand, then sang fervently of how I would serve him and love him for ever. In my mind the flowers were strewn before his feet, it was our wedding day; and wearing my wreath of myrtle I was going to him – half gladly, half fearfully.

My eyes filled with tears as I whispered to him in song of the new joy which lay under my heart, and of how his dear image would soon smile up at me from the cradle beside my bed. I sang of the bliss of nursing his son at my breast – my joy, my delight. Then finally, with painful voice, I sang of his desertion – as he slept the sleep of death, and I, left alone, folded into myself, my whole world at an end.

When I had finished I stood trembling and shaken beside the piano in Frau Gehring's big empty studio. Elsa Gehring rose and came to me. 'Good, little Gräfin, good. But do not cry, your brave lover still lives, and who knows what the future will hold for you? And now it is time for you to laugh again – we will study the "Song of the Flea"!'

At first I was indignant, but then I could not keep from laughing at the tale of the king who so loved his flea that he dressed him in silk and satin and made him a minister.

The snows melted in the mountains and spring came to Munich in the emerald-green waters of the Iser. I would beg Fraulein to take me down to the Luitpold Bridge, and stand there fascinated by the wild abandon of the river as it rushed beneath me.

Frau Gehring told me she would be teaching another English girl. She said firmly, 'Your father is rich, Gräfin,' and I thought of Papa's loud complaints that income tax was now so high he would be ruined – but then I remembered the coal mines, the slate quarries, the Girvan estates in north London and the endless carefully planned investment, and knew Elsa Gehring was right. 'I make the rich pay dear, so that I can help the poor – I am a Social Democrat, you see, but do not tell the Kaiser!' She laughed. 'This girl I do not charge – she has saved every Pfennig she has earned to come to Munich. Madame Goldman recommends her highly – she lives in Manchester – do you know Manchester, Gräfin Elena?'

'Why yes – Hatton is quite near to Manchester, Frau Gehring.'

'Good, good. When you leave Munich you will study with my friend Madame Goldman – we often sang together when we were younger; she is contralto, as is this girl, "Waltraute Jenkins" – is not that a good name for a contralto?' I stared at Frau Gehring, disbelieving. 'I do not tell a lie, Gräfin, there, look.' She held out a letter: it was signed in a strong clear hand: "Waltraute Gladys Jenkins".

'Pa really loves his Wagner, but they call me Wally at home,' Miss Jenkins explained. She was tall and broad-shouldered, with a squashed snub nose and a wispy bun of mouse-coloured hair. Her toothy smile was engaging; her manner so open, that I took to her at once. Everybody liked Wally Jenkins; even Fraulein unbent a little when we met her at Frau Gehring's studio. Wally was twenty-three and strode through Munich in her sturdy black boots with her shabby coat flapping as if she feared nothing. She stood in the pit through the longest of operas, refusing politely but firmly my offer that she accompany Fraulein and myself as our guest. 'Thank you kindly, Lady Helena, but I prefer to be independent.'

Wally had a deep, rich, contralto. Elsa Gehring taught us a little duet, and we sang it together at the students' concert. I was grateful for her company as we waited in the wings, but once on stage my fears melted away. Frau Gehring had taught me well: I knew how to sing.

Mother insisted that I travelled back to London that summer in time for the Coronation. I watched her step gracefully down the staircase at Cadogan Place, swathed in cloth of gold, her coronet perched on her shining dark hair, Fisher holding up the heavy ermine-trimmed velvet behind her. Papa, resplendent in knee breeches and all his decorations, held out his arm, and the two coroneted heads ducked carefully into the gilded state coach, and drove off to the Abbey.

This summer I did make the hot dusty journey out to the streets of west London to see Miss Ling. Her tired face lit up as the little maid-of-all-work ushered me into the stuffy back parlour. My maid slipped away to the kitchen, and for a moment I felt dreadfully shy, but Miss Ling's interest in all the doings of our family was so familiar, so genuine, that the last two years slipped away, and I chatted to her as easily as ever.

Papa had become very friendly with a businessman called Benson. Alice said to me, 'He's never averse to the nouveaux riches. Especially when they *are* rich,' she added tartly. The Bensons certainly were rich. Alice and Hugh had been to stay with them at their place in Surrey: 'Quite palatial, Hellie – totally vulgar, of course, but personally I've nothing against gold taps when the water that comes out of them is piping hot. And do you know, they have *six* bathrooms, just fancy that! With two more just for the servants. And when we were there just after Christmas the whole house was warm! Mother sniped at Lucy Benson and told her how unhealthy central heating was, but I notice she's been sending for catalogues ever since. Don't get too optimistic, though, she'll never instal radiators at Hatton, she's far too mean. That's one of the reasons why the Girvans are "anciens riches" – that and Papa's unfashionable obsession with making even more money.'

I said, 'But Papa insists that this new Liberal Budget will ruin him – I'm sure he means it, he looks quite drawn.'

Alice snorted. 'Wait till you want to get married, Helena, and he has to discuss settlements – then you'll see how drawn he can look when he tries! Hugh told me he got his handkerchief out at one point: he thought Papa was going to break down and sob in the middle of the library. Still, he did cough up in the end, thank goodness – it's bad enough as it is, having to live in London all the year round.' She looked discontentedly round her pretty drawing room. 'I do wish Hugh could get some nice fat briefs.'

Mother told me Mr Benson had been very useful to Papa, and I must entertain Pansy Benson, who was just a year younger than I was. 'It's time you made a girlfriend, Helena, you spend far too much of your time with your brothers.' Pansy – how could I make a friend of a girl called Pansy! I decided to be very cool.

But it was impossible to dislike Pansy Benson. She was sweet and silly and kind, and she gazed at me in awe when Mother told her I was studying music and singing in Munich. 'How brave – I could never go abroad without Mumsy. Oh, you must sing for us, Lady Helena. Do say you will.'

I took her off to the music room and sang my aria, while her eyes went wider and wider in admiration. 'You must meet Lance, Lance is so musical.' Lance was her only brother; she adored him. But she told me that she thought *my* brother the handsomest, cleverest, bravest man in the whole world – after Lance, of course. 'But' – blushing – 'Lord Muirkirk is so different.'

Guy came into the drawing room soon after, and Pansy's round blue eyes followed his every move. He came over to speak to us, and she blushed and stammered inarticulately; I felt a wave of fellow feeling. Guy treated her like a child, but Pansy did not seem to mind; she gazed at him adoringly, even when he was obviously flirting with Eileen Fox. I decided Pansy was like the girl in the second part of *"Frauen Liebe und Leben"*, who looked so humbly at her loved one that she could promise to bless his chosen bride many thousand times. But I hoped Eileen would not be Guy's bride: she was not half nice enough for him.

Pansy's brother Lance arrived. He had the long serious face of a scholar, and he was an excellent pianist; he was soon acting as my accompanist. Plump, kindly Mrs Benson asked me to sing every evening; Mother smiled with her mouth and agreed. The other guests drifted in and out of the music room, but Lance and I were happy with the Steinway. He was exactly the same age as I was: we would both be eighteen in September. He wanted to visit Germany or Austria to study music now he had left school, but Mr Benson was insisting that he go on to Sandhurst. He said to me quietly one day, 'I don't want to be a soldier, Lady Helena, but Father is adamant.' He gave a wry, self-deprecating smile. 'If I'm not brave enough to stand up to my own father – how will I ever lead a charge against the enemy?' He turned his attention back to the piano. 'I don't think my cadenza was quite right in this piece – will you listen and correct me?'

Then suddenly everyone was talking about an international crisis – over Morocco, of all places. We British were very angry with the Germans – the Chancellor of the Exchequer made a speech at the Mansion House – I knew it was serious because Papa actually had a good word to say for Mr Lloyd George. 'Time these Germans were put in their place – who do they think they are, trying to compete with the British Navy?'

The twins became very excited and talked of war. I told them not to be so silly. 'We'd never fight against Germany – besides, you would have to shoot Franzl – you wouldn't want that, would you?'

Eddie put down the billiard cue he was aiming at the stuffed stag's head and said that girls just did not understand.

I went back to Munich as usual at the beginning of August. Nobody seemed at all interested in Morocco; instead the whole town was abuzz with the story of how Herr Mottle had collapsed in the middle of conducting a performance of *Tristan*, and on his very deathbed had married Fraulein Fassbender, the famous soprano. 'How sad,' 'Such a terrible loss,' 'Ah, he was dedicated to Wagner – it was as he would have wished.' I slipped easily back into Fraulein's steady routine as if I had never been away.

Papa told Eddie and Robbie they were old enough now to come by themselves to Munich, so for the third Christmas we went to the theatre and frequented the cafés and skated on the frozen meadows. I begged them for news of Stavey's uncle – they told me he had run down to Windsor on the previous Fourth, with Lady Staveley, Stavey's mother – he had asked after me – but it was hopeless; they could not remember the exact words he had used. They said Stavey thought a lot of him, and he had been no end of a swell in South Africa; he hunted in the Shires every year, was a good sort – and that was all.

I shed tears when the time came in March for me to say goodbye to Munich. I clung to Franzl, and Gretchen, who had maided me; I embraced Frau Reinmar and kissed all the old ladies of the pension; Elsa Gehring hugged me and told me not to forget to practise every day, and even Fraulein unbent to kiss my cheeks before she waved me off from the Central Station.

As we sat back in our compartment at Dover, Fisher said, 'You'll be looking forward to your first Season now, my lady.' It was a statement, not a question, but suddenly I was not sure. For a moment I longed to return to the safe enclosed world of Munich. Once I was Out there would be no going back: my girlhood was over. But then I thought of Lord Gerald, and excitement rippled through me.

CHAPTER THREE

Mother planned my first Season like a general planning a campaign. She made it very clear that she saw herself in the role of an experienced commander saddled with a particularly inadequate subaltern – but she was determined to do her duty. She escorted me to corsetière and dressmaker in an attempt to remedy the deficiencies of my figure. 'I had hoped that eating all those German Kuchen would make some difference to your bosom, Helena – and your neck seems longer than ever: perhaps all that singing has stretched it.'

She engaged a smart French maid for me, who

wrestled with my hair: 'Miladi, feefty 'airpins – 'ow is eet possible? But eet is so slippery!' I cringed. Liliane volubly urged assistance to my complexion: 'Miladi is so pale – a leetle rouge?'

My mother pursed her lips, then regretfully shook her head. 'I think not for a debutante, Liliane. We will just have to bear with it.' I stood, flushed and humiliated, as my mother bemoaned yet again the unfortunate tilt of my nose. 'And the Girvan mouth, Helena, far too full in a young girl – and those eyebrows!' She shuddered. Liliane eagerly seized a pair of tweezers and advanced purposefully, but my mother restrained her. 'No, thinner eyebrows would only draw attention to the size of her mouth. Their shape is not too unsatisfactory, just do the best you can.' She stood up and swept out of my bedroom.

After she had gone Liliane said, tentatively, 'Miladi has long thick eyelashes, and beeg dark eyes – this is good.' I blinked to hold back the tears from flooding my "beeg dark eyes" as the pale oval in the mirror blurred.

My presentation day arrived. I drove with Mother to the Palace, the three ridiculous ostrich feathers bobbing on my hair, swathed in white satin from head to toe. I was rigid with fear; the whole occasion was like a night-mare and I committed the ultimate sin and touched the royal hand with my nose. Afterwards I sat on a spindly gold chair as the other debutantes made their curtseys, longing desperately for the water closet – the long dressing and the three-hour wait had been too much for me; now my belly ached.

When I got back to Cadogan Place I found that Liliane had thrown away my girl's corset. Standing imprisoned in my rigid boned stays I shed tears for the loss of that threadbare old bodice, of my swinging pigtails, of my short free skirts. Liliane shook out my evening frock and I stood like a dressmaker's dummy while she buttoned and hooked and tied; then pushed me down

116

on to a chair and began the endless back-combing needed to make my too-fine hair hold its shape.

A hairpin fell into my soup that night; I looked desperately round to see if Mother had noticed, but with a flick of a napkin and the flicker of an eyelid the footman retrieved it; I glanced back at him gratefully. Then I sat on at the table, tongue-tied and embarrassed between two elegant young men who tossed the odd comment towards my plate before turning back to the cleverer, wittier women on their other sides. Mother spoke to me angrily afterwards: 'Why do you have to look so *sullen*, Helena, whenever you're in company? Young men won't dance with sulky girls.'

I told myself I did not want to dance with "young men", only with one man – I did not care about the others. But I did care when the surge of the crowd carried me back partnerless into the ballroom at the beginning of a dance. Mother had berated me before she left for the card room: 'Why can't you be more *welcoming*, Helena, *smile* – and when you're dancing you must talk to your partner. Goodness knows, I don't expect you to be witty, but at least say something.'

But I could never think of anything. In Munich we had talked of practical matters – the food, the weather, the singers at the opera – it had been so simple there; and besides I could always shelter behind Fraulein. Now I stood alone and defenceless at the entrance to the brightly lit ballroom, watching the be-frilled dresses swirl past, each happy, girlish face smiling up at the man who held her. I turned and almost ran down the corridor to the cloakroom.

It was Alice, arriving late, who found me still hiding there. She shook her head. 'Oh Hellie, you really are feeble! Well, come along with me now and I'll lend you Hugh – I don't want him cramping my style all evening.'

Alice thrust me at Hugh, with, 'Here's a wallflower for you,' then glided past. He stared wistfully after her, before pulling his shoulders back and turning to me with

117

a smile. 'Would you like to dance, Helena?' I gulped a 'Thank you'.

As we danced sedately round the room Alice flashed past in the arms of a broad bronzed man with side whiskers; she was talking animatedly, gazing up into his eyes. Hugh said abruptly, 'Alice is seeing a lot of Danesford these days.' I did not reply. At last he heaved a sigh, looked down at me and said, 'I tell you what, Hellie, I'll take you round and introduce you to some nice young men – how about that?' He smiled at me warmly and I felt a rush of affection for dear, solid Hugh.

Dances got a little easier after that. Hugh must have spoken to Guy; my brother turned up rather shamefacedly in several ballrooms with a covey of fellow officers in tow.

Through the long hot Season I longed for a glimpse of Lord Gerald Prescott. My eyes searched the crowded rooms, and any sleek fair head would set my heart thumping. Then, one evening, he did appear. I was dancing with Lance Benson when I saw him; as soon as the music stopped I steered Lance up to the other end of the room and dived into the throng next to Lord Gerald. But he politely stepped to one side without even looking at me, and I was mortified. I snapped at Lance when he asked for another dance, and went dismally in to supper.

I was pushing a strawberry ice round my plate when a voice said, 'It is Lady Helena, isn't it?' I turned so quickly my ice slipped dangerously; blue eyes were smiling at me and I felt as if I were drowning. He murmured a few words about going down to Eton, to see his nephew, and said my brothers were well – then the band struck up again. I gazed wistfully up at him and he suddenly smiled, saying, 'You look just like your twins when they're standing outside the sock-shop wondering if they can afford strawberries and cream – would you care to dance?'

I breathed, 'Oh, please,' and put my hand on his arm. As we moved away I glimpsed Lance's dismayed face – I had promised him the dance after supper – but I fixed my gaze firmly ahead and walked on.

It was a waltz. Lord Gerald danced stiffly but correctly. 'Do you reverse?' I nodded and we executed a decorous turn. He made the conventional remarks about the heat and the pleasant flowers, then lapsed into silence. I searched desperately for something to say, but my mind was a blank. I could not believe that it was his arm round my waist and his gloved hand holding mine.

When the music stopped he bowed politely. 'May I escort you back to your Mama?'

'No – she's in the card room – she won't want to be interrupted – please just leave me here.'

He raised his eyebrows a fraction, then smiled. 'I see I'm being old-fashioned. You youngsters hardly need chaperons these days. You know, it's so long since I last danced, I had to concentrate on the steps rather hard. I'm so glad you didn't keep chattering, or I should have been quite distracted. Thank you for your understanding – goodnight, Lady Helena.'

I gazed after him in a daze of wonder. My hero, I had actually danced with my god-like hero, and he had thanked me for being understanding!

A hand touched my elbow. 'I thought that was to be *our* dance, Lady Helena.' It was Lance Benson's reproachful voice.

I started. 'Oh, I am sorry – but I . . .'

'Well, may I have this one, instead?'

'Of course – it doesn't matter.'

His face flushed, then he said in a hurt voice, 'Actually, it does matter to me, Lady Helena.'

I felt so guilty I said impulsively, 'Please, do call me Helena, Pansy does.' His sweet smile warmed his face, and he pulled me closer.

A week later Lance Benson proposed. He knelt before me in the drawing room, his eyes shining and hopeful.

At last I muttered, 'I'm sorry, but I . . . oh Lance, I do *like* you so much, but . . .'

'That's a start, Helena.' He reached for my hand.

I drew back quickly. 'No, you see – there's someone else.' He dropped my fingers as though they were red hot. At last he said rather thickly, 'That fellow you were dancing with the other evening?'

'Yes.'

'But, Helena, forgive me – but does he feel the same way about you?'

I could not answer. Finally I whispered, 'That doesn't make any difference, it's how *I* feel, you see.'

'Yes, I do see.' He got slowly to his feet and stood looking down at me for a long time. Then he said, 'Helena, if there's ever anything I can do for you, send for me, wherever I am. I'll always come, always.'

'Thank you, Lance.'

He picked up his hat and gloves and left; I went upstairs and cried.

All through that summer it seemed as if every minute of each day was mapped out. I tried to do my singing exercises, but so often I was interrupted; Mother sent for me to go for another fitting at the dressmaker's, or to make the interminable calls. In the morning I was just too tired, after coming back from a dance at the time when men in rubber boots were hosing down the streets ready for the new day.

I sang my aria and knew that it was no longer pure and true. In desperation I told Mother that I had promised I would go and see Miss Ling; with a bad grace she let me go out to Hammersmith one afternoon, where I poured out my troubles to my old governess. Miss Ling was reassuring: she told me that for the time being I must do as my mother wished, but then, at the end of the Season, perhaps I could go to the lady whom Frau Gehring had recommended in Manchester. I felt calmer as I travelled back to the West End and later Miss Ling wrote and suggested that if I was in London during the winter perhaps I would like to come and sing with her local music circle. I was grateful, and decided then and there that I would go if I possibly could.

I begged Mother to take me down to Eton on the Fourth of June; I longed to see the twins – and perhaps *he* would be there, visiting his nephew. But Mother insisted she had a previous engagement, and all I could secure were vague promises for next year. Next year! That was a lifetime away.

I cried tears of frustration when the twins' next letter arrived: 'Guess who ran down on the Fourth to see Stavey!! Serves you right, Big Sis, for neglecting your baby brothers!' I screwed up the letter and rang for Liliane – it was time for my daily walk in the park.

My depression did not lift; the dusty leaves drooped on the trees and the grass was brown and dried up. I hated stuffy, dirty London – I wanted to go home. I walked slowly, eyes on the ground, and scarcely noticed at first when Liliane touched my elbow. Then she spoke, 'Miladi – a gentleman – signalling to you.' I raised my head and there he was – just a few yards away, coming straight towards me. I gaped at him for a moment, my mind in a whirl: the shock had taken my breath away. Once I understood I was so dizzy with ecstasy I clung to Liliane's arm for support. Then my eyes focused on the elegant female figure beside him, and my joy vanished.

'Good afternoon, Lady Helena. I hope you don't mind my stopping you, but I thought you would like to know how those young rascals of brothers of yours are getting on – I spent some time with them on the Fourth. But first, introductions are in order – Moira my dear, may I present Lady Helena Girvan?' Jealousy stabbed my heart as the cool grey eyes appraised me. I reached out a shaking hand to the spotless kid glove. He continued, 'Lady Helena, my sister-in-law, Lady Staveley.' My legs began to shake and I nearly sank to the gravel path in my relief.

121

Lady Staveley smiled. 'I met your brothers last week – how very like them you are.' I stammered a reply, and then managed to ask after her son. She gave a little frown. 'Poor Arthur's always been a touch delicate – his chest is weak, so he often has a cough.'

I thought of my strong healthy brothers and said quickly, 'Oh, I *am* so sorry, how worrying for you.'

Her eyes warmed a moment. Then she pressed Lord Gerald's arm. 'Gerald, we mustn't detain Lady Helena any longer – but I'm so glad to have met you, my dear.'

With a parting smile he was gone. I stood quite still, giddy with excitement; he had sought me out, he had introduced me to his sister-in-law! A small breeze rippled the green leaves above me and the sun shone in the glorious blue sky. I wanted to sing to the heavens of my love.

Liliane's fractured accent brought me down to earth. 'Miladi, you are going out to dinner tonight – it is time we return.' Obediently I started to move towards the Albert Gate.

I haunted the area around the Albert Gate every afternoon for a week, but I never saw him there again.

CHAPTER FOUR

Town seemed to become hotter and hotter, and I felt more and more fagged, but at last in July London began to empty. The Eton and Harrow match at Lords, the Regatta at Henley, the Goodwood Races – all the signs of the ending of the Season came and went. In August, Mother, indefatigable as ever, moved on to Cowes, and finally I was allowed to go back to Cheshire with my brothers. Never had the park seemed lovelier and more peaceful; I felt like a fish which had for too long been flapping out of water, and had now been tossed back into its familiar lake.

The twins came with me to Manchester and we sought out Madame Goldman. Calm, almost phlegmatic, she was a patient teacher, and as we worked together my voice came steadily back under control. After three weeks I sang my aria for her and when I had finished she nodded. 'Good, that is as Elsa would wish it.' And suddenly I burst into tears and sobbed with relief. Madame Goldman patted my shoulder. 'Silly girl, how could you expect to sing well when you stayed up until all hours in London – dancing in hot stuffy rooms which make your poor head ache? You will be wiser next year.' I vowed to myself that I would.

Papa came back from shooting grouse in Yorkshire, Mother wrote to say she was moving on to Marienbad, and on the first of September the partridge season opened. Alice came up to act as hostess for the shooting party and brought her two boys – it was like old times to run up to the nursery and find Nanny ensconced in her battered wicker armchair.

Letty's governess went on holiday and Letty announced she was going to join in the shoot. Alice argued with her but my younger sister was completely immovable – she said one of the underkeepers had been giving her lessons and the boys had gone out with the guns at twelve so she was jolly well going to do the same. Alice appealed to Papa, but he only said, 'Oh, let her make a fool of herself if she wants to!' So she stumped out to the butts, pigtailed and determined between the twins. When Alice and I arrived with the ladies at lunch Letty was in possession of quite a respectable bag. Alice's lips tightened, but she said nothing – but later I heard a sharp squeal from behind the game cart and saw Alice flouncing back with a look of satisfaction on her face and a red-faced, defiant Letty in her wake.

'Your daughter,' Alice said very loudly to Papa, 'was smoking a cigarette – in the company of the underkeepers!' Her voice rose and she sounded exactly like Mother.

Papa went red and said to Letty quite firmly, 'That's not on, my girl, not on at all – if you want to shoot you must toe the line – otherwise I'll send for your governess.'

Letty still looked mutinous, but she kept her mouth shut until Papa had walked away, then she turned to me, muttered '*Whose* daughter, anyway?' and stalked off. Alice was right: Letty spent far too much time gossiping with the servants.

The twins went back to Eton for their last year, Mother returned to Hatton and Papa left for more shooting in Scotland. Guy bought me a new bay mare for my birthday; I christened her Melody and planned to take her out cub-hunting.

Lady Maud came up to Cheshire; she had taken a small house near Hareford and brought both her daughters with her: tall, square-shouldered Juno and small, giggly Julia. Juno was like her mother, she lived for hunting – whenever I had seen her in London she had been striding across parquet-floored ballrooms swinging her fan as if it were a riding crop, her face sulky and bored. But as soon as the cub-hunting season started she came alive again and we often rode out together in the mist or drizzle of the autumn morning. Lady Maud came out with us sometimes, and Papa's old friend and neighbour Sam Killearn.

Mother talked ominously of taking me on visits, but I begged to stay for the November meets of the Cheshire Hunt; grudgingly she agreed, and left for Suffolk without me. As soon as she had gone, Letty announced that from now on she was going to ride astride. I told her she would look ridiculous, and never be able to keep her seat, but, being Letty, she took absolutely no notice. She had a fall at the opening meet, but that only made her more obstinate. She even boasted of how much more easily she had managed to remount with a cross saddle

– 'None of this hanging around for a man to put me up – or fiddling with lengthening the stirrups when the rest of the field's racing ahead – much simpler.'

Juno said scornfully, 'You'd never have come off in the first place if you'd had your knee wrapped round a leaping head.'

Letty tossed her plaits. 'It won't happen again.' She limped out of the stables.

Juno shrugged. 'Still, at least she's got more spunk than my sister – Julia's always whingeing at the odd bruise or a few splashes of mud. Come on, Helena, where's this tea you offered me? I'm certainly ready for it.'

Conan came up to hunt for a few weeks; he stayed over at Sam Killearn's. He told me one day that Mother had banned him from Hatton while I was there without her. He grinned. 'She's probably right not to trust us – you look very tempting in that habit, young Helena!'

I retorted angrily, 'She need have no fears on *my* behalf.'

Conan was unabashed. He leant forward and whispered, 'You were ready enough in the maze that evening.'

I turned Melody's head quickly away as the hot shame engulfed me. I was different now.

Mother came back before Christmas and told me I was turning into a recluse, so she was drawing up a programme of visits for me. Accompanied by a mountain of luggage and a delighted Liliane, I set off. Every visit was a new ordeal, but towards the end of January I went down to the Bensons' and Pansy asked me to stay on after the main party had left. She and her mother fluttered kindly round me and I felt at ease with them; I sang every evening after dinner and Lance came at the weekend and accompanied me; he seemed almost like one of my brothers. Guy ran down from Town to see me on the Sunday. Pansy hung on his every word and gazed up at him adoringly with her round blue eyes –

and suddenly my longing to see Lord Gerald Prescott was so sharp that it hurt.

In February I did see him. Alice left Hugh in London and took me to stay at Melton with Sir John and Lady Eames. We were there for a fortnight so Papa sent down Melody and one of his own hunters for Alice, and I was thrilled at the thought of hunting with the prestigious Quorn.

We had two glorious runs, but I had to leave each one at lunchtime, so as not to over-tire Melody. Our host saw me looking enviously at the second horsemen arriving and offered to lend me an extra mount for the next meet. I accepted quickly.

We drove over to the next meet; the grooms had arrived before us. Melody whickered as she saw me and I spoke to her and stroked her velvet muzzle before I bent down to check that her girths had been tightened. Then the groom led her over to the block and held her head while I mounted.

The air was crisp and clear. I glanced through the fine silk mesh of my veil at the other riders – several of the ladies were wearing bowlers, Papa would have been shocked; he always insisted on our wearing top hats. And there was a noticeable wrinkle in Mrs Taunton's skirt – just over her right knee; I glanced smugly down at my own immaculately smooth habit. Then, as the riders shifted, I spotted yet another too-short jacket over a too-large behind and shook my head in disapproval.

Alice came up beside me and followed my gaze. 'I know – even in the Shires you see some sights. Papa may have his faults but he's never skimped on our habits, I'm glad to say – nothing but the best Melton for his daughters. Hugh complains now, but I tell him I just am not prepared to look a fright on the hunting field, even if he is a struggling barrister. Oh, Hellie, look at the fit over those shoulders!' She shook her head disapprovingly, then turned her eyes on me. 'I must say, Helena, that Mother can bemoan the boyishness of your figure as much as she likes, but it means you look absolutely splendid on horseback – you're quite the best-looking girl here today. Ah, there's Jimmy.' She clicked her tongue to her chestnut and moved away. I gazed after her, glowing with gratitude. A gentleman with his back to me reined in to let her pass – and as he leant to pat the neck of his horse I saw a clean-cut profile and the glint of a golden moustache. My breath caught in my throat – it was Lord Gerald.

But there was no time to think – the hounds were moving off to the first draw. Silence fell as we waited beside the covert, then there was a sudden flash of tan, the huntsman sounded the "Gone Away" and we were off. I headed straight for the first fence. Melody was over it cleanly and easily and the hounds settled down to a steady pace on the scent. In the next field I spotted the hunt members moving towards the gate in the corner and followed quickly – then I was off and galloping across the pasture in front. It sloped away from me quite steeply but I leant back and gave Melody plenty of rein and took her straight down. We stretched out as soon as we reached the level again, and rode for the thorn fence at the bottom. A voice close behind me called: 'Take care, there's a blind ditch on the other side.' I saw Lord Gerald fly over the thorn ahead of me and gave Melody a squeeze with my leg, then let her have her head. I felt her land a fraction short – her hind legs were in the ditch – I threw myself forward, and it was enough; we were off over the heavy ridge and furrow. The blood sang in my ears in tune with the pounding of Melody's hooves. I was wild with exhilaration as we galloped across country.

The fox ran well but the hounds finally killed in the open, and I was there with the leaders. I closed my eyes as the huntsman's knife flashed and the pack tore the rest of the small brown body to pieces. An amused voice said, 'You can open them now, Lady Helena, it's all over.' It was Lord Gerald, with a smile on his mud-spattered face. As I blushed for my squeamishness he spoke again. 'That's a nice little mare you've got there – well trained.'

At last I found my voice. 'Yes, she was a birthday present from Guy – my eldest brother.'

He smiled again, raised his topper and rode off. I felt as though the gates of heaven had opened for me. Then Alice appeared beside me, looking beautiful and irritated. 'That idiot Jimmy Danesford claims he's twisted his ankle – I might as well have brought Hugh to Melton with me – at least he can stay on a horse. Ah, thank goodness, the refreshments are here.'

I turned and saw that the second horsemen had arrived with flasks and sandwiches. I found Sir John's groom and handed Melody over to him; then he bent to put me up on my borrowed horse, a rangy grey.

The grey stood placidly enough while we waited for the hounds to draw, but as soon as we moved off, I felt a shock of dismay as I realized I could not hold him – his mouth was so hard he took me just where he liked – all I could do was hang on. I jostled a red-faced man at a fence and only had time to shout, 'Sorry!' to his angry glare before my mount was off again, pounding tirelessly up a steep slope.

We ran over several fields without a check; I could not steer my horse towards the gates – he took the timber every time until unwittingly I found myself at the front, close behind the Master. I prayed for a really heavy ridge and furrow, but none came. Instead, as we reached open pasture the hounds bowled their fox over – and my hard-mouthed grey carried me straight into the middle of them! I was buffeted by a torrent of abuse from the Master as I fought for control amidst the snarling, yapping pack. I finally managed to haul my grey out of the mêlée, and now the damage was done he stopped dead under me so I had to sit, head bowed and crimson with shame, while the rest of the field streamed up to witness my humiliation. I knew Lord Gerald had been among the leaders; I could not look up. A tear of utter misery plopped on to my glove. I heard a rider come up beside me and glanced up, then looked hastily down again – it was Lord Gerald.

'You'll never hold him in an ordinary double bridle – you must tell the groom to put him in a segundo next time.' I bit my lip, and to my horror a second betraying blob spread out on my glove. 'Cheer up, Lady Helena – it could have been worse!' I swallowed desperately, but I could not reply. He moved closer still and said, confidentially, 'I'll wager *you*'ve never headed the fox!' Slowly I shook my head, and dared to raise my eyes. He was smiling. 'You know *I* did, when I was about your age – it was over with the Pytchley, right at the start of the run – I thought the Master was going to burst a blood vessel, he was so furious with me! I didn't know where to put myself – and Staveley, my brother, was out too that day and he laughed so much he had to dismount.'

I said slowly, 'I suppose the twins would have done the same, if they'd been here and seen me.' I felt a little warmer.

He grinned. 'And it was worse for me, you know, because I'd just been gazetted to the Life Guards, so old Wroughton wound up his peroration with: "You call yourself a cavalryman – you'd do better riding the washerwoman's mangle!" '

'How awful for you,' I breathed.

'The whole field heard him, and when we embarked for South Africa, just a few months later, a crowd of friends came to see us off, and one of them cupped his hands round his mouth and bellowed out from the quay just as we were casting off: "Staveley, have you packed the washerwoman's mangle for Prescott to ride?" ' He threw back his head and laughed. 'How I cursed them! Come along, the horses are getting cold – can you manage that brute now? I think your party are waiting for you.'

As he turned his horse away. I called quickly, 'Thank

you, thank you so much, Lord Gerald.' He smiled to me, raised his hat and cantered off.

Sir John apologized and said he would speak to the groom. I said quickly, 'It doesn't matter, really it doesn't.'

We set off for home and I rode in a happy dream as the short winter afternoon drew to its close. We jogged through a small village: lamps were being lit in cottage windows, little boys ran out to watch us and rooks cawed overhead as the church bells began to peal out for a practice. I felt utterly at peace with the world.

CHAPTER FIVE

But the next Season I scarcely saw him. Once we were at the same dinner party, but he was further up the table. It was very late before the gentlemen joined us, and then he stayed up at the far end of the big drawing room talking to a dark-haired young man. I longed for him to look in my direction, but he was engrossed in his conversation. I watched the movements of his finely shaped mouth avidly, and wished I were near enough to eavesdrop, but Mother was exchanging gossip with Lady Maud and did not move. They spoke in undertones, but I heard the names "Alice" and "young Danesford", so I guessed what they were talking about. Now I looked over again at Lord Gerald and vowed that I would always be true to him, whether he cared for me or not.

I saw him in the distance at Covent Garden, looking so very elegant. He was talking animatedly to the same young man and I felt a surge of relief that, apart from his sister-in-law, I had never seen him in the company of a woman. I could not have borne it.

I was happier in my second Season. Mother was less

relentless – or perhaps just bored with debutantes' balls. She would let me go out with only Guy as a chaperon, and he was pursuing the sophisticated Eileen Fox, so I often did not see him all evening. But I would dance with his friends or with Lance, or Conan, who was in Town a lot that year. One day my cousin introduced me to a tall, fair young man, 'This is Bron, Hellie – Bron Nichols – we were in the same house at school. He's a ruddy awful dancer but I know you're not that fussy!' Bron Nichols had blond curly hair and guileless blue eyes set in the face of a mournful angel – he looked much too virtuous to be a friend of Conan's but they seemed to be on the best of terms.

I used to dance for as long as I wanted to; then, when I had had enough, I would ask the footman to call a motor cab and set off for home. I would bowl through the dark streets on my own behind the driver and reflect on how stupid it was that in the daytime I was not allowed to step outside the front door without a maid yet after midnight nobody inquired as to how I got back. If Mother were entertaining at home I would call through the letter box, and the footman on hall duty would fetch Cooper to pay the cab, then I would whisper to the butler, 'Please don't tell Lady Pickering that I'm back so early.' He would nod conspiratorially, and throw open the green baize door so that I could creep unnoticed up the back stairs.

Liliane escorted me to my singing lessons early in the morning. Madame Goldman had recommended to me a small fiery Italian, and I generally managed two or three lessons with him each week. Papa paid his bills uncomplainingly, since he knew Mother disapproved.

Pansy came out that year, and Mrs Benson often took me with their party to the opera. In April, Covent Garden celebrated Wagner's centenary with the whole of the Ring Cycle; in May Caruso came to London and I heard him sing in *Pagliacci*.

We applauded Melba rapturously on her twenty-fifth

anniversary, and I managed to persuade Guy to take me to her single performance in *La Traviata*. A Saint-Saëns season followed – we glimpsed the composer himself; then it was five weeks of Russian opera at Drury Lane. Whenever Lance came too, the pair of us would dissect the performance afterwards bar by bar – until Pansy screamed at us to stop.

Miss Ling kept her promise and invited me to join her local music circle. They held a small concert every month, and I rehearsed and sang with them regularly. After my second concert the secretary asked me whether I would be available to sing the soprano part in their *Messiah* next Christmas. I was so thrilled, I said "yes" at once.

Dances were more fun with Conan in Town; it was like having an extra brother. I told him that, one evening, after he had rescued me from a sweaty-palmed German princeling who had pursued me through three dances because I spoke German and he knew no English. Conan bowed and laughed and plied me with champagne, then said that as a brother he must see me safely home. He insisted he preferred an old-fashioned growler and I realized why as soon as we had set off – he slid his arm round my shoulders and began to kiss me. Dizzy with dancing and too much champagne, I savoured his warm mouth on mine and our tongues met, until I felt I was drowning in sweetness. Then, outside, a man spoke to a friend; and something in the clipped tones recalled Lord Gerald's voice. At once I pushed Conan violently away in anger and revulsion: 'How dare you, how dare you!' I hit out at him; he sat back in his corner fending off my blows until I began to cry. Then he said impatiently, 'For goodness' sake, Helena, it was only one kiss between cousins – don't be so childish.'

I hated him – he had made me betray my hero. But in bed that night I hated myself even more.

Towards the end of May the twins wrote to ask if we would be coming down to Eton on the Fourth of June

– it would be their last. I reminded Mother of her promise and she looked furtive, then said she could not go after all. I exclaimed, 'But Mother, you promised – last year you promised!'

For once she seemed almost apologetic. 'But I didn't know the Derby would be on the fourth this year – I'm sorry, Helena, it's really impossible for me to go.'

Just this once I dared to argue. 'But it's the twins' last Fourth!'

'If you're so set on going I'll see if I can find someone else to take you. That's the best I can do, Helena.' She left the room with a swish of skirts.

Two days later she told me that Eileen Fox's mother would take me with her party, and Guy could go with us too. Guy was so pleased at this that he offered to escort me to the Trooping the Colour the day before: his Grenadiers were not involved this year.

I sat in the stands looking down at the hollow square of troops on Horse Guards Parade, my heart thumping as I watched Captain Lord Gerald Prescott, splendid in his scarlet tunic and gold cuirass, commanding his squadron of the First Life Guards on the south side. My eyes were glued to him all through the ceremony; I never even looked at the King, or Lord Roberts. And tomorrow, surely, the Fates would be kind and I would see him again at Eton?

Next day Eileen Fox was dark and dramatic in a sheath of flame-coloured satin, her complexion vivid under an enormous hat, and I felt like a schoolgirl in my pale pink linen. In the railway carriage she and her two girlfriends chattered like a flock of starlings, whilst I sat and watched my brother compete with the other young men for a glance from Eileen's flashing eyes, listening enviously to the sparkling volleys of repartee.

I saw the twins as soon as we drew into Windsor. They were both in Pop now so they were resplendent in gaudy waistcoats, blobs of sealing wax adorning their top hats, and the two of them sported enormous floral buttonholes. I jumped up, wrenched open the door and was out before the train had properly stopped. 'Eddie, Robbie!' I hugged them alternately, dancing from one to the other in my excitement until I heard Eileen's amused drawl, of 'I certainly hope Tommy's not expecting a reception like that from me!' and jumped back, embarrassed.

My twins doffed their toppers, 'Morning Mrs Fox, Miss Fox – young Reynard's down on the field somewhere – he told us to tell you. Come on, Big Sis, we'll show you round.' Feeling very smug I linked arms with my two tall brothers and walked off between them.

When we arrived Eddie said, 'You don't want to bother with speeches, they're pretty dull – we'll show you the sights instead.' Robbie added, 'We've arranged for you to have lunch with us and Stavey – Foxy Reynard's in a different house.' Eddie broke in, 'And guess whose Uncle Gerald came by the earlier train?' as Robbie finished smoothly, 'We do hope that suits you!'

I breathed, 'Oh, yes Robbie – perfectly.'

Eddie raised his eyebrows exaggeratedly. 'You know, Robert John George, I begin to suspect our dear sister had an ulterior motive in coming down today.' 'I do believe, Edwin John Alfred, that you might just be right.'

I blushed furiously. 'I don't know what you mean!'

'We mean that with Guy goggling at Reynard's sister . . .' 'And you goggling at Stavey's uncle,' 'Nobody loves us at all!' they ended in dismal chorus.

'Oh I do, I do.' I hugged their arms in dismay until they both burst out laughing and I began to laugh as well. The bright green leaves of the lime trees danced against the pink bricks of Upper School and my heart danced with them.

Lord Staveley came shyly to meet us at the house. 'Good morning, Lady Helena. Uncle Gerald sent his apologies, he's lunching with the Provost'. ('With the Nobs,' Eddie helpfully explained.) 'He said I must be your host for luncheon.' He paused, uncertain, and I realized my face had fallen at his news.

I pulled myself together quickly. 'That will be delightful, Lord Staveley, and I'm relying on you to show me round properly – these two are hopeless, they just say "That's the chapel over there" and head off in the opposite direction!' The face of the boy in front of me lit up. He was younger and slighter than my brothers and I felt suddenly protective. 'And please, do call me Helena – I feel as if I've known you for years.'

His thin face flushed. 'I'm Stavey to everybody – except Mama, she calls me Arthur . . .'

Eddie was brutal. 'Well, we're not calling you Arthur, like that curly-haired twit in *Uncle Tom's Schooldays*. He'll answer to Stavey, Helena, or a short sharp whistle.' He pulled the corners of his mouth out and emitted a hideous screech until I kicked him hard on the shin bone. He screamed and danced around in an agonized parody while Robbie said kindly, 'Just see how lucky you are, Stavey, not having any sisters.' I put my heel down firmly on the toe of his boot, and slipping my hand through Stavey's arm said, 'Shall we go into luncheon, Arthur?'

Stavey closed his mouth with a surprised click, then with a blushing smile replied, 'With pleasure – Helena.'

Lunch was salmon and cucumber, chicken in aspic and an incredible pie with a ring of pigeons' legs apparently diving straight through the pastry crust. We followed these up with jelly and meringues and a quivering trifle spiked with almonds. I felt warm and happy and ate everything my three squires pressed on me.

Stavey whispered, 'We've got strawberries upstairs in my room for tea.'

I exclaimed, 'Oh, my favourite fruit!' and his face was one beaming smile.

Replete and content we strolled up to Agar's Plough to see the rest of the match between the First XI and the Eton Ramblers. The clouds had blown away now and the sun was shining. The twins installed Stavey and me in two chairs and went off in search of more. 'Lucky we're both duffers at cricket – else we'd be sweating away out there.'

Stavey said, 'They're wet bobs instead, so they'll be out in the boats tonight.' He added, rather sadly, 'I'm useless at sport – I can't play cricket, or row either.'

I put in quickly, 'That's just as well today, I shall need you to keep me company when the boys are on the river.'

He gave a sudden quick grin. 'Then I'm glad I'm hopeless at sport!' I smiled back and saw his face light up as he looked over my shoulder. 'Here's Uncle Gerald.'

Stavey jumped to his feet and his uncle clapped him lightly between the shoulder blades. 'I hope he's been behaving himself, Lady Helena.'

I took a deep breath and said, 'Lord Staveley – Stavey – has been the perfect host.'

'I'm delighted to hear it.' He dropped into his nephew's chair, beside me, and I was overcome with a paralyzing shyness.

Then the twins were back. 'How were the nobs, Lord Gerald?' 'Knobbly, very knobbly!' We all laughed, and I began to relax.

The boys chatted idly. Lord Gerald tipped his grey top hat forward and stretched out his long legs in the sun. I felt a wave of happiness flood through me as I sat between my beloved brothers and the love of my life – and his sweet shy nephew.

It was Robbie who heard it first. He looked up, then jumped to his feet, 'Eddie, Hellie – there's an airship – do you see?' I leapt to my feet and squinted up into the sky and saw the fat cigar shape appearing over the trees.

Eddie exclaimed, 'By George, it's coming this way!'

Lord Gerald smiled. 'I rather think it is. Lucky the cricket match has nearly finished.'

Stavey's eyes goggled. 'You mean it's going to *land?*'

His uncle nodded and the boys began to shout with excitement.

Our ears were filled with the throb of the engines. We watched the enormous dark shape slowly circle the ground, once, twice – a rope flew over the edge of the small boat hanging below – a group of khaki-clad men on the ground ran forward to secure it and then, in a sudden silence, it began to float gently down beside the cricket pitch.

Lord Gerald smiled. 'I heard in Town this morning that they'd probably be over – it's the *Beta* from Aldershot; Maitland's commanding it, I believe.'

As soon as the ship was moored the spectators began to move towards it and in my excitement I picked up my skirts and ran with the boys. Lord Gerald arrived shortly after us, a little out of breath. 'Well done, Lady Helena, you were the clear winner – first lady to the ship, the others are miles behind!'

I blushed with shame – then I saw the twinkle in his eye, and my discarded parasol in his hand.

The rest of the day passed in a blissful haze. We ate strawberries and cream in Stavey's tiny room; he elected me guest of honour and solemnly dusted the one shabby armchair for me with his silk handkerchief. My brothers left to change, and I strolled in the late afternoon sun with Lord Gerald and his nephew until it was time to congregate in the school yard. At the last stroke of six silence fell on the crowd and "Absence" was called. I thrilled as "Mr E. Girvan" and "Mr R. Girvan" were read out and my tall good-looking brothers raised their flower-decked boaters in turn. Then, in white duck trousers and short monkey jackets, flaunting their brightly coloured ties, they moved off to the rafts.

Down by the river we sat on rugs with Mrs Fox's party, watching as the boats rowed upstream then back again minus their jackets on their way to their own supper near Datchet. As we waited for their return our hampers were opened and champagne corks began to pop in the still evening air.

Darkness fell and coloured fairy lamps shone on the banks while the Guards' Band played behind us. I watched the shimmering water falling gently over the weir until with a sudden screech the first rocket took off. It shot higher and higher into the air until it exploded in a shower of brilliant sparks. And just as it did so the "Monarch" leapt out of the darkness, closely followed by the "Victory" and the "Prince of Wales". I craned to spot my brothers, but as suddenly as they had appeared they vanished behind the weir, and the trail of lower boats followed. Then the "Monarch" appeared again, the cox's voice cried out and he rose up with his bouquet in his white-gloved hands; unsteadily each of his crew stood up in turn, as the rowers in the other boats followed suit. Stavey's voice close by my ear said confidently, 'They'll fall in from the "Thetis", they always do.' A wobble, and the water was filled with bobbing heads swimming to shore, the cox still waving his bouquet as he trod water.

The fireworks blazed against the dark velvet sky; I gazed up wide-eyed until the final sizzling set piece portraying the King and Queen heralded the end, and we all rose to our feet to sing the National Anthem as the smoke drifted across the river. The band switched to the Eton Boating Song and my brothers sang lustily as they marched past us with the Boats. It had been a perfect day.

When I arrived back in Cadogan Place, Mother was fuming. She had backed the favourite in the Derby; it had passed the finishing post leading by a neck, and then the stewards had disqualified it and the race had gone to a 100 to 1 outsider. 'It was bad enough that wretched woman throwing herself under the King's horse – the poor jockey took quite a nasty tumble – but then to disqualify the favourite!'

Papa grunted. 'If you ask me, it was that suffragette female's fault – she upset all the horses.'

For once Mother nodded in agreement. 'You're right, Victor, that was when the rot set in.' She frowned angrily. 'As I said to Sir Ernest this afternoon, women like that are a disgrace – they have *no* moral sense at all.' I slipped away to my bedroom to dream.

I only glimpsed him briefly one day at Ascot, but he spoke to me at the Eton and Harrow match. I felt my cup was full.

We went home to Hatton as usual, then in September I went to Scotland with Guy and the twins. Great-Uncle John, their godfather, had died the previous year, and as he had been a bachelor he had made Eddie and Robbie the joint heirs to his large estates; included was a small shooting lodge in the Western Highlands, and they had clamoured to go there to stay. Guy offered to take charge of us, Mother gave in, and we boarded the Scottish Express at Manchester Exchange in a state of bubbling excitement.

Kintonish could only be approached by boat; it squatted at the head of its loch, remote and peaceful. Conditions were spartan, but the ghillie's wife came in every day to cook us large, simple meals which we devoured ravenously after long hours in the open air. We trolled for sea trout in the loch, and cast for salmon in the little river which ran its short way to the sea. Guy fished steadily and with some success; the twins and I took our sport more lightly, but I was thrilled when one evening on the loch I landed a beautiful three-pounder: it was black and gold, with spots the size of threepenny bits. I sat back with aching arms and watched the water and the moorland turn to shades of coral pink and was utterly content.

When we were not on the loch or the river we stalked on the hills. Some days we covered twenty miles on the trail of the deer – and by the time we got back to the lodge my legs were afire and I was so tired that I fell asleep almost before the dessert plates had been cleared.

I did not care whether the rain fell or the sun shone. The world was far away; this easy companionship with my brothers was all I wanted. Together we laughed and sang, chatted or fell silent. It was a golden month.

CHAPTER SIX

Back in Cheshire I travelled regularly to Manchester to prepare my *Messiah* solos with Madame Goldman; Wally Jenkins was brushing up the contralto part so she sang "He shall feed his flock" and I followed on with "Come unto Him, all ye that labour." Madame Goldman suggested that we might like to practise a duet together and we learnt the Barcarolle from Offenbach's *Tales of Hoffman*. I enjoyed working with Wally: she put every ounce of concentration into her music – yet she was always ready to laugh and crack a joke.

Mother had decided to spend the Little Season in Town and, a couple of days after we arrived, Lady Eames came to call, and asked her if she would let me sing in her charity concert. I waited apprehensively for my mother's answer. I knew she did not like Lady Eames; she made malicious jokes about her to Lady Maud: 'Such a worthy woman – but why are worthy women always so dull? Molly Eames is the strongest argument against virtue I know; fancy toeing the line all your life and then arriving at the pearly gates to find her there before you, clutching that great ugly embroidery bag and lecturing St Peter on the benefit of flannel next to the skin!'

Lady Maud had laughed. 'Well, Ria, I shouldn't waste

any sleep worrying about that eventuality – it's too late for you, anyway. How is Sir Ernest these days?'

Mother had arched her fine brows. 'Very well, I believe – and Lord Pickering, is he quite well too?' And, as ever, small complicit smiles had been exchanged.

So now I held my breath as I waited for Mother's reply – but she was gracious. 'So long as it doesn't interfere with her engagement at Hammersmith – young girls today are so very catholic in their tastes.'

It appeared that the German Ambassador was to be the guest of honour, so Lieder were required; Lady Eames had mentioned this to Mrs Benson, who had at once thought of me. Lance was to play a solo, and would later act as my accompanist. I was pleased and flattered and I took out my scores to select my five songs. 'Nothing too long, dear,' Lady Eames had said, 'and do start with something lively – not everyone understands German.'

After earnest thought and anxious consultations with Lance I decided to open with "Die Forelle" – the tune of Schubert's "Trout" was so familiar – and I would follow with Brahms' "Nachtigall" and Schumann's "Mondnacht". I could not resist the drama of "Gretchen am Spinnrad", but I would wind up with the light-hearted song of "The Blacksmith". Lance said I must prepare encores; I shook my head but he insisted – I was to be last of the performers, so he said I must be ready. Lady Eames insisted that no one must know even the names of the participants. It was to be a surprise concert: 'So much more fun, my dear – I'm simply having the cards engraved: "A Concert of Music and Song, by Ladies and Gentlemen of Society, in aid of St Margaret's Hospital". Besides, she added shrewdly, 'more people will come if there's a mystery!'

We were instructed to mingle with the guests in her large ballroom, and not to admit to being performers until the moment we stepped on the platform. I swore my brothers to secrecy and they were there on the night beside me, while a palpitating Pansy hung on Lance's arm. I was nervous too, and sat well to the side of the crowded room, but as the other performers came on I began to relax. They were talented, but only Lady Rhodes' violin playing was outstanding, and Eileen Fox, who to my surprise mounted to the stage and sang two simple ballads in a pleasant mezzo, was noticeably flat in places – though Guy, sitting raptly to attention beside me, obviously did not care.

It was not until the interval that I saw him. He caught my eye and began to stride towards us. My breathing quickened. 'My, *aren't* you the lucky girl tonight,' Eddie murmured in my ear. 'Good evening, Lord Gerald, glad you could come.'

He smiled as he greeted us, and my heart jumped in my breast. 'So the Girvans are out in force tonight: I thought I saw Muirkirk.'

'You did,' Eddie replied, 'but he's just rushed off to tell Miss Fox what an oh-too-wonderful voice she has.'

Lord Gerald gave a small shrug. 'It was quite pleasing – but I'm afraid she was flat. Still, that's the trouble with amateurs. I'm rather apprehensive, I must say; I've heard a rumour we're to have Lieder for His Excellency, and I do hate to hear Lieder mangled – I feel it should be left strictly to the professionals – ah, there's our hostess, I must congratulate her on her masterly organization.' He moved off and I was left rooted to the spot, shaking.

Eddie burst out laughing. 'I can hardly wait to see dear Uncle Gerald's face when Hellie steps up on to the platform – what a crashing brick, and he's always so suave!'

My eyes filled, and I turned and fled into the shelter of a palm and collapsed on to a chair, my fists clenched. Two astonished faces appeared either side of the foliage. 'Whatever's the matter, Hellie, suddenly struck down with stage fright?'

I whispered, '*I'm* an amateur, I'm an *amateur.*'

They stared at me. At last Eddie said, 'You didn't take him *seriously*, did you?'

'Of course I did!' I almost screamed at them.

'Oh Hellie, don't be so ridiculous.' Eddie was scathing. 'He didn't know it was *you*.'

'But he *will*, he *will!*'

'But Hellie.' Eddie spoke more patiently now. 'That's the joke, don't you see – you *don't* mangle Lieder, so he'll have to eat his words.'

I looked up at them helplessly. It was Robbie who suddenly squatted down beside me and caught my cold hand in his. 'Hellie, you have a lovely voice and you sing beautifully, we know that.'

I gazed into his loving dark eyes and whispered at last, 'But – but you're my brothers. I *am* an amateur.'

Robbie smiled at me and said softly, 'When we came to see you in Munich for the last time, Elsa Gehring spoke to us one morning while you were busy with the accompanist – she was complaining that one of the best voices she'd ever trained belonged to a Grafin, who would never be able to sing professionally. It was your voice she was talking about, Hellie, and she's trained an awful lot of voices. So now you're going to get up on that platform with old Lance and you're going to sing as only you know how to sing – do you understand?'

At last I nodded. Eddie clapped me on the back. 'That's the spirit, Big Sis, you get up there and hit 'em for six – and just watch old Prescott's face, it'll be a picture.'

I jumped up. Suddenly I was confident – I knew in my heart my brothers were right: Elsa Gehring had taught me well, I would not let her down. I reached up and kissed their two smooth cheeks, then walked sedately back to my seat.

The string trio bowed, and left the platform. Lady Eames gestured to me and I stood up and walked, head held high, to the short flight of steps and up them. Lance followed me up and went straight to the piano. He flicked out his tails and sat down on the stool, then half-turned a moment to smile at me. I smiled back, before walking forward to the front of the small stage. As the master of ceremonies came forward to announce us, I glanced along the rows and located Lord Gerald's sleek fair head. My opening smile to conceal that first vital intake of breath came quite spontaneously at the sight of the appalled expression on his face. Lance struck the first chords and easily, confidently, I began to sing:

'In einem Bachlein helle,
Da schoss in frother Eil'

and even as I sang the first lines I saw his expression change to rueful amusement, to admiration. I saw him sit back in his chair and lose himself in my song.

I sang to him, I sang to my brothers, I sang to the beaming German Ambassador, I sang to the whole listening audience.

The applause was thunderous, and this was not a small group of Hammersmith enthusiasts, these were cultured sophisticates, men and women who could hear the best voices whenever they chose – and they were applauding me. I knew now why Lance had insisted on encores.

When at last we had finished I held out my hand to Lance; he gripped it firmly and we bowed together. I saw my brothers' hands raised in a boxer's clasp of triumph at the back, then I ran quickly down the steps – and almost into the arms of the German Ambassador.

'My dear Lady Helena – I never thought to hear Lieder sung so outside of Germany, I congratulate you, with all my heart I congratulate you.' He raised my hand to his warm lips as I blushed and blushed.

We talked of Munich and of Elsa Gehring: Sir Ernest joined us with his congratulations, and in my turn I thanked him. And all the time I was conscious of a smooth fair head waiting on the outskirts of the throng, but I did not hurry my conversation with His Excellency;

I knew that the fair head would wait. I was confident, sure of myself – and when at last I was able to turn to him it was I who spoke first. 'Well, Lord Gerald – did I mangle the Lieder for you?'

He put his hand to his forehead in mock abasement. 'Lady Helena, I am utterly confounded! But my only excuse is that I understood this concert was to be given by amateurs, whereas you, you are a professional.' I glowed. He continued, 'I should have asked your brothers what exactly you were studying in Munich, but my reconnaissance was faulty and as a result my nose has been rubbed in the gravel!' He laughed. 'But never have I been corrected with such enchanting grace and elegance – you have a lovely voice, Lady Helena, and you sing beautifully; you must forgive me if my thoughtless remark earlier this evening caused you a moment's pain.'

I said quickly, 'There is nothing to forgive, Lord Gerald.'

'No, I suppose not – you must have been laughing up your sleeve at me.' I smiled, but did not answer. He added, 'But I'm surprised I had not heard of your singing – I don't go about much in Society these days, but still . . .'

'Mother doesn't really approve, she thinks it very old-fashioned to sing for one's supper.'

His blue eyes danced. 'I can assure you, Lady Helena, that if I ever have the good fortune to provide you with supper you will certainly be expected to pay for it – I look forward to hearing you sing again.'

Even as I replied I stood amazed at my own boldness. 'As it happens, I shall be singing in public again this week – on Friday, in the *Messiah*.'

And he actually took out his diary. 'Tell me where, exactly – I have a tentative engagement, but it can be postponed.'

I whispered, 'At Bell Street Congregational Church, Hammersmith – at seven o'clock.'

'Hammersmith?' He raised his eyebrows, then smiled.

'I've certainly never been there before – but I shall find my way. Until Friday, then.'

I said a bemused farewell, then took to my heels and almost ran across to the twins. 'He's coming to hear me – on Friday – at Hammersmith!' I clutched Robbie's arm.

'Oh, well done, old girl – still, I'm not surprised, you really were something special tonight. Even Mother sat up and took notice – and just look at her now, graciously accepting congratulations from the Duchess – after the way she's pooh-poohed your singing in the past!' I looked, and then began to laugh. I had never been so happy.

I watched the clock all day on Friday, agonizing over what I should wear. I longed to sing before him in my newest, smartest evening gown, but I would have looked hopelessly overdressed in a church at Hammersmith. I stood before my wardrobe biting my lip, until Liliane discreetly brought forward a simple dress of midnight-blue velvet, trimmed with satin bands of paler blue. 'Miladi will be warm enough without a cloak in this frock – if she wears her woollen combinations.' I felt my face fall a little; she added, 'Nobody will guess, Miladi is so slim.'

As soon as I was out of my bath Liliane laced me into my corsets. 'Not too tight, please, Liliane – remember I have to sing.'

'Yes Miladi.' The blue dress slid smoothly down over my silk petticoat, the hobble skirt fitted close as a glove round my hips – and the satin bands at neck and hem and cuff shimmered in the light as I moved. I had to force myself to sit still as Liliane worked over my hair. She secured most of it in a bun on the top of my head. 'Miladi will not remove her hat in church,' she said practically, 'and we must make eet safe.'

The simple black hat with its one curving blue feather was eased gently over my soft hair, and carefully manoeuvred into place. I leant forward to peer anxiously

146

into the mirror. Liliane smiled reassuringly. 'Miladi has colour in her cheeks tonight, because she enjoys singing.' I smiled back at her reflection, blushing: I knew it was not the thought of singing which had made my eyes shine and my cheeks glow. I slid my feet into the narrow black shoes that she held out for me, and circled my toes so that the silver buckles glinted. My maid brought my cloak and wrapped it around me, I drew on my black kid gloves and smoothed them over my fingers, then, with a last glance in the mirror, I was ready.

My brothers drove with me to Hammersmith: Papa had lent us the Delaunay-Belleville. I was shaking a little as Miss Ling came forward to meet me at the church, but in the small crowded vestry the contralto greeted me warmly, and I became calmer. As I walked out with the other soloists into the gas-lit church I raised my eyes for a fraction of a second and scanned the front pews – and he was there, beside my brothers. My heart jumped; he would never normally have come to such a place – he had come only because I was singing tonight.

The organ began to play the familiar music; every note of the *Messiah* seemed to become part of my body now.

When the time came I rose for my first recitative: 'There were shepherds abiding in the field, keeping watch over their flocks by night.' The notes wove their magic pattern as I relayed the angels' message of hope, then sang: 'And suddenly there was with the angel a multitude of the heavenly host, praising God and saying:' and the choir swelled out in answer, 'Glory to God in the highest, and peace on earth, goodwill towards men.'

The opening bars of my first air surged out.

'Rejoice, rejoice, rejoice greatly, rejoice, O daughter of Zion!' My voice soared up into the shadowy beams high above and I heard the exaltation in it. 'Shout, O daughter of Jerusalem! Behold, thy king cometh unto thee.' And I rejoiced because this evening my king had indeed come to me.

He only spoke to me briefly afterwards, but it was

enough. Then he turned to the man at his side, 'Lady Helena, may I introduce Edward Summerhays – Edward, Lady Helena Girvan.' The dark-haired young man shook my hand and smilingly congratulated me, then they melted away into the shadows and left me to Miss Ling and the Hammersmith Music Circle. But he had come; he had come so far out of his normal haunts just to hear me, and he had even brought a close friend with him – for I had recognized Edward Summerhays as the young man he had been talking to at the dinner party, and again at the opera and at Ascot. I knew his nephew, I had met his sister-in-law, and now I had been introduced to his friend; I was becoming part of his life. I sang softly to myself as we all drove home together.

Alice and Hugh came to stay at Hatton in February, but I felt rather flat – the twins had gone back to Cambridge and Guy was in London with his regiment. I was toying with a second piece of toast at breakfast one morning when Hugh glanced up from his *Times* and said to my father, 'I suppose Prescott'll have to resign his commission now, sir.'

My head jerked up. Papa grunted and sliced another kidney. I asked, tentatively, 'Lord Gerald Prescott?'

Hugh nodded. 'Yes – my brother Charles was at Sandhurst with him. Brought him down to stay once or twice, nice enough chap – but very tied up with his regiment, he'll miss it.'

My mind was in a turmoil. Why was Lord Gerald resigning his commission? Had he been falsely accused – in a card scandal perhaps? Oh, surely not. At last I found my voice. 'Then why – why is he resigning, Hugh?'

'I suppose he'll have to, now he's inherited.'

'Inherited?' I stared at him.

Hugh explained patiently, 'His nephew's died, it's in the obits – and he's the next heir.'

I protested stupidly, 'But his nephew's Stavey – Stavey can't die, he's too young.'

'We're none of us too young to die, Helena – poor little beggar was only eighteen.'

I could not believe it. Stavey, who had been so shyly courteous at Eton last summer – Stavey dead. And Lord Gerald – he had been so fond of his nephew – however must he be feeling now?

My father swallowed his kidney and put his fork down. 'Is it a big estate?'

'A good slice of Northants I believe, sir – besides the Irish property – and there's something in Scotland, too.'

Papa pursed his lips. 'Not to be sneezed at, eh? Entailed, is it?'

I crumpled up my napkin and scraped my chair back; I could not stay to listen to this cold-blooded discussion. I ran upstairs and flung myself on my bed and wept for fair gentle Stavey and his grey-eyed mother – and for Lord Gerald. But with a sudden unpleasant shock I realized he was Lord Gerald no longer, he was Lord Staveley now – the Marquess of Staveley – and his blue-eyed fair face seemed to slowly fade from my inward vision, and become that of a stranger. I sobbed on.

The twins' next letter was subdued. Stavey had caught a chill, it had settled on his chest, turned to pneumonia – and that was that. They had both gone up to the funeral at Bessingdon; I was glad of that. They said Lord Gerald – Lord Staveley – had seemed very cut up. My heart bled for him, and I rehearsed careful phrases of condolence though I scarcely expected I would ever have need of them.

We went up to Town as usual at the end of March. It was the second week in April and I had been buying gloves in Jermyn Street when I saw him, coming out of his tailor's. His back was as straight as ever, but his face – his face was defeated. I did not stop to think – there was a gap in the traffic and with a peremptory 'Stay there' to Liliane I lifted my skirts and scurried across

149

the street. But my carefully thought-out phrases deserted me and I could only stammer, 'Please – I wanted to say – oh, I am so sorry.' His head jerked up and his blue eyes stared at me bleakly. My small store of courage oozed away, but I *had* to tell him, so I stammered on. 'He was such a nice boy, so gentle, and he was so kind to me at Eton – and you . . .' At last I blurted out, 'If anything happened to the twins I just couldn't bear it – it must be dreadful for you. I'm so sorry, Lord Gerald – I mean Lord Staveley.' I saw how his face contracted with pain at the title and hated myself for my clumsiness – so I turned and darted dangerously across the street and, seizing Liliane's arm, hauled her half-running down the pavement. Back at Cadogan Place I took refuge in my bedroom, and wept with shame for my stupid unthinking impulsiveness – I had only re-opened his wounds and made a fool of myself.

Next week Mother took me to a reception in Grosvenor Square. The evening was long and dull and my head ached. I moved across to the window and tried to fade into the heavy curtains as my eyelids drooped. 'Lady Helena.' My eyes flew open. He was standing in front of me, his face almost as pale as his shirtfront. We stared at each other. At last he said, 'I spoke to Muirkirk, he thought you'd be here tonight, so I came along.' My heart pounded; was he still so angry with me? He suggested, 'Perhaps we could sit down somewhere?' I followed him to a small brocade sofa and sank down on it. He arranged himself carefully beside me. 'The other day, in Jermyn Street, you left so suddenly that I didn't have time for a word with you.' I sat mute and trembling. 'I wanted to tell you how grateful I was for what you said. I know you'd only met Stavey a few times but – he liked you. That day at Eton you treated him like one of your brothers – and yet you made him feel grown up. He was terribly pleased; he talked about you a lot afterwards, you know.'

I felt the blood rising in my cheeks as I stared down

at my shaking hands. Finally I whispered, 'I liked him, too.'

He said gently, 'I know you did – and if I hadn't, I would have realized it last Friday.' He drew a deep breath and then said, his voice tight with pain, 'Lady Helena, you would hardly believe the way condolences have been offered to me. Oh, quite politely and correctly, of course – but all the time' – I sensed his shudder – 'I could see the calculation in their eyes. Subtly, slyly, they were congratulating me.'

I turned and looked at him. 'But, but Lord Gerald – Lord Staveley . . .' and then I understood. I remembered my father and Hugh and I felt sick.

He watched my face and said simply, 'So now you see why I was so grateful to you last week.' We were silent for a moment, then he gave a short, hard laugh. 'No, you would hardly believe how many mothers of marriageable daughters have suddenly clamoured to renew their acquaintance with me – I who was always known to be a confirmed bachelor – but of course I wasn't worth anything to them then – a younger son with a barely adequate allowance – but now I've become the prey of every dowager in town – and poor Stavey's body is scarcely cold in its grave. They behave as if I don't care.' His voice was tortured. He looked at me and spoke urgently. 'After my brother died in South Africa and I came back alone, Moira took me up to the nursery and he was there, playing with his toy soldiers. He called to his mother and then he saw me – he was nervous, I could see that, I'd been away so long, I was a stranger – but he smiled, a brave little smile, and held out his hand, as Nanny had taught him. And I vowed then that I would be as a father to him – and so he became my son – the son I had never had, and never looked to have. And now they tell me how sorry they are, and add up my income behind their greedy eyes.'

I felt the intensity of his anger, but there was nothing I could say. We sat beside each other in the crowded glittering room, in silence, until at last I took a deep breath, turned to face him and said falteringly, 'How is, how is his mother, Lady Staveley?'

'Distressed, of course, but Moira's always been a very religious woman. She seeks consolation in her Church.' He glanced at me and added, 'She spoke several times of her meeting with you, in the park that afternoon. She said you seemed "a nice, old-fashioned girl" '. He paused. 'And you are an old-fashioned girl, aren't you, Lady Helena? You work diligently at your music and practise your singing every day and blush when you are spoken to, and have to search painfully for answers.'

I whispered, 'I'm sorry.'

He said quickly, 'Oh my dear – don't be sorry. I am complimenting you. You know I look round rooms like this sometimes and shudder at the thought that these shrill, giddy little females are the future wives and mothers of England. They can't even stay loyal for more than five minutes to their bosom friends – how will they ever be loyal to their husbands and sons?' I looked up at his pale face as he stared at the noisy crush in front of us. Turning quickly, he caught my gaze and held it. He looked at me for a long moment, then spoke in a low voice. 'You are a very loyal person, Lady Helena, aren't you? I believe you would follow your brothers to the gates of hell itself – if need be.'

I returned his gaze, slowly I nodded. 'I think that once you've given your affections you've given them for a lifetime.' And I knew then that he knew, and I dropped my eyes before him.

He got to his feet and stood in front of me, and said abruptly, 'Obviously I will not be going into Society this Season – and there are the lawyers with their interminable business – but perhaps before your family leaves Town I might see you again. Good evening, Lady Helena.' He turned and walked away and left me shaking on the small hard sofa.

CHAPTER SEVEN

It was June when he came; Mother was receiving at home. Cooper brought in a card and Mother picked it up from the tray and I saw her frown a moment as she looked at it. Then she turned to Mrs Clavering and said, 'How curious – Lord Staveley – I don't believe we've ever met. Show Lord Staveley up, Cooper.'

I sat rigidly beside her as he walked across the room. 'Lady Pickering, please forgive my intrusion – Muirkirk told me you were at home today.' He turned to me. 'Lady Helena, would you be so good as to present me to your Mama?'

Mother glanced at me, her dark eyes suddenly sharp. As soon as I had performed the introductions he said to her, 'I met your daughter some years ago in Munich, Lady Pickering, so I feel we are old friends – and your inseparable twins were in the same house as my nephew at Eton.'

Mother murmured the correct reply, then touched my hand lightly with hers. 'Helena, I believe Juno is signing to you.'

Juno was not, but I obediently walked over to the far side of the drawing room. As I pretended to listen to Juno I watched Mother and Lord Staveley from the corner of my eye. They were talking earnestly together. Then he picked up his hat and gloves and threaded his way through the company to me. His face was serious and he stood looking down at me before he spoke. 'Lady Helena, your Mama has kindly invited me to join her house party at Hatton, at the end of the month. I haven't given her my reply yet – that depends on you.' The blood pounded in my ears, I could only stare at him. He

153

said, slowly, 'I will come – if you will sing for me. Will you do that?'

'Yes, Lord Staveley. I shall be pleased to sing for you.'

Gravely he looked at me. 'Then I shall come.' Turning away, he left the room. I struggled to concentrate as Juno rattled on about the latest exploit of Mrs Pankhurst, but I did not hear a word.

That evening Mother and Papa both dined at home; there were only the three of us. As soon as the servants had left Mother reached for a peach and said, 'Victor, Lord Staveley called today.' Papa grunted. 'I have invited him to our house party at Hatton later this month.'

Papa looked up in surprise. 'But we won't be at Hatton then.'

Mother said firmly, 'We will be, now.' Papa opened his mouth to protest, but Mother continued, 'It appears Lord Staveley has known Helena for some time – and he spoke very highly of her singing.'

Two pairs of parental eyes swivelled in my direction. Then they turned and met, with small mutual smiles of satisfaction. 'Then of course I shall put off going to old Towcester's, Ria. Lord Staveley, eh? Northants, you know – ironstone.'

Mother added softly, 'The Irish estates are rather run down, I believe – but extensive.'

Papa cracked a walnut. 'You know, Ria, I think I'll have a word with Hyde – discreetly, of course . . .'

'Of course,' Mother echoed, 'but it's as well to be prepared, Victor.' They leant towards each other in a rare moment of amity.

I could not bear to listen to any more. I pushed back my chair. 'Mother, if you will excuse me . . .'

'Of course, my dear.'

Papa smiled jocularly. 'You run along, Helena – and practise your singing.'

I thrust the door shut, too hard, as their voices murmured on.

Mother insisted on several visits to Mirette's in Dover Street before she took me back to Hatton; my wardrobe must not be found wanting at this time. I was her ugly duckling who had, suddenly and against all expectations, turned into a swan. I followed her passively, in a daydream of fair hair and blue eyes.

He arrived at Hatton early on Saturday evening, just before the dressing bell. I sat at the table in a daze of happiness; I could not believe he was really here, in our familiar dining room. I kept glancing under my eyelashes down to where he sat, handsome and impeccably tailored, on Mother's right hand.

When the gentlemen joined us in the drawing room he came up to me and asked, very formally, if I would sing for him.

As I led him through to the music room I asked, 'Do you wish for Lieder, Lord Staveley?'

He gave an apologetic smile. 'I'm afraid my accompanying is not up to young Benson's standards – I can't sight read.'

I said quickly, 'I can accompany myself.'

He looked at me, surprised. 'Even Lieder? I didn't realize you were such a proficient pianist – that is good news. I was thinking I'd have to brush up my own technique – or rely on the local organist at Bessingdon.'

He spoke so matter of factly that it took a moment for the implications of what he had said to sink in. I sank quickly on to the piano stool to conceal my shaking legs. He chose the simple, lyrical songs and I played and sang for more than an hour. When Mother came to the connecting door he stood up and thanked me gravely before escorting me back to the drawing room.

All through the night I would drift into consciousness and hug myself with sheer joy at the thought that he was sleeping under the same roof. Next morning I tried on and discarded half a dozen frocks until Liliane was bemused. At last I stood before the mirror in a simple pleated linen in a warm peach shade. As always I wished that my nose were straight and my mouth smaller – but today I knew that it did not really matter.

We spoke little at breakfast; I was grateful for Mother's confident flow of small talk. As we finished our coffee she said lightly, 'You must ask Helena to show you round the grounds, Lord Staveley. The Japanese garden is quite pretty at this time of the year – and of course the orangery is delightful in June.'

Speechless, I led him out on to the terrace. He turned to me and smiled. 'Which is it to be, Lady Helena – the orangery or the Japanese garden?'

I said quickly, 'The orangery is nearer.'

He threw back his head and laughed, and I blushed for my gaucheness.

A gardener slipped quickly out of the far door as we came into the warm scented orangery. I glided in a dream between the waxy white blossoms and dark glossy leaves until he said, 'Won't you sit down, Lady Helena?' I sank down on one of the ornate iron benches and he carefully hitched up the cloth of his elegant grey trouser leg and dropped down on one knee on the stone floor in front of me. He looked up, his face quite still, before he finally spoke. 'Lady Helena, will you do me the honour of giving me your hand in marriage?'

I looked back into his blue eyes, and saw the network of fine lines around them, and the silver threads among the gold at his temples as I whispered, 'Yes, yes – of course I will.'

We stayed unmoving for a few moments, like two statues, staring at each other. Then slowly I held out my hand and he took it and I felt his warm lips brush my skin.

I smiled at him and he jumped up quickly and threw himself down beside me so that the iron bench jerked. Drawing a deep breath he said – suddenly, endearingly, young – 'I've never made a proposal of marriage before – I do hope I got that right!'

I felt a bubbling joy well up inside me, I wanted to laugh, to sing. I dared to tease him. 'Perhaps we should check in the etiquette books, Lord Staveley?'

He turned and looked at me in surprise. Then he began to laugh as he took my hand and squeezed it. 'What a nice child you are, Helena. But, you know, I'm sure the etiquette books will say you can call me "Gerald" now!' I felt the hot blushes rise in my cheeks. He smiled and stood up and pulled me up too. 'I'd better go and see Lord Pickering now, I suppose I should have asked his permission first – but I think I made my intentions pretty clear to your Mama and she didn't seem to see any problems. Where will your father be at this time of day?'

I almost thrust Gerald through the door of the library, then I ran to the back stairs and flew up them. Alice and Hugh had left their sons at Hatton on their way to Wales; now I burst into the nursery and cried, 'Nanny – I'm going to be married – I'm going to be married!' Then I was laughing and crying in the beloved carbolic-soap-scented arms.

Nanny patted my shoulder and said, 'There, there, dear – isn't that nice? Well, I am pleased for you, my chick.'

When Cooper came for me I felt very shy. My heart was pounding as I entered the library. Gerald was standing with my father, talking – but he turned towards me at once. The library floor seemed to shiver as I walked forward, but his voice was quite calm. 'Your father has given his consent, Helena.'

Papa bent over me; his moustaches tickled my cheek. 'I'm delighted my dear, absolutely delighted.' He straightened up. 'She's a good girl, Staveley old man – you won't regret it – does as she's told and never argues. I must go and tell her Mama.' He strode towards the door and we were alone.

I wanted to run to Gerald and throw my arms around his neck, but I was too shy. I stood rooted to the floor, gazing up at him. He said briskly, 'Perhaps we should view that Japanese garden now, Helena.'

On the terrace I held my hand out to him; he picked it up and placed it securely through his arm. I leant against him a moment, for the sheer joy of feeling the hard male strength of him. Then we set off sedately for the Japanese garden. The sun shone, the flower beds were a blaze of colour, and the lawns stretched green and inviting before us. I loved him, oh, how I loved him!

As we came up to the curving wooden bridge over the small still lake he said abruptly, 'Helena, I must leave you after luncheon.' The shadow swooped darkly down on me. 'Don't look so desolate, my dear – it will only be for a few days. But Moira is expecting me.' The stabbing pain of jealousy pierced me. 'Remember, it won't be easy for her, Helena; she's lived at Bessingdon since she came there as my brother's bride, and watched her son grow up there.' And now her son was dead, and I would usurp her place. 'She'll be glad it's to be you, Helena. I dropped a hint, and she was pleased, I know. But I would like to tell her in person as soon as possible.'

And now I was bitterly ashamed of my unreasoning jealousy; he was so kind, so good – how would I ever be worthy of him? 'Of course, I quite understand – Gerald.' My voice dropped as I spoke his name; I scarcely dared use it, even now.

'And there's something I must bring back for you – the Prescott betrothal ring. Though it'll have to be altered before it will fit that slender hand of yours.' With the tip of his finger he gently touched my hand as it lay on his sleeve. I stood very still. 'Du Ring an meinem Finger, Mein goldenes Ringelein' – my dream had come true. Slowly I raised my eyes to his face: he was gazing ahead at the dainty bamboo tea house. I drank in the firm line of his jaw, the curve of his cheekbones, the fine arch of his eyebrows. I loved him, I loved him – and now he was mine. He stepped forward on to the bridge; I followed obediently.

After luncheon I walked sedately out to the Delaunay-Belleville with him; he took my hand, squeezed it quickly and jumped in. I would have liked to have gone to the station, but he had said nothing and I was too shy to suggest it. So I stood gazing after the departing motor, and then walked slowly back inside, quite bereft.

But upstairs Nanny cheered me with plans for the nursery at Bessingdon. 'This one will be old enough for a governess next year' – she patted William's curly head – 'and then I can come to you.' I thought of my child, Gerald's child, safe on Nanny's lap – and the world seemed to have room for no more joy. Until my brothers arrived home just before teatime and slapped me on the back and promised to come and shoot Gerald's partridges every year. 'And his pheasants, and we'll hunt his foxes,' 'and stalk his deer,' Robbie chipped in, 'and fish his salmon!'

I laughed. 'You can come to see me, you selfish wretches.'

Next morning Papa muttered over his *Times*. 'Those Serbs ought to be horsewhipped, the lot of them – they've shot the Austrian Archduke. That country's a disgrace – remember the butchery in '03?'

Uncle Arnold protested, 'But that was their own king and queen, Victor – quite a family affair.'

'Well, they've shot a Hapsburg now, in Sarajevo – it's not on.'

Uncle Arnold shrugged. 'But Sarajevo's in their own Empire – I don't see how they can blame Serbia for that.'

'It says here this feller, this assassin, was a Serb, a Serb Orthodox – they'll blame Serbia all right.'

Lady Maud joined in. 'Quite right too – it's time they were taught a lesson.'

Eddie stabbed his bacon. 'Not *another* war in the Balkans, it's not fair, they have all the luck – one a year.'

Papa put down his paper. 'Well, Serbia's nothing to do with the British Empire, I'm glad to say – we've got enough problems with Ireland.' He began to talk about the real crisis, in Ireland, but it flowed over my head unheard. I sat in a happy dream. This time next year I would be entertaining my brothers at my own breakfast table – and perhaps even leaving them briefly for a visit to the nursery? I blushed and blushed and dreamt my dreams.

Gerald wrote to say that he would not be coming back to Hatton until the beginning of the following week. I felt dismay as I read his small neat handwriting – his letter was brief, he would be spending the weekend with a friend in Leicestershire – but he said Moira Staveley had been delighted by his choice and would be writing to me. He was having the ring altered and would bring it with him. The ring! I looked down at my left hand, and then almost ran to the music room. I played and sang Schumann's *Frauen Liebe und Leben* with a full heart. But I did not sing the whole song – and for a moment the last stanza with its ominous message of loss darkened my joy – so I put it from me and dwelt instead on the time when I would hold him to my heart and tell him of the coming cradle: the cradle from which his image would smile up at me. I remembered how I had first learnt to sing those words in Munich, with an impossible wish in my heart – and now that wish had come true.

It seemed almost an anticlimax to go off to smoky, dirty Manchester for my singing lesson, but Madame Goldman was expecting me. My brothers said they fancied an outing and drove me there in their new Sunbeam. Just as they came back to collect me a very ruffled Wally Jenkins burst in. 'Madame, whatever shall I do? That little wretch Flo Morten has gone down with a bad throat – she can't possibly sing tonight – and we're booked for the Ainsclough and District Co-operative Society's annual concert!'

160

Madame Goldman was soothing. 'Do not fret so, Waltraute, we will find someone else.'

Wally gave an emphatic shake of the head. 'We won't find another soprano who can sing the *Barcarolle* with me – you know there's no time to rehearse it properly – and it was to be the highlight of our programme!' Then her mouth opened in a round 'O' and she stared at me before looking back at Madame Goldman; their eyes met, and Wally moved purposefully in my direction. 'Lady Helena, you can sing the *Barcarolle* – we rehearsed it lots of times last year – we could have a short practice this morning, if Madame is agreeable?' Madame Goldman inclined her head. 'There! And I know you can sing most of Flo's programme – we can always change the odd item – but the *Barcarolle*, we must have the *Barcarolle*, it was a special request.'

I burst out laughing. 'Oh Wally! How can I possibly sing at – where was it? The Ainsclough and District Co-op's concert? Mother would have a fit.'

Eddie broke in, 'Mother wouldn't know. Anyway, you sang at Hammersmith, didn't you?'

I gaped at my traitorous brother. 'But Eddie, that was quite different – it was an *amateur* group. This is a paid concert – I couldn't possibly take a fee!'

'Then put it in the plate on Sunday.'

'Eddie, that's not the point – there's Gerald, suppose Gerald found out? I couldn't, I couldn't.'

It was Robbie who said thoughtfully, 'You could go in some sort of disguise, Hellie – obviously if you walk up on to the platform in a silk creation from Mirette's and are announced as The Lady Helena Girvan, then there would be a sensation – but you don't have to do that, for goodness' sake.'

I protested weakly, 'But . . .'

Wally's face was alive. 'I could lend you one of my sister's dresses, Lady Helena.'

'And you could call yourself *Miss* Girvan,' Eddie jumped in quickly. 'I know, Miss Nellie Girvan, the

161

aspiring young soprano! Well, that's settled – we'll dine early in Manchester and run you both up there ourselves. Can't say fairer than that, can we Robbie?'

Robbie nodded, his eyes alight with mischief. I was still protesting when Madame's accompanist struck up the first bars of the *Barcarolle*, then I gave in and began to sing.

I borrowed a dress and coat from Liliane, though I wore my own string of pearls – I did not think the honest burghers of Ainsclough would come near enough to judge their quality. Eddie made our excuses to Mother and we set off. As we turned out past the North Lodge I felt a sudden rush of excitement; we were a group of naughty children playing truant, and Lady Helena Girvan would be left behind at Hatton Park – Miss Nellie Girvan would sing in Ainsclough tonight! Ainsclough – I did not even know where it was.

Wally was waiting for us at the Royal Exchange. As soon as she had climbed into the car she said to me, 'Now, don't open your mouth more than you have to, Lady Helena.'

'But how can I . . .'

'I mean off the stage, of course. Folks do expect singers to speak differently, but not with your accent.'

'Accent – *I* don't have an accent, Wally!' I was indignant.

'You'll have one to Ainsclough and District Co-op, my lady. Take the left turn for Bolton, Mr Girvan.'

I sat astounded – how could *I* have an accent? Servants had accents, even the middle class gave their origins away, but we, we spoke correctly!

We bumped over the setts of Bolton and out into open country. The Sunbeam growled as Robbie changed gear for the long pull up over the empty moorland. We climbed through small stone villages and up on to the rounded tops until at last we began to run down a steep hill and saw before us a small smoky town, in a valley which sprouted high black chimneys instead of trees. So this was Ainsclough, the scene of Miss Nellie Girvan's first – and last – performance. I began to giggle to myself.

The dignitaries of the Ainsclough and District Co-operative Society welcomed us warmly, with moustaches brushed and quivering, oiled hair plastered down over their round heads and broad smiles on their ruddy faces. 'Glad you could come along at such short notice, Miss Girvan – it were right good o' you. Now don't be frightened, lass – Miss Jenkins here says you've not sung often in public – but we'll not eat you.' The chairman bared a row of gleaming china teeth.

I smiled and shook sweaty palms but said little, as Wally had instructed, and in a very short space of time we were on the platform. I felt a sudden devastating shiver of nervousness, then the strings began to tune up, the conductor raised his baton and the orchestra embarked briskly on Balfe's *Siege of La Rochelle* overture; I forced myself to concentrate.

In a dream I rose to my feet, smiled to the pianist and waited for my cue. When it came I parted my lips and launched into Edward German's 'Daffodils'. As my last pianissimo, 'growing', died away over the packed hall, I felt a surge of sheer joyous light-heartedness sweep through me – I was intoxicated by the occasion.

The tall thin tenor sang 'O vision entrancing! O lovely and light' to the accompaniment of the orchestra. The pianist followed with a Mendelssohn solo and then it was Wally's turn. As I listened to her full, rich voice singing del Riego's 'Slave Song':

> Bright bird, light bird,
> Bird with the purple wing,
> Do you bring me a letter,
> Or do you bring me a ring?

I thought that never had the world been so fair a place – even Ainsclough Co-op Hall seemed a gilded palace tonight.

It was my turn again, Arline's song from *The Bohemian Girl*. With a delicious sense of the ridiculous I sang: 'I dreamt that I dwelt in marble halls' – for though Ainsclough Co-op Society could never guess, I *did* dwell in the marble-pillared hall of Hatton – and soon I would be boasting of an even higher ancestral name. But then the sentimental words caught hold of me, and with a rapturous longing in my heart I sang:

> 'But I also dreamt, which pleased me most,
> That you loved me still the same,
> That you loved me, you loved me still the same,
> That you loved me, you loved me still the same.'

We were a success; the applause for the concluding *Barcarolle* was deafening. All our encores had been demanded before a radiant Wally led me off the platform.

In the Sunbeam afterwards Robbie suddenly burst out into a roar of laughter. 'Oh Hellie' – he wiped his eyes – 'I'll never forget it, never as long as I live – you up there singing,' he produced a squeaky falsetto and parodied: ' "And I dreamt that one of that noble host came forth my hand to claim," and little did that solid Lancastrian audience guess that one of the noble host already *had* made his claim – and it was the future Marchioness of Staveley who was entertaining them in the guise of a humble singing lass! Your face, you looked just like a hen who's laid a double yolker!' He laughed and laughed, and Eddie joined in so that his hands shook on the steering wheel and we veered dangerously for a moment; then we settled down to the long pull out of the grimy little valley and back to civilization.

CHAPTER EIGHT

Hugh and Alice arrived the day before Gerald came back: Alice was profuse in her congratulations. 'Just think, Hellie, you'll outrank Mother – how delicious! Oh why did I make do with a boring old barrister instead of waiting for a dashing cavalry officer to sweep me off my feet and carry me away on his black charger – straight to his ironstone quarries in Northants! Oh, you are lucky!'

Hugh stood behind her, looking very serious; I hoped that Alice's careless words had not hurt him.

In the drawing room later he drew me on one side. 'Forgive my asking, Helena, but – are you in love with Prescott?' I stared at him in amazement and he reddened. 'I mean – you didn't accept him just because you were flattered – an older man, distinguished war record, title and all that?'

I was deeply wounded. How could Hugh accuse me of such a thing? 'I fell in love with him the first time I ever saw him, when I was only fifteen. And I've never changed since.'

Hugh's face was scarlet now. He patted my shoulder awkwardly. 'I'm sorry, Hellie old girl, I suppose I shouldn't have asked that, only – you're so young and innocent, and well, I'm dashed fond of you, you know – I do want you to be happy.'

My face was glowing as I raised it to him. 'I will be, Hugh, I will be.'

That afternoon I wandered out into the garden, dreaming of Gerald. Without thinking I found myself outside the entrance to the maze. I stopped abruptly – I had scarcely been inside it since that summer evening

165

which had resulted in my being sent to Munich; I certainly did not want to go in now. How badly I had behaved that night, and how thankful I was now that Mother had arrived when she did. I remembered Conan's searching hands and probing tongue and trembled. I loved Gerald, I was betrothed to him – yet we had not even kissed. Our love was pure and spiritual, not a greedy, thoughtless, tangling of bodies.

The next day Gerald arrived back only just in time for dinner. I had lingered downstairs as long as I could but Alice finally chased me up to dress with a laughing, 'You want to look your best, Hellie,' and of course I did. When Liliane had piled my hair up high I peered into the mirror and thought it made my neck look longer than ever, so I suddenly tugged it down and told her to dress it low at the back instead. Her fingers moved swiftly but the second bell had sounded before I flew downstairs, and I only had time for a brief greeting before we went in to dinner. At the table he talked of his journey, and asked if I had been singing while he was away. I remembered my excursion to Ainsclough and became tongue-tied – I barely stammered a reply. Mother glared at me and asked him his plans for hunting next season, Alice chipped in and the conversation became general. I sat back in relief and watched him; he looked very pale and tired.

After dinner my brothers and Papa quickly joined us, but Hugh and Gerald stayed on in the dining room. I hung around the tea tray, fiddling with the tea spoons, until Mother told me sharply to sit down. When Gerald finally came in with my brother-in-law I felt so shy I scarcely dared glance at him, but I saw Hugh nod in my direction before he moved over to Alice. Gerald marched straight across the room to me, his face very determined. My heart thumped.

'Helena, it's such a fine evening – would you care for a stroll on the terrace?' Without a word I stood up and took his proferred arm. We stepped out of the long window and into the balmy night air. A shaft of light shone out from the house behind us and I risked a glance up at him: his mouth was tightly set and he was staring grimly ahead. My stomach lurched; what had he and Hugh been talking about for so long? Why had Hugh questioned me? And where had he been this past week? I had never seen him with a woman in Society but there were other women – men became entangled with them – the twins had dropped hints about Guy. A black wave of jealousy engulfed me, my chest heaved and I gripped his arm and dragged him to a halt. He turned, startled. In a voice that was ragged with fear I demanded, 'Lord Gerald – you must tell me – is there, is there another woman in your life?'

For a long moment we stood facing each other; my heart seemed to stop beating. Then he said, very gently, 'No, Helena – I can assure you of that. There is not, and never has been, any woman but you. And there never will be.' His voice was completely decided. My knees gave way and I threw myself against him, clinging to him, burying my hot face in his shirtfront. His strong arm supported me as he gently stroked my hair in the dark garden. I began to cry. 'No tears, sweet Helena, no tears. Come, it's time I kissed you.' Slowly I raised my face and his soft lips pressed against mine. Then he drew back his head and said, 'I will be a true and loving husband to you, Helena, I promise.'

As he spoke the crescent moon shone in the black velvet sky and carved his face in ivory. 'Hold out your hand, my love.' The Prescott betrothal ring slipped easily over my knuckle. I raised myself on tiptoe and kissed his cheek in thanks, and knew I would love him forever.

The next morning Alice and Hugh were moving on to Yorkshire, leaving Hugo and William behind at Hatton. Nanny brought the children down to see them off; William stomped out and climbed on to the running board, saying, 'Me go on train – me and 'Ugo and Nanny on train.'

Alice was impatient. 'Oh, don't be such a silly boy, you can't possibly come with us.'

His small face crumpled and Gerald spoke quickly, 'Lady Alice, Helena and I could escort them to Manchester, and see you on to the York express, if you're agreeable.'

William, scenting success, ran to Gerald and wrapped his short arms round his long leg. My heart turned over when I saw the expression on Gerald's face as he looked down at the child. I called to my sister, 'Yes Alice, we'll come with you to Manchester. Nanny, I'll ring for your hat and coat – there's plenty of time.'

Nanny grumbled a little at the hustle but I could see she was pleased at the idea of an outing with Gerald and myself.

We waved Alice and Hugh off at Victoria. Hugo gazed wistfully after his father's diminishing hand and William's lower lip trembled ominously. Gerald squatted down beside him. 'I say, old man, how about coming and having a look at one of those engines – you'd like that, wouldn't you?'

William's mouth became a round O. 'Yes please, sir.' Hugo was eager.

I glanced across at Nanny. She said automatically, 'Nasty smelly things,' but there was a beatific smile on her face as she looked at Gerald. I could see that the nursery at Bessingdon was enlarging before her eyes.

Gerald led us down the platform to a waiting black monster. The driver was agreeable so Hugo scrambled up the side like a monkey; behind him Gerald swung William safely up into the strong hands of the young fireman, seized the rail, and climbed lithely up on to the footplate. High-pitched boys' questions received rumbling replies. I reached out a hand to stroke the burnished steel hand rail and Nanny said, 'Don't touch, my lady – you'll dirty your nice clean gloves.' To tease her I simply peeled them off and clasped the shining rail

168

with my bare hand. Gerald's sapphire blazed blue fire in a shaft of sunlight. I gazed at it, smiling to myself.

A voice spoke above my head. 'I enjoyed your singing – at Ainsclough last week.' My head jerked up; as the grimy seamed face of the engine driver smiled down at me, my face flamed.

Nanny was peering anxiously up at the chimney. 'Just look at those nasty black smuts – do take care, my lady.' My title seemed to ring out, and I saw behind the driver's head the broad, sweat-streaked face of the fireman; his blue eyes were alight and his mouth was one wide white grin. They both glanced down at the winking sapphire on my left hand, then the driver gestured over his shoulder. 'Don't you worry lass – us'll not let cat out o' bag.' He ducked back into the cab and I was left for a moment looking into the young fireman's blue eyes, then he winked and turned away. I stood, taking deep breaths, trying to cool my burning cheeks as Nanny chattered on.

Gerald climbed down first, guiding Hugo. The fireman vaulted on to the platform after them, held up his brawny arms for William and swung him safely down in turn. Gerald reached into his pocket; there was the clink of coins and the fireman's large fist closed round the silver; with a 'Thank you, sir' and a touch of his cap he sprang back on to his engine.

Hugo and William chattered on to Gerald about fire boxes and brick arches as we walked up the platform; I felt a giggle welling up inside me – Miss Nellie Girvan had been exposed, by a grimy-faced engine driver! I could hardly wait to tell the twins – how they would laugh.

On the train back to Hareford, Gerald lifted William up on to the seat and held him firmly, so that he could look out of the window. William pointed at the horses in the streets and the cows in the fields, and asked endless, repetitive questions. Gerald painstakingly answered every one, until Nanny leant forward and said to said to me in a loud whisper, 'There's not many gentle-men have the patience of my lord here when it comes to the nursery.' I saw the pink flush rise in Gerald's fair skin as his arm steadied William's chubby body. Perhaps by this time next year? A matching blush rose in my throat.

That evening after dinner Gerald led me into the music room again. 'Sing for me, Helena,' he commanded. I went gladly to the piano and my fingers began to move over the keys. Without thinking I found myself playing the opening bars of 'Gretchen am Spinnrad'. I sang as the girl enslaved by her love for Faust, whose peace had been destroyed because she cared only for him. And the passion, the burning desire of Gretchen swept through me as I sang of the touch of his hand, and his kiss. My eyes were fixed on the man sitting opposite me, my body was heavy with longing:

> 'An seinen Küssen
> Vergehen sollt!'

Under his kisses I should die. My heart beat hot in my breast as I sang the last stanza:

> 'Mein Ruh ist hin,
> Mein Herz ist schwer
> Ich finde sie nimmer
> Und nimmermehr.'

As I struck the last note I stood up and moved towards him, my hands outstretched. He was on his feet at once. He spoke lightly. 'Dear me, Helena, how dramatic you are – we'll have you singing Brunnhilde next!'

I stopped, suddenly, feeling very foolish; my arms dropped to my sides. He circled round me towards the piano. 'Perhaps I could persuade you to accompany me, now. Let's see, have you the music for "Where'er you walk?" '

I felt dull and heavy. 'I can play that from memory.'

'I think I would like the score, though – perhaps you would look?'

I went to the shelves and began to search. I was glad my back was to him. When I found Handel's 'Semele' I carried it over to the piano. 'It's my copy, for a soprano . . .'

'That will do for me too.' So he was a tenor. I had not known, but there were so many things about him I did not know. I began to play.

As his light, pleasant tenor sang: 'Where'er you walk, cool gales shall fan the glades,' my own hot cheeks were cooled, and my heaviness began to ease a little. 'And all things flourish, where'er you turn your eyes,' and his own eyes seemed to smile at me in love and forgiveness.

After I had played the final bars I let my hands drop to rest on my lap. 'You sing well, Gerald.'

'Thank you. Perhaps when we are married you could give me a few tips on how to improve my performance. Shall we rejoin the others?' He came towards me.

I slipped my hand through his arm and held it, lightly. 'When we are married', he had said; I was reassured: he was not angry with me. I sat watching him as he talked to Alice. How lucky I was – but I had behaved like a silly impulsive child – it was time I grew up.

Early next morning I was woken by the familiar cramping pains in my stomach. I was too ill to go down to breakfast; I lay in bed clutching my hot-water bottle and wept with pain and frustration.

It was late in the afternoon before I was well enough to get up, and I was still tired and dull at dinner that evening. Afterwards I sat in the drawing room listening as my brothers and Gerald discussed the coverts at Bessingdon, and the prospects for the shooting this season. I sat silently watching them, my twins dark-haired and dark-eyed, so different from my lover. The fine tracery of lines round his eyes was very noticeable tonight; he looked much older than my brothers. But of course, he was much older than they were. I realized with a sense of dismay that I did not even know his age, only that he had been old enough to fight in the South African War. The twins were wrangling a point between themselves so I asked abruptly, 'Gerald, how old are you?' As soon as I had spoken I was aghast at my temerity.

His face was surprised as he looked at me. 'I shall be thirty-seven next April, Helena. I suppose that must seem quite ancient to you.'

'No, no – of course not . . .' I stumbled over my denials, and looked desperately towards my brothers.

Robbie came swiftly to my rescue. 'By the way, sir, I was going to ask you what you thought about the Irish affair – is there any chance of Ulster being excluded from Home Rule? After that massive gun-smuggling exploit in April it certainly looks as if the Unionists mean business.'

Gerald answered, authoritatively; my brothers listened, their faces respectful. I stayed very quiet; my tongue was so clumsy tonight, I dared not trust it again.

But as I watched them, I felt deeply grateful that my brothers were on such good terms with my betrothed. I wanted the twins to come and stay often when I was married: I would miss them so much. And I was frightened by the thought of Bessingdon; would I be able to run it to Gerald's satisfaction? And he would surely want me to entertain big house parties as Mother did at Hatton. I thought of my mother, always so gracious and clever, arranging the day so skilfully for her guests, keeping the conversational ball bouncing lightly across her dinner table with deft pats of wit and charm – I knew I could never hope to be such a hostess. Gerald would be disappointed in me; I would fail him.

He looked across at me. Then he excused himself politely from my brothers and came over to my chair. His voice was kind. 'You look tired, Helena, perhaps you should have an early night.'

I stood up obediently and went to Mother. She scarcely glanced up. 'Yes, run along Helena, if you want to.'

Gerald held the door open for me. 'Goodnight, Helena my dear.'

'Goodnight, Gerald.' I slipped through and heard the door close firmly behind me. I trailed slowly up the stairs to my bedroom; I felt very tired and the pad between my legs was sodden.

Next morning Mother told me that it was time we returned to Town for the remainder of the Season. She said we would travel down after the weekend, on Monday, when Gerald left. It was obvious he had already told her of his plans and I was hurt that he had not spoken to me first. But he smiled across the table. 'Helena, your mama wishes to begin her preparations for the wedding, we shall have to discuss a date.' My heart leapt.

After breakfast we walked down to the lower terrace and sat together in the sun. He told me Mother had talked of September – I felt a flutter of excitement – but then he said, his face grave, that he felt himself to be still in mourning – and there was Moira. So he had suggested next year – my heart sank – but Mother had insisted on December, as she wished the wedding to be at St George's, Hanover Square – so if I were agreeable?

'Yes, Gerald.'

'December it is then – that should give you a chance to get your fripperies together. Where would you like to go for the wedding journey? I wondered if you'd care to revisit Germany, since you spent so long there – Munich, even – what do you say?'

'Oh, yes please, Gerald – I should like that.'

'Good – that seems to be all settled then.'

I asked, a little hesitantly, 'Will you be returning to London, when we go?'

He shook his head. 'No, there's too much to do at Bessingdon at present.' I felt my face fall. He smiled at me kindly. 'But perhaps if Moira wrote to Lady Pickering, you might run up for a few days in August – would you like that? It would be very quiet.'

'Please – oh, yes please.'

'I'll speak to her then. I'll leave you now, my dear. Lord Pickering promised to take me round the farms this morning – one or two points I want to discuss with him – I'm not much of a landlord, yet.' He stood up to go; I held out my hand but he did not see it. I turned and watched him stride up the steps: at the top he paused for a moment and waved; I waved back, then I went to look for my brothers.

The twins decided to stay in Cheshire; they said London was too hot and stuffy now. The last weekend passed very quickly. Mother had invited a party for a Saturday-to-Monday, so the house was full of guests, and she said she supposed it was time she paid off some of her arrears of hospitality to local worthies, so there were two big dinner parties. I hoped Gerald would suggest that we walked in the garden afterwards, but he did not. Mother was pleased with him, because on Saturday he gallantly engaged in conversation with the elderly vicar of Lostherne, and shouted patiently down his ear trumpet for most of the evening. On Sunday he was equally persevering with old Miss Porteous; as Gerald nodded and smiled her withered face became quite pink and animated. I loved him for his kindness, but I would have liked to walk in the garden with him again, alone.

On Monday he left before we did, for Bessingdon. He bent down and kissed my cheek, then strode off to the waiting motor. We followed two hours later. On the train to London I was desolate and tears filled my eyes – but I dared not let them spill over, or Mother would have been annoyed. Then she began to talk about bridesmaids, and I felt a little more cheerful.

Guy came round to see us at Cadogan Place that evening; I ran to him and he hugged me tightly. 'Hearty congratters, Hellie old girl – if you couldn't manage to fall for a Grenadier, then I suppose the Life Guards are the next best thing!'

Lance came round the next day with Pansy and their mother. While Pansy and Mrs Benson were talking to Mother he said to me quietly, 'I hope you'll be very happy, Helena.'

'Thank you, Lance.' I did not know what else to say. Then Guy joined us and they began to talk about the worsening situation in Ireland.

'I hope we don't get sent over there, Lance old boy – it's going to be a nasty business. I've got some good friends among the Unionists – I don't fancy having to order an attack on the streets of Belfast.'

Lance looked serious. 'Yes, civil war's the worst kind – they say the King's suggesting a conference at the Palace – let's hope it comes off.'

My thoughts drifted back to Gerald. I jumped when Lance got up to go – I had forgotten he was there.

Moira Staveley wrote to me; her words were formal, but she said she had also written to Mother, inviting us both to visit Bessingdon in August. Mother's jaw dropped a little as she read her letter. 'How terribly old-fashioned – luckily I've already made a previous engagement – Maud will think of something. I'll write the usual platitudes and send you by yourself with Liliane. Gerald will be a pleasant enough son-in-law, but he's not the most exciting of men. Besides, I've got better things to do with my time than watch you mooning round over him, Helena. Still, you'll come to your senses soon enough once you're married – one man's much the same as another as a husband – providing he's got money of course, and there's no doubt on that score. By the way Helena, it's time I gave you some advice. Don't go hunting the first winter, Gerald will want an heir as soon as possible, and jumping will only joggle your insides. Besides, I've always held that any woman worth her salt should give her husband at least two sons before she begins to relax and enjoy herself. Remember that,

Helena – I don't want a daughter of mine to fail in her duty.' She swept out of the room. I glared at her retreating back – how could she speak so cynically about our marriage? I loved Gerald, and I always would. And he had pledged to be faithful to me; his vow in the garden at Hatton would live in my memory for ever.

When I had calmed down I went up to my bedroom and composed a careful reply to Moira Staveley.

At the end of the week I received a letter from Gerald. I slipped it inside the breast of my blouse, and did not open it until I was alone, but it was very matter of fact. He described what he had done each day at Bessingdon; Moira had ridden round the estate with him every morning – I felt a sharp stab of jealousy, then I remembered poor Stavey and was overcome with guilt. I wrapped his letter in tissue paper and tied it up with ribbon, together with the others I had had from him. I wrote back and told him of the dinner parties and dances Mother had taken me to – I wanted to tell him I cared nothing for them, and could only think of how I loved him – but I was too shy.

Then one day Guy came round to lunch and he and Papa started to talk about the Balkans again. Apparently Austria was determined to teach Serbia a lesson after all. They became excited and forgot their lamb cutlets and began to talk of fighting. But of course Serbia was much too small to take on the Austro-Hungarian Empire – even I knew that – she would have to give in. In the afternoon Mother took me to look at monograms for my trousseau linen.

But that Sunday, Guy arrived at breakfast time, waving a copy of *The Times*. 'War's broken out in the Serb states!' Papa was at his elbow, I heard their excited voices: 'Russia', 'France', 'Berchtold', 'Von Bulow', 'Luxembourg – the Germans are invading Luxembourg!'

I said stupidly, 'But the war's in Serbia – why should the Germans invade Luxembourg?'

Guy began a long tirade about allies – Russia – the

Kaiser – France. I listened bewildered as strong fingers stabbed at the maps in the newspaper.

On Bank Holiday Monday the Regatta was abandoned at Cowes, and Parliament met in the afternoon. The headlines screamed: 'France Invaded', 'Germany's Ultimatum to Belgium'. France, Belgium – but they were so near!

On Tuesday morning I was playing the piano in the morning room when the footman threw open the door: 'Lord Staveley, my lady.' It was Gerald. I jumped up and ran to him. He caught me to him in a quick hug, then set me to one side and began to stride up and down the room; his eyes were shining, his face glowing – I had never seen him so excited.

'It's war, Helena – it must come. We can't stand aside now, our very honour is at stake. I've seen old Birch – I'll be back in uniform this afternoon.' He threw back his head and laughed with joy.

I was in a turmoil. I saw Gerald, Gerald in his red tunic and gleaming breastplate, thundering into battle with the white plume on his helmet streaming out in the wind, his sword shining in the sun – and excitement coursed through me. But then, from long ago came the words: 'Hellie – Jem's *dead*', and fear closed my throat. And as I stood dumb he bent down and kissed me quickly and turned away, calling his farewells as he left.

All day I waited apprehensively – surely something would be done, somebody would act? But it was too late; by the afternoon the newsboys were shouting in the streets: 'British Ultimatum to Germany – War at Midnight!'

I went to bed early that night, and hid my head under the covers. First thing next morning I sent Liliane down for the paper. I opened it with shaking hands and read the stark black capitals:

WAR DECLARED

I handed the paper back to Liliane and went over to the little heap of elegant embroidered monogram patterns on my bureau. I carefully wrapped them in tissue paper before I put them in the back of the drawer and pushed it shut. It closed with a soft decisive click.

PART III

AUGUST 1914
to
SEPTEMBER 1916

CHAPTER ONE

Gerald and Guy went first.

Gerald came round to Cadogan Place in the morning; a strange Gerald in khaki and gleaming riding boots – a soldier now. His blue eyes were sparkling, his face alive. As he talked quickly and confidently to my parents my gaze dropped to his breast, to the scarlet and blue ribbon of the medal he had won in an earlier war. Now his sword hung again by his hip and he was going to war once more.

He stood up – he was making his farewells – and I had said nothing. The words of love and longing stayed glued to my tongue in the formal drawing room before my parents. He came forward and took my hand; I held my face up to him and he kissed me quickly, then turned to go. I called after him, 'Take care – oh Gerald, do take care!' He looked back and smiled, his face amused, and I realized how stupid I had sounded – how could a soldier take care?

I went upstairs and wept until Liliane came to tell me that Guy had come to say goodbye. I ran down, the tears still damp on my cheeks; and now the khaki-clad officer in the drawing room was tall and dark – my brother. He smiled and caught me to him. 'I haven't got long, Hellie – we're off this evening. What luck I'm attached to the Second Battalion – the First are still kicking their heels in the barracks at Warley. There'll be nobody left for them to fight by the time they get over to France!'

My parents came in; I sat down quickly, close to my brother, and gazed at his beloved face, so happy and excited. And as they all talked of the war I realized with a shock that he was already wearing a leather holster –

here, in Mother's elegant drawing room, he was carrying a revolver.

I was still downstairs at the piano when yet another man in khaki came to bid me farewell: Lance Benson. He came towards me shyly, his fair face flushed; there was no light in his eyes – only a stoic determination. 'So it's come, I'm glad it's not Ireland, at least – if I have to fight I'd rather fight foreigners – but, Helena, I wish I didn't have to fight at all.' And as I heard him, for a moment I felt contempt; then it was swallowed up in a rush of affection. Dear Lance, my partner so often at the piano and on the dance floor, who once had even asked me to marry him; Lance who had never wanted to be a soldier, and who now was going to war.

I jumped up and ran forward and flung my arms round his neck and pressed my cheek against his. 'Oh Lance, take care, do take care!'

I felt his arms tighten round me and the brush of his kiss on my ear, then he released me, gently. 'Thank you, Helena. Goodbye.' He turned and walked quickly out, a thin scholarly figure, but a soldier now.

Pansy came round the next morning and burst into tears. I knew I should try to comfort her, but I did not know how. I sat looking at her helplessly while she held my hand and whispered in broken sobs her fears for Lance and Guy.

A couple of days later the twins arrived from Hatton before dinner. They were in tearing spirits; they had pulled all the strings they knew how, and would soon be in receipt of two temporary commissions in the Lancashire and Cheshire Light Infantry. I said, 'But you're not soldiers!'

'We soon will be.' Eddie threw his hat high up into the air, Robbie caught it and waved it triumphantly.

I still tried to protest. 'Papa says it will all be over by Christmas.'

'Oh, don't be such a spoilsport, Hellie.' Eddie jostled

his brother towards the stairs as they went up to get changed.

Papa ordered an extra *Times;* we pored over them every morning. Liége was holding out, there were reports of German losses of twenty-five thousand – surely it would not last long now? Rumours flew about London; everybody had a new story to tell. People rubbed their hands and talked of the Russian steamroller – but Russia was far away and the Germans were in Belgium. I remembered the handsome Kurt; it seemed so strange that he and my brother were riding to war – to fight against each other. Then the head groom wrote from Hatton to say that the horses had been requisitioned, and I wept bitter tears for my graceful, loyal Melody – I had not even been able to see her to say goodbye.

Mother took me to roll bandages at Lady Eames'. Juno was there, her bandages twisted into an untidy bundle; she lit a surreptitious cigarette and the gauze began to smoulder. There were little shrieks and the footman had to come in to put it out.

A letter arrived from Gerald, written hurriedly at Southampton as he was about to embark for France with the Composite Regiment. He sounded very cheerful, and said I was not to worry if I did not hear from him again for some time, as he would be very busy.

That evening Alice and Hugh came round to dinner. Hugh had applied to join his brother's Irish regiment. Alice's eyes were sparkling; she leant across to touch the flowers in the epergne and her breast brushed Hugh's hand, her fingertips moved on to the ferns and her full bosom dipped again. Hugh's eyes narrowed; Alice flashed a burning smile at him.

Conan burst in when we were drinking coffee in the drawing room. He had been with a yachting party in northern Norway – he had only just heard and he was wild with excitement. He badgered Hugh and Papa with questions and when Hugh told him of what he had done he said imperiously, 'Get me in too, Hugh, there's a good chap – I want to fight with an Irish regiment.'

Hugh promised to do his best, then he jumped up and seized Alice's hand. 'We must be going – it's late.' I glanced at the clock on the mantelpiece, it had only just gone ten; but Alice swayed towards him and they left, their heads very close together. I felt an aching longing for Gerald.

Two days later came the official announcement that the British Army had all been landed in France, with no casualties. The French had welcomed our soldiers warmly. I thought of Gerald and of Guy, riding through the streets of a small French town – riding to war.

Next Monday we read that the Russians had won a brilliant victory and the Serbs had defeated the Austrians. But the evening edition carried the news that the great fortress of Namur had fallen – and that British troops had been engaged in battle throughout the previous day. Liliane was red-eyed that evening, fearful for the safety of her family, but I reassured her that the British Army would never allow France to be overrun.

On Tuesday the paper said that the First and Second Corps had fought at Mons, and driven off the enemy – but because of Namur the Allies were withdrawing. We scanned the papers anxiously all week, but they told us little, until on the following Monday the news was better – the Allies had retreated, but only to hold a stronger position. It was the last day of August, and wounded were already being landed at Folkestone and Harwich. I was in the morning room playing the piano when Juno burst in, her face flushed, her hat crooked.

'Hellie – have you heard?' I swung round – had the Germans surrendered? Had we won a great victory? She strode across the room to face me and said, 'Lance Benson's been killed.'

I stared at her, then said stupidly, 'No – he can't have been.'

She shouted at me. 'For goodness' sake, Helena –

there's a war on!' Then she mumbled, 'I'm sorry I – well, it was a bit of a shock. I've always been fond of old Lance – can't take it in. They say Pansy's in a terrible state.'

I remembered all the times we had analysed operas together, all the times he had played for my singing, and I remembered his earnest young face as he had said: 'If there's ever anything I can do for you, send for me, wherever I am. I'll always come, always.' But he would not come now. Lance, Lance who had never wanted to be a soldier had died a hero's death – had given all that he had while I sat in a comfortable room and played the piano. I dropped the lid with a bang and stood up.

Juno looked at me. 'Truth to tell, Hellie, I don't like sitting around doing nothing when all this is going on – what use are a few mouldy bandages? I've been making inquiries; nurses are being called up as well, the hospitals are short-staffed – anyway, the East London in Spitalfields is willing to take paying probationers, for three months at first – I'm seeing the matron this morning.'

I walked to the bell and rang for Liliane. 'You're right Juno, we must do something. I'll come with you.'

I let Juno do most of the talking at the interview, while I tried not to stare at the matron. She wore an elaborately frilled muslin cap: it looked so odd above her lined, leathery face that for a moment I wanted to laugh, then I remembered Lance and felt sick. A doctor was summoned; he questioned us on our childhood ailments, then we were instructed to bare a discreet portion of our chests so he could listen carefully. 'Say "Ah".' As I breathed 'Ah' he commented, 'That's a magnificent pair of lungs, young lady, for such a slender physique.' He prodded again. 'And you've got the diaphragm of an ox.' Matron nodded approvingly. I felt like a cow for sale in the stock market.

Juno muttered, 'That's all your singing, Helena.' The doctor overheard and grunted. 'You won't have much time for singing if you intend to be a nurse.' I felt apprehensive as he folded his stethoscope into his bag and reported, 'Both A1, Matron, strong as a pair of dray horses – just what you need.' He left without a word to us. Matron began to talk about vaccination and uniforms.

My parents dined at home that evening. They were obviously shocked at the news of Lance's death; they spoke to each other in low voices, and I heard them mention Guy several times. I felt a fluttering of panic. Mother glanced at my untouched plate, then said, quite kindly, 'Don't worry, Helena, Gerald is an experienced soldier, he's come through one war unscathed already.'

I thought, but his brother didn't.

Next morning the newspaper reported that eight hundred wounded soldiers had been taken to the London Hospital in Whitechapel; and the doctor arrived at Cadogan Place to vaccinate us.

The matron had told us we could not begin nursing until I was twenty-one, so we decided to enter the East London on Thursday the 10th of September, the day of my twenty-first birthday. I felt that if I did not go at once I would never pluck up the courage to go at all.

I wrote to Gerald and told him of my decision, but even as I sealed the envelope I wondered if my letter would ever reach him.

The Times printed fresh maps every day now. 'The Dash for Paris' on Wednesday became 'The Danger to Paris' on Thursday. The German troops were a thick black line slashed across northern France. Liliane became very quiet, though her parents lived down in the south, in Provence; Provence had not appeared on the maps yet – but Amiens had fallen to the enemy. There was a Press Bureau report headlined: 'British Cavalry Engaged with Distinction' – they had captured ten big guns; as I read it I thought of Gerald, fighting for all of us. On Friday the King and Queen visited the wounded at the London Hospital and on Saturday the Roll of Honour gave the names of ten more officers killed; now the map was entitled: 'The Defence of Paris' – our forces were still retreating.

Papa lunched with a friend at the War Office and came back to tea with a very grave face. He told us the Grenadiers had been in battle at a place called Landrecies in August, and fought again in an 'engagement' they called it, at Villers-Cotterêts on 1st September. Casualties were being shipped back, but as far as he knew Guy was safe. Then he turned to Mother. 'The Germans are still advancing, Ria – they're sweeping across France – and if Paris falls . . .' He shook his head. 'I thought I'd ask Grayton if I could be any use, joining up again . . .'

Mother spoke sharply. 'For goodness' sake, Victor! You'll be fifty-five this year – leave the war to the youngsters.' Papa flushed and left the drawing room.

A special night edition of *The Times* was called on the streets on Sunday evening; the map said simply: 'New German Movement'. On Monday morning it read 'The Germans Across the Marne'; but on Tuesday the headlines began to change: 'German Check in France' and on Wednesday 'German Line Driven Back' and, at last the words, 'A British Victory'. I showed it to Liliane and she burst out sobbing, 'Grâce à Dieu, grâces au ciel.' She began to tell her rosary; I backed away, embarrassed.

Thursday was the 10th of September: my twenty-first birthday. A neat pile of parcels and letters was stacked beside my plate on the breakfast table. Papa kissed my cheek. 'Happy birthday, Helena – we've driven them back twenty-five miles, right across the Marne, Paris has been saved, thank God.'

I sat down and began to open my presents. I recognized Moira Staveley's writing on a flat packet and opened it first; inside were two framed photographs of Gerald. In one he wore his full-dress uniform and his face was serious, the other was a smiling portrait in a morning suit. I held one in each shaking hand, gazing at them alternately. I loved him so much – oh please God, keep him safe. In her letter she said that before he left he had commissioned her to buy my present; it had been ordered and sent from Cartier's. She wished me well and said she was praying every day for Gerald's safety. I found the right package and opened it with shaking hands; inside, sparkling against the red velvet, was a diamond tiara. It was made in a graceful design of leaves and flowers on fine gold stems, with a slim diamond chain so that it could also be worn as a necklet. Now I slipped it on and it lay cool against the back of my neck, the diamond leaves heavy on my breast. I gently touched one brilliant flower with my fingertip – I had hoped, but I had not expected anything. Dearest Gerald, to remember my birthday even as he left for the war.

Guy had remembered too; he had asked Alice to buy me a sapphire necklace to go with my ring, and matching earrings. I slipped out my small pearl studs and put Guy's gifts in their place. Alice and Hugh had sent a corsage watch, set with pearls and diamonds; I pinned it to my blouse by its bejewelled bow. Mother laughed. 'Goodness, Helena, you look like a Christmas tree! Still, you'd better enjoy them this morning, you won't be able to once you're a hospital nurse.'

I felt a tremor of nervousness, but there was a big parcel for me still to open, from the twins, so I began to break the seal. Soon glossy crocodile leather appeared, and when I pulled the paper away I saw it was a dressing case. I pulled up the fastenings and the lid sprang up to display an Aladdin's cave of gleaming bottles with silver tops and shining mirrors nestling against the dark-blue watered silk lining. My fingers twitched to explore it, but Papa was addressing me. 'I'll ring for Fisher to bring in your present from your mother and myself.'

When my mother's maid appeared her arms were full of dark fur. As I saw it, for a moment Mother's fur cupboard closed darkly around me, then I forced myself forward. 'How beautiful, thank you so much.' Miss Fisher hung the cape round my shoulders. I tensed before I touched it, but the fur was deep and soft, and there was no sharp evil face leering out at me. 'Thank you Papa, thank you Mother.'

Papa's moustaches brushed my face, Mother's cheek touched mine. 'Happy birthday, my dear.' 'Happy birthday, Helena.'

Then Miss Fisher took the cape away again and we sat down to read Sir John French's Dispatch from France.

The next post brought two more packets: I recognized Conan's scrawl on one; the other was from Letty. I opened Conan's present first – he had never remembered my birthday before. There was a note with it:

'Happy birthday, sweet Coz, Hugh told me of your plans so I thought you might like this to take into your convent with you – to remind you of the frivolous days of yore.'

I unwrapped the soft tissue: it was a fan. I flicked the slender ivory sticks and opened the dainty semi-circle of Marceline lace. There was a figure painted on the lace – a dark-haired girl in gauzy draperies, reclining under a small green tree. I moved it back and forth, and the air it stirred caressed my cheek. Then I folded it carefully, wrapped it and slipped it into the outer pocket of the bag Liliane had packed for me; I would take a memento with me into my convent.

I was still smiling as I opened Letty's parcel; it was a pen, a fountain pen. I handled it gingerly: I had never used one. Letty had written a careful explanation.

'This is more sensible than fiddling with bottles of ink all the time. I got a Pelican because it has a shut-off valve, so you can carry it upside down if you like – it won't leak.'

It all sounded very technical and next to it in the box was a glass fountain-pen filler – it was sure to be a messy job; I would have to get one of the footmen to fill it for me. I picked up Letty's note again:

'I thought a pen was a good idea for your present, because you will have to write a lot of letters now.'

I felt chilly in the warm bedroom; yes, I would. Those I loved were already scattered, and now I was leaving too. Reluctantly I pushed Letty's gift into my travelling bag as well.

Finally I picked up again the two photos of Gerald; I would take one with me and leave the other here at Cadogan Place, beside my own bed. I hesitated for a long time before I made my choice – the smiling Gerald in civilian clothes would go with me. I knew he was a soldier now but I wanted to think of him as I would see him in the future, when the war was over and we were married and he would come into our breakfast room and greet me each morning with just such a warm, affectionate smile.

Papa took us all to Claridge's for lunch. As I sat at the table with Mother and Alice I could not help noticing how many of the younger men were already in khaki. England was at war, and so Juno and I were going to play our part in the grimy barracks of the East London. Under the damask tablecloth my vaccination scar throbbed and my belly was one tight knot of fear.

CHAPTER TWO

I had just finished my last thank you letter when Juno and her mother arrived. We were all to take tea together at Cadogan Place and afterwards Lady Maud would escort us to Spitalfields. Now she chewed buttered crumpets at top speed while talking excitedly of her plans to get out to France and help the troops. Mother's voice was mocking. 'Dear me, Maud, how brave you are – and Helena here is shaking in her shoes at the thought of merely going to the East End of London!'

Lady Maud said stoutly, 'I'd plump for France any day – much healthier.'

France, where men were fighting and dying: I would never dare to go there. Spitalfields seemed almost welcome for a moment.

Mother and Juno began to argue about Zeppelins: how far they could fly, how big they were. Lady Maud broke in, 'They're so huge they would practically fill St James's Street – Victor swore that was true.'

'Then, Maud, it can't possibly be so!'

Lady Maud blinked, then laughed with Mother. 'But seriously, Ria, they say they could reach Britain, if they tried.'

I remembered the round fat cigar which had hovered over Agar's Plough at Eton before floating slowly down. It was no longer an innocuous ship of the air, it was a Zeppelin – and under its threatening dark shadow our safe island would be safe no longer. I shivered.

Lady Maud brushed the crumbs from her lap and stood up. 'Come along you girls, it's time to enlist.' I rang for my hat.

As we climbed out of the cab the hospital loomed over us and the blank windows stared at us like so many unsleeping eyes. We passed inside the ugly yellow brick gateway and crossed dingy courtyards to the Nurses' Home; the porter trundled our boxes behind us. A pale-faced, unsmiling housekeeper asked our names, then we followed her up several flights of stairs. The housekeeper selected one of a row of identical doors and threw it open; she gestured to Juno who took a deep breath and said to Lady Maud, 'Cheerio for now, Ma – I'll run up and see you when I can.' They shook hands vigorously, then Lady Maud crushed my fingers in turn, 'Good luck, the pair of you.' She swung round and strode off. I gazed after her helplessly, but the woman beckoned me on.

My room was further down; it was like a cell. The porter hefted my trunk inside as I fumbled for a tip. He glanced at it in surprise and touched his forelock. 'Good

191

evening, Nurse.' I started and looked round before I realized he was addressing me, and my legs were shaking as I crouched down and began to tug at the heavy leather straps. I had never unpacked for myself in my whole life and I was surrounded by untidy heaps of clothes and tissue paper when there was a loud rap at the door which was flung open before I had time to call 'come in'. A middle-aged woman in a blue cotton dress and nurse's cap marched in, then stopped suddenly. She stared disapprovingly at the chaos around me before snapping, 'Tidy up at *once*, Nurse. Then dress in your uniform and come *straight* down to my room with the other new probationers. Bring your cap with you and I will instruct you on how to make it up. Put your box *outside* as soon as it's empty and don't waste any more time.' Starched skirts crackled out.

I began frantically to burrow for my uniform. I had not even tried it on before – I had not wanted to look ahead. The frock was a hideous mauve check in coarse cotton, the skirt clumsily gathered at the back only, with sleeves that puffed out over the upper arm and then became suddenly tight at the elbow. It looked ugly and old-fashioned and the housemaids at Hatton would never have worn it, not even for lighting the fires first thing. I struggled to attach the high starched collar to the dress with slippery collar studs; I was sweating with the heat and with fear. The billowing linen apron enveloped me from shoulder to ankle, and when I secured it with the wide white belt it bunched uncomfortably over my hips. My pointed bronze leather toes peeped out below it; they looked surprised. I scrabbled frantically for the thick black stockings and flat black shoes that would complete the whole graceless outfit. I was fastening the last suspender when there were rapid footsteps in the corridor and Juno burst in. 'I never thought I'd have to dress up like a general servant – and what is this supposed to be?' She held out a short white cotton tube.

I suggested tentatively, 'A sleeve?'

192

'But it's not attached to anything – and it's the bottom half!' She threw the object down on the bed. 'Come on, Hellie, locate this cap of yours and we'll get downstairs.' I found a pile of flat white cambric pancakes with tapes running through them, picked one up and followed Juno out.

We found the right room at last. The woman in the blue dress looked impatient and as soon as we came in she pounced on my ring, Gerald's ring. 'Whatever are you doing wearing that?'

I put my hand protectively over it. 'It's my betrothal ring.'

My fingers were prized open. 'No jewellery at all to be worn on the wards, *most* insanitary – it will harbour germs, besides the damage to patients.' She made irritated clucking noises in her throat. 'Here.' She rustled to her desk, scissors snapped and I was handed a length of tape. 'Take it off and tie it round your neck for the time being – *under* your dress.' Slowly I pulled off Gerald's ring, threaded the tape through it and pushed it down inside my camisole. The stone lay cold on my skin above my heart. Then she seized my pancake, tweaked the tapes and converted it into a cotton shovel. 'Bend your head, Nurse. Dear me, no bun? All nurses must part their hair in the middle, lift it *above* the ears and wear it in a bun above the nape – how else can your cap be attached?' She waved the ends of the tapes.

Somehow the shovel was fastened to my hair, then Juno bent her head in turn. We stood uncertainly waiting until there was a tap at the door and two more girls came in, clutching white pancakes. 'Is this the right room?' The leading girl spoke with a marked and unpleasant accent. I glanced at Juno and shuddered.

The next hour passed in a confused mêlée of unfamiliar sights and sounds: the tiered lecture room, the massed ranks of nurses, the frock-coated doctor addressing us – haemorrhage, arteries, tourniquet – whatever did his words mean? Then out again along endless stone passageways and steep bare staircases until Sister's sharp voice pierced my frightened senses. 'You are allocated to Allsop Ward, Nurse.' I was whisked through a lobby and into a long high room which receded into the shadows. The blinds were drawn but a red-shaded lamp glowed by one bed; the humped figure in it shifted restlessly and I heard a low moan of pain – my stomach lurched.

A woman in blue came forward without speaking to me. 'Thank you, Sister. Staff Nurse is in the kitchen.' I was whisked back out again.

Staff Nurse was tall and angular and looked angry. As soon as my escort had left she snapped, 'I don't know what we're supposed to do with you – we've one useless pair of hands already.' She glared at a small mousey girl stirring something at the stove who shrank back over her saucepan, her eyes frightened. Staff Nurse turned back to me. 'What's your name?'

'Lady Helena Girvan.'

Staff Nurse's bony face reddened. 'We don't have any ladies here – or Christian names either. That's the first rule.' She jerked her head towards the door. 'I suppose I'd better show you round. Carry on with that custard, Fraser – at least try and stop the lumps getting any larger or Number Seventeen won't even be able to get them in her mouth. Follow me, Girvan.'

It took me several seconds to realize she was addressing me; then I hastily scurried after her. 'Steril-izer, linen cupboard, Sister's room, bathroom.' She rattled off the names, sprang at another door and flung it open. 'Sink room.' The stench hit me like a blow in the face and I stepped quickly back. 'Patients' WCs and lavatories are at the other end of the ward – though not many use them, they're mostly confined to bed.'

She paused for breath and I ventured a query. 'Where are the WCs for us to use?'

'Officially down three flights of stairs by the side entrance – but you'll be lucky to ever be allowed off long enough to get there, so you'd better learn to hang on, or if you're desperate you can slip into the patients' — but don't let Sister catch you and for God's sake don't sit on the seat — some of our women are as infectious as lepers.' I felt sick, and decided I would 'hang on'. 'I've got to sort out that idiot Fraser — you'd better just stand in the corner there and use your eyes, we're off duty in ten minutes.'

I stood still in the corner of the darkened ward, feeling frightened and useless. I saw the momentary flash of a white cap at the far end, then it vanished behind a screen and I was left alone, while all around me sick women lay sleeping in their beds. A thin white plait stirred on the bed cover nearest to me, and a pair of eyes gleamed in the gloom. Very slowly the bedclothes moved until a claw-like hand emerged and began to flutter above the sheet. The eyes were fixed on me as the toothless mouth opened and gave a low moan; I shrank back against the wall. The moan rose in pitch until it was a keening cry of distress; I was terrified. The keening came again, higher and shriller; I looked desperately round and at that point the ward door swung open and the mousey nurse called Fraser came in. I let my breath out in relief — but she ignored the outstretched claw and headed up the ward. I ran after her and caught her arm. 'Please — an old woman — she's crying . . .'

Fraser pulled herself free. 'For goodness' sake!' Her voice was impatient. She marched back to the bed at the entrance and glared at the old woman. 'Be quiet *at once*, Number Fifteen, you're disturbing the whole ward.' The moan stopped abruptly in mid breath; she clutched at her sheet and stared up at us with crazed, frightened eyes. Fraser was gone; I backed treacherously away from the despairing eyes and half ran to hide in the other corner.

I peered at the hands of the ward clock, willing them to move on, and at last they crawled to twenty past nine, and Staff Nurse came to fetch me. 'The night nurses are here – come and be dismissed.'

I stood at the end of the row while Sister dismissed us; she did not even glance in my direction. We walked sedately out into the lobby and then there was a stampede. Staff Nurse hissed, 'Harris, take Girvan to the dining room with you.' A small blonde girl looked quickly back and nodded; I scuttled after her, terrified of being lost in the maze of passageways.

When we finally reached the dining room another blue-frocked woman sat at the entrance with a register in front of her. 'Number?'

I stared at her blankly. The blonde girl spoke over my shoulder. 'She's new, Sister, she hasn't got a number yet, her name's Girvan.'

The sister's mouth tightened as her finger flicked down the page. 'Twenty-seven.'

There was a jab in the small of my back and a hissed, 'Give her your number.'

I jerked out, 'Twenty-seven'; the blonde said, 'Fifty-two', and we were finally allowed in to the sound of impatient mutterings from the queue behind us.

I was pushed towards a chair and almost fell into it. A panting Juno flopped down beside me. 'What's your number Hellie?'

'Twenty-seven.'

'How strange, I'm Thirty-four, yet we arrived together.'

A nurse opposite glanced up. 'They give you the number of the last pro to go – Thirty-four was Potts, couldn't stick it, I believe – Twenty-seven was Rowley's number, wasn't it?'

Her neighbour nodded. 'Pity; nice girl, I believe.'

Juno asked, 'Did she give it up, too?'

'No, she died last week, tubercular meningitis – ssh, Sister's saying grace.'

A plate with some kind of rissole on it was slapped down in front of me. I picked up my knife and fork, but the rissole tasted of warmed-up grease and I could only force half of it down. I looked around the big bleak room at the hundreds of strange faces and felt very alone. Then Juno muttered beside me, 'What foul food,' and I was a little comforted – at least I had someone of my own sort there beside me.

At the end of the meal we followed the nurses from our table and found ourselves in the wrong Nurses' Home – apparently there were two – it was very confusing. When we eventually found our way back to the right corridor both the bathrooms were occupied, with dressing-gowned queues outside. Juno shrugged. 'I had a bath this morning, I'm going to bed dirty – anyway I want to write some letters.'

So did I, but I found it very difficult to concentrate in that box of a bedroom. I took out the smiling photograph of Gerald and looked at it for a long time before I began to write 'Dearest Gerald', but still the words would not come. In the end I managed a few lines on our arrival, but I could not tell him my fears about this strange new life – not when he was so bravely fighting the enemy. I sealed the envelope and began to write to the twins instead. I was pouring out my anxieties and despondency in this frightening place when the room was plunged abruptly into darkness; it was ten-thirty. I fumbled my way into bed, but it was a long time before I fell asleep.

CHAPTER THREE

The clanging of a handbell shook me violently from sleep; the noise grew louder, the clapper resounded outside my door, then the ringer passed on. Shaking, I pushed myself out of bed; it was a quarter before six.

While doors banged and feet scampered along the corridor I pulled on the unaccustomed uniform; and combed and twisted and pulled at my hair until I had anchored it in some kind of bun at the back of my head. I tied the tapes of my white cambric shovel under it and speared in hairpins until they hurt; I saw with dismay that my face in the mirror looked like a scalped chicken's without any softening dark mass above it.

At breakfast the butter was an odd colour and tasted horrible; the new probationer with the accent squealed, 'Ugh, margarine!'

Juno's voice was indignant. 'Mama's staff would all go on strike sooner than eat that muck – and this fish has seen better days.' We chewed grimly, and tried to mask the rancid flavours with the dark bitter tea.

Breakfast lasted a bare ten minutes, then the nurses began to stream out. We looked at each other – we did not know what to do next – then Juno grabbed a passing arm and demanded instructions. 'You can go back to your rooms if you want, but be on your ward at the stroke of seven, else you'll catch it.'

I decided not to risk going back to the Home; I knew it would take me all my time to find Allsop Ward again. I scanned one dusty courtyard after another and ran all the way up the wrong staircase before I arrived panting at the door of the ward just as the clock chimed seven. I searched desperately through the lobby until I found the other pros on the ward standing in a line in front of Staff Nurse. She glared at me and rapped out, 'Girvan, sweep first and then dust – Harris, show her where the things are kept.'

Harris seemed less impatient than the others; she even smiled at me as she spoke. 'Goody, that's usually my job, now I can make beds instead.'

'Stop dithering and get a move on.' At Staff Nurse's rebuke we shot into the lobby. Harris whispered, 'Staff's not a bad old stick, her bark's worse than her bite.' She handed me broom, shovel, and bucket of tea leaves, pointed to the box of dusters and gave me a push towards the ward.

After an hour I felt battered and bruised and totally stupid. I did not know how to sweep or how to dust; I could not even hold a broom correctly. Staff Nurse shouted at me; the other probationers hissed and pushed me out of their way. I thrust desperately hither and thither with my broom until my shoes and stockings were coated with dirt and the floor of the ward was streaked with dusty tea leaves. The patients who were propped up in their high beds looked at me with amazement. I saw one broad-faced woman glance at her neighbour, raise her eyebrows, then tap her forehead significantly. In my childhood I had seen housemaids perform these very tasks so easily, so efficiently – and now I was being branded as a half-wit by some costermonger's wife. I burnt with shame.

As I struggled with the duster I knocked a bed crooked, so that the woman in it groaned in pain. Staff Nurse scolded, 'Don't be so careless, Girvan – and remember, Number Twelve is a typhoid case, if you so much as shiver her bed you'll kill her!'

Number Twelve lay huddled on her side; my hands shook as I gingerly dusted her bed rail – typhoid, surely that was very infectious? My eyes kept going back to the tiled stand which stood at the foot of the bed, bearing its ominous bowl of disinfectant. As I circled round I saw there was a set of cutlery and crockery stacked on the lower shelf – each item painted with a bright blue 'T'. I shuddered.

When I had finished the dusting, Staff Nurse set me to clean a glass trolley with big bottles of lotions on it – yellow, blue and pink – the colours were pretty in this bleak ward and it was a relief to be able to stay in one place for a while and have a simple task to perform. But I put too much meths on the cloth and the glass smeared, and when I rubbed at it frantically to try to clean it, small threads of lint clung where the duster moulted.

My back ached, so I pulled up a nearby chair and sat down to attack the lower shelf, but no sooner was I seated than a stern-faced probationer swung round from one of the beds and snapped, 'Get up at once! You must *never* sit down on the ward in the daytime.' I leapt to my feet like a scalded cat, thrust the betraying chair away and crouched down by the shelf. Tears stung my eyes.

At twenty-five past eight I was summoned to the central table and handed a cup of tea. 'Drink it quickly, Sister comes on at half-past.' I was embarrassed to be drinking in front of the watching patients, but I felt so sick and shaky I swallowed it gratefully. As soon as we had finished I was sent to return the tray to the maid in the kitchen; I was walking back through the lobby when a door opened and Sister came out. Without thinking I glanced into the doorway behind her and saw a little sitting room, with ornaments on the mantelpiece and pictures on the walls – and realized incredulously that she lived there, on the ward – how ever could she stand it? Her face stiffened as she saw me and she shut the door with a sharp click.

I followed her back into the ward and joined the group of nurses. Staff Nurse whispered, 'Fetch the hassock for Sister.' I looked wildly round – for an instrument? A utensil? 'The *hassock*, don't you ever go to church?' and then I saw the plump needlepoint hassock nestling under the table. I snatched it up and Staff Nurse flicked her apron over it and placed it in the exact centre of the ward. Harris held out bell and prayerbook to Sister, who took them, rang for silence and then creaked down on to the hassock. The rest of us fell on our knees on the hard wooden floor.

'We beseech Thee . . . to bless the work of this hospital . . . We commend the patients to Thy loving care . . . Help all those who are nurses . . .' Sister's voice intoned monotonously on and I found myself repeating silently over and over again:

'Please God, look after Gerald – please God, keep him safe,' until suddenly everyone else was on their feet and I had to hastily scramble up, feeling very foolish.

We were sent back to our rooms for half an hour to clean them and make our beds and to put on fresh aprons. The thought of another struggle with broom and shovel was too much for me; I collapsed on to the mattress and stared hopelessly at the bare walls. I was a failure, before I had even finished my first morning. Then Juno burst in waving a *Times;* she looked as dishevelled as I felt, but she did not seem to care. 'Look, Hellie, the appointments are out from the London Gazette – just look here.' I followed her stabbing finger below the heading 'Cavalry' and read: '1st Life Guards, Captain the Marquess of Staveley to be Major.' My face flushed with pride and my heart beat faster. I thought of Gerald riding at the head of his squadron as he fought for his King and country; of Guy leading his men into battle; and of Lance, Lance with his gentle face a white mask as he lay still on the fields of Belgium. Whilst I, I sat weeping because I could not perform the simplest of household tasks. I stood up straight and began to tug at the crumpled sheets.

Back on the ward I was set to cleaning again: the brass knobs on the beds; the brass taps on the lavatory basins; the brass rims round the tables; the brass trays in the kitchen. My fingers became stained and dirty; my nail broke and caught in the polishing cloth. Harris saw me tugging at it. 'You'd better cut those nails Girvan – here borrow my scissors.'

I managed to cut my left hand, but I could not hold the scissors straight to trim the right. Harris seized them from me and pared the nails down quickly. As she snipped she asked, 'How ever have you managed not to learn to cut your own nails?'

I whispered, 'My maid always manicured my hands.'

She glanced up at me, her face astonished. 'Then I don't know what you're doing here, Girvan, but I think you're wasting your time.' I had to blink hard to keep back the tears.

When I had finished cleaning the bath I had to empty the sterilizer, scrub it out and refill it; my apron was sodden by the time it was done. As soon as I reported to Staff Nurse she hauled me into the vile-smelling sink room with curt instructions on how to deal with bed pans. She seized one, ran the seat under the hot water tap, dried it briskly then rushed me up the ward and made me pull the heavy screens round a bed. 'Don't worry, Granny, you'll soon be comfortable. Watch carefully, Girvan.' Shrinking, I watched her put her right hand under the woman's back and slide the white earthenware pan under the flabby buttocks. We heard the splash of urine and I prayed there would be nothing more.

Staff Nurse tipped the pan down the low glazed sink, then pulled the chain which flushed it. 'A quick dowse with hot water and a drop of lysol, then it can be hung up to dry. We only do a full wash once a day, after the evening round. There, you'll know what to do next time – never keep a patient waiting for a bed pan, it's far more trouble to change a dirty bed. Wash your hands now, it's nearly dinnertime.'

It was only twelve o'clock, but that was dinnertime for the patients. In the kitchen each probationer was given a knife and fork – for one hopeful moment I wondered if we were to eat first – then I saw that the potatoes had been boiled in their jackets and it was our task to skin them. 'Hurry up, Girvan, they don't want them stone cold.' I fumbled and hacked and lost control of the hot slippery potatoes and kept Staff Nurse impatiently waiting.

On the ward Sister herself served the dinners; the pros ran up and down the beds with loaded trays. I repeated the number of each plate frantically to myself as I scuttled along, but I still gave a plate of greasy stew to a gastric case and suffered the full force of Staff Nurse's wrath as she snatched a loaded fork from the woman's lips.

After dinner I had to wash up; I was told to bring the two bowls of soapy water into the ward and put them on the coal box. I had to force myself to plunge my hands into the water and touch other people's greasy knives and forks and plates. As I was drying the pudding plates I heard the patients in the beds nearby tittering. Harris looked up and laughed. 'Oh, you do look funny, Girvan – dabbing at them like that – get hold of the wretched things and give them a good wipe.' My face burned.

By the time I had finished, my six-thirty bread and fish had long been forgotten and I was faint with hunger, but we were still not allowed to go; yet again I was sent for the duster. It was a quarter past one before Sister read the afternoon off-duty list and dismissed us. We washed our hands and left the ward.

At our luncheon, which was called dinner, the boiled mutton was served to us, but the vegetables were put in large dishes on the table – they were almost finished before I realized I had to ask for them to be passed and help myself. At the end of the meal the nurses had to pile up their plates, knife, fork, spoon and glass, and carry them themselves to the hatch in a greasy pile; it was all very unpleasant. Juno and I ate so slowly we were left in the room with the maids clattering noisily in the background; we decided we would have to learn to chew faster. But at least we were off duty for the afternoon, until five o'clock.

I had scarcely looked at the outdoor uniform when I had unpacked; now I struggled into the grey alpaca dress and picked up the hat – it was a bonnet. Juno came in, holding hers in her hand. 'However can we go out in these? Suppose we meet someone we know!'

I said at last, 'I don't suppose we'll meet anyone we know in Spitalfields, and we can't stay in all afternoon.' I raised the bonnet and put it on my head. It was a small square straw trimmed with black velvet, with a floppy bow right in the centre at the front and a long gauze veil hanging stiffly down from the crown at the back. Two wide white ribbons had to be tied in another bow under the chin. When we had finished Juno and I stared side by side into the mirror at our astonished faces peering out from between the two enormous bows.

Juno's sudden grin flashed out. 'Well – lead me to the fancy-dress party!' And we both looked so funny I began to laugh; she joined in and soon we were gasping and holding our sides as we giggled uncontrollably in the hot stuffy bedroom. The horrors of the morning receded as we pulled on our black cotton gloves and set out again, still chuckling.

But beyond the side gate of the hospital our light-heartedness evaporated. This was a very different London from the spacious squares and avenues of the West End. The buildings were packed closely together, the streets were narrow and smeared with horse dung; and an unpleasant miasma compounded of ammonia, sulphur and other odours I could not identify assaulted our nostrils. Above our heads the brightness of the September sun was tarnished by the smoke and fumes of factories and workshops. I pulled my skirts more tightly around me as we passed small grubby children with dirt-encrusted faces playing in the filthy gutter. A group of men lounging against a wall stared boldly at us and before I dropped my eyes, I saw the dark greasy line behind them on the bricks where they had leant and smoked their pipes so often before. There was a rattling on the cobbles and a rickety barrow trundled round the corner towards us; the man pushing it peered out from between the drooping brim of his cap and an enormous walrus moustache. Two wailing cats followed him round and one of the small children cried out, 'Ay, Ma, it's the cats' meat man!' A woman with a shapeless swollen body waddled out of a doorway and headed towards the barrow; as we drew level with it we smelt the stench of half-rotten meat. Another half-starved cat streaked past our ankles and began to jump up at the cart, yowling like a banshee; we hurried past, faces averted from the noisome cargo, and almost ran round the corner.

But the next street revealed the same low, mean houses, the same grubby children crouched beside the pavement and a couple of men lounging by a favoured wall; the only difference was the addition of a group of women gossiping in soiled shawls. As we came towards them one stepped down into the gutter and straddled the grid. She raised her skirts above her dirty bare ankles and we watched in horror as the stream of liquid splashed down into the drain below. One of the lounging men nudged the other and guffawed and his taller companion called out, 'Ow much, Ma – while yer got yer drawers off ready?'

Juno's face turned fiery red, she seized my arm and dragged me, half-running, down the street. I almost stumbled over the children, and jerked hastily away as the sour unwashed smell of them filled my nostrils. Juno panted, 'How frightful, how frightful – how can people live like that?' I could not reply.

We turned another corner and thankfully found ourselves on Commercial Road East. At least here there were some decent-looking men and women among the ragged ones, and most of the females had covered their heads – though some only with their husbands' flat caps. There were shops too, with respectable-looking shop-keepers – I saw a straw-hatted butcher smile at a neatly dressed customer as he reached for a heap of quivering white folds. 'Arf a pound o' dressed tripe, missus – coming up.'

Juno said, 'We had a footman who used to eat that stuff – with vinegar. He let me taste some once – said it was cow's stomach.'

The bloody sides of beef seemed to waver and sway above me; I clutched desperately at Juno's arm. 'Look – a bus, let's get up on top and away from this place.'

We scrambled up the stairs, clutching our flapping cloaks about us, and collapsed on to the hard wooden seat. A slight breeze fanned our hot cheeks as we jolted forward.

Juno tugged her bonnet straight. 'We'll book to the terminus – at least we're resting our feet.' I nodded. I felt tired and sick.

We treated ourselves to tea and buns in a respectable-looking café near Aldgate, then boarded a tram for the return journey. At five o'clock I climbed the stairs to Allsop Ward, my heart sinking.

CHAPTER FOUR

As soon as I pushed open the big ward doors Staff Nurse pounced. 'You're almost late, Girvan – the washing-up's waiting from tea – get on with it, then come and find me.' I steeled myself to tackle the dirty cups and saucers, but at least they were not greasy.

When I had finished I found Staff Nurse in the sink room where she was piling soap and towels and bowls of hot water on to a trolley. I stood helplessly by as she moved quickly from cupboards to sink. 'Come along, we've got a new admission to wash and get to bed.' As I trotted behind her I heard her muttered complaint. 'What a time of day, that wretched Armstrong – always waits till after tea to send 'em up.'

We unloaded our bowls on to the locker beside an empty bed and rushed back to the ward entrance where a small female child crouched on a wooden chair, gasping for breath, her spindly legs dangling. As we came forward the haggard grey-haired woman beside her stirred and sent the smell of stale urine wafting from her skirts. My nose wrinkled in distaste but Staff Nurse appeared not to notice. 'All right, Mother, we'll see to her now – can she walk?'

I stared at the woman as her toothless gums mouthed a 'Yes' – surely she was far too old to be this child's mother? But Staff Nurse was on the move. 'Up you get.' The child slithered off the chair, her head hunched over her chest; the woman reached out a tentative hand but Staff Nurse was already propelling the child forward through the lobby. She called back a curt 'Visiting on Sunday', then snapped at me, 'Screens, Girvan, quickly.' I ran ahead to find the heavy red screens and drag them round the empty bed. Before I had finished she was bundling the child out of her ragged frock and shawl and dumping them on the floor. 'Put those in the draw-string bag – they'll all have to be sent for fumigation, she's got scabies as well as bronchitis.' I picked up the smelly clothes with my fingertips and dropped them as quickly as possible into the bag.

'Help me lift her, Girvan.' Staff Nurse had wrapped the child in an old blanket so I picked up the edge gingerly. 'For goodness' sake get hold of her properly, or you'll drop her.' I tightened my lips and grabbed a larger fold and somehow the child was transferred to the bed. Staff Nurse rolled her over on her back and for the first time I saw her face: I gasped, she was so ugly. Her face seemed to cave in between a bulging, knobbly forehead and a jutting chin and the two frightened eyes stared out either side of a rudimentary squashed nose. Staff nurse glanced at me. 'Take a good look, Girvan – you'll see plenty more like her in this hospital. Some men should be shot for what they do to their children.'

I was aghast. 'You mean – she's been hit?'

'Of course not, she was born like that – specific disease.' Her voice was heavy with meaning and although I had no idea what 'specific disease' was I drew back hastily.

Staff Nurse said impatiently, 'She's not infectious with it now – Armstrong's no fool, he'll have checked her over pretty thoroughly – he'd have warned us to take the usual precautions if they'd been necessary. No, it's the scabies we've got to watch out for.' She pulled back the blanket and revealed the child's arm – it was a mass of red blotches. 'I'll have to pare her fingernails down, she's been scratching – look at that!' I could not take my eyes from the arm where patches of skin had been ripped off to expose the raw red surface below; in between the patches, foul sores oozed pus. I wanted to gag as the child wheezed on. 'Armstrong's dug the mites out with a needle – thinks he got most of them.'

I breathed, 'The mites?'

'That's what causes it – they burrow under the skin to lay their eggs, then of course it itches so the patient scratches and Bob's-your-uncle. We'll tie gloves on her as well.' Staff Nurse worked quickly, washing the child and patting her dry in sections. My skin crawled as she handed me back the towel and I flinched away. 'For goodness' sake, Girvan, scabies is nothing – we can soon cure it with cleanliness and plenty of ointment – it's the bronchitis that'll cause the trouble, poor little so-and-so.' She bent down over the child. 'What's your name?'

At last a thread-like whisper came: 'Edie.'

'Now, Edie, don't worry, we'll soon have you better.' Staff Nurse rubbed the ointment briskly on – how could she bear to touch this child? 'Now it's your turn, Girvan – you can do the head, it's sure to be alive.' I stared at her blankly. 'Nits, of course – I'll tell you what to do.' I stood as if in a nightmare as Staff Nurse tied a mackintosh cape round the child's shoulders then handed me the second bowl. 'It's the right temp now – remember always to test it, especially with children. I've put the soda in already, you rub in the soft soap then give her hair a good wash before you go through it with this.' She held up a metal comb with narrow teeth very close together. 'Do it bit by bit, but you won't get them all out today, and you'll have to pull, the little beggars stick like glue. Keep dipping it in the carbolic as you go.' She pushed through the screens and left me.

I looked desperately round, but there was no help for it, so I took a deep breath and pulled the child to the edge of the bed. I got the matted hair washed somehow as the water in the bowl went darker and darker in colour. Then I dipped the comb in the dish of carbolic and began to tug at the tangles. The child whimpered and moaned, but I tugged grimly on. As I withdrew the comb I saw that tiny round whitish objects were caught between the teeth; I plunged them into the carbolic. When I spotted the small brown creature clinging like a crab to the comb I choked as I jumped for the disinfectant. But I had managed to comb almost the entire head by the time Staff Nurse came back. She stood watching me finish, then she laughed out loud. 'For goodness' sake, Girvan, don't look so scared – after all, they can only bite you! And to think you're paying that skinflint of a matron a guinea a week for the privilege!' She laughed again and I winced at her jeering tone. 'You picked the wrong hospital for your Lady Bountiful act. The East London works on sweated labour – it's well known for it – I knew that when I started, but at least I'm not such a fool as to pay to be sweated! Towel her dry properly – we'd normally saturate the lot in carbolic solution now, but as she's got bronchitis already we'll have to rely on you tooth-combing her twice a day.' She smirked at my horrified face. 'After the first year you'll wonder why you made such a fuss! You can try meths next time.'

Meths? I thought wildly, am I meant to set fire to the child's head?

'It dissolves whatever the little devils stick themselves on with – remind me tomorrow.' I gave a weak nod. 'And let's have a bit more of the "Thank yous", Girvan – mind your manners.'

Manners! How dared she speak to me so, she with her

common accent and coarse laugh? But I managed to get out, 'Thank you.'

'Thank you *Staff*. I thought you lot all had nannies to teach you your Ps and Qs.' She rustled off; angry and resentful, I stumbled after her. My feet were on fire and the backs of my calves were taut with pain; tears began to fill my eyes – how could I ever stand another three hours in this hellish place? Staff Nurse glanced round and I saw the triumph in her expression. I forced my tired legs to move faster and my face became a rigid mask – I would not break down before a woman of that class.

I ran backwards and forwards on my burning feet carrying the patients' supper trays. I offered soup to a patient who wanted bread and milk then gave an egg to a woman in the middle of the ward who instantly began to spoon it greedily into her mouth. Another woman asked for her egg; I ran back to the kitchen where Harris exclaimed impatiently, 'There aren't any more, Girvan, patients bring their own – why ever didn't you look? I pencilled the right number on it. You'll have to go and tell Number Nine what you've done.'

Number Nine's lips tightened as I faltered through my explanation. Then she glared at the yolk-smeared mouth of the woman in the next bed and whined, 'I wouldn't 'a minded so much if you'd a given it ter one o' me pals – but *'er!*' I limped back to the kitchen with burning cheeks.

After supper I was set to sweep again while Fraser washed up. The ward seemed to grow longer and longer and wider and wider – I felt as though I were sweeping the Mall, and I still could not collect the dust together in one place for my shovel.

As soon as I had finished Staff Nurse ordered, 'Harris, take Girvan to the sink room – she can empty and wash out the bed pans for the rest of you. Tell her exactly what she must do.' In the stench of the sink room I tipped away the unspeakable contents of the heavy bed pans as they were thrust into my hands and as I clumsily scrubbed them clean I tried desperately to focus my nostrils only on the smell of the disinfectant I had poured into the soapy water. Harris came in with yet another reeking burden; teeth clenched I reached out for it but she shook her head. 'It's the typhoid's stools – they'll be teeming with germs.' She lifted the carbolic solution and tipped some in, then she rammed down the lid again and swished the whole pan round before she placed it on the shelf. 'Leave it for *at least* fifteen minutes before you throw it away.' She seized three more empty pans and disappeared.

I gazed in horror at the rounded white earthenware pan as it stood on the shelf, decorated with its menacing blue 'T' and 'teeming with germs' – and *I* would have to empty it and plunge my bare hands into the sink to wash it clean. It was too much; I could not stay here in this prison any longer – I had been a fool to think I could ever learn to nurse. I began very carefully to dry my work-reddened hands, and as I did so I excused myself to the uncaring walls: 'I don't want to be a nurse, I don't want to be a nurse,' and an echo answered me, Lance Benson's gentle voice: 'I don't want to be a soldier, Lady Helena – Helena – Helena.' I stood and wrestled with the memory – how could I desert now?

My tears dripped into the sink as I forced my hands back into the dirty water.

I kept my face averted as another pile of stinking pans was thrust into my outstretched hands, but I heard Harris' cheerful voice, 'Thanks, old thing – I must say it's nice being able to dump them on you, it's speeding us up no end.' Her starched skirts rustled out as I began to empty each one in turn. At the end of fifteen minutes I took hold of the typhoid bed pan with both hands and forced myself to tip the contents away. When it was white and clean and drying on the rack I felt a little better; I stared at it hanging there and whispered, 'I'm sorry, Lance – I will stick it, I promise.' Then I went out to the ward for prayers; it was eight o'clock.

So once again I fell to my knees on the hard floor and heard Sister's flat voice pray for the hospital and all within its walls. I tried to picture Gerald so that I could pray for him, but his face was a blur behind my closed lids and receded further and further from me, until in desperation I turned instead to my brother. 'Oh Guy – please God keep Guy safe,' and his friendly face and loving dark eyes seemed to smile at me in reply, and I was comforted.

In a daze of tiredness I stood with the other probationers while Sister walked from bed to bed in the darkened ward, inspecting each chart in the flickering light of the candle carried by Staff Nurse. Then I was ordered to do the inventory. 'Mind you find *every* piece of silver, Girvan – one knife, one fork, one dessert and one teaspoon per patient – and there's thirty patients, in case you haven't noticed – lay them all out on the coal box in fives.'

I searched and counted and searched again until at last I was only missing one teaspoon. I stared round the kitchen helplessly – two of the probationers were making custards, chattering as they stirred, I kept murmuring, 'Excuse me, excuse me,' as I peered again and again into the grill pan and under the oven and back again to the empty sink. At last Harris broke off her conversation and glanced up from her saucepan. 'What are you short of?'

'A teaspoon.'

'Try the pig bucket.' She gestured behind the door and turned back to her companion: 'And do you know what Sister Corley said to her? – I would have died honestly – she said . . .' But I had seen the faint gleam of silver; recklessly I plunged my hand in among the slimy potato peelings, thrust the spoon at the dishcloth and scuttled off to the coal-box lid.

Staff Nurse counted carefully then gave a nod. 'Put

them away now and then go and tidy the linen cupboard.' In the close little cubbyhole I fumbled with the coarse sheets; I tried to refold one but it flapped away from me and went crooked until in desperation I bundled it up any-old-how and leant crouching against the hard edges of the wooden shelves, waiting for release.

It came with the padding footsteps of the night nurses. Sister dismissed us and I followed the other probationers to the dining room, gave my number and slumped into a seat. Juno arrived panting and angry after grace. 'The cow kept us late, now we've all got black marks – God, what on earth are we doing in this place, Helena?' A maid rammed two plates down on the table in front of us. On each was a square of tripe. My gorge rose as I looked at it. They had bullied and harassed us all day, and now they fed us with cow's stomach – I closed my eyes. A shrill cockney voice opposite asked, 'Dontcher wannit, then?' I looked at the round red face and silently shook my head. 'Give it 'ere, ducks – you'll get in trouble with Sister else.' A rapid glance to right and left, a piece of deft sleight of hand and my cow's stomach had vanished from under my nose.

'Thank you,' I said weakly.

'Pleasure's mine, duck – pass us the vinegar again, would yer be so kind?' I passed the vinegar.

Over the bowl of porridge which followed Juno made plans for securing a bath. At the end of supper she used her large frame to jostle her way to the doorway, then as soon as we were out of sight of the Home Sisters she broke into a trot, calling over her shoulder, 'I'll book it for you after, Hellie.'

In the thankfully piping-hot bath I scrubbed and scrubbed myself; I felt dirty all over. I wanted to wash my hair in the basin but there was a banging at the door. 'Come *on*, there's two of us waiting.' I thrust my damp arms into the sleeves of my dressing gown and came out. As I walked down the corridor I heard the shout behind me, 'And empty the bath next time, you slut!' I threw myself into my bedroom.

I was struggling into my nightdress when Juno thumped on the door, burst in and flung herself down on the bed. She kicked her slippers off and began to massage her toes. 'My feet, Hellie, my feet! And that bloody Home Sister went through my drawers and pinched my cigarettes – she's emptied the whole case – how dare they do things like that?' She glared at me, then asked, 'What was your evening like, Hellie? I swear mine was even worse than the morning. The ghastly staff nurse trapped me in that foul-smelling sink room all evening. I was only allowed out to the kitchen – and that was crawling with cockroaches. I never got near any patients after the washing up.'

'I wish I hadn't.' I shuddered. 'I had to help Staff Nurse wash a little girl who'd just been admitted – she was so dirty, and she was covered in vile sores. And Juno, she was such a hideous-looking child – Staff Nurse said it was her father's fault, she was born with a "specific disease".'

Juno's eyes widened. 'Good God, Hellie – we've not got to nurse patients with *that*, have we?'

I repeated, 'She didn't say what it was, just a "specific disease".'

Juno said grimly, 'I can guess what they mean by that all right.' She shuddered, then, as I stared at her blankly she leant forward and hissed, 'Syphilis!'

'Syphilis?' I echoed – I had dim memories of Miss Ling's stories of the Greek myths. 'You mean the man who had to push a rock up a hill, and every time he got it to the top it came rolling down again?'

Juno gave a short bark of laughter. 'Lord, Hellie, you are dumb sometimes – that was *Sisyphus* – no connection, though for all I now he may have had it too. No, syphilis is what men get off tarts.'

'Off tarts?'

'Tarts, whores – women men pay to let them *do* things

214

to them – come on, Hellie, you must know what men do with women, after all, you'll be getting married soon.'

My face was burning hot. 'You mean some women let men do that to them – just for money – not because they, they care about them?'

'Oh Hellie – I forget you're so much younger than me – they can't *care* about them, they pick up strangers – Mama told me – it happens all the time.'

My belly lurched. 'How horrible!'

Juno went on, 'But sometimes the tarts have got this loathsome disease – they get it off sailors and such like – and then they pass it on to all the men they go with.'

And suddenly I remembered Munich and the pretty girl I had seen on Papa's arm – she must have been one of those, he had *paid* her to do that . . . 'But Juno, when Papa came to fetch me once from Munich – I saw him, with a girl like that . . .'

Juno grunted. 'The old so-and-so, I bet he kept that dark from Mama! But don't worry, Hellie, men of our class can afford to buy women who are clean – but I suppose they don't have much choice in the East End.'

I was still very shaken. 'But – why do they *do* it?'

Juno looked at me and said patiently, 'For the money, of course. It's got to be easier than slaving away in a place like this, for instance. Though I don't suppose any man with halfway decent eyesight would pay much for that beast of a Staff Nurse,' she added thoughtfully.

'No, I mean the *men*, why do they want to do something like that with a strange woman?'

Juno stretched her arms until her shoulder joints cracked. 'Oh, why do men do anything, Hellie? I suppose they just feel like it.'

We were plunged into darkness; it was ten-thirty. 'This bloody place!' I heard Juno swearing in the gloom. 'Wherever are my slippers?' We both began to scrabble on the floor and bumped into each other. 'Ouch, mind where you're going, Hellie. I hope they haven't switched off the lights in the water closet or I'll be pissing all over their lino – ah, got them.' She muttered and swore as she pulled them on. 'I'm going to have to find some way of hiding my cigarettes – I'll never stand this place otherwise. Goodnight, Hellie, see you in the morning, worse luck!' The door banged behind her and I heard an indignant cry of 'Nurse' as Juno cantered down the corridor.

As I lay in bed that night I recalled the child's ugly face, and thought of what Juno had told me. Then I remembered Gerald's clean-cut profile as he had stood on the terrace at Hatton and said: 'There is not, and never has been, any woman but you.' And I was comforted, and fell asleep clasping his ring.

CHAPTER FIVE

The next few weeks were an endless humiliation. In a world where every move had to be made at the double I could not keep up. I tried to scuttle like the other nurses, but I could not scuttle fast enough and if I broke into a run a passing voice would sharply pull me up. Often I hesitated through ignorance and uncertainty, only to bear the brunt of the anger of a harassed staff nurse or head probationer. For the first week Sister Allsop only spoke to me once; as I rushed past her with three stacked bed pans I stumbled, and the contents slopped dangerously through the hollow handles and splashed my apron. Spotless starched skirts drew to one side and I heard a carrying voice ask Staff, 'Who *is* that filthy probationer?'

'Girvan, Sister.'

I threw myself and my stinking burdens into the foul sink room, tears of shame filling my eyes.

All day I felt soiled as I sweated in the ill-ventilated

sink room; on the ward I had to move so quickly that I was perpetually damp at neck and armpit and groin. And the sickly scent of disinfectant overlaying the all-prevailing smell of urine, faeces, vomit, and pus filled my nostrils.

My mind was never free of my fears for Gerald and for Guy; I searched the post every day until at last a letter arrived from Gerald. I scanned the scribbled lines with a fast-beating heart; he had obviously written it in a great hurry and he said little, only that he was well and the enemy were on the run. I raised the flimsy paper to my lips then tucked it down inside my camisole where his ring hung from a fine gold chain.

Every day, in the snatched minutes when we were sent back to clean our rooms, we bent tensely over the newspaper, and read yet more familiar names in the casualty lists – the names of men we had dined with, danced with, laughed with – and who would dine and dance and laugh no more. Paris had been saved, but the price had been a high one, and was daily growing higher. Even Juno's hand trembled as she opened the paper each morning.

On the 2nd of October I leant over her shoulder and saw the headline: 'Heir to Peerage Among the Killed' – and the words: 'Grenadier Guards' below. I began to gasp and cry until Juno shook me roughly. 'Pull yourself together, Hellie – it's not Guy, it's not Guy.' I sobbed helplessly but Juno slapped my hand, hard. 'Show a bit of backbone, Helena, for goodness' sake. Come on, we're due back on the wards.' I stumbled out of the room after her.

All through October the Roll of Honour lengthened, but by the time the paper reported heavy casualties among the Grenadiers, Guy was already back in London – wounded, but not seriously. A bullet had gone through his arm but missed the bone, and he was well enough to be sitting up when I went hurrying round to see him at King Edward VII's Hospital for Officers in Grosvenor

217

Crescent. Guy looked at me in astonishment as I came rushing in. 'Good God, Hellie, what a fright you are in that rig.' I was suddenly conscious of the peculiarity of my bonnet and cloak but then my brother grinned. 'Still, I suppose I'm not much to write home about at the moment, either.' He held out his good arm and I clung to him, weeping, while he patted my shoulder.

A week later, when I arrived for my visit I saw that his face was alight with joy. 'Congratulate me, Hellie – Eileen's agreed to have me!'

I felt a sharp stab of pure jealousy, but I managed to smile and stumble through the correct words as the sleek, glossy creature uncoiled herself from the armchair and extended a beautifully manicured white hand. She arched her eyebrows as her fingers touched the rough skin of my disinfectant-scoured palm and drawled, 'Goodness, Helena – you *are* taking the war seriously – ruining your hands and dressing up in that, er – quaint outfit. I do hope dear Muirkirk doesn't expect me to sacrifice myself like that – I just couldn't bear to look such a sight.' Her mouth curved towards Guy, and for a moment my handsome brother looked just like a codfish on a slab.

He muttered, 'Good God no, Eileen – you're far too beautiful for that.' She drew in a deep breath of smoke, exhaled it very slowly, then removed the cigarette from between her scarlet lips, bent down, and brushed his cheek with her mouth. But as her head moved up Guy's hand shot out and seized her wrist and pulled her down once more. He was breathing heavily, his eyes intent on hers.

She stayed quite still for a moment, then drew back a little. 'Really, Guy, whatever will your little sister think?'

Guy's glance flicked in my direction, then to the door. I stood up as calmly as I could and muttered, 'I – I must go, I'm due back on duty shortly.'

Eileen smiled her cat-like taunting smile. 'Leaving so soon? Don't get too *earnest* my dear – it's a terrible bore.'

She blew an exquisitely formed kiss in my direction and my cheek muscles tightened into a rictus as I smiled back, and left.

At the end of six weeks on Allsop Ward I had learnt to use a thermometer, chart temperatures, make beds, wash helpless patients and, fighting my revulsion, give an enema. But I was slow and clumsy: I dropped bowls and chipped their enamel; I threw away urine specimens that should have been preserved; I broke things – like the two china sputum mugs which oozed their foul slime over the clean floor. I spilt milk on the sheets when I fed patients, my fomentations were soggy and painful and my linseed poultices coagulated into sticky, useless lumps. I was a failure, I knew I was a failure – but like a broken-winded cab horse I still staggered grimly on.

One day Juno told me her sister was getting married. 'Dick's got five days' leave before he goes to France, so it's a special licence for him and Julia tomorrow.' As she spoke I felt a wave of envy wash over me – if only Gerald had not had to go so quickly, I might have been his wife by now. Then I touched the small hard shape of the Prescott betrothal ring and reproached myself; Gerald was a soldier, a regular officer – naturally he had gone to war at once and as his betrothed I must accept this.

Early in November we heard of the destruction of Lord Hugh Grosvenor's C Squadron of Life Guards at Zandvoorde Ridge; the order to retire had not reached him, so he had fought on to the death with all his men. My heart turned to ice as I thought of my love. Every night, sick with fatigue, I knelt beside my narrow bed in my small room and prayed for Gerald's safety. Often I dropped into a stupefied sleep in the middle of my prayers and woke later, stiff and dazed, still huddled against the hard edge of the bedstead.

He wrote in November that the Composites had been disbanded and so he was now back with his own regiment. His letter was a letter from a man in the midst of a great adventure. It was clear that he was happy, and

219

totally absorbed in the task on hand; never had he seemed so far away from me as he did now. He was fighting for his King and country while I – I struggled uselessly with squalor and grime in the slums of London. He had praised me for what I was doing, but it was obvious that he had no real idea of what hospital nursing involved. As I battled to cleanse an incontinent senile old woman I prayed fervently that he would never find out.

The twins wrote cheerfully from their training camp: their only fear seemed to be that the war would be over before they could join in; and the occasional postcard which arrived from Conan showed that for him too war was the greatest of games. Only Guy was not happy; he had wanted Eileen to marry him as soon as he came out of hospital but she had made a string of excuses and finally announced that she was not ready to lose her figure yet – London was just too exciting at present. Guy looked hurt and miserable as he told me, then he repeated, 'She's the only girl for me, Hellie – the only girl in the world.' I hated svelte, selfish Eileen – how gladly would I have married Gerald if he had been in London now.

Towards the end of November I was moved to a men's medical ward. At first I shrank from having to handle male bodies so intimately, but there was no time for such delicacy at the East London. And then there were the delirious cases; with their vacant staring eyes and sense-less incoherent mutterings – I had to nerve myself to go near them.

One of the beds had its warning bowl of disinfectant, and neat stack of marked crockery at its foot, but this case was not one of typhoid. Staff took me on one side and told me what Number Six was suffering from and my skin crawled, but his bed had to be made and his needs attended to, just like the others. 'Remember, Girvan, even if you only just touch his bed, wash your hands in disinfectant at once.' I remembered, and my hands became red and chapped with constant washing. How I loathed the East London.

CHAPTER SIX

By the beginning of December we had saved the Channel ports. Brave little Belgium had not been completely overrun, as we had beaten off the German attack at Ypres, and the French had regained some of the land they had lost early in the war. Gerald was resting in billets well behind the line and he wrote me a long cheerful letter recounting his daily routine and that of his fellow officers: he said he found it strange to realize he was fighting as an infantryman now – but war was like that, you never knew what it had in store for you. As I folded up his letter to go back to the ward to do the washing up I smiled in wry agreement.

I had a day off due, and I went up to Cadogan Place the night before. At breakfast next morning Mother announced that she was taking me to Mirette's to order a new winter outfit. 'Suppose Gerald comes home on leave? You can't possibly meet him in last year's costume.'

As we came out of the dressmaker's I suddenly saw Guy strolling towards us with a girl leaning on his arm. I called out, 'Guy!' and ran forward, but he looked up and his jaw dropped, and as he hustled the girl past I saw it was a strange pretty brunette with lips painted an improbable red. I turned and stood staring after him – he had not spoken a word to us, he had not even raised his hat!

Mother bundled me into our cab. 'Helena – how gauche of you, embarrassing your brother like that.'

I exclaimed, 'But who was that girl with Guy? It wasn't Eileen, and he didn't offer to introduce her.'

Mother leant forward and checked that the glass behind the driver was fully closed before she turned to me. 'Guy is a young man come home from the war – of course he wants female company.'

'But he's got Eileen, he loves her.'

Mother gave an impatient snort. 'Helena – he can hardly use a girl of his own class.' I still stared at her blankly. 'Really, after three months as a hospital nurse!' She explained very clearly, 'Helena, that girl was a whore. Your brothers are normal, healthy young men – thank God – naturally they need to make use of women like that from time to time. It means absolutely nothing to them. Stop gaping like a fool.' She sat back in her seat with lips compressed and it was clear the subject was closed.

I tried to grapple with the idea that Guy was engaged to Eileen; he had said he loved her – he did love her, I knew he did – and yet he paid another woman to let him do that with her – and Mother said it meant nothing to him. Then I thought: Gerald is engaged to me, but – oh God – does he, does Gerald . . . ? He had said no other woman, but if Mother's right – this would seem of no account to him. I sat racked with jealousy while my mother talked of the Red Cross Hospital Mrs Benson had set up at The Pines.

When I got back to the hospital that evening Juno told me she was not signing on for another three months. 'I can't stand being perpetually harried by these viragos, Hellie – and Mother's got a scheme for taking a canteen over to France to feed the soldiers – it sounds a lot more fun. Besides, I'll go mad if I don't get the stink of this place out of my nostrils.'

I knew Matron would be calling me in next and I did not know what to do. I was getting through the days somehow and I was no longer permanently sick with tiredness, but the thought of another three months filled me with revulsion. I was still undecided when I received Matron's summons. 'Now, Nurse Girvan, I've no doubt you're longing to get out to France to nurse our brave boys, but remember you're still far too young to go – so wouldn't it be better to stay here and gain more experience?' I hesitated. Her heavy body creaked forward a fraction. 'Suppose I send you to Foldus Ward for the next three months? It's a men's surgical – and it has taken in some wounded soldiers so you will gain the *best* experience there.' She bared her strong teeth and held out the pen; weakly, I took it. As I signed I wondered how on earth I would manage without Juno to commiserate with.

But on Foldus Ward I was kept so busy there was scarcely time to notice her absence. Yet, busy though we were, the harassed frenzy of the first months was not repeated here. Sister Foldus was an organizer. Every minute of every probationer's day was allocated, so we knew precisely what we had to do and when, and we were never called away from one incomplete task to start another. Sister sat in the centre of her ward like a great squat spider spinning the web of her daily routine, a web which was perfectly formed and strong.

The wounded soldiers were Belgians and one of them had lost a leg. I felt sick the first time I had to hold the stump for Staff to dress – he was a young, good-looking chap and it seemed such a terrible mutilation, the slim hips and strong muscular thigh ending abruptly – in nothing. But Staff Nurse's fingers moved as skilfully as ever. She spoke sweetly to the man, whilst I translated in my halting, schoolroom French, and when we had finished we all exchanged comradely smiles of relief.

I learnt to trust Sister Foldus – she was kind to the men and patient with us probationers. At last I began to gain a little confidence, and to feel that I was really nursing. Sister Foldus was a good teacher. Her heavy body would waddle to the side of a bed, her pudgy hands would move swiftly and surely and her gravelly voice explain. 'Now you do it, Nurse.' She would watch patiently, tireless in her corrections or praises. She had a collection of dog-eared nursing textbooks in her sitting room and she sent each pro off with a chapter to read every day, and next morning we probationers were examined in turn. At last the twice-weekly lectures which I had been nodding through in a haze of exhaustion began to make sense.

Four of the Belgian soldiers lay paralysed in one corner of the ward. To Sister Foldus they were not young men to be pitied – they had fought for their country, they had been unlucky, she wasted no time on emotion – now the care of these men was a challenge to her nurses. We must learn to tend them: to feed them, to cleanse them, to shave them and, when necessary, to wash out their bladders and empty their bowels for them.

One of them had had an operation on his throat and he could not swallow so Sister Foldus showed me how to oil india rubber tubing and ease it up through his nostril and down into his stomach. Then I carefully poured the beaten eggs and milk and brandy into the glass funnel until he was fed. One day the man next to him closed his mouth against the feeding cup and turned his face away. Sister pursed her lips and sent me for the rubber tube again, but this man resisted and she had to hold him firmly still with her fat capable hands as I fed the life-sustaining liquid down the funnel into the broken body. He looked up at me, and his eyes were resentful and despairing, and for a moment I questioned the morality of what we were doing – but only for a moment; Sister Foldus' square face brooked no doubts – her patients must live, whether they wished to or not.

Now Juno had left, I often found it difficult to obtain a daily paper so most of my war news came from the patients. The French were making gains and the Russians were fighting around Warsaw – though news from the Eastern Front filtered through very slowly. In the third week in December we heard that the Germans had attacked at Ypres again, and there had been fierce fighting to hold them off. I waited in fear for my next letter from Gerald, but it came – he was still safe. Then we heard the shocking, unbelievable news that five enemy battle cruisers had bombarded the coast of England itself – Hartlepool, Scarborough and Whitby had all been attacked in turn; hundreds of civilians had been killed and many more injured. We talked in whispers that day, and looked at each other apprehensively – how could the enemy ships have so easily given ours the slip? Was our navy no longer invincible? Our men were fighting in France and Flanders to keep us safe on our island – but now it seemed our island was safe no longer. That evening I took out all Gerald's letters and read them yet again – and took comfort from his cheerful confidence.

The twins wrote regularly: they told me that Letty had given her governess the slip at Hatton, caught the train to London on her own and persuaded Papa to agree to her going away to boarding school. Mother was furious with her, but my sister had apparently insisted that she wanted to go up to Cambridge, and so needed better teaching. I remembered myself at fourteen and was awed by her daring.

Miss Ling wrote to tell me that her invalid mother had died – and her small annuity with her – so my old governess had had to find a new position. We drank tea together in the Nurses' Home before she left London, and reminisced about the old days at Hatton. Back on duty I collected a Higginson's syringe and a bowl of soapy water and went to give an enema to one of the paralysed Belgians. 'Soon have you comfortable, old man.' I began to oil the rubber catheter. I was grateful to Sister Foldus – it was she who had tipped me off about filling my fingernails with soap before passing the tube into a patient's backside, and it really was much pleasanter like that.

By the beginning of January I had read all Sister

Foldus' textbooks, so in my off-duty time I ventured along the Strand to Southampton Row to buy one of my own from the Scientific Press there. I moved along the shelf in the nursing section, taking down each book in turn and flicking through the pages, until the next book fell open at a drawing of a baby – a beautiful, perfect baby. It was curled up with its arms and legs neatly crossed and its round head pointing downward. I stared at the picture in fascination and then I suddenly realized that this was a baby waiting to be born, still cosily nestling in its mother's body. I slid my hand down over my flat stomach and pressed it against my belly, and thought of a baby growing there. An assistant moved towards me and I shut the book hastily and seized two others off the shelf, put them on top of it and began to search for my purse with shaking hands.

Nobody was in at Cadogan Place. I ran upstairs to my bedroom, threw myself down on the bed and began frantically to rip open the brown paper parcel to release my midwifery textbook. As I turned over the pages of small round bodies curled up in their mothers' wombs I felt an aching longing grow in the pit of my belly. I looked up at my photo of Gerald, so tall and stern and strong in his breastplate and tunic – and knew that I wanted him. I wanted him to take hold of me and thrust himself forcefully into the softness deep inside me, and plant his seed there, so that my womb could slowly swell and grow and become heavy with child.

As I sat trembling before his picture I heard quick strong footsteps running up the stairs and banging the book shut I looked round desperately for a hiding place, but Guy had already tapped on the door and burst in. 'Cooper said you were at home, Hellie – I've just heard – I've been gazetted, I've got my company.'

'Oh Guy – congratulations, I'm so pleased!' But then I realized what this meant.

'I'm going out again next Friday.' He dropped suddenly down on to the bed beside me, his face taut.

'I've just seen Eileen, but she won't budge – still on about her blasted figure.'

'But, Guy, she can't . . .' Then I remembered my book and with a telltale exclamation of guilt I tried to push it underneath my skirt.

'What's that you're trying to hide, Hellie?' He reached across and caught at my hand. I tried to wriggle away from him but he clamped me firmly to his chest with one arm and began to tug the book from my grasp with the other hand. After a short tussle the prize was his, and I pulled away from him, my cheeks flooding crimson as he flipped over the spine and began to laugh. 'Well, well, little Helena – and I thought you were supposed to be nursing wounded soldiers!' He opened the book and began to turn over the pages; I stood up and walked over to the dressing table and fiddled with my hair brushes. There was silence behind me.

At last I heard the book slam shut. 'Damn and blast Eileen – damn her.' I turned round; my brother's face was brick-red. We looked at each other until at last he burst out, 'But that's what a woman's figure's for! Hellie – if – when Gerald comes home on leave . . .' He stopped and watched my face, then he said, 'But I don't need to tell you, do I, little sister?'

I said, 'No, Guy, you don't.' He stood up and pulled me tightly against him for a moment, then he quickly kissed my cheek and we went downstairs together.

The next morning Sister kept me back after prayers and told me that the junior night probationer on Foldus Ward had reported sick with a septic throat. 'I have spoken to Matron, Nurse Girvan, and she has agreed to let you take her place. You may go off duty at midday and report to the night nurses' corridor after lunch.'

I was apprehensive, but I also felt a stirring of pride. Sister had asked for me – she trusted me on her precious ward at night – I must not let her down. Besides, on night duty I would be sure of free time every morning so I would be able to spend it with Guy at Cadogan Place until he left for the Front again.

I scarcely slept that afternoon, so the first night passed in a fog of exhaustion; but Bowers, the night senior, was steady and efficient – somehow she prodded me through the routine tasks until at last it was nine the next morning and Sister Foldus' hoarse voice was dismissing us.

I chewed my way mechanically through the meal then tied on my bonnet and cloak and headed for the main gate. The porter whistled me a cab and I sat slumped into the corner, my eyes aching. Guy had only just finished his breakfast when I arrived at Cadogan Place. He poured me a cup of coffee and I sat hunched over it while he read me the latest war news from the paper. There were dark circles under his eyes and he kept yawning. 'Lord, I'm tired, Hellie.'

I muttered resentfully, 'Anyone would think you were the one who'd been up all night.'

'I was – I didn't get home till after five.'

I exclaimed, 'Surely Eileen's mother . . .'

He grimaced. 'I escorted Eileen home before midnight, like a good little boy – you'd best not ask me how I spent the rest of the night, Hellie. Still, she was the one who wouldn't get married.' He shrugged, his face bitter. 'So what's a man supposed to do when he's about to go back to the front line? Eat, drink and be merry – there may not be a tomorrow.'

I was so weak with tiredness I could not hold back the tears. Guy looked up from his paper. 'Poor old Hellie – I'm not being very tactful this morning, am I? Come on, tie the ribbons of that awful bonnet and I'll take you back to your front line. You'll feel better when you've had a sleep.'

I wept on his shoulder all the way to Aldgate, then he handed me his own handkerchief. 'Mop up, Hellie, and lets have "a nice big blow", as Nanny would say.' He half-lifted me out of the cab at the hospital entrance. 'I'll be better company tomorrow, Hellie, I promise.' He patted me on the shoulder and I staggered across the courtyard to the Nurses' Home.

Yet after a few days I got used to my topsy-turvy life: breakfast at night and dinner in the morning seemed normal now, and on the day I said goodbye again to Guy I was grateful for the crushing tiredness which closed my eyes and transported me instantly into the oblivion of exhaustion.

Some nights were very busy, but I found Bowers easy to work with; she never lost her temper however rushed we were – and when I heard the irregular breathing of the most badly wounded Belgian slow and stop, and the uncanny silence which followed, I was thankful she was there beside me, calm and capable. As soon as the houseman had been she took me behind the screens and began to instruct me on the performance of the last offices. Together we removed the pillows and laid the wasted body flat. Together we undressed him and straightened the thin limbs and closed the staring eyes. Low voiced, she told me how to tie up the dropped jaw with a slit for the chin so that in death his mouth would look almost life-like – though no relatives would see poor Leopold to be comforted by our carefulness. Then we plugged the openings of his body with cotton wool, covered him with a sheet and left him for an hour. As I packed dressings for the sterilizer my eyes veered again and again to the screened bed, but Bowers' round face was composed and steady.

At last she lifted her watch and nodded, and we filled bowls of warm water and for the last time washed the emaciated body and packed and rebandaged the familiar wounds. His jaw was fixed now, and as Bowers bared his face it looked for a frightening moment as if he were about to open his mouth and address us in his halting, guttural French – but of course he was quite dead. We walked either side of the bier to the ward door as the porter wheeled him away, but as I heard the rattle of the lift gates outside I turned on my heels and ran straight to the sink room and vomited into the bed-pan sink. When I had finished I flushed it all away and cleaned the white surface with disinfectant and walked on trembling legs back to the ward. Bowers glanced up and said, 'You can start cutting the bread now, Girvan.' I dipped my head in acknowledgement, made my way silently to the kitchen and began to saw at the loaf. I had found cutting bread very difficult when I had first come to the East London – now I did it easily, automatically. I wondered if the day would come when I would lay out dead bodies automatically, too. I supposed it would, if we did not win the war soon.

After a month the regular junior had recovered, and I was allowed a day off before going back on days, so I travelled down to spend it at The Pines – Pansy had written and begged me to come. I shrank from going because I knew she would weep for Lance and I did not know how to comfort her. But as we sat together before lunch and Pansy cried softly, talking of her brother, my embarrassment eased and I searched my memory and told her of everything Lance had ever said to me, and found myself crying too and sharing her grief.

Later she took me to visit the soldiers in their hospital. She looked very pretty in her VAD uniform, but she told me her mother would not allow her into the wards to nurse – 'But I help with the washing up, Helena, every day. Do you help to wash up at the East London?'

'Yes, yes I do.' She seemed satisfied with my answer, so I did not tell her any more. She asked me to sing to the patients, so I sang 'The Last Rose of Summer' and 'Home, Sweet Home', and they all clapped vigorously before a corporal with a strong Scots accent thanked me on their behalf. The men were mostly convalescent and the double row of beds neatly laid out in Mrs Benson's gilded ballroom seemed a far cry from Foldus Ward.

I caught the underground from Victoria, came up into the street at Aldgate and made my way to the bus stop. Snow had begun to fall and a thin layer of dirty slush was already coating the pavements, so that I was glad to be wearing my stout nurses' shoes. Once upon a time I had never stepped outside our house in London without my maid to escort me; now I was alone at night in the slums with the snow falling silently around me. My life had changed so much over these last few months.

On my next day off, a month later, I went up to Cadogan Place. Juno's sister, Julia, dined with us; her body was already swollen with child. Up in my bedroom I could not look at the drawer where I had hidden my book of babies. I made myself think instead of Juno and Lady Maud – 'somewhere in France' – serving endless cups of tea to tired soldiers. When I was calmer I knelt and prayed for Gerald's safety, as I always did.

Hugh and Conan were posted a fortnight later. I had a half-day off due, so I managed to dine up at Cadogan Place during their embarkation leave. Alice was unusually subdued, and Hugh kept looking at her with the face of a child who finds himself unexpectedly on the wrong side of the pastrycook's window. But Conan came in like a whirlwind: he rushed up to Mother, caught her round the waist, and danced her round the drawing room, humming a waltz. She was flushed and smiling when he deposited her back on the sofa. 'Now it's your turn, Hellie.' I protested, but he pulled me up and twirled me round like a dervish until I was panting and begging for mercy.

I had to leave before the dessert to get back to the Nurses' Home on time. Conan jumped up with me and said he would take me in a cab. He seized my cloak from Cooper and wound it round and round until I was cocooned and helpless, then ran laughing out to the taxi as I struggled free.

He stopped the cab before the hospital and walked with me down the darkened street. Before we reached the gates he pulled me to him. 'I'm off to the wars, Hellie, so you must kiss me goodbye.'

I protested, 'But I'm engaged to Gerald.'

'Oh, Gerald won't mind – I am your cousin after all.'
His voice became coaxing. 'Come on Hellie, be a sport.'

I exclaimed, 'Oh, Conan – I can't!' But I saw his
shoulders slump a little in the gloom, and suddenly the
endless black printed lists swam before my eyes and I
reached out to him and we clung together – and it was
I who found his lips and opened mine beneath them. I
was panting a little when at last we drew apart.

Conan said, his voice rather breathless, 'Well, lucky
old Gerald. Goodbye, sweet Coz.'

I turned and ran towards the high gateway.

On 10 March Matron called me in and I signed on for
another three months; as long as Gerald fought the
enemy in the trenches of France and Flanders, then I
too would wage my war on disease and squalor in this
ugly barracks in the heart of London's slums. There was
no other option.

CHAPTER SEVEN

A week after I had signed on again I opened my weekly
letter from Gerald with the familiar throb of excitement
– and found it was just a short note to say that he was
coming home on leave for five days – in forty-eight hours
he would be in London. I began to tremble.

When we were sent back to sweep and dust our rooms
I rushed through the work, dragged on my clean apron
and hurried to Matron's office. She seemed quite
sympathetic; she almost smiled at me as she said, 'Of
course you must take the full time off while your fiancé's
on leave – enjoy yourself, my dear.' I thanked her
gratefully.

I waited all morning at Cadogan Place, and sent my
lunch back barely touched; it was nearly teatime before

he came. He strode into the drawing room in his khaki tunic and riding breeches – his pale skin had weathered, he was lean and tall and handsome – and he looked like a stranger. I was overwhelmed with shyness and it was obvious he felt the same. He barely touched my outstretched hand as he greeted me very formally, 'Good afternoon, Helena.'

All the words of love and longing which had coursed through my mind over the past long months fled from me. At last I stammered, 'Did you – did you have a good journey?'

He shrugged his elegant shoulders. 'Good enough.' I dared not ask him why he had not come sooner – he was so spick and span he must have been to his club first. So we sat and talked of the weather until Mother came in to pour the tea. She took the reins of the conversation into her capable hands and they laughed and chatted together while I sat silently by, like a girl still in the schoolroom; but I did not mind, he was here and that was enough.

After tea Mother made her excuses and left us; Gerald sat down again and smiled at me.

'Well, Helena – and how are your brothers?' So I talked of the twins and Guy as we sat together in the darkening drawing room, and we were at ease now. I gazed at the shape of his beloved mouth and happiness surged through me. Cooper came in to draw the curtains and light the lamps, but Gerald waved him away. 'The firelight's quite adequate – you don't mind, do you Helena?' Of course I did not – it was such bliss to sit with him like this.

We began to talk of other people – he had heard of Lady Maud's canteen in France – I told him Julia's new husband had just gone back from sick leave. 'She was very upset, but of course, soon she will have . . .' I faltered then gathered all my courage together and blurted out, 'Gerald – couldn't you – couldn't you get a special licence – so that we could be married now?'

I saw the dark shape of his head jerk suddenly upright. He sprang to his feet and moved to the fire before he spoke. 'But you wouldn't be able to carry on with your nursing, then, Helena.'

I said at once, 'I could go to a Red Cross Hospital – besides – I might – I thought . . .' The memory of the little round babies curled up so safely in their mothers' wombs swam before my eyes and at last I managed to say, 'I want to bear you a son, Gerald.'

A glowing coal fell, the fire blazed up and I saw his face – and the longing in his eyes. I jumped up and ran to him and flung my arms around him. I pressed my empty womb against his hard flat stomach and suddenly, desperately, I wanted him to fill it. I whispered, 'Gerald, please,' and he held me tight as his lips found mine. And as his arms gripped me I felt the sweetness rise in my belly preparing myself for him, and I began to moan a little as my hands clung to his back. Then he took his mouth from mine, his strong hands moved up to seize my elbows – and he pushed me away.

I stared at his heaving chest as he took several long, deep breaths and heard him say, 'No, Helena – no.' His hands fell so abruptly from my arms that I staggered a little, and almost fell on to the sofa. He strode across to the window and stood with his back to me and there was silence until I began to cry with the searing humiliation of his rejection. He came back and stood over me and turned on the light beside my seat, but I could not look at him – I was sobbing now. He knelt down in front of the sofa. 'Helena, dearest Helena – I'm so sorry to have distressed you like this.' He put out a gentle hand and turned my chin up to the light. I fought to control my sobs, but I could not stop the tears from trickling down my face. He looked at me for a long time, then said, 'You're just a child, Helena, aren't you?' His voice was very kind as he took out his handkerchief and began to dry my cheeks. I sat still, sniffing a little, until he handed me the handkerchief, 'Blow your nose now,

Helena.' For a moment he sounded just like Nanny, so I did as he told me.

He got slowly to his feet and returned to the armchair opposite; he leant back until his face was in shadow, then he spoke quietly. 'Helena, you must realize that I'm a soldier now, under fire – I may be killed or wounded at any time.'

I swallowed, and whispered at last, 'But if – the worst – did happen, then I should still have . . .'

He said flatly, 'Nature is not always so obliging, Helena. You might find yourself a childless widow.' I opened my mouth to protest but he went on, his voice stronger now. 'Besides, death, that is at least clean and final – but in this war – you have no idea of the damage an exploding shell can do, and yet still leave a man alive.'

I said quickly, 'If you lost an arm or a leg, Gerald, I would still . . .'

'Helena,' he cut me off in the middle of my declaration, and stood up, looming over me. 'I'm not talking about arms or legs, Helena. This morning I went to see a corporal-trooper of mine – he was wounded at Warneton, I saw him as they carried him out – the whole of the lower half of his face was blown away – just a great gaping hole, with his eyes, looking very puzzled, above it. I knew he was in the 3rd London and he was a good NCO – so I thought I'd look him up. I had some vague, stupid idea that they'd have patched him together again.' He shuddered. 'God forgive me, when I saw him I could scarcely look into those eyes of his.'

I asked at last, 'Was he – was he conscious?'

'Oh yes – quite conscious – he knew everything that was going on – even that his wife was already carrying another man's child. She'd only been to see him once – ran screaming out of the ward in hysterics – but some officious neighbour had taken it upon himself to write and tell him what she's been up to since – the sister had told me beforehand. I emptied my notecase on to his bed and I left – came straight back to Town – what else could I do?'

I drew a deep breath and said, 'Gerald, even if . . .'

He broke in roughly. 'Don't be silly, Helena, you don't know what you're saying.' I could not speak again. At last he sat down again and said, more quietly, 'I'm sorry Helena – I know you meant that. You would make your vows, and keep them, whatever it cost you. But I won't accept that kind of promise from a young girl.' His voice was final and I knew there was nothing more to be said.

He came after lunch each day. I did suggest, timidly, that he might come earlier, but he said, 'A chum of mine's in hospital, Helena – he's very down, poor fellow – I like to spend the mornings with him.' I dared not try to argue with him; besides, I did not want him to think me selfish. So each afternoon we walked in the Park and I hung on his arm in pride and joy. Then he would bring me back to Cadogan Place and sit in the morning room while I played and sang to him. One afternoon I heard a faint snort, and when I turned round he was sprawled on the sofa, asleep. He began to snore, softly, and I felt a wave of love and tenderness wash over me – my handsome, immaculate Gerald – sprawled out and snoring. I sat quite still, just watching him, until he began to shift and groan, then I swivelled quickly round and began to play again – I did not want to embarrass him.

In the evening we would dine early at Cadogan Place before going on to a show. I would drive back in the dark cab with my shoulder resting against his, and feel that for a little while I was in heaven. After he had gently kissed me goodnight I ran up to my bedroom and sat curled up in a chair by the fire – I did not want to go to bed and fall asleep until I had remembered every word he had said, every expression that had crossed his beloved features, every movement of his fine hands as he had helped me into my cloak and escorted me through the crowded foyer.

But on the fourth evening he said, 'Goodbye, my dear Helena – I'll write to you as soon as I get back.'

I stared at him, aghast. 'But – I thought – you wrote *five* days.'

He looked away, towards the heavy velvet-shrouded windows. 'I'm afraid that nothing can be guaranteed in wartime.' Then I realized that he must have known all today that he would have to return early – but he had said nothing, he had kept it to himself, rather than spoil my pleasure in the day. And in my disappointment I loved him even more for his thoughtfulness – I must not be less brave.

I went to him and raised my face to his and kissed his lips, then said, 'Goodbye, Gerald,' and ran out of the room. I heard the front door close as I was on the stairs, and I sank down and clutched the bannister rails and wept.

Next morning I knew I should have gone back to the East London early, but I did not; I was too unhappy. Instead I buttoned on my walking boots and set out. I did not turn back until I had gone far beyond Kensington Gardens, but as I returned I realized my feet were taking me to the Albert Gate, to the place where I had met him unexpectedly, and he had introduced me to his sister-in-law. I retraced my steps and stood on the very spot where he had stood on that long-ago afternoon of peace – and thought of him today, on the train to Folkestone, or even, perhaps, already steaming across the Channel.

There were tears on my cheeks as I walked down to Hyde Park Corner, but I felt a little calmer as I passed St George's and turned into Grosvenor Crescent. I came level with the entrance to King Edward VII's Hospital for Officers, and glanced across at it, remembering my visits there to Guy – and stopped dead. Gerald was coming down the steps. I told myself, 'No, it can't be,' but I recognized his companion too, so I knew it was. Edward Summerhays was leaning heavily on Gerald's arm, his thin face very pale. A cab drew up, and through the grimy window I saw Gerald carefully help Edward in; then he sprang in beside him and the motor quickly accelerated away. I stood staring after it, my mind in turmoil.

He had told me he was going back, early this morning! But then I remembered his exact words, as I remembered every word he had ever spoken to me – and knew he had not said that, but he had spoken as if . . . No, perhaps there had been some last-minute alteration of plan: he was just taking Edward Summerhays to the station, and then he would come straight round to Cadogan Place . . . I broke into a trot and ran all the way round Belgrave Square, into Chesham Place and down Pont Street, to arrive home panting, my hand clutching the stitch in my side.

I sat all day in the drawing room, but he did not come. Straight after dinner I said goodbye to Mother and Papa and caught a bus back to the East End.

I waited for his letter; he would explain. But when the letter came it was just the same as usual. I scanned the neat handwriting – there was no explanation. He wrote that he had had a good crossing, mentioned that the trains in France were as slow as ever; he had ridden up to the transport lines, left his horse with his groom and then made his way to the support trenches where his batman had soon had a hot meal ready for him – but there was not one reference to dates or days. He had deceived me.

I felt a surge of blazing bitter jealousy; I knew what he had done – I pictured him, waving goodbye to Edward Summerhays then going straight to Piccadilly and accosting one of the gaily dressed tarts there – a girl like the one I had seen hanging on Guy's arm in Dover Street – and then he had used her. He had rejected me, but like all soldiers, he wanted to take his pleasure before he went back to the front. In a blaze of fury I picked up my pen and wrote to him of my bitterness and humiliation, my anguish and despair. I heard footsteps in the corridor – I was already late back on duty. Crushing my letter into an envelope, I ran down the stairs and thrust it into the postbox.

I woke the next morning sick with remorse, but it was too late, the box had been emptied. Sister sent me off duty in the morning and frantically I picked up my pen and wrote again – I wrote that I trusted him, that whatever he did I would always trust him, I understood – nothing mattered as long as he loved me. Then I put on my outdoor uniform and took it to the nearest post office.

Four days later, I was pulling the beds out and dusting the back rails, when I heard one of the men rustle his newspaper and call to his chum. 'One of the nobs bought it, Charlie – shot by a sniper, nobody's safe in this 'ere war.'

As I dusted the end of the bed I thought idly, knobs – no, nobs – and remembered Eddie's voice at Eton, 'How were the nobs, Lord Gerald?' and the amused reply, 'Knobbly, very knobbly!' and how we had all laughed together. Now I felt very cold as I bent down and asked quite quietly, 'Who has been shot, Number Twenty-four?'

He grinned up at me from under his walrus moustache. 'Oh, just some Markis or other, Nurse.' So I asked him very politely if I could borrow his newspaper and standing there amidst the bustle and clatter of the busy ward I read that my love was dead. Then I folded the paper up neatly, and said quietly, 'Thank you, Number Twenty-four,' and picked up my duster and began to rub at the brass rail. I did not know what else to do.

A few minutes later Staff came up the ward. 'One of the office sisters has come for you, Girvan – to go over to Matron.' She hesitated, then added, her kind face

239

grave, 'She said your father is here – I hope it's not bad news.'

I said, 'I'm afraid it is bad news, Staff Nurse,' then I folded up my duster and put it tidily in its box and carried it down the ward to the kitchen.

The telegram had gone to Moira Staveley at Bessingdon. She had immediately telegraphed to Papa at Hatton, but both my parents were in London, so it had lain there unopened for some time until a maid had noticed it and sent it on. Gerald had already been dead two days by the time I had read of it in the newspaper.

Papa put me in a cab for Cadogan Place, but halfway there I asked him to take me to Alice's instead. He said Alice was away, but I insisted. When we arrived I climbed very slowly up the steep flights of stairs, like an old woman. Nanny looked up as I came into the nursery and I said, 'Gerald has been killed,' and she opened her arms to me and I collapsed in a flood of tears on her broad bosom.

When I got back to Cadogan Place that evening I went straight to the morning room, opened the piano and began to sing. I sang the Maiden's Lament:

> 'Das Herz is gestorben,
> die Welt is leer'

My heart was dead, my world was empty – my lament would not be able to waken he who had died, my tears would flow uselessly.

And now at last I sang to him the final stanza of *Frauen Liebe und Leben*:

> 'Du schläfst, du harter, unbarmherz'ger Man,
> Den Todesschlaf.'

Cruel, pitiless man – you sleep the sleep of death – and now I have no more life. So I sang of my dead love in German, in the language of those who had killed him.

240

I played and sang until my voice was hoarse and my fingers numb – and the house was silent around me. Then I climbed stiffly off the stool and went out into the hallway. The drawing-room door opened, and Mother stood there very tall and straight. 'I'm sorry, Helena.' Then she added, 'When my sister Alice died I thought it was the end of the world – but I lived on, and so will you.' The door clicked shut and I climbed the stairs to my bed.

In my room I picked up his photograph and stood gazing at it – and it was only then that I remembered my angry, jealous letter. I threw myself on the bed in an agony of guilt and remorse. For two days I stayed in my room and wept. My parents came to the door but I screamed at them to go away; Fisher brought trays but I thrust them outside untouched – I could live with myself no longer. Then Nanny came panting and puffing through the door. 'Now stop being a silly girl and have a taste of this nice soup.' I swallowed, dumbly; then she said, 'My lady, my chick – we didn't know how to give these to you – they came back yesterday.' She held out two letters, my two last letters. I took them from her and turned them over and saw that neither flap had been unsealed. Someone had written across the back of each: 'Much regret this officer has been killed – returned to sender.'

I began to cry again, but more quietly now – God had not completely abandoned me after all.

Chapter Eight

I did not go back to the East London. I had been defeated, and I knew I had been defeated, but I did not care – nothing mattered now. I roamed round Cadogan

Place and out to the Park; I could not stay still, except at my piano, and there I sang every day of my heartache and grief. Mother forced me to answer the letters which came, otherwise I might not have done so. Moira Staveley wrote inviting me to come and stay with her at Bessingdon. Part of me wanted to accept, to see the places where he had grown up, to see his home – but then I thought that it would never be my home now. Moira's son had grown up in that nursery, but mine never would – so I could not bear to go.

Eddie and Robbie both came up to see me. They were in camp at Gainsborough now – it was a long journey to make for a few brief hours – and they were not both allowed to be away at once, so they had to come separately. But because they knew I would need them they each came and sat with me patiently while I wept and stormed at the cruelty of fate. I told Eddie what I had told no one else – of my terrible angry letter. He listened quietly, then said, 'Hellie, perhaps he went straight back, after you saw him – and if he didn't – men are different, it wouldn't have meant anything to him if . . . You must accept that. The important thing is that he never knew that you saw him and how you felt – remember that. Now wipe your eyes and we'll go for a walk in the Park before I catch my train.'

When Robbie came he said, 'We've decided that you must destroy those two letters, Hellie – go and fetch them now.' Slowly I brought them down to him, and my brother took out his matches and set fire to the corners and dropped the burning paper into the grate where the flames flared up among the glowing coals, then died down. 'There, all gone now Hellie – and no one will ever know.' He put his arm round me and I began to cry again, but it was a little easier now.

A couple of weeks later they arrived together. 'Four whole glorious days in Town – how about that, Hellie?' I smiled at them and said, 'How nice.' But I guessed why they had come together – it was their embarkation

242

leave. I lunched and dined with them and accompanied them to several shows – they wanted so much to cheer me up, and they were so excited at the prospect of going to France that I pretended to enjoy the glittering silly musicals they chose. And afterwards we came back through streets that were always dark now – for fear of air raids – and they would sit with me in the drawing room over their whisky and soda and then we would all go up to bed. But later I would hear them tiptoeing past my room as they crept out again, and the whistle for a cab far below. As soon as they had left the house I would turn my face into my pillow and lie weeping, for Gerald – my lost love.

Before they went back they told me which evening they would be passing through London with their territorial battalion; they knew they would have to stop at Liverpool Street to change engines, so I decided to go and wait there. I tipped a porter to smuggle me on to the right platform, then stood hiding behind a pile of trunks, under the smoky, cavernous roof. No one would see me in the shadows, now that I was dressed in mourning.

The troop train clanked into the station, and at first I was bewildered: there were so many khaki-clad figures crammed into the compartments, so many caps waving from the open windows as men shouted to the refreshment sellers and newsboys on the platform. Then my eye found the first class, and I peered at the sleekly groomed officers until at last I saw them – Eddie's laughing face with Robbie's mirror image opposite him. I ran forward and two pairs of eyes became round in surprise, then they were pushing through the door and out on to the platform and we were all hugging each other at once. 'Hello, Big Sis – are you going to be a stowaway? We'll wrap you in a greatcoat as disguise', 'and pull a cap down over your face, like this.' Robbie rammed his own cap down over my eyes; I was half-laughing, half-crying as I clung to them. Then there was an angry bellow from the train and the twins snapped smartly to attention. 'Must go, Hellie, that's the Colonel – we're setting a bad example.' They kissed me quickly, one on each cheek, then wheeled round together and marched back to their compartment.

I stood watching as the excited soldiers waved their caps and returned the cheers of the crowd on the station concourse; my throat tightened – they were so full of spirit, so eager to be on their way to the war – and down at the other end of the train the fresh engine was already being backed on. I saw a young lance-corporal push the whole of the top half of his body out of the window and raise his hand in a salute. Then he dragged his cap from his tow-coloured hair and waved it – in my direction. I half-turned and glanced over my shoulder, but there was no one behind me and I realized that I was the object of his attentions. For a moment I was indignant – how dare he presume? Then he gave a wide, hopeful grin, and looked so young and carefree that my indignation vanished and I raised my hand to him in acknowledgement and saw the delight on his face just as the train gave a warning jolt. At once my eyes searched frantically for my brothers and locked on to theirs, and I waved and waved until their faces merged with the white blur of all the other faces of that battalion going to war.

I realized that I was praying as I walked back up the platform: 'Please God, bring them back safely, please God, bring them back safely,' but God had not let Gerald come back; and the smoke stung my eyes and I could not see, and blundered into a newsboy, so I pretended I had wanted to buy a paper from him. I read it when I got back: the Germans were attacking again at Ypres, the Canadians had held the line after French colonial troops had been driven back by a new weapon – poison gas. My brothers, oh my brothers.

They wrote to say that they had had a very calm crossing that evening, but from Boulogne their men had had to march some distance uphill to a rest camp. Apparently the soldiers had crammed their packs full of last-minute purchases from Britain, and as the going got steeper and steeper, a variety of strange objects had been tossed either side of the road; everything from patent periscopes to knuckle dusters and tins of anti-vermin powder, Eddie wrote. Then Robbie described the misfortunes of the Transport Section: 'Imagine a cold, wet night – one team of mules baulked at a wooden bridge – behaved as if they'd never seen one before and tried to throw themselves and their limber into the canal – they'd only just been restrained when a wagon in front turned turtle in a ditch and old Rayner (the TO) dismounted to see what was going on and landed straight in a quagmire! Then the pole of one limber ran through the tailboard of the one in front and the whole procession ground to a cursing halt – so here we are on active service!

Look after yourself, Big Sis,
Your loving brothers,'

And the two familiar signatures were scrawled across the page – identical except for the fact that one sloped to the right and one to the left.

Cadogan Place was desolate now, so I wrote to Mrs Benson and asked if I might come down to Surrey to act as a VAD in her Red Cross Hospital. When I told Mother I was going she said, 'It's just as well, Helena, as I'm going back to Cheshire to set up a convalescent home at Hatton, so I shall be leaving London shortly myself.' I looked at my elegant beautiful mother, leaving Town in the Season – even she could not remain impervious to the War any longer. Most of Cadogan Place was put under dustsheets and a pair of maids stayed behind as caretakers. Papa was vague about his plans; he said he might put up at his club.

Pansy and Mrs Benson were very kind and they were so blessedly simple and uncomplicated. I spent hours sitting with Pansy talking about Gerald, though I never told her of my insane jealousy or the letter I had written;

she would not have understood. When I had exhausted myself, she talked of Guy. Her eyes were soft and shining as she said how wonderful he was – so kind, so brave, so clever. 'Eileen is *so* lucky, Helena.'

We did very little in the way of nursing. The men were well on the way to recovery and they cared for their own needs; there were some bed pans in a cupboard, but I never saw one which had been used. Every day the vicar's three sturdy daughters came cycling up the drive and went rushing round the ward with trays and medicine bottles, like a gaggle of cheerful geese. I swept and dusted and scrubbed lockers. Sometimes I felt rather bored, but mostly I drifted about in a daze.

By the middle of May the French had gained land near Ypres, but the papers were more excited by the British landings on the Gallipoli peninsula – so now we were fighting the Turks as well, far away at the other end of the Mediterranean. Then a letter came from Guy: he was in hospital in London – nothing serious, he assured me, just a touch of fever – he felt rather a fraud being evacuated back to England for it. I rushed up to London at once; he was in a nursing home in Park Lane and he did not look particularly ill – but his eyes had a beaten look. I asked him if he had been in action recently and he replied abruptly, 'Forget it, Hellie.' Then he stared at the flowers on his locker and said, 'Eileen's given me the push. She married Jimmy Enscombe last week.'

I whispered, 'Oh Guy, I'm so sorry.' He sat in a glum silence. 'Look, why don't you come and convalesce at The Pines? Mrs Benson's still got the same cook, and Pansy will be thrilled to have you.'

He looked more interested, then muttered, 'I don't know if I can stand Pansy mooning round me all day.'

'She's a very sweet girl, Guy.'

'Quite. Eileen wasn't sweet at all – Christ – I wish she'd married me last time.'

But he came the next day, and was quite ready to let

Pansy wait on him hand and foot. He would sit in the drawing room while she knelt at his feet lighting his cigarettes and pouring his whisky for him.

After a week he went up to the Medical Board, and when he got back he came to find me in the garden and told me they had passed him fit; he was going back in ten days. I stood very still and thought that I could hardly stand the anxiety of having all three brothers at the Front again, but there did not seem to be any choice. Then he stubbed out his cigarette and said, 'I'm going to marry Pansy.'

I gaped at him. 'But I've just been talking to her — she didn't say anything . . .'

'Oh, I haven't asked her yet, but I know she'll have me.'

He did not sound particularly pleased, so at last I asked, 'But why, Guy?' He turned and stood looking at me for a long time, his eyes dark. Then he said, 'Because it's bloody awful over there — I'll probably be wiped out by some shell — blown to smithereens, or buried alive like . . .' He began to shake; I put my arm through his and held him close until he got control of himself again. 'I just want to leave something behind — I want to beget a son, Helena.' He added, 'I'm not bothered about the bloody title, the twins can have that — it's me, I want to leave something of myself.' His face contorted, then he lit another cigarette with hands that shook.

As we turned to walk back to the house I asked hesitantly, 'But, what about Pansy?'

'I'll be doing her a favour, Hellie. She's always been besotted with me, ever since she was in the schoolroom — just like you were with Gerald. Well, now she can have me.' Then he added, his voice bitter, 'I suppose she's a better bet than Eileen — since I've got to leave her on her own — Eileen's not cut out to be a faithful wife.' I remembered the pretty girl on Guy's arm that day, but I did not remind him — as Mother had said, it was natural for men.

247

Pansy was radiant, Mrs Benson fondly thrilled, Mr Benson beamed with pleasure. Mother and Papa came down; they were pleased too. As Mother said to me, 'Pansy is her father's sole heir now – and he's a very wealthy man.' To be fair to Guy, I do not think he had given the money a thought.

It was a quiet wartime wedding in the local church, not the fashionable London affair we had expected for Guy and Eileen. It was only too obvious he was making the same comparison; his mouth was an angry line as he stared straight ahead, and he scarcely seemed to be aware of the bride by his side. Pansy looked as velvet-soft as her namesake in a white silk afternoon dress; she wore her mother's lace veil over her curling brown hair.

As they left for their honeymoon she was clinging to Guy's arm, and her blue eyes shone as they gazed adoringly up at him; but my brother's face was bleak and his square jaw jutted ominously. When he delivered Pansy back to The Pines the following week her eyes were no longer shining, and she flushed as her mother embraced her. Her small hand trembled in mine as Guy said abruptly, 'Pansy offered to come up to Charing Cross to see me off, but I told her not to bother – she'll only start howling.' Then he muttered, without looking at me, 'How about you, Hellie – do you fancy a run up to Town this afternoon?'

Pansy whispered, 'Please go with him, Helena,' so I rang for my hat and coat. Pansy was crying as he quickly kissed her goodbye; I could scarcely bear to look at her.

At Charing Cross I put my arms round Guy and he held me tightly against his chest; his heart was beating very fast. Then he muttered, 'God, Hellie – I wish I had more guts – I don't want to go back.' He kissed me quickly, then pulled away and I watched him stride over to the train. He waved as it drew out and I waved back, then I forced my shaking legs to walk away.

Guy had gone back on the last day of May, and next morning we heard that Zeppelins had bombed north-east London that evening. The official communiqué stated that the number of casualties had been small – but one had been a child, and one a babe-in-arms. Mrs Benson kept repeating, 'I can't believe it, I can't believe it – not London, they can't have bombed London – oh when will it ever end?' Pansy sat at the table with swollen, red-rimmed eyes; she had scarcely spoken since she had come back from her honeymoon. I went up to her room later, with a wedding present which had just arrived, and she was lying on her bed, sobbing. I was going to slip away, but she heard me and called me back, so I went slowly in and sat down. At last I said, 'Guy – Guy will be all right, I'm sure he will.'

She looked at me vaguely, her blue eyes blurred, then she reached out and seized my arm, her nails biting into my flesh. 'Helena, I'm so ashamed' – her face flushed scarlet – 'I can't tell you what Guy did to me – he was like an animal, it was horrible, horrible.' She was panting and distraught; I sat stunned, not knowing what to say. 'But I must tell someone, I must – or I shall go mad – and I can't tell Mumsy, I can't.'

She looked at me desperately until I swallowed and asked, 'What did Guy do?' She whispered, 'In the hotel, he came into my room, when I was in bed – and started taking all his clothes off, in front of me – and he was so hairy and . . .' She was sobbing again, Pansy, whose mother had not even allowed her to see soldiers in their pyjamas.

I felt very old and tired as I asked, 'Did your mother not, well, say anything to you beforehand?'

She gulped, then whispered, 'Mumsy said Guy might – might do something I didn't like – and I was to close my eyes and not complain. But Helena' – her voice rose in a wail of distress – 'I didn't close my eyes soon enough! He came towards me and I saw . . . I didn't know men looked like that, I couldn't look away, and then he – he pushed my nightgown up and – oh, Helena,' she began to sob again. 'And it hurt, it did hurt so much, but I didn't say anything, I bit my lip very hard, but I didn't complain. And afterwards I lay there, waiting for him to go away, and I thought, 'Well, at least it's over now, it's done, and then, Helena – he did it again!'

Poor, innocent, ignorant Pansy. 'But why didn't you tell him, that he was hurting you?'

'How could I, Helena? I was so embarrassed. I didn't know how to face my maid in the morning, and there was blood on the sheets – whatever must the chambermaid have thought? I felt as if everyone was looking at me.' She sighed, very heavily, 'It happened every night, and once he wanted me to go upstairs in the afternoon – in the afternoon! I couldn't, I just couldn't, so I said no and he was very angry and swore at me and went to play golf.' She gave another long, shuddering sigh. 'So when it was time for him to go back, for a moment I was pleased, and now I feel so guilty, because I do love him so much.'

I looked at my small sad sister-in-law with pity. Then I pulled myself together and tried to explain. 'Pansy, what Guy did is quite normal – all husbands do it with their wives.'

She stared up at me, then said very firmly, 'Not Mumsy and Papa – they wouldn't.'

I looked at her helplessly. 'But they must have done, Pansy – otherwise you wouldn't be here.' She still looked up at me, in total disbelief, so in desperation I said, 'I want to show you something, I'll be back.'

I ran to my room, delved in my bag and found my midwifery textbook. I took it along to her and showed her the pictures of the small, curled-up babies, and explained why Guy had done what he had, and finished, 'And that's why he did it so often, because he wanted to make sure.'

She gazed in fascination at the pictures, then put her hand on her flat stomach and said, her voice awestruck, 'Oh, Helena, do you think . . . ?'

But suddenly I did not want to talk about it so I thrust

the book into her hands and said brusquely, 'Read it – keep the book, it's no use to me any more.' I left her quickly and went down to the ward in the ballroom and began to scrub the already-gleaming glass trolley.

Pansy was very quiet and thoughtful for the next two weeks, then one day she came to me, her face radiant, and I knew what she had to say. She asked me to tell Guy when I wrote to him; she was too embarrassed herself. I had difficulty in writing the words to my brother; my monthly cramps had started, and when at last I crawled into bed I lay and wept with my womb for Gerald's unbegotten sons.

Chapter Nine

I could not bear to stay and watch Pansy's body swelling with child. A notice had come round that the big military hospitals in London were taking on VADs now, and as I had passed my First Aid Certificate at The Pines I applied at once. Before the end of July my orders had come through from Devonshire House: I was to report to the 6th London General Hospital at Wandsworth. An asylum for orphans had been requisitioned at the outbreak of war; the orphans had been dispatched elsewhere and the building was now at the hub of a vast sprawling encampment of hutted wards, erected to receive the never-ending stream of casualties from France.

I found it very easy to slip back into nursing. The routine of a military hospital was sometimes different, but the sisters and staff nurses were almost all on the Territorial Force so they had trained in hospitals very like the East London and I knew what they expected of me. In return Sister treated me like a civilian probationer and answered my questions and told me what I needed to know.

My life narrowed, and I became totally absorbed in my ward and in my patients. When they won their evening tussle with their neighbours in the next hut for possession of the gramophone I was glad – even though it meant that the sentimental favourites blared out incessantly, and we had to bandage to the tune of 'If you were the only girl in the world', and give out cocoa to the words: 'Hold your hand out, naughty boy'. When they lost their battle, the packs of cards appeared and endless games of solo whist and cribbage were played for cigarette stakes. Occasionally a group of men would slip off to the latrines together, and we knew the Crown and Anchor board was in use; but we pretended not to notice, since dice counted as gambling, and gambling was strictly forbidden.

This time I surrendered myself willingly to the institution, not wanting to think of the outside world. I wrote to my brothers every week and prayed for their safety, and felt superstitiously that if I spent all my time and energy on my patients then this would somehow keep them safe.

I did practise my scales in my off-duty periods – I had been doing this every day for so long now that it was as much part of my daily routine as cleaning my teeth – but I did not offer to sing to the men in Hut 33. Whenever the weather was fine I would take my writing case out on to Wandsworth Common and lie on the dusty grass writing long letters to my brothers. I would describe to them the small daily events and jokes of the ward, or relay the odd snippet of gossip that Alice had fed me, together with buttered scones, when I made my occasional visit to Town. I liked to hear how Hugh and Conan were getting on, but I was not much interested in anybody else – still, I thought the twins might be, so I carefully recorded all Alice's news for them.

Sometimes when they wrote back it was of trench raids

and wiring parties, and I felt sick with apprehension, but more often their letters dwelt on the domestic side of war. When back in their billets they too wrote letters and played cards and ate to the sound of a wind-up gramophone.

Over the months the officers in their mess and the men in their platoons became personalities to me, so that I could picture the two contrasting subalterns: small dapper Ormsby and tall swashbuckling Gardiner. Ian Ormsby was the soft-spoken son of a solicitor – he had gone straight from school into the army, whereas Frank Gardiner was an American rancher in his thirties, who had been visiting Britain in the summer of 1914. As soon as war broke out he had applied for a temporary commission, swearing he was a Canadian by birth. Now he was serving beside my brothers in the Lancashire and Cheshire Light Infantry – 'just for the hell of it', he had told Robbie.

I also looked forward to hearing more of the sayings of sturdy, lugubrious Sergeant McTavish – a Glaswegian who said he had only joined an English regiment because he had been too drunk at the time to know the difference. McTavish complained all the time about the English, but had only ever been heard to refer to the enemy once. Robbie wrote that a shell had exploded nearby and all the men had ducked except for McTavish, who sat stolidly through the explosion stirring his tea; but when he took his first mouthful his face had gone purple with rage and he had shouted: 'Bluidy Gairmans have put mud in ma tae – it shouldna be allowed!' The other men had rocked with laughter, Robbie said, but McTavish had simply stared at them saying, 'What's yer joke, mon, what's yer joke?' Big steady Sergeant James; small perky Private Jackson; with his friend, the red-eyed Pertwee whose nose quivered like an albino rabbit's; stocky Lancastrian Corporal Holden with an eye as quick to spot a good estaminet as a sniper's hideout – these men became known to me from my brothers' letters, so that I rejoiced when Pertwee's long-delayed leave came through, and wept when McTavish was carried in dying from a trench raid.

Several times I woke up in the early morning and found myself wondering when Gerald would be home on leave – and the grief when I realized he would never come again was as sharp as ever. Then I would lie in my narrow cubicle and force the edge of the sheet into my mouth to stifle my sobs, longing for the maid to bang on the door with our jugs of hot water. Pansy's happy letters were a torment to me, and it was an effort to answer them, but I felt a spurt of anger with Guy when his birthday greetings to me arrived a week early, from Paris. He wrote quite casually that he had had leave, but had not fancied coming back to England. 'You waste so much time on the journey it's hardly worth it.' It was only in a postscript that he had bothered to scribble: 'Don't tell Pansy, Helena – there's no point stirring it up, is there?' The letter was written on a fine cream notepaper, quite unlike Guy's normal choice, and when I held it up to my nostrils I could distinguish the scent of orris root – it was only too clear how my brother had spent his time in Paris. I felt so sorry for gentle, trusting Pansy.

Other VADs went down with poisoned fingers or septic throats, but I seemed immune. They went up West in the evening, and some of them even crept back through the basement windows after the hostel's door had been locked; I saw them on the wards next morning red-eyed and yawning – but I had no wish to join them. I did not want to find pleasure in trivial amusements now – I was a nun vowed to my convent – at twenty-two my life stretched bleakly ahead of me, an arid desert. As long as my beloved brothers were safe I asked nothing more.

I came alive for a while in November when the twins came home on leave, Eddie first, then Robbie. I spent every minute I could with them: I dined out, and went to musicals – I would go anywhere they wanted me to: my brothers must have every wish fulfilled. They did not talk much of the fighting, and they looked older – but their faces were not bleak like Guy's face had been. Eddie said one day, 'You know, it's got its ghastly moments, but there's no doubt this war business is exciting – and you feel as long as you're with the other fellows you can stand anything.' He grinned. 'Cambridge'll seem very tame when we eventually get back there.'

At the beginning of December I was transferred to night duty. It was a wrench leaving Hut 33, but I did not mind nights: I almost preferred the upside-down routine. Life was so odd now it seemed only fitting that it should become even odder.

In the early hours of Christmas morning a man with a suppurating chest wound finally died. His eyes would not close but I remembered Sister Foldus telling us to use wet lint, so I cut two pieces and dampened them and pressed them firmly over his eyelids for a few minutes. As I stood waiting I was aware of a sombre sense of satisfaction – Night Sister was busy, but I knew exactly what to do and how to do it.

It was only much later, as I trekked over the dark common to the hostel that it struck me how strange it was that I should have spent the night before Christmas laying out a corpse – and not even thought of it as strange. I remembered the tall dark girl who wore three bobbing ostrich feathers in her hair and had almost fainted with horror because she had dared to touch the royal hand with her nose, and suddenly I began to laugh. By the time I got to my cubicle I was crying; the ice around my heart was melting, but I did not want it to go.

CHAPTER TEN

Guy's son was born at Cadogan Place on Boxing Day. I did not want to see the baby, but in the end I had to go. Pansy was feeding him when I went in – the small dark head was still against her breast, only the round cheeks moving in and out with fierce concentration. Pansy looked up, her tired face glowing. 'Isn't he beautiful, Helena?' I looked at him and felt only relief; he was so obviously Guy's son and there was no answering tug in my breast. My brother had the son he had wanted, and I was glad.

Guy came back to England soon after. It was not very clear why, and even Pansy seemed uncertain. Guy himself muttered something about 'training', but he was so bad-tempered nobody dared to question him further. The glow died out of Pansy's eyes, and by the time Guy went glowering back to France at the end of April, Nanny was feeding young Lance from a bottle; Pansy's milk had dried up because she was pregnant again. I had learnt much in the past year, but I suspected that Pansy had learnt even more.

My leave was due as soon as Guy had gone back, so I went up to Cheshire and spent the time very quietly at Hatton. It was strange to see men in their blues and not be responsible for their welfare, but Mother had organized a team of local VADs who did just as they were told, so I walked in the park each day and then came back to play and sing in the music room, which had been kept as the family sitting room.

The week after I got back a letter arrived from Mother – she had come down to Cadogan Place because Conan had been wounded. She wrote that he was recovering quite well – he had been caught in the head by a piece of shrapnel on his way up to the line with a carrying party. That wound had been relatively slight, but the impact had knocked him off the duckboards and he had fallen awkwardly and broken his leg above the ankle. I wanted to go up and see him at once, but the other VAD on my ward had gone sick and her replacement was a girl from a small Red Cross Hospital in Dorset – she was badly shaken by her first experience of the 6th London, so Sister asked me to stay on duty longer for several days.

When I eventually arrived at the luxurious private hospital for officers overlooking the Park, the small VAD hovering outside the spotless sink room was doubtful about letting me in to see him. 'Doctor said, as Lieutenant Finlay is a head wound he should be kept quiet – only relatives are allowed to visit.'

I said, 'I am a relative, I'm his cousin.'

She still seemed uncertain, until a second girl came, and after a whispered consultation she said, 'Well, since you're a VAD – I suppose I can take you along to his room.'

'No, Sybell – I'll take her . . .' They wrangled in soft pretty voices; the first girl waved a pink-tipped elegant hand and I wondered how she managed to keep them so well – finally they both decided to take me. After a slight scuffle Sybell reached the door first and flung it open. My cousin was lying back on his bed while a shapely girl with silver-blonde hair bent over him, holding a medicine glass to his lips. Her eyes were fixed on his face, his were riveted on the swelling curve of her bosom.

Sybell announced, 'Lieutenant Finlay, your cousin has come to see you.' Conan's glance flickered in my direction and he raised a languid hand in greeting. My two escorts stood gazing at him, then Sybell's friend glanced at me and said, 'Isn't it curious – you look much more like him than either of his sisters.'

I looked over at Conan whose eyes were now fixed

again on the full breasts suspended above him and said, very distinctly, 'Lieutenant Finlay does not have any sisters.'

There was a chorus of little gasps, and an indignant trio of skirts rustled backwards through the door. Bereft of his entertainment Conan looked across at me: his blue eyes snapped, 'Thanks, Hellie – thanks a lot!'

I smiled sweetly at him. 'You really must introduce me to your sisters some time, dear Cousin.'

His sudden grin flashed out. 'Give me a chance, Hellie – I haven't introduced them to each other yet!' I began to laugh, and he reached out and seized my hand. 'Anyway, after the damage you've just done the least you can do is give me a cousinly kiss.' He pulled me towards him and I bent down to put my lips to his cheek, but he was too quick for me and it was his mouth which met mine – before I could move away an arm was clamped round my waist and I was sprawling halfway across the bed in a long, breathless kiss.

There was a click behind us, and an indignant squeak of 'His *cousin!*' before the door closed again and I was able to break free. Conan began to laugh. 'That serves you right – that just serves you right!' With my cheeks on fire I swept to the furthest corner of the room and sat down with my hands primly folded. Conan lay back on his pillows, looking at me, then he grinned again. 'I'll tell you something, Hellie – I like kissing you even more than I do my sisters!' He started to laugh again, and at last I joined in.

At the end of May, Conan's father took him back to his estate in Ireland to convalesce, and I began to look forward to the twins' next leaves – I knew they were due shortly, and opened each envelope with its distinctive black circle with a throb of anticipation. But the news had still not come when, in the middle of June, the hostel housekeeper met me with a telegram. I opened it with shaking hands: 'Eddie wounded. In 1st London General at Camberwell. Pickering.'

I rushed upstairs and scrabbled for money, then ran all the way back to the cab rank outside the hospital gates. I sat in the cab, clutching the stitch in my side and gasping for breath, 'Eddie – please God, don't let it be too bad.' All the worst and most mutilating wounds I had ever seen flashed before my eyes and I wanted to scream at the driver to go faster, faster. I jumped down and ran to the porter, waiting impatiently as he consulted his records. 'Lieutenant Girvan, Miss? B Ward, Officers' Row, turn right by the X-ray hut . . .' I was running again.

At the entrance to the hut I stopped, very frightened, looking along the rows of beds. A staff nurse came towards me. But I had seen him, and I plunged forward and there was Eddie, lying back smoking, his face quite unmarked, with his left leg strung up in a Balkan beam and his right arm in a sling. He looked like a schoolboy as he grinned up at me. 'Hello, Big Sis – aren't I the popular one today! Papa's only just left.' My legs were shaking and I collapsed on to a chair, then threw my arms round him and buried my face in his neck. 'Hey, watch it – I'll be setting your hair on fire.' I straightened up, still clutching his uninjured arm. 'I'm afraid I wasn't quick enough at the station – got taken to the rival establishment – so you won't have the pleasure of carrying my bed pan! Still, it is the same side of the river.'

At last I managed to find my voice. 'Conan was in Park Lane – it was very luxurious – and he had three terribly pretty VADs waiting on him hand and foot.'

Eddie snorted. 'Typical! Still, I'm damn glad to be anywhere, frankly,' he shuddered. 'Christ, Hellie, I thought I'd had it! They sent us out on one of those bloody stupid trench raids – crawling about in No-Man's-Land with blackened faces clutching knobkerries, like a crowd of drunken Irishmen on St Patrick's night – "Just get out there and capture a couple of the enemy, Girvan." "Certainly, sir," I said, my knees knocking

259

like a pair of tapdancers. "It makes all the difference to know whether we're being shot at by a Prussian regiment or a Saxon one." "Of course, sir." And that was it, poor little Edwin for the big heroics.' He took another pull at his cigarette.

'What happened, Eddie?'

'Oh, the usual – a flare went up and someone didn't freeze fast enough so the next minute a load of grenades were being lobbed in our direction. It was like being hit by a bloody steam-hammer. When I came to in a shell hole there was just me and Private Dobson – and he was dead. I was so stunned I kept whispering in his ear – until I realized it wasn't actually attached to the rest of his body any more. Then I tried to crawl back, but they'd smashed the other ankle as well; I couldn't get out of the bloody hole – I was as weak as a kitten. So I just lay there, thinking very gloomy thoughts about the dawn – I've never been very keen on seeing the dawn, as you know. We'd gone over too late because it'd been moonlight earlier – the whole operation was a botch-up from start to finish – old Pearson didn't like it above half, but orders are orders, so he had to send us.' His face was grim. 'I kept thinking about Robbie, if he'd been in the forward trench he'd have come looking for me – and I cursed the fact that he was in support, then I thought about it a bit more and thanked God he was further back.' He fell silent.

At last I asked, 'But how did you get back, Eddie?'

He shook himself, then winced with pain. 'Light me another cigarette, Hellie, and I'll tell you.' My hands shook as I struck the match; Eddie inhaled deeply. 'Well, I lay there, watching the pearly glow in the east, feeling pretty sick, when a voice with a strong Lancashire accent whispers, "Is that you, Mr Girvan, sir?" and there, peering over the lip of the hole, was Sergeant Holden. I thought I was hallucinating, but I managed to yelp, "Yes, but I'm afraid Dobson's had it." He says, quite calm, "Then I'd best get you in, sir, it's a bit chilly out here." I hissed back, "You're mad – it's nearly daylight and I can't move." He slid down into the hole and said, "That's all right, sir, I can carry you." Hellie, I've heard some poetry in my time, and I thought it was pretty smart stuff, but that simple phrase, "I can carry you" – I tell you, Shakespeare never wrote words like that. Then he picked me up and carried me in, just like a baby.'

I shivered. 'Didn't they – didn't they fire at you?'

'Yes, they did – but Holden assured me they couldn't see properly, not with the dawn rising behind their trenches, and by that stage I'd have believed him if he'd told me the moon was made of green cheese. Anyway, they missed us, or perhaps they let us get away with it – they do sometimes – and there I was back in our trench waiting for the stretcher bearers. Pearson said Corporal Smith had come back in a blue funk so Holden picked him up and shook him like a terrier with a rat until he'd told him more or less where we'd been. Smith insisted that Dobson was dead, but then he admitted he didn't know about me. So Holden said he'd go out and see what had happened. Little Ormsby offered to have a go, Pearson told me – very decent of him – but Holden said I'd be too heavy for him to manage, whereas he was used to heaving coal around so he'd better do it.'

'Oh Eddie – how kind, how very kind, I'll write and thank him today.'

'Good idea Hellie, I can't scribble a thing at the moment. God, was I glad to see him – I've always had nightmares about lying out in No-Man's-Land, ever since we found old Sawley' – he shuddered – 'the rats had made a pretty fine mess of him – I only hope he died first.' I could not speak; I just sat and clutched his arm.

As soon as I had scribbled a note to Robbie I wrote to Sergeant Holden, and posted both letters before tea. When I saw Papa the next day at Camberwell he said he had written too, and sent a box of Havana cigars. On the third day I managed to get over in the morning.

261

Eddie lay listlessly in his bed; he looked rather feverish and said his leg was hurting a lot. On the fourth day I just sat with him, holding his hand. His pulse was racing, and as I bent over to kiss him goodbye I smelt the sickly scent of decay from his wound. He opened his eyes and said, 'Hellie – I feel lousy.'

I whispered, 'It's just a reaction, old man, you'll feel better in a day or two.' He tried to smile and began to shake. When he had stopped, his eyes were closed again. I tiptoed away.

Matron came to my ward early next morning and said I must go over to the 1st London at once; a cab was waiting at the door. Papa had telegraphed to Mother at Hatton and she had caught the midnight sleeper from Manchester. When I arrived at the hospital Eddie was already delirious; he did not recognize us. They had taken his leg off in the night, but it was too late, he had absorbed too much of the poison. The three of us sat beside his bed until he died.

I went back with my parents to Cadogan Place. Miss Fisher was waiting in the hallway; she hurried forward, 'My lady . . .' Her voice trailed away.

My mother's tone was quite steady and she held her back ramrod straight as she requested, 'Please lay out full mourning for Lady Helena and myself, Fisher.'

The maid bowed her head in assent and turned towards the servants' door. I muttered something to my parents and ran to the stairs and up to my bedroom, where I began to take off my uniform; my hands were trembling so much I could scarcely unfasten the buttons.

When she had dressed me in the black I had worn for Gerald, Fisher handed me a letter – I had put it in the pocket of my frock that morning at Wandsworth, unopened. It was from Sergeant Holden, saying that he was glad to hear Mr Girvan was going on so well. I sat down at my desk, picked up my pen and began to write.

Dear Sergeant Holden,

I am sorry to have to tell you that my brother died this morning.

It looked very bald, so at last I added:

He told me how much he had dreaded the possibility of lying wounded and dying in No-Man's-Land, and thanks to you he did not have to endure that.

Yours very sincerely,
Helena Girvan.

I sat staring at the letter, then I wrote underneath: 'Thank you for enabling me to be with him at the end.' I folded the paper and put it into an envelope, then I began to weep – for Eddie, for Robbie, and for myself.

They let Robbie come back on leave. He had been in the support trenches with A Company; he had not even seen Eddie before he was taken down the line. His face was a grey mask. He kept whispering, 'I knew, I knew – my leg hurt and hurt and then it didn't hurt any more – there was just nothing – so I knew he'd gone.'

We took Eddie back to Hatton to be buried. I watched Robbie carry the flag-draped coffin of his brother out of the old grey church at Lostherne. Together with the other khaki-clad pallbearers he lowered it gently into the open grave, then he threw a handful of soil down on to the body.

' . . . earth to earth, ashes to ashes, dust to dust . . .'
I stepped forward and stood close beside him.

'Grant, we beseech Thee, O Lord, Thine Eternal Rest to all who have died for their country, as this our brother hath . . .'

Our brother. We stood shoulder to shoulder as the firing party raised their rifles and the volley crashed out over the grave, and I felt his fingers reach convulsively for mine as the bugle sang its wailing lament over the peaceful hillside – the Last Post, for our brother, our brother who was dead.

That night as I lay dry-eyed and sleepless I heard the soft click of the door. 'Hellie?' My brother's tall shape came towards me, his shoulders shaking. I went to him with hands outstretched and led him over to my bed. I pulled him in beside me and we lay clasped in each other's arms and cried ourselves to sleep.

I went to see him off at Victoria. Robbie said, 'He was the strong one, Hellie – he always looked after me, all the time. Now he's gone I don't know how I can stand it.'

I looked up at his white face, then I said, 'Robbie, I'll be old enough for active service in September – I'll put my name down the minute I get back. I'll soon be in France, with you.'

His face lightened a fraction, then he hugged me very tightly and strode off to the waiting train. I went home and wept.

CHAPTER ELEVEN

But there was no time to grieve. Two days after I got back to the hospital the great British offensive on the Somme began, and soon the wounded were flooding in. The whole ward stank of the thick yellow pus which poured out as we unwrapped the blood-caked bandages. We probed and delved for pieces of broken bone, then packed the gaping holes, thrust in the draining tubes and quickly bound them up again. In bed after bed men lay desperately ill, and my wrists ached from wringing out fomentations, while the skin on my palms became permanently wrinkled from handling the hot cloths. The rubbish bin in the annex was full to overflowing with reeking dressings and I had to ram my pail down hard on to the filthy mass to empty it. Then I ran back to the bubbling sterilizer, on to the sticky lysol-filled sink to dunk the bloodstained mackintoshes, and out again to the ward where face after face swayed beneath me as I slid my arm below pillow after pillow, and tipped up the feeding cup with the repetitive, meaningless words, 'Come along now, old man, have a nice drink . . . a nice drink, . . . a nice drink . . .'

There were feet that no longer looked like feet, hands that had been torn into shreds, and faces that were only eyes above holes – pathetic, despairing eyes which had to be met with a calm smiling face: 'Soon have you right, old man – right old man – right old man.'

When we sat down to our cold meat and pickles each evening there would be another face missing.

'Where's Elton?'

'On leave – her brother . . .'

'Andrews?'

'Her fiancé, I believe . . .'

In a couple of days they would be back again, tight-lipped and red-eyed as they delved and packed and bandaged.

Sometimes we gathered in one of the larger bedrooms to drink cocoa and grumble about the rudeness of a staff nurse or the tyranny of a sister or the dreariness of our meals, until one by one we crept yawning back to our beds to fall into a stunned sleep. There was no time to grieve.

In August the pace began to slacken a little, and we were occasionally sent off duty again. I dragged myself up to Alice's one afternoon and she poured me cup after cup of tea, and kept refilling my plate as I ate in a daze. I showed her the last pencilled note from Robbie; he was still alive, and so was Guy. As I stood up to go she told me Conan was back in Town, and wanted to look me up one day. I stared at her vaguely. He must have trekked down to Wandsworth shortly after, because there was a note from him, delivered by hand while I was on duty. He asked when I would be free; I crumpled it up and trudged down to my room in the basement. There was no time.

Two days later, a broad-shouldered officer was hovering by the railings as we came back off duty. He spoke to the VAD in front; she turned and pointed at me. Cap in hand he drawled, 'Say, are you the Lady Helena Girvan?' I nodded and a great grin split his sunburnt face. 'Am I glad to hear that – you're the fiftieth girl I've spoken to – and each one prettier than the last. Your brother Rob said I'd find you here when he waved me goodbye yesterday afternoon – I left him sunning himself in a pretty little village called Vignacourt, way behind the line. The battalion have been pulled out for a rest – he said I must be sure to tell you.' Relief flooded through me; Robbie would be safe for a while. 'Now, you just wait here while I call a cab and I'll take you someplace where you can rest those dainty little feet of yours.'

'But we haven't been introduced!'

He thrust out a large hand and seized hold of mine. 'Frank Gardiner at your service, ma'am. I reckon that'll do for an introduction – you just come right along now.'

He was so determined it was easier to follow him than to resist. He sat opposite me in the small restaurant and talked of Robbie and I drank in every word. Then he told me how sorry he had been about Eddie's death. 'He was a good buddy – always ready with a laugh and a joke. I'm from the mid-West myself – now a lot of your Limey officers are just bank clerks and such like – they barely know one end of a horse from the other. And stiff! My God, when you clap 'em on the back they go and wash their hands. Now your brother, he was a real man, he could ride and he sure knew how to handle a gun.'

I told him, 'We hunted from the time we were children, and Eddie shot his first partridge at nine.' I remembered his pride, and Robbie's generous delight in his brother's success – oh God, please keep Robbie safe. I shivered in the warm room and the man opposite leant forward and picked up the wine bottle and held it over my glass. 'No more, thank you, Mr Gardiner – I don't have a very good head for alcohol.'

'You should try it – sometimes I reckon it's the only thing that stands between me and the madhouse.' His greenish eyes dulled, and we stared at each other bleakly. I saw his hand on the tablecloth tremble and put mine over it; his fingers were strong and warm. He shook himself like a dog coming out of a pond and said, 'No use feeling sorry for ourselves, Lady Helena – I guess we've just gotter make the best of it while we can.' He leant forward. 'Let's you and me paint the town red together, tomorrow night – how about that?'

I wanted to go, but I hesitated. 'I'm not off duty until eight – and they lock the doors at ten-thirty, so I'm afraid we'd only manage a very pale pink in that time.'

He threw back his head and laughed. 'Don't you believe it – between us we'll leave London as scarlet as an old-time soldier's tunic.'

He escorted me back to the hostel and shook my hand very formally, but his face as he bent over me and whispered 'Tomorrow!' had the lean dark profile of a hawk and his eyes gleamed in the light of the dimmed lamp; I felt a mingled rush of apprehension – and excitement.

The ward was hot and stuffy, the sun beat down mercilessly on the iron roof and the men's faces shone with sweat. Little Johnnie Lambert lay in his corner bed, slowly wasting away. The bones jutted out of his thin body as I sponged him down and his soft spaniel eyes watched me, helpless and supplicating. After I had tucked the single sheet securely round him I placed my hand against his downy cheek and he smiled and turned his face into my palm and closed his eyes. I stood beside him for a little while, then I heard Staff calling me, so

I gently withdrew my hand and pushed the trolley back to the sink room.

Frank Gardiner was lounging against the hostel railings when I came round the corner. He sprang to attention and called, 'Hiya, Princess – get your gladrags on and we'll start painting.'

I did not want to go now, my head ached, but it was too difficult to refuse, so I quickly got changed, swept my hair up on top of my head and thrust my tired feet into soft kid shoes. As he helped me into the cab he said, 'We'll eat first, then go on to a little place I know, where we can dance.' I tried to protest that I must be back by ten-thirty, but he only laughed, 'Plenty of time, Princess – plenty of time.' There was a predatory glint in his eye as he spoke and I felt a momentary flash of panic when he jumped in after me and his big rangy body sat close beside me on the seat. Then the smell of tobacco and shaving soap and healthy male sweat filled the cab and overwhelmed the traces of lysol and iodoform which always lingered in my nostrils, and I breathed in deeply and felt my senses stir. Without thinking I moved closer to him; he grinned ferociously and my breath caught in my throat.

At dinner I automatically put my hand over my glass again, but he gripped my wrist and lifted it off and poured in more wine. 'Drink, Princess, drink.' His greenish eyes mesmerized me so that I picked up the glass with my left hand and drank deeply; his broad fingers still pinned my other hand to the table; his palm was very warm. The wine took away my tiredness, I relaxed, I laughed, and the other diners receded and left me alone with a big square-shouldered man with narrowed green eyes and a wolfish grin. 'The club first.' He stood up and I wondered giddily – why first? surely the meal had been first – but my head seemed curiously light and my headache had quite vanished, so I laughed as I stood up on legs which had turned to cotton wool and swayed against him. He put his strong arm around my waist and helped me from the restaurant – Mother would have been shocked, but then, Mother was not here. I giggled as Frank Gardiner helped me in to the cab and he laughed with me. In the close intimacy of the cab the male smell of him was utterly desirable and I leant towards him and said, 'I want to smell you – you smell so nice.' I knew I must sound ridiculous, but he did not seem to mind – he grinned and pulled me over to him until I was sprawling against his shoulder. I rubbed my cheek against the harsh cloth of his tunic.

He bent forward, muttering, 'My bootlace is undone,' but it was my shoe he was fumbling with and I giggled – fancy not knowing my foot from his! His hand slid up over my ankle and I realized he was stroking my calf, low down where the driver could not see. Dimly I knew I should not let strange American officers stroke my leg, but it did not seem to matter any more.

The cab drew to a halt and Frank Gardiner slowly withdrew his hand. As the driver called, 'Here we are, sir,' and jumped out, strong fingers squeezed my knee. 'Hey, Princess – are you sure you want to go to the club first – 'fore we go home?'

I nestled against him for a moment – I did not want to go home yet – then I slid over to the open door. 'OK, Lady – you're in charge.'

The fresher air outside gave me a little shock, but he was at my elbow, guiding me down some steps. I said stupidly, 'It's a cellar – how can we dance in a cellar?' but he did not answer. In the dim passageway his hand touched my thigh and it was like an electric shock. He stopped and pulled me against him.

'We won't stay long, Princess – just time for another drink and a dance – then it's home to bed.' I smiled up at him drowsily; we were alone in the passage and suddenly he caught me to his chest and bent down to find my lips. His tongue was in my mouth, and I wanted it there – I sucked at the salty taste of him, pressing myself against his body. Then there was the quick tap of high heels and he released me and tugged me on.

We came into a dark, smoky room; there were only a few lights up in the shadows but they hurt my eyes so I looked down at the table. He called for drinks – the liquid in my glass burnt my throat, but he made me drink it. Then he hauled me to my feet. 'Time for one dance, Princess, before I take you home.' He led me on to the tiny floor and pulled me tightly against his chest. It seemed a strange way to dance, but there were so many other couples I supposed it was the only way. We did not seem to move at all – we only swayed backwards and forwards in time to the strong rhythm – and every inch of his hard lean body pressed against mine.

A girl's face swam before my eyes – it was painted like a doll: small pearly teeth gleamed as she laughed up at her companion, her curls were very blonde, too blonde. I recognized her for what she was and was vaguely wondering what she was doing here when Frank Gardiner was suddenly wrenched away from me. I stood, swaying, bereft of my support. Gardiner was shouting, 'Hey – mind your back!'

A voice replied angrily, 'What do you think you're doing with my cousin?' I recognized it – it was Conan's. The yellow-haired girl stood, mouth agape, as Conan squared up to the burly American; she reached for my cousin's arm, but he shook her hand off impatiently.

Frank Gardiner shouted, 'She's my girl for the evening.' His voice was belligerent; I had to calm things down. But I had to think hard before I spoke and my tongue would scarcely form the words as I said, 'It's all right, Conan, Mr Gardiner was just about to take me back to the hostel.'

Gardiner's head jerked up. Conan said scornfully, 'Like hell he was.'

I repeated, 'He said he'd take me home.'

Conan's dark-blue eyes held mine for a moment; his expression was unreadable, then he breathed, 'Christ,

Hellie – whatever do they teach you at that ruddy hospital – knitting?' He stepped in front of me. 'Sorry, chum, but she's my cousin and I'm taking her home.'

'You Limey bastard – trying to snatch my girl – you with your fucking sneering voice – you think you own the whole bloody world!' A fist swung out, Conan staggered back against me, the blonde squealed and clutched at my arm with long red talons. A space was forming on the crowded dance floor and the two men were circling round each other like a pair of dogs, fists balled – my mind refused to take it in. Then the doormen were elbowing their way through the crowd; one jumped for Gardiner just as the American launched a blow at Conan – Conan leapt aside as it slammed into his cheekbone – straight into the clutches of the other doorman.

'Now now, sir – what's all this about? We don't want any trouble, do we?'

Frank Gardiner was swearing, a monotonous monologue of blasphemy. Conan took several deep breaths, then twisted round to smile at his captor. 'Just a slight disagreement – this lady is my cousin' – he jerked his head back to where I sagged behind him, clutching a chair – 'the colonial gentleman's language was becoming a trifle – ' he raised his eyebrows in a rueful grin, 'so she asked me to escort her home. Perhaps you'd be so good as to call a cab.' The doorman had released Conan's right arm and Conan was already feeling for his notecase.

The man smiled. 'Hang on to yours, Fred,' he called to his fellow, then he set Conan free and began to brush down his tunic. 'No trouble, sir, no trouble at all.'

Conan swung round to me and held out his arm. 'Helena?' It was a command, and his blue eyes were hard as he looked at me. For a moment I was frightened; then I obediently put my hand on his sleeve.

A female voice shrilled out, 'Con – where are you going – you said you'd give me a good time!'

He did not even look back. 'Hard lines, Mona – you'd

271

better try your luck with the New World.' He thrust me out of the basement.

In the warm darkness of the cab I began to giggle, helplessly. Conan said, 'Hellie, you're tight as a newt.'

I could not stop giggling. 'You looked so funny – fighting in the middle of a dance floor.'

Conan grunted; I could tell he was still annoyed. 'I've got enough on my plate fighting the Germans – I prefer not to have to take on the blokes on our side – especially ones that size.' He raised his fingers to his face and gingerly touched his cheekbone, and I saw the dark shadow of a bruise.

'Oh, poor, poor Conan.' I put my hand up to his face, then found myself stroking his uninjured cheek – it felt warm and alive, and my fingers slid down to caress the rougher skin of his jaw – he had such a nice jaw, I wanted to kiss it so I moved closer and before I knew what I was doing, my arms were around his slim firm body and I was clinging to him, my head buried in his neck. And I felt the forgotten sweetness rise in the pit of my belly, and began to quiver against the throbbing beat of his heart.

He slid his arm round me and held me clamped to his chest, then leant forward, rapped on the glass and called, 'Change that, driver – Cavendish Mansions, Langham Street.' I raised my head in surprise and saw his mouth curve up in the dim light of a street lamp as the driver reversed, then he checked that the glass was closed and said, 'It's not just drink that's the matter with you, is it, Hellie? No wonder that Yank was putting up such a fight – I feel rather sorry for the bastard now. Anyway, I can't take you back to that nunnery in this state – it's lucky Russell lent me his rooms.' He laughed and lifted me so that I was lying across his lap with my head on his shoulders; I clung to him mindlessly for the rest of the short journey.

Conan had to half-carry me out of the cab, and he bundled me quickly into the lift before the porter could reach us. In the small box I sank to the floor in a heap and gazed up at him. He leant against the panelled side and hummed tunelessly; he did not once look down at me. He held the lift door open with one foot and hauled me up. 'Come on, my girl – you'll have to try and walk, my gammy leg's still playing me up.' I stumbled into his rooms and stood swaying in the bright light. Conan went over to a standard lamp and switched it on, then the centre light mercifully went out.

'Conan?'

'I'm here, Hellie, don't worry. Come on, let's have you on the sofa.' He steered me over and I collapsed into the cushions. He stood looking down at me for a long time, his face inscrutable, then he straightened up and turned away.

'Conan, please don't leave me!'

'I'm not leaving you, Hellie.' He spoke shortly. In a minute he came back in his shirtsleeves and breeches. 'Now, let's have some of this rigging off.'

I kept trying to cling to him as he undressed me, but he turned me briskly from side to side, dealing quickly with buttons and tapes until I was down to my camisole and drawers. Then, at last, he knelt down beside the sofa and put his arms round me and kissed me. At the feel of his lips on mine, my body caught fire, but then he drew back, until I writhed and pulled him hard against me – I knew I was moaning aloud but I did not care. His hand moved over the thin cotton of my camisole and came to rest on my belly, low down where the delicious sweetness was – he began to caress me there, and the pressure mounted until I was sobbing with the exquisite unbearable torment of it. Then, quickly, his lips came down on mine again and I felt the quick darting probe of his tongue in my mouth just as his hand pressed down, hard – and I exploded in an ecstasy of release. As I felt the slippery wetness between my legs I began to cry with relief.

He wrenched my clinging hands from his neck,

jumped up and strode away from me. I heard the door slam and I lay still, limp and lost. But he was soon back – he came and stood over me. 'I suppose I'd better put you to bed now, Hellie.' He pulled me up and just managed to carry me into his bedroom; he was panting as he rolled me between the sheets.

I lay there, looking up at him, and at last I whispered, timidly, 'Don't you – that is . . .' I turned and hid my face in his pillow.

He said roughly, 'There wouldn't be much point in my stopping that Yankee swine sending you to France with a bastard in your belly if I went and did it myself.' I began to cry and his voice softened a fraction. 'Don't worry, little cousin – I've seen to myself – since by now Mona is no doubt tucked up with your erstwhile suitor. I'd spent good money on that girl, too.' He sounded aggrieved, so I murmured, 'I'm sorry, Conan,' and fell suddenly asleep.

I woke with a raging thirst and a splitting head; it was already light. I could not think where I was at first, then I suddenly remembered and jumped out of bed. My head bounced painfully, and I staggered a little, then my stomach heaved and I stumbled out in search of the bathroom.

I was retching over the bowl of the WC when a voice behind me said, 'Well, well – so retribution has struck.' Conan stood in the doorway, a cigarette in his hand, watching me. I huddled back against the wall, trying to pull my camisole round me. He grinned sardonically. 'It's a bit late for modesty now, fair Coz – you'd better get back to bed – my bed – and sleep it off.'

I swallowed, then asked, 'What time is it?'

He took out his watch. 'Nearly a quarter to seven – why?'

I dragged myself up by the edge of the bath, and stood swaying. 'I'm on at half-past.'

'You're surely not going back in that state?'

'I must, Conan – there was a convoy due in last night.'

He leant across me and turned on the shower jets. 'Get under that then – I'll fetch your clothes.'

I pulled off my camisole and drawers and scrambled into the bath; I yelped as the jets hit me, the water was icy cold – but I knew he was right, so I stood shivering and let them wash over me. A hand came round the door and my clothes were unceremoniously dumped on the floor. I reached for the towel. As soon as I began to struggle into my clothes I realized that he had forgotten my corset – but I was too embarrassed to call out for it, and besides there was no time, so I knotted my stocking tops and hoped for the best. I ran through the doorway still jabbing in hairpins; Conan was waiting in the hall. He held out my hat and ran to open the door. 'There's a cab waiting downstairs.' I fell into the lift.

I told the driver to stop round the corner from the hostel, with a prayer of thankfulness that my room was in the basement. I swayed as I climbed over the railings – but others had done it and so could I. There was no time to look for a clean corset as I threw on my uniform – I tied elastic above my knee and flew out of the bedroom. The housekeeper was at her desk; I cried through the open door, 'I'm sorry – I overslept,' and ran to the waiting cab.

I felt sick and shaken all day – I could scarcely keep up with my routine. Johnnie Lambert caught hold of my hand but I snatched it away – 'Don't be so silly!' – then waves of shame engulfed me as I saw the look on his face. But somehow I got through the day, and pulled myself up the hill to the hostel by the railings.

A carelessly wrapped brown paper parcel had been left for me – I knew what was in it as soon as I saw Conan's scrawling handwriting. I picked up the note which fell out.

Helena, my pet,
This gets a trifle monotonous. Why don't you just throw
the damn things away? With your figure nobody'll notice.
Your loving cousin,
Conan.

He was right, nobody had noticed. I picked up my
abandoned corsets and rammed them into the waste-
paper basket. Then I looked back at Conan's note —
there was a P.S.:

If you can't hold your liquor like a gentleman,
my sweet, *keep off it.*

Then he had added a second PS:

The medical board passed me fit this morning, but I'm
sick of slogging it out on the ground, so I've applied to
transfer to the RFC.

I sat down on my narrow bed and began to cry — for
Eddie, for Lance, for all who had died and all who would
die. And painfully, rackingly, and in shame I wept for
Gerald — Gerald, my pure strong lover.

I bought a sateen band with suspenders hanging from
it to keep my stockings up — it was much cooler. Conan
came to see me, before he went off to learn to fly; he
was just the same as ever. We had tea together and
walked on the common, then he kissed my cheek, just
as my brothers always did, and waved to me as I went
back to the hospital. The next day I looked at the notice-
board as usual and saw my name was down for an over-
seas posting. Just two days after my twenty-third
birthday I left for France.

PART IV

SEPTEMBER 1916
to
MARCH 1919

CHAPTER ONE

Two sleek destroyers raced beside us, their sterns cutting the green water in a froth of curling foam. I stood at the rail in my unwieldy lifejacket, watching them. It was difficult to believe that we on the Channel steamer needed them, to protect us from the swift secret launch of a torpedo. I turned quickly away, and looked down instead at the deck – but there was no escape there. Excited youngsters, obviously going out for the first time, laughed and joked alongside groups of dull-eyed men huddled into their lifejackets in weary resignation as they returned from leave. I remembered the last time I had made this journey, happily anticipating the welcome awaiting me from my friends in Munich – my friends who had become my enemies, who would destroy me if they could.

I was part of the British Army now. Although I had moved away from the other VADs and come to stand by the rail I, like them, carried an army identity certificate in my pocket. It bore my unsmiling photograph, and recorded my name, age, army rank and the number of my detachment. It was only that number, repeated in brass on my shoulder straps, which singled any one of us out from her fellows. Otherwise we were all alike: all labelled by our white shirts and black ties, our ugly hats and dark-blue coats and skirts, and the wide Red Cross brassard encircling our arms as VAD nurses going on active service.

Twenty of us had left that morning in a group from Victoria. Alice had come with me to the station in a cab, ready to wave me off, just as she had waved goodbye to her husband the week before, at the end of his leave.

Dear Hugh: I had been off at five the day after he came home, and Alice had invited me to dinner. I had gone straight up to Eaton Terrace in my uniform – I would change later – and Hugh and Alice were in the drawing room. Hugh's face was tanned and his chest had seemed broader then ever, stretching the leather strap of his Sam Browne belt; but otherwise he was the same as always, my warm friendly brother-in-law. He held out his hand in greeting, but I ran to him and threw my arms round his neck, and he gave me a great bear hug in return. When he had kissed me, he set me back a little and looked me over, smiling. 'You're looking as lovely as ever, Helena – just as beautiful as your sister!' I knew my face was too pale and my hair was lank, but I smiled back gratefully. 'And what's this – your first stripe, eh? Well done.' He patted the white stripe on my sleeve.

'Why Hellie – so they've made you a lance-corporal at last!' Alice was laughing.

Hugh said seriously, 'No, Alice – nurses count as officers, you know.'

I had laughed at that. 'I'm afraid I'll never make an officer, Hugh. I'm hopeless at bullying the orderlies – I leave all that to Sister. No, this is just a service stripe – everyone gets it after a year as long as they keep going and behave themselves.'

As she lit her cigarette Alice winked at me. 'I'm so glad to hear you've been behaving yourself, Hellie.'

My face flamed. I looked desperately round for distraction – and caught sight of the two stars on my brother-in-law's cuff. 'Oh Hugh – you've got your second pip up – I am so pleased. Alice didn't tell me.'

My sister broke in. 'I'm only going to start boasting when he gets those pretty little red tabs on his collar – first lieutenant is nothing.'

Hugh's face reddened, and I flushed again, for him. But he said firmly, 'I wouldn't accept them if they were offered to me, Alice. I'd rather stay at the front with the men. Staff officers are good for nothing but saving their own skins and sending a fine bunch of fellows out on useless raids.'

I felt the blood drain from my face, and Hugh saw and looked stricken. He reached for my hand and patted it clumsily as I whispered, 'Like Eddie, like they did to Eddie.'

Hugh muttered gruffly, 'Poor old Eddie – God, I was cut up when I heard. It seemed worse somehow – I mean, if anything happened to me, I've had some good years – and there's been Alice and the boys – but these youngsters . . .'

Alice stubbed out her cigarette; her voice was angry. 'He was twenty, just twenty.'

My eyes blurred with tears. I stared out to sea and prayed that none of the other VADs in the draft would come and try to speak to me now. I glanced quickly sideways – none of them were near – but a young Flying Corps officer was looking straight at me. He caught my eye and began to edge forward, his mouth curving in a tentative smile. I swung round and fixed my eyes on the grey destroyers.

But seeing his uniform had made me think of Conan. Hugh had talked of my cousin, saying how much he had missed him after he had been wounded – they had been subalterns in the same company for several months. 'Come to that, the whole battalion must miss him – the Colonel made him billeting officer and we've never lived so well out of the line, before or since. That famous Finlay charm – the most obdurate Frenchwoman was putty in his hands – and it's the women who count in France now, with all their men at the front.'

Alice smiled and blew a smoke ring. 'But I seem to remember he spoke the most atrocious French!'

Hugh replied seriously, 'Oh, he knew enough to do the trick. I remember one occasion – we'd been warned by the battalion before us that this spinster schoolmistress ran the village and she hated the English, she'd made life bloody uncomfortable for these poor devils.

She had a chest like a washboard and the moustache of a Grenadier – yet Conan went straight up to her, clicked his spurs, bowed – and then kissed her hand.' Hugh shuddered. 'Then he announced: "Irlandais, nous sommes officiers Irlandais, les anciens alliés de France. Mais nous n'aimons pas les Anglais, Madame." His eyes flashed as he said that, then they went all mooning and he whispered, "Ah, les belles dames de France – elles sont ravissant, et si charmantes – madame, nous sont dans ta mains, nous prieons ta secours." I don't know about his grammar but his delivery was impeccable. She nearly swooned at his feet. We lived in the lap of luxury for the next two weeks. The schoolmistress insisted on giving up the best bedroom to us, then waited on us hand and foot. Conan was very decent – he never forgot I was his cousin-in-law – that time he persuaded her to borrow another bed, so I could share with him and Bron Nichols.'

I interrupted. 'I remember Bron Nichols, I used to dance with him before the war – he has that lovely curly blond hair, and such a sweet face. He used to go around with Conan a lot.'

'That's right – they'd been in the same house together at school. They were inseparable in France – but those baby-blue eyes were deceptive, Hellie, old Bron was as much of a young devil as Conan when they were together – the japes they got up to, the pair of them!'

I said, 'Conan will miss Bron Nichols – I'm surprised he's transferred.'

Hugh looked up. 'That's why he did transfer, Hellie.' I saw the expression on my brother-in-law's face, and shivered, although the room was quite warm. Hugh stared at the empty grate. 'We were due to be relieved that night, we'd had a quiet time, only a couple of casualties in our company, nothing to speak of – then there was the usual screeching roar and an almighty crump, and I heard the shout go out for stretcher bearers. A corporal came round the traverse, I asked,

"Someone hit?" "They got Mr Nichols, sir." I pushed along to see if I could do anything – a shell had caught the back of the trench, damned unlucky. They'd pulled old Bron out; he was lying on the duckboards, with his head pillowed on a sandbag, looking very surprised. Conan must have got there just before I did; he was squatting down beside him, chatting, his voice as cheerful as ever. "Well, Bron old boy," he said, "It looks as if you've put one over on me. This should just about get you to Blighty, I reckon – with a bit of luck." Then he lit a cigarette for Bron and put it between his lips, and while Bron smoked it he went on talking, about what Bron would do when he was on sick leave – he mentioned a tart they'd had in London before we came out – they'd both shared her, apparently. Conan said, "You lucky bastard, Bron – what a girl – and now you'll be able to have her all to yourself." He took the cigarette butt out of Bron's mouth and began to light another one, and I saw Bron smile at him, and he managed to speak – his voice was very low, but quite clear. "I'll always share with you, Con – you know that." And Conan smiled at him. Then Bron's face seemed to change, and he said "Only, Con, I don't know about tarts – I can't feel anything down there – would you have a look, old man?" So Conan leant forward, and his face never changed – God, not an eyelid flickered, then he smiled back at Bron, "Don't worry, old chap – it's all still there, one cock and two balls, just as the Good Lord provided. The damn shrapnel got you in the leg, a nice clean wound." '

Hugh stopped. I whispered, 'Did he – were his, were they injured?'

Hugh looked straight at me. 'Hellie, there was nothing there – nothing, except a few pieces of torn gut. The bloody shell had scooped the whole of his middle out, how the hell he survived as long as he did I don't know. I went back to stop the stretcher bearers – there was obviously no point. I had to steel myself to come round the bay again, I can tell you. But Conan was still there, still chatting and making jokes, though Bron wasn't answering any more, he just lay there looking up at him; then he whispered, "It's getting dark, Con," and Conan replied, "There's a storm brewing up, the sky's as black as ink – that's all we need for the relief tonight. Still, you'll be down the line long before that." And just as he said it Bron stopped breathing, just like that. He was still staring up at Conan, but there was nothing there any more. The sergeant came forward and said, "I'll fetch the stretcher now, sir," and Conan got up and walked away and was sick over the edge of the duck-boards. I went up to him; I didn't know what to say, but I had to try, and he just stared at me and said, "I wanted to hold his hand, Hugh – I did so want to hold his hand – but he'd have guessed then, wouldn't he? So I couldn't." I put my arm round his shoulders – he was absolutely rigid – then he asked, "Do you think Anderson'll let me go down with the burial party?" "I'm sure he will, old man – I'm sure he will." A couple of months later Conan got his Blighty one, thank God. And now he's transferred to the RFC – but he should do well in it; they say good horsemen make the best pilots, and Conan's a damn good horseman. I'd better go upstairs, Alice, and get changed for dinner.' He walked out without looking at us.

Alice spoke viciously: 'What a bloody war!' She lit another cigarette.

I had spent my embarkation leave with Pansy and her mother at The Pines. Then I came back to London for the last night as I had been told to report to Victoria at 7.30. Alice got up early the next morning to see me off. 'I've said fond farewells to so many men, now it's the turn of the girls. Good luck, Hellie.' Her perfumed cheek brushed mine. 'My dear, you look *hideous* in that ghastly hat.' She gave a mock shudder then turned and walked away over the station concourse. I saw several backs straighten as men returning dejected from leave stopped to watch her swaying hips and the poise of her beautiful head.

I had looked down at myself: my coat was hideous too, and my shoes were almost flat, but it would not matter where I was going. So I pulled the unaccustomed weight of my knapsack more securely on to my shoulders and beckoned to my porter to follow me on to the platform.

The destroyers began to wheel about; we were coming close to the coast of France. I heard excited squeals of mirth behind me and saw that two of my fellow VADs were either side of the young Flying Corps officer, talking and laughing up at him. I was shocked; how could they have allowed themselves to be approached like that – without an introduction? I looked at them disapprovingly – until I remembered my own voice protesting to Frank Gardiner: 'But we haven't been introduced!' – and such a short time after, I had permitted his intimacies in the taxi, and kissed him in the night club. Bitter shame swept over me. Gerald – oh Gerald, how could I have so forgotten you? And as I stared through a mist of tears at the harbour of Boulogne coming steadily nearer I vowed I would never dishonour his memory again.

CHAPTER TWO

Six of us were posted to Rouen, to a tented hospital on the edge of a great forest. I shared with a VAD called Innes: her father was Master of an Oxford College and she had graduated herself before enlisting, so I was rather nervous of her: but she was shy and softly spoken, and in the forced intimacy of the tiny bell tent we became friends.

The grey-haired matron, who wore a regular army cape and the ribbons of the South African War, welcomed us pleasantly the first morning – but her face was stern as she recited the strict list of rules we must obey. We were very subdued as Home Sister escorted us to the big marquees which were to be our wards.

But I was lucky; as I stepped through the canvas porch a tall handsome woman with striking black hair framing her face rustled forward. 'Pleased to meet you, Nurse.' As soon as she spoke she betrayed her origins, but she gave me a warm smile with a flash of very white teeth, and I smiled gratefully back.

Sister Jennings was from Birmingham; she had trained in a Poor Law infirmary there. She was very tall, taller even than my five foot nine, and her hair was blacker, her cheeks pinker, her figure fuller; so that at first I felt like a mere shadow in her surging wake. But she was kind. She seemed to like everyone, and everyone liked her. With the men she flirted relentlessly; I was shocked until I began to realize that flirting was like eating and breathing to her. She flashed her eyes at the CO; her hand would rest lightly on the orderly officer's arm as he did his round, and when he patted her full behind in the sisters' bunk one day she turned and laughed at him and wagged her forefinger in front of his nose – 'Now, now, behave yourself!' and then the rebuking finger descended and she stroked his lapel and straightened his tie as he smirked back at her.

We had the hardest-working orderlies in the hospital, because Sister flirted with them too, and the patients adored her. She laughed and chaffed, and as she took the medicines round she sang, 'Hold your hand out, naughty boy,' in a deep warm contralto. If we were not too busy in the evening she led the men in sing-songs, and I would join in too. One evening as we went off duty together she said, quite seriously, 'You know, you've got a really nice voice there, Girvan – plenty of body to it, despite your being so slender. And, dear, if you don't mind me suggesting it, why don't you borrow some of my rouge when you go down into town next time? You could be a real stunner if you dolled yourself up a bit. Why, with your voice you could even go on the stage!'

I did not know how to reply, so at last I said, 'So could you, Sister, I'm sure.'

She said seriously, 'No, dearie, – I'm a nurse. Never wanted to do anything else and never will, it's my job, you see.' And I did see. She was deft and kind and clever, and like a true professional she made the most difficult tasks look easy. The only duty she was unhappy with was writing to patient's relatives. 'I've never been very sharp with a pen, it doesn't come natural to me. When I write the words they seem too stiff and formal, and I know they're not right but I can't think of any others. So I'd be grateful if you'd do it when you've got the time dearie – ever so grateful.'

From the tales the other VADs told, it was obvious that Sister Jennings did not take Matron's rules too seriously. They said she often slipped back into our compound late at night, skirting the edge of the forest and ducking under the barbed-wire fence behind the latrine hut. She had never actually been caught yet, and the general opinion was that Matron suspected, but chose to turn a blind eye because Sister Jennings was such a good nurse.

I wrote to relatives, as Sister had asked me to, and I wrote long letters to Robbie. He became quite interested in my fellow VADs and nurses, and would even ask after them by name. But in every letter he referred to Eddie; the loss of his twin ran through his words, like the counterpoint to a tune. As I read them my heart ached for him, and for myself – I still could not believe that Eddie would never laugh with me and tease me again. But I noticed that Robbie often mentioned an officer called Ralph Dutton; they seemed to spend a lot of time together when they were out of the line and he wrote, 'Ralph's a very decent sort,' so that I was glad he had found a new friend. In another letter Robbie told me that Sergeant Holden had been awarded the Military Medal for his work in bringing in the wounded under fire after the failure of the attack on Thiepval early in September. I remembered Eddie's loved voice as he had said, 'Then he picked me up and carried me in, just like a baby.' Sergeant Holden had earned the gratitude of other men's sisters now. At the end of that letter Robbie wrote, almost casually, that he had been given his company. It was with pride that I addressed my reply to 'Captain Girvan'.

A brief scrawl from Conan told me that he was back in France, his all-too-short training period over. As I answered it I remembered Hugh's tale, and thought that at least my cousin would never again have to squat in a muddy trench while his chum died at his feet. It was Nanny's cramped, seldom-used handwriting that informed me of the birth of Guy's second son. She had written: 'Lady Muirkirk is well, but very tired.' I suspected that even Nanny thought the births had come too close together. When I next wrote to Guy I congratulated him, but Guy's letters were very short now – he never mentioned Pansy at all, only the weather in the front line, and how sick he was of the incessant hammering of the guns.

Gradually I learnt to gauge the strength of the wind by listening to the rush and slap of the heavy walls of the big marquee, and got used to calling sugar boxes medicine cupboards, and the bell tent at the end of the ward, the sluice room. I soon realized that emptying bottles and bed pans was much more complicated in a tented hospital, but luckily Sister Jennings' way with the orderlies ensured that I hardly ever had to do this job, and the only time I visited the incinerator was when I slunk there after dark to push in my own sodden pads. I was ill the second week in Rouen, but Sister filled me a hot-water bottle herself and placed a footstool beneath my feet and left me to doze behind the screens that made up Sister's bunk. Afterwards, when I tried to apologize for my incapacity, she said, 'Oh, dearie, don't think of it – I know what it can be like – I have the occasional bad do myself. But generally I'm so glad to see it that I don't mind. I always try to be careful, but you never quite know, do you dear?' She went off with the medicine tray, humming, as I gaped at her. But it was impossible to be shocked: she was so open and cheerful.

Once Innes and I had mastered the mysteries of the guy ropes and tent pegs, living under canvas was fun – rather like a continuous picnic – but the one thing I did not like about camp life was the rats. I was terrified of them – with a terror out of all proportion to their size and activities. Innes spent hours trying to explain that as long as I did not interfere with them they would not interfere with me – she seemed to be quite fascinated by their mentality – but as soon as I heard the telltale scuffle under the floorboards of the marquee I would go rigid with fear. And at night I would huddle with my head under the bedclothes while Innes shooed the intruder away.

One day the Colonel decided the rats were getting too obstreperous, and declared a rat hunt in our marquee and the one next to it. The patients were wild with excitement that morning; and Sister obligingly told the orderlies to roll up the canvas sides so that everyone could have a grandstand view. A fatigue party arrived armed with spades and tent-peg mallets, and accompanied by a very small white terrier bitch from the infantry camp across the road. Her owner was a brawny red-faced sergeant-major who was boasting of her talents to anyone who would listen. Most of the MOs appeared, their canes held hopefully in their hands, and I even spotted the red flutter of Matron's cape next to the Colonel.

I longed to go and hide, but I was on duty, so I edged very close to Sister for protection. She flashed her white teeth at me in a broad smile – and I saw she had a broom handle concealed in her skirts. Two orderlies tugged up the linoleum at one end of the marquee, and prised up the floorboards, while a couple of others began to bang on the wooden floor and shout – and suddenly pandemonium reigned. The white terrier streaked forward – her sergeant-major owner bellowing encouragement – the patients shouted, the orderlies banged, the MOs pressed forward, and I threw myself back against the wall of the next marquee, shaking. I watched mesmerized as the terrier sprang on to rat after rat, snapping her teeth into its neck before tossing it contemptuously aside. But one was too fast for her – it escaped while its predecessor was still in her mouth – the orderlies' mallets and spades thwacked the ground but the sharp-nosed animal zigzagged frantically through the obstacles and headed straight towards me. I screamed in terror and Sister shot forward, broom handle raised. The rat turned, Sister gave chase – one hand holding her skirts above her shapely calves, the other wielding the broom handle like a hockey stick. There were excited yells and shouts, 'After it, Sister, after it,' and incredibly, Sister was gaining on the frantic grey form. There was a slicing blow, two quick thuds – the rat rolled over and the terrier pounced. Cries of congratulation rent the air: 'What a goal!' 'Holed in one!' 'Well held, Sister' and, louder than the rest, the sergeant-major's betraying bellow: 'Well done, Connie, old girl.'

As I walked back into our marquee on trembling legs beside the heroine of the hour, she said, quite seriously, 'You know, you could ask Tom to lend you that bitch of his at nights – he's a really nice chap and a tremendous sport. Just flutter those long lashes of yours and flirt with him a little and you'll have him eating out of your hand.'

In my relief at the end of the rat hunt I could hardly suppress the giggles welling up inside me as I imagined the Lady Helena Girvan flirting with a brawny sergeant-major!

The main road to Rouen ran between us and the infantry camp opposite. When Innes and I were both off duty we would slip out to the little booth at the camp gate, where a plump Frenchwoman sold chocolate and eggs and any fruit which was still in season. When we had made our purchases we would perch on the railings and linger a while to watch the traffic go past. The long strings of mules always made us laugh – one of the six was generally trying to break free and when it succeeded it would kick up its heels and set off down the road with its harness trailing, leaving its fellows dancing and shying. In the evening a long line of soldiers would pass us, marching back from the Bull Ring at Rouen, grimy and sweaty and tired but still singing. Their deep voices filled the air as they sang: 'It's a Long Way to Tipperary', 'Mademoiselle from Armentières', and all the other well-worn favourites. But best of all I liked to watch the Indian cavalry ride by on their gleaming horses, the afternoon sun shining on the points of their lances and turning to gold the khaki of their tunics and turbans, so that they seemed like the bronzed warriors of long ago.

One afternoon Innes and I were off at the same time, so we both crammed into the tiny tram car which ran past the camp. We creaked and groaned down to the city, swung across the bridge over the Seine and plunged suddenly into the Middle Ages. It was good to stroll through the narrow cobbled streets, peer into the diamond-paned windows of the cramped little shops, and breathe the sweet scents of the wares in the flower market in the centre. We ate a fresh cooked omelette and salad in a little café and then began the tramp back to the hospital.

But camp life was too crowded for me; I needed to spend time on my own. So whenever I could I would duck under the barbed-wire fence behind the sanitary hut and walk silently on the soft mossy carpet through the tall straight trees, with their bark that was almost pink and their dark-green heads. At first I would hear voices, and see the flash of a white nurse's cap at an impromptu picnic, but soon the camp was left behind me, and only the high firs stretched ahead. Then I would find my chosen clearing, and practise my singing.

I went into the forest one day in October. The bracken was turning, to brown, to red, to yellow, to gold. Tiny white parachutes spun and danced in shafts of sunlight and then drifted slowly down to rest on the purple heather. I stopped in my clearing and began to sing: first my scales, then my aria, and finally my sad, longing Lieder. As I turned to leave I saw a little group: a couple of French peasant women with young children close to their skirts, and a small hand cart piled high with sticks and bracken. They smiled at me and called, 'Merci, mademoiselle – merci beaucoup,' and I realized they had been standing there silently, listening to me. I smiled back and slipped away between the tree trunks – and hoped that they would never know that I had been singing in German. Behind me I heard the high-pitched voices of the children as they continued their search for sticks: firewood and kindling to store against the cold of winter.

That night I woke in the dark; I was shivering and cold. I heard Innes slide out of bed, so I got up too, and we both fumbled for our coats to add to our bedding. I dozed off again, but next morning we saw the thick frost on the ground – winter had come too early that year.

CHAPTER THREE

Cold October gave way to a colder November. At the beginning of the third week we heard that our men had finally captured Beaumont-Hamel – which they had hoped to gain long ago on 1 July. Beaucourt had been taken too, together with thousands of German prisoners; after this success the numbers of casualties began to dwindle. The army had exhausted itself in the huge Somme offensives, and now it crouched in its trenches like a great spent animal, licking its wounds.

Life under canvas was not so pleasant these days; the winter saw to that. I would wake up very cold at nights, when my blankets came adrift, so Innes and I sent to Harrods for sleeping bags, and they helped a lot. But it was still getting colder and colder. We kept the oil stove burning in our tent all evening and huddled in our sleeping bags either side of it, so for a while at least we were warm. But it became more and more of an effort to haul ourselves out of bed in the morning and struggle to unlace the frost-hardened ropes with numbed fingers, so that we could scuttle through the icy air to the sanitary hut.

We began to admit men suffering from frostbite and trench feet. Privates from a Highland battalion arrived who told us they had been holding a sector which was knee deep in mud. They said their feet and then their legs had gone quite numb as they stood on sentry duty – it had almost been a relief – but when they got back to the support trenches and took off their water-logged boots and puttees their feet had turned dark blue, and were swollen and agonizingly painful. When we unwrapped their dressings we often found toes blackened by gangrene; then Sister called the MO, the men were taken off to the theatre, and when they came back they had only two or three toes left. One burly Scot stared in dismay at his mutilated foot, then shrugged his shoulders and smiled: 'I canna play "This wee piggy went to market" now, Sister, that's for sure.'

Some cases were less serious; their feet were still numb and white. We rubbed them gently with warm olive oil and wrapped them in soft cotton wool until the feeling came back – and with it, the pain. The men said their soles were on fire, and they shrank from our touch – but we had to touch them.

We took in a lot of chest cases; the wet open trenches were taking their toll in this way too. It seemed so ludicrous to try to nurse them in this draughty marquee, but we had no alternative; I was glad now of all the time I had spent at the East London learning to make my linseed poultices smooth-textured and nicely sticky. Some of the men were wheezing from bronchitis, others became delirious with pneumonia, and young boys came in doubled up with rheumatism so that they shuffled up and down the ward like old men. We evacuated all those who were well enough to travel, but others soon came flooding in to take their places. It was a bad winter.

We did manage to celebrate some kind of Christmas for the men in the wards. Sister and I and the night VAD pooled our resources and brought small gifts back from Rouen. I had written to Pansy and she and her mother sent a great hamper of food from Harrods. The men were thrilled at this gift from 'Lady Muirkirk' – I did not tell them that she was my sister-in-law, and they never guessed because of our different names; one of the men in at that time was a Lowlander from Muirkirk itself, and by virtue of association he was awarded the credit for this patronage and preened himself all morning. On Christmas Day the kitchens provided chicken and ham, with plum pudding to follow, and our men spooned it down with lashings of brandy butter from Pansy's hamper. In the bell tent that was the ward kitchen, the night VAD and I mixed jellies and made trifles with our chilblained hands.

The medical staff organized a concert for those of the men who were well enough to get about. They all crammed into the orderlies' mess, which soon became warm and smoky, and listened to comic recitations and attempts to impersonate Harry Lauder. Sister and I had been asked to perform. Sister chose Marie Lloyd's old favourites – the men nearly fell off their chairs with laughter at her suggestive smiles and saucy gestures as she sang: 'There was I, waiting at the Church,' and they all joined in with a rousing chorus of, 'But my wife, won't let me!' As they finished the last echo a cockney voice from the back shouted, 'Cor, Sister – I wish mine would!' There were roars of agreement and the Colonel hastily leapt on to the stage at Matron's frowning nod and began to thank Sister Jennings warmly. I had to follow – I was rather nervous – how could I possibly compete with Sister's flamboyant delivery? But of course, that was not what they expected or wanted from me. I sang for them the sentimental favourites in a girl's clear high soprano – of the last rose of summer, blooming alone, and of home, sweet home. There was a reverent hush as I began:

> 'Mid pleasures and palaces though we may roam,
> Be it ever so humble there's no place like home!'

And then, in a message of thanks and hope to these men wounded in our Empire's service, I sang of how their loved ones back in England were keeping the home fires burning as they waited for their return. And the low male voices joined me softly in the final chorus.

But soon there were very few fires burning in No.15 General; the miners went on strike and there was no coal; coke supplies dwindled, but coke was a poor substitute at the best of times since it was almost impossible to light and never blazed up.

In the New Year the cold intensified. Snow and rain had been falling alternately, then they suddenly stopped; an icy wind blew and the long frost set in. For six weeks we stared at the thermometer in disbelief as it fell to twenty and even thirty degrees below. We seemed to be always shivering, and it was agony to force our chil-blained hands into the bowls of disinfectant we had to use. As I scrubbed the lockers each day, the soap suds froze in the basin where they stood: the lotions froze in their bottles, the milk froze in its churn; the eggs froze in their shells; and all the water pipes in camp froze until there was only one tap for the whole of the hospital.

We learnt to sleep with our vests on, otherwise in the morning they were too stiff to pull over our heads. We piled on jersey after jersey over our blue cotton dresses and took our gloves off only when we had to work with water – we even ate with our gloves on, else the metal cutlery burnt our fingers. I wrote to Mrs Hill at Hatton and asked her to send me the pairs of ankle-length drawers I had used for hunting. As soon as they arrived I pulled them on and sighed with relief as the black cashmere clung warmly to my legs. But the biggest battle was the one to keep our patients warm in canvas marquees that were coated with ice. And as I boiled up kettles and endlessly refilled hot-water bottles I thanked God daily for whoever had invented the Primus stove.

My heart ached for Robbie, for Guy, for Hugh – shivering in the exposed trenches on the front line, or in makeshift billets further back. Robbie's letters became shorter and shorter, pencilled scribbles from numbed fingers. Conan's brief scrawls still came from time to time, but there was a dullness in them now – as if he doubted the effort of writing being worthwhile. I always answered them quickly – it was all I could do.

The French said it was the coldest winter for fifty years, and I believed them, as I stood on the bridge at Rouen and watched the huge packs of ice float slowly down the Seine towards the sea. Yet the forest was more beautiful than ever: a white still world in which I walked through the soft dry snow – and listened to the distant rumble of the guns.

At the end of January, Papa wrote to say that Guy had been slightly wounded. He assured me so strongly that there was no need to worry about my brother, that at once I did. I wrote to Alice and asked her for more news. She said that Guy's wound was not serious, but he had been blown up and buried for some hours. 'I suppose he's shell-shocked. I don't think he can take any more, Hellie. Papa is pulling every string he can at the War Office.' Then she had added, 'Frankly, Guy's in a pretty ugly mood these days – only a woman like Pansy would put up with him.' I thought of Guy, my loving, loyal elder brother – always so steady and even-tempered, 'in a pretty ugly mood these days', and I prayed that Papa's strings would be long enough.

Somehow we endured February but by the time March came I had forgotten how it felt to be warm. April arrived and winter still showed no wish to release its iron grip, but the news broke that America had declared war on Germany, so now we had a powerful new ally. At the same time rumours of revolution and the forced abdication of the Czar filtered through from our old ally, Russia. But soon events nearer at hand filled all our thoughts as we were told that any man who could stand the journey was to be evacuated, and we must clean our wards and wait. So we knew that a new push was in the offing – a spring offensive, except that there was no spring. As we sat polishing probes and forceps in the quiet ward the insistent throb of the guns seemed to swell and fill my ears. I prayed silently for Robbie, for Hugh, for Conan.

Then a blizzard struck northern France: gales howled through the lines of tents and snow stung our faces as we dashed from bell tent to mess to ward – and at the same time convoys of wounded began to arrive. It was Easter 1917, and our men had gone over the top at Arras – into the teeth of that blizzard. We worked for hours on end in the dark, shadowy wards, then went to the mess and asked if there was any news – there were stories of an advance, but nobody dared to believe them. We did hear at last that the Canadians had captured Vimy Ridge, but their casualties had been heavy. Down in Champagne the French attack had failed, and their losses had been enormous. In her latest letter, Alice wrote that in London it was being rumoured that the earliest date at which the Americans could put a trained army in the field was 1919! I stared at that date in dismay – it was two whole years away – how could we wait another two years? I folded the letter and put it away and went quickly back to my ward. As far as I knew Robbie was safe; I would cling to that.

It was the middle of April before the bleak cold ended in a last flurry of snow. The first casualties from the battle of Arras began to be evacuated, we became a medical ward once more, and off-duty time was reinstated. As I prepared a poultice for a dark-haired Glaswegian one morning I realized that I would be able to spend my half-day off in the sunlit forest. I smiled at the man – 'Here we are, Jock – a nice warm poultice' – and slapped it on his chest. He muttered incoherently and his eyes rolled; he was delirious in the grip of pneumonia – spring meant nothing to him now. But it did to me, and I said goodbye to Sister and went off to lunch with a lift in my step.

I slipped under the barbed-wire fence and walked in between the tall firs. It was very still, with only the raucous caws of the rooks sounding above me. As I came into my clearing a pale cold shaft of sunlight gilded the withered grass and the tussocks of heather; the straight rows of trees stretched away until they merged into blue shadows in the distance. Even the far-off vibration of the guns seemed to fade away, and for a little while I was at peace.

Softly I began to sing my scales, until my voice was full and flexible in the crisp still air. I chose the pastoral Lieder today: those poems that spoke of bright sunshine stealing through sleeping woods. But then my voice rose up as I sang of my longing for peace.

> 'Ruhe, ruhe, meine Seele:
> Deine stürme gingen wild'

Rest, my soul, after the raging storms.

> 'Ruhe, ruhe, meine Seele
> Und vergiß, was dich bedroht!'

Oh let me forget, forget what threatens.

I stared into the blue-shadowed forest, and for a moment I was at peace. Then I heard the rustle of footsteps behind me, and slowly turned – and saw Conan. He stood watching me from the edge of the clearing. Then he called: 'An orderly told me which way you'd gone, but I thought I'd never find you – then I heard your voice, and it led me to you.'

As he began to move forward he trod on a dead twig – it broke with a sharp retort like the crack of pistol shot and his head jerked up like a puppet's on a wire. He stood there, in the clearing, shaking. I ran to him and seized his hands – even through his leather gloves I could feel how cold they were.

'Conan – what are you doing here?'

'I'm on my way to Paris, Hellie – they gave me local leave.' He tried to smile, but only one side of his mouth moved. 'I'm something of an embarrassment to them – the only one of my draft left – the replacements aren't due for a couple of days. I'm the only one left,' he repeated. He looked away into the forest. 'Giles, and Hemingway, Baker, Thomas – all gone. Even jolly little Dawson – I saw him go, he jumped out – but he was already on fire – he went down blazing like a torch. He was so near we could hear him screaming – so when it was his turn Thomas stayed in his machine – it spun round like a top. They took their spades and dug him out later – to get his identity disc, you see.'

He turned and stared at me; his face was grey and the vivid blue of his eyes was blank and hard. Then he said simply, 'I need you, Hellie.' I bowed my head in acquiescence and we walked hand in hand out of the clearing and down through the aisle of trees.

He pulled up as we came near the camp. 'Hellie – I don't want to get you into trouble with your matron, I know what they're like. I'll go on ahead, it'll give me time to find somewhere – I'll see you in the cathedral.' I nodded, and stood watching the tremor in his shoulders as he strode off.

I suppose he got a lift down into Rouen, because there was no sign of him at the tram-car stop. I went straight to the cathedral and pushed open the heavy wooden door. My eyes searched the dim incense-laden interior, where the small sanctuary lights glowed red above their altars. I saw my cousin sitting slumped in a chair; he was staring at a crucifix. He stood up slowly, his eyes still on it, and said bitterly, 'But His didn't last three years,' then he took my arm and steered me out.

The patron of the small hotel looked at me knowingly as he handed over the key. The room was stuffy, but the stove in the corner was alight, so at least it was warm. Conan threw his cap on the floor and slumped down on the bed – he was shaking uncontrollably. I knelt down and unlaced his boots and pulled them off, then I stood up and unbuttoned his greatcoat and eased him out of it. He held up his arms like a small child so I could unbuckle his belt and holster; I put his revolver carefully down on the worn rug. Quickly I slipped off my own coat and hat, kicked off my shoes, swung myself up on to the high bedstead – and held my arms out to him. With a convulsive shudder he threw himself into them. I hugged him to me, then his heavy body slipped down until his face was buried in my lap and he began to cry – great heaving, gulping sobs. I held him tightly and stroked his soft black hair. At last, at long last, the shuddering of his body lessened, his breathing slowed, and he fell asleep. I sat on through the long afternoon, until the sun went in and the room darkened.

The man on my lap stirred, heaved himself up and yawned. He looked at me with Conan's blue eyes and familiar smile and said, almost jauntily, 'What a rotten day off for you, Hellie – a regular busman's holiday!'

As I replied I tried to match his light tone. 'Oh, we

don't nurse our patients on our laps, you know – Matron wouldn't like it.'

'Then she's a fool – a woman's lap is the finest medicine in the world.' He looked at me and smiled a little ruefully. 'I should certainly know that. But today I wanted it to be a woman who cared for me, not one I'd paid for. Thanks, Hellie.'

He jumped up and bent down for his holster and began to buckle his belt round him. I asked, 'What will you do now, Conan?'

He looked up from tugging on his boots and his grin flashed at me. 'I'll catch the first train to Paris and when I get there I'll buy the prettiest whore, the finest dinner and the largest bottle of champagne I can find – in that order! Eat, drink and be merry!' He shrugged himself into his greatcoat and came back to me, his face quite still for a moment. 'For tomorrow *will* come, I know that now. Goodbye, Hellie.' He bent and kissed me gently on the lips, then turned and pulled open the door. I heard him whistling as he ran down the stairs.

I pushed myself slowly off the bed and peered into the spotted mirror, tugging my hair into place. Then I put on my hat and coat, retrieved my shoes and went slowly downstairs. The proprietor gave me a sly grin as I passed. 'Au revoir, mademoiselle – madame!' I ignored him, and stepped out into the busy street.

Next day at lunch there was a rumour flying around that a VAD had been seen slipping into a hotel in Rouen, with an officer. 'And going upstairs!' Oliver exclaimed, her eyes round with horror. She said Matron was questioning each of us in turn. I swallowed another spoonful of soup.

The young dark-haired Scot got steadily worse that afternoon. I boiled water and sprinkled in linseed meal with one hand while I stirred briskly with the other. I spread the mixture out on its tow mat and applied it firmly to his chest, but it was too late, poultices were no use now – he had spent too long in waterlogged trenches.

He was delirious, but for a brief moment before the end I saw sanity in his eyes. He screamed like an animal, 'I dinna wanchter dee! I dinna wanchter dee!' as he fought like a madman against my restraining arms. Sister came running and between us we managed to hold him in his bed until his unnatural strength ebbed as quickly as it had come. His eyes rolled and he began to mutter incoherently again. He died at teatime and Sister helped me to lay him out.

After tea Matron sent for me. I stood in front of her, my hands neatly clasped behind my back as I had been taught so long ago at the East London.

'Nurse Girvan, I must ask you on your honour – did you enter a hotel room in Rouen yesterday, in the company of an officer?' Her pale eyes were tired and anxious as they held mine.

I looked straight back at her. 'No Matron, I did not.'

She dismissed me and I went back to our bell tent and took out my writing case. I found the scrap of paper on which I had noted down the young Jock's home address and wrote it on an envelope. Then I began my letter:

Dear Mr and Mrs McPherson,
I am so sorry to have to tell you that your son William died this afternoon. I expect you will have had the usual telegram from the War Office, but I wanted you to know that he died quite peacefully. His last words were of you, and then he simply fell asleep.

I stopped and rubbed my aching eyes before I re-read what I had written. Then I picked up my pen again and signed it. Truth had no place in this war.

A picture postcard of Paris came from Conan. He had scrawled across the back: 'Mission accomplished – but I'd rather she'd been you, Sweet Coz!' I smiled a little as I put it away in my writing case. Two weeks later a letter came from Papa:

Dear Helena,

> I am very sorry to have to tell you that Conan is posted missing . . .

Robbie's letter gave more details. Conan had flown out over the enemy line, a fellow flying officer had seen his aircraft hit – it had lost height, wavered and begun to drop – then the other pilot had had to bank to evade the AA fire, and when he had wheeled round to look for Conan again the sky was empty.

I took out the last postcard, and read again the scribbled message. Then I said aloud: 'Yes, I would rather it had been me, dearest of cousins.' I pushed the card back into my case and walked stiff-legged over to the ward.

Chapter Four

For days I worked like an automaton; my hands seemed to move as though they had no link with my brain. On duty I dared not think, or I could not have continued. At night I tried to weep silently, so that I would not disturb Innes: Innes who tried to comfort me, but who could not understand, with her strict middle-class code, that part of my grief was regret, regret for what I had not done. I had never loved Conan as I had loved Gerald, but we had been young and happy together, and he had come to me in his anguish and taken only a sister's comfort – he had not asked for more. But now I wished I had offered myself to him, that on that last afternoon I had gone down the stairs of the hotel beside him, and caught the train to Paris – and accepted the consequences of dismissal and disgrace. But then, another VAD went sick, a second refused to renew her contract, and a staff nurse went home to marry her fiancé who had been blinded at Arras, so we were short-staffed again. My body was strong, my hands were skilful now. I was needed here in France. Conan was dead – but my patients were still fighting to live.

One afternoon Sister came to fetch me from the end of the ward; she was smiling. 'There's a visitor for you outside, dear, a lady.'

I could not imagine who it was as I hurried between the beds, but as soon as I came through the flaps of the porch I saw her: there, in a long fur coat incongruously worn over riding breeches, was Lady Maud. She strode forward and wrung my hand. 'Good to see you, young Helena. I've just brought my unit to Rouen – we've set up our canteen at the railway station and the customers are pouring in.' She showed her large strong teeth in a broad grin. 'Your papa suggested I came and looked you up, so here I am. You must come down for a cup of tea and a good old gossip – Juno's with me. Go and fetch your hat.'

'But I'm still on duty!'

'It's all fixed, Helena, I've seen your matron – bearded the old trout in her den, fearsome creature, they should never put women in positions of authority. Hey, you there,' she bellowed at a luckless orderly, 'run and tell my staff car to drive round – it's at the main gate.' The orderly lumbered resentfully off. I asked how on earth she had managed to comandeer a staff car. 'No trouble, Bobby Mason's a friend of mine – glad to do me a favour – for old times' sake.' She dug a sharp elbow into my ribs. 'Not a word to your papa, eh, Helena – we girls must stick together. Got to do your bit for the war effort – as I say to Juno, keep the troops happy and they'll soon have those Boches on the run.' She laughed again, and I had to smile back – there was something so attractive about her boisterous vitality – and her novel idea for winning the war. I ducked back into the ward to ask Sister's permission for my outing.

'You go off and enjoy yourself, dearie, a little bit of a chat with your friends'll do you the world of good.'

And I did feel better, having tea with them in the corner of their hut, talking of people and affairs far away from the hospital, and it was good to see Juno again. Before she sent me back in the borrowed staff car Lady Maud announced that she was getting up a concert. 'Just a simple little do, give some of the men a treat.' She looked at me meaningfully, and weakly I offered to sing in it.

Lady Maud's 'little do' filled one of the largest halls in Rouen; Bobby Mason had obviously come up to scratch. He shook me warmly by the hand: he was a small wiry man with a bald head, and as we talked his gaze kept straying longingly to Lady Maud – she looked very handsome tonight.

I sang: 'The Girl I Left Behind Me', 'When Irish Eyes are Smiling' and the inevitable 'Home, Sweet Home'. When I had finished, the audience roared and clapped deafeningly – but then so they did after Lady Maud's off-key rendering of 'Land of Hope and Glory'.

I was whisked back to the hospital in the borrowed staff car again. As the long lines of marquees appeared in the moonlight I was relieved to be back; it was easier to keep working. Innes was waiting for me in the mess, her face anxious. 'Girvan – there's a cable for you, from England.'

My hands were shaking so much I could not get the envelope open, so she took it from me and tore up the flap and handed back the buff form. I stared at it until at last the dancing letters formed words in front of my frightened eyes: 'Conan slightly wounded. Recovering in captivity in Germany. Victoria Pickering'.

My eyes blurred and I felt Innes' hand on my arm. I could not speak so I handed the telegram to her to read. 'Oh Girvan, I'm so glad, so very very glad.'

I whispered, 'So am I,' and stumbled off to the bell tent.

Alice wrote later that Mother had broken down and wept when the message came through from the Red

Cross: 'She always did prefer Conan to her own children! I am so glad, though, at least someone's safely out of it. Hugh will be pleased.'

Soon after I had another visitor – Robbie. We hugged each other tightly, then he gestured over his shoulder. 'I've got old Ralph with me.' I felt my face fall as the pleasant-looking subaltern came forward and his shy smile wavered. I quickly pulled myself together.

'Mr Dutton – Robbie's written so much about you – I am so pleased to see you.' He looked a little happier and shook my hand vigorously.

Robbie said, 'They've just pulled us out – we've had so many losses from sickness we've got to wait for a new draft – so Ralph and I are on a couple of days' local leave; we're on our way to Paris. Go and tackle your old battle-axe and see if she'll let you off a couple of hours early and we'll take you down to Rouen for a decent meal.'

I shook my head. 'I'm not asking Matron – I'll only get a long lecture on dining in the company of an officer who's not a close relative! No, I'll see Sister, she's a good sort.'

'Then I'll come and ask her myself – besides I'd like to meet her, after your stories!' He strode purposefully into the ward. Sister Jennings flashed her smile at my handsome brother and shooed me out with orders to enjoy myself. I trod on air as I went to fetch my hat and coat.

We ate in a hotel in Rouen and the food was delicious: lobster thermidor, followed by an enormous omelette aux champignons served with a salad aux fines herbes, and crêpes with lemon and sugar to round it all off. I savoured the freshly made coffee as Robbie and Ralph Dutton lingered over their brandies. Then Robbie pushed his cup away and lit a cigarette. 'By the way, Hellie – a curious coincidence, Sergeant Holden – you remember?' I nodded, my eyes prickling. Yes, I remembered Sergeant Holden. 'Well, he's been made up to

Company Sergeant-Major, and he's coming to my company – so we'll be working together.'

I said hesitantly, 'It'll – remind you . . .' then I stopped.

Robbie's face was very still, then he said, softly, 'He can't remind me of what I never forget.'

There was silence. Ralph Dutton coughed. 'Holden's a very steady man.'

Robbie said quietly, 'Yes, I'm lucky to get him.' Then we began to talk of other things.

A couple of days later Matron called me in and told me I was being transferred to nights. I was sorry to have to say goodbye to Sister Jennings – she had been the best of sisters to work under, so efficient, and yet so warm and cheerful. As I thanked her for all she had taught me, she said she was going to nag Matron about a posting to a Casualty Clearing Station. 'I like to be kept busy, dearie, and to be in the thick of things.' I wished her luck and went off duty at lunchtime to try to snatch a few hours' sleep.

The two marquees under my care were right at the end of the lines, and when I came back from the mess tent after our midnight meal I lingered outside for a moment, listening to the night. The firs swayed and whispered, then slowly fell still again; a bird cried out among the trees and further away a hound bayed in the forest. As my ears sharpened they caught more distant sounds: the whistle of a train running into Rouen; the wail of a siren from a ship going down the river; and, underlying all these, like the bass of a mighty organ, the unceasing vibration of the guns playing their oratorio of death. I shivered in the cool air and ducked under the flap of the porch.

The forest was beautiful now, and if the weather was fine when I woke up I would pack a basket with bread and cheese and fruit, on top of the small meths lamp and kettle I had bought in Rouen, tuck in a packet of tea and a tin of milk and scramble under the barbed wire with it and out of the camp. I would picnic in my clearing, then doze a little until it was time to trail back for supper.

It was a full year since Eddie had died. On the anniversary of his death I took my writing case into the forest and wrote a long letter to Robbie. Although we were separated I knew we would both be looking at despair today. Our brother. Please God keep Robbie safe.

Although I was coping I seemed to have little energy. One night one of the amputation cases – he came from Moffat so we had named him Mack – called out to me in the ward. I was tired and it took me a moment to realize where he was; then I ran to him and threw back the covers and saw the fresh red blood staining the bandaged stump where his leg had been. I fumbled as I began to unfasten his bindings – it must only have been for a moment but it seemed an age as the man's life blood drained away beneath my hands – then I tugged the tourniquet from my belt and was tightening and tightening it until at last the bleeding stopped. A man further up the ward slid out of bed – 'I'll go for the orderly, Sister' – I saw him limp quickly away as I stood, panting, my hands slippery with blood. Mack opened his mouth, but it was several moments before I heard what he was saying. 'I'm sorry to have frightened you, Sister – I could see you weren't feeling so grand this night.' I stared down into the concerned brown eyes and felt the tears slide down my cheeks. He reached out and touched the edge of my apron. 'It's no job for a young lassie, this.'

I could not reply and I was still silently weeping when the orderly came back with Captain Bevan, whose pyjama sleeves were showing under the cuffs of his tunic. I could not stem the flow of tears even as I prepared Mack for another visit to the theatre. But when Sister came bustling in, just as he left, she frowned and beckoned me down behind the central screens; she spoke sharply: 'Stop that, Nurse – you're upsetting the patients.'

I said weakly, 'But he's lost a leg – and yet he was able to worry about my looking tired.'

She looked at me steadily. 'Nurse, if you are not able to match the courage of these men, then at least have the grace to pretend. I never want to see you crying on the ward again.'

'No, Sister.'

Captain Bevan came back with the stretcher; Mack was still under the anaesthetic. 'Had to take off a bit more before I could tie the artery – the walls had rotted, but he's still got a reasonable stump there, should be OK for a tin leg. Come with me, Nurse Girvan.'

I followed him down the ward to Sister's bunk and waited dully for another lecture. Instead he rummaged in the medicine cupboard, found the brandy and filled a medicine glass to the brim. 'Drink that, Nurse.'

'But . . .'

'All of it – doctor's orders.' He smiled at me and I forced the harsh burning liquid down my throat. 'You'll feel better now – goodnight.'

He was right, I did. The brandy warmed me all over and nothing seemed to matter as much. I went about my work in a dream, and I started to sing softly as I wrung out a fomentation for a painful swollen leg. The leg's owner looked up at me and whispered, 'That's a nice tune, Sister – what is it? I couldn't catch the words.'

I started guiltily, then looked him straight in the eye and whispered back, 'It's a song about a fish – a trout. You wouldn't recognize the words because it's in – er,' – I thought frantically – 'Portuguese – they are our allies, you see.'

I was hunched over my breakfast a few days later when Home Sister came into the mess tent and handed me a type-written form. I stared at it disbelievingly.

MISS Girvan   RANK Nurse
CORPS VAD   HOSPITAL 15 General

has been granted fourteen days' leave from 6/7/17 to 21/7/17.

N.B. She should report her arrival in writing to the Matron-in-Chief, War Office, London, SW, immediately on arrival in England, on attached form.

The Colonel's signature blurred before my eyes. I was so very tired, and here at last was my release.

I packed my knapsack for the journey and joined the other two VADs who were going on leave as well. They burst out laughing as they read the printed instructions we had been issued with. 'Look, Grey – it says we mustn't take on leave: "bombs, shells or shell-cases", nor "trophies captured from the Enemy". Oh dear, you'll have to unpack them all!'

All I could do was hold my travel warrant tightly between my fingers as I thought longingly of escape.

We collected yet more documents from the RTO at Rouen, and my companions laughed again at our apparently being designated as: 'chevaux et mulets' on the large 'ordre de transport pour l'expédition d'Armée Anglais', but I slumped silently in my seat, and thought that they could call me an ass if they wanted – just so long as they let me go. When the train came in a group of English officers insisted on helping us in with our luggage, and one asked eagerly, 'May we travel with you? We haven't spoken to a British girl for months!' But I had been up all night and nothing was going to keep me awake now, so I left the other two to entertain them and fell instantly asleep.

It was lucky I was not alone – I had to be hauled out of the compartment for changes, and pushed back in again when the next train arrived. At Boulogne they found me a space in a cabin and I slept until we docked at Folkestone. I woke up just as the train was drawing into Victoria, and suddenly I was alive again, and realized it was well on in the evening. The other two left me at the cab rank: 'Goodbye, Dormouse!' 'See you in a couple of weeks, Girvan.'

'Where to, Miss?'

I said, 'Cadogan Place,' and sat back on the tobacco-smelling leather seat.

A maid showed me into the drawing room, where Pansy stared at me as if I were a ghost. 'Helena – I didn't recognize you – you look so different.' As I unslung the knapsack from my shoulder and dumped it on the Aubusson carpet the mirror between the windows caught my reflection – and I realized I did not recognize myself, either. For a moment I wondered who this creature was, in a badly-fitting navy-blue coat, peering out from under the brim of an ugly straw hat, and anchored to the ground by solid, sensible shoes. It was so long since I had seen myself I had lost my bearings. Then I heard a soft gulping, and saw that Pansy was crying – and pregnant yet again.

She made a great effort to pull herself together. 'I'm sorry, Helena – Guy isn't in.'

I sat down in the armchair and promptly lost my balance – it was so unexpectedly deep. 'That's all right, Pansy – I never said I was coming. I'll see him later.'

She said in a very small voice, 'He may not come in later – he often doesn't come back at all.'

At last I said, 'Perhaps he doesn't like to disturb you – he probably sleeps at his club.'

Pansy just looked at me. Her round blue eyes were those of a child who discovers too late that Santa Claus does not, after all, exist. Then she began to talk of her babies, and after a while she took me up to the nursery to see them. I did not look too closely at the sleeping babies – instead I sat in the day nursery and let myself be clucked over by a dressing-gowned Nanny.

Guy did eventually come home that night. For a moment he looked pleased to see me, then a shutter came down over his face. I ran to him, but he gave me only the briefest of hugs. 'Hello, Hellie.' He did not acknowledge Pansy at all. She sat on the sofa, a pitiful swollen figure, but with a kind of dignity. Guy asked me short, staccato questions, but I knew he was not really listening to my replies, and his eyes never met mine as they roamed restlessly round the room. His mouth was a hard thin line.

Pansy eventually spoke to him, very timidly, about some slight domestic matter – a fellow officer had called – but he rounded on her savagely: 'Can't you stop nagging me, you bloody woman?'

I exclaimed, 'Guy! She only – ' But he had already gone. We heard his boots crashing down the stairs and the slam of the front door.

Pansy looked at me helplessly. At last she said, 'He can't help it, Helena – I really don't think he can help it.' Tears rolled down her cheeks. 'Nanny spoke to him, but he wouldn't listen, not even to Nanny. She's very kind, Helena, she lets me sit up in the nursery for hours, with the children. And – I've got him.' She put her hand on her swollen abdomen in a small, loving gesture.

I went to see Alice next morning, and then I travelled up to Hatton. Mother was still running it as a convalescent home and there were Canadian and Australian accents everywhere. They seemed a cheerful bunch, and a group of local VADs waited on them hand and foot. The dining room was being used as a ward, so we ate dinner in the morning room, but otherwise it was the same as always – the white damask tablecloth, the gleaming silver, the fresh-cut flowers. Mr Cooper had maids to help him now – the footmen had all joined up – but he had trained them well and the service was as deft and silent as ever. I stared down at the fragrant consommé in its delicate, gold-rimmed porcelain bowl, and felt as if I were dreaming.

Each day when it was fine, I took a rug and a packed lunch and walked far out into the park until I found a secluded spot, and then I lay down and slept. When it

312

rained I took my rug into the almost deserted stables, climbed up into the sweet-smelling hayloft, and curled up on it there. As soon as I had dined each evening I went up to my bedroom and nodded over a novel for a little while before climbing into my clean soft bed and sleeping the night through.

Papa came up from London for a visit, and told us that Guy was going back to France – but as a staff officer at Fifth Army HQ. As he told me I felt sick with relief – my brother would have to go up to forward positions occasionally, but most of the time he would be safe at the base. I went up to my bedroom and wrote at once to Robbie; he had written before I had come on leave to say that his battalion of the Lancashire and Cheshire Light Infantry were in a quiet sector at present. I prayed they would stay there.

When I had put on my uniform on the last morning, Mother looked me up and down at the breakfast table and said, 'For God's sake, Helena – do something about that hideous uniform. Buy some better-looking approximation of it and charge it to my account.'

I murmured, 'Yes, Mother,' but I knew I would not bother – what was the point? But when I went upstairs after breakfast, on an impulse I went to the chest of drawers and took out a dozen of my silk petticoats, rolled them up small and stuffed them into my canvas knapsack. I would wear them each day as some small gesture against the dirt and the blood and the ugliness.

CHAPTER FIVE

I stayed the night with Alice at Eaton Terrace, then set off for Victoria in the morning to catch the leave train. There was a great press of people round the barrier:

women saying goodbye to their husbands, their lovers, their brothers. White faces, tear-stained faces, faces trying bravely to smile with their mouths while their eyes were wide with fear – I tried not to look at their private grief as I threaded through the crowd. As I climbed on to the train my stomach twisted; I did not want to go back.

When we docked at Boulogne I trudged down the gangway and went to report to the Embarkation Sister in her office at the Hôtel de Louvre. As soon as I told her my name she picked up a piece of paper. 'You've been transferred to No.23 General at Étaples, Nurse Girvan. Your kit has already been sent on from No.15.' I stared at her, my heart in my boots. Her face softened a fraction. 'These things happen in wartime, you know. And I do have a little treat for you – you won't have to go by train. An ambulance from Étaples brought an American MO down to Boulogne this morning, so I told the driver to wait and pick you up – I'm sure you'll enjoy the ride.'

I managed to reply, 'Thank you, Sister,' before going out on to the quay to look for my transport. There were fewer Tommies about than I remembered from last September – the men unloading the stores from the steamer were wearing khaki, but their tunics and trousers were made of baggy cotton, and their faces were brown. As I watched them a girl's voice behind me said, 'It's the Egyptian Labour Corps – and we've got Chinese coolies back at the camp. Isn't it exciting – the whole world has come to help us.' I turned round and saw two girls in blue tunics and skirts, wearing sturdy boots; I could not place them for a moment, then I saw the VAD badges and the oil stain on one sleeve and realised they were my ambulance drivers. Yes, all the available men were needed at the front these days.

My drivers were jolly, friendly girls, but I did not feel either jolly or friendly today. They insisted I must sit between them on the front seat, 'Safest place, Snaps is a terrible driver!'

Snaps brayed with laughter; she did not look at all put out. 'It wasn't *me* who reversed into the general's staff car last week, was it Bim?'

Bim giggled happily, 'But it didn't matter, he was simply ripping about it – such a good sport! And Jack said the more staff officers I ram the better.'

She turned to me to explain. 'Jack's my brother, he's a first lieutenant now. He's just come out to France for the second time – after sick leave – he brought a draft over and spent a fortnight with them at Étaples – they had to train in the Bull Ring, although they'd mostly been out before.'

I said, 'How nice for you to see your brother.'

Bim's freckled face was serious for a moment. 'Yes, it was – I miss him awfully, you know. We used to have such topping times together when we were young.' She did not look much over twenty now, but I knew exactly what she meant.

Snaps steered the clumsy vehicle skilfully through the crowded streets of Boulogne, and as we began to climb she changed gear as smoothly and efficiently as our chauffeur always had in the Delaunay-Belleville at home. I realized Bim had been chaffing her friend.

As we came up out of the town, beside the downland rising to our left, the two girls continued to chatter. Bim said to me kindly, 'How sickening for you, coming back from leave like that and finding you've been pushed off somewhere else.'

'Yes, it is rather.' I did not want to talk about it, and Bim turned the conversation to the vagaries of the ambulance; I was grateful to her.

We drove past the twin chimneys of the cement works at Dannes and through the big camp at Camiers, where the incessant rattle of the machine guns at the training school temporarily drowned out the noise of our engine. We ran out into open country again and Bim said, 'Not

315

long now to Étaples – Eatapples, that's what the Tommies call it. It is simply the most enormous place – we kept getting lost there at first, didn't we, Snaps? And it's crawling with redcaps – Jack says it's no wonder they need so many policemen, the way the men are treated – Jack was so angry. That wretched Bull Ring! I feel so sorry for the men, pounding around with all their packs weighing them down, and being bullied by permanent base NCOs who wouldn't recognize the front line if they fell over it, Jack says.'

Snaps broke in, 'We can see the Bull Ring from here – look, over by the estuary.'

I stared at the enormous sandy parade ground where company after company of men were moving in formation, like so many well-drilled ants. Bim jabbed her elbow into my ribs. 'And do you see that stockade over there?' I looked at the high wooden stakes and the sentries standing to attention outside. 'That's where they put the deserters before they shoot them.' I shivered.

'And that,' said Snaps' ironic voice as she took her hand from the wheel and gestured in the other direction, 'that is where they put the deserters *after* they've shot them.' The cemetery at Étaples had grown since I had passed by it on the train the previous autumn; it sprawled over the hillside in row after row of wooden crosses. And my anger boiled up at their flippancy and I said, speaking very distinctly, 'I think there are very many men buried there who did *not* desert, men who did their duty and paid for it with their lives.'

In the silence that followed I realized that I had spoken to the two girls in the tone of voice my mother would have used to rebuke a careless housemaid.

Then Snaps replied, sounding very embarrassed, 'I'm sorry, one shouldn't joke, I know – especially not to a nurse. It must be very upsetting for you, seeing them carried out under their Union Jacks. It upset us, too – while the Arras push was on the buglers seemed to be sounding the Last Post all day on that wretched hillside.

Look, Nurse, that's No.23 over there. The Sisters' compound is on the right-hand side of the road, tucked in beside the railway, the ward huts and marquees are on the left.'

'Thank you so much.' I was sorry now for the way I had spoken to them – they were young girls doing a difficult job; cracking jokes was probably their way of coping with it. I should have let them be.

The Home Sister was harassed but kindly. She escorted me to the hut I was to share with another VAD. 'Your kit's already arrived from Rouen, Nurse. At least I won't have to watch you throw your hands up in horror at the lack of a wardrobe, like the girls fresh from England.'

I looked round the small wood and canvas hut and said politely, 'This looks very spacious, Sister – we were still quartered in bell tents at No.15 – although there were rumours that we were going to be hutted sooner or later.'

'Later rather than sooner, if I know the army.' Sister smiled. 'Tea will be served in the mess in ten minutes. Oh, by the way, it's Nurse Aylmer that you're sharing with, I'm sure you'll both get on.'

Aylmer had been scrupulously fair about keeping her gear to one half of the hut, and it had a neat, almost homely, appearance. She had curtained the window with a pair of yellow cotton dusters and there was a straw mat on the floor. A shelf had been put up over the camp bed and there were several books standing on it, but my eyes dropped in surprise to the space below where two framed texts were hanging side by side: 'God is Love', and 'The Lord Will Provide'. Sister followed my eyes and said, 'Nurse Aylmer is a Strict Baptist – a *most* reliable girl.' She sounded very approving. As she rustled away I wondered if Sister would consider me to be 'a most reliable girl'; I remembered Conan and the hotel at Rouen and decided that she would not. I began to feel rather apprehensive about the unknown Aylmer.

As soon as I started to unpack I found my dozen silk petticoats; I decided I must have been mad to think of bringing them to this grim place. I thrust them back and went in search of a cup of strong tea.

I slipped into a seat at the end of the trestle table. The girl opposite smiled at me briefly then turned back to her companion. 'Where's Tilney?'

'Gone Paris-Plaging with MacLeod. I'm reliably informed that two personable young officers from the Machine Gun School at Camiers would just *happen* to overtake the pair of them as they just *happened* to be strolling down by the estuary.'

'Lucky devils – I could just murder one of those scrumptious chocolate cakes the Blue Cat serves up.' She looked disconsolately down at her thick slice of bread and butter.

The first girl laughed. 'Never mind – at least you can eat that with a clear conscience. I've told Mac she'll be in hot water one day. Matron will march in and catch her and Tilney in flagrante delicto – with the chocolate not dry on their lips – but she doesn't seem to care!'

The other girl sighed as she reached for her bread. 'She doesn't need to worry, as long as she sticks with Tilney – Tilney will talk her way out of it – that girl could argue her way out of hell itself!' They both laughed, then the girl opposite looked over at me and asked, 'Who are you sharing with?'

'Nurse Aylmer.'

She pulled a face. 'Now Aylmer *never* Paris-Plages, not ever.'

'Don't be bitchy, Sears – she is engaged, remember?'

'Don't I just! – after all, haven't I often admired the socks she knits for her dear Tom?' They both began to giggle and I felt homesick for Rouen. Then I looked down at my chipped enamel plate and felt even more homesick for Hatton.

I was quite nervous by the time Aylmer appeared in the hut, but she turned out to be no older than I was, with a pretty face and fair curly hair; she asked me about Rouen, and as we compared notes on our experiences I began to relax a little.

I went to bed early but did not sleep well. I tossed and turned and crept out to the latrines in the middle of the night – they were over by the railway line, and a train came trundling along as I came out. A huge shape loomed up against the sky – and one after another the menacing barrels of the big guns rolled slowly past. I went back to the unfamiliar hut and lay awake there for a long time, feeling very alone.

I reported to Matron the next morning. She was big and broad and red-faced, and she looked me up and down with small, sharp eyes. 'Your cap is crooked, Nurse Girvan.'

I raised my hand to adjust it. 'I'm sorry, Matron.'

'Report to L.3, Sister Oates.'

'Thank you, Matron.'

L.3 was a large hut, but only half a dozen beds were in use. Sister Oates was grey-haired and very tall. 'We're evacuating every day at present – there must be another big push due. Matron said we'd better take our half-days off now, while we're not busy, so I'll send you off today and go myself tomorrow, when you've had a chance to find your way around.'

Even the thought of such a rapid off-duty failed to cheer me up. I carried out Sister's instructions automatically, and tried not to think about where I was.

After lunch I wandered out on to the main road; there was a lot of traffic – ambulances, lorries, cars, horse-drawn limbers – the entire army seemed to be on the move in Étaples today. In Rouen I would have gone into the forest, but here there was not even a blade of grass to be seen – apart from the tired-looking square in the Sisters' compound. The sense of the huge crowded camp all around me was very oppressive – I began to walk along the road to escape.

At last I did see the bright colours of flowers – they

319

were growing on the lower graves of the great cemetery. But behind the wooden crosses at the top of the hill I saw the dark green of pine woods, so I turned in and began to walk towards them, keeping my eyes fixed on the trees above.

But just as I was about to slip between the scaly brown trunks a voice hailed me. I looked around and it was a military policeman. He came panting up to me. 'Miss, you can't go wandering in there.'

'Why ever not?'

'Because it's not safe, that's why. There's deserters 'ang out in them woods, all round Eetapps they do.'

I protested disbelievingly, 'But I always walked in the forest at Rouen – it was perfectly safe.'

'I dessay Rouen's different – it's inland, see – they comes 'ere 'cause it's on the coast – they 'ang around in the sand dunes or chalk caves up 'ere – trying to get 'ome like – though 'ow they think they'll ever get their-selves on to a leave boat's beyond me.'

I turned back to the shade of the trees. 'I'm not afraid of a few wretched deserters.'

His eyes began to bulge. 'Them's thieves and robbers – they break into officers' quarters and steal, they do – besides, deserters are cowards.'

I remembered the men I had nursed, who had told me of their fear; I remembered Robbie's letters, and I remembered Guy's eyes that could no longer meet mine. I looked at the man in front of me, safe in his base camp, chasing cowards, and I asked, 'How long is it since you were in the firing line, Sergeant?'

'That's none o' your business!' He was very angry now. 'But I'm telling you, you keep out o' them woods, or I'll report you to yer Matron, and then you'll be in trouble, young leddy.'

Without replying I turned and walked back to the top row of graves, and along to the rough wooden bench that had been built beside it. I sat down and stared ahead of me. I heard the policeman clump away, still muttering

320

angrily to himself. I felt the breeze on my burning cheeks, cool and comforting.

I looked down over the road and the railway line towards the estuary, and saw between the sand dunes the wide bare expanse of the Bull Ring and the khaki-clad ants scurrying there; companies of ants, battalions of ants, regiments of ants – all marching and wheeling and drilling at the word of command, all bowed down by the weight of their heavy packs. And as I watched, I wondered how many of that multitude would survive the next few months; and of those who survived, how many would have lost an arm or a leg or a jaw or a face. How many would be irreparably damaged, just like the men I had seen in the streets of Rouen – one with a lone leg, balancing on crutches, another with an empty sleeve neatly pinned to his jacket? The French had a name for them: they called them 'les mutilés': 'un mutilé de la Marne', 'un mutilé de Verdun', 'un mutilé de guerre'.

And as I watched I knew that I too would become like them; that if I stayed in this terrible place some part of me would be damaged beyond repair. Not my body – my body was strong, even as their bodies were now – no, my mutilation would be of the soul, of the spirit. For I had seen too much already – too much suffering, too much death, too much despair; but as yet I was only wounded, I could still recover, the scars would fade and turn silver with time and do me no harm. But I must leave now – there was no time to lose.

I looked down in compassion at the men below me. They had no choice – for them the only way out was the hand-to-mouth existence of the outlaw; the flight, the capture – and the judicial execution. So they were trapped, there on that bleak sandy plain. But I had a choice, for I was a woman, a temporary volunteer, so I was free, free to break my contract and go today – back to the greenness, the safety, the sanity of Hatton.

I was about to rise, when I remembered Robbie – I would be deserting Robbie. But Robbie would forgive me. No, not forgive – that word implied limits, the awarding of blame – and there were no limits, no blame between my brother and me. Whatever I did Robbie would always love me, whole-heartedly, unquestioningly. Just as I would him, if, by some unbelievable chance he deserted his post and became a hunted man in these woods behind me. Then I would lie for him, cheat for him, steal for him – and know no limits. No, I did not have to answer to Robbie – and there was no one else alive now to whom I owed such an answer.

I was free, free to go now before that irreparable damage had been done. And I closed my eyes and felt a great weight fall from my shoulders, and sat at peace. But when I opened my eyes again, still I saw those men marching and drilling below, so I spoke aloud in my pity: 'You, you were born at the wrong time – you and I.' And I. And even as I spoke I felt the breeze fan my cheeks again, but there was no comfort in it now, for it blew away my illusion of choice, and I knew there was no choice for me either. I too had been born at the wrong time. And I felt the weight of their packs on my shoulders, and bowed beneath the burden. But as it was for them now let it be with me. I too would become 'un mutilé' – 'une mutilée de guerre'. So be it. And I stood up and began to walk down, down into the dead forest of crosses.

CHAPTER SIX

I went back to the Sisters' compound, unpacked the rest of my kit and arranged my belongings in meticulous order in my half of the hut; then it was time for tea. I walked rather nervously into the mess, aware I was still a stranger in this place, but as soon as she saw me Aylmer smiled and patted the seat next to her and I slipped into it gratefully. She introduced me to the others at the table and as I caught the names 'Tilney' and 'MacLeod' I looked at their owners with interest. Tilney was small and slight with a narrow inquisitive face, MacLeod tall and freckled with shining auburn hair escaping from under her white cap. They talked quickly, in the short-hand of two people who know each other very well, then Tilney began mimicking Matron's portentous manner – despite her small size she managed to give an impression of pompous gentility which was clearly recognizable. ' . . . a very serious matter *indeed*, Nurse Tilney. Infor-mation has reached my ears, that you and Nurse MacLeod were in the process of actively encouraging certain' – Tilney paused, then delivered with maximum effect – 'certain *officers* . . .' 'Harrumph, harrumph,' MacLeod began to play the Colonel. 'Steady on now, Matron – girls will be girls, you know, and boys – harrumph – boys!' The whole table burst out laughing.

It became clear that their 'Paris-Plaging' of the previous afternoon had ended in near-disaster, but there had apparently been a sufficient element of doubt for them to have escaped with a strong reprimand. 'Such a wigging, my dears.' Tilney's eyes rolled. 'Poor Mac and I just *slunk* away, heads bowed in shame. Not a dry pillow all night, eh, Mac? Hey, Pargeter, leave some tea in that pot, you greedy hound!' They did not seem at all cast down by their experience. I glanced under my lashes at Aylmer; she was steadily munching her bread and jam.

As soon as we had finished Aylmer turned to me and said, 'I'm off for the evening now, so I'm going to walk down to the sea – would you like to come, if you're free?'

'Thank you, I should like that.' We went to put on our hats.

Aylmer set a good pace and I strode out beside her over the bridge and down through the muddy square of

323

Étaples village. As we crossed the second bridge, over the river Canche, Aylmer began to tell me about her fiancé. Her Tom was a Baptist minister, but he had a club foot and could not walk far, so he had had to find work with the YMCA instead of enlisting as an army chaplain. Aylmer said, in a matter-of-fact voice, 'I used to feel so sorry for Tom – we grew up together and he couldn't join in most of the games my elder brothers played because of his foot – but now, I thank God for it. Only I wonder sometimes if I'm being selfish, because Tom feels he should do more.'

I stared at the empty sky and said abruptly, 'My fiancé didn't have a club foot, so he was killed, just after Neuve Chapelle.'

'I am so sorry, Girvan.'

We walked on together in silence for a while, then she began to talk of the hospital and the other VADs – where they came from and how long each one had been at No. 23. I tried to concentrate on what she was saying.

We drank coffee together in a small, pretty café in Paris-Plage, and the brisk walk back beside the estuary, breathing in the sharp salt air, cheered me up a little. But as we came back over the bridges and saw the great camp with its barbed wire, its endless rows of dull brown huts, its acres of dirty grey bell tents, the clattering unresting railway – it all seemed to press in on me and quench my spirit.

That night, as Aylmer prayed for her Tom, I lay on the hard army mattress and remembered Gerald – and knew I was no longer the girl he had loved; the war had stolen not only my dear one but also my innocence. I turned my face into my pillow and wept for my lost dreams.

Over the next ten days we evacuated our patients as soon as they were well enough to stand the journey; they left, jubilant, for Blighty – except for those unlucky few who were ordered instead to the convalescent camp up on the hill. Trainloads of ammunition and guns rumbled through the camp, night and day, while draft after draft of men from the big infantry camp on the hill marched down to the station each morning. The rumours said the offensive would be at Ypres, where so many men had died already. Aylmer was quite calm. 'God will never desert us, if we trust in Him,' she said to me one evening.

I looked at her earnest face and could not help my reply. 'But presumably there are those who trust Him in Germany, too.'

She flushed, then said quietly, 'God is good, Girvan.'

I envied her her confident faith but I did not share it. I spent my off-duty time writing long and determinedly cheerful letters to Robbie. His replies were briskly reassuring, but I was not reassured.

The attack was launched on the last day of July, just as the weather changed and the rains began. By the following afternoon the wounded were flooding in. As I came out of the ward to watch the first ambulance of our convoy arrive from the hospital siding I saw Snaps at the wheel. She jumped down to roll up the canvas curtains for the orderlies and saw me. She whispered, 'I'm sorry, there's only two – I had to stop at the mortuary to unload the others.' Her face was so distressed, as if it were her fault, that I found myself replying in a ridiculous attempt at comfort, 'Never mind – you couldn't help it. They shouldn't send them down like that.'

She shook her head. 'They say they've put the CCSs further up and they're being shelled – so they have to fill all the trains.' She dropped the curtains as soon as the men had been carried out, and ran round the front to go and collect another load; a second ambulance backed up and I hurried into the ward.

By the end of the day the hut was full, and men lay on stretchers down the centre. But next morning the centre aisle was clear again – sufficient men had died in the night, so now everyone could have a bed. One of Aylmer's texts ran through my head: 'The Lord will provide' – and, indeed, the Lord had provided beds. I heard the faint wail of the Last Post sounding from the hillside above – God had given us the cemetery and that was big enough – why, over these last few days had we not seen the gravediggers taking in a new section – digging the deep trenches, ready – as the men had marched down from the camp to entrain for the front? Yes, the Lord had provided. I stared at the cleared centre aisle, at the long rows of beds holding pain-racked men – and I began to giggle. Loos, the Somme, Arras – I had seen them all – yes, God was good.

I slipped away into the kitchen so that I could laugh aloud. I was still laughing when Sister came in, closed the door, raised her hand and slapped me, hard, across the face. I stared at her, stunned. 'Go back to the ward, Nurse Girvan, and start the dressings on the left-hand side.'

'Yes, Sister.' I went.

But as I prepared the dressings trolley I made my decision – I would not look upon these broken bodies and see them as men – I did not want to suffer any more. From now on they would be objects – parcels to be unwrapped and probed and squeezed and bundled up again. I had no more pity to spare.

For days I worked like a machine. Some died at once, some were soon fit to be evacuated, others lived on for a week, eyes bright with pain, and then died despite our efforts. I resented these – how dared they waste all our work?

Once, long ago, I had been frightened when I dressed a wound, frightened that I would not have the courage to cleanse it adequately, to thrust the drainage tube in deep enough – but now they were not men so I was determined and uncompromising, and Sister praised me for my thoroughness. And now I only spoke in the meaningless platitudes of the ward, 'Not long now, Sonny – hang on', 'Turn over, Taffy, soon have you comfortable',

'Soon be finished, old man, and then you'll feel better' – but I never met their eyes.

An amputation case had a pocket of pus in his wound and it had to be emptied every day; he whimpered as I came towards him, but I ignored his frightened panting, and as the orderly held his stump steady for me I put my two strong thumbs squarely down on the tender flesh and squeezed as hard as I could. He screamed, and I was annoyed and said sharply, 'It has to be done – it's for your own good.'

Then I moved on to deal with a jaw case. I tugged out the sodden dressing and poured peroxide through his head and out of his ear – he tried to catch my eye, to make contact, but I did not look at him. And at the next bed it was easier as there was no eye, only a gaping socket where it should have been. Swiftly I pulled the rolls of stinking gauze out of the hole, syringed it and pushed the clean dressing through into the cavity behind. I was very quick these days, as quick as Sister, but then I needed to be – there was so much to be done.

None of the men asked me to write letters for them any more, and I was glad, for we had no time off duty now and after supper I only wanted to write to Robbie. Brief letters still came from him, but he had given up trying to reassure me. He and his men had not gone over the top yet, but I knew from the way he wrote that it would not be long now. And finally a short, mud-stained note arrived one afternoon. It ended: 'Take care of yourself, Hellie – and remember, I love you.' My flesh went cold in the clammy mess hut, then I gulped down the rest of my tea, put his message safely into my pocket, and went back to the ward.

As I rebandaged the Australian corporal in the second bed it was obvious that he was dying; Bourne had put up a strong fight – there was a girl he wanted to get back to in Queensland – but his body had suffered too many wounds. I wondered if he would last out until eight o'clock. If he died after eight then it would be the night staff's responsibility to lay him out – it would be a nuisance if he went earlier because there were still some dressings I must do, and a man was due back from the theatre any minute – and Sister simply had to catch up on her paper work. I pinned the last bandage and turned away from the bed – and a thin hand reached out and caught my skirt. 'Sister, don't leave me – I'm frightened.'

I said briskly, 'I'm sorry, old man, but the orderlies are just coming back from the theatre.' I detached his hand and went down the ward to the bed I had prepared. It was another amputation, so as he was being violently sick into the bowl I was holding, I looked to check that the tourniquet was hanging ready from the bed rail. It was – good, everything was quite satisfactory. I went to empty the bowl.

On my way back from the sluice the Australian opposite Bourne called me over. I went to his bed impatiently. 'Yes, Walker – what is it?'

He whispered, 'Jack Bourne – he's going, isn't he?'

I glanced across at the irrigation in the next bed – what a nuisance, the receiver had overflowed and the bed was wet – we really did not have time to cope with irrigations at the moment, but Captain Adams had insisted we try with this one and now I would have to change all the bedding.

'Sister, Jack Bourne . . . ?'

I glanced down at the face in front of me, then my eyes slid away again as I said formally, 'Corporal Bourne is not very well,' and turned to go. Suddenly I felt my hand seized in a tight grip – I was jerked down and the man's unshaven face was only inches from mine as he spat out, 'You callous bitch!' Then he threw my hand aside. I backed away, staring at him – then I turned around and half ran down to the linen store. I was shaking.

I made myself reach up for a sheet – I had a bed to change. But the words reverberated in my ear, and the

328

contempt I had seen in his eyes as he flung my hand away scorched into my brain. I tried to take hold of the sheet, but my hand – the same hand – would not close on it. A man lay dying in pain and fear; a young man who had loved his girl and fought bravely to live and go back to her, but instead he was dying here, thousands of miles from his homeland – and I had not spared him even a single minute. For a moment I hated him for the guilt and pain I felt, then I turned and walked up the ward, found a chair and carried it to his bed and sat down beside him. 'There, I'm not so busy now – I'll sit with you a while if I may – and rest my feet!'

His bloodless lips managed to smile, then he said simply, 'I'll not keep you long, Sister.'

I kept back my tears and my voice was quite calm as I offered, 'Would you like me to write to your girl at home?'

He looked up at me in naked defeat. 'What's the use? I been thinking this afternoon – remembered what blokes have told me about their wives – not even faithful when they're married. I used to believe in my Jenny, but now – even if she does cry for me when she gets the cable – I reckon she'll have forgotten me by the next day.'

So I had to speak, to tell him. 'No, Bourne, she won't. My fiancé was killed more than two years ago now, and I've never forgotten, never. I love him still, and I always will.'

His eyes were fixed on mine and he gave a small sigh as he read the truth in them, and then he whispered, 'Thank you, Sister. I'd like to think she'd remember me – we've been sweethearts a long time. Please write that letter for me – and tell her I loved her.'

He died just before eight, so Sister and I had to come back after supper to lay him out. I copied the address I needed out of his pocket book; there was her photo there, too – she was not a pretty girl, her nose was too big for that – but her large anxious eyes were trying to smile for her Jack. Back in the hut I began to write:

'Dear Miss Foster, It is with the deepest regret . . .' But at least this time I could tell her the truth: that he had died bravely and with her name on his lips. I hoped it would be some consolation.

And now they were men again, with faces and personalities and eyes that looked at me for comfort, and I gave them all I could. But as I stood by the bed while Captain Adams told a young cockney that his leg would have to come off and saw the boy's nostrils quiver like a frightened rabbit's, and his dry furred tongue trying desperately to moisten his flaking lips so that he could whisper, 'All right, sir,' then I wished I was a machine again. But it was too late now.

A few days later a scribbled note came from Robbie; as I held it in my hand my whole body was shaking with relief. He had survived, but the Colonel and adjutant had both been killed, and my brother wrote that when the battalion had finally been relieved and had lined up for roll call only five officers and a hundred and twenty men had answered to their names – more than five hundred had gone into the attack. 'And we've been luckier than some. The stretcher bearers just can't cope in these conditions; it's taking eight of them to carry one man out, and anyone who slips off the duckboards simply disappears into the slime. Still, I know Ralph managed to get back – he was hit in the arm, thank God – so perhaps some of the others have been lucky too. And I've still got Sergeant Holden with me; it makes all the difference having an NCO as unflappable as he is, in this kind of show.' I read that last sentence and was glad – Sergeant Holden had rescued Eddie and brought him back to me, however briefly – surely he would look after Robbie if he were wounded? I clung to the thought as a talisman. But I would not have to worry for a while, because Robbie's battalion would have to wait for new drafts and a refit before it could go into action again. Surely they could not even be sent to hold the line after such a mauling?

At the end of August I had a letter from Innes at St Omer. She had written to tell me she was going home on leave, and as soon as she had arrived back she had been transferred, just as I had been. She wrote philosophically of the change, but it was obvious that, like me, she missed Rouen. As I answered her letter I felt glad that she was still in France.

Early in September we heard that the hospital site at Camiers had been bombed. No. 11 General had suffered badly, medical staff had been killed and wounded and men had received fresh injuries. The men were British soldiers, but the nurses and doctors and orderlies were Americans – they had come over ahead of their main armies to tend our wounded, and this was their reward. Camiers was only a few miles away – I wondered uneasily if it would be our turn next; it seemed so unfair that men already wounded should not be safe even in their hospital beds, but the railway that ran through our camp would provide an easy target and it carried supplies and ammunition day and night.

Some kind of food poisoning was going the rounds of the Sisters' compound and most of us were affected. Sister and I had to rush out to be sick in a basin in the sluice several times a day, and we discovered that one of the patients was running a book on how often each of us turned green and took to our heels. Sister was disapproving, but I thought it was really rather funny – Tilney and Mac screamed with laughter when I told them – but I knew my face was scarlet every time I came back from the sluice afterwards.

Then, before we had recovered, the bookmaker was evacuated, along with half of the ward, and after a frantic rush in the morning we were able to relax a little. I was tidying the linen cupboard after lunch when Sister called me out; she was smiling. 'Nurse Girvan, your brother-in-law is here to see you.'

'Hugh! Oh how nice.' Then I felt my face fall. 'But I'm not off until teatime.'

'Don't worry about that – we're not busy at the moment – you can finish the linen cupboard tomorrow. Run along now.'

I thanked Sister and ran. There, outside the hut, was Hugh – Captain Knowles now – looking as kind and solid and dependable as ever. He held out his hand and I clasped it between both of mine. 'Hugh – how lovely to see you! Are you going on leave?'

He shook his head. 'No, Helena – worst luck. The Colonel wanted an officer to come down here to fetch a draft, and as soon as he said Étaples I volunteered – I told him I had a beautiful sister-in-law there and he put me down for the job at once! Now, where would you like to go – can I buy you a nice tea in the village?'

'No – Matron might spot us – we could risk Paris-Plage – but, well, actually Hugh, I'd rather not go anywhere to eat in public. I've got a touch of ptomaine poisoning – it's nothing, we've all got it, it's the weather I think – but I may have to be sick.'

'Poor old Hellie. Then let's go down and find a quiet spot among the sand dunes.'

The quiet spot was not really very quiet since we could hear the machine guns clattering away on the Bull Ring, but it was private; Hugh spread out his greatcoat and we sat down on it.

He said, 'I suppose you've been very busy, down here.'

'Yes, yes, we have. Hugh, we only hear rumours – has anything been gained?'

Hugh shrugged his square shoulders. 'We are a bit further forward, but we haven't got the ridges yet, and that's what the brass hats are after. I suppose they're right – Ypres'd be a safer place if we could capture them, but . . .'

Ypres, 'Wipers'. I said, 'The men – the ones who go to the convalescent camp – they dread the thought of being sent there.'

'So do I, Helena. It's one vast charnel house – acre after acre of rotting corpses.'

My stomach heaved. 'Excuse me, Hugh.' I jumped up and stumbled through the sand to be sick in a hollow. Hugh came floundering up beside me and held my shoulders steady. When I had finished he wiped my mouth with his own handkerchief.

'I'm sorry, Hellie – I shouldn't have spoken like that – how tactless of me.' His voice was guilty.

I looked up at him, surprised. 'Oh, it was nothing to do with what you said, Hugh – I'm always sick about this time in the afternoon – just before tea. I'm very lucky, poor Sister gets it afterwards and wastes all her bread and jam!' He hugged me tight, and as I leant gratefully against his broad chest I said, 'But it is good of you to take care of me like this, Hugh – most men would run a mile.'

He replied simply, 'I can remember what Alice was like when she was carrying the boys.'

He led me back to his greatcoat and we sat down again. I slipped my arm through his and said warmly, 'What a nice brother-in-law you are, Hugh!'

His face reddened and he looked pleased, then he suddenly said, 'I have tried to be, Hellie, but once – I don't know whether I did the right thing by you – perhaps . . .' I stared at him; I could not imagine what he was talking about. He took out his pipe and began to fiddle with it, then he turned and smiled at me. 'It doesn't matter, Hellie – that was a long time ago. But I did my best, I really did.'

He looked so anxious that I said quickly, 'Of course you did, Hugh – always.'

We sat and chatted together, easily and comfortably, and then it was time to go back. He walked me to the hospital entrance and bent to kiss me goodbye. Then he said abruptly, 'Helena – I told you – this show's not going too well – in fact it's a bloody shambles up there. So if anything happens to me, will you write and tell

Alice that I loved her? I know I wasn't fit to black her boots but I loved her, I always did.'

I whispered, 'Yes, Hugh – but – don't talk like that – you'll be going on leave soon, you can tell her yourself.'

He gazed at the long line of huts and said flatly, 'No. My number's up this time, I can feel it in my bones. So tell her, Hellie, please.' He turned and walked away, just one square-shouldered figure in khaki amidst all the others.

It was Papa who wrote to tell me: 'Hugh is posted missing, but after what happened with Conan, Alice has not given up hope.'

But I had. We had had our one miracle; I doubted that we were due for another.

Papa wrote again three days later. A corporal who had been with Hugh had come round in a CCS and reported that the same shell which had wounded him had blown Captain Knowles to bits. I picked up my pen and began to write my letter to Alice.

CHAPTER SEVEN

Nanny wrote to tell me that Guy's third son had been born and he was to be called Hugh. I thought of Pansy with her three babies in the nursery – Lance, Edwin and now little Hugh – and I wondered bitterly how many more sons she would have to bear in order to replace the men who were being killed.

Rumours from the battlefront talked of advances – but pitifully small ones, and the men who had paid the price were carried into us day and night. Then one Monday morning there were different rumours – of events much closer at hand – there had been a riot at Three Arch Bridge just outside Étaples – that bridge which was always guarded by redcaps to stop men from the camp entering the village. It was said that stones and sticks had been thrown at the sentries the previous afternoon – the New Zealanders were involved and a Gordon Highlander corporal on the fringe of the crowd had been shot in the head by one of the police. We knew this last story was true because he had been brought into Tilney's ward just as she had been going off duty that evening; by next morning he was dead. Later the rioters were supposed to have come back and stormed the bridge and forced their way through into the village. We were still discussing it all when Matron came into the mess; we listened in silence as she announced that we were confined to the hospital compound until further notice. As she finished speaking we looked at each other uneasily – so it was true.

Tilney set herself the task of discovering exactly what was going on; she had read history at Oxford before volunteering as a VAD and she had a sharp, inquisitive brain which revelled in ferreting out information. Each evening in the mess, she regaled us with the fruits of her research and we listened eagerly – it was a diversion from the war. Most of us had a sneaking sympathy for the men who had finally turned on their tormentors after enduring the sadistic bullying of the Bull Ring, and I was angry when Tilney argued that technically they were mutineers. We all knew the French Army had mutinied after the agony of Verdun, but our men were still fighting and dying in the hell around Ypres.

Matron kept us confined to camp until the middle of October, though the whole affair seemed to have died down after a fortnight; but by then it made no difference to me as I had been transferred to the theatre and had no off-duty anyway.

The two theatre huts squatted close together in the centre of the hospital, next to the reception hut and near to the acute surgical wards. It was raining as I slithered over the slippery duckboards the first evening and the weather seemed to reflect my mood – I was miserable as well as nervous. But there was no operation in progress and Sister was in there alone, cleaning instruments. She was young and brisk and showed me how to operate the sterilizer before setting me to pack drums of dressings. When I had finished she said, 'You'd better turn in early tonight, Nurse Girvan – there's a convoy due first thing, so we'll be very busy.'

I did not sleep well that night – I did not know what would be expected of me – and suppose I was too slow and got in the way of Sister and the surgeons – or made some dreadful mistake? I was dozing uneasily when the theatre orderly banged on our hut door. 'It's five-thirty Nurse, Sister Saunders says you're to come over at once.'

Sick with apprehension I fumbled for my clothes; it was still dark and I had to dress by the light of my electric torch. Aylmer stirred. 'Girvan – there are some biscuits in the tin on my shelf – eat a couple now.'

I whispered, 'I'm not hungry, thank you.'

She swung her legs out of bed, reached down the tin, opened it and thrust two biscuits into my hand. 'Don't be silly – you may not be able to get over to breakfast, it's bound to be hectic at first.'

Obediently I began to nibble at a biscuit, and I was still swallowing the last mouthful as I came into the brightly lit theatre hut. Sister glanced up from the sterilizer. 'Had something to eat? Good girl, I meant to warn you. I've lit this thing and sent the orderly for water, so there's just time to snatch a cup of tea in the night bunk.'

The bugles were sounding as we swallowed our last mouthfuls of tea and came out into the cold morning air, and the first ambulance was already backing up to the reception hut, while another was being waved on to the wards. I knew only the most serious cases would come straight to the theatre, and my stomach lurched. I tied on my clean overall with trembling hands, wiped out a bowl with meths, set a match to it and watched the flame spurt up, then I put it ready on the trestle.

The MOs came in in pairs: surgeon and anaesthetist together – Captain Adams and Mr Casson, Captain Blaymire and Mr Morris. 'They're on their way, Sister.' Mr Casson pulled out his stool and perched on it at the head of the table, waiting. The orderlies brought the first stretcher alongside. I saw the man's eyes, staring and frightened, as I moved forward to help the orderlies slide him off the stretcher – his left leg was a mass of stained bandages, and it stank.

'All right, old man, just breathe in now, easy does it.' The mask in Mr Casson's hand came down as Sister told me to unroll the bandages. The flesh exposed was swollen and green. 'Slit the rest of his trouser leg, Girvan.' I picked up the scissors and laid bare the travesty of a leg.

'Must have been lying out some time – poor bastard – it'll have to come off, then . . .' Captain Adams shrugged as he eased on his gloves. 'Nurse, get hold of that foot and play tug-of-war with it – pull back as hard as you can.'

I took a deep breath and reached out for the green foot; it squelched unpleasantly under my fingers, but I tightened my grip until I felt the bone under the gangrenous flesh and then I pulled hard. At the next table the orderly was unwrapping another stinking leg as Mr Morris crooned, 'Easy old man, easy,' and Captain Blaymire pulled on his gloves.

Sister stood between the two surgeons, eyes swivelling from one to the other. The scalpel flashed as she handed it to Captain Adams, and I watched a scarlet slit appear in the green of the leg. 'I can't go any further up, dammit – he must have been out there for days. I suppose we've been driven back again.' He was slicing into the muscle as he spoke, and Sister was handling artery forceps with the speed of a juggler, soon they dangled from the gash like an obscene metal fringe. I watched the sweat bead on the surgeon's forehead as the saw grated through the bone. Foul yellow pus began to pour out of the leg, and

337

then the saw on the other table picked up the refrain. Captain Adams began chanting the bawdiest version of 'Mademoiselle from Armentières' with his eyes fixed on the bone, 'Oh, yes, I have a daughter fair – pull harder, Nurse – With lily-white breasts and golden hair . . .' I pulled until my arms ached and then there was a sickening crunch and I reeled back and thudded into the wooden wall, the severed leg clutched to my breasts. I pulled myself upright again and ran to stuff the leg in the dustbin in the corner. When I got back to the table Captain Adams was sewing up the severed veins and arteries with quick delicate stitches. At the next table the orderly staggered back, grunted and took a second leg to the dustbin.

The stretcher bearers were ready to empty the table; a second frightened-eyed man was waiting his turn. As the voice ordered, 'Take a deep breath old man, easy does it,' I began to unwrap the swollen bandages from another rotting leg.

All the early cases were gas gangrene – the CCSs had dressed them, injected anti-tetanic serum and morphia, then sent them down in hope while they concentrated on the chests and the heads and the abdominals that must be operated on at once – the urgent cases – but by the time they reached us these men had become urgent cases in their turn.

The stretchers followed each other relentlessly: I became light-headed from the fumes of the chloroform, and my feet slipped in the blood and creosote on the floor – but still the stretchers came in. The sterilizers hissed and bubbled over their Primus stoves and the hut became hotter and hotter. We did rush over for food – we had to – but we swallowed without tasting, and as soon as we got back another man was lifted on to the table.

By mid-afternoon there was a slight slackening in the pace, because the desperate cases had been dealt with; now those from the wards were being carried over. I could catch my breath while the surgeons peered at X-ray plates, then scrubbed their hands with perchloride before beginning their careful cutting and probing.

It was nearly midnight before we finished, then Sister and I and the orderly had to stay behind to prepare the theatre for a six o'clock start next morning. Tired though I was, I stumbled to the ablutions hut and scrubbed myself all over – I felt as if I would never be clean again.

On the morning of the fourth day I realized that the cases coming in were less serious, and then there was only one more stretcher waiting outside. As I bent over him he said, 'My lady.' I looked round, my tired brain not understanding. Then he spoke again: 'It is Lady Helena, isn't it?' And I realized he meant me. There was something familiar about the fair young face and I smiled at him and nodded, 'Yes – yes, it is.'

'I've often seen you, my lady – my father's the stationmaster at Hareford.'

'Why, of course – I recognize you now – I am so glad to see you.'

Then I realized the boy was lying on the floor of a stinking, slimy hut – and that I must have sounded absolutely ridiculous. But he looked quite pleased. As we lifted him up on the table I said quickly, 'I'll write to your father and tell him I've seen you.'

As Mr Casson's mask came down the boy said, 'Thank you, my lady . . .' and trailed off into a gurgle as his eyelids dropped.

Captain Adams reached for his scalpel. 'Nothing like a bit of social chit-chat to start the op on the right footing, eh, Nurse – or should I say "my lady"?' His red-rimmed eyes grinned at me as I began to unpin the bandage.

Luckily there were only a few small pieces of shrapnel in young Shepherd's buttock and I was able to write reassuringly to his parents; they sent me a touchingly grateful reply.

We lived to a different rhythm in the theatre hut:

several frantic days would follow each other, then there would be an oasis of calm while we cleaned instruments and packed drums and went early to our beds to prepare for the next onslaught.

At the end of the month Matron called me into her office and presented me with a strip of braid; it was one of the new scarlet proficiency stripes. That evening as I sat unpicking the white service ones from my sleeves to replace them with the red braid I thought of Hugh. I remembered how he had noticed my first white stripes and congratulated me on it; I remembered his comforting arm round my shoulders as I had been sick among the sand dunes – and I remembered his courage as he had walked away, back to the charnel house of Ypres, knowing he would never leave it. Dear Hugh. My tears dropped on the red braid and darkened it, before it was even attached. But two days later my tears were of relief; Robbie had written to say he had been moved back from Ypres.

Later in October they shifted us into more sturdy wooden huts for the winter; Aylmer and I chose to stay together. Several sisters and staff nurses had left for Casualty Clearing Stations: they went cheerfully, undeterred by the stories of bombings nearer the line. One wrote back to Mac and in her letter she had drawn a little sketch of a stick nurse in gas helmet and steel hat – underneath she had written: 'The latest Paris fashions – we all wear them here.'

But it was not just the CCSs which were under attack – on 1 November we heard that St Omer had been bombed the night before, and there had been casualties at No. 58 General Hospital – Innes' hospital. I was busy in the theatre all day; the numbers of cases were tailing off now, but we still had plenty to do – so it was suppertime before Tilney told me, in a shocked murmur, that eighteen patients and a staff nurse had been killed – and two VADs. The staff nurse had been singing to a frightened patient, trying to calm him, when she had been hit, Tilney said. I shivered as I thought of Innes' pale face and gentle smile. I wrote at once, and waited sickly for my letter to be returned unopened – but it was Innes' own handwriting on the envelope which came back.

She said simply that she had been very frightened and they were all distressed by the deaths, but there was nothing to do except carry on. Her father had written that day ordering her to come home – 'I have never disobeyed Papa before, but on this matter I feel I must do so; after all, he has other daughers.' She finished her letter with the hope that we might sometime be able to arrange a meeting.

Soon after, the Canadians captured the village of Passchendaele, and I gathered from Robbie's letters that the bloody campaign fought in the mud in front of Ypres was finally over. 'God knows what this show was supposed to be worth, Hellie – I just don't care any more. Those of us that are left sit around in the mess and argue about which mud was the stickiest, Wipers or the Somme. I'd like to pick up the brass hats by the scruffs of their necks and roll them in both to let them decide – except that they'd sink without a trace and then we'd never know the answer.'

The news was not good: the main body of troops of our new ally, America, still had to be trained and cross the Atlantic; in the meantime our old ally, Russia, had stopped fighting after a second revolution. Now the Kaiser was free to concentrate all his forces on the western front – on us.

With the coming of winter and the ending of the Ypres battles, two theatres were no longer needed, so our hut was closed down and I was sent to a surgical ward. B.4 was housed in a marquee, and Tilney had been sent there on nights the previous week, so I was able to have a few minutes' chat with her evening and morning – and find out all the gossip. I was glad to get back to the familiar routine of washings, temperatures, pulses, medicines, dressings – and bed pans. There was only one orderly now and he was surly and unco-operative. Sister's nagging had little effect so I did not even try. Besides, he was rough and careless with the men, so I preferred to do everything for them myself, with the help of the occasional obliging convalescent.

CHAPTER EIGHT

We were still nursing the last shocked survivors from Flanders when a ripple of excitement ran through the camp – the enemy had been driven back at Cambrai – we had gained several miles in a single day. Mac, arriving back from leave, said the church bells had been rung in London, and people were saying the war would soon be over. I wanted to believe this, but I could not. And as December opened the rumours were bad again: the Germans had counter-attacked, we had lost the land so recently captured – and more. When orders came that all those men who were fit to travel were to be evacuated to Blighty then we knew the rumours were true – the brief period of victory was over.

As soon as we had said goodbye to our patients we began to prepare the empty wards: scrubbing out lockers, making beds, putting up fresh charts. Sister told me the day staff would be called back in the night when the convoy arrived, so we knew things must be bad up the line if the wounded were coming to us unwashed and still in their khaki. As I started laying the brown reception blankets over the clean sheets my skin began to itch in anticipation. I reached up to scratch a tickle at the back of my neck, and saw Sister doing the same as she picked up one of the planks for a fracture bed. She caught my eye and smiled ruefully, 'I'll douse myself in Keating's tonight – but I think those wretched lice just eat it!'

I grinned back. 'That's what my brother says – you can always tell a louse that's been fed on Keating's, because it looks so fat and healthy!' I tucked in the edge of the brown blanket tightly.

We were sent off duty early, but it was too cold in the hut to go to bed at once, so Aylmer and I huddled either side of the stove writing letters until it warmed up. As I addressed my envelope to Robbie I wondered where he was now – I knew he had gone back up to the line, but not to Ypres – I prayed it was in a quiet sector. He and his men had surely suffered enough.

At last the hut was warm and cosy, so we began to undress – with luck we should be able to snatch several hours' sleep before we were called out. I sat on the edge of the bed, brushing my hair with slow, rhythmical strokes – it was very soothing – then the bugle sounded. It was 'Fall in'. My hand stilled and my hairbrush stood suspended, its oval shadow motionless against the wall, then, clear in the night air came the second call: 'At the double'. I began to plait, frantically, as Aylmer reached for her vest. We scrabbled for coats and gumboots, turned out the stove and shivered as the cold air came to meet us.

The camp was already alive as we scurried over the duckboards; two acetylene flares streamed up into the blackness outside the reception hut and an ambulance was crawling forward – as it swung round to back up to the waiting orderlies I caught a glimpse of the set face behind the wheel and recognized Bim. By the time I came level her cargo had been unloaded and with a burst of acceleration she sped off into the darkness to collect another load.

The walking wounded were already staggering out of the hut towards the marquees: grotesque, blundering figures in the shadows cast by the flares – hung around with packs and gas masks and steel helmets they stum-

343

bled towards the shelter. One huddled trio stood out for a moment as they passed under the light – two men with a useless arm apiece slung up under their greatcoats, both supporting a third who hopped between with one leg stuck out stiffly in front of him – a leg which ended too short in a dirty bandage.

Aylmer swung away to 'H' lines, and I quickened my pace to 'B'. Inside the golden gloom of the marquee Sister was at the entrance directing the men while Tilney scuttled round with hot-water bottles. Sister gestured over her shoulder at the half-dozen walking wounded already sitting slumped on the edge of their beds. 'Get them moving, Nurse Girvan.' I went to them and began to shake bowed shoulders: they were exhausted but I had to rouse them – they must get themselves undressed and into bed – we had so little time before the stretcher cases began to arrive. I had not finished serving them with hot Bovril when the orderlies carried in the first of the stretchers – and the discarded clothing was still littering the floor. I thrust the last mug into the waiting hands and picked up a muddy tunic, and as I did so I caught sight of the shoulder title – it was that of Robbie's regiment. My hand froze a moment, then I pulled the dirty khaki closer and read the battalion number – Robbie's battalion number. I began to shake. Then I heard Sister calling me sharply so I bundled the tunic into the sack along with its trousers and seized another one to thrust in as I ran – but even as I did so I read the title, and on that shoulder too were the familiar markings. Oh Robbie, oh my brother.

But there was no time to think; stretcher after stretcher was being carried in until the floor of the ward was covered with long brown shapes. Sister was walking down the rows of wounded studying the labels, and Tilney was ready waiting at the other side. Sister gestured to me and I climbed on to the first of the rigid mattresses and knelt there. As the orderlies brought the stretcher alongside I lifted the man's arms and pulled them round my neck so that he could hang on, then I slipped my own hands beneath his buttocks and with muscles straining helped to haul him on to the bed. The orderlies moved off for the next stretcher and I jumped down, quickly tugged the blanket round the befouled khaki and rushed to the next bed. On the opposite side Tilney's slight figure was hauling in her turn.

We got the fractures settled, then the next man managed to roll himself over on to the mattress; his eyes closed with the effort of it as I wrapped him up. On again – a boy now, with white glistening face and open, unfocused eyes. He muttered and moved restlessly as we slid him on to the bed; I slipped my hand out from beneath his back and saw that it was smeared scarlet with fresh blood. I called to Sister, holding up my dripping hand, and she rushed to my side. 'The dressing tray, Nurse – quickly.' I flew down the ward for it.

As I came back she was speaking to the boy, soothingly, quietly – his eyes looked up at hers and he stopped muttering and managed to smile. I helped roll him over and we saw that the bright blood was swiftly colouring the darkness of his back. Sister began to cut away the stained bandages. 'There's no time to fetch Captain Adams – wring out that gauze for me, Nurse.' As soon as I had put the Eusol-soaked pad into her hand she thrust it hard into the hole in the boy's shoulder and pressed down. 'Bandage, now.' The orderly lifted the boy's trunk so I could loop the bandage round him, Sister eased her hand out as I tightened it and then together we pulled and pulled until at last the bleeding slowly began to lessen. We stood watching it, then Sister gave a nod of satisfaction, tied the bandage as tight as she could and laid the boy back against the folded blanket. 'I think he'll do now, but the minute we've got these last two in bed, run over to the reception hut and ask Captain Adams to come as soon as he can.' The orderly ducked his head in assent and went for another stretcher.

The next man was square-shouldered and heavy, and

I had to struggle to lift him. His eyes stayed closed and his face was so drained of blood it was blue-white under the grime – I could scarcely hear his breathing. By the time I had bundled him up in his blankets, Tilney was already putting the last man to bed. Sister came over to me. 'I'll have to go over to the next marquee – they're short of a VAD and they've just started taking in. You can go off now if you want to, Nurse Girvan – thanks.'

Tilney started down to the kitchen to make drinks. 'I'll give you a hand with those before I go.' I brushed aside her thanks – I did not want to go back to the hut yet and have to think about Robbie, under attack.

The man with the blue-white face did not stir when I offered him a drink; I went on to finish the rest of the side – perhaps he would be awake by then. When I got back to him his eyes till stayed closed, although I felt sure he was not unconscious. I raised my voice and lifted his good arm, but his hand would not take hold of the mug so I slipped my arm under his neck and raised his face a little and put the rim to his mouth – still it would not open. I stood for a moment, baffled. Captain Adams came up beside me. 'Sister did a good job with that haemorrhage – I've left the dressing in place until the morning. What's the matter with this one?' He picked up the red-bordered field card and scanned it quickly. 'He's been knocked about, but I've seen worse.'

'He won't drink.'

The MO lifted the limp wrist and held it for a minute, looking down at the man with narrowed eyes, then he motioned me away. He spoke softly. 'The poor blighter's given up, he's been in France too long and lost too much blood – you must get him to drink, Nurse Girvan, otherwise he's had it.' He looked round the crowded ward before turning back to me with a bitter smile. 'The American medical units are giving blood transfusions, so I'm told – but we haven't the time or the equipment. They've had him on a saline drip at the CCS, but that's not going to be enough – he must be made to drink.

God knows we need every experienced sergeant-major we've got.'

I went back to the bed and saw this time the small crown above the sergeant's three stripes – I had been so conscious of the Lancashire and Cheshire badges that I had not noticed them before. The man still lay unmoving, and I stood uncertainly holding the mug – I was very tired, perhaps Tilney . . . ? The patient in the next bed stirred and a hoarse whisper asked, ''Ow's Ben, Sister?'

I moved across to him. 'Is that his name, Ben?'

'Aye, Ben – Ben Olden.' On his shoulder, too, I saw the titles of Robbie's battalion, and shuddered inwardly. Olden – an uncommon name. Then with a sudden tearing shock I realized – it was not Olden, but Holden, Sergeant Holden – Robbie's company sergeant-major. I turned round and stared down at the ghastly face above the filthy khaki and a fierce irrational anger swept over me. He had left my brother, he had deserted Robbie. Who would carry Robbie in now if he were wounded? Then I took hold of myself, and felt very ashamed. This was the man who had risked his life for Eddie and now it was he who lay dying in front of me.

I bent down over the dirt-smeared face and held the mug to his mouth again. 'Please – you must drink.' His eyelids did not waver, but I saw the bloodless lips close more tightly. Captain Adams was right, he had given up – he did not want to live. I spoke to him softly but very clearly. 'I'm damned if I'll let you die, Ben Holden.' There was no flicker of life on the muddy face.

I took to my heels and ran down to the kitchen. I warmed milk and recklessly threw in eggs, sugar, brandy and beat them quickly together in a jug. Then I rushed into Sister's bunk and began to look for the rubber tubing and glass funnel – I would force him to drink; I knew how to do it from long ago on Foldus Ward. I remembered sliding the wriggling red tube down the nostril of the paralysed Belgian – but then I remembered the Belgian next to him and hesitated – that soldier had resisted, just as this man would resist. Sister and I had had to hold him down as he struggled – and if this man struggled he would wear himself out and die anyway – so that could not be the answer. I stood still and searched my memory, and thought of Robbie – oh God, was he even now lying in another of these great tents, perhaps dying, without even the strength to ask for me to come to him? The pain stabbed at my heart as I thought of my brother's white face and dark eyes and saw them in my mind's eye – not Robbie as he was now, a man and a soldier, but Robbie as he had been long ago, a frightened child lying on Nanny's full bosom as she had coaxed him to drink. And I had the answer. My own small breasts under my stained white apron could not match Nanny's, but they would have to do.

I ran back to the kitchen and took down a white china feeding cup and put it on a tray with the jug. When I got back up the ward I saw he had not moved – he lay so still that for a heart-stopping moment I thought he was already dead. Then I saw the faint beat of his pulse at the temple and put my burden carefully down on the locker. I went to fetch the screens and carefully arranged them round the bed, so that the two of us were enclosed in a little private room of our own. Then I took off my apron, unfastened my cardigan and unbuttoned the bodice of my frock. I glanced down at the curve of my breasts under the soft cashmere of my vest and prayed they would be good enough as I began to slide myself carefully into the bed on his uninjured side. He was heavy, too heavy – but I managed to wriggle my way sideways until I was kneeling with his shoulders on my lap – and his muddy brown hair resting on my chest. I put my hand gently under his stubbly chin and turned his head until his cheek lay against the fullness of my right breast, then I curved my hand round his face and held him there as I whispered, 'Ben, you must drink, Ben.' He did not move, but I knew he was listening –

unwillingly perhaps, but he was listening. I spoke softly, soothingly, as Nanny had done to a tired, unhappy child. 'Ben, in a little while I'm going to give you a drink, a nice warm drink, and you must be a very good boy and drink it all down, just for me.'

I touched his cheek, then I reached for the feeding cup and held it ready while I put my finger between his pale lips and gently parted his teeth. I felt the soft warmth of his tongue on my fingertip as I slid in the china spout. I whispered, 'Drink, Ben – please drink,' as I tipped the liquid slowly into his mouth. The muscles of his throat tensed under my hand – and then he began to swallow. I murmured to him, 'Good boy, Ben, good boy. A little more now, just a little more.' As he finished each cupful I refilled it, and he drank again, until the whole jug was empty.

My hand was shaking as I put the empty feeding cup back on the locker. I sat holding him for a while and then, at last, I felt him move – slowly he turned his head and pressed his face into my breast. I sat quite still, gently stroking his hair. Then I whispered, 'Sleep now, Ben Holden,' as I slowly slid out of the bed and eased his head back on to the pillow. I bent over him, my legs trembling with tiredness and relief, and murmured, 'Goodnight, Ben.' And as I watched, his eyelids flickered and slowly opened; bloodshot grey-blue eyes stared up at me, and for a moment his mouth moved – then his eyelids dropped like a shutter and he fell asleep.

I carried the tray in shaking hands down between the rows of beds; exhausted men groaned and grunted in their sleep as I passed them. Tilney was bent over the table, her white cap gleaming. 'I'm just going off,' I told her.

She looked up at me, grinning. 'I don't know what on earth you were doing up there, Girvan, but Sister said to leave you to it, so I did. You'd better get straight to bed now – you look like a ghost.'

Aylmer was already fast asleep; she had put a hot-water bottle in my bed – it was lukewarm now – but I clutched it gratefully to my chest and thought of Robbie, until my tired body slept.

When I began to dress next morning I found a louse on my vest. I tumbled all my clothes together and took them to be disinfected. There was no time to wash my hair – I only hoped that it had been safe in its tight plait.

By the time I went on duty, all the men had been washed and changed: Tilney had worked hard. I went straight to the kitchen and mixed more eggs and milk, and took my jug and feeder up the ward. Ben Holden was a better colour this morning. I spoke to him and gently touched his cheek, and when his eyes opened I held out the feeding cup, but he turned his head a little and his mouth worked and I realized he was trying to speak. At last, with a great effort he got the words out. 'Captain Girvan – 'e were back with Transport when they come – so 'e should be all right.' I caught at the rail of the bed – my legs would scarcely support me – and it was some time before I could whisper my thanks. Then I put the spout into his mouth and began to feed him. His eyes had closed again, but he swallowed all that I gave him.

As soon as I took my tray back Sister said briskly, 'We've got to get these dressings changed, Nurse Girvan – and Captain Adams will want to see them to decide who's got to go to the theatre.'

Captain Adams' face was impassive as he studied each wound and marked notes for the theatre, but when we arrived at Ben Holden's bed he gave a pleased nod. 'You're looking much better, Sergeant-Major, much better.' Ben Holden smiled at me as I reached to unpin the bandage holding his splint in place. The dressing had dried in the hole in his left arm and I had to pull the gauze away from the torn muscle. His face went rigid, but he did not move. I put in fresh packing, bound it up again and moved down to his thigh. Captain Adams made his inspection and then said, 'You've been lucky,

350

Sergeant – no bones broken there.' I looked down at the jagged, gaping tear and thought how the war had changed our definition of luck. The MO moved over to Sister's side of the ward, and as I re-packed the wound I asked, 'How did you know who I was, Sergeant Holden?'

'I saw you at Liverpool Street, when we went out first time. And I saw your photograph, the one the Captain carries – he showed it to me, after . . .' His voice trailed off and I knew he was thinking of Eddie.

'Thank you for bringing Mr Girvan in – it would have been terrible for him to die out there – alone.' I finished off the dressing in silence and then helped him into a more comfortable position. 'That's all for now, Ben – I mean, Sergeant Holden.'

He said gruffly, 'You can call me Ben if you want, Sister – seeing as I don't have a nickname like Ginger, there.' The red-haired man in the next bed grinned at me; Ben Holden looked suddenly anxious.

I was grateful to him for living, so I said recklessly, 'Then I will, Ben,' and pushed my trolley on.

It was impossible to call the boy who had haemorrhaged anything other than Lennie – he told me he was nineteen, but he had the manner and speech of a small child, and he sobbed like a child when I dressed the quite small wound on his foot. Captain Adams told me not to disturb the dressing on his shoulder – he would look at it under the anaesthetic in the theatre first. When he heard this the boy began to whimper.

Ben Holden called across the space, 'Don't tha mither thisenn, Lennie lad, we'll a' go together – mekk a proper musical turn like.' The sweat was standing out on his forehead by the time he had finished speaking, but his words seemed to soothe young Lennie, and the whimpers ceased.

Captain Adams started operating an hour later, and once the stretcher bearers arrived Sister and I had to race up and down the ward all day. Lennie came back dribbling blood from his mouth; I wedged a kidney dish under his unconscious cheek and ran to inject the next theatre case. Another was carried out before he had had his injection, and Sister chased after the stretcher, skirts flying, the hypodermic clutched in her fist like a gun. I turned to laugh at her, then a small middle-aged Lancs and Cheshire corporal began to vomit and I darted back to him; he was shuddering violently and as I held him still I saw Sister come back again and help to lift Ben Holden on to the bed opposite. He looked very pale, but his chest was rising and falling steadily.

Later in the evening I saw he had come round and was watching me as I steadied the corporal through another bout of racking sickness. I smiled at him over the wiry grey head and he grinned back and dropped one eyelid in a wink. For a moment a memory tugged at my tired brain, then a chest case began to gasp and choke down the ward so I laid the corporal quickly back, rammed the bowl into his pillow and took to my heels again.

When I sat down next to MacLeod in the mess at supper, her freckled face was unusually gloomy. 'I've been transferred to nights, Girvan.'

'Hard lines,' I replied, 'but at least you'll be able to see something of Tilney.'

'That's true – and I don't mind nights all that much, it's just – well, it's on the German wards.'

Sears said, 'How rotten. I didn't know you could speak German, Mac.'

Mac shook her head. 'I can't, that's why Matron's sending me – no fraternization with the enemy – as if *I'd* fraternize.' Her voice was bitter; we all knew that Mac's only brother had been killed on the Somme last year.

It was Aylmer who broke the silence. Her face was rather pink as she said, 'God tells us to love our enemies.'

Mac turned round and snarled, 'Then let Him damn well nurse them – I don't want to.' She got up and stalked out and there was a shocked silence. But whether it was in response to Mac's blasphemy or to Aylmer's text I could not tell.

CHAPTER NINE

Within a few days our new patients had become our old patients, and we began to wonder when they would be evacuated; but the hospitals in Britain were still busy with the casualties from Ypres, while in France the long autumn of battles was finally over and no new convoys were likely – so for the time being they stayed with us. Then Captain Adams told us that the high command were getting worried about the shortage of experienced men. 'Apparently the hospitals aren't to send any more back at the moment unless they've bought it for good – and not even some of those – so it looks as if these poor devils'll be here for Christmas.'

I was sorry for the men's sake that their hopes of Blighty were receding, yet for myself I was glad. I had got to know them – they were familiar personalities now, friends even, and knowing how each man would react, and how he wanted me to behave in turn, made the morning dressing round so much less of an ordeal. The middle-aged L & CLI corporal who had suffered so badly from sickness when he first came back from the theatre was Lofty – his real name was Makins but he was so short his nickname was inevitable. And I knew that Lofty liked to hum steadily all the time that I dealt with his arm – when I dressed the wound on his leg then he was ready to chat about his wife and family, and his eldest son, already at the front. Ginger, in the bed next to Ben Holden, liked to engage me in flirtatious banter: 'I bet you're going to have tea with the MO today, Sister – lucky so-and-so.' His body tensed and he groaned as

I pulled the last sodden twist of gauze out of the hole in his buttocks, then he managed to twist his head round on the pillow and wink at me. 'Ah, the soft touch of a woman's hands is music to a lonely soul.' I smiled back at him as I picked up the syringe of Eusol. 'Just imagine this is best champagne I'm using, then it won't sting so much.'

'If it were, it'd break my heart to have it wasted on me backside – ouch! It's cold. Come on, Sister – hurry up with me clean nappy or I'll catch me death.'

'Coming up, Sergeant.'

'Ah, now you have hurt me.'

'Ginger, I'm so sorry.'

He gave a big complacent grin. 'That's better now – it were me feelings what was hurt – you not calling me by me proper name – us red-heads are very sensitive.'

'I am sorry, Ginger, I wasn't thinking, Ginger – Ginger how could I have been so thoughtless – all finished now, Ginger – Ginger you can put your pyjamas back on . . .' He started to laugh and I laughed with him, then moved on to Ben Holden's bed.

Ben Holden never tried to flirt with me. He always said a polite 'Good morning, Sister.' Then he would lie stoically still as I worked over him, only the quickening of his breathing betraying the pain I had to cause him. When I had finished he would thank me gravely, and I would smile and move on. We followed this pattern for several mornings, and then one day I was clumsy. I felt tired and ill and I had heard nothing from Robbie for a couple of days, so I was careless and caught the exposed ending of a nerve hard with my forceps. His face went into a rigid spasm of agony. I watched, horrified, and felt the tears come into my eyes, but he said nothing and I could not speak. I made myself carry on, and then, when I had finished binding him up I managed to whisper, 'I'm sorry Ben, I'm so sorry.'

He put out his uninjured arm and rested his hand over

mine for a moment. 'It's all right, Sister – you're doing your best.'

Young Lennie was asleep, so I went past; I could not face his shoulder yet. I began to unwrap the slimy bandages of the man with the smashed jaw. I knew I should say something – he could not speak and he looked forward to my chatting to him as I did his dressing, but today my numbed brain could not form the words, and I watched the disappointment dawn in his patient eyes. All I could say as I finished was 'I'm sorry – I'm sorry.' And he too touched my hand in understanding and comfort. I felt very ashamed.

As I dressed Dennison's foot the cramps squeezed my belly, but I had not finished: there was still Young Lennie's shoulder and he was awake now. I looked over at Sister but she was busy on the other side, so I took a deep breath and fetched what I needed for Lennie.

He lay with his cheek pressed into the pillow, but one eye stared up at me beseechingly. I managed to smile back and began to unwrap his shoulder. He started to whimper at once, and Ben Holden called across to him – he always did, he was very skilful at distracting Lennie – asking him simple, childlike questions which Lennie would answer falteringly. The foul-smelling pus poured out of the wound and the bile rose in my throat – I tried to tell myself what a fool I was to mind after all this time, but I did mind today: I felt so dreadfully ill and the pain in my belly was mounting – my monthly cramps were worse than usual. Somehow I got the drainage tube in and managed to pack the wound with the clean dressing, but my hands were shaking as I pinned the bandage in place and whispered, 'There, Lennie – all over now, you've been very brave.' Then I stumbled away, clinging to the trolley for support.

Dimly I saw that the orderly had pushed several screens to one side, against the wall of the marquee, and now I blundered behind them and dropped crouching on the floor beside the reeking trolley, thrusting my nails into the palms of my hands as I tried to stop myself moaning aloud.

It was Sister who slipped through the screens. 'Nurse Girvan, you silly girl – why didn't you say? I could have managed without you for a while. Come along now.' She put her hand under my arm and helped me up. As I came out of my refuge I saw Ben Holden look at me anxiously, then quickly turn his eyes away. I walked very slowly down the ward – it seemed to stretch into infinity – but at last I was huddled in a chair in the bunk while Sister filled a hot-water bottle and shook out the aspirin. She was still scolding, 'Goodness knows how long you would have been there if Holden hadn't had the sense to call me over and tell me you were ill.' Even in my pain I felt my face crimson. Sister glanced at me and said robustly, 'Don't be silly, they've got wives and sisters at home. Besides,' she smiled, 'he was very discreet. Stay here until you feel better, I must get back to the ward now.'

By the middle of December winter had set in and it was very cold. I began to sleep in my vest again and we shivered in the darkness as we dressed in the morning. Bundled up in layers of jerseys, I tramped to the ward in my overcoat and boots – but underneath I wore my fine petticoats, and enjoyed their soft silken rustle as I moved.

In the marquee the orderly poked ineffectually at the stove and it would splutter and sulk until one day I found Ben Holden had struggled out of bed and was hunched on a chair in front of it. His large square hand was delicately feeding in pieces of coke, and I watched him manipulate irons and damper until a small blaze flared up and he sat back with a grunt of satisfaction. 'You shouldn't be out of bed yet, Ben.'

He swivelled his body round carefully to face me, then said, 'Don't you worry, Sister, I can manage.' I opened my mouth to argue with him, then realized I would be wasting my time.

Over the next few days Ginger and Lofty also staggered out of bed and into their blues, and began to
make themselves useful, too. When Lofty received a
photograph from home of his son on leave, posing in his
spick-and-span uniform with the rest of his family, he
met me with it first thing in the morning. 'Look, Sister
– he's a fine young shaver – and me missus – she's still
a good-looking lass for all she's given me six healthy
childer – there's me two eldest girls, see.' I took the
photograph and admired it and asked names and ages
and Lofty beamed with pride. Ginger came up and I
asked him if he were married.

He grinned. 'Nay – me and Ben are having a good
look round first – we're choosy, like.'

Lofty winked at me. 'They don't know nowt yet, do
they, Sister? They'll find out – when it comes down to
it it's lasses as do the choosing!'

I left them wrangling by the stove; I knew they would
keep it nicely glowing and there was no problem with
running out of fuel these days, since Ben Holden had a
firm way with the orderly – I had never seen him work
so hard.

I was off that afternoon, and at lunch I discovered
Aylmer was too, so we decided to go for a brisk walk
down by the estuary. Before we set out, Aylmer picked
up her basket. 'I must buy some potatoes on the way
back – for the men,' she explained, seeing my puzzled
look. I still looked puzzled so she laughed and said, 'I've
promised them some chips after tea; Sister doesn't mind
and they love them.'

I began to unearth my basket. 'I'll get some for my
ward, too – if you'll tell me how to cook them.'

'Don't worry about that, Girvan. Just walk in with
the frying pan and one of the men will take it off you in
a trice; all you need do is supervise.'

It was Ben Holden who took the frying pan off me. As
I did the temperature round, I watched him set Ginger to
the peeling and slicing while he melted the dripping over

the stove. A delicious aroma soon filled the marquee and I could hardly stop myself laughing at the look of satisfaction on Ben Holden's face as he deftly flicked and turned the chips to a golden crispness. I said teasingly, 'My, what a good cook you are, Ben!' And Ginger chipped in, 'Aye, Ben'll make some lucky lass a fine 'usband one day – fully trained he is – you could go further and fare worse, Sister!' One eye dropped in a wink and his expression was so full of mischief that I burst out laughing. Ben Holden's face turned brick-red and Ginger said quickly, 'By the colour o' you Ben I reckon that job's too hot for you – fancy a swap?'

Ben growled, 'Tha'd slice them taters a sight faster me lad if tha'd shut thy gob and stopped cackling like a parrot. Lofty, bring us plates, an' you can tek 'em round – these first'uns are for Lennie.'

Young Lennie's face lit up and he touched the hot chips delicately with his fingertip as if he could scarcely believe they were real. Lofty offered some to Sister and myself and we ate them guiltily – of course, it was against the rules, but they were delicious. When he had finished frying, Ben Holden limped over to Lennie's bed and played simple, childish games with him; they were like two little boys together over their cards.

Sister sent me to early supper and Tilney came across to the mess to get warm before her night duty. She asked me how Young Lennie had been over the day, and I told her that although his shoulder was no better he had seemed more cheerful in the evening. 'He and Ben Holden were like a pair of children together over their game of snap – the men are so easily amused, aren't they?'

Tilney looked at me with her small, sharp eyes. 'Don't be so patronizing, Girvan. They all know Lennie's not more than ninepence in the shilling and so they make an effort – that doesn't mean the rest of them are without intelligence.'

I tried to protest, 'I never said . . .'

'But you think it, don't you? Officers are brave and clever, other ranks may be brave but they're not very bright – good enough for footmen or gamekeepers, *but* – there's always a but with women like you, isn't there?' I stared at her angry face; she stood up and shook out her skirt and bent over me. 'It was quiet last night so I was catching up on my reading – Carlyle's *French Revolution* – Holden got up to fetch a bottle for Lennie and when he'd taken it back he stopped to have a word with me, and before I knew it, there we were arguing the rights and wrongs of Robespierre, in whispers. He's read his Carlyle, you know, and understood it.' She stumped off.

I looked down at my enamel bowl of stew; Miss Ling had suggested Carlyle to me once, but I had never got beyond the first page. As I chewed another gristly mouthful, I wondered uneasily if there could possibly be any truth in what Tilney had said of me.

Next morning Captain Adams came round with us as we were doing the dressings. He studied Ben Holden's arm as I uncovered it, then said, 'It's healing quite nicely, Sergeant.'

Ben Holden asked hesitantly, 'I were wondering, sir, if I'd get back full use o' me arm – you see I'm a left-handed shoveller, it's important in me job.'

Captain Adams pursed his lips a moment, then said, 'I don't see why you shouldn't, by the look of it now – what did you do before you enlisted, Sergeant-Major?'

'I were on the footplate – a fireman with the Lancashire and Yorkshire Railway.' And as he spoke his glance swivelled to me for a moment – and then I knew.

After I had finished the dressings I went back to Ben Holden – he was sitting on his bed writing a letter. He looked up as I approached and I said abruptly, 'I saw you, just before the war – you showed my nephews round the footplate at Manchester.'

He nodded. 'Aye, that's right – I were firing to old Jacky Spence.'

And as he spoke, for a moment I was back again under the echoing cavern of Victoria with Gerald tall and straight beside me, tipping a grimy young footplateman before turning to me and holding out his arm, smiling his beautiful, ethereal smile. Then I returned to the gloomy marquee with the canvas flapping dolefully, and pain and sickness all around me. I said at last, 'He was killed, my fiancé, in the spring of '15.' There did not seem anything else to say so I turned and walked away, fighting to control my tears.

Young Lennie was very feverish that day, so Sister sent me to sponge him down in the afternoon. He was childishly pleased with the extra attention and I pretended to splash him and he squealed with delight. But his small store of energy was soon exhausted and he was already half-asleep by the time I had towelled him dry. Then I heard Ben Holden's voice: 'Sister, look who's here!' He sounded excited so I pushed the screen quickly aside, 'Who is . . . Oh!' There, at the end of the ward, with a dusting of snow on his greatcoat and his cane tucked elegantly under one arm – was Robbie. I picked up my skirts and ran between the beds, my eyes never leaving the smiling face until I was safe in his arms.

He told me he had been sent down to Boulogne, and had managed to wangle a lift in a staff car to Étaples, and now he was here. Sister smiled and said she could manage alone for a couple of hours, so I began to tug him towards the porch, but he pulled me gently back. 'Just a moment, Hellie – I must have a word with the men.' I clung to his arm as he walked round the ward. He chatted to all the L&CLI patients – he seemed to know each face and the name which went with it. He delighted Ginger by chaffing him about his tie being under his ear, and brought a pleased glow to Lofty's face as he asked after his son. He talked very gently to Young Lennie, who gazed up at him adoringly, and then he went on to tell Dennison that his great pal had sent his best wishes – and thanks for the food parcel which had arrived after Dennison had been wounded, which they had all enjoyed – especially the contents of the tobacco tin! Dennison went scarlet: I guessed there had been illicit liquor concealed in that tin, and laughed with my brother at the private's discomfiture until Dennison began to grin as well. All the way round the ward Ben Holden limped beside my brother, every inch a sergeant-major; he should have looked ridiculous in his ill-fitting hospital blues, and with his arm in a sling, but he did not.

I looked up at Robbie, my Robbie – Captain Girvan, an experienced company commander, with his men. I could scarcely contain my pride and joy – then I saw the hollows in his cheeks and the tiredness in his eyes, and remembered that he was only just twenty-two. I shivered. He finished his conversation, shook hands with Ben Holden and then looked down at me, with his old sweet smile. I smiled back and thrust the war away from me and thought only of the next two hours.

A few snowflakes were tossing gently in the wind as we left the camp and wandered down to the dunes near the estuary. Then we plunged over the shifting sand until we came to a sheltered hollow. We slipped and slid down to the bottom of it, and just as we sank down on to a hummock of rough grass the wintry sun broke out from between the clouds. I was so happy.

We did not talk much as I sat in the shelter of Robbie's arm and breathed in the cold salty air. It was enough that he was alive and warm and whole beside me; but all too soon he took out his watch, rose to his feet and pulled me up. We clung to each other for a moment, and then began to trudge back to the camp.

Next morning Tilney called me into the kitchen before she went off. She had a copy of *The Tatler* in her hand, and she pointed at one of the photographs. I stared down at a pre-war picture of myself – in riding habit and glossy top hat, mounted on my beautiful Melody. The caption underneath read: 'At a meet of the Cheshire at Hatton Park. Lady Helena Girvan is the second daughter of the Earl of Pickering, and is an enthusiastic follower of hounds. She is at present serving as a VAD in France.'

Tilney said, 'Dennison's aunt is a lady's maid – when he wrote to her he told her our names – and Auntie's mistress kindly parted up with this. The men have been passing it round all through breakfast; they're quite stunned at the idea of an aristocrat in their midst.' She smiled at me maliciously: 'Well, Girvan – it looks as if I'll have to practise my curtsey before I dare speak to *you* in future!' She went off to breakfast, and I put the magazine down as if it had burnt my fingers, then walked on to the ward.

I could sense the change in the atmosphere at once; the usual morning greetings were very subdued, and eyes followed me warily as I moved about. I knew I should make some casual reference to that wretched photo – toss off a joke, let them see I was their nurse, just the same as ever – but I did not know how to do it, and the quieter I became, the more self-conscious they were. I felt a spurt of bitter anger at Dennison's aunt and her interfering mistress, as Lofty carefully talked about the weather all through his dressing, and would not meet my eye. Ginger, lively Ginger, blushed scarlet as he dropped his trousers to let me dress his backside; he was totally tongue-tied – and so was I.

I caught Sister in the sluice and asked her what I should do, but she was busy and only shrugged as she replied, 'There isn't anything you *can* do, Nurse Girvan – titles do make a difference.' As she left she threw over her shoulder, 'I'd rather not have known myself.' I felt quite devastated.

As I followed her out Ben Holden limped past on his way back from the latrines; although he smiled he did not speak, and now I was angry with him – he at least had always known who my family were – so why could he not treat me as usual? Then I felt ashamed of my anger – Ben Holden was acting no differently – he had never had the flow of easy chatter with me that Ginger and Lofty had.

Aylmer was off duty with me that afternoon. 'Are you coming to buy potatoes, Girvan?'

I filled my basket too, but as we walked back I wondered whether they would be used – would the men be prepared to cook chips in front of a lady, an earl's daughter? After tea I dragged on my mackintosh and picked my way reluctantly over the slippery duckboards to B.4.

Dumping my basket in the kitchen I walked out into the ward – and sensed the suppressed excitement at once. All the men who were up were grouped round the stove in the centre, and the others were alert and watching from their beds. I stepped forward, hesitantly – and caught sight of Young Lennie's eyes peeping over the edge of the blanket, round with delight. The screens were alongside his bed and as I stepped forward Ben Holden emerged from behind them – but it was a very different Ben Holden. His brown hair had been parted in the centre and ruthlessly sleeked back with water so that it clung to his square head; in place of his red tie he had knotted an enormous white bow, and two ridiculous trailing tails of gauze had been sewn to the back of his blues jacket. Pinned to the sling on his injured arm was a neatly folded white pillowcase, and in the other hand he was carrying one of the water buckets which had been burnished until it shone like silver – a fine wisp of steam rose from it. I stood astounded, and Ben Holden stepped foward, very stiff-legged, lifted the shining bucket and said, in a voice of the utmost solemnity, 'Would you care for some tea, my lady? We have Indian or China – the Indian is a little strong, so if you would prefer China the footman will add more hot water to the pail.'

A grinning Ginger, with another large white bow at his neck, appeared with the big ward kettle. I glanced at the men agog either side, and then looked again at

Ben Holden's parody of a butler and felt laughter well up inside me. I knew the charade they wanted me to play, but I had an even better idea. I stepped forward, pulled out the cotton skirts of my uniform dress and swept down to the polished linoleum in a full-scale court curtsey. My forbidden silk petticoat rustled in the silence as I slowly rose again. Then I extended the tips of my fingers to Ben Holden and said, in an exaggerated drawl, 'My dear Lord Benjamin, how delightful to see you – such an unexpected pleasure! And I see your friend, Mr Rufus Auburn, is with you, how do you do?' I shook the bemused Ginger by the hand, and his face broke into a broad freckled grin. I swung back to Ben Holden, and we stood facing each other. Our eyes were exactly on a level, so I saw the momentary surprise in his, then he dropped the bucket, put his hand to his waist, bent in a deep bow – and as he straightened up, seized hold of my hand and swept it to his lips. There was a roar of appreciation from the ward, then an expectant silence fell – all eyes were on me, but for once I was not disconcerted.

I retrieved my hand from Ben Holden's grasp and extended it in a regal gesture towards the row of iron bedsteads. 'But Lord Benjamin – I see you are entertaining a large house party this weekend – do introduce me to your guests, and I shall pour tea for them.'

Lofty rushed forward with an enamel mug and I dipped it into the steaming pail and glided over to Lennie's bed. His eyes shone. I turned to Ben Holden, 'Do, please, introduce me, Lord Benjamin.'

He glanced at me, then back at Lennie, and carefully lengthening his Lancashire vowels he said, 'Sir Leonard Smith-Brown-Jones, Lady Helena.' Lennie's white face beamed at me as he held out his thin hot hand. I took it in mine.

'How do you do, Sir Leonard – I believe I saw you at Henley recently, such a beautiful afternoon.'

We progressed solemnly from bed to bed. The titles

Ben Holden manufactured became more and more improbable – the men were rocking with laughter, but Ben and I managed to keep our faces straight. A flood of Society chit-chat fell from my lips with an ease that I had never possessed at the real Hurlingham or Goodwood. Dennison, in the guise of the Duke of Anaconda, claimed a series of incredible wins at Ascot, and I congratulated him gravely and moved on to ask about the health of the Emir of Elongate's thirty-seven children. Lofty answered delightedly. Finally I spoke graciously to a blue-eyed private of the Devons masquerading as a Danish prince, and then I had circumnavigated the ward.

Ben ushered me politely out of the entrance with a series of bows; I waved goodbye and dashed into the kitchen and leant over the table and laughed until my sides ached – I could hear the excited shouts and laughter of the men in the ward – but however was I to make my reappearance? Then I caught sight of the basket I had dumped earlier. I picked it up, marched into the ward and held it aloft with both hands: 'Chips tonight!'

There was a yell of delight followed by a storm of clapping. Ben Holden called, 'Fetch pan, Ginger – you're a working lad again now,' took the basket from me and headed towards the stove. I went into the bunk and began to prepare the evening medicines. As I came out with my tray the delicious smell of frying potatoes met me; and I realized that I had not felt so light-hearted for months.

CHAPTER TEN

Lofty's arm was healing well and the concentrated humming of the early days had ceased now; instead he talked of his wife and family all the way through the dressings. I listened and smiled and nodded as I wielded my forceps. 'Had a letter from the missus this morning – she says eldest lass is singing in *Messiah* at chapel this year – front row of the altos, and she's only fourteen.' He added wistfully, 'I'd like to have bin there, I likes a good *Messiah*.'

'Aye, me too.' Ben Holden had just come back from doing the washing up with Ginger. 'There's nowt like *Messiah* for getting folks ready for Christmas. I'll push trolley back for you, Sister, while Ginger gets his trousers down.'

Ginger looked almost serious. 'Me old Mam, bless 'er, she used to take me to *Messiah* every Christmas when I were a youngster – I didn't allus fancy goin' then – too long for me it were, an' chapel seats's powerful 'ard – I'd start wriggling and she'd clip me one right across shin, low down where minister couldn't see – she knows what's right, me Mam does. But now, well I'd like to be 'earing it this Christmas, truth to tell.'

He climbed on to the bed and lay face down for me. 'Slide across a little, Ginger, there's a good boy.'

He turned his head and grinned at me over his shoulder. 'Here I am, at feet of most beautiful nurse in the world – and all she does is tell me I'm a good boy.'

I was quick with my reply, 'Ah, but we're both of us flatterers!' And laughed down at the comic face he pulled.

Ben Holden had taken his outer bandages off ready

for me. I dealt quickly with his thigh, then he shifted slightly so that I could tackle his arm. He did not speak, but his eyes watched my face all the time I worked over him. I had grown used to his steady scrutiny – it seemed to help him bear the pain and discomfort. When I had finished he said, 'Thank you, Sister,' and reached for his blues.

I moved on to Lennie; his pitiable whimpering began before I had even touched him. As I began to unpin the bandage, Ben Holden pushed through the screen and took a firm hold of Lennie's left hand. I looked down at the ruins of his right shoulder; it was not healing. The foul yellow pus stank more each day, and Captain Adams had said it might have to be dressed in the evening as well. Sister and I had looked at each other in horror – as it was, the daily dressing was more of an ordeal than he could stand, but he was too weak to be anaesthetized for it. Today as I pulled out the slime-coated rubber tube he began to scream – a thin, high-pitched noise like a rabbit caught in a trap. Ben Holden's grip tightened and his voice deepened as he talked on steadily – he had lapsed into a dialect so thick I could not understand what he said. But it seemed to bring Lennie back from the brink; the terrible screaming stopped, though his breath still came in frantic, hunted gasps.

By the time I had finished the boy lay white and shaking on the bed.

Ben Holden said, 'I'll get the clean sheets – Ginger, fetch bowl.'

I washed my hands and then took hold of Lennie's good one and stood gripping it until he gradually calmed. Ben and Ginger came through the screens, Ginger put his burden on the locker and slipped away, but Ben Holden stayed to help me. In the pain and terror of his dressing Young Lennie was incontinent now: it happened every morning. I wiped between his buttocks with a handful of tow as Ben held him steady, then, very carefully, we eased him on to the edge of the soiled drawsheet so that I could wash his behind. Ben swung him over a little so that I could soap and rinse and towel dry his small floppy genitals, then, between us, we pulled out the dirty drawsheet, slid in a clean one and tucked him in. Ben said, 'Back in a minute, Lennie,' and the simple, childlike eyes followed his movements trustfully as he hefted the soiled linen in his one hand and set off down the ward. I followed with my bowls.

In the sluice I could not help myself. I burst out, 'He should never have been sent out, never! How could someone like him possibly understand what was happening?'

Ben Holden shrugged. 'We all knew that, Sister – and Captain Girvan tried everything he could to get him sent home, but it weren't no use. He'd volunteered see, like the rest of us. But the Captain kept an eye on him – and Lennie worships him, he does.'

I looked at the stocky man beside me. 'And I think he worships you too, Ben.' Ben Holden's face reddened, and he limped back into the ward without another word.

It was a Sunday, so the night VADs came in to tea. MacLeod threw herself down beside me and stared at her bun. Tilney called across. 'How are the enemy, Mac?'

Mac said shortly, 'Dying – just like the rest,' and picked up her cup. When she had drunk she turned to me. 'God knows, I didn't want to go on the German ward, but,' she sighed impatiently, 'they're frightened and in pain just like the others – and with no Blighty to look forward to. And, do you know, when they first come in they flinch as they see us walking towards them, as though they think we're going to stab them with a scalpel. God knows what they've been told about the British. But when all's said and done, they're only men – except the ones who are still boys.' Her face twisted. 'Oh, Girvan – I was so angry with Night Sister last night. We've got this boy in, he really is only a child – he can't be more than fifteen, and he's had both hands and both feet blown off by a shell. He just lies there all day, looking up at the roof, but whenever I go near him he keeps trying to ask for something. In the end I got one of the other prisoners to translate – he'd been a waiter in London before the war, so he speaks good English – and it seems that this poor child had had a row with his mother before he left – something quite trivial, the man said – but the boy's desperate now to tell her he's sorry. The other man offered to write a letter for him, so I spoke to Sister – we all know he can't live much longer – and after she'd bawled me out for even daring to ask, she went on about security, and suppose he was a spy sending information – I ask you, the state he's in! In any case I could have found somebody to censor it. And the worst thing was, he guessed I'd been asking – and his face when I had to say no!' She bent her head down and stared at her empty plate.

I spoke quickly, 'Mac – I'll do it if you want. I could come over tonight.'

Her face shot up. 'Oh Girvan, would you? I'd be so grateful – I didn't know you spoke German.'

'I spent two years, more than two years, studying in Germany before the war – in Munich.'

She gave a short laugh. 'Whatever you do, don't tell that to Matron – she'll have you arrested. Munich, that's one word I do know – this boy keeps sobbing, "Mutter" and "Munchen" – that's Munich, isn't it? He must come from there. Look, Sister's generally done her first round by ten – slip over after that and I'll smuggle you in. We'll have to be careful, there'll be all hell let loose if she finds out.'

'I'll come.' Then suddenly I thought: Munchen – it's little Franzl – it must be little Franzl! My stomach lurched and I hurriedly scrambled over the bench and out into the cold air. 'Oh, please God, not little Franzl!'

It was not little Franzl. A strange face looked hopelessly up at me from the pillow – a downy-skinned, child's face. He was attached to some kind of frame like a crucifix and only his eyes moved as I sat down beside him.

I spoke softly. 'Guten Abend, mein junger Freund, Ich bin gekommen den Brief zu Schreiben.' I saw the tears well up in his eyes and overflow to trickle down his thin cheeks. I wiped them gently away and took out my pen and writing case. 'Wie is die Adresse Ihrer Mutter?'

He began to sob, then with a great effort he got control of himself and started to dictate his letter. It was a jumbled, scarcely coherent catalogue of real and imagined misdeeds such as a boy would commit: a stolen spoonful of jam, a lie about a fishing expedition – I wrote down each word of the pitiful little confession and the anxious, pathetic apologies.

'I shouted at my mother, Sister.'

I whispered, 'She will understand, Karl, she will forgive you – I know she will.'

When he had finished he lay exhausted for a while, with his eyes closed. Then they opened again and sought mine. 'You speak good German, Sister.'

'I studied in Munich, before the war.'

'Sister, please talk to me a little of Munich, my home.'

So I talked of his home – of how I had stood on the Luitpold Bridge in the spring and watched the tumbling green waters of the Iser; of how I had stopped every day on my way down the Schellingstrasse to look at the Fürstenhaüser with their brightly painted scenes of knights in armour on prancing horses. 'Ah, yes, Sister – do you remember the knight on the left, waving his sword? I used to pretend I was he – I was only a child, then,' he added hastily. And I smiled at the child still, as I told him I did remember his knight, and the beautiful maiden below.

'Munich is a beautiful city, the most beautiful in the whole world – what did you like best in Munich, Sister?'

I pursed my lips and pretended to think a little. 'That is a difficult question, Karl – there are so many lovely buildings in Munich.' I saw his face flush with pleasure. 'But I think I liked best the Residenz Theatre – and all those plump golden cupids with their flowers – I visited the opera often in Munich, Karl, for it was singing that I was studying there.'

His face stilled and he whispered, 'My mother sings – when I was a little boy she would sing me to sleep every night.'

He did not ask, but I saw the longing in his eyes, so I bent over and touched his cheek. 'Then I will sing you to sleep tonight, liebe Karl.'

As I straightened my back I glanced down for a moment at that broken body under its coarse grey blanket – then my gaze returned to his fair young face and, softly, I began to sing.

> 'Guten Abend, gut Nacht,
> Mit Rosen bedacht,
> Mit Näglein besteckt,
> Schlüpf unter die Deck:'

Good evening, good night; slip under this flower-strewn coverlet, bedecked with roses – and I watched the cradle song of his countryman bring peace to this dying child. His eyes were fixed trustingly on mine:

> 'Morgen früh, wenn Gott will,
> Wirst du wieder geweckt.'

Tomorrow morning, if God wills it, you will wake again. If God wills it.

His eyes closed obediently at the final bidding:

> 'Schlaf nun selig und suß,
> Schau im Traum's Paradies.'

Sleep sweetly now and be blessed – and in your dreams may you see Paradise.

But after the last note had faded away his eyelids quivered and he gazed up at me again – but I knew it was not I he saw as he whispered, 'Mutter, liebste Mutter, kuss mich!' so I bent down and kissed his cold forehead, and he was smiling as he fell asleep.

I picked up my writing case and turned away, and as I walked down the ward I heard the voices in the darkness, whispering: 'Danke schön, Schwester,' 'Vielen Dank, Schwester', 'Gott segne sie, Schwester'.

And there in the entrance to the hut stood Night Sister, her face very cold. 'I shall report this to Matron first thing in the morning, Nurse Girvan.' She drew her skirts aside with a crackle of starch as I came towards her. I could see Mac's agonized face behind her shoulder, but I walked on. There was nothing to say.

But before I went to bed I huddled over my torch and wrote a quick note to Guy and then put the two letters together, addressed the envelope and crept out again to the post.

I was in the ward next morning when Matron came – I had just finished settling Lennie, and Ben and Ginger were still with me. She swept up the ward, her face mottled red with fury. 'Give me that letter, Nurse Girvan.'

I stood facing her, and said as calmly as I could, 'I have already sent it, Matron – to my brother.'

'To your brother! And where is your brother? I insist on knowing.'

I looked straight back and said, very distinctly, 'Major Lord Muirkirk is attached to General Gough's staff at Fifth Army Headquarters. He will ensure it is censored and sent on to the Red Cross in Switzerland.'

She was almost gobbling with fury now, but I managed to keep my gaze steady, grateful for the presence of Ginger and Ben Holden close behind me. Then I saw the flicker of cunning cross her face – she glanced beyond me and raised her voice so that it could be heard right the way across the ward. 'And do your patients here know that you visited the German hut last night?' I heard a sharp hiss of breath behind my shoulder, quickly suppressed. As I felt the blood drain from my face I knew what she would say, I knew how she had chosen to punish me. Her voice rang out again. 'So you, Nurse Girvan – a British nurse – not only chose to write a letter for a German prisoner, but you also sang to him – you sang to a Hun! And then, Nurse, you were so far lost to all human decency that – you – kissed – him – good-night!' She turned on her heel and left the field of battle triumphant.

With churning stomach and shaking hands I bent over the locker to pick up the bowl; there was silence over the entire ward. I straightened up and stared full into the set faces of Ginger and Ben Holden; they looked at me, expressionless, and then, with one accord they turned their backs and walked away.

I was weeping as I cleaned the trolley in the sluice. Sister came in. 'Nurse Girvan – why ever did you do it?'

I whispered, 'He was only a young boy, Sister – a dying child, crying for his mother.'

She sighed, and then she patted my shoulder in comfort. 'Well, it's done now – and if it's any consolation, I don't think Matron'll take it any further. She's had her revenge.'

Yes, she had had her revenge. I dreaded going back into the ward again, and when I did the men were polite; far too polite. I saw that Lofty had come back from the latrines, and Ben Holden and Ginger had got him in a corner, talking heatedly. I knew from their expressions that they were retailing my sins. I ran into the kitchen and tried to hide there for the rest of the morning.

At lunchtime I swallowed my meal hurriedly and ran back to the privacy of the hut. I found a brief note there from Mac, to say that the German boy had died at five o'clock that morning – he had never regained consciousness. I took out my pen and to the address I remembered I wrote in German: 'Dear Frau Sussner, It is with the deepest regret that I write to tell you . . .' Guy would be kept busy with the Red Cross this week.

When I got back to the ward Sister said, 'Several of the men want to speak to you, privately, so I told them they could wait in the kitchen.'

I took a deep breath and pulled my cardigan more tightly round my shoulders as I went in. Ben Holden and Ginger were there, with Lofty's small wiry figure standing foursquare in front of them. He began to speak at once. 'Sister, these youngsters want to have a word with you.'

I looked at them apprehensively. Ben Holden stared fixedly at some point over my left shoulder and blurted out, 'Me and Ginger – we're sorry, right sorry – we reckon we didn't understand – and we should have trusted you.'

Ginger added, 'Aye, I'm sorry, too – real sorry.'

They both looked at me desperately until at last I whispered, 'That's all right,' and the two of them blundered out.

Lofty said apologetically, 'They're only youngsters, those two – they don't think. I went for them, and Sister told them how it was when you went off to dinner. They've been right upset since, they really have.' He leant towards me, his small seamed face very serious. 'I reckon – if my lad's ever captured an' lying like that – well I hope there's a girl over there as'll do for him what you did.' He half turned away, and then asked, 'How is he, this German youngster?'

'He died early this morning, Lofty – it was better that way – he had lost all his limbs, you see.'

Lofty reached out and patted my arm, then he shook his head sadly and left.

I was still nervous when I went out on to the ward; Ginger was trying hard to be his usual self, but Ben Holden was very quiet, and I knew I was just as constrained. Lofty said to me later as he helped with the washing up, 'Don't be too hard on 'em, Sister – a lot of it were jealousy, you see – that you'd never sung to them.' He grinned a moment: 'Or kissed them good-night, for that matter.'

I stopped and looked at Lofty, then I managed to smile. 'I don't know about the kisses – but I can certainly sing to you all, if Sister agrees.'

His face lit up in a beaming smile. 'Then I'll ask her now – we'll have a little concert like, tonight – that's just the ticket.'

Lofty reported that Sister was agreeable, and when I came back from tea there was a pleasant air of antici-pation in the ward. I walked in, running through a list of the trite old favourites in my mind. But when I stood in the centre of the hushed marquee looking at the expectant faces I suddenly knew I could not begin with 'Hold your Hand out, Naughty Boy'. I remembered Lofty's daughter – Christmas was very near now – and these men deserved better.

I stood still and let the opening chords play through my head, then took an imperceptible breath and let my voice soar up into the shadowy canvas in the age-old message of hope:

'I know that my Redeemer liveth, – and that He shall stand at the latter day upon the earth.'

As my voice died away in the final 'earth' I sensed them hearing with me their familiar chapel organs playing the intervening bars, until I raised my voice again at the terrible:

'and though worms destroy this body – yet in my flesh shall I see God, yet in my flesh shall I see God.
– I know that my Redeemer liveth, and though worms destroy this body, yet in my flesh shall I see God.'

I sang the final triumphant:

'for now is Christ risen from the dead, the first fruits
of them that sleep.'

No one stirred until the chords of our memories had
ceased to play. Then there was a low murmur of appreciation and a voice asked hesitantly, 'Can tha sing "How
Beautiful are the Feet", Sister?'

So I sang of the gospel of peace to men maimed and
wounded in this most terrible of wars.

Then it was the joyous song of exultation:

'Rejoice, rejoice, rejoice greatly, rejoice, O daughters of
Zion! . . .
Shout, O daughter of Jerusalem . . .
behold, thy King cometh unto thee . . .'

And finally, at Sister's mouthed; 'Only one more now,
Nurse,' I sang that short and beautiful message of
comfort:

'Come unto Him, all ye that labour, come unto Him, that are
heavy laden, and He will give you rest . . .
Take His yoke upon you and learn of Him,
for He is meek and lowly of heart,
and ye shall find rest, and ye shall find rest unto your souls.'

We waited together until the final chords died away in
our memories, then I turned away from the centre of
the great marquee and walked down between the beds,
and heard the voices calling softly, 'Thank you, Sister',
'Thank you so much, Sister', 'God bless you, Sister'.

I remembered Elsa Gehring's words – the words of
my friend whom fate had made my enemy: 'You must
be able to sing anywhere – in the tiny cell of a monk,
or the great Schloss of a king,' and thanks to her, I
could. But never, never had I thought that I would one
day sing in this huge camp of weary, suffering men; all
of us caught up together in the greatest and most terrible
war the world had ever known.

CHAPTER ELEVEN

Three days before Christmas I was transferred to night duty, but to my surprise and relief I was to stay on B.4. Tilney had gone down with flu and been sent to Sick Sisters, so I was to take her place. Sister said to me, 'I expect Matron doesn't want to upset the men too much at this time – it's bad enough they're being kept in France over Christmas, without too many new faces as well.'

She may have been right, but I suspected she had misunderstood Matron's motives – there had been a gleam of spite in the latter's protruberant eyes as she had told me of the transfer, and she had seemed disappointed when I did not protest, so I decided I was being left on B.4 as a punishment. I smiled a little to myself as I left Matron's office; I did not want to face the upheaval of nights, but if it had to be, then I would rather go to friendly, familiar B.4 than anywhere else.

I went off duty at lunchtime and slept through the afternoon, but I still felt tired and drained as I listened to Sister's report that evening: she said Young Lennie was worse – his wound was so bad now it had been dressed in the evening too. I felt a cowardly relief that it was no longer my responsibility, but I was so sorry for him. The orderly began to cover the main electric lights with red handkerchiefs and I went to sit down at the screened table in the centre of the ward. When the orderly went on to one of the other marquees I felt very alone. Either side of me the beds receded into darkness, the chimney of the stove jutted up like a long black elbow, and the shadows moved menacingly as the canvas rose and fell, hissing and flapping like a sail in the wind.

For a moment I was frightened; then Ginger turned on his back and began to snore in a steady, familiar rhythm, and I smiled and bent over the case book.

It was not long before my ear caught the whimpers from Lennie's bed; I went to him; he was restless and frightened, his brown eyes bright with pain. I put my hand on his cheek and whispered, 'I'll fetch you a nice hot drink, old man, that'll make you feel better.'

I gave him two aspirins with his hot milk, but I knew they would be almost useless. Captain Adams had had to start giving him morphia; I would have to ask Night Sister about an extra dose. He drifted into an uneasy doze at last, and I was able to go back to my table and begin a letter to Robbie.

As I was writing I heard a rattling noise from the direction of the kitchen; I put my pen down and went nervously to investigate – but there was no one there. When I came back I saw there was a dark shape crouched on the floor by Lennie's bed: it was Ben Holden in his pyjamas. The boy was clinging to Ben's hand while Ben talked to him in a low rumbling monotone. I went over to Ben's bed, pulled off the top blanket and took it and wrapped it round the pyjama-clad form. As I tucked the corners in he looked up with a word of thanks, and I saw the tiredness in his face; but I knew it would be no use telling him to go back to bed; he would do what he felt he had to, regardless of any orders of mine. I took Young Lennie's hot-water bottle to be refilled, and brought one back for Ben as well. As I slipped it inside the blanket against his chest he smiled at me gratefully, but his words to Lennie never paused.

I finished my letter to Robbie and forced myself to begin one to Conan – it was dispiriting writing when I never knew if it would get through, but I felt I had to try. I noticed Ben finally clamber back into his bed and lie there breathing heavily, and saw he was watching my table. I moved softly over to his side and murmured,

'I'm just going to make myself some tea – I'll bring you a cup.'

While the kettle was boiling I decided to get out the bowls I would need in the morning; I reached into the dark cupboard – and my hand touched something alive, and furry. There was a clatter and a large rat jumped out, straight at my face. I gasped and twisted frantically away from its vicious white teeth and felt its body brush my cheek. I clung to the table, terrified, as it scurried away into the shadows behind the far cupboard. Mesmerized, I stood watching the corner where it was hiding, feeling the hysteria rising. Then footsteps limped down from the ward, the flap was pushed aside and a face peered in. 'Anything wrong, Sister? I thought I heard you call out.'

I licked my dry lips and managed to whisper, 'A rat, Ben – in the cupboard.'

I saw the beginnings of a smile, hastily suppressed as he took in my panic-stricken state. 'You get up ward – I'll see to him.'

I pointed to the dark corner and then almost ran to the screen and round it. As I cowered behind its flimsy protection I heard sounds of scuffling from the kitchen, a rattle of tin plates and then two heavy thwacks. Ben Holden appeared again, his face very smug. 'Here he is – dead as a doornail.' He swung the large grey creature by its tail, and I backed away. He began to tell me again that it was dead, but when I kept on backing, he shrugged and turned and took his trophy away. I sat down at the table, legs trembling. So it was Ben who made the tea, and brought it to me. He leant over the table and said, 'They won't hurt you, you know – they're more frightened of you than you are of them.'

I looked up at him and shook my head firmly. 'No, Ben – it just is not possible for any rat to be as terrified of me as I am of it.'

He said, 'Ah,' and retreated with his mug.

Next evening Ben Holden got out of bed as soon as

Sister had gone, and I saw he was still wearing his blues trousers. 'I've got summat to show you.' His voice was conspiratorial. I followed him into the kitchen and there, sitting on the dresser top, comfortably ensconced on one of our best blankets, was a large ginger tom cat. Ben went over to it and rubbed its ear and it rose, arched its back and gave a loud rumbling purr. He explained, 'I made a few inquiries, see, and Jones won it for us – from the Canadians. We've given him a good feed an' he's happy as a sandboy. Give him plenty o' grub and a bit of a stroke now and then and there'll be no more rats on this ward.' He looked at me hopefully, just like a small boy waiting for praise.

I mumbled, 'But – Sister . . .'

He was firm. 'Sister likes cats.'

How could I tell him I did not? I pulled myself together and said, 'What a good idea, Ben – how kind of you.'

His plain face glowed. The tom leapt down from the dresser and began to explore the kitchen; we both stood watching it. When it reached the table it turned its back on us, displayed two large round balls and then neatly sprayed the table leg. I looked at Ben; his face was on fire. He mumbled, 'Um – I'll leave you to it, then, Sister,' and backed hurriedly out of the kitchen without looking at me.

The cat sprang up on to the table top and butted my chest with an imperious yowl. Tentatively I scratched its head and it immediately began to purr again. Then I thought of Ben Holden's crestfallen face and clutched the edge of the table and giggled and giggled until my belly ached with suppressed laughter. Poor Ben – what a return for his chivalry! I could hardly wait to write and describe the scene to Robbie.

I grew quite fond of the cat over the next few days; as Lofty said, there was nothing like the smell of a tom cat for keeping the rats at bay. Sister told me that during the day Ben took it up the ward and it slept on Lennie's bed; he liked to stroke it with his good hand and its presence seemed to comfort him. 'Of course we have to keep it out of Matron's way otherwise she'd read me a lecture on the dangers of infection, but we all know it's not going to make any difference to Young Lennie now.'

On Christmas Day the night VADs got up for lunch, but I was so tired the afternoon passed in a daze. Sears told me Ginger and Ben Holden had been very amusing with the mistletoe. 'One of them would creep up behind me with it, then at the last minute the other one would cough loudly, so that I'd got time to dodge away – then they would pretend to fight each other over it! It was hilarious, Girvan, all the men roared.'

I listened dully and wondered how I would ever keep awake all night. But I had no difficulty, because Lennie was crying and moaning; Night Sister got out more morphia, but it took a long time to act and she said I might have to call out Captain Adams next time, to write up a bigger dose.

On Boxing Day night Lennie was crying; tears of pain and weakness dribbled down his cheek – the second dressing in the evening had taken him far beyond his small stock of endurance. Night Sister came in to look at him, but she told me she could not stay, as the VAD in 'Heads' was hysterical – she was weeping and laughing alternately. 'I've got to go and take her off, otherwise she'll be as crazy as all her patients by the morning.' I held back the canvas curtain as she ducked underneath, and watched her hurricane lamp bob off over the duck-boards, then I went back up the ward to Young Lennie's bed.

I snatched a few minutes to go over to the night bunk for my meal. Ben Holden was with Lennie; he insisted I went, and I told the orderly to stay on call. But when I came back Lennie was screaming – a thin, animal sound that was torn from his wasted body. His eyes were terrified, so I sent the orderly to wake Captain Adams.

Captain Adams came quickly. He took Lennie's pulse

381

as he twisted and turned in Ben Holden's grasp, then said abruptly, 'Come with me, Nurse.'

I followed him down into the sister's bunk and he opened the medicine cupboard and took out the phial of morphia tablets. He looked at the record sheet for a moment and asked, 'Are Wall and Sanders asleep?'

'Yes, both sound asleep.'

'Right, I'll put the other doses down to them.' He drew water up into the hypodermic syringe and then began to add the tablets. As I saw the quantity, a ripple of shock ran through me and my hand was barely steady as I held it out for the syringe. But Captain Adams shook his head. 'No, Nurse Girvan – this had better be on my conscience. It won't be the first time – when you've been at the front as a regimental MO you learn not to be too sparing with the morphia.'

I followed him back up the ward. Lennie was frantic now; Ben was struggling to prevent him from banging his shoulder against the mattress. I rolled up Lennie's pyjama sleeve and Captain Adams stepped forward with the syringe; I saw Ben Holden glance up at him in surprise, then he looked at me, and I knew from his face he had guessed what was happening. 'Come on, Lennie lad – just a little prick now, and then pain'll all go away – and you'll feel right as rain in morning.'

I held Lennie's arm still and Captain Adams pushed in the needle and pressed down the plunger. When he withdrew it I gently rubbed the place where the needle had gone in and said, 'There, Lennie – you'll soon feel better now.' The frightened eyes caught at mine for a moment, and I smiled back into them and saw a second of comfort. Then his face twisted and his eyelids screwed up, and he jerked forward on the bed and lost his balance and fell hard on to his bad side before Ben or I could stop him. He screamed again and again.

I ran to the head of the bed and slipped my hand under the bony body. 'Ben!' and his warm hand clasped mine and together we pulled Lennie up until he stopped screaming. Soon he began to mumble, and I knew that the morphia was taking effect.

When his breathing finally slowed and then stopped, I straightened my aching back and said, 'Thank you, Ben. Go back to bed, I'll see to him now.'

I walked down into the privacy of the sister's bunk and slumped into the chair, my hands pressed to my eyes. I could not stop the tears. Lennie had been a child, a simple pathetic child, who had looked up at me with his guileless eyes and trusted me, trusted that I would help him, even when I had had to hurt him again and again in his daily dressing. And now, how had I repaid his trust? Captain Adams had put in the needle, but it was my hand which had massaged the prick in his arm to spread the drug more quickly, my face into which he had looked in the extremity of his pain and fear, and my voice which had lied to him in those last trite words. I sat huddled on the chair and knew I could take no more.

There was a short cough and I raised my face and looked up through swollen eyelids. Ben Holden stood in the entrance. 'I brought this for you, Sister.' He held the lid of a packing case in his right hand, carefully spread with a clean towel. On it sat Sister's battered brown tea pot and enamel jug, and my cup and saucer. There was a plate of bread and butter, too – and each slice had had its crust neatly cut off. I felt my throat tighten. He put down the makeshift tray and began to back out.

'Ben, please – stay – bring a mug – there's enough for two.'

'I can't drink tea with you, Sister – not in here.' He was shocked.

'Please,' and we both heard the ragged edge to my voice. I swallowed, 'Sister's busy in "Heads" – she won't be back. Sit down, Ben.' Suddenly I could not bear to be alone.

He fetched an enamel mug and poured the tea for

both of us. I said, 'Ben, he trusted us – and we did that to him.'

'It were the only thing to do – he'd had enough, more than enough – you know that, Sister.' Yes, I knew that, but I felt my face tighten. 'Sister – do you fancy a cigarette? I've got some in me locker – it might help you like . . .'

'No, thank you – I don't smoke.'

'I didn't either, afore the war – me old dad leathered me for it when I were a lad so I kept off it after that.'

'Where do your parents live, Ben?'

He said woodenly, 'There's neither of them living now, Sister.'

'I'm sorry.' My voice broke.

He went on steadily, 'It's not surprising– I were a late babby, see – my old dad were well over fifty when I were born, and he died just after I started as a cleaner on railway. Me mam – me mam died not long afore we went over at Ypres in the summer. She were took ill, and Captain Girvan got me home on leave, but it were too late. I went to funeral, though, I were glad of that. There's just me two sisters now, they're a sight older 'an me but we always got on all right. They're both married to decent blokes and got families of their own – nice youngsters they are – I'm fond of childer.'

'Then you must marry too, Ben – when the war is over.'

He looked back at me steadily. 'Aye, happen – but like Ginger said – I'm choosy.'

I could think of no reply and we both sat on in silence. My mind went back to Lennie's terrified face and I felt my breath begin to quicken again. I had said: 'When the war is over', but the war would never be over. I saw myself, years ahead, bent and grey – after a lifetime of deathbeds. I whispered hopelessly, 'Ben, I don't think I can go on – I can't stand any more.'

His shadow loomed over me as he leant forward. 'Of

384

course you can – you're a bit upset now, it's only natural – but you'll be all right tomorrow, you see.'

I shook my head. 'No – I can't take any more, I just want to go away and – '

'Don't be so daft, lass – you're not type as runs away, not while you're still needed. You're like your brother – he looked like a thin mardy lad at first, but he's got a backbone o' steel, and so have you.' The blue-grey eyes held mine across the table, until at last I straightened my back, took out my pen and began to indent for a shroud.

The following evening I walked into an almost empty ward. Only the men with fractured femurs remained, suspended gloomily from their Balkan beams. The powers-that-be had finally relented and the Blighty orders had come through.

Over the next few days the letters of thanks arrived from my former patients: Lofty was in Oswestry and Ginger in Newcastle, and Ben Holden wrote from the 2nd Western at Manchester. I also received an awkwardly written, misspelt letter from Lennie's mother – she said she was glad to hear he had passed away so peacefully.

CHAPTER TWELVE

After Christmas the weather became colder still, and then I went down with a flu-like fever and had to be warded in Sick Sisters. I was just creeping about again when Robbie arrived on a twenty-four-hour pass. I began to cry as soon as he came into the ward to see me, and I scarcely stopped all day – I felt so weak and tired. Sister said if I wrapped up well I could go out with him, and he half carried me out to the car he had hired and drove me down the straight white road to the sea. We sat in the lounge of the best hotel in Paris-Plage and he talked to me while I wept on his shoulder. After tea he drove me back to the hospital and I clung to him hopelessly when the time came to say goodbye. That evening I cried and cried until my eyes were so swollen that I could scarcely see out of them; the next morning I felt bitterly ashamed of myself for spoiling Robbie's precious leave. I wrote a long letter of apology and self-recrimination, and he replied at once – 'Don't be a silly donkey, Big Sis – that's what brothers are for. Besides, if you hadn't been ill I wouldn't have seen so much of you – now keep your pecker up and don't work so hard.'

When I was passed fit again Matron put me on days in a light surgical ward, where the work was much easier. When I came off duty I slept a lot in our small stuffy hut and Aylmer kept the stove going and fed me with biscuits and cocoa. We did not talk much, but we were comfortable with each other and I began to feel stronger again.

In February I had a letter from Innes, to say she had been transferred to No. 11 General at Camiers – if she walked down to Étaples one day perhaps we could see each other? I spoke to Sister and we eventually agreed on an afternoon. I walked out along the Camiers road to meet Innes: she looked thinner, and her face was very pale, but her smile was the same as ever. We decided to catch the tram to Paris-Plage and stroll beside the sea and then have tea in the Blue Cat.

As the tram trundled along beside the estuary, Innes told me the news of Rouen after I had left: Sister Jennings had gone up to a CCS, so had Captain Bevan – 'Not the same one,' Innes added hastily, her face rather pink, and I smiled to myself at the memory of flirtatious Sister Jennings. Then I told her about Hugh and she whispered, 'I'm so sorry, Girvan – so very sorry.'

We walked by the sea and drank coffee and ate chocolate cakes together, but she never referred to the raid on St Omer, so I did not ask her about it. When we got off the tram at Étaples I said I would walk part of the way up the road to Camiers with her. It was dusk by now and her face was in shadow as she told me, her voice intense, 'I can only keep going now by planning what I shall do when the war is over – I think of it in part of my brain all the time, whatever I'm doing. My old college have offered me a junior fellowship and I cling to that like a life raft; I'm going to study the work of poets who wrote of green, living things, and who died long ago, peacefully in their beds. And I shall train my mind never, ever to think of the war again. You must turn back now, Girvan – you've come more than halfway.'

As I walked back alone in the darkness I thought of what Innes had said. I almost envied her, for I knew I would never be able to have my mind under such control. But then, it was different for Innes – she had never lost a sweetheart, or a brother.

We managed to arrange a second afternoon together, early in March. By then the camp was heavy with rumours that the Germans were planning an attack in the spring. Men who should have gone back to Blighty were sent up the hill to the convalescent camp, miserable and resentful. We in the hospitals clung to our bleak corner of France and waited.

It was a Thursday, the third Thursday in March. I was sitting over an enamel bowl of greasy soup when I realised that the VAD on my right was talking in a quick, urgent voice. I began to listen – the rumour had come that the German attack had been launched. I thought of Robbie and closed my eyes for a moment. When I opened them again I pushed the bowl away untouched; I felt sick. By that evening we knew that the rumour was true – and that our line had broken before them. Sister and I were hastily erecting extra beds and making them up, even as the bugles sounded for the first convoys.

Day followed frantic day as the ward became foul with the smell of blood and pus and human excrement. There was no time now to be frightened of what lay beneath the filthy blood-soaked bandages, there was only time to work – to work harder and faster than I had ever done before, even in the worst days of the Somme. And all around us was the scent of fear – our armies were being pushed back.

Some men sobbed aloud as they heard of the loss of the places we had fought so hard to gain. Others tried desperately to explain, to excuse. 'There were so many of them, Sister, and only a few of us – what could we do? We didn't have a chance, we didn't have a chance.' All those who were fit to travel, and many who were not, were evacuated, while the others went straight to the cemetery and their beds were filled again by grey-faced, unshaven men.

As Étaples village teemed with refugees, and yet more wounded flooded in, in lorries, cattle trucks and anything that could carry them, the litany of losses lengthened: Péronne, Bapaume, Beaumont-Hamel – and Albert. The Somme battlefield which we had fought so desperately to gain in 1916 had fallen to the enemy. Paris itself was being shelled, and early in April we heard the dread news that the Germans were entering Amiens.

Men from the convalescent camp, many still wearing their bandages, went limping off back to the front, their faces masks of despair. And we too felt despair as, for the first time, we began to fear that we might lose; that all those terrible four years of fighting, all those lost and broken lives, might have been for nothing. The exhausted sisters fleeing back from the bombed CCSs, with tales of patients barely evacuated as the Germans came over the next field, confirmed our worst fears – we were on the run, and we would be trapped in our narrow strip of land, caught between the advancing enemy and the sea. I worked on, waiting each day, heart in mouth, for those short notes which told me Robbie was still alive and holding the line further north. Somehow, I managed to scribble even briefer replies.

One evening as I came off duty between convoys a scrawled note was delivered to me. It was very short:

Dear Helena,
My YMCA team has been evacuated to Étaples, I can't get away myself but do come over if you can. I've seen your brother. Isn't it all too exciting?
                                        Yours,
                                                    Juno.

I read again the flamboyant: 'Isn't it all too exciting?' – how typical of Juno – and how typical too that she had not said which of my brothers she had seen. I put on my coat and began to fight my way through the mêlée the camp had become.

When I arrived at the YMCA hut, Juno was behind the counter, slapping endless mugs of tea down in front of huddled, dispirited men. I stood watching them as they queued – men with thin pasty faces and bowed legs, with hollow chests and sloping backs – men who would probably never have been accepted for service earlier in the war, and certainly never sent up to the front line. How could men like this stem the German tide? As I watched them, defeat took hold of my heart.

Juno saw me and signalled; she spoke over her shoulder and another pair of hands took her place at the urn. She began to push her way through the crowd, carrying two mugs of tea. 'Over here, Helena.' She tugged the cloth from her belt, gave the smeared table a perfunctory swipe with it and dropped heavily into a chair. 'Good timing – I was just about due for my fifteen-minute break. How goes the nursing, Helena? God, I never thought, when we signed on for three months at the East London, that you'd still be at it after all this time. Lucky I didn't lay any bets on the end of this war – it would've been money down the drain.' She lit a cigarette and drew in a lungful of smoke. 'That's better – it's against the rules, of course – but I'd like to see any of that lot stop me. By the way, I saw Muirkirk last week.'

'Guy – so it was Guy you saw.'

'Yes – he was going back up the line with the First Battalion. Said he'd had enough of Headquarters – so he's wangled a transfer. Good luck to him.'

So Guy was back at the front. As I picked up my mug, I realized I was almost glad. Guy had lost his self-respect; now he had the chance to regain it. Juno went on, 'I saw Pansy in London a couple of months ago – she's preggers again. Each to their own form of war work, I suppose.' She threw back her head with her typical braying laughter and I felt my stiff muscles relax as I smiled back. Juno leant forward. 'I must say, I got pretty fed up before I signed on for this unit – kicking my heels about in London for a couple of months after Mama's little outfit got deported. You know, I was walking across Piccadilly one day and I noticed three Jocks on leave, arm in arm – then a couple of tarts picked up two of them, one right after the other, and I saw the third Jock left all on his own and looking pretty wistful and I said to myself, Juno, old girl, you'd better take the last one home yourself – at least you'd be doing something for the war effort.'

I looked at her in horror and asked weakly, 'You didn't, did you?'

There was a pause as Juno took another long pull at her cigarette, then she winked at me. 'No – one of the regulars got there first, so I toddled off to the club and started ringing up everybody I knew with any pull at the YMCA.' She added, 'I wouldn't be much good as a tart anyway – I don't really like that sort of thing.' I wondered how on earth she knew, but it was better not to ask – being Juno she would probably tell me, at the top of her loud voice in this crowded canteen. She looked me up and down and said kindly, 'Hellie, you do look a mess – your mother would have a fit if she could see you now.' Then she grinned again. 'Funny, we neither of us take after our respective mamas, do we? And he was quite a well-set-up Jock, too!' And suddenly I began to laugh, and Juno laughed with me as she stubbed out her cigarette and lit up another one. Then she glanced over my shoulder. 'Somebody's trying to attract your attention, Hellie – that stocky sergeant-major over there.'

I swung round – it took me a moment to distinguish the man she meant amid the milling khaki throng – then I recognized him. It was Ben Holden. I smiled and he began to push his way through to us; I noticed he still had a trace of a limp.

He stopped beside the table, rather red in the face. 'I don't like to intrude, Sister, but I thought . . .'

'Sit down, Sergeant,' Juno interrupted, 'we're all democrats in this hut – here, have a cigarette.'

Ben sat stiffly down on the third chair. 'Thank you, miss.'

I asked, 'Ben – why are you back in France? Surely your arm's not right yet, and you're still limping.'

He shrugged. 'They'll do. I walked well enough for Medical Board – and I can fire me rifle.'

And then I understood. 'They're not sending you up to the front again – not so soon?'

His blue-grey eyes looked steadily back into mine, and I saw that his cheekbones still showed gaunt in his face as he said, simply, 'Someone's got to go.'

I sat desolated – whatever was the point of nursing men back to health, if they were only to be sent, still limping, back up into that maelstrom again? Juno was speaking: 'They say our men are on the run, Sergeant.'

Ben Holden brought his fist down hard on the greasy table top. 'I'm not running! And I tell you, I'll keep the swine back even if I have to strangle them with me bare hands.'

Juno's eyes shone. 'That's the spirit, Sergeant-Major!' She lowered her voice a fraction. 'I got hold of a rifle, as soon as I came out this time – I'm keeping it under my mattress. I can shoot as well as any man – if they break through to here I'll give the blighters something to remember me by.' She and Ben Holden leant towards each other, bodies tense and eyes locked.

Then he nodded to her and turned slowly to me. 'Don't you worry, Sister, we'll keep you safe – we'll hold 'em back somehow – you'll see.' He stood up abruptly. 'I'd better collect me draft together. Good evening.' He ducked his head to us and was gone before I had even had time to wish him luck.

Juno looked after him. 'That's the right sort of man – as long as we've got chaps like him in our army we can't lose.' She ground out her cigarette in the over-flowing ashtray. 'I'd better be off – so long, Helena.'

As I walked back to the hospital, lorries and ammu-nition wagons were rumbling after each other along the road in a continuous stream; a loaded train rattled and clanked its way up to the front and I saw the distant flash of the guns against the night sky. My ears were filled with the clamour of war. And yet my sense of defeat had lessened: between them Juno and Ben Holden had heartened me and given me strength – we would hold out, we must. And back in the mess Tilney told me that Amiens had not fallen after all; so that vital city, at least, was still in our hands.

But the other news from the front got steadily worse, and in London the age of military service was raised to fifty – fifty! German aeroplanes were coming nightly to the coast now, and one evening the lights in the mess went out and we heard heavy crashes nearby. A veiled shape appeared in the doorway and ordered us to scatter – in Matron's voice. Aylmer seized my hand and we ran back to our hut. I sat on the bed shaking while Aylmer prayed in a low calm voice, and the flashes of the exploding bombs lit up the small window.

Next day we heard that Étaples village had been bombed and the bridge over the Canche destroyed: for a morning no trains ran on the main line through the camp, then the engineers completed their work, and the men and shells began to pass by once more.

Then the Germans attacked again, the Portuguese gave way and the enemy broke through in a second place, further north, near Neuve Chapelle. We looked at each other with fear in our eyes, then hurried to the wards where the wounded were filling the beds and overflowing into the centre aisles. On Thursday 11 April, just as we felt we could cope no longer, Sir Douglas Haig's Special Order of the Day was pinned up on the mess notice board – addressed to all ranks of the British Army in France and Flanders – addressed to us. I stood and read it through until the last paragraph:

> There is no other course open to us but to fight it out. Every position must be held to the last man. There must be no retirement. With our backs to the wall and believing in the justice of our cause each one of us must fight on to the end.

And even as I read it I knew it was true. We had no choice. We must fight on to the end, whatever that end might be.

A couple of days later the rumour in the mess at lunchtime was that Ypres had been taken; I felt sick with fear until Mac came flying in, her voice high-pitched with excitement. 'The Americans have arrived – I've just seen them, hundreds of them, marching up the road to Camiers. They've come, they've come!' And as we looked at her she burst into tears. Tilney jumped up and took her arm and pushed her into a seat, and I heard Aylmer's low voice beside me: 'Thanks be to God, thanks be to God.'

Three days later I received a postcard from Guy: he was in the thick of it, but the few scribbled words radiated confidence and determination. I was glad, for his sake. And they said in the mess that Ypres had not fallen after all: we were still hanging on. Then Robbie wrote and told me that he and his men were being pulled out of the Salient and were to be sent to a quiet sector down in the south; I felt a deep thankfulness.

At the end of April spring came, but we were so busy we scarcely had time to notice the new green leaves on the trees. Casualties still flooded in through the first weeks of May. One evening as we were chatting in the mess there was a sudden crash and the ground shuddered; Aylmer and I looked at each other blankly – there had been no air-raid warning – another crash, then another; and we were frantically scrabbling for tin hats and ramming them on as we ran to the slit trenches which had been dug for us. We huddled in them for two hours as crash succeeded crash – they seemed to be all around us.

When we eventually got to bed I lay trembling in the darkness for a long time before I could sleep – although I was very tired. Next morning we heard that it was the No. 1 Canadian General which had taken the brunt of the attack: twenty-two of the bombs had landed on their hospital, half of their personnel were casualties and three of their sisters had been killed. We talked of it in shocked whispers, and hurried to our own wards as soon as we had finished our breakfasts.

Several new patients had been brought in from the raid of the previous night and one of them was a tall, broad man with a broken arm and leg. As I talked to him I discovered he was a Lifeguardsman who had just finished a course at the machine-gun school at Camiers. A group of a dozen or so NCOs had been under canvas at Étaples, across the railway line from the hospital, when they had been bombed in their tents – only two had survived. My patient told me he was a regular, and he had been out since 1914. I looked down at his weather-beaten face as I dressed his wound and ventured to ask, 'Did you – did you know anything of Major Lord Staveley?'

'Yes ma'am – Sister I mean – he was a good officer, he knew his job and he looked after his men, a fine man, and a sad loss.'

Before lunch I ran to the hut and took out my photograph of Gerald and sat looking at it for a long time. 'A fine man, and a sad loss.' I felt the tears on my cheeks as I mourned him still.

A week later we heard that the Germans had launched a third great offensive, in the south, against a quiet sector on the river Aisne – and our line had been broken again. Robbie, oh my Robbie.

Two nights after, the bridge over the Canche was bombed again, the village was hit and French civilians injured. This time the engineers took only seven hours to make their repairs, then the traffic of war was roaring past us again. I had heard nothing from Robbie.

The following evening, the last night of May, we heard the whistle blow and from the north came the menacing throb of aircraft engines. We tumbled into the trenches as the sudden blinding flash of a magnesium flare turned night into day. I crouched like a small frightened animal, listening to the steady crump of the bombs exploding. A couple of hours later I unlocked my rigid limbs and we went back to the hut and lit the stove – although it was nearly June we were shivering and cold.

Next morning we learnt that it was St John's Hospital, next to us, which had taken the weight of the attack this time; another four sisters had been killed while caring for their patients. Again any of us who could be spared were sent off duty to walk in their funeral procession; Tilney and I met at the mess. We were early, so Tilney insisted we must go and look at the bomb damage.

I followed her listlessly, but as we walked towards the wreckage of the camp my listlessness stiffened into shock. The rows of huts at the Camiers end had collapsed like a house of cards; now they were simply a heap of splintered wood. Debris was scattered all around – shattered beds, torn blankets, lockers smashed by the blast. Men were still searching the rubble, and as we watched, they disturbed a pile of broken beams and a piece of paper was set free and was tossed about in the wind until it came to rest at our feet. Tilney picked it up and smoothed it out. It was a letter: 'Darling Ma, Just a quick note to let you know that . . .' but at this point the writer had broken off – called to the wards? or worse? We did not know, and nor perhaps would 'Darling Ma'. Tilney folded the piece of paper, bent down and anchored it carefully under a twisted tube of metal, then we turned and picked our way back over the rubble in silence.

We stood by the side of the road waiting for the funeral procession. The wind tugged at the padre's white surplice as he led it; an RAMC sergeant marched ramrod straight behind him. The flag-draped coffin of the first sister followed on its high bier, drawn easily along the level road by the four orderlies marching at its corners. The spokes of the large light wheels etched their delicate shadows in the morning sunlight and the pale-pink petals of the wreath on the coffin clashed with the harsh red and blue of the Union Jack.

Kilted Highlanders stood to attention each side of the road as the matron and sisters followed the bier; we moved forward and fell into step behind them.

The forest of crosses was growing daily now, advancing steadily over the bare hillside.

'Grant, we beseech Thee, O Lord, Thine Eternal Rest to all those who have died for their country, as this our sister hath; and grant that we may so follow her good example that we may be united with her in Thine Ever-lasting Kingdom . . .'

And as I listened to the words of the chaplain I knew that whatever faith I had once possessed had gone now. Almost without my noticing it, it had seeped away in the blood and pus of the last months. If there was a God, then He was the God of the Old Testament, a jealous God who scourged His people for their sins and exacted an impossible price.

As I walked back with the other mourners I felt something akin to relief; it would be easier now, now that I had come to the end of hope.

CHAPTER THIRTEEN

The news I had for so long dreaded came the next day: Robbie had been in the 'quiet sector' where the Germans had launched their third onslaught and had been seriously wounded. He was already back in London and Papa wrote that a shell had exploded in front of him: the shrapnel had caught him full in the chest and also broken his right arm. The surgeons at the CCS had managed to remove the jagged fragments from his lungs, but as usual, infection had set in and now everything depended on Robbie's natural powers of resistance. My father said he would write again as soon as there was any more news. I folded up his letter and walked back to the ward. Robbie, oh my Robbie.

For two days I waited, praying to a God I did not believe in, and on the next morning three letters were waiting for me. I opened Papa's with hands that shook – Robbie was still alive, and Papa said he was holding his own; now it was just a question of time. So that first dangerous week was over – surely I could begin to hope a little?

Alice had written as well; she had visited Robbie the previous afternoon and he was talking again now, though rather wheezily – and he sent his love. She said Letty had run away from school and had badgered Mother to let her serve in a soldiers' canteen at Victoria Station. I looked down at the letter and thought, but she's only a child! Then I realized my younger sister was nearly eighteen – I had not seen her since Eddie's funeral. In the last paragraph Alice said she was marrying again: an industrialist called Clayton. 'He's quite a bit older than I am, but he's very well-heeled, and he's made a lot more money because of the war.' There was an added note scribbled in the margin, 'He's not a profiteer, I haven't sunk that low!' She explained that Hugh had not left her and the boys in very good circumstances – 'and I don't want to sponge off Papa all my life, so when Fred asked me I said "Yes". The wedding will be very quiet.' There was no word of love or even affection in her account. I shrugged. For all her faults Alice was not a hypocrite – and nobody could say that Hugh was barely cold in his grave, since he had no grave. But I wished she had waited a little longer; because Hugh had loved her.

The third letter was in a hand I did not recognize. I opened it and looked at the signature – it was from Ben Holden. It was quite short and almost painfully respectful. He had heard of the bombings at Étaples and that sisters had been injured and killed – was I safe? He asked would I send him a line? 'Just a postcard with your name on it, Sister, that's all, just so that I know.' I was touched that a man who was in the midst of the hell of the front line should have the time and energy to think of my safety, so when I had written to Robbie and Alice that evening I picked up my pen again and wrote him a letter, thanking him for his concern and telling him the latest news of my brother. Then I forgot about him again until a straggly pencilled note from Robbie himself lightened my heart – and told me that Ben Holden had been awarded the DCM. 'It was a good show, and from what I've heard he earned it several times over.'

The news from the front became less black: the Germans had been held back from Paris and the Americans had fought their first battle, counter-attacking fiercely at Château Thierry – their troops were fresh and vigorous. There were stories too, that the advancing Germans had stopped to loot the cellars of Champagne, and that drunken soldiers were no longer obeying their officers – we hoped that they were true.

One day Sister came to fetch me from the end of the ward. 'Nurse, your brother is here to see you.' I swung round and there was Guy. I ran to him, but as I came near I slowed my pace, and hung back, remembering him as I had last seen him when I had been home on leave in the summer of '17. But his smile was the smile of the old Guy, though his face was leaner and older, and I threw myself into his arms and hugged him very tightly.

Sister said I could be spared from the ward for a couple of hours, so we walked down towards the estuary together. Guy told me he had been sent down to Montreuil to give a report, so he had seized the chance to come on by train to Étaples to see me. We talked of Robbie – Papa had written that he was still very weak and in some pain, but that he was eating solid food again now. Then Guy spoke of his three small sons, so I nerved myself to ask, 'How is Pansy, Guy?'

He answered quite naturally, 'She's tired, of course – but otherwise reasonably well.' Then he looked away from me, out over the sand dunes to the coast, and said at last, 'She's been a brick, Hellie – and I've been a swine to her – you've no idea. When I think of what she's had to put up with over these last years – I usually didn't bother to write when I was in France, and then, when I was home those months – I don't know how she stood it. The way I spoke to her and the things I said. I wanted to hurt someone, and she was there, and – she's easy to hurt.' He turned and looked at me for a moment, then braced himself as he went on, 'One day she was out, in Bond Street, and she saw me – I was with a whore I'd just picked up. I don't think she realized at first, and she came towards me, smiling – so I called

399

a cab and bundled the woman into it and jumped in myself and drove off. I saw her as she stood there looking after me – she looked like a child that's been hit – and, God forgive me, Hellie, I was glad. She never said anything when I got home, she never reproached me, she just opened her arms to me that night and let me' – his voice broke – 'let me use her like a whore too.' There were tears on Guy's face as he stared out over the dunes. 'And it wasn't until the morning that I realized what I might have done. I'd taken that girl straight off the streets, and not used anything – Papa always warned us. I lay in my dressing room sweating – I could have given my wife a dose of the clap, and she was carrying my child. Even then, it was only the child I cared about – I kept remembering old Foster's youngest,' he shuddered. 'But I was luckier than I deserved. So after that I only used the reputable establishments – and thought I was being a considerate husband!' His voice was tormented with self-disgust.

I waited and at last he said, 'When I'd decided to go back up the line it was like a weight dropping off my back. I wangled forty-eight hours' leave – you can pull any strings at HQ – and I went home. I arrived at teatime and she was there in the drawing room with the children around her. She looked dreadful: her ankles were puffed up, her body all shapeless, and her hair was a mess – the baby had tugged it down. I stood in the doorway, looking at her – she didn't see me at first, the boys were making such a racket – and I thought, I love this woman, I love her.'

He fell silent, until I whispered, 'And was she pleased?'

Guy's face as he looked at me was suddenly very young and bashful. 'I don't know, Hellie – I was too embarrassed to tell her.'

I cried, 'Guy!' I wanted to hit him.

He fended me off, laughing, 'It's all right, Hellie, I wrote – all the way back on the steamer I just wrote and wrote. I told her everything: that I knew what a vicious brute I'd been – how wonderfully patient she was – and how I felt now. I've never written so much in my life before.' He looked out towards the sea, towards England, and said softly, 'I think she was pleased.'

I reached up and kissed him, then I slipped my arm in his and we walked back to the camp together.

Several days later, Alice wrote to tell me that Guy had been awarded the MC for the part he had played in the March retreat. I wrote to my brother to congratulate him, and then I wrote to Pansy. Her reply overflowed with love for Guy. In thoughtless anger Guy had rushed into a hasty marriage; had done everything to turn Pansy's love to bitterness – and incredibly he had failed. My brother had been very lucky.

The impetus of the German offensive was slowing down: we had lost ground but we were no longer being pushed back; we could breathe more easily now. But still the casualties flooded in, and the men I was nursing could scarcely breathe at all – I had been moved to the gas marquees. There were four of them, pitched side by side, with a VAD in each and one sister and one MO in the dressing tent that stood at right angles to the four. They were there if I needed them, but most of the time I was alone with my forty gassed men: men who were burned, who were blind, and who were gasping for breath.

The gas had seeped into the cloth of their uniforms as they had stumbled to the aid post, and now they were all on fire, with festering sores on their bodies where the gas had eaten away their flesh. Their eyes had been scorched as though by a flame, and hid behind eyelids gummed together with sticky pus. And they panted and choked on their pillows as the gas destroyed their lungs.

Each day, after the routine ward cleaning was done, I injected the strychnine that forced their weary hearts to keep beating. Then I lugged the oxygen cylinder to each bed in turn to give relief to labouring chests, before

I cleansed the dried pus from their eyelids and dropped lotion on to staring eyeballs. And finally there were the dressings; the MO did some, I did the rest – and learned to soak the lint in castor oil as well as picric so that next day it could be more easily peeled off the scorched raw flesh.

The effort of drawing air into their gas-filled lungs took all their strength and they were frightened and alone in their dark worlds, so all day they lay and listened to me. They needed my voice; as long as they could hear me they knew I was there and that they had not been abandoned. They could tell when I came towards them, and be ready for my touch. At first I talked of the weather, but there was not enough to say, so I told them stories from the nursery, of days outside in the park at Hatton, of long-gone rides to hounds – and then I began to sing. I sang all the childhood favourites, I sang all the familiar hymns, I sang arias from the Italian operas and catchy tunes from pre-war musicals – but I did not sing Lieder, and I could not sing the message of hope from the *Messiah*, for I would not sing a lie. All through that long hot summer the foetid smell of burns and sweat invaded my nostrils and seeped into my pores and forced its way down my throat, but still I sang my song of war.

Dimly I realized that the balance of the fighting was changing: Étaples was bombed again in August, but at the front we were the attackers now – slowly, very slowly, the enemy were retreating, and slowly, very slowly, the numbers of gassed men dwindled, until by September three of the marquees had been transferred; and then my leave came through.

As soon as I arrived in London I went straight to the hospital to see Robbie. He was very thin and pale, but his face lit up as I came into the room. I sat with his hand in mine and we talked together in disjointed murmurs; he wheezed and spoke slowly, but he could speak. As I was sitting there I just fell asleep. I woke much later, stiff and cramped, still holding Robbie's hand. He managed a short gasping laugh at the expression on my face as I woke up, and I laughed too and stood up and kissed him goodbye. 'I'll see you in the morning, Robbie,' and I stumbled out and down the stairs and asked the porter to call a cab. Pansy was at Cadogan Place; she was enormous but she hugged me as best she could, and then Nanny appeared and clasped me to her swelling bosom and said, 'Bed, my lady.'

I staggered out every day to see Robbie, but otherwise I slept. I even slept when I was with him. It was a luxurious hospital for officers and he ordered an armchair to be put in his room for me, so that I could curl up in it, and sometimes I dropped off in the middle of a sentence. Once I woke up and Ralph Dutton was there, talking softly to Robbie. I was embarrassed for a moment, but he jumped to his feet and came forward with his hand outstretched and his pleasant open smile lighting up his fair face, so I relaxed and smiled warmly back. We chatted easily together for a little while, and then Robbie sent me home to bed.

Pansy's baby was born while I was in London; it was another boy. It was strange to think of Guy as the father of four sons – at least he had something good to show for the years of war. I gently touched the small crumpled red face and felt a great sadness.

Papa came to Town for a couple of days to see his new grandson. My father's hair was sprinkled with grey now, but he was still very upright. He said Mother was busy running the Red Cross Hospital at Hatton, and she hoped I was not ruining my hands. I looked down at them, red and roughened by years of disinfectants and winter chilblains, and I laughed, because there was no point in crying. Then I went upstairs and lay down on my bed and slept, until Nanny roused me with a tray. She sat over me while I ate and then she helped me undress, tucked me up between the fine linen sheets and kissed me goodnight. I slept again.

Ralph Dutton invited me to the theatre one evening

during his leave. I sat down beside him in the warm stalls and woke up in the interval with my head on his shoulder. He smiled my apologies away and went to fetch me some coffee, then as the next act started he pulled my head down against his neck in the darkness and I slept until it was time to go home. He joked about it to Robbie next day, calling me a dormouse, and I said lightly, 'Next time you'd better just invite me out to bed, Ralph,' and watched in dawning horror as his face crimsoned. But my brother burst out into wheezing laughter, and managed to gasp, 'You don't change, do you Hellie? Mouth open and foot straight in it!' And then Ralph and I began to laugh too.

I met Alice's new husband. He was tall, but very thin, with sparse grey hair and ever-flickering eyes. I did not like him much, and Alice obviously felt the same way. Letty was living with them – she at least had not changed – going her own way as always, impervious to those around her. She told me she was going to go up to Cambridge to read Natural Sciences and I protested. 'But Mother will never say "yes"!'

Letty shrugged. 'Then she can say "no", can't she? It won't make any difference to me, I shall go in any case.'

When I arrived in Boulogne I was sent back to No. 23 again. Aylmer welcomed me warmly to our hut and I chatted to her and Mac and Tilney at supper and felt as if I had never been away. Next morning I was sent to a light surgical ward. The work was easy; few of the men would be permanently disabled and we had all begun to realize that the war was finally drawing to a close, so my patients knew they would probably never have to go back.

At eleven a.m. on the eleventh day of November the bugles sounded and we knew it was over at last. I was with Sister in the bunk, and we turned and looked at each other, then she said flatly, 'So it's finished, then,' and bent down again to her forms. I went back to laying out a fresh dressing tray. Even the men seemed scarcely to realize what had happened; they were as stunned as we were by the ending of the long years of war.

Tilney bought a couple of bottles of wine in Étaples that afternoon, and half a dozen of us crammed into her hut and shared it in the evening. The alcohol made me feel giddy, and when I tried to stand up to leave I swayed and fell back on to the bed. The others all laughed and then Mac said, 'You'd better stick to cocoa next time, like Aylmer.' She and Aylmer helped me back to our hut and next morning I felt rather shaky when I woke up.

I felt even more shaky a week later when I read Papa's letter – he said the Grenadiers had been in action in the first week of November and their casualties had been high. Guy had fought to the bitter end. He had come through unharmed, but I mourned for those other women who had had their loved ones snatched from them even at the moment of victory.

But victory scarcely seemed an appropriate word for us now, because we were in the midst of a camp of dying men. The light surgicals had all been sent home and our ward had become a medical one – Spanish flu had invaded Étaples. More and more men went down with pneumonia, and Sister herself collapsed with the symptoms and had to be warded. There was no replacement – too many other nurses and orderlies were sick – so I soldiered on alone among men who were delirious and incontinent, watching their faces turn the dreaded dusky blue before they died. As I laid out corpse after corpse I thought bitterly that we must have won the war too soon – we had cheated the God of Vengeance, so now He had played His ace.

For the first weeks, while I changed soiled beds and sponged fevered bodies in a desperate attempt to lower their temperatures, I worried about Robbie. As I carried the oxygen to one gasping man, and tried to erect a steam tent round another before going to mix a poultice to slap on a third heaving chest I thought of my brother's shattered lungs and felt sick with fear.

But then I got a letter from one of the gamekeepers' cottages in the middle of the woods at Hatton and found I had underestimated my mother. As soon as the number of flu victims had begun to rise she had ordered the chauffeur to disinfect the Delaunay-Belleville, and driven straight down to London. In the teeth of all War Office regulations she had extracted Robbie from his hospital and taken him straight back to Hatton. Robbie said it was the funniest thing, to be lying across the back seat watching Mother's ramrod back in the front, actually sitting next to the chauffeur. They had driven directly to the cottage and he was installed there with the stern-visaged Fisher to care for him, in a state of total isolation. I was not even allowed to write a reply to him. But he sounded perfectly content, although I could not imagine what he and Fisher said to each other in the long evenings. I put his letter away and went back to my blue-faced men who were drowning in their own sputum.

Very slowly the epidemic began to wane, but it was the middle of March before my papers came through; Tilney and Mac had already left. I laid out my last corpse, washed my hands carefully, then walked over to the mess. For the last night I slept on my low camp bed under coarse army blankets. In the morning I dressed in my uniform for the last time, said goodbye to Aylmer, threw my kit into the back of the waiting ambulance and left the hillside of wooden crosses behind me.

My war had finally ended.

PART V

MARCH 1919
to
JUNE 1920

CHAPTER ONE

I stood on the deck and gazed out over the grey sea at the white cliffs of England coming steadily towards me. My gloved hands gripped the rail and for a moment I looked down at the inverted Vs on my forearm – those two blue chevrons that marked my years of active service. In France I had simply been Nurse Girvan, with a job to do and a role to play. But today, when I took off my uniform for the last time – who would I be then? Lady Helena had been a girl, an ignorant carefree girl, who had obediently gone with her mother to Court and theatre and ballroom, to Ascot, Henley and Ranelagh, and asked for nothing as long as she could laugh with her brothers and daydream of her tall handsome lover.

But my lover was dead now, and through his death he had taken with him my dreams for the future, even as the loss of my brother had overshadowed my memories of the past. Over these years of war I had learned to live only in the present – but the dead were lost for all time. And gone also was my innocence and my faith, because I had learned what should never have been learned, and seen what should never have been seen – and now I would carry that knowledge with me always, as a scar upon my soul.

But when I climbed on to the train to London I forced these gloomy thoughts away from me; I was going home. And Robbie was waiting for me when I arrived, and as his face lit up at the sight of me, my heart sang.

But that evening I listened to the catch in his voice as his damaged lungs laboured to give him breath, and saw how his body was bent, and watched him walk heavily from the dining-room table, like an old man. Then I reminded myself how gravely wounded he had been, how long he had fought for his life – of course he would not recover from such an illness all at once – and after his being an invalid for so many months I could surely rejoice that now he was able to lead a normal life in London. I had so much to be thankful for.

I soon discovered that I need not have worried about my role now – Mother had no such doubts – Lady Helena Girvan must be returned to Society as soon as possible. My uniform was consigned to the dustbin, an off-the-peg outfit was quickly purchased from Selfridges, and then for a week I scarcely saw Robbie while I was subjected to a ceaseless round of dressmakers, milliners and bootmakers. Even my pre-war gloves and shoes had to be discarded for, to my mother's annoyance, my feet and hands were broader now. 'How could you have been so careless, Helena? Mary Eames served as a VAD at Hatton, but she took the trouble to rest on her bed every afternoon, with her feet up on half a dozen pillows.' I thought of the expression on Matron's face if I had suggested lying down each afternoon during the March Retreat – then replied weakly, 'But we only had one pillow, Mother.'

She was somewhat appeased when, at Bertholle's, Madame exclaimed enthusiastically about my figure – apparently I had at last come into fashion – straight narrow shapes were decreed by Paris now, 'And miladi has such a shapely calf and ankle – so important, now that hems have risen.' I noticed my mother unobtrusively tuck her own thick ankles and heavy calves under the spindly gilt chair, and felt a spurt of mean gratification.

Frocks for day and evening wear were modelled in front of us: Mother and Madame Berthe held earnest discussions on the merits of shining satin charmeuse over clinging silk stockinet, on the benefits of the coat dress versus the suit, on the stability of the new fashion in waistcoats, and the charms of the curious pegtop outline of the latest coats.

410

We moved on to the Maison Lewis and the parade of hats began: wide-brimmed picture hats; close-fitting toques; the newest fashionable cloche shapes – hats trimmed with ribbon, hats adorned with ostrich feathers, and hats alive with dainty, dancing tassels.

I sat in warm salons breathing in the scented air and remembered how only last week I had walked between beds of coughing, spluttering men, carrying bed pans whose noisome odour my nostrils had long ceased to register. I found myself smiling at the oddness of my transition and Mother, seeing me, said sharply, 'Helena – it really is time you learnt to take life seriously! Which *do* you think will look better with that midnight-blue embroidered coat dress – the ivory satin toque or the ruched cream cloche?'

But only when it came to my feet did I feel any interest. I was still luxuriating in the feel of sheer silk stockings clinging to my legs, now so daringly exposed to mid-calf, when the sensation of the glove-like fit of my newly made shoes, so soft and supple and elegantly high-heeled, became a further joy to me.

Parcels and boxes began to arrive at Cadogan Place, and the frown on Mother's face slowly faded as she sat in my bedroom and instructed Norah, my new maid, to array me in outfit after outfit. I walked and turned and stood before the long mirrors and my sense of unreality deepened, as a fashionable stranger stared back at me, dark-eyed and pale-faced in all her finery. Mother pursed her lips. 'Luckily painting is quite acceptable in Society these days – besides you're no longer a young girl. By the way, some mamas are attempting to reinstate chaperonage of their elder daughters – quite ridiculous. Why, Molly Eames has taken Mary back under her wing as if she were just out of the schoolroom – and she smoked like a trooper while she was at Hatton! I have no intention of wasting my time chaperoning you, Helena – I've got quite enough to do organizing Letty's début – thank God that'll be the last one. Besides, no doubt you'll be running about with your brothers, just as you did before the war.'

In my head the words formed an answer – 'Except that I had another brother then, Mother' – but I did not speak it; my mother lived in the present, that was her great strength.

And I was glad of my restraint later, when she sent for Fisher and took out of her hands a jewel case and brought it to me. 'I've had these cleaned for you, Helena – you will be able to wear them now.' And there, sparkling up at me in all its brilliant purity, was the diamond tiara Gerald had given me for my twenty-first birthday. I stood very still, looking at it, until my mother spoke again, her silvery voice almost gruff. 'He was a brave man, Helena – wear it and be proud of him.'

Reverently I lifted it from its velvet nest and carried it to the mirror. I set it gently on my head and saw the diamonds shine against the darkness of my hair. And my eyes shone below with unshed tears. Mother slipped quietly from the room and I sent Norah away and sat down before my dressing table still wearing Gerald's tiara, and took his photograph in my hand – and remembered.

I remembered him still, later in that month, as I stood on the balcony of Devonshire House. Robbie was propped against the balustrade at my side, as we watched the Victory Parade of the Household Cavalry and the Guards' Division. The bands played and crowds cheered as the men who had helped to save us marched tall and proud down the length of Piccadilly. Beside me, Pansy's cheeks were wet with tears as Guy marched past with the Grenadiers. Nanny held little Lance up higher. 'Wave to your Papa, dear – your brave Papa.' The chubby hand waved, and the childish voice called, 'Papa, Papa!' For a moment Guy turned, and his eyes looked up to his wife and his son. Pansy clasped my hand as she whispered, 'I've been so lucky, Helena, so terribly, terribly, lucky.' The tall straight men marching past blurred into one khaki mass, and I gripped the edge of the balcony until my fingers hurt. I felt Robbie's arm round my shoulders and heard his wheezing breath in my ear. 'Good old Guy – out at the very beginning, back at the very end.' Yes, so few of that first army had ever returned, but at least my brother had been among those who had.

Pansy and Guy dined with us that evening at Cadogan Place before driving back to Richmond. They had taken a house there for the summer, since Pansy thought it was more healthy for the children. They left early, and as he kissed me goodbye Guy said cheerily, 'You must come down and stay with us, Helena, now you're back.' As he spoke his eyes turned possessively to Pansy, and his hand touched her shoulder in a small, loving gesture.

Pansy smiled back at him, her eyes adoring, 'Yes, do, Helena – we'd love to have you.' But I sensed that they would not. After four children they were at last having their honeymoon. I would go down for tea occasionally, but that would be all; I would not intrude. Besides, it hurt me to see Pansy's baby on Nanny's lap – where Gerald's son should have been.

Alice and her Fred stayed much longer – he was fidgeting to be off, but my sister deliberately ignored all his hints. There was a brittle edge to her voice now, and when she addressed her husband her lovely eyes were hard. I remembered Hugh's kindly face, and almost hated her – how could she have forgotten him so quickly?

By April the Season was in full swing: the first postwar Season. The whole of Society seemed determined to get back to normal – or more than normal. There was a demented gaiety in the air: everyone danced more frantically, drank more deeply and shrieked more loudly with mirthless, high-pitched laughter. I learned to smoke and began to drink wine again, but as I stood watching the frenzied multitude, I felt like a haggard, gaunt, outsider – a leftover from an earlier era. The men I had danced with were buried in France and Flanders; the girls who had come out with me had children in their nurseries now – I had spent more than four years away at the war, and the world had moved on without me.

I thought longingly of the friends I had made over these last years – surely they would be feeling the same? I wrote to Innes and she invited me down to Oxford for the day. I set off hopefully in the morning, but it was no use. The real world we had shared was the war – and Innes only wanted to forget it. She was kind and polite and introduced me to her college friends over tea: their eyes flickered over my outfit as soon as they saw me, resting for a moment on my too-high hemline before returning to gaze with obvious astonishment at the large ostrich feather on my fashionable picture hat. Decked in my fine plumage I stood out like a bird of paradise among a flock of domestic hens – and we had about as much to say to each other. I sat holding my cup and saucer and listened to them discussing poets and novelists of whose writings I had barely heard, and planning their work for tutorials and lectures I knew nothing of. Innes had her old life now, and I had no place in it.

A couple of weeks later, when I went to see Aylmer, I dressed in one of my prewar skirts, and wore my plainest coat and a toque trimmed only with ribbon. My heart sank when the cab drew up outside a narrow grimy terrace of yellow brick, one of thousands in the outer suburbs of London; I would be even more out of place here.

And yet, in a way, it was easier. Aylmer's mother was firm in addressing me as 'My lady', and as she ushered me into the small front parlour she said quite openly, 'I'll be the envy of the neighbourhood, entertaining an earl's daughter to tea. Jean, fetch those scones out of the oven before they burn.'

Aylmer was placidly welcoming, and though we called each other 'Jean' and 'Helena' rather awkwardly at first, as soon as I asked after her Tom her whole face glowed and she began eagerly to tell me of the wedding plans –

it was only a few weeks off now. 'If it's not presuming, my lady, we wondered . . .' Mrs Aylmer beamed with pleasure as I told her I would be delighted to come.

I was glad I had made my visit, and as I sat on the train on my way back, I thought of how fortunate Aylmer was, with her Tom, her family, soon, no doubt, her babies – and her faith. I would choose a delicate, costly present, and go to her wedding dressed in the finery appropriate to an earl's daughter and be talked of later in Laburnum Road – but I could no more become part of Aylmer's postwar life than I could of Innes'. My class, my upbringing, my very manner, set me clearly and surely apart from them. I felt very lost and alone.

I tried to talk of this to Robbie, but even Robbie had changed. He went out every night as usual, but he had to carry a stick, and a cab was always called to the door. One evening he seemed at a loose end, so I suggested he come with me and Letty to a dance at the Eames's. He turned on me, his face twisted, and wheezed angrily, 'What the hell would I do at a dance? It's as much as I can do to walk to the other side of the Place!' He pulled himself to his feet and thrust open the door even as I was stammering my apologies. I cursed my careless tongue – but he was so often irritable now, he lost his temper easily, and had no patience.

He always stayed out very late, and some nights he did not come home at all. I was on my way down to breakfast one morning when I saw Cooper helping him out of a cab. He was panting for breath, his face was grey and he could hardly walk. As soon as he was in the hall he slumped down into a chair – and I noticed the dusting of cheap face powder on his shoulder. I stood at the foot of the stairs and said nothing – but when he reached into his pocket with shaking hands and took out his cigarette case I could not keep quiet any longer. 'Robbie, no – it'll make you worse.'

He turned his bloodshot eyes on me and gasped, 'Mind your own bloody business, Helena,' and began to flick his lighter. I stood there, helpless, as he drew in the first lungful of smoke and burst out into a paroxysm of coughing. And I stayed where I was, not daring to go to him – to my own brother in his suffering. When at last he recovered himself he stared down at the floor and wheezed, 'Nothing'll make it any worse.' I knew it was a kind of apology.

It was Conan, when he came back from Ireland, who told me that Robbie's girl was an actress of sorts, in the chorus of a musical comedy. Then he said, 'Leave the poor sod alone, Hellie – he's had four years of hell – let him catch up now.' Conan was certainly catching up now. Letty said he had been unbelievably thin when he had first come back from Germany and he was still lean, but now he had the lithe strength of a coiled spring. His recklessness seemed to pervade the very air around him. He was sharing rooms with a fellow officer he had met in the prison camp; they had both resigned their commissions now, but my cousin was flying again. He had gone straight back to it and I knew he took risks, but it was the only thing that seemed to satisfy him. The rest of the time he danced and drank and smoked.

I saw him twirling a slim ash-blonde around the floor at a dance I had gone to with Letty. Mother had given her consent to Letty going up to Cambridge if she spent one Season as a debutante first. My sister, who did nothing by halves, flung herself into it with gusto. She was not pretty – her jaw was too heavy for that – and she made no effort to flirt or entertain, yet she was always in demand. I stood watching her bounce around the room while I sipped at my glass of champagne.

'Drink up, Hellie – drink up!' Conan was beside me, summoning the waiter to fill my glass. I protested, but his blue eyes flashed at me, so I shrugged and drank again. As I drained my glass, the band struck up the opening bars of a tango; he seized the glass from me, thrust it into the hands of a startled dowager, caught me round the waist and propelled me on to the floor. The strong rhythm caught hold of me as we swung into the routine of the steps: the scissors, the heel-clicking, the sudden turns – he threw me round and under his arm and I twisted and turned at his bidding – giddy with champagne and excitement.

He danced me down the length of the crowded room, dodging and feinting between the fast-moving couples, and then we were through one of the long windows and out on to the terrace. He danced me on, twisting and turning, until we reached the top of the steep flight of steps down to the lawn. He swung me down them, step by step, in time to the fading music from the ballroom. When we reached the bottom I collapsed against him, laughing – but he would not let me rest; seizing my hand, he tugged me half-running into the shadows of the garden. We stopped, panting, close by the dark wall – and his eyes glittered as he pulled me nearer. As I felt his hands hard on my bare arms I swayed towards him, and lay unresisting against his heaving chest as he began to tug urgently at the fastenings of my dress. 'I want you, Hellie, I want you!'

There was a soft laugh close by, and we both froze and watched another couple stroll past, arms decorously linked – and realized we were in an open garden, within sight of the blazing ballroom. Conan set me away from him and fumbled for his cigarette case. I watched his face, sharply etched for a second in the flare of the match – and knew that I wanted him too – I wanted his strong male body on mine, hard and determined.

With an effort I kept my voice casual. 'We could find a hotel.'

He drew in a deep lungful of smoke, and exhaled it slowly before he replied. 'We could, Helena – but I'd be paying for it with your mother's money, and I'm not quite such a bastard as that.' He pulled on his cigarette again and said, 'My dear father said he wouldn't allow me a penny unless I stayed in Ireland, but I can't face that great barn of a house. So I blew my gratuity, and

417

Aunt Ria guessed I was skint – she's opened an account for me, letting me draw what I like and do what I like with it. She's been bloody generous, Hellie – sometimes I think she's the only person who understands. So now I've sobered up, the answer's no, thanks all the same.'

He ground out his cigarette and ran back up the steps to the crowded ballroom. I called a cab and went home.

Next day he dropped in at Cadogan Place at teatime. He sat chatting and smoking with Mother. I asked for a cigarette and he said casually, 'It won't do your voice any good, Helena.' I held out my hand and he shrugged and gave me one. Mother went upstairs and we sat smoking beside the tea tray without speaking for a while, then he said, 'Sorry about last night, Hellie, but you do see . . .'

I could not think of any reply, so I smoked on in silence. Eventually he got up and reached for his hat and gloves, then he turned towards me, and his sardonic grin flashed out for a moment as he said, 'Christ, Hellie, over the years you've cost me a fortune in whores!' and he swung out of the room.

I thought, not your fortune, my cousin – it's my mother who pays now. There seemed a certain poetic justice in the idea.

As I came out on to the landing I heard the front doorbell ring, and Cooper ushered in Mother's latest admirer – a square-shouldered, grizzled general with a barking voice. 'I'll go straight up, Lady Pickering is expecting me.'

I drew back into the drawing room as his heavy footsteps pounded past on his way to her sitting room. A silly picture began to form in my head: this evening, while Mother was dressing for dinner, I would go up to her room and nestle cosily at her feet and ask her advice. 'Dear Mother, how can I get a man? Any man, I'm not fussy – just for the one night.' And she would bend over me with a motherly smile on her still-beautiful face and tell me exactly how to do it.

I pulled myself up suddenly and thought, quite rationally: Helena, you're going mad. I lit another cigarette and went up to my room.

Ralph Dutton invited me out to lunch the next day, and as I sat toying with my smoked salmon I realized that I was not listening to a word he was saying – instead I was steadily appraising the set of his shoulders, the strength of his hands – looking him over as if he were a stallion ready for stud. Suppose – but no, Ralph would not do. He was too respectable, he would be shocked – or if I persuaded him he would feel guilty afterwards, perhaps even want to marry me. I gave a small shiver. 'Are you in a draught, Lady Helena? I'll call the waiter.'

'Thank you, Mr Dutton, that would be so kind.'

I walked in the Park after I had left him, and wondered again if I were going mad. At least it would make a change.

There was the jingle of harness and the rattle of spurs behind me – I glanced round automatically – it was a troop of Life Guards. The officer in charge was a young boy with a fair moustache. I swayed and ran to a seat and sat with my face in my hands while waves of shame and humiliation washed over me. Gerald – Gerald who had died when the war was young and heroic, Gerald who had stood in the moonlit garden at Hatton and told me, 'There is not, and never has been, any woman but you. And there never will be.' Gerald had loved me, and yet here was I now, behaving like a bitch on heat – besmirching his memory and soiling the girl he had honoured.

I sat there for a long time, my mind in turmoil. Then I walked to the Stanhope Gate and took a cab to Signor Bianchi's studio. He did not seem surprised to see me. 'Ah, Lady Helena – you're back. Good. Let's hear some scales.'

I sang very badly; my voice was rough and cracked on the high notes. He held out his hand, 'Your cigarettes, please.' I handed them over and he threw the whole lot, silver case and all, into the empty grate. Then he said, 'You have a lot of work to do. Come back at this time tomorrow.'

As soon as I got in at Cadogan Place I went to the morning room and sat down in front of the piano.

CHAPTER TWO

Life was a little easier now that I was singing and playing again; each day had a purpose and a structure which had been lacking over the past couple of months. Now I forced my fingers to re-learn their dexterity, and listened to myself carefully and critically as I sang – trying to coax my voice back to its former suppleness.

But I still worried about Robbie. One evening he did not go out. I found him in the drawing room, hunched over the paper. 'Not going out tonight, Robbie?'

He did not look up; he just shook his head. Then he burst out, 'What's the point? I'm a bloody crock now – I'm no use – I can't even act like a man any longer!' And as he spoke I knew he was repeating someone else's words – and I hated the girl who had said them to him. He shifted in his chair, to turn his back on me, so I left him.

A few days later Ralph Dutton dropped in – he had decided to stay in the army as a regular and they sat talking about the war together; it seemed to cheer Robbie up. Ralph had gone back for the last months, and through into Germany with his men; they spoke about who had survived, so I asked after Lofty and Ginger and Ben Holden. Ralph thought Ginger had been wounded again – he was not quite sure – but he knew both Lofty and Ben Holden had gone on to the end and been demobilized. I was glad of that.

For a while Robbie seemed more cheerful; then Ralph had to leave Town and my brother's temper shortened again and he began to go out every evening on his own – and to stay out.

My voice was improving; Signor Bianchi took it very slowly at first, saying that I had nearly destroyed it in the war – and I remembered the gas marquee and shivered. But it had not quite gone because Elsa Gehring had laid such strong foundations. Dear Elsa – I wondered how she was coping in Germany today: did people still learn to sing there? But Elsa was a survivor; she would not go under.

I was playing and singing one day in the morning room when Conan came in. 'Stop that racket and go and put your hat on, Hellie – I'm taking you out to lunch – I want to talk to you.'

We sat in the small restaurant, chatting casually over our meal. Then, when he had finished his ice, he put his spoon down, leant forward and said, 'I'm going to China.'

I stared at him and repeated stupidly, 'To China?'

'That's right – big place where they're all yellow with eyes like this.' He pulled his eyelids up into a grotesque slant and leered at me. 'Haven't you noticed I've been letting my hair grow long, ready for the pigtail?' Then he was serious again. 'A chap I met at Hendon – he's going out, a flying job – so I thought I might as well go too. I asked around and it's all fixed up. I can't sponge off Aunt Ria for ever, and I feel like a change.'

I was too stunned to speak. He picked up his wine-glass, twirled it, and then said casually, 'Do you fancy coming with me, Hellie?'

'With you?'

'We'll do it legally, of course. Get a special licence, have a damned good honeymoon, then be off at the beginning of next month.'

'You're proposing – you're suggesting we get married?'

421

'That's right.' He added, 'Look, Hellie – I can't promise I'd be a faithful husband, you know me better than that – but, well – I wouldn't ever let you down.'

My mind was in a whirl. At last I stammered tritely, 'But – it's so sudden!'

He gave a great shout of laughter. 'So sudden! Oh, come off it, Hellie'. He leant across the table until his lips were close to my ear and whispered, 'I've had my hand up your skirts ever since I was seventeen!'

'Conan!'

'Well, not all the time, but you know what I mean – and I'm fond of you, Hellie – you know that.'

I still sat silent, uncertain, so he lit a cigarette and said, 'You needn't make your mind up today – sleep on it, and I'll come round and see you in the morning.'

I reached out and touched his hand: it was very warm. I slid my fingers up under his cuff and began to caress the fine dark hairs on his wrist; my breathing quickened. But he pulled away. 'None of that, Hellie – I know your tricks.' He grinned. 'If I give in to you now you'll hustle me off to a room somewhere, have your way with me – and then abandon me – ruined!'

He was laughing, and he looked so young and carefree that I could not resist retorting, 'It was nearly me that was ruined – in the maze that evening.'

'Ah, but I didn't, did I? And I behaved myself afterwards. Aunt Ria appealed to my boyish sense of honour – then she came down to earth, pressed a ten-pound note in my hand and told me to go home to Ireland and seduce a housemaid.' He smiled reminiscently.

I could not help it, I had to ask. 'And did you?'

He looked at me with the devil in his blue eyes. 'You bet I did, Hellie – you bet I did. She was a pert little thing and very free with her favours. I thought I was in paradise that autumn – I was drunk with it!' I thought bitterly: While I, I was put under guard and exiled to Munich. 'Then I had to go back to Eton, and Father turned up a couple of months later in a raging fury –

he'd had to pay to marry her off to a groom. He really tore a strip off me, the old hypocrite. I can't stand that harridan he's got living with him now – that's one reason why I'm not keen on going back. Come on, Hellie, I'll take you home.'

I was very restless that evening. I refused to go out with Mother and Letty, and sat playing the piano for hours before I went to bed. But I still could not sleep: the temptation to go with Conan was strong – there were too many memories in England now. Then I remembered Gerald, kneeling at my feet in the orangery, and Conan's casual, careless proposal suddenly repelled me. I got out of bed and walked restlessly to the window and stared out over the dark gardens. A cab drew up further down the street and a man got out – he staggered to the railings and was violently sick through them; my lip curled, and then something about the way he was clinging to the iron uprights alerted me. It was Robbie.

I threw on my wrap and dashed down the stairs. By the time I got the door open an ashen-faced Robbie was on the step, supported by a brawny taxi driver. ''Ere you are, lidy – bit worse fer wear fer 'is night aht – but I got 'im back ter you.' He looked at me expectantly. I rummaged through my brother's pockets and the man took the coins and said, 'I'll give you a lift inside wiv 'im. Come on, now, chum, upsadaisy.' He heaved Robbie into the hallway and dropped him into a chair. 'Cheerio, lidy – don't be too 'ard on 'im – we all tikes a drop too much sometimes.'

I closed the door behind him and ran back to Robbie; he stank of whisky and vomit. 'Sh, I'sh – couldn't find the key.' He began to heave again and I held him steady while he was sick into the umbrella stand. Then he sagged back against me, his breath rasping in his chest – I couldn't shift him alone, so I rang the bell. Cooper came so quickly I knew he must have been waiting up for my brother.

Between us we managed to get him up the stairs and

into the bathroom. He slid down on to the floor and Cooper helped me take off his soiled suit, then I washed his hands and face. His underwear reeked of cheap scent. We got him across to his bedroom and put him on the bed. The butler stood panting beside me; he was an elderly man now. 'That's all, thank you, Cooper. I can manage.'

'Are you sure, my lady?'

'Yes, quite sure.' He slipped noiselessly out of the room.

I looked down at my little brother, wheezing in a drunken stupor, and reached for his pyjamas. I saw the ragged scars on his chest and his arms as I took off his vest and covered them quickly with his pyjama jacket, then I turned to slip off his underpants and draw on the silk bottoms. While I was tying the cord he opened his bloodshot eyes and looked up at me – and as I saw the despair in them I knew I would not go to China with Conan.

Next morning I shook my head as soon as my cousin came into the drawing room. He looked suddenly absurdly disappointed, and for once he was speechless. I felt I owed him an explanation so I began to talk of Gerald – how I had loved him and how I always would. I found myself repeating Gerald's vow to me – I had never told anyone else, and now there was a painful pleasure in telling it, even to Conan. But my cousin looked at me with a strange expression, as if he did not believe me. I spoke almost angrily, 'He meant it, Conan – he meant it.'

Then Conan said, 'Yes, Hellie – I'm sure he did. I couldn't make that declaration to you, and you know it – there's no point pretending. But . . .'

There was a discreet tap at the door and Cooper appeared. 'My lady, Mr Robbie's come round – I mean, woken up – and he's asking for you.'

I said quickly, 'I'll come – tell him I won't be a minute.'

424

Conan watched my face as the door closed, then he said, 'It's because of Robbie, isn't it? That's the real reason.'

I hesitated for a moment – I did not want to give my brother away – then I told him of the state Robbie had been in last night. He picked up his hat. 'Poor old Robbie. I'm not going to try and persuade you, Hellie – I would have done if it had just been . . . But I know you won't leave Robbie now. Give me a kiss and say goodbye.'

I clung to him and began to cry. 'Come on, Hellie, old girl – I'm just going to China – it's only the other side of the world, you know! Besides, I expect I'll be back some time.' He kissed me again and left, and I went upstairs to Robbie.

My brother looked dreadful; as I came towards him he tried to apologize for the night before, but I put my finger to his lips and smiled at him. He managed a faint answering smile, then his eyelids dropped and I saw he had dozed off again. He stayed in bed all day. I went upstairs after dinner and he lay propped up on the pillows with his eyes closed while I read the newspaper to him. When I reached the foreign news he began to cough. I waited but his coughing became worse; he was gasping for breath with his handkerchief clutched to his mouth. As I ran to him my nostrils caught the foul odour of his breath and I saw his handkerchief was already soaking. I sprang to the washstand and seized the bowl and just managed to get back to him in time as with a great convulsive heave a stream of thick brown pus erupted into the bowl. I stood with my arm round his shoulders until he had emptied his lungs, then I put the bowl down with shaking hands and eased him back against the pillows, wiping his lips with my own handkerchief. 'All right now, Robbie, all right. I'll send for the doctor.'

By the time the doctor came Robbie's face was a better colour, and his breathing much easier. The doctor was bluff and cheery. 'You'll feel a lot better now you've got all that off your chest, young man. Stay in bed for a few days to get your strength back. I'll be round again in the morning.'

Next day the doctor told Robbie firmly he must give up smoking. My brother accepted his decree, and although he was edgy and irritable for a few days he agreed his breathing was much better for it. By the time he came downstairs he looked fitter than he had done for months; I felt so relieved. Now he had got rid of the infected pus his lungs could begin to heal.

Robbie was able to walk in the square gardens by the time Conan came to say his formal goodbyes. Mother sat very upright as she wished him good luck; her face and her voice never faltered – sometimes I had to admire her. My own eyes were full of tears, but I did not let them spill over. I hoped my cousin would find what he wanted in China.

Guy went next. He had accepted a position as ADC to the Governor-General in Canada. He had told me he could not settle in England now – and London made him bad-tempered. I knew how he felt. Pansy was content to go with him wherever he wanted: her round blue eyes followed him everywhere, and her face lit up at every remark he made to her. My brother was very gentle with her now. She told me she wanted another child, but Guy said four children in four years were already too many for her – she must have a rest. 'But I've been either carrying his child or nursing his baby for so long now, Helena, that I feel quite lost – I like to have part of him with me, always.' She spoke with such simple child-like faith that I suspected Nanny would be engaging yet another new nursemaid before very long.

Before he left England, Guy said to me, 'Helena, if you can, take Robbie back to Hatton – London's not doing him any good.'

I knew he was right, so I spoke to Robbie that evening. He sighed, then he said, 'Yes, Helena, we'll go back –

just the two of us – it'll be like old times, won't it?' He tried to smile, but we both knew that in the old times there had been three of us. He swallowed painfully, 'God, Hellie – how I miss him – three years, and I still miss him every hour of my life. We were part of each other.' I sat with his hand in mine as we remembered our brother.

Mother was annoyed at first when we told her we were going back before the end of the Season. 'But the staff are all in London and Hatton's under dustsheets – it's most inconvenient, Helena.'

Robbie began to speak, then a fit of coughing caught hold of him. We sat by helplessly, and as soon as he had wheezed into silence Mother said, 'I can manage without Mrs Hill – I'll send her back ahead of you, with the head kitchenmaid. I gather she's quite competent – no doubt she'll jump at the experience, it'll stand her in good stead later. I'll see that her wages are raised over that period – remember that, Helena, when you're running a household of your own. I hear so many fools of women complaining about the servant problem – but I've never had a servant problem and I never will because I pay for good service. Always be prepared to do the same, it's well worth the few pounds a year extra.'

I said meekly, 'Yes, Mother,' and wondered whether she would have advocated treating Chinese servants in the same way.

'That footman who's been valeting you, Robbie – John, is that his name? He can go too. Mrs Hill will see to everything else; I'll ring for her now.'

We left London at the beginning of the second week in July, just after the great peace celebrations. At Euston, John took charge of all our luggage, and Norah hurried along beside him with my jewel case safely chained to her wrist; I strolled down the platform with Robbie, carrying my parasol. Robbie had been much better these past few days, and now I was going home to Hatton with him – at last the world was getting back to normal.

427

It was very peaceful at Hatton; we walked in the gardens and sat together in the sun. At teatime we would saunter to the summerhouse and wait for John to arrive with the tea tray. I would lift the elegant silver pot and watch the delicate amber stream flow into the fine white porcelain – it was a far cry from the mahogany brew and thick china crockery of the last four and a half years. For a moment I would think that those years had been nothing more than a nightmare – then I would see my slim young brother reach for his stick, and hear the catch in his breath as he slowly rose to his feet – and I knew that the nightmare had been real.

But by the time the Season ended and my parents and Letty came back, Robbie's breathing had improved in the fresh country air – he coughed less frequently, and he could walk further. Guests arrived and departed – I was glad when it was time for them to leave; my tongue had never been fluent in the easy chit-chat of Society, and now it creaked like a gate in want of oil. For years my conversation had been confined to the narrow familiar world of hospital and camp – now it could not break out again. My mother became impatient and told me I should forget the war – but how could I, when every difficult breath Robbie took and every slow movement he made was a constant reminder? And when Eddie lay dead in the churchyard at Lostherne, and I had to brace myself before I could enter the orangery?

My brother was more adept than I. He laughed and joked and even flirted with the short-skirted narrow-hipped little flappers Letty brought home with her. I felt rather jealous of them – they had been born too late for the war and it had not cast its long shadow over their lives. In September, when Ralph Dutton came up to stay, Robbie drove out to the butts and spent the morning shooting partridges at the stand between Ralph and Letty. I went out at lunchtime and my brother's eyes were shining – propped casually on his shooting stick he looked his old self again and my heart lifted.

But as I left, I walked past the game cart with its racks of bloody corpses and the sight of it made me feel very sick. I did not go out to the butts again.

A couple of days before Ralph was due to leave, Robbie came into the music room while I was practising. He sat down beside the piano and when I had finished my scales he said casually, 'You know, old Ralph thinks a lot of you, Hellie.'

'I like him, too – he's so easy to talk to.'

'But no more than that?'

I looked at my brother in surprise. 'Should there be more than that?'

Robbie shook his head. 'I didn't think there was, but – well, Ralph wanted me to ask.' I felt the blush rising to my cheeks as I understood. 'Shall I give him any hope, Hellie – perhaps tell him to wait and see?' Robbie's dark eyes were steady.

But I did not need to think about it. 'No, Robbie – I like Ralph a lot, but – no.'

'I'll tell him, then – he didn't want to be a nuisance.' He gave a wry grin. 'You know, Ralph's one of the best, but – still, I suppose no brother thinks another man's good enough for his own sister.'

The rail strike early in October disrupted one of Mother's house parties and she was furious. She was even more angry when Letty announced her support for the strikers. Mother's colour rose as she attacked Letty in short, biting sentences, and I cringed – but Letty stayed stolidly calm and insisted on propounding the basic tenets of socialism until Mother sprang to her feet and left – with an audible slam of the drawing-room door. Papa mopped his brow and looked at Letty with something approaching awe.

The following week he left for Scotland with Lady Maud, and Mother departed for the Riviera, to stay at Sir Ernest's villa there. It was almost like old times again, except that now it was my sister who was cramming for Cambridge. She went into Hareford every morning to work with a retired schoolmaster there, and sat over her books in the evening. Robbie said, 'Good God, Letty, you don't have to work that hard – they're not very fussy, you know.'

Letty glanced up. 'They might not be, but I am. What I do I do properly.' She made another note in her small neat handwriting. As she did it she looked absurdly like Uncle Arnold, when he came on a visit and sat in the library poring over his ministerial dispatches. I caught Robbie's eye and knew the same thought was going through his mind. We smiled at each other in shared amusement.

Robbie spent time at the desk in his room, too; I put my hand on his shoulder and noticed the letter he was reading – it was an appeal for help. His face flushed, then he said, 'A lot of the men are not finding it easy – since Ralph's a regular now he passes things on to me. Goodness knows, I've got more than I'll ever be able to spend – it might as well benefit some other poor blighter who's in trouble.' He reached for his pen and I squeezed his shoulder and slipped away.

His Colonel had written a history of my brothers' battalion; as he finished each chapter he sent the manuscript on to Robbie, who checked it through diligently. I said to him one day, 'Oh Robbie – do you have to do that – doesn't it bring it all back?'

He looked up at me. 'You know, Helena – it's a funny thing, but that's all I seem to be interested in these days – the war. When Ralph came up I really enjoyed thrashing things over with him – and I miss the men.' He bent over the sheets again.

The local doctor had long chats with him every time he came up to listen to Robbie's chest. Dr Craig was a big-boned Scot and Robbie usually brought him down to the small drawing room for tea when he had finished his examination, but although he conscientiously addressed a few commonplace remarks about the weather in my direction I sensed he disapproved of me for some reason. I did not mind because his visits cheered Robbie up, so as soon as I had poured the tea I would retreat to a corner with my music scores while they sat over their buttered crumpets, yarning. But once I heard Dr Craig saying 'And then they sent me back to the St John's Hospital in Étaples.'

I looked up, surprised. 'How curious – we were alongside them then.'

He stared at me. 'What were *you* doing at Étaples, my lady?' His tone was almost rude, and I flushed in embarrassment.

Robbie said quietly, 'Helena's entitled to her active-service ribbons, Craig, just like you and I. She was nursing all the way through, from September 1914 – and nearly three years of that in France.'

The doctor's face changed, and he said very formally, 'Then I owe you an apology, my lady.' I did not understand what he meant, but he shook my hand very vigorously when he left, and his manner towards me after that was much warmer.

The stables at Hatton were full again now, and Papa had bought a new mare for my use; she was coal black and lively and I called her Gavotte. I took her out when the Cheshire Hunt met at Hatton – it was a fine autumn day, my blood raced and Gavotte went beautifully. But as I galloped down a slope and saw the pack gaining inexorably on the small frantic tan body I felt a wave of revulsion. I was there at the kill, but I turned my mare aside and walked her into a copse and only just managed to slide off her back before I was violently sick. Dr Craig rode up to me and sprang from his horse. 'Are you all right, my lady?' I looked up into his bony face and then turned my eyes back to the yapping hounds. I was crying. He spoke quite gently. 'Aye, you'd best get back to your brother.' He cupped his hands for my foot and I mounted and rode back to Hatton. I did not hunt again.

CHAPTER THREE

As soon as we had come back to Hatton I had arranged
a weekly lesson with Madame Goldman in Manchester,
and as the autumn wore on I fell into a habit of singing
to Robbie before tea; he liked to lie back in his chair
and listen, and sometimes he fell asleep. I was glad when
he did, because now that the colder weather had come
he was often awake at night, coughing.

In mid November Mother came back from France and
assembled a large house party. Mary Eames came with
a streaming cold and Robbie caught it. I was furious
with her as I tended my feverish brother upstairs. Dr
Craig came twice a day and we slipped easily into the
nurse-doctor relationship. Although Robbie was very
weak he did seem to be coughing less now, and I was
glad of that. Cooper detailed John to sit outside the
bedroom to wait on us; the young footman was cheerful
and willing, and I felt that Robbie could safely be left
in his care while I went down for my meals. When I
came back one evening they were playing cards together;
John jumped up, his face very red, but I told him to sit
down and carry on with his game. I took out a pair of
Robbie's socks that I was darning and it was very cosy
in the warm bedroom, with just the quiet murmur of
voices from the two men. I slept in Robbie's dressing
room with the door open, and if he was restless I would
get up and sing him lullabies – they usually worked and
sent him back to sleep again.

But one night he was very hot and uncomfortable, and
I had to send for the doctor; as soon as he arrived Robbie
went into a paroxysm of coughing and began to bring
up the foul sputum again. It eased him at once, but he

was still coughing up more pus, so Dr Craig and I worked out the best position for Robbie to lie in, and by the third morning he had brought up all the poison; his breathing became easier and his temperature went down. Soon he was able to get out of bed and sit up in the chair in his bedroom. But I was still angry with Mary Eames – her carelessness had given my brother a very unpleasant week.

Papa had put a head round the door each morning: 'How's the invalid today? Better? Good, good. Mustn't let the draught in.' His head disappeared again. Mother came in for fifteen minutes before the dressing bell every evening and sat very straight while she retailed the gossip of the day. She was careful never to smoke in Robbie's room, and I was grateful for that. Letty had gone down with Mary's cold as well, so she stayed away.

It was December by the time Robbie was downstairs again, and Letty was already planning her Christmas presents. She asked me to go with her to Manchester one Saturday – I knew she only wanted my company because if I went too, Papa would let us have the Delaunay-Belleville – but Robbie was busy with his battalion history and I was at a loose end, so I agreed.

As soon as we turned out of the park gates Letty leant forward and rapped on the glass partition. Barnes pulled up, but before he could get round to open the door my sister had jumped out and was heading for the driving seat. The chauffeur got back in beside her. I slid back the glass to protest, but it was too late. 'It's all right, Hellie – Barnes has been teaching me.' The car gave two massive judders and then surged forward; I sat back in resignation – Letty was so stubborn it was a waste of time arguing with her.

Once under way she began to chat to the chauffeur – the conversation centred on cams and crankshafts and I did not understand a word of it – but I noticed that although Barnes spoke politely enough it was with an ease of manner he never displayed to Mother or to myself. As we ran into Altrincham Letty demanded, 'Light me a fag, Barnes.' He took out his own packet of Woodbines, put one in his mouth, lit it – and passed it to my sister. She thrust it between her lips: 'Thanks.'

As soon as we had left the car at the Royal Exchange I rounded on my sister. 'Letty – you should never do that!'

'Do what?' She looked at me in surprise. 'Come on, Hellie, I wasn't that bad – the bus did cut me in, and I barely touched it anyway.'

'I'm not talking about your driving – but Barnes – that cigarette . . .'

'But Helena, I could hardly take my hands off the wheel, and you don't smoke now – oh, I see – you think I was being too familiar?'

I said firmly, 'Yes, far too familiar.'

'For God's sake, Helena – they're all human beings, just the same as us.'

'I know that, but they are servants – you should keep them at a proper distance.'

Letty stopped dead and turned to me. 'Helena, you amaze me, you really do. You must have spent years wiping the backsides of men like Barnes – perhaps you even did wipe Barnes' backside, I know he was wounded at Arras – and then you come out with a comment like that, and sound just like Mother.'

I flushed, but I knew I was right. 'Letty, it's most unwise . . .'

She interrupted me: 'If you think I'm going to elope with Barnes – like that stupid Derlinger female and her chauffeur, then you can think again. If you'd ever bothered to stop and talk to him like a human being you'd know he's head over heels about a girl in Hareford – he's invited me to the wedding. Come on, let's see what Kendal's can offer in the way of useless gew-gaws.'

My cheeks were burning as I followed Letty – I was right, but what she had said had made me feel rather ashamed – I had not known that Barnes was getting married, nor even that he had been wounded at Arras.

When we came out of Kendal's later there was rather a crush on the pavement. We drew back a little – a group of young men were passing – working men in their Saturday afternoon best. I gazed at their flat cloth caps without really looking, until one of the caps lifted. I shifted my gaze lower, to a large brown moustache – there must be someone behind me he was acknowledging. The man hesitated, then moved on, and as he did so something about the set of his shoulders tugged at my memory. I spoke uncertainly, 'Ben – Ben Holden?' He swung round so quickly he bumped into a boy behind him, and I saw that it was indeed Ben Holden. I smiled, 'Goodness, I didn't recognize you with that moustache – how are you, Ben?'

He shot out a large hand and shook mine vigorously. 'Very well, Sister, very well. And Captain Girvan, how's he getting on?'

'He's still rather wheezy, Ben, but then, it was a serious wound – and he's getting around again much better now.'

'Good, I'm glad to hear that Sis – I mean, my lady.'

His face reddened, and, conscious of Letty at my elbow, I said recklessly, 'Oh, please call me Lady Helena, Ben – after all, we're old friends. And do let me introduce you to my sister – Letty, this is Sergeant Holden – Ben, my sister, Lady Violet Girvan.'

Letty said warmly, 'How do you do?'

'Pleased to meet you.' They shook hands. There was a short silence and then Ben said, 'Well, I'm right pleased to have seen you. Give my best regards to the Captain and tell him I hope . . .'

I suddenly broke in, 'Ben, why don't you come to visit him at Hatton one afternoon? He'd be delighted to see you – and it would be a great kindness to him, he can't get out at the moment – he had a nasty bout of chest trouble recently, and he does so like to talk over old times.'

Ben looked at me for a moment, then he took a deep breath and said firmly, 'I'd like to do that, my lady – Lady Helena – I'd like that fine.'

'The station's at Hareford, it's only half an hour from Manchester.'

'Aye, I know.'

'Tell them to ring for a car for you, it's a long walk through the estate. We'll look forward to seeing you – you must take tea with us.'

His face broke into a grin. 'Aye, I'll be there.' He raised his cap again and clumped off to his waiting friends.

Letty began to giggle. She was still laughing as she said, 'Really, Helena – you are an old hypocrite! One minute you're scolding me for being too familiar with the chauffeur, and the next you're calmly inviting other ranks to tea – saying, "Oh, please call me Lady Helena – and this is my sister, Lady Violet"!'

'You didn't mind, did you, Letty?'

'Of course I didn't – but I'd love to see Mother's face when he starts "Lady Helenaing" you all over the drawing room carpet! Oh, Hellie – was he one of the ones you put on a bed pan?'

'I suppose he must have been – I really can't remember, there were so many, and we did have male orderlies.'

'Naturally – much more proper!' Letty laughed again, then she suddenly stopped. 'Helena – Sergeant Holden – but that's the man who . . .'

'Yes.'

'Poor old Eddie – he must have been hard work to carry – he was taller than your Ben Holden. Oh well, I suppose Mother will have to forgive you this time.'

All the way home in the car I remembered Eddie's loved face and his voice as he had said: 'Then he picked me up and carried me in, just like a baby.' But it had been too late.

Although I had stopped hunting I still rode regularly. Robbie would chase me out with, 'You need some fresh air, Hellie – and that mare will grow fat as a pig if you don't exercise her.' Letty came with me once or twice, looking very ungainly on her cross-saddle, but we did not have a lot to say to each other. I had seen so little of her over the last years that sometimes I felt she was a stranger. Alice had come up to stay for a few days in the autumn, but although we had become closer during the war I could not forgive her for her hasty remarriage – her new husband was a barrier between us. Besides, I had always chosen the company of my brothers. So now I rode alone.

The week before Christmas I turned Gavotte's head to bring her back across the drive from the Hareford Gate – and saw a small dark figure trudging up the slope beyond the lake. As I came nearer to the drive he stopped, and stood motionless on the gravel, staring at the point where the Hall rose above the trees. Then he pulled his shoulders right back and set off again; he walked with a barely perceptible limp, and now I was closer I realized who it was – Ben Holden. He stopped again, looking ahead, and seemed to half turn away. I urged Gavotte into a canter on the springy turf and as he heard the beat of her hooves he swung round and dragged his cap off – then stood very still, watching me. As I reined in beside him I noticed that his square face was clean-shaven again now. 'Hello Ben, so you have come – Captain Girvan will be so pleased to see you. But surely you're not lost – you can see the Hall from here.'

'Aye, that's what I've been looking at.' He paused, then burst out, 'Truth to tell – I were near turning round – going straight back – afore I saw you.' He stared up at me, his face set, then he turned and looked ahead again. I followed his gaze: Hatton glowed golden above its ranks of green terraces, the long lines of windows

437

glinting in the pale winter sun. It looked just as it always did. He flung a hand towards the rolling parkland. 'I seem to have been walking for miles, since I come through that gate.'

I smiled at him. 'But it *is* miles, Ben – that's why I told you to ring for transport. But it's not far now, so why . . .'

He drew a deep breath. 'It were stupid of me – I knew you were a lady, an' all that – but I only ever saw you in uniform, save that once – so well, I never thought it 'ud be like this.'

And at last I understood: Ben Holden, Sergeant-Major Holden, D.C.M., M.M. – who had marched calmly across No-Man's-Land carrying my brother and ignoring German bullets – was afraid – frightened by Hatton. I wanted to laugh, it seemed so silly – but I managed to stop myself. 'Look Ben, it's just my home.' He still looked so unhappy that I had to make him feel better, so I leant forward and patted Gavotte's neck. 'And you know, I'm nothing but a pauper, really – I haven't a penny of my own. This mare, everything I'm wearing – they're all provided by Papa – and the way he rants on about the income tax he won't be able to do that much longer!' I smiled down at him, and his face lightened – but then he glanced towards the hall again, and his eyes were uncertain, so I said, 'I've finished my ride, I'll walk in with you.'

He moved quickly to the mare's head, then hesitated, 'I don't know how to . . .' I had been going to dismount on my own, as I usually did, but now I held out my hands to him. 'Hold her head steady, Ben, and give me your other hand.' I caught hold of his broad palm with my gloved fingers and jumped quickly down.

As I rearranged the apron of my habit I saw that he was studying my saddle. He glanced round at me. 'I never seen one of these afore – I didn't know how you kept on.'

'Oh, it's much safer than a cross-saddle – especially

when you're jumping. Look, I put my right leg round the near head, here – so it's flat on the horse's shoulder.' I touched the saddle, explaining as Gavotte stood obediently still, 'and then I tuck the other knee well up under the leaping head – there's only one stirrup, of course.'

Ben Holden had relaxed now, absorbed in the technicalities. He moved his capable hands over the saddle, testing the strength of the heads and scrutinizing the fastenings of the stirrup. Then he stood back and nodded, satisfied. 'I reckon I've got th'idea now – let's be getting on, then.'

I could not walk very fast in my tight-fitting riding boots, and Ben looked down at them and said, 'Those are hardly meant to go on ground, I reckon.'

'No, hardly. But I do like them to be well-fitted – I'm afraid I'm rather vain about my feet!'

He turned and grinned at me. 'Aye, I remember at No. 23 you always walked lighter than t'other sisters – so we knew when it were you coming in dark. That leather were over fine for them wards – must have worn out quick.'

I laughed. 'They did – but they were still heavier than I liked. Do you know, when I was very young Nanny told me once I was going to have a pair of "glassy" slippers. Cinderella was one of my favourite stories, so I was convinced they'd be made of real glass. I was so excited – I couldn't sleep all night for thinking about them! And of course, when they came they weren't glass at all, just glacé kid.'

'Were you right disappointed, then?' He sounded quite worried.

'Only for a moment – and then I thought they were so beautiful – they had silver buckles.'

Ben said thoughtfully, 'Aye, I reckon shoes made of kid must be real dainty. I don't recollect ever having seen 'em. How's the Captain been since I saw you in Manchester?'

We walked on together, talking of Robbie and of No.

439

23 until we reached the garden gate. 'Now I must take the mare round to the stables – you go through and ring the bell, Ben, and the butler will show you to Captain Girvan.'

Ben stared across at the massive double doors between their tall flanking pillars, and beads of sweat appeared on his forehead. Then he offered, 'I'll come to stables with you – give you a hand with her.'

'Come with me by all means, Ben – but the groom will see to the horse.'

He reddened. 'Of course – stupid of me.'

I wanted to ease his embarrassment so I asked casually, 'Do you ride?' And then cursed my tactlessness – of course the working classes did not ride! But luckily he took my question at its face value. 'I got me leg across the horses pulling the ammunition limbers once or twice – just to see what it were like, and I managed to hang on – but I didn't feel too safe.'

I laughed, 'There you are, Ben – it's as I told you, side-saddles are much better. Though my sister's always telling me I should change – that I'm being old-fashioned.'

Ben paused a moment, then said loudly, 'Don't you take no notice of 'er, Lady Helena. When you came galloping towards me there you looked just like a princess – I've never seen anything so beautiful.'

By the time he had finished speaking his face was a dusky red. I was warmed by his simple compliment – and the obvious effort it had cost him to deliver it. 'Why, thank you, Ben. Here she is, Jenkins – I've walked her already, so she's cooled off by now.'

'Thank you, my lady.'

I took Ben Holden in by the family entrance. Seen through his eyes I suppose even that seemed rather awe-inspiring. I rang for Cooper. 'Please take Sergeant Holden to Mr Robbie – he'll be in the small drawing room – and then send Norah up to me.'

'Very good, my lady.'

'I must go and get changed – I'll be down shortly, Ben.' For a moment his face looked like Daniel's at the entrance to the lions' den, then he straightened his back still further and marched resolutely after Cooper. I found I was smiling a little as I ran up the oak staircase.

As Norah helped me off with my habit I said, 'Bring me my silver glacé kid slippers, please.'

'But my lady . . .'

'I'm going to wear them with my afternoon frock – just for today.' When she brought them to me I eased them gently on, and twirled one shining foot – admiring it.

Robbie and Ben Holden were already deep in conversation when I came into the small drawing room. Ben looked quickly round and began to rise, but I motioned him down before Robbie could try to get up too. As I advanced across the carpet I took little dancing steps, and then held out my right foot. 'There you are, Ben – a glassy slipper!'

He flushed and put out one tentative hand, then drew it quickly back. 'Well, I am learning a lot today, and no mistake. First it's side-saddles, then slippers. Were them what Cinderella really wore?'

Robbie shook his head. 'I don't think so, Holden. Our governess told us there was some confusion in the translation from the French to explain that story – the English got muddled between "verre" meaning glass, and "vair" that meant fur. Cinderella wore fur slippers – and Hellie would never even touch those, let alone wear them.'

Ben Holden raised his eyebrows in a silent question. I answered it. 'Because of our first governess.'

Robbie grinned. 'I'll tell you the whole story, Holden – but I must warn you that it doesn't reflect much credit on my lady here! It was when Nanny had to go away unexpectedly and we were pitchforked into the arms of this wretched Frenchwoman.' He shuddered. 'She was a sadist of the first order and she bullied all three of us, but especially me – so in the end big sister here decided to act.' He grinned across at me affectionately. 'You wouldn't believe this, Holden, to see her sitting there looking so demure – but she literally threw herself at this woman and sank her teeth into her hand – she hung on like a terrier with a rat – Eddie and I were petrified by her daring. But when the woman had finally prised Hellie's jaws apart she marched her off' – Robbie closed his eyes for a moment. 'We thought she'd taken her away to kill her – stupid of us, but one's not very rational when one's young and frightened.' He stopped for breath, then went on, 'Anyway, to get back to the slippers: Mamselle shut Hellie up in Mother's fur cupboard, and showed her one of the neckties – with a head and teeth – and told her it would bite her if she dared to move. So my sister's never been very keen on fur since – or small furry animals.'

Ben said, 'Like rats.'

Robbie grinned. 'Yes, she wrote and told me how you'd helped her out there, old man – did you ever manage to house train that ginger tom?' And now we were all laughing together.

Ben and my brother sat chatting to each other about men they had known and sectors they had fought in. I listened with half an ear, glad to see Robbie so engrossed and happy. After a while Cooper came in, and told us her ladyship would be pleased to receive Sergeant Holden for tea in the main drawing room. Robbie pulled himself up. 'Just time for your usual sing-song then, Hellie – we'll go through to the music room.' He staggered a little as he reached for his stick and Ben Holden moved forward, but he saw the slight shake of the head I gave him and stopped at once. It was only too obvious Robbie could not both walk and talk and I was grateful when Ben Holden began to speak, telling us he was on the footplate again, firing trains into Manchester sometimes, or driving on shunting turns.

Once he was safely sitting down Robbie asked, 'Where are you living now, Holden?'

'I'm back where I started – though I'm in lodgings now – otherwise it's all t'same, same job, same shed – up at Ainsclough.'

Robbie caught my eye – Ainsclough! Ainsclough where Miss Nellie Girvan had once sung so light-heartedly. I sat down at the piano and, almost without thinking, began to play the opening bars of Edward German's 'Daffodils' – and now I sang again that song I had sung a lifetime ago. As I played the last notes I saw that Ben Holden's gaze was riveted on me. 'Are you fond of music, Ben?'

It seemed to take him a long time to find an answer, and then he said simply, 'Aye, I am.'

I turned back to the keyboard and began to play Arne's lively setting of Ariel's song. I heard the door open as I was singing the last: 'Under the blossom, which hangs on the bough.' My fingers continued to travel over the keys in the closing notes and then we all stood up.

We followed Cooper to the big drawing room, where both my parents were waiting beside the tea things. Papa was affable, Mother gracious, Ben awestruck. Mother knew what was due to Eddie's Sergeant Holden and though it must have cost her an effort to pour tea for an ex-NCO footplateman in her own drawing room she knew the debt we owed and paid it scrupulously. After tea Papa insisted that Ben Holden must be driven back to the station in the Delaunay-Belleville, and when, as he took his leave, Mother heard him say, 'Goodbye, Lady Helena,' she scarcely winced. I was sorry Letty was not there to see her.

After Christmas my young sister decided to go to Paris for a few weeks with a schoolfriend, and Robbie handed her a cheque before she left. She flung herself on him in delight, but as she hugged him I saw his face stiffen in pain, and felt a sharp pang of fear. But Ben Holden came to see him twice in January, and his visits seemed

443

to do Robbie good. I did not see Ben myself as each time I was in Manchester at a singing lesson; I was sorry to have missed him on the second occasion – it was bad luck as Madame Goldman had had to change my usual time at the last minute.

At the end of January I received a letter with a German stamp – I held it gingerly in my hand, as if it would explode. When I opened it I found that it was from Frau Reinmar, in Munich. She was very distressed to trouble me, but she said there was no one else she could turn to: little Franzl had lost an arm in the war – they were very badly off now and they could not afford an artificial one – not even a hook – could we, please, help?

I showed it to Robbie and he wrote out a money order at once; when I replied I enclosed a short note to Franzl – it was difficult to write to him, even just simple news – but I did so want to make contact with him again; he had been like another brother to me. Frau Reinmar sent my note back unopened. She had not dared to even show it to Franzl – he was so bitter against the English; she had lied to him as to the source of the money. It was not for himself that Franzl minded so much, but for Kurt, Kurt his beloved elder brother who had been killed on the Somme. She was so very, very grateful – but please, I must never ever write to Franzl again. After I had read it out to Robbie he looked at me tiredly and said, 'They did lose, Hellie – it makes a difference.' I remembered Franzl, laughing on the ice beyond the Englischer Garten with my two tall twins – then I crumpled up the letter and threw it on the fire.

CHAPTER FOUR

Letty came back from France early in February. She seemed to have spent most of Robbie's present on clothes, some of them very odd indeed. She boasted that she had rationalized her underwear and showed me a curious garment which was like a chemise, but with a loose flap which buttoned between one's legs so one could dispense with wearing knickers. She pressed three pairs on me, made of satin: one in peach, one in pale blue and one in eau de nil – and she insisted that I take a set of black lace garters as well. I thanked her and put them away in a drawer. As I pushed it to, I began to laugh to myself – if I'd been wearing these frivolities when I was a girl, instead of my corset, I might have escaped three years of banishment! I wondered where Conan had got to – I could not even pronounce the names of the places on his postcards.

Robbie was due for a medical board in London soon after Letty got back. Dr Craig asked to see me one day when he had left Robbie upstairs so I took him into the library. He said abruptly, 'Look, are you going up to London with your brother?'

'I haven't really decided – it's only for a couple of days . . .'

He picked up his hat, said, 'Go with him,' and left. I felt very cold.

Robbie would not let me accompany him to Millbank. 'I don't want to look the kind of fool who's always tied to some woman's apron strings – no, you go and have a nice stroll round the shops and I'll see you later.'

It was much later when I heard John letting him in. I jumped up, but he ignored my greeting as he came into the morning room; he went straight to the side table, opened the cigarette box and took one out. As he snapped the lighter I said, 'Robbie – no – they'll make you worse again.'

He turned and looked at me with the lighted cigarette in his hand. 'It doesn't matter now, Hellie – it's not going to make one iota of difference.'

'But . . .' Then I looked at his face and understood. 'No, Robbie – no!'

'I'm sorry, Hellie – I've been driving around for hours wondering if I'd got the courage to keep it from you – but I haven't. Besides, you'd only guess – just as Eddie would have guessed if he'd still been alive – but he isn't.'

I said desperately, 'You must have misunderstood – medical terms are so confusing – I should have come with you . . .' My voice trailed away as I saw the expression in his eyes.

'Helena, you listen pretty carefully when a man's delivering your death warrant. Besides, he spelled it out very thoroughly, showed me the X-rays, the lot. Apparently it was a miracle I survived at all after what that shell did to me. He said some surgeon at the CCS performed "heroic surgery" – those were the words he used, "heroic surgery" – they opened my chest up to get the shrapnel out – even dug a piece of the bloody stuff out the heart muscle itself – Christ, I wish they'd never bothered! I could have gone out then, clean and finished, instead of hanging on as a bloody cripple for a couple of years and then having to face it in cold blood.' He drew at his cigarette again and began to cough.

When he had stopped I demanded, 'Tell me exactly what he said, Robbie – every word – there might be some chance.'

He leant back in his chair and said quite calmly, 'Colonel Thompson thinks it's probably the lung infection that'll finish me off – he said I've got a chronic abscess, low down – it's boiled over twice already, you

446

know that. Well, next time, or perhaps the time after . . .' He shrugged.

'But – an operation – '

'They can't operate on something like this, it would only speed things up – besides, my other lung's so shot to pieces I'd never stand an anaesthetic. I asked, Hellie – God, I'd be willing to take any risk, but apparently they aren't – he said I wouldn't get a surgeon in the whole country to touch me, it'd be murder.'

'Drainage then' – I was becoming frantic – 'they can drain it, under a local anaesthetic – I nursed men like that.'

'They did drain me, Hellie – for weeks – you were still in France. But that was outside the lung; this is inside, so they can't do a thing. Besides, I might as well tell you the whole story while I'm at it – they think my heart's been affected by the infection as well – one of the valves is practically gone – so it's heads the lungs get me, tails the heart. You can lay bets on it if you want to – but you'll have to collect against my estate, I won't be around to pay up.'

'Robbie – '

His face twisted. 'I'm sorry, Big Sis – but it's the only way I can talk about it. Like when you're in the front line – you have to joke or you'd be finished. And Hellie, I don't want anybody else to know – it'll be our secret, right? And we won't talk about it after today.'

I whispered, 'Yes, Robbie.' But I had to ask, 'Did they say – how long?'

My brother stared out of the window. 'It could be months – but not years. The Colonel said I'd have "time to put my affairs in order".'

I felt bitter anger against this unknown, faceless doctor. 'He should never have told you!'

'But I asked him, Hellie – I asked him point blank. I've had a feeling, you see – I knew something was wrong. I hoped he'd tell me it was nothing that wouldn't eventually improve – but he didn't. Look, why don't we

447

go to the theatre tonight? Nothing highbrow – something that'll make us laugh.'

I barely slept all night and in the morning I told Robbie we must get a second opinion.

He shook his head. 'It'll be a waste of time – Thompson's a good man – one of the best when it comes to battle injuries.'

'Please, Robbie – doctors do make mistakes.'

He gave in at last, but only to please me, and the report was exactly the same. So the day after, we went back to Hatton together. On the train Robbie said suddenly, 'I wish Conan were here.'

I looked at my brother – we had only had those scribbled postcards. 'He couldn't do anything.'

'Not for me, no. But although he can be a wild so-and-so at times, he'd never let you down, Hellie, I know that.'

I supposed that was true. But at the moment all I could feel was overwhelming relief that I had not gone to China with Conan; at least I was here with Robbie now.

When we got back I began to sleep on the bed in his dressing room, otherwise life went on as normal. One night when I looked in on him after he had gone to bed I suggested, tentatively, that perhaps I should write to Guy. Robbie shook his head decisively. 'Guy's always been a pretty decent elder brother, but I don't want two of you hanging around looking at me as though I were an ox waiting for a particularly messy slaughter.'

The blood rose in my face as I said with difficulty, 'I'm sorry Robbie, I don't mean to.'

'Oh, blast my wretched tongue – I should never have said that. Hellie, I'm sorry!' He seized my hand and pulled me to his side. 'It's just that you look so sad sometimes. But I couldn't do without you, you know I couldn't.' I stood beside him, with his warm hand clasping mine, then he slowly released it and said, his voice studiedly casual, 'By the way, Hellie, I had quite a chat with Craig last week, while you were out riding. He was a damned good MO in France you know – he was with old Teddy's battalion for a while, and Teddy thought very highly of him – I remember his saying once he admired a doctor who had the guts to reach for the morphia and let his conscience go hang.'

And now I realized what he was trying to tell me – I remembered Young Lennie – but my brother, my little brother!

'No, Robbie – no!'

But his face was tired and old in the lamplight as he looked up at me. 'I'm sorry, Hellie – but I think I used up all my courage in the war. I used to keep telling myself, if I can only hang on until it's all over, then I'll be all right. But it is over, and I'm not all right, am I? I keep feeling as if I'm going to choke – and this damn pain, it's getting too much for me. Each time I get nearer to losing control, and I think, if it's like this now, what will it be like when it finally happens? So I asked Craig outright, and he didn't mince his words. If I'm lucky my heart'll go first, and it'll be pretty quick – I won't know much about it – but if I'm not lucky – well, it'll be bloody unpleasant coughing up my lungs. So I told him I'd rather not leave it to luck, and he agreed right away. I don't want to go out screaming and cursing – if I know he's coming then perhaps I can hang on.' I could not speak. But Robbie had not finished yet. 'I've been trying to pluck up the courage to tell you all week, Hellie – he'll only do it if you swear to keep your mouth shut – obviously you'd know. And it means we can't get a nurse in, either – but he said you should be able to cope, after spending so long in the base hospitals.' He paused. 'But, Hellie – you can say no, if you want to.' But I saw the pleading in his eyes.

I swallowed, and then said quite clearly, 'I swear to keep my mouth shut, Robbie. You can tell him in the morning.'

'Thanks, Big Sis.'

I had to break the silence, so I tried to make my voice light. 'Goodness – all this talk about coping – when I've only got one patient! Why, you're talking to a woman who had forty men under her sole command night after night – you won't dare to disobey me – when I've got my apron on I can outdo Catherine the Great herself!'

Robbie looked at me with a startled expression, and then, incredibly, he began to laugh. 'Oh, Hellie, Hellie,' he managed to gasp, 'history never was your strong suit, was it? Don't you know that Catherine the Great – well, compared with her, our late lamented King Edward was a celibate monk. She supplied Poland with kings for years – from her discarded lovers!'

'Oh no, Robbie! But that was one of my favourite jokes when I wanted to get the men to go to bed at night.'

Robbie lay back and wiped his eyes. 'Helena, you are priceless sometimes. Well, we'll just have to trust that Russian history isn't on the syllabus of the council schools. But I hope you never made that joke in front of Holden – I found him once in the sergeants' mess on the last volume of Gibbon's *Decline and Fall*, and he told me he read every history book he could get his hands on – said it gave him a sense of proportion.'

I smiled back at my brother. 'I expect I did, you know – but Ben would be far too polite to even *think* about such a thing.'

Robbie grinned up at me. 'Go on, he's only human – I expect his tough little Lancashire heart went pitter patter for weeks afterwards, every time he saw you coming up the ward!' I bent down and pretended to box his ears, and heard him still chuckling to himself as I left him.

The following afternoon Dr Craig called and asked to speak to me. As soon as Cooper had closed the library door behind us the doctor reached into his pocket and brought out a pill bottle. He held it out to me. 'My lady, your brother spoke to me this morning. You'd better

450

keep these safe somewhere, under lock and key.' His manner was as brusque as ever. 'They'd best be here ready when I need them. There's a hypodermic upstairs already.'

I had difficulty in keeping my hand steady as I took the glass tube from him. 'Thank you, Dr Craig. How do you think he is today?'

He looked at me and shrugged his shoulders. 'As well as can be expected – what do you want me to say? You can relay the usual platitudes to Lord and Lady Pickering.' He turned and stalked out, his red hair on end.

I carried the bottle upstairs as though it were a live grenade, and locked it away in the dressing room. When I came down again Robbie asked, 'Did he give them to you?' I nodded and turned away, but not before I had seen the relief on his face.

At dinner that evening Mother said, 'I gather Dr Craig called to see *you* this afternoon, Helena – and that you saw him alone. Please remember that it doesn't do to treat the man as though he were a social equal – especially as it's rumoured he's some sort of socialist.'

Letty looked up from her plate in interest. 'But in that case he *is* our social equal, in his eyes, that is.'

'Don't be ridiculous, Letty.'

'No, Mother, you're failing to understand a basic philosophical concept – what *we* believe and what Dr Craig believes are two quite separate things . . .'

They wrangled on, Mother's voice becoming higher and sharper while Letty adopted a tone of exaggerated reasonableness which was calculated to raise the temperature even further. My father sat watching with a small, satisfied smile: it was ironic that only Letty, of all her children, dared to cross my mother. I looked over at Robbie, but it was clear from his withdrawn expression that he had shut his ears to them. I tried to do the same.

The following day Ben Holden came. Robbie and I were sitting in the small drawing room together, just the

451

two of us. I had played and sung all morning. I sang to Robbie a lot now – he liked me to, and that way we did not notice so much his increasing shortness of breath. After lunch he had stretched out on the sofa and gone to sleep; neither of us slept much at night now. Elsa Gehring had been right, when she had taught me to sing softly – though it was not the bedroom of a king I sang in night after night. It was difficult to sing when there were tears in my eyes – I was forcing my voice now and all my skill would not keep it true much longer – but I knew I would not need it for much longer.

I stood at the window looking out over the green parkland and thought of how Hatton had narrowed to a prison for my brother – a prison with only one way out; and I was trapped here too, with him. Just a year ago I had come back from the war thinking that it was over; but I had been wrong, for the war still wheezed and panted on the sofa behind me. 'Hellie?' I went quickly to his side and helped him raise himself a little higher on the cushions.

The door opened. 'Mr Holden, my lady.'

I turned in relief. 'Ben! I'm so glad to see you.'

He marched forward, very broad and solid. 'I would have come before – but I thought the Captain were away.'

'We both were, in London – but we came back.' I saw his eyes move to Robbie's face, but there was not the flicker of a change in his expression. He came up to the sofa, hand outstretched.

'It's good to see you, Holden. What's the news?' Robbie's eyes had brightened.

The two men sat talking together quietly. I lapsed into a near-doze, scarcely listening – but I was still aware of how skilfully Ben Holden guided the conversation, so that Robbie never had to use more than a few words at a time. Later I poured tea for them, and then Ben got up to leave. He refused Robbie's offer of a car. 'I enjoy the walk, sir – thanks all the same. This is a different sort of country for me – makes quite a treat.'

Robbie turned to me. 'Why don't you walk a little way with Holden, Hellie? You haven't been out of the house for days.' I opened my mouth for the automatic refusal, but then my brother added, 'I feel like another nap.' So I arranged him on his cushions and rang for my coat and outdoor shoes.

We walked in silence until Ben Holden finally asked, diffidently, 'Did they say owt at medical board?'

'Yes.' I could not go on, but I knew he understood.

We walked on further. At last he said, 'Look, lass – I mean Lady Helena – if there's ever anything I can do, you know where I live: Clegg Street, Ainsclough – you drop me a line and I'll come soon as I can.'

'Thank you, Ben.'

We walked on without speaking until we drew level with the larger lake; then he sent me back.

CHAPTER FIVE

The day after Ben Holden's visit Robbie seemed a little better. He was sleeping peacefully when I looked in on him in the morning, so I dressed quickly, crept out through the dressing-room door and went down to breakfast. Only my father was there. He lowered his *Times* and muttered to the butter dish, 'How is he today?'

'He's still asleep, Papa – and he had a quiet night.'

'Good, good.' *The Times* moved up again.

After breakfast I walked out on to the terrace; the sun was shining and I felt more hopeful – perhaps the infection would clear up after all – doctors had been wrong before. But my small burst of optimism quickly evaporated as I saw my brother coming towards me – leaning so heavily on his stick, and with his breath coming in small anxious pants. And as I reached up to kiss his cheek the freshness of the morning air was tainted by the scent of decay from his lungs. Yet his old smile was on his face, as he greeted me, and looked around with pleasure. 'What a lovely day! You must go for a ride, Hellie – or perhaps we could go for a little trip in the governess cart.'

I smiled. 'If you'll trust yourself to me, Robbie – I'll try not to tip you out this time, like I did in front of Sir Ernest!'

He gave a reminiscent chuckle, and we went slowly into the house. As soon as we sat down in the music room Robbie reached into his pocket and drew out a small leather case. I knew what was in it before he flicked open the clasp. We both sat in silence, looking at Eddie's watch. I remembered the smile on Uncle John's face when he had held them out, one in each hand, 'Twin watches for twin godsons.' I had looked at the boys' faces, so pleased and proud. Although Mother had said the twins were far too young to have gold watches they had never been broken: they had both come back from France, whole and unmarked, unlike their young owners.

Robbie gently stroked the smooth gold with his fingertip. 'I always meant to send it to Holden – Eddie would have wanted him to have it. Only I couldn't bear to part with it before, but now . . .' He shrugged his thin shoulders, then abruptly held it out to me. 'You take it, Hellie, and see it gets delivered.'

I took the watch in silence and ran quickly upstairs to put it safely away. When I came back down he was cheerful again, and picked out odd notes on the piano as I sang. But that afternoon, even the slow governess cart was too much for him, and we had to turn back before the West Lodge. At dinner, when Papa talked of the prospects for next season's hunting, Robbie said nothing, and I found myself blurting out that I thought it was wrong to kill anything – even a fox. Papa's face was hurt and uncomprehending, while my mother, slicing neatly through a peach, said in her beautifully modulated tones, 'But Helena, you only ever had two social accomplishments – singing and hunting – I don't think you can afford to give one up.'

The old sense of failure tied my tongue, but Letty, bold Letty, said pertly, 'You never used to consider her singing a social accomplishment anyway – don't be inconsistent, Mother – it's a sign of old age.' Mother flushed angrily and drew breath, but her retort was checked by the entrance of Cooper with the coffee, and Letty winked at me, unabashed. Robbie looked down at his untouched plate, his face very tired. I felt a rush of hatred for my bickering family.

The next day Robbie was fighting for breath, and the pain attacked him that night. He had twenty-four hours of peace, and then it came again, and after that he was never free of it. Three nights later he was racked with great tearing coughs and even as I reached him with the bowl he choked up foul-smelling pus; there was blood and shreds of tissue mixed with it, and I wanted to cry, but I did not. When he had finished I eased him back against the pillows, my arm around his shoulders. As he looked at me I saw the desperate apology in his eyes and I stroked his hair with my free hand and whispered, 'It's all right, little brother – it's all right.' He rested his cheek for a moment against my palm and I thanked a God I did not believe in that I had spent four long years holding men's heads in just such a way – and so now I could hold my beloved brother's without flinching.

I hoped that bout would relieve him, but it did not. I spoke to Dr Craig in the corridor, but he said bluntly, 'It won't make any difference – there's more than one abscess now.' And I realized that my brother's lungs were simply rotting away. Cooper asked to see me the next day and told me, his eyes fixed on the shining toes of his shoes, that John had suggested he should sleep in the butler's pantry, instead of Robert – so as to be near the bells. 'I was ready myself, my lady' – he looked up, his eyes anxious that I should understand – 'but I'm not as spry as I was, I can't move very fast – John's a reliable youngster, and since he's been valeting Mr Robbie . . .'

I touched his sleeve with my hand. 'Thank you Cooper, and thank John for me. We're very grateful to both of you.'

I felt the tears prickling behind my eyelids as he left the room, and then anger came to me at the thought that the servants had guessed, while our own family seemed so unaware. But at dinner that evening I saw both my parents glance in turn at Robbie's empty place – then each looked quickly away – and I wondered whether they were so oblivious, or just too frightened to face reality.

In the night I heard him call me; and even as I awoke I heard the new note in his voice – high-pitched and afraid. I ran through the door, pulling on my dressing gown. 'I'm here, Robbie – I'm here.' I fumbled to turn up the light and press the bell with one hand while he gripped the other like a vice.

He was gasping and panting and I could barely hear him as I bent down, 'Hellie, don't leave me.' His eyes closed as the tears forced their way from under his lids.

'I won't leave you, Robbie – I'll never leave you.'

There was a soft tap and the footman slid noiselessly through the door. 'Phone for the doctor, John – tell him to hurry. But it must be Dr Craig – only Dr Craig – no one else will do. Wait downstairs for him – have the door ready open.'

My brother writhed white and sweating on the bed, but he did not cry out as I talked to him, repeating over and over again, 'John's gone to phone the doctor – it won't be long now, hang on old man, the doctor's coming.'

But the footman came back too soon – and there were only his footsteps in the corridor. I felt Robbie's shoulders go rigid against my arm as John came alone through the doorway. The footman whispered, 'He's been called out for a confinement over Hallam way, so I got Barnes up and told him to go for him there – was that right, my lady?'

'Yes, quite right, John. Would you wait outside the door in case I need you?' But as I spoke I was already thinking – a confinement, how could he leave a confinement? Oh why had not John asked how long he had been there? But even if we knew – a difficult confinement could take hours . . . And my brother's body arched up and he choked and the blood and pus spurted from his mouth before he fell back against my arm – and as he stared straight up at me I saw the desperation in his eyes – and knew he could not wait.

I would not let my brother scream his life away in pain and filth – and the agony of defeat. I knew now why the glass bottle had been left with me. I put my face close to his and said, 'It's all right, Robbie – I know what to do, I can help you,' and I saw understanding dawn, and with it a great relief. But then he moved his head in a little gesture of renunciation, and I sensed rather than heard him say, 'I can wait.' But my mind was made up, and I replied quite loudly, 'You don't have to wait, Robbie. Lie still, I won't be a minute.' And I ran for the bottle.

My hands were quite steady as I unscrewed the needle and drew the water into the syringe. How much? It suddenly seemed very important not to give him more than he needed – yet that was absurd, enough was too much – my head began to spin – then I had a sudden sharp memory of Captain Adams' lean face as I had watched him fill his syringe, and I remembered and put in the same number of tablets. But now it was my hand that drove in the needle, my fingers which pushed down the plunger, and my own brother who looked up at me from eyes tortured with pain – and gratitude.

I drew the needle out gently and rubbed my warm

457

palm over the mark it had made, whispering, 'It's all right, Robbie – not much longer now, little brother.' I put my arms around his shaking body and held him close, telling him again and again, 'I love you, Robbie – I love you.' Gradually the shudders weakened and his breathing slowed, and I felt him begin to sag against me. Still holding him I laid him back against the pillows, then drew away a little so that I could search his face. His eyes were already dulled, but desperately I watched his lips, willing him to speak. But he could only move them slightly in one last attempt at a parting smile – then I felt him slump into unconsciousness.

I sat gripping his hands and listening to the irregular rhythm of his breathing, and watched the final tremors shake his body until the room went suddenly very quiet. Then I lifted his hands and placed them neatly, one above the other, on his chest, and looked down at him for an eternity. From long ago, in a vanished ballroom, I heard Gerald's voice: 'I believe you would follow your brothers to the gates of hell itself.' Tonight the gates of hell had opened for me, and I had passed through.

I knew I could not live with myself any longer, now. And the remaining tablets seemed to wink at me through the glass, and I looked at them gratefully and reached out my hand for the bottle and slipped it into my dressing-gown pocket. It lay there, cool and comforting to my touch. I sat on by the bed until I heard the faint slam of a car door, and knew that the doctor had come – too late. He arrived panting, and shut the door quickly behind him, but he slowed as soon as he saw the still form on the bed. As he put the stethoscope down he looked across at the empty syringe. 'So you did have the guts – I wondered. How much did you give him?'

And without thinking I answered, truthfully. He glanced at the syringe again then his eyes narrowed and he came round the bed and stood looming over me. 'Then I'll have the rest back.' He held out a large square palm.

I shook my head. 'No – please – let me . . .' The little glass bottle clung lovingly to my hand.

'Oh no you don't, my girl – I've put my head on the chopping block once already tonight.'

I was begging now. 'No – I want them, I must have them!'

And suddenly he lost his temper and hissed, 'Look, my lady, if that's what you want you can go and fling yourself under a train. But you're not playing silly games with my morphia. Give them to me.'

Slowly, reluctantly, I took my hand from my pocket. Roughly he seized hold of it, prised my fingers apart and took my friends away. Then, as I looked up at him, his face softened; he put a heavy hand on my shoulder for a brief, clumsy pat and said, his voice more gentle now, 'Don't be a fool, girl – you only did what you had to do. You had no choice.'

He went to the door and sent John for hot water and towels and fresh bed linen and began to tear off the soiled sheets. I stood up to help him and together we washed Robbie and dressed him in fresh pyjamas and laid him between clean sheets until he looked smooth and young again. I stood gazing down at my brother until the doctor gave me a little push towards the dressing room. 'You'd better get changed before we call your parents.' I looked down in dull surprise at my stained robe and went to do as I was told.

When I came back I went out to the patient John. 'Go and ask Taylor to wake Lord Pickering, please, and send Miss Fisher to her ladyship.'

He ducked his head. 'Yes, my lady.'

It seemed a long time before my parents came, and I was grateful for the doctor's fidgety presence. My mother and father were suddenly shocked and old. They stood apart, looking at Robbie's still face, then Mother turned to me, her voice sharp and reproachful. 'You should have sent for us, at once. He would have wanted to speak to us.'

'He never spoke, Mother – he was unconscious.' The lie slid easily off my tongue. She was not appeased, but I did not care. I realized with a pleased relief that soon nothing would matter any more.

Back in my room I thought of how much simpler it was this time. I had had to mourn for Gerald, and for Eddie – dear Eddie, I had missed him so much – but now I would scarcely have time to grieve. Why, if I could just keep my mind empty for a few short hours, I need never feel sorrow at all. I was pleased with the idea, and I smiled to myself and hummed a little tune as I waited for Norah.

She came very quickly, her eyes red-rimmed from weeping; I saw the sympathy in her face and wanted to tell her there was no need to feel sorry for me, no need for the black clothes she was dressing me in – but I thought she might not understand.

As soon as my hair was pinned up I went to my jewellery drawer and took out the fine diamond brooch that Robbie had given me on my last birthday – how long ago that seemed! But I must wear it today, of all days. But as I stood with it in my hand I noticed an unaccustomed red leather case in the drawer. Its presence puzzled me for a moment, and then I remembered – it was Eddie's watch. I would take that with me too, today, and remember both my brothers. But as I picked it up a flicker of unease touched my mind – it was not mine to take, Robbie had wanted me to give it to somebody – but to whom? My mind was very slow today; I stood, cudgelling my brain, then it came back to me – of course, Sergeant Holden – that was who Robbie had asked me to give it to, only just the other day. I held it, uncertain, I had not got the time – I had something else to do – yet Robbie had asked me, so how could I refuse? Then my mind cleared. I would take it first, I would deliver it on my way – after all it did not really matter where – perhaps it was better if I went further away, then nobody would know me and try to stop me.

'Bring my hat, Norah – any will do.'

My maid looked startled. 'You're not going out, my lady?'

'Yes, yes I am, and I'll be away all day, so don't wait up for me.' Then seeing her concerned expression I added, to reassure her, 'I have a little package to deliver, Mr Robbie asked me to – as soon as possible.' Her face cleared and as she reached for the hatbox I thought how clever I had been not to arouse her suspicions – and it was the truth.

I sent her for Barnes at once – there was no point in waiting for breakfast – I would catch the first train to Manchester. When it came in there was an empty compartment, and I felt I was in luck. I hummed a strange little tune to myself – it kept going round in my head, over and over again, yet I could not place it – normally I could always place a tune, and I felt a little spurt of irritation, then I smiled at my foolishness – as if it mattered today!

I had to wait at Victoria, so I strolled up and down the platform, breathing in the smoky air and smiling to see the porters scurry around with their absurd, bustling gait. We left the station into brilliant sunlight, and I was so pleased because it was going to be a fine day. How lucky I was!

A pleasant-faced woman with a small boy got in at Bolton – I wondered idly why they were both out so early, and without Nanny. The little boy kept rushing up and down between the seats and his hands were getting dirtier and dirtier. His mother became flustered; he would not obey her and she kept darting apologetic glances at me. I smiled reassuringly back. Then he fell heavily against my knees so she picked him up, with an, 'I am so sorry!' and swung him on to her lap and held him there, as he wriggled. Suddenly I felt a piercing sense of loss – but I thrust it ruthlessly from me; my way was best, I knew it was. I looked away from the

461

child, out of the window at the small stone cottages and round green hills.

There was a moment of confusion at Ainsclough, when the cab driver asked me where I wanted to go. I stared at him blankly for a moment, then out of the air around me came the words 'Clegg Street', and I said, confident now, 'I have a small package to deliver, to a Mr Ben Holden who lives in Clegg Street. Perhaps you would be so good as to inquire for the number?' He raised his hand to his cap and climbed up on to his perch. We set off with a jolt down the steep slope and I gazed, in mild interest, at the tightly packed grimy stone houses.

There was only a short delay while he questioned a group of quick-voiced schoolchildren, and then we drew up in front of one of the flat-faced terraces. The driver opened the door. 'It's Number Six, miss, just 'ere.' I thanked him and asked him to wait, then I lifted the gleaming brass knocker, admiring the clean varnish and freshly whitened front step. Ben Holden's landlady must be a good housewife; I was pleased for him: he was a nice man.

A thin-faced woman with grey hair opened the front door. She looked surprised to see me – of course, it was far too early in the morning for a call – but then I only wanted to deliver a package. She asked politely, 'Yes, miss, and what can I do for you?'

I smiled at her. 'I'm so sorry to inconvenience you by calling at this hour, but I have a small package to deliver. Would you be so kind as to give that to Mr Holden, please?' I held out my little parcel, ready to turn away – but she did not take it. Instead she swivelled her head round and called back into the dark passageway, 'Ben, there's a lady at door, with summat for you.' She turned to me again and explained, 'He's on nights – but he's not gone to bed yet.'

I was disconcerted. 'Please don't trouble him – if you would just be so kind . . .'

But Ben's face appeared behind her, blinking in the

bright sunlight. The woman stood aside and he pushed quickly past. He was in his shirtsleeves and braces, with no collar on, and I noticed the telltale smear of egg yolk on his chin. I was embarrassed at having taken him unawares like this. 'Oh, Ben – I didn't want to disturb you at your breakfast – I am so sorry to have been such a nuisance.' He just stood there staring at me – the expression of astonishment on his face was so comical I only just managed to stifle a giggle. I held out the small parcel. 'This is for you.' But he did not take it. I began to feel impatient; after all I had delayed my plans especially to deliver the watch, and now no one would take it from me. I spoke again. 'Captain Girvan wanted you to have this. It's Mr Girvan's watch – my brother always intended you to have it, but you know how it is' – I gave a little shrug – 'he couldn't bring himself to part with it before.'

I thrust my package forward again, but Ben still did not take it. He was behaving very oddly this morning – perhaps he was tired. But he did, finally, speak. 'Before *what*, Lady Helena – he couldn't bring hisself to part with it before what?'

I smiled at him; he really was being obtuse today. 'Before he died, Ben,' I explained patiently.

I saw his eyes narrow; he must be understanding at last. Good, I wanted to get on, I had something important to do. But he still would not take my package; instead he asked me another question, quite quietly. 'And when did he die, Lady Helena?'

'Why, last night, of course – or was it early this morning? Yes, that's right – it was actually this morning.' I smiled at him again, but he did not smile back. I thought, of course, he liked Robbie, he must be quite distressed – it's not as easy for him as it is for me. Poor Ben, he will have to grieve. I wanted to comfort him. 'He didn't suffer for too long, Ben – not at the end.' Then I bit my lip; that was not quite true. 'That is, it was bad for a while, but . . .' How could I explain?

Then I had a sudden inspiration – of course, I could be discreet, but Ben would understand. 'Do you remember Young Lennie, Ben? How he was in such pain – and then Captain Adams came?'

He said quietly, 'Aye, I remember.'

'Well, that's what happened with my brother – at least' – I paused for a moment, anxious to be quite truthful – 'it didn't happen exactly like that because the doctor had been called out, you see, so he couldn't come soon enough – but it was quite all right, Ben, because he'd given me what I needed, so Robbie didn't have to suffer for too long.' I felt pleased with myself as I finished. I had explained it all very neatly – I had not given anything away, but Ben would understand, and realize there was no need to worry. And I was so tired of holding out my little package, so I bent down and placed it carefully on the snowy white step, saying firmly, as if I were talking to a rather slow-witted child, 'That's for you, Ben. Goodbye.' Then I turned back to the waiting cab.

But before I could get in Ben suddenly leapt forward and barred my way, and when I tried to step round him he seized me by the arm; so hard, that it hurt. I looked at him blankly. The cab driver tried to interrupt, but Ben spoke to him quickly, in some kind of dialect – I could not follow it – and the man stood back. Ben turned to me again, and asked loudly, 'Where are you going to now, Lady Helena?'

I felt a sudden spurt of irritation – first he had refused to put out a hand and take my package, and now he was trying to stop me going. 'You don't need to shout at me, Ben. I can hear perfectly well.'

'I'm sorry.' He spoke more softly now, but very distinctly, with little pauses between each word: 'Where – are – you – going?'

But I knew it would not be wise to tell him – he might not understand how clever my idea was, so I decided to be evasive. I smiled again. 'I haven't quite decided yet.'

'Then wouldn't it be nice if you was to come in for a cup of tea?' His voice was cajoling.

I replied quickly, 'But it isn't teatime, Ben. Why, it's still the morning – I can't pay a call before lunch!'

Ben's reply was quick. 'Ah, but it's different here in Ainsclough, Lady Helena. If you come to door in Ainsclough, whatever time, then folks expect you to come in and have a nice cup of tea. Mrs Greenhalgh here, her'll be right upset if you don't come in for a cup of tea – right upset, her'll be.' I stole a glance at the woman in the doorway. Her thin face did look quite anxious – perhaps Ben was right. He seemed to sense my uncertainty, and lowered his voice confidentially. 'She won't be able to face the neighbours if you don't come in – they've all seen you calling, a young lady in a cab – and then, if you don't come in! Why, they'll all be talking – and she sets great store by neighbours, does Mrs Greenhalgh.'

He was confusing me – things did not seem so beautifully clear now. At last I said reluctantly, 'I will then, Ben – but only for a few minutes.'

For the first time he smiled at me. 'That's champion.' He raised his voice, 'Just show Lady Helena into the parlour, Mrs Greenhalgh.'

As she ushered me in I heard the jingle of coins, and a 'Giddup' behind me. I turned quickly, 'Oh Ben – I wanted the cab to wait!'

'We can soon call another cab, Lady Helena – no point in keeping him hanging about now, was there?'

I looked at him doubtfully, but he seemed very certain. 'Only five minutes though, Ben.'

He nodded. 'Only five minutes.'

Satisfied, I entered the small crowded parlour and sat down on the hard slippery sofa. A clock was ticking loudly, and the woman had vanished. I heard Ben's voice outside, and a boy's voice answering; there was the distinctive chink of coins followed by the clatter of clogs on the cobbles, and then Ben put his head round the door and said reassuringly, 'Mrs Greenhalgh is just putting the kettle on.' The door closed again and I sat listening to the tick of the cheap clock. Then the clogs came clattering back up the street and there was a rat-tat at the door and a breathless voice speaking to Ben. His footsteps went past into the kitchen and to my relief I heard the sound of a spoon on china; I had to be on my way as soon as possible.

Ben brought the tea tray himself, with a cup ready filled. He handed it to me carefully and then sat down opposite on a straight-backed chair. The tea tasted very sweet and syrupy, and I felt rather sad that Ben had forgotten I did not take sugar – but No. 23 was a long time ago. I sipped it slowly at first as he sat watching me, but it was not very hot so I decided to swallow it down quickly – after all, I wanted to be on my way – but when I tried to replace the cup on the saucer the saucer moved – and it kept on moving until Ben jumped up and took it and the cup from me and went to the tea tray again. I tried to tell him I did not want another cup, but the words would not come out and my head was spinning and then Ben was kneeling on the floor in front of me holding the cup to my lips – I turned my head away but the cup turned with it and he made me drink, and when I swallowed the tea burnt my throat but I kept on swallowing because his face was very close to mine and his voice very loud in my ear as he ordered, 'Drink up, lass, drink up.'

So I drained the cup as he bid me, and then he moved aside and I saw that the shadows were coming towards me, dark with menace. I cried out, but no sound came; and they were coming closer and closer. I threw myself back against the hard sofa, but still the shadows came on – and now I saw there was to be no escape, so at last, helplessly, I surrendered myself to them, and guilt and sorrow overwhelmed me as I slipped away into the darkness.

CHAPTER SIX

I opened my eyes and the ceiling was too low above me. My mouth was dry and my head was pounding so that I could only move it very slowly – and as I did so I saw a man sitting slumped in a chair, asleep. The chair was wedged across the doorway, so that I was trapped inside the small stuffy room. And as I looked at him I knew why he had trapped me here, and I hated him for what he had done – because now it was too late.

The stocky figure blurred and in its place I saw Robbie's thin body, shaking on his bed, and Robbie's dark eyes gazing up at me as I bent over him with the needle in my hand – the needle which I had driven without faltering into his very flesh. My brother, oh my brother. I cried out in pain and guilt and the other man's head jerked up and now it was Ben Holden's blue eyes which watched me, warily.

I pulled myself up, but as I moved my stomach churned and the bile rose in my throat and desperately I was lurching forward, my hand over my mouth. He kicked the chair aside and wrenched the door open and I ran through the dark kitchen and tiny scullery and out into the narrow yard. I looked frantically round until he pushed past me and flung back a door – I threw myself down on the hard stone and seized the cold white sides as the sickness took me over.

At last my retching shuddered to a stop and I knelt panting with the smell of it all around me. He hauled me to my feet and held me up as he leant across to pull the chain, then he half-carried me back into the kitchen and lowered me into a chair. A cold damp flannel was pushed into my hands and I wiped my face, then dried it on the towel he offered. Neither of us had spoken a word.

I sat huddled in the chair watching Ben Holden raise the lid of the range and poke the fire up before he put the kettle on it. I whispered, 'Just tea this time, Ben.'

He turned and his smile was very gentle, 'Aye lass, just tea.'

The room was warm but I began to shiver. He saw me shaking and went to the door and took an old shawl from the peg behind it and brought it back to me. 'Sit forward, lass.' I bent forward obediently and let him wrap the shawl around my shoulders and pull it close across my chest and tuck the ends in securely. I clutched the woollen folds to me as he turned back to the kettle and began to make the tea. His calm, deliberate movements steadied me, and when he handed me the cup I took it from him and gulped down the scalding liquid, gratefully. There was no sugar in it this time. As soon as I had finished he refilled my cup, then sat down opposite me cradling his own mug in his large hands, waiting.

I drew a long painful breath and said loudly, 'I killed my brother, Ben. I killed Robbie.'

He shook his head, his expression set. 'No, lass, the Germans killed him. You only eased his passing.'

I said, my voice still far too loud, 'But it wasn't a very easy passing.'

'Easier, lass, easier.'

I had no answer, and he fell silent again, yet I could see he was searching for words. At first, when he began to speak, I was bewildered by what he was saying, then I understood. 'At Wipers, in '17, we were next to Suffolks afore we went over – not that there were much to go over, by then – we just scrambled through mud. I got separated from company – most of them had gone by then, happen, I don't know. Any road, I slipped down a shellhole for a bit of cover, and there were one of Suffolks there, with his insides all spilt out. I thought

468

he were dead at first, but he weren't – and when I leant over him I could see he'd only got half a face, t'other half were missing. But he were still alive, and looking right at me with his one eye. I knew what he wanted. So I put me hand over his face – what were left of his face – lifted me revolver and blew out rest of his brains. Then I climbed out th'ole again and went back to try and find me men – to keep them moving forward, see.' He stopped, then went on, 'I never told no one. I didn't even think about it at time – there weren't any time. But I thought about it a lot later, and, well, – I reckon he were grateful.' Ben's low voice ceased; in the dark kitchen his face looked like that of an old man.

At last I whispered, 'Thank you, Ben.'

He pulled himself out of his chair, moving very heavily. 'You're welcome, lass.' Then he straightened up square in front of me, and added, quite matter of fact, 'You'd best get some sleep now, you must be worn out, what with being up all night as well. Mrs Greenhalgh had to go out – her elder lass has just had a new babby, up valley, and there's another young 'un to see to – otherwise she'd have stayed. She lost her own lad in war, see. Now you come and lie down on sofa again.'

I stood up stiffly, and felt the pressure of my bladder – I glanced towards the back door, my face flushing. Ben spoke quickly, 'There's soap and towel in scullery – I'll go up for pillow.'

The small closet still smelt faintly of vomit, and as soon as I had finished I reached for the jar of carbolic and shook a few drops down. Back in the scullery I washed my face and hands carefully at the single tap and dried them on the worn towel.

The door of the little parlour was open, and Ben had drawn the curtains and arranged the sofa with pillows and blankets, just like a bed. My jacket had been hung neatly over the back of a chair and he said, without looking at me, 'You can take your skirt off if you want – save it getting all crumpled – I'll go outside.'

Slowly I undid the buttons of my skirt and slipped it down over my hips, then I crept in between the blankets and pulled them tightly round me. I felt desperately alone. Ben's voice came from outside the door. 'Have you got everything you want, Lady Helena?'

Quickly I called back, 'Ben, please – ' His head came round the door; he looked very tired. But I was so frightened of being alone in the small, still room – alone with the dark threatening shadows, so I begged, 'Ben – would you, would you stay with me, please?' I could hear the panic in my voice.

He did not hesitate. 'Of course I will. Wait while I fetch me things – I'll be right back.'

He was very quick. I lay watching him as he moved about the room, pulling the bright rag rug into the centre of the floor and placing his pillow carefully at one end. He bent to take off his slippers and put them neatly inside the fender, then he rolled himself up in the grey blanket and lay down, facing the sideboard, with his back to me.

'Goodnight, Lady Helena.'

'Goodnight, Ben.'

I only slept in snatches, waking again and again with my heart thudding and my chest tight. But I fixed my eyes on the brown head above the grey blanket, and forced myself to concentrate on the steady breathing of the man on the floor, until slowly my panic subsided and I dozed off again – until the next time.

As I lay between sleep and waking I heard him moving about the room. Then he softly opened the door and slipped out – but I knew he was still in the house. I did not sleep again; I lay gazing up at the network of fine cracks on the plaster ceiling until I heard the front door pushed quickly open, and the thud of clogs in the passageway. A girl's voice called out, 'Ben – ' to be quickly shushed, and followed by the murmur of voices outside. Then there was a soft tap on the door panel.

'Come in.'

The door swung open and a girl came shyly into the room. She wore a shawl over a crumpled cotton working dress and there was a pair of dusty black clogs on her feet. Brown curls framed a round face that was rosy with health; her blue eyes were solemn as she came towards me. 'How are you, my lady? Ben thought you might be awake – he's only just come down himself – he's been on the night shift. Mam sent me back from our Annie's to start his tea and see how you were – she says she'll be in later when she's given our Wilf his meal – but he's helpless like when Annie's laid up – a proper man – still, he's pleased with babby – a bonny little lass she is . . .' She bubbled on while I slowly pulled myself up and began to look vaguely round for my skirt and jacket. The girl went quickly to the chair. 'Here they are, miss – my lady – what lovely soft cloth, and all sewn so beautiful! Did you sew them yourself?' She stopped suddenly, her pretty face very pink. 'I'm not thinking – of course a lady like you wouldn't make her own clothes – I'm sorry I spoke.'

I said quickly, 'Oh, I can sew – but not well enough to tailor. I'm afraid I don't know your name?'

'I'm Emmie, Emmie Greenhalgh – you met our mam this morning. I was at mill, but it's half day on Saturday so I slipped up to see the new babby . . .'

Ben's shout interrupted her. 'I've brewed up, young Emmie.' I reached quickly for my skirt.

Emmie was still chattering as she led me through to the kitchen. Ben was wearing a waistcoat and jacket now. 'Why Ben – you're all dressed up today – he normally wears his braces round the house, my lady . . .'

'Emmie, get that tea poured!' Ben's face was red as he broke in.

Emmie picked up the tea pot, saying proudly, 'I talk too much, our mam's always telling me – like a babbling brook, our Emmie, she says.' She pursed her lips in concentration as she carefully added the milk. Ben put his hand over the sugar bowl with a shake of his head and Emmie carried the cup to me. 'Now sit down with this, my lady – it'll make you feel better – there's nothing like a nice cup of tea, mam always says.'

'Thank you, Emmie.'

I sipped the tea in silence, listening to Emmie's soft voice extolling the virtues of her new niece. But when she had finished her tea she put her cup down and her face became serious as she said, 'My lady, I were right sorry to hear about your brother. I know how you feel – when the telegram came to tell us our Joe had passed away I cried and cried – I couldn't stop for a whole week.' She paused a moment, then went on, 'He were gassed, you see. But we had a lovely letter from the nurse, she said he died so quick and peaceful. "His last words were of his family," she wrote, "then he laid back his head and fell asleep." Did you nurse men who'd been gassed, my lady?'

'Yes, yes, I did.'

'And did they all die quick and peaceful, like our Joe?'

I looked at the girl, remembering the big marquee, and my useless efforts to help men who were coughing their lives away in agony through all those endless days of dying. And after the last desperate wheezing gasp, when the contorted purple face had finally fallen back upon its pillow, then I too would reach for my pen that evening, and write. 'I'm sure you will be relieved to know that your son – your husband – your brother – passed away quite peacefully . . .'

'Yes,' I said, 'yes, they all died quickly and peacefully.' And Robbie's voice rang in my ear: 'God, Hellie, I'd have to stand and watch while the sergeant shovelled the pieces into a sandbag, then I'd sit down in the dugout and write, "He died at once, just a clean shot through his chest – his face quite unmarked – he looked very peaceful." ' Robbie, my brother, who had not died peacefully – but who at least had died more quickly than he might have done, because I – and I heard my voice sharp with bitterness saying, 'Yes, Emmie, all soldiers die quickly you know – and if they don't, why, we try to make sure – '

But Ben Holden spoke loudly, drowning my angry words, 'Emmie, lass – Lady Helena'll be wanting a bit of a wash and brush up. Run upstairs and tidy the front bedroom, now – there's a good girl.'

After Emmie left us, I sat staring down at my trembling hands, ashamed now. At last I looked up, and saw that his face was drawn and tired – the face of the man who had filled the sandbags. 'I'm sorry, Ben.'

He said heavily, 'There's no call to upset the lass – it's best they believe what they do.'

'Yes.' We sat in silence until Emmie came running back down the stairs.

Up in the small bedroom with its double bed neat under a snowy white counterpane I stripped and washed myself from head to foot, and then pulled my black clothes on again and went slowly downstairs. Emmie's chatter broke off as she saw me come in, and she put her arm round my waist and led me to the rocking chair. Her plump dimpled hand squeezed my shoulder in silent sympathy.

Ben cleared his throat. 'Lady Helena, I'm due on again this evening, so I were wondering – I thought I'd best see you safely back, first.'

'Back?'

'Back home – to Hatton.'

I stared at him, and began to shake. 'No – I can't – I can't go back' – back to where Robbie's body lay waiting – waiting in its coffin, waiting for me. 'No, no . . .'

Emmie put her arm round my shoulders and pressed me to her. 'You can stay here, as long as you want. You've upset her, Ben Holden, going on like that!'

'But Emmie – '

'I'll sleep in chair – she can have my place – but no, there's Mam. Why, that's what we'll do – you can have Ben's bed, my lady – I'll put clean sheets on it for you.

473

He'll not be back while morning. There, I'll ask Mam when she gets in, she'll understand.'

I subsided into a frightened huddle in the chair as Ben said doubtfully, 'But, her family – they'll not know where she is . . .'

'Then you can telephone, Ben, and tell them.' Emmie's voice was triumphant. 'A grand house like that'll have a 'phone – won't it, my lady?' I nodded. 'That's settled then – and there's Mam's step at door – I'll ask her now.'

It was soon settled – I would stay in Ainsclough that night. I murmured my gratitude as Mrs Greenhalgh took clean linen from the cupboard beside the range and sent Emmie upstairs with it. Then she lifted saucepan lids, peered into the oven, gave a 'hm' of satisfaction and told Ben to take me down to the post office.

I followed him along the street in a daze. He called the operator for me, pushed in eight pennies then stood to one side so that I could give the exchange and number. But when Cooper answered I could barely speak at first, and only just managed to whisper, 'May I speak to Lady Violet, Cooper?'

'My lady' – even over the line I could hear the anxiety in his voice – 'I'll fetch her at once, my lady.'

Letty's voice came loud and clear: 'Helena! Where *are* you? You left no message – Mother's furious – and Dr Craig's called twice already asking for you and he's insisted he's coming back again this evening – that made Mother even more annoyed. So where on earth are you?'

I felt sick and giddy; there was a long pause before I managed to get out, 'Ainsclough. I'm in Ainsclough.'

'Ainsclough! Whatever are you doing there?' Letty's voice shrieked over the line; Ben, standing close behind me, shielding me from the shop, must have heard every word. My sister spoke forcefully: 'Well, when are you coming back? The funeral's arranged for Monday – two o'clock.' I began to tremble; I could not answer. 'Hellie? Are you there?'

474

Ben reached over my shoulder and took the earpiece from my shaking hand, then he nudged me gently aside so that he could speak directly to my sister. 'Look, my lady, she's staying in Ainsclough over weekend, but tell your ma she'll be back in time for funeral.' Letty's voice squeaked in protest but Ben ignored it. 'I said she'll be back in time, that's all – oh, and you'd best tell that doctor she's quite safe.' He slammed the phone back on the hook. 'Not that he deserves it.'

I whispered, 'It wasn't his fault, Ben – he was out at a confinement.' I began to cry. He took my arm and guided me out of the shop, still using his body as a shield against the curious glances of the other customers. Outside he swung me round and pushed me into a narrow alleyway. I shook with sobs, fighting for control. At last I said, 'I can't go to the funeral, Ben.'

'You'll have to. It'll look downright strange if you don't.'

'I don't care, I won't go.'

'Look, Lady Helena.' His voice was low, but very serious. 'What you did, you could be put away for it, if it ever gets out.' His eyes held mine; I stared back into his stern face as he said, 'You were right to do it – it were only thing to do – but law's law.'

I repeated, 'I don't care – I deserve to be punished.'

'Oh no you don't. Anyroad, what about doctor? He were ready to help Captain – to take a chance – you don't want to put him behind bars, do you?' At last I shook my head. 'Well, then – you've got to go to funeral and act normal. And no more letting cats out of bags, like you nearly did with young Emmie. You'll have to keep your mouth shut.'

'But – I told *you*, Ben.'

'That were different.' His tone was final. 'I'll take you back meself Monday morning. 'Sides, I want to pay me last respects to Captain Girvan – he were well liked.'

Back in the small kitchen I swallowed a few mouthfuls of potato pie. It tasted like sawdust, but under Mrs

Greenhalgh's stern gaze I dared not refuse it. Then she sent Ben into the front room to sleep on the sofa before his shift. He tried to argue. 'I've got to see to me plot, and – '

'You can do that later, Ben Holden. I doubt you've had enough sleep today, and if you're staying up on Monday you've got to get what you can, today and tomorrow. Off you go now.' And meekly, he went.

I sat listening to the clatter of saucepans in the scullery as Emmie and her mother washed up – Emmie's voice murmured on unceasingly, with only the occasional punctuation from Mrs Greenhalgh's short replies. When they had finished they came back and sat down at the kitchen table, and Mrs Greenhalgh lifted a large basket on to the red chenille tablecloth. Emmie's face fell. 'Oh Mam, not the mending – not when we've got a guest.'

But her mother was inflexible. 'You've barely a whole stocking to your foot, my girl – and there's Ben's socks.' She turned to me and said, half-apologetically, 'We've been a bit tied up getting ready for the new babby, my lady – else I'm not one to be getting behind with my mending, though I say it myself.'

I watched her shake out a sock and reach for the wooden mushroom and suddenly I was begging, 'Please – do let me help.'

Mrs Greenhalgh looked shocked. 'Certainly not, my lady, it wouldn't be fitting. Besides . . .'

'Oh, but I can darn. Nanny taught me, when I was a child. I *like* darning . . .'

'Like *darning!*' Emmie's face was amazed.

Mrs Greenhalgh still shook her head. I said desperately, 'Please – if I had something to do – I can't bear just to sit . . .' My hands were beginning to tremble again. The woman's stern face softened for a moment, and silently she held out the skein of wool. I threaded the needle, positioned the mushroom and began to pick up the worn loops.

I was still darning when Ben pushed open the door

later – bleary-eyed and stretching his brawny arms until they cracked. Emmie said quickly, 'Ben, Lady Helena's mending your socks for you – she's a beautiful darner – look how neat hers is, next to my stocking.' Emmie generously held out her own puckered darn.

Ben flushed red and Mrs Greenhalgh said sharply, 'Put that away Emmie – showing a young man your stocking! Whatever will you do next?'

Emmie said, 'It's all right, Mam – my leg's not still inside it,' and winked at me.

Her mother reared up. 'Into the scullery with you my girl, and fill that kettle at once.' Emmie dumped her mending on the table and scuttled off.

We drank more strong hot tea and then Ben went up to his plot. 'He's growing lots of vegetables – he's really worked hard, my lady. Old Alf Whittam had let it get all overgrown with weeds and suchlike, and Ben spent all autumn clearing it. I helped too, didn't I Mam?' She leant close to me and whispered, 'But Mam wouldn't let me go up with Ben too often, she said it wasn't respectable – and I'd get under Ben's feet and keep chattering all the time. But when I told Ben he said he didn't mind. "After all," he said, "I don't have to listen, do I?" ' She smiled happily as she reached for another coarse black stocking and stabbed awkwardly at it.

I offered, 'I'll mend those for you tomorrow, Emmie, when I've finished Ben's socks.'

'Oh, would you? I'd be ever so grateful – I hate mending.'

At eight o'clock I heard Ben come in and go straight upstairs. When he came down again he was wearing a pair of grubby overalls. He picked up the haversack Mrs Greenhalgh had packed ready for him and left for work, with only a glance in my direction. I darned on.

At half-past nine Mrs Greenhalgh put away her needle. 'I'll make you a nice cup of cocoa, my lady – it'll help you to sleep.' As she came past me I felt the light touch of her hand on my shoulder, and the tears stung my eyes.

Emmie took me up to Ben's bedroom at the back of the house. It was very neat and tidy; the only furniture was the bed, a chair and a chest of drawers, though one alcove was curtained off. I looked at the other alcove which was spanned by three sturdy shelves, filled with books. Emmie followed my gaze. 'Ben put those up himself – he's a great reader is Ben, when he's not up plot or down pub on a Friday night. It's not just paper he reads, he gets books regular from the Co-op library – but all them's his own. Mam thinks they're a waste of money, but he saved a lot in war, see. His old mam she kept on working, and though he made her a good allotment she wouldn't use much of it, she put most of it in Penny Bank – he said it made him wild but she would do it, and of course she were well over seventy, so she had a bit from pension, too. She had Ben very late, you see – Edna Fairbairn told me Mrs Holden thought it were change – didn't know she was expecting, and one day she thinks she's just got a touch of indigestion and she stands up to ease it like and next minute Ben pops out on the rug and sets up a howling fit to wake the neighbours! There was only his sister Ada there to help – she were my age then – gave her quite a turn it did – she were courting Albert Small, him she wed, but she called off banns then – said she didn't fancy it if that's what it were about – but he talked her round and she's got five of her own, now – he's got a good job, Albert, clerk at Bolton Town Hall.' She paused for breath, and before she could carry on there was a call of 'Emmie!' from downstairs. Emmie's hand flew to her mouth. 'Oh, miss – my lady – don't tell Mam what I told you – she'd have a fit. She thinks I still believe babbies are found behind cabbage patch!'

Emmie looked so funny in her round-eyed dismay that for a moment I almost laughed. Then I promised, 'Don't worry, I won't tell her, Emmie.'

She flashed me a quick smile, said, 'Chamber's under bed,' and was gone.

I sat down on the chair and looked round the cell-like room. I knew I would not sleep – I longed for the mending basket. There was a photograph of an elderly woman on the mantelpiece – Ben's mother, I guessed – there was a look of him around the eyes. She was half-smiling, and she had a kind face – but she was dead – they were all dead. I gripped my hands together until they hurt. When I had controlled myself I stood up and walked over to the alcove and made myself concentrate on the books there. I forced myself to read the titles on the top row: *Locomotive Management from Cleaning to Firing* – in a purple binding; next to it a shabby green volume proclaimed itself to be *Continuous Railway Brakes;* and it was followed by a fat *Textbook of Mechanical Engineering*. I put out my hand and took down the last one – I would see what Ben read – but there was page after page of working drawings and diagrams and close-packed text. Then I came upon a picture of four men – in waistcoats and close-fitting caps, working at a bench – I looked hopefully at the page opposite: 'If the surface is to be further trued, recourse is had to the scraper.' The words meant nothing to me, and they blurred and danced before my eyes until I slammed the book shut and pushed it back on the shelf.

I looked down at the next row and saw more familiar authors: Carlyle's *French Revolution*, Burke's *American Speeches and Letters*, Macaulay's *History of England*, Gibbon's *Decline and Fall of the Roman Empire;* followed by Hobbes' *Leviathan*, More's *Utopia* – and Marx's *Das Kapital*. How shocked my mother would be if she saw that! Tucked in, incongruously, at the end of the bottom row was a modest green volume entitled *How to Grow Vegetables*. I looked at the choice hopelessly; then at last I took down the first volume of the lowest shelf and opened it; it was Gibbon. I would read that. I pulled the chair under the gas mantle and forced myself to read:

'In the second century of the Christian era, the Empire of Rome comprehended the fairest part of the earth, and the most civilised portion of mankind. The frontiers of that extensive monarchy were guarded by ancient renown and disciplined valour . . .'

And suddenly I wondered whether one day a woman would be reading a book which began just like this one, but that was entitled *The Decline and Fall of the British Empire?* And would all our sacrifices of these last terrible years have been in vain? I thrust the treacherous thought from me and read grimly on.

CHAPTER SEVEN

It was very late when at last I closed Ben's book, undressed, pulled on Emmie's starched calico nightdress and climbed into the bed. I fell asleep at once, but as I slept I dreamt. I was back in the nursery with my brothers tumbling and laughing at my feet; I felt their soft baby hair brush my bare leg – and woke weeping. When I dozed off a second time I dreamt again: I was very young and small, clutching tightly at Ena's hand as I stumbled along the shadowy passageway. Nanny sat in her chair with a big white bundle on her lap; Ena lifted me up, and Nanny smiled, her loving smile, and turned back the fleecy edge of the shawl – I leant forward, eager, excited, to see my present, my babies. But there were no babies' dimpled cheeks on Nanny's lap – only deep holes and gaping sockets – I was looking down at two tiny skulls – my babies, my babies! I woke sobbing, and knew that both my babies were dead now; I had sat and watched Eddie die in his delirium – and Robbie, Robbie I had killed myself. I lay weeping and dared not sleep again, until the early church bells calling across the valley told me it was morning.

Mrs Greenhalgh tapped at my door soon after. 'I've brought you a cup of tea, my lady. Ben'll be back soon and needing his bed.'

Ben returned while we were breakfasting. He smelt of oil and coal dust and his tired face was smudged and grimy. He went straight through to the scullery with a pail of hot water from the range and we could hear him splashing out there. As her mother riddled the fire Emmie leant forward and whispered, 'Ben washes every day, as soon as he gets in – there's some I could name in this street as don't bother, but Ben – he's fussy like that.' She smiled as she spoke and I realized that in her eyes Ben could do no wrong. I was glad for his sake – Emmie was sweet-tempered and lively – and so young.

But when Ben came back into the kitchen he only returned her greeting absently before turning to me. 'Did you sleep all right, Lady Helena?'

'Yes, yes thank you,' I lied.

Mrs Greenhalgh reached down her pan. 'I'll fry you a rasher of bacon with your egg this morning, Ben – seeing as it's Sunday. Now, my lady, if you've finished your slice of toast perhaps you'd like to go through to parlour, while Ben's having his breakfast.'

I got up obediently and went to sit in solemn state in the small front room. I heard Ben go up to bed and then Emmie came in and told me we would be going to morning chapel later. I asked her for the mending basket and she looked quite shocked. 'But it's Sunday, my lady – still, I'll ask me mam.' She came back rather long-faced. 'Mam says it's all right, just for today – but I mun help you.' She sighed and took out a coarse flannel petticoat and began to repair the hem.

As I began to set the first delicate stitches in one of Emmie's thick cotton stockings I remembered how she had admired the soft cloth of my suit the day before and offered, 'Emmie, my sister's about the same size as you

481

are, and she's just brought lots of new clothes back from Paris, so she'll be going through her wardrobe – would you like me to send you some of her old frocks?'

'Oh miss – my lady – that'd be lovely!' Her face was alight. 'Why, perhaps Ben'ud take me to Co-op dance, if I had a nice new dress.'

'Would you like to go dancing with Ben, Emmie?'

She blushed and looked down at her hem. 'Mam says he's a steady enough chap, and a good worker.' She sewed on in uncharacteristic silence for a minute or so, then asked, without looking up, 'Don't you think he's handsome, my lady?'

I stared at her – Ben, handsome? Ben with his tow-coloured hair and bluish-grey eyes and very ordinary face. 'He – he's a very well set-up young man.'

'He's not young – he's nearly thirty!' Emmie exclaimed. 'Why, he mun be near as old as you, my lady.' I did not bother to correct her; I had seen my face in the mirror that morning. But Emmie had not finished. 'He told me about you, my lady, after he saw you in Manchester a bit back. He said' – she drew a deep breath – 'he said as you saved his life!' Emmie gazed at me, and for a moment her frank admiration warmed me. 'I'm ever so glad you did, my lady.' Her rosy face bent back over her sewing.

I went with them to chapel; how could I tell the upright Mrs Greenhalgh that I had lost my faith? Afterwards we sat in the stuffy little parlour through a long afternoon. Mrs Greenhalgh did not go to her elder daughter's. 'Wilf's home today,' she had told me as we walked back from the chapel. 'A man likes a bit of peace and quiet on his day off. I've left a pie for him to heat up, and taters peeled ready.' Emmie's whisper had enlightened me further: 'Wilf don't always see eye to eye with our mam.'

As the memories crowded in I fought them back with my desperate needle. 'You've given us a real lift with the mending, my lady – basket'll soon be empty. I'll go and see to Ben's tea – he'll be hungry when he gets up.' Mrs Greenhalgh rolled her last stocking and put it neatly on the pile of work the three of us had completed.

After he had finished his meal Ben came into the front parlour and suggested, rather hesitantly, that Emmie and I might care for a walk. Emmie jumped up eagerly, but Mrs Greenhalgh frowned. 'It'll be evening chapel soon, Ben. Minister were asking after you – reckon he's forgotten what you look like, and you used to be in choir, and all.'

Ben looked squarely at me. 'I thought you might fancy some fresh air, Lady Helena – we could go up on tops, perhaps walk along to tower.'

I put down my needle. 'Yes, Ben – I should like that.'

I slipped on my jacket, Emmie wrapped her shawl round her shoulders and we were ready. It was fresh and clear outside and I breathed in deeply. Emmie chattered happily to Ben and he answered her with the occasional grunt. I did not speak.

At the foot of the path leading up to the tower Emmie spotted a couple of girls ahead. 'There's Lily and Elsie – hey, Lil!' The girls heard her and turned and waited and she ran heavily ahead, her plump calves flashing amidst her petticoats as she scrambled up the stony slope.

Ben paused and turned to me. 'Can you manage, Lady Helena? Them shoes of yours aren't made for walking.'

'None of my shoes are made for walking, Ben, but I can walk in all of them.' I saw his smile and added, 'The secret is to have them properly fitted. Gerrett's in Sloane Street have my last; I never buy footwear anywhere else.'

There was a silence, then Ben asked, 'Do they make your glass slippers?'

I smiled at him, then my breath caught in my throat as Robbie's thin face swam before my eyes. I could not go on; I stopped still on the stony track and began to weep. The high-pitched girlish laughter of Emmie and her friends rang out ahead and I felt Ben's hand touch my arm in apology. 'I'm sorry, Lady Helena, I'm sorry – I should have thought before I spoke. Emmie,' he called, 'come back down a minute.'

Emmie swung round and came stumbling down the path, panting. Her warm arms came round me and hugged me as I wept. At last I whispered, 'It's all right, Emmie – I'm all right now, thank you. You go back to your friends, they're waiting for you. I'll just sit down for a moment – and look at the view.' My legs were shaking so much I almost collapsed on to the flat-topped boulder beside the path. Emmie hovered over me, her face concerned, until Ben said, 'Leave her to rest now, lass,' then she squeezed my shoulder and walked slowly back up to the other two girls.

Ben squatted down beside me and together we gazed out over the smoke-smeared valley. My breathing gradually slowed. A party of Sunday walkers passed us, chattering and laughing, and then, as their voices receded, there was only the singing of a solitary bird. 'It's peaceful up here, Ben – I'm glad we came. I couldn't have stayed in that parlour any longer – I had to get out.'

'That's what I reckoned.' He was quiet for a while, then he said, 'When I came back from France I couldn't settle. I know I were one of the lucky ones – with me job waiting for me, and Company counted me war service as seniority – but still, I couldn't settle. And I ran wild like – drinking too much and – anyroad I were generally playing the fool, so me driver, Stan Roberts it were then, he spoke to me, straight from shoulder. I didn't like it at first – with me having been a sergeant-major and all – but then I began to see sense. What he said to me was, "You go up and walk on tops, Ben – walk till you're fit to drop and then walk some more – that'll get war out of your system." He were right, not that you forget – you can't forget – but you learn to live with memories. The hills, these hills – they give you a sense of proportion, like.'

I was grateful, and I understood what he was trying to say – but it was too late for me now.

Next morning Ben dozed in the chair for an hour after he had eaten his breakfast, then he went upstairs to change and came down in his best suit, wearing a black tie and with his cap in his hand. Even then I tried to refuse, to say I could not go, but his face was like granite and my words trailed away and I picked up my handbag. I thanked Mrs Greenhalgh, scarcely knowing what I said, and Emmie hugged me at the door, but still I was numb.

At the station Ben went ahead to the booking office, and when he came back I realized he was apologizing because he had forgotten and taken third-class tickets. I kept whispering, 'It doesn't matter, Ben, it doesn't matter.'

At Manchester he was fussing about the tickets again and I spoke sharply: 'Get third, Ben – don't waste your money.' He looked hurt because he had offered to pay for first – but I was glad I had hurt him – he had forced me to come and I hated him for it: I wanted to hit out in my grief and anger.

The wheels pounded in my head – I had to fight to stay still in my seat – I wanted to throw myself against the walls of the compartment, against the hard shining windows – to bruise myself, to inflict pain on my numb body. But I did not move. The man opposite was watching me, so I dared not move.

Mr Shepherd came out on to the platform at Hareford, his face grave. 'I'll ring for the car, my lady – there's a good fire in the waiting room.'

Ben sat awkwardly by my side, his flat cap on his knees. When the stationmaster came in and told me the car had arrived Ben stood up and held out his hand. 'I'll have a look round the town, and walk up to the church later. Goodbye, Lady Helena.' I shook the hand he offered, but I could find no words of thanks. My throat had closed.

485

Norah had a bath waiting for me, and then she dressed me again in black and I went down to lunch. As we walked into the dining room Letty muttered under her breath, 'I told Mother you were staying with a friend from the war – she thinks it was another VAD.' I looked blankly back at my sister – what did it matter what my mother thought or did not think? What did anything matter now?

We ate our meal in silence; Papa barely touched his food and even Mother's careful make-up could not conceal her red-rimmed eyes. Alice and Letty looked only at their plates. And then it was time to leave.

We were in the car driving slowly behind the carriage carrying my brother's body, and for a moment I thought it was Eddie's funeral, and I turned to comfort Robbie beside me – but Robbie was not with me now – he travelled ahead of us, screwed down in his brass-handled coffin.

The bearers hoisted their burden on to their shoulders and began to walk slowly towards the church. Letty gripped my arm and forced me to follow.

'I am the resurrection and the life, saith the Lord: he that believeth in me . . .' But I did not believe, not any more.

'I know that my Redeemer liveth . . .' And from long ago I heard a girl's clear voice sing these words – and knew with a sick certainty that I would never sing again. My voice was dead: it had died with Robbie.

'I will keep my mouth as it were with a bridle . . .' In my head I heard Ben Holden command: 'You'll have to keep your mouth shut.' I bowed my head.

'I became dumb, and opened not my mouth: for it was thy doing. Take thy plague away from me: I am even consumed by means of thy heavy hand.' But I did not ask for the plague to be taken from me. Let me be consumed. And the terrible cadences rolled on. 'Thou turnest man to destruction . . . In the morning it is green and groweth up: but in the evening it is cut down, dried

486

up and withered . . . Thou hast set our misdeeds before thee; and our secret sins in the light of thy countenance . . .'

As we stood in the churchyard beside the open grave I remembered Robbie, young and happy, running with Eddie over the green lawns of Hatton – laughing and calling – 'Man that is born of a woman hath but a short time to live . . . He cometh up and is cut down, like a flower . . .' And at the last it was I who had cut him down.

The coffin sank slowly into the deep hole. My father moved forward with a handful of earth. ' . . . earth to earth, ashes to ashes, dust to dust . . .'

I could see no longer; as Letty pulled me back from the graveside I thought in despair that at least Robbie and Eddie had each other now – but I had no one, no one.

We sat in the drawing room, waiting. The church had been full, and Papa had stayed at the lych gate shaking hand after hand, acknowledging the low-voiced condolences. Alice's husband had brought us back and then we had sat and waited.

Mr Hyde came in with Papa; after the lawyer had greeted us he sat down and took out a piece of paper – Robbie's will. His dry clipped voice read steadily on, retailing a series of bequests: to servants, to Miss Ling, to men from his regiment who were disabled or in difficulties – oh my little brother, even at the last you had thought to do this . . . 'And all my real and personal estate not otherwise disposed of by this my will I bequeath unto my beloved sister, Helena, with grateful thanks for all that she has done for me.'

'Done for me, done for me – she has done for me.' Oh Robbie, forgive me – but I could not let you suffer so. And for a moment I remembered the gratitude in his eyes as I had plunged the needle home – and knew that I would rather suffer my guilt for a lifetime than that he should have endured such agony for a single minute longer. And for that moment I felt strong – but only for that moment. Then I stood up and ran from the room and blundered upstairs and threw myself on the bed and wept and wept. Alice came in, but I screamed at her to go away, and after a while she went, and left me alone. Alone.

The next day Dr Craig came to Hatton and asked to see me. As soon as the library door closed I told him: 'I have held my tongue, as you wished – except for one man, and he did the same himself once, in the war – so he will not speak.'

I heard his loud sigh of relief. 'I'd have denied it, in any case – sworn you were off your head with grief and didn't know what you were saying, on oath if necessary – but I prefer not to have to.' He paused, then his bony face flushed as he added, 'If there's anything I can do for you now, my lady, you've only to say the word.'

'No, there is nothing, thank you.' There was silence. Then he turned and left me.

Ben Holden wrote to ask how I was; he said Emmie sent her best wishes. I remembered my promise and went to ask Letty if she would let me have some of her last season's clothes. She produced quite a sizeable armful – she brought them to me herself and said her maid was not too pleased about it, but she had been given several frocks already. I wrote a brief note to Emmie and told Norah to parcel the clothes up and send them off.

Emmie wrote back a very effusive letter of thanks. She said that Ben was working very hard on his plot – it took me a moment to remember who this Ben was – my mind was so slow these days. Miss Ling wrote as well: she was painfully grateful for Robbie's bequest; she said it would enable her to purchase an annuity for when she became too old to teach – but she was so sorry, so very very sorry. I remembered her patient kindness to my brother when she had first come to us, and was proud that he had remembered too.

488

There were so many other letters, but Mother and Papa answered those. They had decided not to open Cadogan Place for the beginning of the Season – Mother said she might go up to Town later, but for the present they would remain at Hatton, and perhaps invite a few guests to stay. My mother suggested that Letty go on a visit to Alice, but my sister said she had plenty of reading to do before going up to Cambridge in the autumn, so she stayed in Cheshire too.

But other people irritated me, and I hid from them whenever I could. The next weeks passed in a dream: I knew neither the day nor the hour. Norah got me up in the morning and I sat long hours in my bedroom, staring at the wall, until she came to tell me it was lunchtime, and then I ate only enough to curb my mother's angry glances.

One day I drifted into the music room; the piano lid was raised and I went to it and struck a chord and opened my mouth as if to sing my scales – but my voice cracked and broke – as I had known it would. I dropped the lid and turned away. I remembered from another world the words of Elsa Gehring: 'You must not sit and fruitlessly weep, no, you must turn your sadness into song – how fortunate we singers are.' But I was a singer no longer; my voice had been buried in the grave with my brothers. 'I became dumb, and opened not my mouth.' It was a fitting punishment.

I put on my hat and coat and walked down the wide tree-lined avenue and out of the Lostherne gate and across into the narrow country lane that led to the churchyard. I pushed open the weathered lych gate and climbed up between the gravestones until I came to the one I sought. And there I stood, gazing at the inscription.

Sacred to the Memory
of
Lieut the Hon. EDWIN JOHN ALFRED GIRVAN
L&CLI

Who Died of Wounds Received in the
Service of His Country
19th June 1916, aged 20 years
'Faithful unto Death'

And also of his Twin Brother
Captain the Hon. ROBERT JOHN GEORGE GIRVAN
L&CLI
Who Died as a Result of Wounds Received
in the Service of His Country
27th March 1920, aged 24 years

They were lovely and pleasant in
their lives, and in their death
they were not divided: they were
swifter than eagles, they were
stronger than lions.

II Samuel i.

'And in their death they were not divided'; but I, I was left alone.

CHAPTER EIGHT

One day Mother told us at luncheon that the Eameses were staying with Sam Killearn, and they were all coming over to Hatton that afternoon. I did not want to meet other people, so as soon as we had left the table I put on my brogues and mackintosh and slipped out of the family entrance. There was a blustery wind and squally bursts of rain beat into my face, but I was grateful to the weather for it meant that I could let the tears run unchecked down my cheeks, and no one would notice. My legs carried me mechanically in the direction I wanted to go – I had no need to think, only to weep as I walked up the lane to Lostherne.

I stood for a long time in the churchyard, but I could not feel my brothers there; so at last I turned away from their grave and trudged slowly back to Hatton. But I had only just taken my wet shoes off when Letty came bursting into my room. 'Hellie, thank goodness you've come back – you must come down to the drawing room at once.'

'No – I don't wish to meet the Eameses – or Sam Killearn.'

'Don't be silly, Helena – of course you can cut the Eameses as often as you please – it's not that – your engine driver's here.' I looked at her blankly, so she added impatiently, 'You know – Ben Holden. For goodness' sake pull yourself together, Hellie – Mother's eating him alive downstairs, and the poor man's only come because of you.'

'Because of me?'

Letty mimicked Ben's Lancastrian accent mercilessly: ' "To see 'ow Lady 'Elena's keeping" – Come *on*, put some shoes on.' Helplessly I obeyed her. 'And splash your eyes, Helena – you look a fright.'

Mother was with her guests in the big drawing room – the room was full of smartly dressed, clever people, talking in drawling, confident voices. Ben Holden sat among them perched uneasily on an elegant gilded chair – and looking as out of place as a heap of his own coal would have done if dumped on the Aubusson carpet. As soon as he saw me he reared up and the delicate gold chair rocked dangerously. All the careless eyes turned to stare a moment in our direction, before averting blank, well-bred faces from the sight of his ill-cut suit and my tear-stained cheeks.

As Ben blundered towards me Mother's voice hissed in my ear. 'Perhaps you would like to take *your* guest somewhere else for tea, Helena.' I turned without a word and Ben followed me through the door and into the hall. But at the foot of the staircase I stopped – I could not go into the small drawing room now.

John stepped forward. 'The library, my lady.' He swung the door open and I walked in, Ben at my heels.

We stood in the centre of the room and looked at each other. The sweat stood out on his forehead like tiny beads as he pushed his damp hair back with his large work-roughened hand. 'I asked for you – but they didn't know where you were.'

'I was in the graveyard.' And as I spoke the tears slid smoothly down my cheeks, but now there was no kindly concealing rain and the man in front of me stepped forward, his face appalled.

He began to rummage in his jacket pocket. 'I've got a clean handkerchief, somewhere.'

I shook my head and reached into my sleeve. 'It's all right, Ben – I always carry one ready now.'

He said, 'I shouldn't have come – I've only made it worse for you.' His face was drawn and disturbed, and I felt pity for him in his clumsy dismay.

'No Ben, nothing can make it worse.'

The door opened silently; it was John with the tea tray. The drawing up of chairs, the silver gleam of the tea pot, the discreet, 'Shall I pour, my lady?' – all served to restore my composure a little and I managed to smile my dismissal and keep my hand steady as I reached for the curved silver handle. 'Milk and sugar, Ben? Oh, but you don't take sugar, do you – how silly of me to forget. Do have a scone.'

It was very quiet in the library; the heavy connecting door muffled the low murmur of conversation from the drawing room – nearby, there was only the steady champing of the jaws of the man opposite. At last he swallowed, took a deep gulp of tea and said baldly, 'I were worried about you.'

I felt a faint flicker of warmth touch me. 'Then it was kind of you to come, Ben.'

He leant forward, his voice urgent. 'I don't reckon it's good for you to stay here, Lady Helena – what with memories and all. Isn't there anywhere else you could go – your brother – the one in Canada – couldn't you go an' visit him, mebbe?'

And as he spoke a longing for Guy took hold of me, and for Nanny – but no, not Nanny. The hope shrivelled and died. 'How could I go there – and not tell them?'

'Aye.' His lips tightened.

The words of the priest echoed in my head: 'I will keep my mouth as it were with a bridle . . . I held my tongue and spake nothing.' And I must speak nothing, least of all to Guy who had loved Robbie, and Nanny who had nursed him at her breast. 'I must keep silent, Ben.'

Ben Holden's eyes fell before mine. Then, with an effort, he spoke again. 'But you don't have to keep silent with me – I thought, it might help you – if I came – me knowing . . .'

He floundered on and I felt sorry for him in his distress so that the lie came easily: 'Yes, it does help – thank you Ben.'

His expression as he looked up was that of a dog who has received an unlooked-for pat, and now he spoke more confidently. 'So I were wondering, if mebbe you'd like to come to Ainsclough one day – and spend afternoon with me.' His last words came out in a rush.

'To Ainsclough, with you?' I was bewildered.

'Just for a break, like. I told clerk I were available for next few Sundays, so I've not got full day off – but in week I'm on earlies for a while, I can be home soon after ten some days – mebbe you could come one of them?'

I did not reply, so he went on, 'We could go for a walk on tops – on moors. Moors helped me when I first came back from war. I could meet train – all trains, say, from eleven while one. If you're not on, well, no matter – I'll be having a chat with Jim on platform. So you needn't feel bound – just if you want to. I'd be going up on tops meself, anyroad – you can come if you fancy – but only if you do.'

'That's very kind of you, Ben – but I'm not sure – '

He broke in, 'I'll give you a choice – I'll write soon as I know more about me shifts and tell you dates – then you needn't decide like until morning itself. I'll wait, just in case. Don't feel bound, but I'll be there.'

And now I was touched by his simple, uncomplicated kindness. He had told me how the moors had helped him, and had come to offer his own solution to me. 'Thank you, Ben – I'll remember.'

He stood up quickly. 'Then I'd best be off.'

'I'll ring for John to see you out' – but he was through the door before my hand had touched the bell. As I went back upstairs I felt a little warmer; I could not go, of course – but I was grateful for his well-meant kindness.

At dinner Mother vented her annoyance at Ben's untimely arrival on me. She was angry too at my distraught appearance before her guests: 'Really, Helena, you're behaving like a child – it's time you pulled yourself together.' I fought back the threatening tears with difficulty.

She was even more angry with me a week later, when Sir Ernest asked me to sing for him and I told him I could not. He accepted my refusal without protest, but later that evening Mother berated me for my lack of social accomplishments. I sat dumb before her until her face sharpened and she said, 'Molly Eames has a secretary now – you can act as my secretary, Helena – it will do you good, and be better for you than mooning around in a dream as you are at present. Come to my room at ten o'clock tomorrow. If you won't sing at least you can write. I presume you *can* still write, Helena?'

'Yes, Mother – I can still write.'

When she left us later Letty asked, 'Whyever didn't you say "No", Helena? It's quite simple, when you know how.' I did not reply and she went on, '*I* never have any trouble with Mother – but you see she knows you're frightened of her. But I admit it's easier for me – I can always play my trump card. You're not so fortunate there.'

No, because Papa was my father, and I took after him – I was a coward and dared not challenge Mother. At ten the next morning I tapped on the door of my mother's sitting room, my writing case in my hand. She dictated rapidly as she leafed through her correspondence, and I was glad of the chance to put my pen down when Mrs Hill came in for her daily orders. As Mother consulted with the housekeeper I sifted idly through my own letters, and found Ben Holden's invitation. He had written and offered me three dates; I felt a momentary pang as I noticed that the first had already gone – I hoped he had not waited too long on the draughty platform at Ainsclough. I put the piece of paper down again as Mother turned back to me. 'You can arrange the bedrooms for the guests arriving tomorrow, Helena – but bring the plan to me so that I can cast an eye over it before you give it to Mrs Hill.'

I had forgotten there were more guests coming tomorrow – or, more probably, I had simply failed to listen when she told me. I allocated the bedrooms, and Mother rearranged them. Then I drew up a seating plan for dinner as she had told me to do – and she tore that to pieces as well. It seemed to give her some satisfaction; and I could scarcely bring myself to care.

The new guests were young and smart: the women narrow elegant tubes, brandishing elongated cigarette holders and wearing thin arched crescents where their eyebrows had been. I moved amongst them narrowest of all – but I did not smoke, and I saw Mother glaring at my unplucked brows. Chameleon-like, my mother had adapted to the fashions around her – I wondered wherever she put her bosom these days. It was a relief when Letty bounced in, plump calves quivering, hair tossed carelessly up. I played my own part dully, only waiting until the hour when I could escape to the empty loneliness of my room.

At dinner the next day I was beside Rory Foster – I knew him slightly, as I had met him several times in the company of Conan the previous summer. They had both trained as pilots together in the RFC, and he had flown in France for two full years before the crash which had broken his nose and stiffened his leg. 'Rory had the luck of the devil,' Conan had said, and he certainly looked devilish tonight in the yellow glow of the candles – his dark curls tumbling and his full lips twisted in a cynical smile. 'Come, Lady Helena – you must enter into the spirit of the party! I've watched you sipping tamely at the same glass through the last three courses – it won't do, you know.' He deftly switched his own full glass with mine and tossed off the wine I had left. The glass was instantly refilled and his dark eyes dared me. 'Drink, Helena, drink.' I reached for his glass and drank. He threw back his head and laughed – he was already a little tipsy. 'There – that's the way to do it. When I squatted in that sandpit on the Peninsula, parched with thirst and waiting for Johnny Turk to take a potshot at me every time I twitched a muscle, why, then I swore that if I ever got out alive I'd drain every glass I could lay my hands on. It's the only way – the only way.' His curved mouth mocked me, yet I saw the sympathy in his dark eyes and recklessly I raised the glass again and drained it.

When I stood up after the dessert my legs were trembling; I swayed towards Rory and felt his strong hand grip my elbow. Someone cried, 'To the fern house – and we'll settle that bet once and for all.' I did not know what bet they were talking about, but I was relieved that the younger men were leaving the table with us – I doubted whether I could have walked unaided.

Outside on the terrace it was suddenly cold; I shivered, and Rory took off his jacket and threw it round my shoulders. I held its warmth to me, and then there was a shout of 'This way!' and as the noisy crowd took to their heels Rory seized my hand and dragged me after them. Inside the fern house the heavy air smelt of greenery – warm and exotic. Voices rose in heated argument and Rory pulled me into a side aisle and held me to him. I leant against him, careless of who might see us. But the noisy mob were intent on their own affairs: they turned together and surged past us, out of the conservatory, and all at once we were alone, safe behind a rampart of green foliage. A voice called, 'Everybody out?' Neither of us spoke. A switch clicked and we were enfolded in soft darkness. Without thought I moved into his seeking arms and pressed myself against his hard chest. His lips found mine and we swayed together in common need. His hands were urgent on my body and as the excitement rose within me I opened my mouth under his. But as I clung to him mindlessly, his head jerked away and sudden light beat against my closed lids. We stood frozen in our green hide until a woman's silvery voice called, 'Rory darling, are you lost in there?' His arms fell away from me and I staggered back. With a shrug and a rueful grin he scooped up his jacket and moved smoothly forward. 'Margot, my dear – I've been waiting for you – we planned to jump out and surprise you in the dark – Helena here swore you'd never be able to find the switch, but you were too clever for us.'

Margot, Margot Janes – Mrs Margot Janes: 'Denny Janes won't be coming, of course,' my mother had said, 'Margot has other fish to fry.' And I remembered her rapid alteration of the bedroom plan. Now as I stumbled towards Margot Janes her eyes narrowed under fine arched crescents – and the painted mouth curved into a thin contemptuous smile as she wriggled her sharp white shoulders into Rory's black jacket. He bent over her in an exaggeratedly protective gesture, and they left me without a backward glance.

The bile rose in my throat and I tripped and almost fell as I ran across the dark lawn until I could collapse, retching, on the cold stone seat. I hated her, I hated him – but, most of all, I hated myself.

When I got up to my bedroom I sat before the mirror and tried to pull and push my disordered hair into some sort of shape – I tried not to look into my eyes – my eyes that were ringed with dark shadows, and dulled with pain and grief. And now I had to go downstairs again, and face the man who had discarded me – and his clever, confident mistress.

I tried to walk in casually, as though I did not care, but I felt myself cringe at the drawing-room door – the air was thick with cigarette smoke and malice. I caught snatches of screeched protestations: 'My dear, you should have seen her!'

'It's too bad the way Ossie watches her every move . . .'

'A private detective – oh, that's *not* cricket . . .'

'And her eldest daughter – like a great fat lump of lard – knocked down to the highest bidder . . .'

'If only Papa had been a war profiteer . . .'

As I listened I knew I had no place here – I could not stay. I threaded my way through to where Mother held court and blurted out, 'I must go upstairs now – I don't feel very well – I think I'm starting a cold.'

As I spoke, the words seemed to catch and stumble on my tongue, and Mother leant back against the cushions and blew a perfect fragile smoke ring before saying in reply, 'Nonsense, Helena, you're merely drunk.' Alongside Mother Margot Janes' lip curved, and she gave a small, malicious titter – beautifully timed, impeccably executed. I stood defenceless before her, then I turned and walked from the room, my head bowed and my cheeks flaming.

Back in my room I tried to take comfort from the fact that they were all leaving tomorrow – and only four of them would be staying to luncheon; but because of my unwilling servitude I knew the names of the four who were staying. I could not, I would not face them – but there was no escape; Mother had so cleverly pre-empted any false appeal to ill health. If I pleaded a headache tomorrow and stayed in my room I would be a laughing stock, and I had nowhere else to go. It was then I remembered Ben Holden's invitation.

I fumbled desperately in my writing case – when was the next date? I was not sure – then, in blessed relief, I saw that it was tomorrow's. I had my excuse.

I could not face my mother again, so I wrote a hurried note: 'Forgotten prior engagement' – 'an acquaintance made in France' – 'some distance north of Manchester' – 'must leave on an early train'. Ben Holden, like the footplateman he was, had given the times of the suitable Blackburn trains, had made everything so easy for me – kind, simple Ben.

I rang for Norah and asked her to deliver the note to my mother in the morning – 'After I've gone, please.' She took it from me with a small understanding smile.

I slept restlessly, and woke in the night to the sound of tapping footsteps and stifled giggles going past my door. I shrank back under the bedclothes, then remembered with thankfulness that for tomorrow, at least, I had an escape. I clung to that thought gratefully as I fell into a dreamless sleep.

CHAPTER NINE

I did not wake again until Norah came in with my early-morning tea, and as she drew back the curtains the sunlight streamed into the room. She turned to me with a smile. 'It's a beautiful day, my lady.' I smiled back, drowsy from the comfort of a good night's sleep. 'Such nice weather for your day out with your friend.' My friend? Of course, I was going out today – I was going to walk on the breezy hills with Ben Holden. Not a friend, exactly – more a comrade – yes, that was the word; we had been comrades together. Ben would escort me, steady and patient and undemanding, and Emmie, cheerful Emmie – how lucky it was a Saturday, she would be able to come with us too. And I would listen gladly to their strong accents and clumsy grammar and occasional dropped aitches: I had had enough of clever, sophisticated people who tied my tongue in knots – and humiliated me. And when I got back to Hatton this evening Rory and his painted mistress would be gone.

I thrust the thought of them away and ordered, 'My tweeds, please, Norah. I shall be going walking. And just bring me a tray with toast after you've run my bath – that's all I need.'

But when I came back from the bathroom the sun was still shining and my tweeds looked sober and dull. I would dress up more smartly today. I sat planning my costume as I ate my toast, and it was good to be thinking of something frivolous again. I became almost excited, like a young girl once more – just like Emmie must be in Clegg Street at this very moment, thinking of her afternoon with her beau. I laughed, and said to her in my mind, 'Emmie, you must share your beau with me today!' Emmie was loving and generous; she would not mind, just for today. Between us we would make Ben proud to be our escort, because Emmie would have fine clothes to wear too – Letty's clothes. How lucky that my sister had 'rationalized' her wardrobe in Paris: Emmie's plump figure would never have been able to squeeze into any of my old frocks. And thinking of what Letty had bought in Paris reminded me – if I wanted to be truly frivolous today then there were those absurd garments she had brought back for me to wear. I felt a little spurt of rivalry with Emmie – Emmie who was so young and who saw me as a woman past thirty. I would show her: in one of Letty's flimsy chemises no one could class me as middle-aged!

I found them tucked into the back of my underwear drawer, and my hand touched the pink one first, so I picked it up and shook it out and felt very daring as I

500

dropped my nightgown and wrap to the floor and slipped the smooth satin over my bare breasts. I buttoned up the narrow flap but the satin strip swung so loose and low that the soft damp warmth between my thighs was free and open. I stepped back, and as I moved, the satin lightly brushed my skin, and then fell away again. Excitement rippled through me – I would be a Parisienne today. Recklessly I reached for the black lace garters and pushed my suspender belt to the back of the drawer – and the touch of it reminded me of Conan; it was Conan whose skilful hands had removed my last corset – I had never worn one again since that night in his rooms. The hot blood flowed into my cheeks and I was giddy with the memory of his lean male face above mine, of his warm lips and probing, darting tongue. My whole body flushed hot and heavy in longing for him – then there was a tap at the door; it was Norah, come back to do my hair. I called hastily that I was not ready yet, and pulled the sheer silk stockings up my legs and slipped the black lace garters on to hold them in place. I did not want my maid to see me in my scanty underwear so I ran to the wardrobe and took out the costume I had decided on: a dark brown cashmere dress with a matching jacket trimmed with tan – it would go with my tan calf brogues. I did not really like wearing brogues, but I supposed I would have to today, and being my brogues they were lightweight leather, with a definite heel. I would look smart, even if we were only walking 'on tops'.

I went to my dressing table and sat down and called Norah in. While the curling tongs were heating up she put away my discarded tweeds, then with deft fingers combed and coiled and teased out my fine hair until it was soft and full around my face. Finally she gently positioned a small tan toque far back on my head, and I was ready.

'You look lovely, my lady – I do hope you enjoy your day out. Are you going far?'

501

'Thank you, Norah. Not too far – only to Ainsclough.' But as I spoke that name the memories came crowding in on me: I remembered the concert before the war – and my brothers, so young and carefree – and my singing, singing of Gerald's love. I battled with the memories, and forced them back into their cage – for this one day I would escape. But the face that looked back at me from under its fine hairstyle and smart hat was shadowed and drawn – Emmie was right, I was young no longer. I felt suddenly very foolish in my black lace garters and scanty Parisian underwear – but there was no time to change, the car was at the door, and besides, no one would ever know that I was wearing it.

As I sat on the train to Manchester I told myself again that for this one day I would escape, and live only in the present. I caught my connection easily at Victoria, and relaxed in my seat as we rattled northwards – but at the great yellow-brick cavern of Bolton the memories attacked me again, and I had to suppress them ruthlessly to prevent weeping at the memory of the mother with her child, on that terrible morning – but no, I would *not* remember. I forced myself to stare out of the window and study the high square mills with their towering chimneys, the grimy gasworks, and the crowded rows of soot-blackened terraces.

It became easier as we ran into open country, because these were not the lush green pastures of Cheshire – this was a different landscape, with its rough tussocky fields and low grey walls. The wayside stations were built of square-hewn stone now and they looked like nursery toys. Far below me a wide sheet of water shone in the sunlight as the train clattered on, ducking under small stone bridges and panting up the steady climb into the hills.

Soon I would be walking on those hills with Ben and Emmie – bright sweet Emmie with her bubbling voice that dropped from time to time into words quite unfamiliar to my ear. She would amuse Ben and leave me free to be quiet – but then I thought, it does not matter anyway, Ben does not expect me to entertain him – I can speak or not as I choose. While for Emmie my presence is enough – to her I was a heroine – 'He said as you saved his life!' – and I wanted that simple uncomplicated admiration today: I needed it.

I watched the grubby sheep feeding in the fields, and saw how the trees had bent before the wind, and noticed the way the small stone cottages took shelter in the hollows of the hills. I too would take refuge in these hills today, and escape for a little while. Suddenly we ran into a tunnel and as I travelled through the dark heart of the hill it seemed as though I were shedding my old life, like a snake shedding its skin. I had left it behind on the other side of the tunnel – I knew inside me that I would have to put it on again when I returned this evening, but for the moment I had escaped and become another person. Who should she be, this new Helena?

And I knew the answer at once – for she was going to meet a man: a sturdy, well-set-up man who was a native of this foreign town, a man who had invited her to spend the day with him. But he was a working man, so she would have to be a working girl – a mill girl from one of those big square buildings in Bolton, a mill girl going on a Saturday afternoon to meet her sweetheart. And then I could be young and silly again and pretend to be in love. And no one would ever know – Ben Holden would never guess – to him I would always be 'Lady Helena': but secretly I would play my part. I would pretend that my satin chemise was a petticoat of cheap artificial silk, that my fine cashmere jacket was a knitted woollen shawl, and my shoes – I held out my foot, shod in its expensive leather – why, I would walk as though I were wearing Emmie's best black-buttoned boots. And as I imagined my different self we came out of the tunnel into a deep rugged cutting, and I looked around and smiled, and shifted my shoulders to get the feel of my new skin.

503

Now black terraces huddled close to the railway line, crammed into the narrow valley and clinging tightly to the steep sides where the hills rose up. Today I would walk between those small houses, and up those steep streets, hanging on the strong arm of my sweetheart – a man with a good steady job, – on the footplate even – while I, I was only a poor mill girl. I laughed softly to myself as the train slowed down for Ainsclough.

I looked out at the platform eagerly, just as a little mill girl would have done – and he was there, waiting at the barrier. He was talking to the ticket inspector, but all the time his eyes were scanning the carriages, searching for me. I felt a surge of triumph as I saw his smile of satisfaction; I had given no pleasure to anyone these past weeks – but he, he was pleased that I had come today.

I jumped down from the compartment and almost ran to meet him. 'Good morning, Ben.'

'Morning, Lady Helena.'

His large hand was warm as I shook it. The sun was shining and I was a new person, in a foreign country, so as I smiled back at him I slipped my hand through his arm. I felt his start of surprise, and laughed a little to myself – he did not know that I was his mill girl sweetheart; he only saw a lady in fine cashmere, but I knew better. We passed through the barrier and on to the ramp sloping away from it, and I held his arm tightly and leant against him as he strode down.

As we came out of the ticket office he suggested a cup of tea. I smiled again, 'That would be lovely, Ben.'

He looked pleased, but he spoke rather diffidently. 'I always go to Bert's, he's very clean – but there's tea rooms down t'other end of Blackburn Street, if you'd rather – they're more classy like.'

I did not want him diffident; a man such as he was would not be hesitant in the company of his little mill girl. 'Whatever you think best, Ben – you decide.' And as I spoke I felt myself sway against him.

'Right, we'll go to Bert's.' I clung to him submissively as we began to walk down the steep street.

He pointed out the library: 'Opened in 1908, copper dome and all, by Sir Andrew Carnegie 'isself.' I gazed at the stone building, a pleasant enough design, but rather small and squat in comparison with what I was used to – but I was a mill girl today so I murmured, 'It's lovely, Ben,' and he seemed satisfied.

'I spend a fair amount of time there when I can – I like reading, 'specially politics and history.'

I knew he did; Robbie had told me. I thrust the memory to the back of my mind and sealed it in – I was a mill girl today. I remembered the other mill girl, the real mill girl, who would take my place when the fairy godmother waved her magic wand – I had borrowed her Prince Charming for the day, but I felt sure she would not mind. As we sat over our cups of tea in the small café I asked, 'Isn't Emmie coming with us today, Ben?'

He looked surprised. 'No, Lady Helena – she's still in weaving shed, hooter don't go while half one. We'll be well up on th'edge by then. She were right pleased with them clothes you sent – said I were to thank you again.' He chuckled. 'Prinking and preening herself for days, she were, an' told me I mun take her to Co-op dance.'

'Did you both enjoy it, Ben?'

'No, I were lucky – I were booked two o'clock start that Saturday. I'm not a great one for dancing.'

'Oh, poor Emmie!'

He shrugged. 'She's a bonny lass – there's plenty of others ready to partner her. If you've finished your tea we'll get started – I've got a bit of summat here for our dinner, so we'll not go hungry.' He hefted his knapsack on to his shoulder and stood up. As he came behind me to pull back my chair I sensed the warmth of his body, and moved towards him – he was so solid and strong. Outside the café he held out his arm, confident now that I would take it; compliantly I did so.

505

My chemise whispered as I walked up the sunlit street – the true unmistakable whisper of silk. I smiled to myself: I was a mill girl with a secret, a Cinderella in reverse – but midnight had yet to come, so I could enjoy my pretence a little longer. We threaded our way through the crowds and came out into a small square. Opposite stood an ornate tram shelter, with a pair of public conveniences under a small dome behind it, and I realized I had not thought to visit the cloakroom while still in Manchester. Normally I would have been embarrassed to make my needs known to this man, but today it was easy. I slid my hand from under his arm and glanced shyly at the green dome, then back at him. He flushed and stood still, and I crossed the square and went up the short path to the open door.

As I came out of the cubicle the woman emerged from her cubbyhole with a clean towel. I washed my hands carefully, then patted my hair in the mirror. My face was flushed and excited, my eyes large and bright – I was prettier as a mill girl. I smiled at my reflection, and smiled again in greeting to the man waiting outside. I reached out for his arm once more and he clamped my hand firmly to his side.

Almost at once the street began to rise steeply. 'Best hang on to me tight, lass, in your fancy shoes.' He had called me 'lass' – he was playing my game. In response I leant the full weight of my body on to his strong arm. A group of children playing in the street stopped as we passed and nudged each other, staring at us. I smiled to myself; they had not seen through my disguise – they thought I was a fine lady on the arm of a working man – but I knew better, for today.

The last part of the street was so steep I was amazed that houses had been built either side of it – surely the floor of one family's home would be halfway up the wall of the next? It did look so odd. 'You'll have to anchor me, Ben – or I'll slide right back down again to the bottom.'

'You'll not do that, not when I've got hold of you. Stand still a minute.' As I stood still he came round behind me and gripped my elbows so that he could propel me up. 'Up you go then, lass.' I leant back a little, teasing, so that he had to use all his strength, and he half-lifted me up the last steep cobbles to the place where the street became a rough track and veered off to the left. He stood behind me, panting, still holding my elbows – and for a moment I swayed back against his broad chest and felt his warm breath tickle my ear. Then he let go of me and came round to take my arm again.

We walked on as the track swung up and round the curve of the hillside, and came to a place where the ground dropped sharply away beneath us. We were above the roofs of the last houses already, and he stopped so that we could look out over the valley. The drifts of smoke from the tall mill chimneys shifted and blurred and I exclaimed, 'It makes me feel quite dizzy!' I felt his arm drop mine and come instead quickly round my waist; he pulled me close against him.

I wanted to giggle as we stood there looking down over Ainsclough – we must look just like a pair of lovers! I knew I should break away and put him in his place, but I did not want to – I liked the warm strong male feel of him, it reminded me of someone, then I remembered – it was Conan he reminded me of, my cousin who held me close – but Conan was in China and . . . My past loomed up and threatened me and I thrust it down and pulled away and cried, 'Come along, Ben – you're too slow – you said we'd walk on the tops, and we're nowhere near the tops yet.'

I began to run ahead and he followed me and came level, panting, and caught up my hand and drew it through his arm again. 'You'd best hang on to me – track's a bit rough for them dainty shoes of yours.'

I laughed, for he did not know what I was really wearing – I tried to tell him – 'I should have borrowed Emmie's clogs, Ben.'

He turned to smile at me. 'Dress you in clogs and a shawl and you'd still walk like a duchess!'

I wanted to correct him, to cry out, 'No, like a marchioness – I should have walked like a marchioness' – but I bit back the retort – I must not remember, not today – let me at least have today free of memories. And the fresh breeze came up and blew my memory away, and I was a mill girl once more.

The track became steeper and the sun was warm, so he stopped and took off his jacket and slung it over his shoulder, then reached out to retrieve my hand. But this time he did not draw it through his arm; instead he clasped it with his warm work-hardened palm, and drew it towards his side. And as he pulled me close to him I caught the sharp tang of his sweat and breathed it in.

Then suddenly we came out of the shelter of the lane and on to the open moor: all about us was high and light and empty. We paused, and I saw a thousand white flowers dancing in the breeze. I tugged him after me to the side of the track and bent down to look more closely – and saw that they were not flowers at all, but soft furry tufts. I picked one and held it soft against my cheek.

He looked down at me and smiled. 'That's cotton grass – I always think spring's come when cotton grass is showing. And look here.' He squatted down beside me and parted the mat of green leaves. 'They're like little fruits, but they're not, not yet.'

I looked at the small round pink bells. 'What are they, Ben?'

'Whinberries – they make a lovely pie. When I was a youngster our mams'd send us out wi' an old pail apiece to pick 'em. Took ages it did – and we ate as many as we picked. But me old dad were powerful fond of whinberry pie.' He looked down at the small pink bells in silence for a moment, then he straightened up and pulled me to my feet. A skylark was singing high above us, and he pointed to the black dot it made against the blue sky; we watched it drop and there was silence – then another bird trilled out and we began to walk on, round the brown-green slope of the moor.

The path dropped down, into a sunken, rutted track, and I slowed as I picked my way over the tumbled stones. He eased his pace. 'Take your time, Lady Helena.' But when we turned the next corner the track dipped, and water filled it, right up to the earth bank on either side. We stopped and looked at it, and I glanced doubtfully down at my smart leather brogues. 'Perhaps I could creep round the edge.'

He twisted round to push his jacket under the flap of his pack, then he held his arms out to me. 'You mun be joking, lass – there's no edge. No, best idea is for me to carry you over – you don't weigh owt.'

For a moment I hesitated, then I remembered that I was a mill girl this afternoon and smiled my acceptance. His arm quickly encircled my waist. 'Put your hand round me neck.' His broad shoulders swung down as he gripped me firmly behind the knees and I was swinging up into the air; I clung to his shoulders and his eyes were very close to mine – I saw his mouth relax into a smile, then he was looking ahead as he strode forward carrying me easily and confidently over the water. His ear was very close to my eyes – I had never noticed before what well-shaped ears he had, delicately moulded and lying flat against his head. I felt warm and safe and drowsy. From long ago a loved voice told me: 'Then he picked me up and carried me in, just like a baby.' And like a baby I dropped my head on to his shoulder and closed my eyes. His boots were no longer splashing through water, his pace began to slow, then he came to a halt. I lay still in his arms. 'I doubt I can carry you all way over tops.' His voice was amused.

I opened my eyes; I could see the sheen of sweat on his face, and feel his heart beating against mine. He was breathing heavily. Slowly I began to unclasp my hands as he eased me gently to the ground. As I turned, his hand brushed my thigh; he pulled it back as if he had been stung – then our fingers came together again and we set off, walking side by side.

At the end of the sunken lane we began to climb up over the springy heather. He pulled me up the slope, and then it levelled off and the going became easier. He raised his free hand and pointed. 'There's a nice sheltered spot up along here. That's where we'll eat our butties.'

'Our butties? What on earth are "butties", Ben?'

He glanced round at me. 'Them's same as what'ud be called sandwiches, by folks of your class.'

'Of your class' – my class, which was so very different from his – because I was not really a mill girl at all. And as a cloud blotted out the bright sunlight I went suddenly cold, and my silly charade blew away with the strong breeze. Whatever was I doing – walking over these rough, alien moors hand in hand with a working man? I who last weekend had been strolling on the smooth green turf of Hatton, hearing the sharp crack of the croquet mallet and listening to the high-pitched, confident voices of my own kind – while above me on the terrace the liveried footmen silently laid out the shining silver tea service.

All at once I was terribly embarrassed, and I tugged hard to free the hand he held. He let me go, but turned to ask, 'Is owt troubling you, Lady Helena?'

As he spoke he moved closer and to fend him off I replied quickly, 'I was remembering last weekend, at Hatton – Mother had guests to stay.'

'Oh. Ah.' He drew back and I slipped my hand in my pocket; he did not reach for it again. And as he trudged steadily on in silence my embarrassment faded; he had taken my hand merely to help me over the rougher ground – there had been nothing odd in that. Now I could walk more easily, he was keeping his distance, as was right and proper. I stole a glance at his face, and he looked no different from the way he always had done:

Ben Holden, my wartime comrade, who expected nothing from me.

My mind drifted back again, to my own world, and I found myself exclaiming bitterly, 'I don't like house parties, especially Saturday-to-Mondays. All those smart, clever people – I can never think of anything to say, and then they look at me as if they despise me.'

'I reckon you say enough for me.'

'Maybe, but you don't expect much, do you, Ben?'

There was a pause before he replied. 'No – happen I don't.' After a moment he added, 'I didn't think you'd be on train this morning.'

I told him the truth. 'I came because Mother had guests staying to luncheon – and I couldn't face them – I had to get away.'

He did not reply at first, then he said, 'Well, you're away now. We're nearly at spot – it's just over here.'

We came to the lip of a hollow; it was a small quarry, overgrown now, with just a few scattered boulders and a rock wall at one end. 'Mind how you go.' He held out his hand to help me, but I pretended not to see it, and he drew it back and clambered a short way down. Then he stopped, and looked back up at me as I picked my way over the loose stones, and I flushed under his intent gaze and lost my footing and almost fell; as I threw out my hand to balance myself he sprang back up and caught it hard in his. 'You see – you can't manage without me.' His eyes looked full into mine and I teetered on my heels, and then swayed towards him. His face was very close now, and his fingers gripped so hard that they hurt. 'Don't worry lass, I'll look after you.' Then he seized my other hand in his, so that I could not break free, and backed carefully down over the stones, guiding me.

There was a short drop before we reached the bottom and he stopped on the edge of it. 'I'll have to jump you down here.' He let go of my hands and sprang down, then reached up again for me. Obediently I held out my hands to him, but he did not keep them in his; instead he lifted them to his warm neck. 'Hang on to me, there's a good lass.' As I twined my fingers together I felt his own large hands grip my waist inside my jacket, then slide up under my arms and hold me so tightly I could scarcely breathe. For a moment we stood locked together, then he swung me down to the springy turf at the bottom. But as he took his hands away they brushed my breasts and I broke free from him and ran to the rock face and stood with my back pressed against it, watching him.

He did not look at me as he swung his knapsack off his shoulders and set it down on one of the flat rocks. I watched him as he began to roll up his shirtsleeves, and saw the brown shadow of the hairs on his forearms, clear in the bright sunlight. I watched the thin cloth of his waistcoat pull tight over the strong muscles in his back as he bent over the knapsack and began to delve into it. My legs trembled, and my body shivered, and he looked up at me and said, 'Best sit down in sun, lass, while I unpack.' He gestured to a boulder fully in the warm sun. 'That'n 'll do. Sit yourself down there.' He did not raise his voice but he was sure and confident, and I resented his power over me even as my unsteady legs obeyed him.

He was a very methodical unpacker. First he unfolded a rug and shook it out on a flat piece of grass near the rock face; next he spread out an old newspaper, and then he began to position each item he took out carefully on it: one knife, two enamel mugs, butter and cheese wrapped in greaseproof, and a loaf of bread. He was just as precise in his movements as the footmen at Hatton. And now I saw my weapon and so I pitched my voice very high and mocking and exclaimed, 'Why, Ben, you'd make a perfect footman – serving tea on the terrace!'

His face went a dull red and I saw he was angry. He said flatly, 'It's not a job as ever appealed to me – I'm a skilled man meself,' and as he glowered at me I became nervous, and anxious to propitiate him.

I leant forward and said quickly, 'Oh, don't take it amiss, Ben. Why, when I was a child I thought the world of our nursery footman – Jem was my hero.' He still looked at me, his face angry, so I explained to him: 'That governess – the French governess who locked me up with Mother's furs – it was Jem who rescued me, and he threw the necktie on the floor and stamped on it, right on its head – and killed it for me.'

He asked slowly, 'And what happened to this Jem – this footman?' He stumbled over the last word, as if it hurt him to say it. 'Is he still at your house?'

I turned my head and looked up to the open moors. 'He went away, to the South African War – he was a reservist, you see – and he didn't come back.' My voice dropped as I remembered Ena, throwing her white apron up over her head as she fell on her knees beside the coal bucket. 'He died of enteric. Our nursemaid loved him, and she cried and cried.'

He said softly, 'Poor little lass,' and for a moment I thought he meant me.

When he had finished laying out his tea table, he sat back on the rug and ordered, 'Come here, lass, and sit on rug by me.'

Slowly I stood up and came towards him; I was breathing too quickly, as the strength of his body drew me to him – but I made myself sit on the very edge of the rug. But then he said, 'You're nearly off rug – come closer.' And he sat quite still while I very slowly inched towards him, nearer and nearer, until I touched his bare arm. I felt the warmth of him and knew I should move away – but even as my mind told me to do that so my body had moved again, until my shoulder pressed against his. 'That's better, lass – we'll keep each other warm, like.' But it was already very warm in the bottom of the small quarry, and I could see the sweat glistening on his face. 'You're breathing so fast lass, you mun be thirsty – here, see what I've got for you.' He pulled the knapsack to him and reached inside it. I heard the chink of glass and watched as he took out two bottles – one large and dark brown, the other smaller and a pale green. He bent forward and set them on the newspaper beside us. 'There, you've got a choice.' He flicked the green bottle with his fingertip. 'This one's ginger pop – Emmie likes that, she's not much more'n a babby, see – but here' – and his hand clasped the neck of the larger brown bottle – 'I brought some beer – it's more thirst-quenching like – an' I reckoned with you being a grown woman, you might fancy a try of it. But if you want the babby's drink – '

And his blue-grey eyes dared me, so that I reached forward recklessly and took the brown bottle from his hand, saying, 'I'll try the beer, Ben – it'll make a change for me.'

'Aye, happen it will.' He took the bottle off me and his broad strong fingers jerked the opener and flicked the cap off, then he poured the shining brown liquid into one of the mugs until the pale crown of froth rose and spilled over the edge. He laughed and bent his head and licked the froth from the rim before handing the mug to me. Then he poured his own drink and raised it, 'Your very good health, Lady Helena.'

'And yours, Ben, and yours.' I lifted the mug and swallowed. It tasted strong and bitter and strange, but I drank it all down. He handed me a thick cheese sandwich, and we sat and munched together; then he refilled my mug and I drank another draught of the alien brew.

It was warm in the sheltered hollow, and the humming of the bees in the whinberry bells lulled me to a soft drowsiness. My eyelids drooped, and he said, gently, 'Lie down, lass – you're tired. Take your hat off now, and use my jacket as a pillow.' So I took off my smart toque as I watched him fold his jacket carefully for me, and leant forward so that he could put it behind my back. Then I slid down until I lay on the rug, with my head resting on the silky lining of his jacket. I gazed up into the blue sky and smelt the male scent of him and smiled. He bent over me saying, 'I could do with a nap myself – I were on afore two this morning. Can I join you, lass?' I smiled again as his warm body slid down beside me, and turned to press my head against his shoulder – and fell asleep.

CHAPTER TEN

I slept, and as I slept I was young again, running over the springy turf at Hatton in the clear moonlight, hand-in-hand with Conan. My cousin bent to kiss me, but our lips scarcely touched and then we were running again, laughing and carefree. The dark maze loomed above us and his warm hand pulled me in; we twisted and turned and by the time we reached the centre I was breathless with excitement. He drew me closer and his lips brushed my hair and now his hands were at my breasts and as he stroked them I felt the compelling sweetness slowly rise and fill my belly. I moved towards him – and then I awoke.

But my body was still in my dream and I felt it jerking and shaking with the exquisite, overwhelming pleasure deep in my belly. I gazed up and saw a pair of blue-grey eyes looking anxiously down at me. A man's hand was stroking my hair, and his voice was trying to comfort me, 'Easy there, easy – my poor little lass.' But it was not comfort I wanted now. I reached frantically for the hand and pulled it down and held it hard on my belly, pushing myself up against it until I saw comprehension dawn on his face and heard his low exclamation of under-standing. Then I closed my eyes and waited for him to press down on me. But instead his hand slid down over my thigh, and then I felt him touch my knee as he lifted my skirts, and his fingers were between my legs, tugging open my flimsy chemise. I shuddered and moaned aloud as I felt his warm hand brush the skin of my thighs and then he was kneading and pressing my bare belly. I squirmed and gasped as the exquisite pleasure mounted, but just as I was ready to burst with it his hand left me.

I cried out, 'Please, please,' and a rough voice answered, 'It's all right lass, I'm ready for you.' My eyes flew open and he was standing in front of me; his trousers were already around his ankles, and now he was dropping his coarse underpants. As I stared up at him my belly knotted in panic and I wanted to cry out in protest, but even as my mouth opened I saw it was too late – and his heavy body blotted out the sun as it came down on me. I felt his strong hands take hold of my thighs and pull them fully apart – then I gasped aloud at the sharp stab of pain as he pushed hard against me, and my fingers fanned out and I reached up in panic and caught at his strong buttocks – and clung to them even as he lunged forward, full into my belly.

He was too big, he was splitting me – there was no room, no room – but he made room for himself. And because he had entered my body he was in control; I had no choice any more, and now I could only lay quiescent beneath him and accept the strong rhythm of his steady thrusts as he used me. His pace soon quickened – he began to hurt me again, then I felt him thrust harder and deeper than ever before and I whimpered in pain even as he gave a last powerful lunge and slumped forward on top of me. And as his heavy weight pinned me to the ground the steady throbbing between my legs told me that he was done.

We lay together, still joined, and I felt a soft smoothness fill my belly and knew that he was deep inside me – and was glad. When at last he slipped out and rolled off me I moaned softly in protest, and his flushed face bent over me and he kissed me hard on the lips and gathered me to him. His arm held me tightly against his chest and I felt his heart throbbing under my breast –

516

and his manhood soft and damp now on my bare belly. We lay clasped together until I felt it quiver and begin to swell and knew that he needed me again. I was pliant and ready for him so I shifted a little to open my legs for him and he understood and hung poised above me for a moment, looking down into my face – and then he drove into me again. Although I was still sore it was easier now; he was softer and slipped smoothly back and forth. I put my hands on his buttocks and when I felt him thrust deeper and begin to quiver I lifted myself a little under him, so that he could fill me again.

At last he slid off me, and we lay side by side as my damp belly dried in the sun. Then he shook himself and sat up, and almost I wanted to smile – to see him like that in his shirt and socks with his strong legs bare between. He leant over me and studied my face for a long time; I stared mindlessly back. Then his gaze dropped to my crumpled skirt, pushed high up round my waist, I saw his eyes narrow, and he suddenly swore, 'Christ!' He looked up at me quickly and now there was a desperate apology in his face. 'Lass – I didn't know it were first time for you – I've never had a virgin before – I didn't realize!' Slowly I raised myself and looked down at the smears of dried blood on the inside of my thighs and the stains on my satin chemise. 'Did I hurt you?' His voice was urgent, but nothing much seemed to matter now.

I whispered, 'Only a little, Ben – only a little,' and dropped back on to the rug again.

His eyes were still riveted on the bloodstains. 'I thought you were ready for it – I could have sworn you were ready for it.'

I confessed softly, 'I was ready for it, Ben,' and thought for a sweet fleeting moment of the silver pavilion hidden in the heart of the moonlit maze. Oh Conan, why did they stop you? But I was exposed in the bright sunlight now with another man – a man with a red face and an uneducated voice who said flatly, 'I could have brought you off with me 'and – you wouldn't have needed much.'

'It doesn't matter now, Ben.'

He opened his mouth and protested, 'Of course it matters – ' Then he stopped in mid-sentence, and said loudly, 'No, you're right lass, it doesn't. We'll get banns called tomorrow – or even get one of them special licences – that way we'll be wed afore anyone's had time to notice.'

I looked up at him blankly, 'Wed, Ben – *wed?*'

'Aye lass, wed. It's only right after what's been between us.' I could not believe what I was hearing. ''Sides' – his broad face reddened, then he put his warm hand flat down on my belly – ''Sides, I've put my seed in you.' His face flushed a deeper red. 'There'll likely be fruit from this day's work – I've heard it said that when a woman's – well, anxious for a man, she quickens easier.' His face was brick-red now; I was dumb.

He stood up, reaching for his underpants, and then bent down for his trousers. As he pulled them on he asked with his back to me, 'When did you last bleed?'

I whispered, 'I've only just finished – and I'm often late.'

'Good – I'll see you've got ring on your finger afore you've time to fret.' He fastened his braces, swung round and dropped on his knees beside me. 'Here, I've got a clean handkerchief – I'd best tidy you up.' He shook out the large white square and solemnly spat on it – just like Nanny used to do when I had a smut on my nose – then I felt him rubbing hard at my thighs. 'There, that's better.' He leant forward and I felt the roughness of his hands on my bare skin as he fumbled with my chemise. He buttoned the low flap awkwardly, then frowned. 'And what do you call – this – ?' He waved his hand down at Letty's present.

'It's an envelope chemise – from Paris.'

'I might have guessed.' His lips tightened. 'Well, you can get rid of these – these flim-flams – they're not

518

decent! Anyroad, you'd catch your death o' cold in them in Ainsclough. Now we're being wed, lass, you'd best get yourself a proper pair of drawers. My missus isn't walking streets half-naked.'

And at his words the full enormity of what I had done hit me like a blow, and I cringed away from him on the old rug and drew my legs tightly together as I turned to hide my face. Behind me I heard the rustle of greaseproof paper and the chink of bottles as he re-packed the knapsack, then he said, 'I'll just step behind boulder, lass, afore we move on.' I sat up and began to tug at my crumpled frock and saw him standing with his back to me on the other side of a large block of stone, and heard the splashing spurts of liquid hitting the ground. As he swung round and came towards me he was still busy with his trouser buttons, and the casual intimacy of his behaviour hammered home the message. With shaking fingers I began to plait my dishevelled hair.

As soon as I had pinned on my hat he came and stood over me, holding out his large, work-roughened hands. 'Up you get then,' I did not offer him my hands but he took them all the same and pulled me to him and kissed me hard on the mouth. I stood, waiting, while he packed away the rug, then he swung the knapsack up on his shoulder, seized my hand and led me out of that 'nice sheltered spot'.

He began to whistle as we set off down the slope, and he did not ask before swinging me up and carrying me over the flooded path. And I knew that this time his hand had not touched my thigh by accident – instead it lingered a moment then slid up and began to stroke my behind. I pulled away from him and ran ahead, tears blurring my eyes – but he caught me up again and seized my hand and held it fast; and so we walked on together.

We came down by another track, and into a cobbled street – it was Clegg Street. Ben said, 'Mrs Greenhalgh'll be surprised, seeing us back so soon – still, reckon she'll not begrudge us a cup o' tea.' I hung back a moment –

I did not want to face that sharp-eyed woman – but I lacked the words to protest, and at his tug on my hand I gave in and followed him numbly.

He pushed the door open and called. Mrs Greenhalgh, straight-backed and neat, came out of the kitchen, wiping her hands on her apron; I spotted the young face of Emmie behind her. 'Hello, Ben, so you're back then. Did you go far?'

'No, not that far – just up top and over bank.' His voice was steady, matter of fact. Her glance turned to me, a smile lighting her stern face, then I saw her eyes narrow as she took in my creased frock and untidy hair. As her smile faded, the hastily wound plait tightened like a steel band around my head. Beside me I heard Ben take a deep breath, and then his voice, too loud, announced, 'Lady Helena and me – we're getting wed, Mrs Greenhalgh.'

There was a gasp of pain behind her, and I glimpsed Emmie's round face, drained of colour – but it was the landlady's pale gaze which held mine, and I felt the betraying tide of red sweep over me as her eyes stripped me bare. Her mouth tightened, then the words snapped: 'That's very sudden, Ben Holden.'

His reply was determined. 'Not so much, Missus – we've known each other nigh on three years now.'

She drew herself up and spoke in measured tones. 'Then indeed you must marry, if you have known each other – ' she paused, deliberately, before she added the 'so long'.

I cringed inwardly as the Biblical phrase tore away the last shreds of pretence, but Ben was still talking, his tone level, apparently unaware. I did not listen to what he said, I only knew I had to get away, to leave this spotless, accusing hallway. I interrupted, addressing the polished linoleum at her feet. 'I must take my leave of you, Mrs Greenhalgh – I have a train to catch . . .' My voice died away and I tugged desperately at Ben's sleeve.

He glanced round, and for a moment I thought he

was going to refuse me, then he said, 'Aye, aye, we mun be going. I'll be out for me tea, Mrs Greenhalgh.'

I turned and almost ran out into the street and the door shut behind us with a decisive thud. My whisper was agonized. 'She knew, Ben – she knew.'

'Don't be so daft, lass. She might be a bit suspicious, but how could she ever know what we'd been up to – she weren't hiding behind a boulder in quarry, I'm sure of that – Fanny Greenhalgh never walks further than shop at end of street.' He sounded almost amused.

'But . . .' I stopped, helplessly; he could not, he would not understand. I stumbled on the smooth setts and he pulled me against him to steady me, holding my arm firmly to his chest. The sudden jolt increased the pressure on my full bladder, and now physical discomfort added to my distress. 'Ben . . .'I was hesitant; all the silly pretence of the morning had vanished and with it my assurance; now I was in an alien place, walking beside a stranger. I faltered, 'Ben, I need to – couldn't we go past . . . ?'

Then he understood and gave a small grunt, half impatient, half indulgent. 'All right, lass, I'll take you round there. But why ever didn't you ask to go down yard at Mrs Greenhalgh's? You know where it is.'

'How could I, after what she said – the way she looked at me?'

He stopped on the steep slope and pulled me round until I was facing him. I stared fixedly down at his waistcoat buttons as he said, 'Look, lass, we've done nowt that's not been done a thousand times afore, and will be a thousand times ahead.' He paused, then added, 'And that's only Ainsclough I'm talking about! Anyroad, it's me as has to face Fanny Greenhalgh tonight, not you, so stop this fretting. We'd best get you sorted, then us'll 'ave a nice cup of tea at Bert's. We've a lot to settle, you and me, afore you catch that train of yours.'

He started forward and obediently I followed. I dared

not think ahead; instead I concentrated all my mind on the immediate need of emptying my overfull bladder.

Yet when we arrived at the small red-brick building under its tiny green dome I simply stood gazing at the curly metal sign until he gave me a little push. 'Go on then – I'll wait for you over by railings.' I walked up the flagged path and went inside. The tiny room at the rear looked warm and cosy in the glow of a gas mantle, and the fat overalled woman looked up from her knitting and glanced inquiringly through the half-glass partition. I quickly fumbled in my purse for a coin and thrust it down into the slot. The heavy door banged shut behind me and I leant for a moment against the cold marble wall, thankful for the small privacy. But as my fingers began to undo the flap of my chemise I came on the odd button left over at the end – it was crooked because he had re-fastened it, and my heart jumped in my chest and I looked down and saw the bloodstains and remembered – and could scarcely stop myself from crying out. And as soon as I sat over the bowl, the burning was another sharp reminder, and I knew that, were it not for the fat woman's presence I would have stayed crouched in there, weeping and ashamed.

The woman had put out the soap and held a clean towel ready, and as I thanked her and dried my hands she asked, 'Has tha been far, Miss?'

'Yes – I've been walking on the moors.'

She smiled. 'Well, it's been a fine day – we mun make the most of it.'

I gave her the coins and a polite smile and turned and walked towards the open doorway. But as soon as I had stepped off the tiled floor my body stopped – I could not go on down the flagstones and out into the world beyond. A few yards away Ben Holden was leaning over the railings with his back to me, apparently engrossed in the scene further down the street, busy with Saturday shoppers and small-town traffic. And as I watched him I was conscious of him as I had never been before: a broad figure in an ill-fitting suit, the brown hair under his cap curving into the short broad neck which was set so square on those strong shoulders – this was the man who had set his mark on me. He had entered me, and by entering me he had branded me – indelibly, permanently; and now I was exposed and vulnerable to him. An uncontrollable shudder ripped through my body, and, as if in confirmation I felt the soreness between my legs rise to burning pitch. The pain thrust me forward, jerkily – and as I moved he turned round. At once I saw the new confidence, almost a jauntiness, in his manner as he looked at me. Just as I knew that I had been entered, so he knew that he had possessed; subtly but irrevocably our relationship had changed and as I walked forward I lowered my eyes before his.

He spoke, and there was the familiar concern in his voice, but now he spoke as a man who had a right to be concerned and who expects a truthful answer, so that the simple query 'Are you all right, lass?' assumed a weight out of all proportion to its words.

The ground at my feet was no longer solid – it shivered and shifted – I was on the brink of a quagmire and I was terrified. Just for this once I must find the quick easy words of my sex and class and use them to throw a brittle span across this treacherous morass so that I could cross safely over it and go back to Hatton, and be free once more; then this afternoon would turn into an unbelievable dream and become unreal, and the mark he had set on me would diminish and fade – and be forgotten. I made myself look on the man in front of me as merely a shape – a stocky form in a badly-cut jacket with the calloused hands of his class, a working man in a small grimy town far away. But even as I looked at him it was too late. My picture dissolved and re-formed, and it was the same shape, but different, because it was Ben Holden's face that looked at me now, Ben Holden's eyes that held mine: Ben, who had turned his cheek to my breast as he came back from the dead for me; Ben, who had stood in front of me with my cup and saucer carefully arranged on a packing case lid on the night that Young Lennie had died; Ben, to whom I had told in pain and grief the terrible secret of Robbie's death. There was too much between us – not the conventional love of a man and a woman, but the shared emotions of sorrow and despair – and the trust which had grown out of them. I was frightened and ashamed now of my reckless, wilful behaviour – for I knew full well that my actions had been decisive; his, merely the inevitable male response to them. The blame was mine, yet he had offered at once to shoulder the consequences of my folly, in the best way he knew how. I could not reject a gift tendered with such simple generosity.

He repeated his question, 'Are you all right – Helena?' And the slight hesitation before he used my name, shorn of its customary title, broke through the last barrier. I shook my head and let my face crumple before him. He came forward and took my arm, and his voice was gentle in my ear. 'Does it hurt, lass?' I nodded dumbly, not knowing or caring whether he referred to the soreness of my body or that of my spirit, and began to shiver. He guided me up into the small park behind the green dome and found an empty bench, and I sank down on to it, and he sat beside me, holding my hand in his until my shaking stopped. When I was still he said, 'You need a nice hot cup of tea. Come on, now.'

I stood up, but as he drew my hand inside his arm and steered me down the street I sensed again his confidence, the taking possession – and, helplessly, I yielded to him.

CHAPTER ELEVEN

I sat sipping strong hot tea in Bert's, and watched Ben eat three toasted teacakes, one after the other. He had ordered one for me, but I could not face it, so he munched through that as well. When he had finished he sat back and wiped his mouth with his handkerchief, then said to me, 'Look lass, I've got a steady job with good prospects, I'm a passed fireman already – shouldn't be long afore I'm driving reg'lar. And I've got a fair bit put by, so I can keep a wife and family. I know you've got nowt of your own, but that's all right by me – any wife of mine – I wouldn't expect her to bring owt.' I knew this was the time I should tell him about Robbie's will, but it seemed to be too much of an effort even to speak, so I simply listened. 'Now we'd best be getting to see parson. I'm chapel meself but I know you'll not be, so we'll get banns read proper.'

In a daze I accompanied him to the vicarage. Even the vicar's obvious surprise as he took my details barely registered in my numbed mind. Then somehow we were back at the station – I did not know how we had arrived there. At the booking office I realized that he was offering to come back with me to Hatton there and then – 'to face music'. I shuddered and refused him vehemently.

'If you're sure, lass.'

'Yes, yes, I'm quite sure.'

He began to steer me up the ramp. 'Train's due shortly, we'd best get you up there ready.' Up on the platform he led me down to the end of it, so that we stood a little apart from the other passengers. 'Now you see about banns as soon as you get back – tonight it'll have to be, as they're being called here tomorrow for first time. Go this evening, then we can fix wedding for two weeks on Monday.' Two weeks! Panic took hold of me and I protested, 'But, Ben – I shall have to tell my parents first – I'm not sure if I'll be able to arrange for tomorrow . . .'

He pursed his lips, then agreed. 'Aye, I suppose it does look a bit of a rush like – an' I'll have to find house, too. We'll say three weeks on Monday, then – but no later. I'll have to ask shedmaster for day off but I reckon he'll let me have it – after all, you only get married once.' He laughed, then raised his voice as the train came rumbling into the station. 'I'll write, lass – let you know when I can come and see your father like – '

I broke in desperately, 'Not too soon, Ben – let them get used to the idea.'

He frowned. 'I don't want them thinking there's any doubt of me doing me duty by you.'

'No, Ben, I'm sure they won't – but please, not too soon.'

'I'll give it a week or two then – see how me shifts fall.' He pushed me towards the waiting train – I turned automatically from the third-class compartment he was heading for. 'Aye, of course.' He flushed. 'Here, wait a minute.' He pulled me back from the step, took a firm grip of my arms and kissed me, full on the mouth. As soon as he released me I swung round and jumped up into the compartment: he slammed the door shut behind me and I heard the guard's whistle blow. 'Look after yourself, lass.' His hand was raised in farewell as the train began to pull out.

We stopped once, and then we ran into the tunnel. The tunnel! It was all I could do to prevent myself bursting into hysterical laughter as we rattled under the hill. Then I began to tremble as I remembered my foolish, pitiful little charade of the morning – I had shed my skin, left it casually on the other side of this tunnel, to be picked up as I came back again, once the afternoon was over. But this afternoon would never be over now – I was trapped in it. I had pretended too well: since I had behaved like a mill girl going to her lover, and, like a mill girl, I had let him take me in a squalid, casual coupling on the floor of an abandoned quarry – and now I must play that role for ever.

I felt a surge of bitter hatred towards the man who had done this to me – unthinking, arrogant man, he could not be entered and filled – it was I, the woman, who was weak and vulnerable before his manhood. And then I was ashamed, I knew the blame was mine: I had teased him and led him on, and at the last my very underwear had flaunted an invitation. It was I who had offered myself to him – I had not realized what I was doing, but I had done it. He had used me, but he had used me in the belief that I had wanted him – and I had wanted him, then, and so my reckless body had trapped me. But then I thought in despair, what does it matter, now? What has anything mattered since Robbie's death? Hatton had become a prison to me – Ainsclough would be a prison too, but a different prison, at least. I huddled into the corner, my mind numbed and uncaring.

The train filled up as we ran down the valley. A young woman sat down opposite me at Bolton. She wore a pretty hat, but as she eased herself back into the seat I saw the swollen belly below the high waist of her frock. I tried not to stare at her but my eyes kept returning to that swelling curve under her full breasts. In a few months I too would be misshapen like her – rubbing my back and surreptitiously easing my swollen feet out of shoes that had become too tight. Ben Holden had said only – 'There'll likely be fruit' – but I felt a dull certainty that there would be – he had covered me as vigorously and effectively as a stallion covers a mare, and now I carried his seed in my womb.

As the train slowed for Hareford I began to shake. Barnes was waiting for me with the motor – incredibly I had caught the very train I had planned to catch, long

527

ago this morning. But I shrank from returning to Hatton – and facing my mother – and suddenly I knew what I would do. As the car drew out of the station I picked up the speaking tube. 'Barnes, I want a word with Mr Staines, at Lostherne – and would you drive round by the road, please, not through the park.'

'Certainly, my lady.' His voice was incurious. I huddled back into the seat. Old Mr Wilkins would have questioned me – wanted to know more, voiced his concern – but the new man only fluttered his hands before reaching for his pen. When he had written down what was necessary he asked, 'What day are you planning the wedding, my lady?' I told him and he admitted he was free. 'Does Lord Pickering . . . ?'

I said tightly, 'I am over age, Mr Staines.' And he subsided, pink-cheeked.

As the motor stopped outside the front entrance I glanced quickly at my watch and saw that it would soon be time for the dressing bell. I knew I must tell Mother now, or I would never be able to bring myself to do it.

She was in her sitting room alone, writing letters. 'Yes, Helena, what is it?'

I said flatly, 'I'm going to be married, to Ben Holden – Sergeant Holden.'

She put her pen down very slowly. 'Have you gone mad?'

'The banns are being read tomorrow.'

Her dark eyes glittered dangerously as they swept over me, in a long comprehensive examination, then she hissed, 'You little slut!' I tried to keep my head up as she repeated, 'You – little – slut!' Then she took a deep breath, snapped her address book shut and said briskly, 'How many months have you missed?'

I stared at her blankly, and then at last I stammered, 'None – I – it was only this afternoon.' I hung my head.

'For goodness' sake, Helena – and you've agreed to marry him!' Her voice almost screeched. 'You little fool – you might be lucky. Though God knows, men of that

528

class are like bulls – they quicken every cow they mount.'
I was shaking now but her voice went ruthlessly on, 'But
still, even if the worst has happened, there are ways.
Maud told me of somebody – he dealt with the Derlinger
girl after . . . I'll take you down to London tomorrow –
I'll have to put off my guests . . .'

'No, Mother, even if – I couldn't bear to do that –
besides, Ben Holden has offered to marry me.'

She said crisply. 'No doubt – a meal ticket for life
must be very attractive – and if you told him of Robbie's
will too . . .'

'No, no – he isn't expecting anything, he said – ' I
stumbled before I went on, 'He told me he could support
me . . .'

She was pacing up and down the room now; she
turned an angry face in my direction. 'Support you! In
a filthy back street with a pack of squalling brats at your
feet and him filling your belly with another every year –
my daughter! He should be put in jail for doing this –
I'll see he's punished!'

I forced myself to confess. 'It wasn't his fault, Mother
– I – the blame was mine.'

She stopped in her steady pacing and turned to look
speculatively at me. Then she spoke very coldly. 'Yes,
no doubt it was – I should have read the signs. And I
haven't forgotten that evening in the maze, when you
were still in the schoolroom. So, Helena, you went to
this man like a bitch on heat – and he served you.'

There was a gasp from the door – neither of us had
heard Letty slip in. Now she came forward. 'Hellie –
whatever have you been doing?'

My mother spat the answer: 'Your sister – your sister
– has opened her legs to Sergeant Holden – and with
typical lower-class morality he's offered to make an
honest woman of her.'

Letty said, 'Oh.' She looked at me with interest and
asked, 'Are you expecting a child, Hellie?'

Mother broke in, 'She hasn't even bothered to wait

and find out.' She turned back to me: 'Helena, why on earth did you say you'd marry him when it was only the one time?' As my eyes fell I saw she had read the message of my burning cheeks. She drew a deep breath. 'Oh, what a slut you are, what a *slut*.' She flung herself through the door.

Letty sat down in her chair. 'Well, Helena, you do surprise me sometimes.' She leant forward, her face eager. 'But Hellie, you must tell me – Dora swore she would when she got back from her honeymoon, but the little rat went all coy – what was it *like*, Helena?'

I looked at her in bewilderment. 'What was what like?'

'Doing it – what Ben Holden did to you – what was it like? I thought it was supposed to hurt the first time, but if you went and did it again, the same afternoon . . .'

I ran to the door and slammed it hard behind me.

But I knew I had to face them again at dinner, and I saw by Papa's appalled expression that Mother had told him. I tried to swallow a spoonful of soup but it nearly choked me, and after that I gave up any pretence of eating as the meal dragged on. When at last the servants left us Mother glared at Papa until he cleared his throat and began, 'Helena, your mother tells me – '

He stopped, and in the silence I whispered, 'I'm going to marry Sergeant Holden.'

Papa spoke again: 'Look, if there's any question of blackmail – '

I only shook my head and it was left to Letty to spring angrily to Ben's defence. 'Papa! How could you even suggest that? You're talking about a man who risked his own life to bring Eddie in – surely as a family we owe him better than this?'

There was a silence, then Papa looked across at Mother. 'Letty's right – we do owe a debt of gratitude to this man. If Helena is determined to marry him we must put the best possible face on it and go ahead.'

Mother asked sharply, 'Is the chapel in the house licensed for weddings? We could hold the ceremony there and nobody need know beyond the immediate family.'

Papa said, '*No*, Ria, no.' My mother looked at him, startled. He went on, 'You're talking of our daughter's wedding, and besides, Holden is a brave man, and we have no reason to suppose he's not an honourable one – indeed, from what you told me before dinner, he is.' His face reddened. 'So we will not have a hole-in-corner affair – there's no use crying over spilt milk, we'll put a decent face on it – it'll be the church at Lostherne and that's final.'

Mother looked back, her eyes blazing. 'Very well, Victor, if you insist. Then I shall send out invitations to all our friends and acquaintances – and the whole county besides. No doubt they'll be delighted at the opportunity to come and gawp but "we'll put a decent face on it",' she mimicked him derisively. They looked at each other until my father's eyes dropped. 'If that's how you want it to be, Ria.'

'Yes – that *is* how I want it to be – after all, "there's no use crying over spilt milk", as you so wittily put it. And let's look on the bright side – after what's happened today it'll be as well to get Helena married off quickly – we don't want all the grooms and gardeners trampling mud into the carpet on their way up to her bedroom!'

There was an appalled silence which stretched on and on. Even Letty was speechless. I looked at my mother with hatred in my eyes until at last, slowly, I spoke. 'But of course, Sir Ernest was a gentleman – he always wiped his boots.'

Mother stood up and leant right across the table, and I felt the stinging pain on my cheekbone as she slapped me, hard. Then her other hand threw her napkin down on the table and she stalked to the door. After a moment my father scraped back his chair and followed her out.

Letty's eyes were bright with excitement as she leant towards me. 'So it is true, Hellie – worms do turn at the last.' She threw back her head and laughed. I jumped

531

up and ran from the room and along the passageway and just managed to get into the closet before I was violently sick.

I had to haul myself upstairs by the bannister, and as I half-fell through the door into my bedroom the curtains billowed and by a trick of the light Gerald's eyes in the photograph on my dressing table seemed to come alive – and to stare accusingly at me. How could I have betrayed him so? Gerald – so noble, so fastidious – I had thought I had lost him before, but now I knew he had really gone from me. I picked up his photograph and turned it face down, opened a drawer and pushed it inside. Then I thrust the drawer to, ran to my bed and threw myself on it in a storm of weeping.

I fell asleep at last, and dreamt I saw Gerald, striding tall and strong along Jermyn Street, swinging his silver-headed cane in his hand. I ran to him, calling his name, and he turned and looked at me – but in his eyes was an expression of such disdain that I stopped and fell back, and as I did so I glanced down and saw that I was wearing the tawdry finery of a woman of the streets, and felt my cheeks taut with the paint that was caked on them. I backed away from him in shame, and he swung round and strode on until he turned the corner – and was gone. I woke with the tears streaming down my face and did not sleep again.

I stayed in my room the next morning until it was time to go to church, then I put on my hat and coat and went straight down. Letty came running out to the motor. 'I'll come with you, Helena – Mother's still sulking and Papa's gone into hiding in the library.' My face was hot and ashamed, but my sister did not seem to notice.

The second lesson was read and then, there in the grey stone church of my childhood, the rector intoned: 'I publish the Banns of Marriage between Helena Alexandra Feodorovna Girvan, of this parish, and Benjamin Holden of the parish of St Matthew, Ainsclough – ' I heard the little gasp from the servants' pew at the back, and my face flamed again under my veil. As we came out Letty said casually, 'Well, that'll have given them something to talk about in Hall tonight!' I could not reply.

My parents barely spoke at luncheon, and I was silent. Afterwards I went to the library and hid in a corner with a book, but I did not read it. My head began to ache and I went upstairs and lay on my bed. I did not go down to dinner.

Next morning only Letty and Papa were in the breakfast room. There was a letter by my plate and I recognized Ben's even writing on the envelope – and shrank from picking it up. I looked across the table and saw that my father was reading a letter in the same hand; I watched him until he put it down. Then his glance flickered in my direction and he said, 'Holden has written a very fair letter, very fair under the circumstances. I must confess I'm surprised – he writes like a man of education.'

Letty exclaimed, 'What a triumph for the council schools! Don't be so patronizing, Papa.'

Papa floundered, 'I didn't mean – that is, for a man of his class . . .' His voice trailed off miserably and I felt a twinge of sympathy for my bewildered father.

I said tiredly, 'I believe he reads widely.'

Papa's face lightened a fraction. 'Then it should be possible to find him a better type of job – the Ship Canal Company always have openings for clerks, and with his war record . . .' I listened to his plans dully; this morning I did not care what Ben did for a living – he was simply the man with whose body I had so carelessly betrayed Gerald. And soon my own body would change and swell, and I would carry an ever-present reminder of my treachery in my belly. I crumpled up my napkin and hurried out of the room.

Letty overtook me in the hall. 'You left your letter in

the breakfast room, Helena.' Her sharp tone rebuked me, and I supposed I deserved it.

I went through into the deserted library and forced myself to tear open the envelope. He wrote about his visit: he had two weeks of daytime shifts, and had promised to work this Sunday, but he would definitely be free to come to Hatton the Sunday after. In the meantime he was looking for a house, and he would also be visiting his sisters – so would I send him a photograph to show them? I got up and went to the albums on the bottom shelf. I began to turn over the leaves but the pictures of my laughing brothers caught at my throat, and as the tears threatened I seized one at random and pulled it out. It had been taken before the war and my face looked very young and hopeful under a ridiculous flowered hat – there was a feather boa round my neck – but when I looked closer I saw the faint droop of my lips, as if I had had some presentiment of what was to come. I looked up at the mirror over the side table and now my hollowed cheeks looked too thin for my full, singer's mouth – but then I was not a singer any longer.

After lunch my parents wrangled over *The Times* announcement. Papa submitted to the simple, 'of Ainsclough' – 'I will not have the whole world knowing that my daughter is marrying a man from Clegg Street,' my mother spat. Papa continued with his draft and handed it to her. She exploded. 'DCM, MM – do you have to proclaim to every casual reader that my future son-in-law was a common soldier? Cross them out.' Papa might have given in, but Letty was adamant, and Mother finally retreated, worsted. So the notice was sent off with Ben's decorations intact.

The day it appeared Mother called me into her sitting room and thrust the open newspaper in front of me. ' "Of Ainsclough", Helena – "Benjamin Holden of Ainsclough!" Think what you are doing – while there's still time to stop this nonsense. You may not have conceived – and even if you have, something can be arranged.' I did not answer, and she moved closer to me. 'Write to him and tell him that you have changed your mind – do it *today*, Helena.' Her dark eyes glittered fiercely and I backed away; but I would not let her bully me. 'No, Mother – the banns will be called again this week.' As soon as I had spoken I turned and half-ran from her room.

After that all her energies were directed towards arranging the largest possible wedding in the short time available. I did not know whether she intended to shame me into surrender at the thought of this massed congregation of Society's leaders – or whether, in her own cruel but courageous way, she was indeed 'putting a decent face on it'.

Papa summoned me next. He stood behind his desk, ill at ease. 'Helena, are you quite sure . . . ? If you want to stop this whole business now, you've only to say the word.' But I lowered my eyes and said no word. I heard his sigh, then the rustle of papers, and when he spoke again his voice was confident and businesslike. 'I've been looking into Robbie's affairs – your affairs now, Helena. Wilson, his agent, seems a good man – he acted for John, previously, and I know he thought highly of him. I would strongly advise you to retain his services.'

'If you say so, Papa.'

'Yes, I do. I've been through all the accounts and reports most carefully, and they're in apple-pie order. Hyde has sent one of his assistants to inspect the properties, and he's very satisfied. But of course, I'll continue to keep an eye on things for you.'

'Thank you, Papa.'

'I shall arrange a current account for you to draw on at Ainsclough – if you insist on going ahead . . . ?' I said nothing. 'I'll see to that then, and have the chequebook with you before the seventh.'

I said baldly, 'Ben doesn't know about Robbie's property. I didn't tell him.'

'No, no – but that doesn't matter at present. When

the next tax year starts, if you're still together, he'll have to know then.' I murmured an acknowledgement; that was a long way off – anything could happen . . . Papa continued, his voice low, almost as if he were speaking to himself. 'Of course, your having this estate does make a difference. A woman takes her social status from her husband, there's no avoiding that; but a substantial income does confer independence – except where the settlements have been carelessly drawn up – or the woman's a fool and the man's a bounder.'

I said tightly, 'Papa, I may be a fool, but Ben Holden is not a bounder.'

'No, no Helena – I've no fears on that score – in any case . . .' In any case, Papa had tied up this estate very securely, and there would be no carelessness of settlements where he was concerned; he had all the shrewd ability of a trained lawyer.

I waited, but he seemed to have nothing more to add, so I asked, 'May I go now, Papa?'

He hesitated a moment before he replied. 'Yes, Helena – I think that's all. There will be some papers for you to sign, but we'll see about that later.' Then, as I began to move, he added, without looking at me, 'As your mother says, divorce is becoming much more acceptable these days . . .' I ran to the door and outside in the corridor I had to fight off the threatening hysteria. The wedding had not even taken place yet – and already my mother was talking of divorce! Sometimes I felt as though I were caught up in a nightmare – but then I would visit the graveyard and know that the nightmare had already come true – and that nothing mattered any more.

As the days drifted past other people made decisions for me – it was a relief not to have to think for myself. Papa gave me papers to sign; Mother talked to Letty of the wedding arrangements; Ben wrote to say he had found a house. I had no interest in any of these things – events had passed out of my control and I did not care.

536

Then, on the second Saturday, the day before Ben was due, a cable arrived from Canada. It read simply: 'Helena, come to us and share our nursery. Guy, Pansy and Nanny Whitmore.' The last name blurred before my eyes – Nanny – Nanny would forgive me, Nanny would take my child and nurse it and scold it and love it, just as she had nursed and scolded and loved myself and my brothers. But even as I longed for her I hesitated – my brothers, Robbie – could I weep on her broad bosom and not tell her of what I had done to Robbie? I wanted to go, oh how I wanted to go – to Guy, so loyal and loving; to Pansy, who would be uncomprehending, even reproachful at first – but she would forgive me – and there was Nanny.

I would go. Ben would be relieved; he had done what he thought right, but now I could release him. Little Emmie was there, waiting – she would soon take the place I had so briefly usurped, and I would become only a fleeting memory; it was better so. I folded the cable and put it safely into my pocket; I would tell him tomorrow, before I telegraphed my acceptance.

But at lunch when Mother said, 'Maud has sent a very handsome present – and she's bringing Juno and Julia,' I felt suddenly confused – the wedding had gained a momentum of its own now. And the afternoon post brought yet another letter from Ben, asking anxiously after my welfare – and I was touched and realized again that this man had every right to be concerned. Then I remembered his silent sympathy as he had held my hand in the little park in Ainsclough and became even more uncertain.

CHAPTER TWELVE

But when I read the cable again next morning, I knew I would go. I felt its comforting presence in the pocket of my dress as I sat in the drawing room watching the hands of the clock crawl round. Then Letty looked in at the door. 'Isn't it time you left, Helena?'

'Left?'

'For the station – to meet Ben.' I looked at her in surprise and she said, 'For goodness' sake – you *are* going to meet him, aren't you? The poor man must be shaking in his shoes – it's the least you can do. I'll ring for your hat.'

I dragged myself to my feet; I did not want to go and meet Ben, but it was always easier to give in to Letty than to try to argue with her.

She was soon back. 'The motor will be round in five minutes – you should just make it. Get a move on, Hellie.'

Ben was first out of the station entrance – he looked about him, spotted the car and came quickly towards it. Barnes sprang to attention and swung the door open, Ben climbed in and the door closed on us with a subdued click. I stared through the glass partition as the chauffeur jumped back into his seat, fixing my eyes on his gauntleted hand as he reached for the gear lever. I could not look at the man at my side; waves of embarrassment washed over me. Neither of us spoke.

We were running through the park gates before Ben cleared his throat with a rasping sound and asked, 'How are you, La – lass – Helena?'

I whispered, 'I'm – quite well, Ben – thank you.'

'Oh – ah – good.'

The Delaunay-Belleville purred to a halt outside the front entrance. Barnes came quickly round to open my door and I stepped out; Ben shuffled across the seat and followed me – out of the same side. I glanced at the chauffeur's face but it was impassive. Cooper had the tall front door already open. 'Luncheon will be served in five minutes, my lady.'

'Thank you, Cooper.'

'Your hat, sir.' Ben surrendered his cap and stood awkwardly in the hallway. Then Letty came running down the stairs. 'Ben – how nice to see you. How do you do?' She put out her hand and he shook it vigorously. 'How was your journey – did you have to wait long for your connection at Manchester?' And as she chattered I saw the overwhelming relief on his face – suddenly I felt bitterly ashamed of myself.

I stepped forward and put my hand through his arm. 'Mother and Papa will be in the drawing room – I'll take you through.' And so we walked in side by side.

Mother did not speak after her frosty, 'How do y' do?' but Papa was polite. 'Pleased you could come, Holden – good journey? Good, good – I expect you fancy a spot of lunch now, and here's Cooper to announce it.'

It was Letty and Papa who kept the conversation moving. Ben's answers were monosyllabic, Mother swallowed every mouthful as though it were laced with arsenic, and I barely touched each course.

At last the ordeal came to an end. As he stood up Papa said, 'Perhaps you'd care to come to my study for a little chat, Holden?'

Ben answered baldly, 'Yes, sir – I would,' and followed him out without a backward glance. We ladies retired to the drawing room. As soon as the footman shut the door Mother rounded on me. 'Helena – how could you, how could you?' Her nostrils flared as she flicked out her skirts and sat down, ramrod straight, with her back to the door.

Letty, her cheeks flushed with anger, exclaimed,

'Helena – you should be ashamed of yourself – why on earth couldn't you be more gracious to the poor man? After all, on your own admission you virtually seduced him!' I stared down at my shaking hands – I had no answer for either of them.

After what seemed an interminable time Ben came back, his mouth set. Mother turned her head away, but Letty smiled warmly at him before saying to me, 'Hellie – it's such a lovely afternoon, why don't you take Ben for a walk in the garden?'

Mother's voice stung like a whiplash. 'Yes, Helena – why not show him the maze?' I almost ran to the door.

I took Ben out through the side entrance and we walked in silence along the gravelled path and down into the rhododendron garden. I was desperate to hide from the Hall, with its rows of blank, accusing windows.

When we reached the first hidden seat I dropped down on to it and began to cry. Ben sat quickly down beside me and put his arm round my shoulders and pulled me close against him. He held me tight and stroked my hair until I was still. 'I'm sorry, lass. I suppose your ma's been putting you through it.'

I drew away from him and dried my cheeks and then sat up straight. I knew I should say something about Guy and the cable from Canada, but I did not know how to begin. Then he began to speak, telling me about the house he had found. 'The foreman at shed put me on to it – I were lucky, it's not easy to find houses these days, and this 'un's a nice sound little place, rent very fair considering. They moved on Sunday so I've been in already – I got Mrs Scholes from next door but one to give it a good scrub-out – not but what it were clean, no bugs or owt like that, I checked careful afore I took it. And Royds Street's a good street, very respectable. I've been round to Bert's – he has a little second-hand business on the side and he let me have some odds and ends of furniture, just to be going on with – he said his missus 'ud see to kitchen, fetch in what you'll need like. It's got a scullery built on – I've whitewashed that, and closet – and range is a good 'un, Mrs Scholes says, she had it lit for hot water and it drew well.'

As I listened to the tale of his careful preparations Guy's cable burnt a hole in the pocket of my frock. At last he stopped, and seemed to expect a reply. 'You've – you've been very busy, Ben.'

'Well, we 'aven't got much time. There's something else – ' He looked away from me, red in the face. 'When I spoke to your dad just now, I told him straight out – I can't keep her in the manner to which she's accustomed, I said, but I have got a good steady job. Why, last week I drew over five pound – I were lucky, I got driving turns, and of course I did full Sunday shift. I'll not be offering for Sundays once we're married – there's plenty of others as'll be glad of money. But even without much overtime I can get three or four pound every week, regular. And I got a fair bit put by – I saved up me wages in war, and then there was me DCM gratuity. So I can support a wife, no doubt about that – and any youngsters that come along.' I flushed and looked down at my lap. 'Your dad started to talk about his money, but I told him I'm not taking any cash with you and that's final. If you bring a few towels and sheets that's fair enough – but I'm not expecting even that.'

I said helplessly, 'But settlements are quite normal, Ben – even if, even if I had married Lord Staveley – Papa would have settled an income on me.'

'They may be normal here, but they're not normal where I come from.' His tone was final.

I remembered Mr Hyde's clipped voice as he had read: 'And all my real and personal estate not otherwise disposed of by this my will I bequeath unto my beloved sister . . .' and ventured, 'Did he – did he say anything after that?'

'Only to suggest as he could get me an office job. What would I be wanting with an office job? – I'm a skilled man. So I told him "No" and he knew I meant

what I said, so he shut up after that.' Yes, he would –
Papa had always been a coward, just as I was.

Ben began to fumble in his jacket pocket. He looked
at me, and his eyes had softened. 'So that's enough of
business – and now I got something for you.' He took
out a small box and held it out to me. I did not move,
and he repeated, 'It's for you, lass, here, I'll show you.'
He carefully pressed the catch and pushed up the lid,
and there, nestling on its satin bed, was an engagement
ring. I looked down at the three small diamonds and my
eyes blurred with tears. 'Put it on then, sweetheart.' I
pushed the ring over my knuckle and it glinted on my
finger – where Gerald's sapphire had once flashed fire.
'Give us a kiss then, lass.' I held up my face to him and
his warm mouth covered mine. He was breathing heavily
as he drew back, then he jumped quickly to his feet.
'How about showing me that maze your Ma spoke of?
I've never been in one of them afore.' I opened my
mouth to refuse, then closed it again and stood up –
after all, what did it matter now?

He stopped me at the entrance and said, 'I want to
see if I can find me own way in. Don't you say nothing.'
He took my hand and tugged me forward and backward
through the narrow green aisles, frowning when he came
to a dead end, and beaming with pleasure when we
progressed. He never made the same mistake twice, and
quite soon we were in the centre.

He stood warily by the hedge, looking carefully round
the clearing – and suddenly I realized I was seeing him as
my brothers had seen him – Holden, the careful sergeant-
major, sizing up the ground, inspecting the available
shelter – and I felt a slight easing to the tightness in my
chest and smiled as I asked, 'Will it do, Ben?'

He grinned back at me. 'Aye, it'll do – come and sit
down, then.'

He pulled me forward and dropped down on to the
carved wooden seat outside the small pavilion – and

before I realized what he was at I was tumbled on to his lap. 'Ben!'

He laughed. 'We got some courting to catch up on, lass.' He bent to kiss me and my body felt the warmth of his and responded to the male scent of him. When he took his mouth away I put my arms around him and pushed my face into his neck. He said simply, 'I've missed you, lass – and I've been worried about you. I nearly came over one evening unexpected like – but, well, I thought it might make things worse for you.' Then he put his large hand on my behind and pulled me round a little, so that my belly pressed against his. He whispered in my ear, 'And he's missed you, too.' For a moment I was bewildered, then I felt it, his maleness, swollen and throbbing – for me. I lay against him, feeling the steady beat pushing at my belly. His breath tickled my ear as he murmured softly, 'Now he knows way in he wants to pleasure himself again.' I lay very still. Then he lifted his damp cheek from mine and looked straight down into my eyes. 'Can I take you now, lass?' I did not answer, I could not answer. His gaze held mine. 'Tha can tell I'm more 'an ready for thi – but tha can say "nay", Helena. Will tha say nay?' He bent his head and found my mouth, and now I felt the pressure of his tongue on my lips, and I opened my mouth under his so that he could fill it. And as I felt the urgency of his need I knew I could not deny him.

But at last he drew back away, and held me a little from him. He was panting, and his face was damp with sweat. 'Aye, tha' wouldna' stop me – but it wouldn't be right – not a week afore wedding. It's not so long now – I mun be patient. I'll have to put you away from me now – I'm that worked up I can hardly control myself.' He pushed himself up, dumped me down on the seat, walked away and stood looking at the pavilion. And as I gazed at the breadth of his shoulders and remembered the powerful thrust of his hips as he had taken me before,

I shivered, but I did not know whether it was in fear – or excitement.

It was a long time before he turned to look at me, then he smiled and said, 'I'd best let you face your mam with a clear conscience. Come on, my lass, let's see if I can get you safe out of this maze.' He held out his hand and I went to him and took it. He led me towards the exit from the clearing, turned the right way and set off. At each choice he stopped, narrowed his eyes, then moved on again. And we came straight out of the maze without one false step.

I exclaimed, 'No one's ever done that before – not the first time!'

I saw the pleasure in his face, then he said, 'I reckon I learnt a trick or two in France. Come on, let's get back afore your mam sends out a patrol.'

We walked up through the shrubs hand in hand, and I sensed his confidence now. He had made his choice in the centre of the maze, and he had chosen not to take me – but he knew full well that he had had the choice, and that knowledge squared his shoulders and lifted his chin. And I, I who had been submissive before him, moved closer to his side and clung to his hand. I need not agonize any longer about facing Nanny, because I knew I would not be going to Canada now.

We wandered in the garden, walking slowly and talking little. Ben asked me from time to time the name of a flower or shrub, but generally I had to confess my ignorance. We went out into the park a little way and down to the small lake and then I heard the stable clock chime and turned and led him back towards the Hall. And at the head of the terrace steps, right in front of the watching house, he pulled me to him and kissed me full on the lips. I knew he was demonstrating his possession of me – but I did not draw away.

The tea things were already set out in the drawing room, and my parents and Letty were all there. Mother curled her lip at the three small diamonds on my finger and opened hostilities at once. 'I trust you don't belong to one of those dreadful trade unions, Mr Holden.'

Ben reached for a sandwich. 'Of course I do, Lady Pickering, and so should every working man.' He looked her straight in the eye and added, 'And I were on strike last year, and I'll strike again if me mates are cheated out of a fair wage.'

They sat bristling at each other until Letty intervened with a question about Ainsclough. As they talked I pushed my plate with its uneaten sandwich away from me.

'Eat that, lass.'

I jumped, then said quickly, 'I'm not hungry, Ben.'

'Eat it – I saw what you were up to at dinnertime. The way you are now a gust of wind 'ud bowl you clean over, so you do as you're told.'

I picked up the sandwich and forced myself to chew it. When I had finished he took my plate, filled it, and handed it back to me again – then he turned back to Letty. Although he was not looking at me I ate everything on the plate – and the scone he tipped on to it next. Letty glanced over at me and I flushed at the amusement in her eyes. Mother was still staring at Ben as if he had two heads, but when he stood up to take his leave Papa spoke warmly. 'I'm very pleased to have met you again, Holden – very pleased. We'll see you on the day, then?'

Ben shook his hand vigorously. 'Aye, my lord – I'll be there.'

It was Letty who suggested, 'Why don't you drive Ben down in the dog cart, Hellie – he'll see more of the park that way.'

I did not argue and I felt a little tingle of pleasure as I climbed into the driving seat and took the reins from Jenkins. I shortened them and felt Star's mouth respond. As we trotted out of the stableyard Ben said, 'She's a thoughtful lass, your sister. I've got nothing against that choffer but I'm not used to flunkeys jumping about all round me.' Letty – *thoughtful?* But we all knew how tactless she was! Then I remembered my own thoughtlessness of that morning and was ashamed.

We swung round the front of the house and Ben said, his voice slightly puzzled, 'But I can't get over how she looks so different from rest of you.'

I pulled on the bit to turn and replied, without thinking, 'Oh, she takes after her father.'

'Her father? But he's dark, like you.'

I realized what I had said now, but Letty's parentage was hardly a secret, so I explained, 'Her *real* father – he's very fair, too.'

Ben turned right round in his seat and stared at me. 'But – she's youngest,' then louder: 'Are you telling me her high and mighty Ladyship dropped one?'

I shrugged. 'It's not unusual, with the younger children of a family.'

'Not *unusual!*' He was brick-red now. 'Not unusual! But what about your father – does he know what she's been up to behind his back?'

I wanted to smile at his horror – how naive he was, with his lower-class morality. 'Don't be silly, Ben – of course he knows. But he has – companions – too. Whyever not?'

'Whyever not! I'll tell you whyever not, my girl. You've got a thing or two to learn if you want to stay out of trouble as my missus. Stop that horse a minute.'

'But Ben – '

'Stop her, I say!'

And I heard the anger in his voice and quickly laid my whip against Star's shoulder. She pulled up and stood patiently waiting. Ben put his hand on my arm, and I turned my eyes to his as he shouted, 'Look, my lass, I'm warning you now – if I ever catch you lifting your skirts to another man I'll take my belt to you and give you the thrashing of your life.' I cringed away from his furious face, but his fingers bit into my wrist above my glove. Then he added, flatly, 'And I'll kill him. Do you understand?'

I whispered, 'Yes Ben – I understand.'

'Good. You can start her up again, then.'

We drove on to the station in silence. As I drew up in the forecourt he put his hand over mine. 'I'm sorry lass, I shouldn't have shouted at you, but well, I were a bit put out. I been feeling right guilty towards your ma and then you tell me this – and you sounded so casual about it, too. But I shouldn't have shouted. Only lass, I meant what I said. I'll not lay a finger on another woman, but in return you mun play fair with me.' I nodded; I could not speak. 'Signals are off – give us a kiss then, and I'll write how I'm getting on with the house.'

His lips were warm on my cold mouth, then he had sprung down and was striding over to the station. He turned back in the doorway and waved before he went in. I waited until the train had left then I jumped down, tied Star's reins to the railings and went into the booking office.

'Yes my lady – what can I do for you?'

'I wish to send a telegram – to Canada.' I looked down at the form and at last I wrote: 'Will stand by original arrangements. Stop. But thank you. Stop.' Then I picked up the pencil again and added: 'Thank you' and signed it.

The clerk behind the counter pointed out, 'You've written "Thank you" twice, my lady.'

'I know, I meant to.' I put down the money and walked out.

When I got back to Hareford I took refuge in the library. I picked a book off the shelves and sat staring mindlessly at it until Letty came in. 'Oh, Hellie – do put the lamp on, it's far too dark to read in that corner.' I blinked as she flicked the switch. She trundled the steps beside the shelves until she found the one she wanted and then climbed up them and sat on the top.

As her glance travelled along the row she asked casually, 'Did you have a nice drive to the station?'

'Yes – no – ' Then I blurted out, 'He spent the time telling me that if he ever found me with another man he would thrash me – and kill the man.'

Letty glanced in my direction. 'I wonder how that subject came up? Oh, you don't need to tell me – I can guess. Well, Mother deserves to be exposed, if you ask me.'

She was quite calm. I said desperately, 'Letty, he said it as if he *meant* it!'

'Oh, Helena, I'm quite sure he did mean it – every word.' As I looked back at her she suddenly grinned. 'You've never even bothered to read his citation, have you?'

I flushed. 'He was decorated for bringing in wounded – Robbie told me.'

'That was the *first* medal – wait.' She backed down the steps and ran a practised eye over the shelves until she found the volumes she wanted. 'I looked it up in the *London Gazette* as soon as we met him that time in Manchester. I was curious – June 1918, Holden, Holden – ah, here it is.'

She thrust the page in front of me and turned back to the shelves. I read: 'Coy. Sjt.-Maj. Benjamin Holden, 2/5th Bn L&CLI.

'For conspicuous gallantry and initiative on 29/4/18 near Vierstraat. During a counter-attack, all his company officers having been killed or wounded, he showed the most consummate coolness and skill in collecting the survivors under intense shellfire. He then led them forward to capture a machine-gun emplacement which was causing great hindrance to the advance, and to clear an enemy trench held by a superior force. Heavy losses were inflicted on the enemy and it is estimated that he personally accounted for more than a dozen of the defenders.'

The bland, euphemistic 'accounted for' danced before

my eyes, and I heard Ben's voice again saying flatly: 'And I'll kill him.' The words of the citation blurred and I dropped the book and ran from the library. Upstairs in my room I felt very sick.

CHAPTER THIRTEEN

But that evening after dinner I slipped out on to the terrace, and stood looking down over the rolling green parkland; and I remembered the huge barren camp at Étaples – the huts and tents crammed with wounded, dying men in the terrible days of the retreat. Each morning we had woken in fear and despair as the enemy came ever nearer. We had watched our last men trudge up to the front – the too-old, the too-young and the wounded returning yet again – and with them had gone Ben Holden. He had sworn to me he would keep the enemy back, and he had kept his promise. I had been grateful then and I was grateful still.

I drifted through the next days in a dream letting others make the decisions. Letty insisted on taking me to Manchester and I stood listlessly by while she selected tablecloths and napkins, sheets and pillowcases – and a glowing rose-pink eiderdown. She dispatched them to Ainsclough, along with a telegram demanding Ben's measurements; as soon as these came she set the sewing-room maid to alter a pair of Guy's grey-striped trousers and morning coat for Ben to wear at the wedding. Then a letter came from Ben to say that the linen had arrived – and that Ralph Dutton had agreed to be his best man – 'I thought it would be easier for you, lass.' In my memory I heard Robbie's voice asking: 'Shall I give him any hope, Hellie?' And I began to cry.

Presents began arriving. I looked at them helplessly:

549

silver, cut glass, crystal, bone china – all for a small terraced house in Royds Street, Ainsclough. Mother tightened her lips and said, 'They'd better all be put in store, once this wedding's over.'

But Letty said firmly, 'I'll select a sample, Helena, and send them on to you – it's only fair to Ben.'

I looked at the elaborate cut-glass decanter in her hand and imagined Ben solemnly pouring his bottles of bitter brown beer into it, before quaffing the foaming brew from the delicate-stemmed wineglasses on the table – and I felt hysteria rising. But I managed to fight it down before I went upstairs to write yet more letters of thanks.

The wedding dress arrived from London, and Norah brought it upstairs for me to try on; Letty came barging in to watch. My maid slipped the cream satin over my head and it slid smoothly down to fit closely over my breasts and hips, and then fell straight to the floor. Letty walked round me, surveying it from every angle, before she said, 'With that fashionable dropped waistline you look rather like a very expensive cigarette – but it does suit you – Mother was really rather clever to choose this style. You are lucky to be so slim, Helena.' But I would not be slim for much longer: my breasts were full and tender, and I walked slowly and languidly now – like a woman already heavy with child.

Alice arrived with her desiccated husband; his fussing irritated her and she snapped at him mercilessly. She came to my room later and said carelessly, 'God, how that man bores me! He's like an elongated stick insect – and about as much use when it comes to the bedroom. Yet he's so jealous I swear he has me watched.' She shrugged. 'Mother can rail on about you as much as she likes but I've got to admit there's something to be said for sampling the wares beforehand – though God knows I think you must be out of your mind to go through with it.' I did not answer, so she began to talk of her two sons. Hugo was at Eton now, and she had been down the previous day for the Fourth of June. When she had gone I remembered with a sharp stab of pain the last time I had been to Eton – on that sunny Fourth the year before the war. Five of us had laughed and chatted and teased each other – and of that five I was the only one still alive. Seven years ago – another lifetime. And now I had betrayed Gerald. But I remembered his kindness that day and thought, surely he would forgive me? I went to my dressing table and opened the drawer and took out his photograph. And as I looked at it his eyes gazed back into mine – gentle with understanding. Dearest Gerald – I would take him with me to Ainsclough; I slipped both my photographs inside the twins' dressing case.

Ben was arriving at Hareford late on the Sunday evening, and would be taken straight to the Mere Lodge where Mrs Davis was putting him up. I knew Ralph was staying with those guests who were at Sam Killearn's – both houses were full. I sat through the long dinner party and the silver gleamed in the candlelight while the air was heavy with the scent of roses. But Hatton bore too many memories now – memories that pierced my heart. I could not have stayed here much longer.

In the morning I woke up feeling listless and heavy. Norah ran my bath and as soon as I was back from it she carried in my breakfast tray. I ate slowly, and as I did so I became aware of the dull ache in my stomach. As soon as I had finished I got up and walked down to the closet – and when I got there, I found I was bleeding.

It took some time for my numbed mind to comprehend, then at last I understood. There was no child in my womb – there never had been. For once I was early. I went back to my room, opened the lowest drawer of the small chest, took out my belt and buckled it around my empty belly. I looked across at my valise, already packed, then I bundled up the pads and went to push them inside it. But then I realized that I did not need to take them with me to Ainsclough – because I did not need to go to Ainsclough at all now. This wedding was unnecessary. But what of the houseful of guests, the tables already laden with their displays of presents – what could I say? However could I stop all these careful arrangements in their tracks?

And although I was bleeding now, so had I in the quarry on the moors, when Ben had broken my maidenhead, entered me, and filled me; and I remembered his voice saying: 'It's only right after what's been between us.' Yet surely I should tell him – but how could I? He was closeted in the Mere Lodge, far beyond my reach – besides, how could I tell him this intimate personal thing? I thought suddenly, I will ask Robbie, Robbie will tell him for me – but Robbie was dead. I began to tremble and there was a tap at the door and Norah came in, brisk and efficient. 'Are you ready, my lady?' She did not wait for my reply but went straight to the wardrobe and lifted out the confection of cream satin and lace which was my bridal gown. I stood, unresisting, while she dressed me in my finery. I felt the dull cramping in my belly and as she fastened the last satin button I whispered, 'Please bring me my usual tablets – and a glass of water.' Her face was concerned as she did as I asked, but she said nothing.

One of the housemaids brought up the bridal wreath, and I smelt the heavy scent of orange blossom.

I wanted to cry out in protest – how could I wear these white waxy flowers when I remembered Gerald dropping on one knee at my feet, his pale hair shining golden in the sun? But the wreath had been placed over my veil and securely pinned into position – it was too late, too late.

Like a puppet I walked down the wide staircase and came into the high spacious hall, where my father stood waiting. Norah whispered, 'I'll come back ahead while you're signing the register, my lady – it's all arranged.' I put my hand on Papa's arm and Norah picked up my train again as we walked out to the car. As my maid

552

carefully arranged the heavy satin folds, Mrs Hill herself carried out the sheaf of lilies that was my bridal bouquet.

I sat in silence beside my father as we drove between the straight rows of tall beeches that led to the Lostherne gate – just as we had driven to my brothers' funerals. We wound on through the heavy summer hedgerows and between the rows of estate cottages until we turned sharply left to stop outside the lych gate – just as we had stopped while their coffins had been carried in. Eyes lowered behind my veil I walked up the steep path to the church – even as I had walked up to hear the words of the burial service read over my beloved brothers.

Letty was waiting in the porch, decked in her brides-maid's finery; her maid came forward to arrange my train and my sister took up her place behind me while the choristers formed their procession in front. The deep tones of the organ swelled out, the choristers moved forward and, leaning on Papa's arm, I followed. We walked slowly between the pews of waiting guests, down the aisle – and over the place where my brothers' coffins had lain on the bier. At the sanctuary steps, I stopped. The choristers were dividing to fill the choir stalls as I heard Letty's urgent whisper, 'Gloves, Hellie – gloves,' and I fumbled to peel them off as she took my bouquet from me.

I heard the soft rustle of my sister's skirts as she moved to stand behind me and then the opening words of the marriage service rang out:

'Dearly beloved, we are gathered together here in the sight of God . . .' But as I listened the words became faint and distant, and I heard instead, strong in my ears: 'We brought nothing into this world, and it is certain we can carry nothing out. The Lord gave, and the Lord hath taken away . . .'

And even as the priest spoke the words of the marriage ceremony, so the terrible cadences from the burial of the dead echoed around me. He proclaimed, ' . . . which is an honourable estate, instituted of God in the time of man's innocence . . .'

But I had not innocence now and I heard only, 'I held my tongue and spake nothing: I kept silence, yea, even from good words; but it was pain and grief to me.'

Behind today's words of hope: 'It was ordained for the mutual society, help, and comfort, that the one ought to have of the other . . .' – the echo sounded louder: 'For man walketh in a vain shadow, and disquieteth himself in vain . . .'

The command rang out: 'Let him now speak, or else hereafter for ever hold his peace.' 'Hold his peace' – as I had held my peace: 'I became dumb, and opened not my mouth.' But my silence had brought me no peace. And now even the words of the marriage service accused me: ' . . . ye will answer at the dreadful day of judgement when the secrets of all hearts shall be disclosed . . .', and the menacing reminder came: 'Thou hast set our misdeeds before thee: and our secret sins in the light of thy countenance.' I would never escape from my sin.

But then he spoke directly to the man at my side: 'Wilt thou have this Woman to thy wedded wife, to live together after God's ordinance in the holy estate of Matrimony? Wilt thou love her, comfort her, honour, and keep her in sickness and in health; and, forsaking all others, keep thee only unto her, as long as ye both shall live?' And the strong voice replying 'I will' – drove the fearful echoes a little away from me.

But when the priest turned and asked of me: 'Wilt thou have this Man . . .' his voice was drowned by the returning shadows and I trembled to the words in my head: 'Man that is born of a woman hath but a short time to live, and is full of misery . . .' 'So long as ye both shall live?' 'In the midst of life we are in death.' And my heart was heavy in the silence that grew and deepened, until I felt the man stir beside me, and his warm flesh touched my icy hand and brought me back to life, so that at last I whispered, 'I will.'

Hand linking hand we repeated our vows, then he put his ring on my finger and held my hand firmly in his as he spoke: 'With this Ring I thee wed, with my body I thee worship, and with all my worldly goods I thee endow: In the name of the Father, and of the Son, and of the Holy Ghost. Amen.'

His arm supported me as we walked from the church into the vestry, and I took the pen from his hand and signed my name for the last time. I stood looking down at the register for a moment and there, in the last column, was written for my father: 'Peer of the Realm' and above, for his, the one word: 'Labourer'. But we were man and wife, now.

Letty pulled back my veil, Ben's lips met mine and others kissed my cheek. My husband held out his arm. 'Ready now, lass?' I dipped my head in answer and he led me back into the church. The opening chords of the wedding march crashed out and we began our slow walk back down the aisle, together.

But the sunlight outside dazzled me and I stopped, and my eyes turned as they always did to that white marble stone high up in the graveyard. My heart lurched in my breast and I wrenched myself free of him and ran towards the graves and began to clamber between them. My thin satin shoes slipped on the green turf, and my train caught behind me – but I stumbled on. At last I reached the familiar grave, and bent and placed my bouquet in front of the white stone.

'They were lovely and pleasant in their lives, and in their death they were not divided.' My brothers, oh my brothers. I fell to my knees on the damp grass and wept.

Ben and Ralph Dutton pulled me up from the ground, and I crouched between them, racked with sobs, looking down at my white bridal lilies lying on the bare brown earth at my feet. 'Easy now, lass, easy.' Ben held me tight against his side or I would have fallen. As my sobbing slowed he swung me round, and began to guide me down to the path where the guests stood whispering in small huddles. I did not look at them as Ben led me past. There was a ragged uncertain cheer from the crowd of villagers waiting outside the lych gate, then they drew back in silence – and I sensed their compassion.

Ben had almost to lift me into the car, then we set off under the green flickering arch of leaves, back to Hatton. His warm hand reached out and took my cold one, but he said nothing.

Norah was waiting for me in the marble-pillared hall, just as she had promised. She took my arm and led me along into the small cloakroom off the family entrance. 'Sit down, my lady.' Cold water splashed my cheeks and cool pads covered my eyes while her hands deftly arranged my hair and veil. 'There, my lady.' Very slowly I forced myself to my feet, and clutched the chair as I swayed – the pain was getting worse now. 'Do you need more tablets, my lady?'

I shook my head. 'I've had too many already, thank you, Norah.' She gave a small sympathetic smile and ushered me out.

Ben stood waiting, a carved image, in the high light hall. My parents and Letty had arrived back. My mother looked towards me – and for a moment I thought I saw compassion in her eyes – then she was marshalling us all into position.

The guests came in a steady stream, one close behind the other; Ben shook their hands and I offered my cold cheek. The effort to stay upright and force myself to smile was so great by now that their faces merged into a blur as their lips mouthed the conventional, inappropriate platitudes. Lady Maud's ginger hair wavered before my eyes, and I heard Juno's ringing voice as she shook Ben vigorously by the hand. 'We meet again, Sergeant – but perhaps you don't remember the YMCA canteen at Étaples, when you were going back up the line.'

'I remember,' Ben replied, 'you brewed a fair cup of tea.'

Juno threw back her head and her familiar laugh brayed out. 'Well, you chaps went up and sorted out those Huns for us, thank God.' She gave way to Pansy's mother who folded me to her soft, violet-scented bosom; I saw the tears in her eyes.

The wedding breakfast passed in a haze of pain and distress: the colours and voices confused my eyes and ears. My plates sat untouched in front of me – Ben glanced at them once or twice but I whispered, 'Please . . .'and he let them go back as they were. I managed to stand unaided to cut the cake, but my legs were trembling as I sat down again. Speeches were made: Ralph's carefully witty – a reference to the bridegroom's gallant war record, but with no hint that it had been as an NCO. He spoke of our meeting in a base hospital in France as though it were the Forest of Arden – no mention of the smell of blood and pus and my desperate struggle to force Ben to live. Skillfully Ralph converted a rushed and over-hasty wedding into a long and faithful courtship. My father spoke the conventional words – and I glimpsed my mother's still-beautiful face, calm and controlled, showing not the faintest shadow of the turmoil and anger I knew she was feeling. Then Ben stood up; I tensed, but I need not have done. Though the Lancashire accent and over-loud tone betrayed him as the sergeant-major he once had been, he spoke slowly and carefully, in grammatical phrases and without one dropped h.

The final toast was drunk, then Mother gave the signal and Ralph Dutton's hand at my elbow helped me up. The cramps in my belly were so strong now I could scarcely stay upright as we circulated slowly among our guests. I clung to Ben's arm, and Letty walked close beside me, answering the conventional queries and parrying the occasional overly-inquisitive probe with a quip and a laugh – so that all I needed to do was smile and murmur empty phrases.

In the library I was left alone for one blessed moment, and in that moment I looked out over the sunlit terrace down to the shining lake and the rolling green parkland stretching away to the horizon. The sunlit vista of Hatton clutched at my heart in a piercing pang of regret – but then Ben swung round to speak to yet another guest, and the view was blotted out by the broad shoulders of my husband.

CHAPTER FOURTEEN

At long last Letty sent for Norah, and I was delivered into the hands of my maid. The hated orange blossoms were removed from my hair, the smooth satin dropped to my feet and I stepped out of the creamy pool. My silk petticoats slipped over my head and then I was ready to be dressed in my going-away costume. Norah fastened the dark green shantung at my back and held out the matching jacket. She pressed me gently down into a chair and knelt at my feet to ease on the narrow strapped shoes of bronze kid; the dark green cloche with its single shining feather came gently down over my tidied hair. I was breathing heavily; the cramps were coming regularly now, and getting stronger. Norah spoke quietly. 'My lady, I slipped a hot-water bottle into your overnight bag before John took it down.' I whispered my thanks, then she added, 'But don't you think you should delay your departure, my lady? You're hardly fit to travel.'

'No, no – I must go now.' I dragged myself upright and stumbled over to the lowest drawer of the chest. In the water closet I saw that I was bleeding very heavily now and my hands were shaking as I attached the loops of the clean pad.

Ben was waiting for me at the foot of the oak staircase, dressed now in his own ill-fitting ready-made suit. We slipped out of the family entrance and into the waiting car. Ralph had gone ahead to the station, and only Letty and Norah waved us off. As the car swung round and down the long drive I kept my back rigidly upright, trying to hold in the pain.

At Hareford we went in through the booking hall and came out on to the platform – and saw all the clerks and porters lined up with their buttons gleaming and their caps held stiffly by their sides, while Mr Shepherd advanced to meet us, in his best suit and carrying his glossy top hat in his hand. I longed to shrink back in my pain and embarrassment, but instead I had to force my shaking legs to walk forward, and hold out my hand to the stationmaster.

Mr Shepherd shook it warmly. 'My lady, I wish you all health and happiness in your married life.' I just managed to smile, then his voice dropped a little. 'I've not forgotten how you helped my son, and took the trouble to write and set our minds at rest – and my lady, I know what you nurses did for our lads out there – they'll never forget it, never.'

The tears stood in my eyes as I murmured my thanks. Then the train began to rumble into the platform and the stationmaster sprang to attention. 'His lordship has reserved a first-class compartment for you both.' Ralph Dutton stepped forward to shake Ben's hand, his duties as best man now over. He turned to me and I reached out and clung to both his hands for a moment – Ralph who had been my brother's friend – then he gently disengaged my fingers so that Ben could help me into the carriage. As the train drew out I raised my hand in acknowledgement of my impromptu guard of honour, and heard their answering cheer as I slumped back into the corner. I doubled up, whimpering, as the pain clawed at my belly.

Ben jumped to his feet and bent over me. 'What's matter, lass?' I pressed my hand into my side and panted for breath. 'You've been as white as a sheet all day – I knew there were something wrong.' He stood straddling the floor as the train jolted over the points, watching me, then he said, 'You need a doctor. Look we'll get you off – next stops are nobbut halts, but it's not long to Altrincham, we'll find one there.'

Weakly I shook my head. 'No – no Ben – it's nothing serious.'

'Not serious! You weren't so good afore, but lass, look at state of you now! I'm taking you to doctor.'

His voice was decided, and I knew I had to explain. I stared down at his highly polished boots and muttered, 'It's only – woman's trouble, Ben. It'll pass – eventually.'

I sensed the stillness of the man in front of me, and in the brief respite between cramps, guilt flooded through me. He knew now that there was no child, that there had been no need for this marriage – whatever must he be feeling? Somehow I should have told him this morning and given him his release. But it was too late now and the narrow gold band tightened on my finger. Then the pain came again and I almost welcomed the temporary oblivion it brought with it.

Ben spoke at last. 'I don't know what to do to help you. My niece – Fanny that is – she had troubles afore she were wed – our Ivy used to put her to bed with a hot brick.' He looked helplessly round at the empty compartment.

'Really, Ben – I'll be better in a minute. Please – sit down – there's nothing you can do.' He sat down beside me in silence and I forced myself to breathe evenly and slowly.

He got me off the train very quickly at Manchester and half-carried me out to a cab. 'Victoria – quick as you can. There's a Blackburn leaving on th'our and me missus is not so good – I want to get her home.'

'Right y' are, mate.' The driver trod on his accelerator and we shot forward.

At Victoria Ben dropped me on to a bench and ran full tilt to the booking office. As soon as he was back he hauled me up and put his arm round my waist, and my feet moved mechanically towards the platform. With a mighty heave he lifted me bodily into the compartment where smiling faces made room for me and I sank down on to the rough horsehair seat. He leapt in just as the whistle sounded, tossed my valise up on to the luggage rack and subsided, red in the face, opposite me. 'I'm sorry lass – I meant to get first class – just for today.'

'It doesn't matter, Ben – it doesn't matter.' And I gave myself up to fighting the pain.

By the time we got to Ainsclough I was losing my battle. The grimy town flashed past the cab windows as we bounced over the setts, then the engine note changed and we growled up the steep street until at last we stopped outside one of the identical small terraces. I sat slumped in the corner while Ben paid the man, then he came back and leant right into the cab. 'Put your arms round me neck, lass.' I did as he bid me and closed my eyes as he swung me up into his arms. I heard the heels of his boots strike the pavement, then he was easing me through a narrow doorway, and in seconds had put me gently down on a chair. When I opened my eyes I was sitting in a small kitchen, close to the warmth of a range. Ben stood looking down at me. 'Well, I carried you over threshold – an' some more beside.' The cab driver came in with our hand luggage, and then I heard the front door slam behind him. We were alone together.

Ben's face softened. 'Mrs Scholes said she'd make up the bed, lass – we'd best get you up there, I'm thinking.'

But as I began to move I became conscious of the fullness of my bladder – and the sodden pad between my legs. I looked round for my overnight case and saw it standing on the table – beside Ben. My mind would not function properly, and I sat on the edge of the chair looking at him, my face hot. He said gruffly, 'Closet's out back – there's soap and a towel in scullery.' But it was the fresh pad I needed. I stood up and reached for the handle of the case. 'That's over heavy for you, lass – I'll take it upstairs in a minute.' My brain was too slow to provide an answer and as I hesitated I felt the gush of blood between my legs and I knew I could wait no longer. I turned my back on him as my shaking fingers unfastened the case and groped inside. As soon as they touched the pads I slid one out and pressed it against the green silk of my skirt, then I edged past him with my eyes on the floor. He jumped suddenly out of the way.

Thankfully the closet was a water closet. I collapsed with relief on to the scrubbed wooden seat, my legs shaking, and began to attend to my needs. But then I was left with the blood-soaked pad, and I sat helplessly, holding it until I caught sight of the squares of newspaper hung on a nail beside me – they were too small but they would have to do.

I walked back in with my messy bundle, praying that he would be upstairs, but he was in the scullery filling the kettle at the single tap there. I pushed past him into the kitchen and darted frantically to the range, but I was still pushing my sodden bundle into the depths of the glowing coals as he came back holding the kettle. 'There's a bucket under . . .' He stopped, then went on, 'I thought you needed – me sisters used to soak their rags . . .' I dropped the poker and headed towards the door, and the stairs went straight up on my left so I began to drag myself up them. 'At front,' he called out after me, and I pushed open the door and almost fell into the small bedroom. The brass bedstead was ready made up, the pillow high and plump, and Letty's eiderdown glowed a warm pink in the late afternoon sun – but I could hear his footsteps on the stairs so I pulled myself round the foot of the bed to stand at bay beside the narrow window.

He put my bag down on the wooden floor. 'I'll bring a jug of hot water up for you, so you can wash like – lucky Mrs Scholes lit range – and then I'll pop round and see if she's got a hot bottle for you.'

'I have one – already. My maid packed it in my case.'

'Then you get it out while I'm fetching jug.' I pulled it out, then collapsed on to the single, straight-backed chair. He was soon back with the jug and he put it carefully down on the washstand and then took the bottle off the bed, saying over his shoulder, 'I'll leave it on top step for you when I come back.' He went out, latching the door firmly behind him. I trembled with relief at the privacy and began to tussle with the tiny buttons of my dress. I had just got it off when I heard his footsteps again – and stood frozen in my petticoat. But he kept his promise and did not come in.

The pain was lessening slightly now into the aching lethargy that always followed the sharpest bouts. But when I had washed I felt a little fresher, and the satin nightdress was cool and comfortable on my skin – though I still tied my wrap around me before venturing out to retrieve my hot-water bottle. As I bent to pick it up I heard a door open downstairs and I sprang back into the safety of my bedroom like a startled rabbit. I waited, trembling, but he did not come up again. I turned to the bed, but my green shantung dress and jacket were lying carelessly over the foot, and I knew I must hang them up myself since there was no maid in this household. I pushed the bottle between the sheets and picked up my costume and carried it to the alcove – but when I pulled back the curtain which hung across it I stood still in astonishment – there were men's clothes hanging there. Slowly I let the curtain fall back, then thought, I suppose there are no hooks in the other bedroom – how very inconvenient. I wondered if he had stored anything else in my bedroom, and went to the chest and began to pull out the drawers – and found that the bottom two held neat piles of men's shirts and underpants and socks. They had been so carefully arranged that they looked quite at home there – and now I began to get frightened. I pushed the drawer back with shaking hands and crept over to the door. Very quietly I unlatched it, put one slippered foot on the tiny landing and gently eased open the door of the back bedroom. Once glance sufficed to show that there was no bed in there – only my piled-up boxes and trunks.

I slipped back and sank trembling on to the bed in my refuge – but it was a refuge no longer. I had known, of course I had known, that Ben would need to come to me sometimes in the night – but foolishly, unthinkingly, I had never dreamt that we would share a bedroom, let alone a bed. Another rush of blood drained out of my body and I thought, no – not now, not tonight, when I'm like this – how can he bear to do that? And he knew – but of course he had to know, I thought wildly, otherwise he would try to – a voice called up the stairs, 'Are you in bed yet, lass? I've got a cup of tea made for you.' I heard his heavy footsteps and jumped up and threw myself under the sheet and clutched it tight to my chin. He pushed the door open – he did not knock, but then why should he – since it was his bedroom too? But he barely looked at me as he put the cup down on the bedside cupboard and went out again.

I gulped down the hot tea gratefully, then slid down into the bed, clutching the hot-water bottle to my belly. My mind was in a turmoil, but I was so exhausted I fell asleep almost at once.

When I woke up the sun was already low through the lace curtains, and I knew it must be well into the evening. I lay still for a while, not knowing what to do. Where was he? Should I go downstairs and find him? I shrank from that but I shrank too from lying in my nightdress, waiting. At last my bladder decided for me so I got up and dressed in the summer frock that Norah had packed in my valise, then hung a towel over my hand to conceal the fresh pad I was carrying and crept softly down the stairs. Ben was sitting in the kitchen reading a newspaper; he glanced up as I came in and my face burned and he looked down at his paper again as I slid through the scullery door. He was out of the kitchen when I returned, and he reappeared only after I had closed the lid of the range again.

We stood looking at each other until he said, 'I'll put kettle on. Mrs Scholes has left a pie and some bits and pieces. I'll set table.' He turned away and asked, without looking at me, 'Are you better, lass?'

'Yes, thank you, Ben.'

'Good.'

I told him I was not hungry, but he made me eat. 'You had nothing at wedding breakfast – you'll be wasting away at this rate – you're too thin already.' I remembered plump Emmie and hung my head.

As we ate he said, 'Lass, I'll have to leave you tomorrow, but I'll be back for the evening. Foreman's played right fair – given me day shift all this week, since I were getting wed, and said he'll try and make sure I don't get caught with any overtime.' He seemed to expect me to be pleased, so I smiled at him, and he appeared to be satisfied as he cut himself another slice of pie.

The round-faced clock on the mantelpiece said half-past nine by the time we had finished. As I put my cup down Ben asked, 'Would you like me to show you round the 'ouse now?'

He looked at me expectantly, but I shook my head. 'No thank you, Ben'. I felt very tired – besides, what would there be to see in a house as small as this?

'Well – perhaps you had best get yourself straight to bed – you look as washed-out as an old dish clout. You go up now – I've got to run up plot to water me seedlings. I'll not be long, but I'll wash in scullery so as not to disturb you.' He stood up and reached for his jacket, then stopped in the doorway and said, with his back to me, 'By way lass – I know it's our wedding night, but of course I'll not be bothering you tonight.' For a moment I hoped he meant that he would be sleeping downstairs, then he added, 'I'll come up quiet in case you've dropped off.'

Up in the small square bedroom I lay rigid on the very edge of the mattress, my face to the window. When I heard him coming up the stairs I closed my eyes firmly – but they flew open again as he cannoned into the end of the bed. I heard the muttered, 'Sorry, lass,' and the sight of his large hairy maleness stayed with me even after I had screwed my lids tightly together again. I pulled the sheets up over my hot face.

The bed springs creaked as he sat down to take off his socks, then the mattress dipped as his heavy body slid in beside me. The edge of the bed dug into my hips as I eased myself another half inch away from him, so that he need not touch me.

'Goodnight, lass.'

'Goodnight, Ben.'

I slept, but I woke later with a crick in my neck from the unnatural position and I was chilly, because the bedclothes now barely reached me. Very gently I eased myself round. He was sprawled across the bed, giving the soft, grunting snorts of a man asleep, while I lay beside him in the dark, fighting the needs of my bladder and my womb. But at last I knew I had to give in so, very slowly, I inched my way out of the bed and fumbled in my bag for yet another clean pad. He snorted loudly and I dared not wait to find my slippers and wrap but fled down the stairs and into the warm kitchen. I saw with relief the glimmer from the range – he had made it up. Outside the stone flags of the yard were cold under my bare soles, and in the tiny closet I began to shiver.

When I got back to the foot of the stairs I hesitated – there was a glow from the bedroom and, apprehensively, I realized he must have woken up and lit the gas. But I had to go back, so I went quickly up and into the room

– skirting the end of the bed and climbing in on my side without looking at him. I felt very exposed and vulnerable in my clinging satin nightdress with barely a sheet to cover myself with, and I lay quite still with my back to him until he turned the gas out. Then I could not stop myself from shivering. In the dark I felt a large warm hand clasp my shoulder. 'You silly lass – you're starved. You should have used chamber – or leastways put summat round you.' I tried to control my shivers, but I could not, 'Oh, don't be so daft – come here.' And he hauled me bodily across the bed and into the warmth of his arms.

He hugged me tightly to his chest until at last my shivering stopped. Then I lay with my cheek against the coarse fabric of his nightshirt and let my body relax against his – as I realized with overwhelming relief that he was not shrinking from my bleeding woman's body – rather he was pressing me closer. And I gave a sudden start of surprise as I felt it – his swollen manhood full and throbbing against my belly. He chuckled in the dark. 'Aye – I thought as how you'd like to know that there's someone down below as wants to renew his acquaintance. But don't fret – he knows he's got to wait. But lass' – his voice deepened – 'you'll tell me when you're ready, won't you? I know women vary like, so you mun tell me.' Then I felt his lips on my cheek, and I turned my mouth to his and we clung together in the darkness. At last he pulled away a little and whispered breathlessly, 'Aye, you're a warm lass, you are – but I'll have to let you go else I'll never be able to drop off.' He rolled away from me and I lay in the warm space left by his body and drifted easily into sleep.

But in the bright morning light I felt very shy of him, and lay with my eyes closed as I heard him getting up. He must have guessed I was feigning sleep because he said, 'I'll bring you a cup of tea afore I go, Mrs Holden.' As he ran down the stairs I realized with a jolt that he must think I had lost my title on marriage – would he be annoyed when he discovered the truth? I pushed the thought away from me and lay patiently waiting.

When he came up again and put the cup and saucer down on the bedside cupboard I sat up without thinking, forgetful of my flimsy nightdress – until I saw how his eyes were fixed on the curve of my breasts as they hung forward against the satin. I sat still with my hand on the cupboard – seeing the blood rise in his face as he watched me. Then he abruptly turned and left the room. As I picked up the cup my hands shook.

He was soon back, and now he was in his bibbed working overalls, with a dirty jacket slung over his shoulder. I felt a moment of revulsion as he came towards me, then I realized he was pushing something into my hand. 'That's for th'ousekeeping while Friday.' I looked down and saw the three grubby ten-shilling notes – and felt very ashamed of myself. He had earned these with hours of sweating, back-breaking labour – and now he was giving them to me.

I whispered, 'Thank you, Ben.'

He looked at me for a moment, then he sat heavily down on the bed and pulled me to him. I put my arms round his neck as his mouth came down on mine. But as he kissed me he freed one of his arms, and I felt him push his hand inside the low neck of my nightdress – and begin to fondle my breast. My skin tingled under his touch and slowly I opened my mouth under his until our tongues met. It was a long time before he raised his head from mine and then, with one hand still inside my nightdress, he eased me gently back on to the pillow. I lay there, gazing up into his intent face while both his warm hands slowly explored my breasts.

At last he pulled himself upright and said thickly, 'Mebbe it's as well you're on rags – else I'd be climbing back in bed with you instead of getting to work.' He pulled the door to with a bang and pounded down the stairs. I curled up like a cat in the sun and fell instantly asleep.

PART VI

JUNE 1920
to
DECEMBER 1920

CHAPTER ONE

When I woke up again the small room was already warm;
I lay in a mindless contentment, unwilling to move –
but my womb and bladder drove me out. I dressed
quickly and ran downstairs and out through the small
scullery into the sunlit yard. As I came out of the closet
I heard children's voices on the other side of the wall,
and the blank windows of the neighbouring terraces
seemed to be staring at me so that I felt suddenly exposed
and bolted back into the small house like a frightened
rabbit.

The tea pot and caddy had been left out on the kitchen
table, and the kettle standing inside the fender was ready
filled, so I had only to lift it on to the top of the range
and set the tea pot to warm. The milk jug was carefully
covered with a little net hat, weighed down by a fringe
of green beads – when I touched one with my fingertip
it tinkled against the white china side. The morning sun
came streaming in through the one window and the small
kitchen looked bright and cheerful. There was a gaily
coloured rag rug in front of the range; I bent down and
lifted one corner and saw that the hessian backing was
clean and new – someone had only just made it, and I
wondered whether it was a gift from one of Ben's sisters.
To the right of the range the alcove was filled in with
varnished cupboards; I opened one side and peeped in
at piles of neatly folded linen, while on the shelves above
there were basins and flat tins and a round wooden
rolling pin. I took the rolling pin out and ran my fingers
over its smooth surface – I had seen one used in the
kitchen at Hatton, but I had never handled one before
– everything was so new and strange.

There were two straight-backed chairs at the table in the centre and two wooden armchairs with padded seats and backs, one at either side of the range. One was large and heavy, the other smaller and lighter, and when I touched it, it dipped forward and I realized it was a rocking chair. The big male armchair was obviously Ben's – the small feminine rocker was for me. I sat down in it experimentally and rocked myself backwards and forwards and then laughed before I got up and crossed to the other one and sat in that. I felt as though I were playing in a doll's house. The fairy story came into my head and I recited: 'Father Bear, Mother Bear, Baby Bear' – but I pulled myself up short; there had been no baby bear after all, and I had been given this doll's house under false pretences. I jumped guiltily up from Ben's armchair and took his used cup and saucer out to the scullery to rinse under the tap. The shallow sink was of yellow fireclay – there was only the one tap over it and the window was set rather high in the wall above it, so that I could only just peak out through the lace curtain. There was very little to see – only the top of the yard wall outside and the lintel of the window of the scullery of the next-door house. I looked down at the sill inside: laid out neatly on it were a comb, a toothbrush and a tin of toothpowder. I picked up the comb and there was a light brown hair caught between the teeth – one of Ben's hairs from when he had last used it. I imagined him standing here in his grubby overalls neatly combing his hair and then inspecting it in the small mirror hanging on the wall above the draining board. There was a wooden box nailed to the window frame, containing a bar of soap and a nail brush, and I realized with relief that he must attend to his daily toilet down here – so I would have the washstand in the bedroom to myself – but how odd it must be to wash in a scullery.

I bent down and peered at the shelves under the draining board. A deep wooden tray held blacking and a couple of brushes – of course, Ben liked to keep his boots brightly shining – then there was a dustpan and brush next to it and a galvanized iron bucket under the sink – presumably the one he had thought I needed last night. I blushed and stood up and swung round – and saw that what I had been taking for a long narrow table had iron claw feet. I grasped the wooden top and lifted it and there it was, a bath – set neatly against the back wall. I began to giggle as I dropped the wooden lid back into place – how very extraordinary – a bath in the scullery. Whatever would I find next?

What I found next was a piano. It stood in the pride of place in the small parlour, against the wall opposite the window; I backed away from it as though it were about to explode. It was an upright, of course, but a good-quality upright and shining with newness – it must have cost Ben a lot of grubby ten-shilling notes. I had to force myself to walk forward and raise the lid – my fingers played a scale – it had a pleasing tone. He had obviously chosen it with care and I remembered his rapt face in the music room at Hatton – and wondered how I could tell him his gift was worthless. I looked down at the gold band on my finger and thought, poor Ben – your chivalry on the moors has cost you dear: a wife who has not the slightest notion of how to keep house, whose only talent, only skill, was her singing – and now she has lost her voice. The blood gushed between my legs and I began to laugh hysterically – my very body had thwarted him and I had been useless to him, even on his wedding night. My silly laughter turned to tears and I stood sobbing, hopelessly, until I heard the hiss of steam from the kitchen.

Making the tea and drinking it steadied me: that at least I could do. I began to list on my fingers the tasks I could perform: I could make tea – and cocoa; I could sweep and dust and scrub lockers; and I could wash up. There did not seem to be a lot more that was of any use; then I thought, I can make beds, so I drained my cup and went up and made ours.

It seemed strange to think of a bed as 'ours' – and yet the idea was not unpleasing. As I tucked in the blankets and shook out the pink eiderdown I remembered Ben's warm strong arms hugging me in the night, and I felt calmer as I went downstairs again in my dolls' house. This time I noticed another door at the end of the scullery, and when I opened it there was a larder, with a bread crock and the last piece of Mrs Scholes' pie between two plates. Against the wall at the end of the bath was a mangle, and a built-in copper with a small grate underneath it – I would have to light it on wash days. Looking at the copper reminded me of the range; it would need attending to soon and I had always had such trouble coping with the coal and coke stoves on night duty in the camp hospitals. As I went reluctantly back into the kitchen I noticed how stuffy it was becoming, with the range glowing sullenly there. And I dreaded the thought of having to cook a meal on it – what little cooking I had done had been on the gas stove in Foldus Ward kitchen. Gas stove! Of course, that was the answer – there was already gas laid on in the house for lighting – it would be a simple matter to instal a stove. I would see to it at once; then I could let the range go out and the kitchen would be so much pleasanter in this warm weather.

I ran upstairs and rummaged through my boxes for hat and coat and gloves, and scrabbled in my valise for the new chequebook Papa had given me, and then set out for the centre of Ainsclough. It was a sunny day and I felt as though I were on holiday as I strolled down through the unfamiliar streets; they had a delightful air of foreignness about them – I could have been a thousand miles from Hatton. People were smiling and helpful, and I soon found what I wanted; I did not need my new chequebook, as apparently gas stoves were hired – I could pay monthly, and the cost of the installation would come comfortably out of my purse, so I left the bank for next time. But I was glad I had the chequebook – I would have hated to be dependent on Ben for every penny I spent – I would have felt trapped.

I came straight back to wait for the workmen, and went to sit down in the small parlour – the padded armchair was surprisingly comfortable. I glanced up at the shelves in the alcove, and recognized the titles of the books from Ben's bedroom in Clegg Street – they brought back memories, so I looked quickly away and concentrated on the three photographs placed neatly at one end of the piano top. I stood up and went for a closer look. I recognized the one of Ben's mother; next to it two women smiled out of the frame at me. They were wearing their best frilled blouses and their arms were linked and the family likeness told me they were Ben's sisters. They looked a lot older than he did – but of course, he was the Benjamin, the last child come late to elderly parents, arriving on the hearthrug, unheralded and unplanned for. I wondered which of the two women was Ada, who had been given 'quite a turn' – but had still gone on to have five of her own.

I picked up the third photo – and felt a slight shock. It was of Ben, sitting in a chair holding a toddler in his lap. Although the child was so young Ben looked completely at ease with it, as if he were used to holding young children – and liked doing so. Guy sometimes patted his sons on the head, but I never remembered seeing him pick one up – that was Nanny's job, or Pansy's pleasure. And then I looked closer at the two other children in the picture – a boy and a girl. The boy's head was leaning trustingly against Ben's shoulder, whilst the little girl was looking at him with adoration plain on her face. I wanted to know who these children were – the photograph had obviously been taken quite recently, since Ben was wearing the moustache he had been sporting when I had seen him in Manchester, so I opened the frame and eased the picture out. On the back was written in a child's careful hand: 'To Great-Uncle Ben, with all our love, from Benjamin' then, more straggling, 'Edie and Baby' and three large wavering crosses. I pushed it back into its frame and replaced it on the piano. It disturbed me – he looked so very at home with those children, and they with him. I had not realized, but when I had believed I was carrying a child I had never thought of it as Ben's child. Men were men and would take a woman if they could – and because he had broken my maidenhead and entered me he had done his duty and married me – but I had never thought of him wanting a child of his own. I shifted uneasily on my seat; the photograph had confused me.

Then I noticed the way he had arranged them again – he had obviously intended to leave room for my photographs, so I would find them and put them there. I ran upstairs and came back down with four of mine: one of Guy and Pansy at their wedding; another of Conan, standing between Alice and Letty, his arms casually draped over each pair of shoulders; then there was Papa and Mother and Maud, all together; and finally my photo of Gerald. I placed each one carefully on the piano top – my photos were larger and the frames were more elaborate than those of Ben and his family. I edged his a little further towards the end, so that I could place Gerald in the centre, where I would remember him always.

The mottled blue cooker was established in the alcove to the left of the range by lunchtime; it looked rather ugly but as I made a cup of tea on my new acquisition I felt quite smug. I ate the last piece of pie then set out again for the town, clutching Ben's three ten-shilling notes – 'for th'ousekeeping'. I decided to shop in the market hall – that way I could have a covert look at the goods before deciding what to buy. I studied the butcher's stall as I waited in the queue – at least I knew when meat was fresh – I had seen so much that was rotting. Then I thought, but that was not meat, that was human flesh – and I felt quite sick and pointed at a piece with my eyes averted. I held the bloody parcel away from me, I had not thought of needing a shopping bag;

but I managed to spot a stall selling baskets, and hastily bought one of those.

I headed for the greengrocer's and requested, 'Some potatoes, please.'

''Ow many, missus?'

I explained, 'Enough for dinner for two.'

He looked at me rather oddly. 'I don't sell potatoes under five.'

'Then five, please.' He picked many more than five out of the sack and it was only when he put the iron weights on the scales that I realized, feeling a fool, that vegetables were sold by weight – at Étaples they had just filled our baskets. I hazarded a single pound of carrots and lugged my booty outside.

A woman jostled me outside a baker's window and I remembered the empty bread crock in the larder at Royds Street and went in to buy a loaf; I bought two jam tarts as well, in the hope that Ben would like them. By now my basket was quite heavy so I asked two women waiting at a tram stop whether I could catch one to Royds Street. They both looked at me blankly, and I had to repeat my query; then one of them answered, but her accent was so broad that I could not understand what she was saying; the other interrupted, and I became even more confused. At last I smiled and thanked them and set off walking down the street. But I was at the other end of the town from where I had been that morning and I took a wrong turning and came into a completely strange street – I thought I could cut through but everything looked so similar that soon I became completely lost. I began to panic – I did not know how long meat took to cook, suppose Ben was back before his meal was ready – would he be angry with me?

Then in the distance I glimpsed a familiar green dome; I shuddered a little at the memories it brought back but I knew that I could at least understand the woman there, so I stepped out briskly. I had to brace myself to go in but she waddled out of her lair at once and I asked my way.

'Royds Street? There's a short cut you can take, up backs – but it's ever so steep,' she glanced doubtfully down at my shoes.

'Oh, I'm sure I can manage.'

She gave me the directions, clearly and concisely, and then, as I was turning to leave she said, 'You're Ben Holden's new missus, aren't you?'

I was surprised. 'Yes – yes I am.'

She chuckled. 'Aye, I heard tell he'd married a lady, and remembered you coming in 'ere a few weeks back, so I put two and two together.' I felt myself blushing and she smiled, baring two blackened stumps. 'There's not much as gets past Edna Fairbarn. I've known Ben since he were a babby – he's a well-set-up lad is Ben – there's more 'an one lass as has had 'er eye on him. I heard tell you nursed him in war?'

'Yes, yes I did.'

She wiped her hand on her apron then held it out to me. 'In that case I reckon you deserved to get him – I wishes you all the best.'

I shook the firm plump hand. 'Thank you, Mrs Fairbarn.' We parted with mutual smiles.

Turning out of the steep back alleyway into Royds Street I noticed several women watching me as they stood in their doorways gossiping in the sun. I walked past with my head held high, my cheeks rather flushed. As I unlocked the front door I wondered if any of them were the ones who had had an eye on Ben. Then I remembered Emmie Greenhalgh and felt very guilty.

I knew potatoes had to be peeled, because I had seen Ginger doing it at No. 23, so I hacked away at them with a small knife I found in the kitchen table drawer. I had a dim memory of seeing the VAD cooks chopping meat and vegetables into small pieces and throwing them all into one big cauldron, so I found the largest saucepan I could in the scullery and began to attack the carrots.

When they were in, together with the meat, there was still plenty of room in the pan so I threw the potatoes on top, too. Then I ran some water over the lot and put it down on the lighted gas ring. I decided cooking was not so complicated as people liked to pretend and sat down in the rocker for a moment – and suddenly fell asleep.

A voice saying, 'What's *that* for?' woke me up. It was Ben, in his overalls, his face grimed with sweat. I gazed up at him, half awake, as he asked again, 'What's that for?' and pointed at my new gas stove.

'It's for cooking, Ben.'

'For burning, more like.' He picked up the saucepan and lifted the lid. 'This is all dried up! But anyroad, you've got a range – this contraption'll only be costing extra when there's no need.'

'Gas is much easier to use – and I'll pay for its hire, Ben, my father arranged – '

'I don't want none of your father's money!' He hit the table with his fist and the tea cup jumped. 'I told him straight – I can support you – but I don't expect you to go off behind me back first morning we're wed and run us into debt. How much is it costing?' I whispered the answer and watched his lips tighten before he said grudgingly, 'I suppose I can cover it – but me old mam never needed a gas stove – she'd'a' been real glad of a lovely range like this.'

I blinked and brushed my hand over my eyes while his back was to me, then took my dried-up stew out to the scullery and ran more water over it. As I turned off the tap I heard his angry shout. 'You've let range go out!'

I tried to keep my voice steady. 'It was too hot in there.'

'Lass, that were me hot water for me bath!' He sounded outraged. 'How am I going to get this muck off with cold?' I stood in the scullery and salt tears slid down my cheeks and dripped into the stew. There was

579

a clatter of fire irons, then he muttered, 'There's still a drop of warm – that'll have to do. Bring me pail, lass.'

I picked up the bucket and took it into the kitchen; he reached a hand back without looking at me and wedged it under the tap of the range boiler. I pressed myself into the corner with my gas stove and began to scrape at the bottom of the pan before putting it back on the light. He stood up slowly and I heard him moving towards me and turned my face away. He began to lumber off to the scullery, and there was the splashing of water. I kept on stirring with my back to the kitchen as he refilled his bucket. The bath creaked in the scullery, then he called out, 'Helena – will you fetch me a change of clothes – from bedroom?' I did not answer, my throat was too tight, but I went upstairs and found what he wanted and came back and thrust the bundle through the scullery door, trying not to see the naked shape of him in the bath. 'Thanks, lass.'

I attacked the stew again; the potatoes had gone grey and begun to break up. I could hear him blundering about in the scullery, then pushing the door open. I kept on stirring, my head bent. He cleared his throat. 'Look, lass – Helena – I – well, I suppose I were a bit hasty – ' I blinked hard, but it was too late; a large tear plopped into the stew. We both stood frozen, then he sprang forward. 'Oh, lass – I didn't mean to – Here, leave that saucepan and come here.'

I felt his arms come round me as he swung me off the floor and then sat down heavily in his armchair, with me in his lap. I began to sob. 'I'm sorry, lass, I'm sorry.' He held me very tightly against him, and began to stroke my hair. Slowly I stopped shaking. He pulled my head gently back from his shoulder, but I kept my swollen lids closed. 'Will tha give us a kiss now, lass? To show we're friends?' I moved my head towards his and felt his warm lips come down on mine, then there was a spluttering from the stove and he put me down and jumped up, reaching for the stew. 'Looks like tea's ready.'

The stew was horrible. After forcing my way through two mouthfuls I put my knife and fork down and said hopelessly, 'I'm sorry Ben – and I forgot the salt.'

He smiled across at me. 'I reckon there's enough from your tears, eh?' I tried to smile back, and sat watching him manfully eating on – he even mopped his plate with a piece of bread. I fetched the jam tarts and he brightened. 'Did you bake these, lass?' I felt my face contract and he said hurriedly, 'No – of course not. I'll mash some tea and we'll take it in front room – I don't like parlours as are only used of a Sunday.'

As soon as we were sitting either side of the fireplace he nodded towards the piano, his face expectant. 'Mebbe you could give me a song, eh?'

My throat tightened and it was a long time before I managed to whisper, 'My voice – I – my voice – after Robbie died – it's gone – it's left me.'

I saw the disappointment wash over his face, then he drew a deep breath and said, 'never mind, lass – piano won't be wasted. You can still play.'

'Yes Ben, that's true – I can still play. And it's a very good piano – with a nice tone.'

He said eagerly, 'You've tried it, then?'

'Yes, yes Ben – I've tried it. I'll enjoy playing on it.' But I knew as I spoke I was lying. For me, playing was only the means to an end – I played to sing, and now I could not sing. Without my voice the piano was useless to me.

We sat and sipped our tea in silence; we seemed to have nothing to say to each other.

At last he cleared his throat. 'Ivy and Ada made a rug apiece for us – one for each room.'

'That was kind of them Ben – they're very pretty.'

He gestured down to the blue and red stripes at his feet. 'This 'un's Ivy's – she said the youngsters asked if they could help – me niece, Fanny's childer – they only live down street from Ivy. They said as how they wanted to make a rug for their new auntie, so Ivy let them –

but they couldn't get stripes straight – you can see at your end.' I looked down; he was right, the stripes were almost a zig-zag at the corner. 'Ivy were a bit put out, but I told her it didn't matter – young'uns were doing their best, and our Benjamin, he's only eight, and Edie's a couple of years younger. So I reckon they did well to stick at it – they made most on it theirselves, Ivy said.' He paused, and I smiled politely. 'That's their photograph up on piano.'

'Yes – I know, Ben – I noticed it this morning.'

I saw his glance travel along the line of frames – to my pictures. It lingered on Gerald, tall and handsome in his gleaming breastplate with his sword at his side. 'I see you put some of your photos up – I left a space for you.' He stood up and went to the end of the line and picked up the one of Mother and Papa. 'Who's that with your parents – I seem to recognize her.'

'Lady Maud was at the wedding, Ben – she's Juno's mother – you remember, at – '

'Aye, at Eetapps, in canteen.' He studied the photo again. 'Funny how she's got her arm through your pa's – and your ma hasn't.' I looked at it – he was right, but I had never noticed it before. I felt my face blush as I murmured, 'Maud's always been – a good friend of Papa's. And of Mother's too,' I added hastily.

His head jerked up and he stared at me for a moment – then quickly put the picture down as if it were redhot. I remembered the way he had shouted at me in the dog cart, and from the colour of his face he did as well. He picked up Guy and Pansy. 'Is that your elder brother and his wife – one who's in Canada now – whose suit I wore?'

'Yes, that's right – goodness, what a good memory you've got, Ben.'

He grunted. 'She looks a nice quiet lass. Have they got any childer?'

'Four sons – and another baby on the way.'

Ben stared at the photo. 'But he's already in uniform there – when were he married?'

'In 1915 – May, 1915.'

'They don't waste much time in your family, do they?' He shook his head disapprovingly. 'I reckon meself that's too quick for a woman – and she's only a little dab of a thing. No one thinks more of youngsters than I do, but I'm going to be more careful with you, lass – I'll tell you that now.' My face flamed. He put down Guy and picked up the photo of my sisters with Conan. 'I recognize our Letty all right – and that's your other sister, isn't it – her who was at wedding?'

'Yes, that's Alice. Hugh – her husband – was killed in the war. But she's married again now.'

'And who's that?' His stubby finger splayed out over Conan's laughing face.

'My cousin.' He waited, so I went on. 'He transferred to the RFC and was shot down and taken prisoner. He's in China now – flying.' Ben examined the photograph carefully. 'He certainly favours you and your brothers.'

'His mother was Mother's twin sister.'

Ben glanced up at me and smiled. 'So twins run in family, do they? Wonder if we'll get two for price of one?' He put the photo down and came towards me; I saw his eyes were fixed on my breasts. 'Have to see what I can do for you, lass, eh?' His voice dropped. 'I know you like double rations!'

I jumped up and dodged round him and went to the piano – suddenly I did not want him to touch me – not now. I spoke in a rush. 'And this photograph in the middle is of the Marquess of Staveley – my fiancé, who was killed in the war.'

He subsided into his chair, and his voice was flat as he said. 'Aye, I recognized him, too. I'll have a read of paper now, if you don't mind, lass.'

'Please do.'

I sat with my hands in my lap as he turned the pages.

When he had finished he folded it neatly up, bent down for the tray and asked, 'What did you get for me bait?'

'Your bait – you're going fishing?'

'For me snap tin – to eat at work.' He read the answer in my guilty silence and heaved a sigh before he said, 'It's all right lass – I suppose I should have told you. Old Sammy Whittle'll still be open round corner – I'll fetch some boiled ham on me way up to plot.'

As he put his jacket on to go out I asked, 'Does he – this Mr Whittle – does he sell butter?'

Ben looked at me, then he nodded and muttered, half to himself, 'I reckon I'll be visiting Sammy Whittle's regular of an evening with you in charge of house-keeping.' My face flamed and I turned my mouth away when he came to kiss me goodbye and his lips only brushed my ear. As soon as he had gone I went out to the kitchen and put the kettle on for the washing up; I would leave the kitchen clean and tidy before I went to bed – how dared he criticize me?

I was just finishing washing myself when I heard him come in; I scrambled quickly into my nightdress and turned to the window and closed my eyes. He bent over me and whispered tentatively, 'Helena?' but I pretended to be sleeping, and after a few moments he went back to his own side and eased himself very carefully under the covers. After a while his steady breathing told me he was asleep.

CHAPTER TWO

I slept fitfully all night, but managed to keep still and not disturb him. I kept my eyes closed while he got dressed in the morning, but he still came back with a cup of tea. I whispered, 'Thank you, Ben,' and turned my face into the pillow. His hand touched my hair briefly and then he left. As soon as I heard the front door close I sat up and drank the tea; I felt tired and ill.

He had cleaned out the range and re-laid it and I succeeded in getting it alight; then I swept and dusted, and made the bed. It was an effort to walk down to the town, but I managed to find the market hall and buy some more meat, and a cabbage instead of carrots. I dragged myself back up the hill.

At midday several boxes and a trunk arrived from Hatton – Letty had sent on the wedding presents as promised. The van boys carried them up to the back bedroom for me but it was getting so crowded in there I thought I had better go up and start unpacking. Letty had put my operatic scores in the top of the trunk; I lifted the top one out and a photograph slipped out and fell to the floor. I picked it up and turned it over and my whole body went rigid: I was on the lawn at Hatton, before the war – standing between my handsome twins, proudly holding an arm of each. I sank to the floor, clutching it to my breast, and crouched huddled against the hard boxes in a stupor of misery.

I was barely conscious of Ben lifting me up much later. He carried me downstairs and put me in the rocker next to the range and began to re-lay it. I sat watching him as he peeled potatoes and chopped cabbage and cut the meat into thin strips and put them under the grill.

He came to me and held his warm palm against my cheek for a moment. 'I'll get meself washed – water's still hot.' He picked up my lunchtime cup and saucer, then paused, 'Helena – what did you eat for your dinner?' I just looked at him. 'Did you have any breakfast?' He repeated the question until I had to answer.

'A piece of bread and butter.'

He drew in his breath sharply, then came and squatted on his haunches in front of the rocker. 'Look, lass – I'm going to fetch some eggs from Sammy Whittle's and you mun promise me to have an egg every day – *two* eggs –

when I'm not here.' His eyes held mine until at last I nodded. 'That's a promise – right?'

When he came back from the scullery he put the cabbage on and went out for the eggs; then he dished up the meal. 'Come to table now.'

'Ben I'm not . . .' The words died away in the face of his implacable expression, and I had to eat everything he had put on my plate. It was an effort to swallow it, although it was all very tasty – he was obviously a much better cook than I was. Afterwards I crept out to the scullery to help him with the washing up.

He wrung out the dishcloth and hung it neatly to dry over the edge of the sink, then said, 'Go and put your hat on lass – I'm taking you out.' I opened my mouth to refuse, but I could see it would be a waste of time arguing so I pulled myself upstairs and did as I was told.

Outside the door we turned away from the town and went up the street and round on to a rough path that led to a steeply rising cart track. He held my arm firmly all the way; I stumbled several times, but he made me go on. My legs were shaking with the effort by the time we came out on to the open hillside. 'Not much further now, lass.' He led me down off the track to a slight depression in the hillside, then he took off his jacket and lowered me down on to it. He put his arm round my shoulder and held me against him, and we sat looking down over the untidy patchwork of allotments to the smoking chimneys of Ainslough in the valley below. We sat there for a long time in silence, then he turned and kissed my cheek and said, 'Lass, if I'd been with you I'd have put that needle in his arm myself. But I weren't and you had to do it – and now you mun live with it. Come on love, I'll take you home.'

I hung on his arm down the steep track and we came to the path through the little allotments. There was a goat in one of them, with a kid frisking beside her, and I stopped to watch them. Ben said, 'That's Jack Holleran's kid – it's a bonny little thing.'

'Yes, yes it is.' Then I managed to ask, 'Which is your plot, Ben?'

He squeezed my arm. 'Come over here and I'll show you.' We threaded our way between the low fences and came to a neat little gate. He led me in. 'I need to do a bit of sticking with me peas. Come and sit on bench outside of shed – it catches sun in th'evening.' I sat and watched him moving among the pea sticks, delicately lifting the fine green tendrils and curling them round the branching twigs. It was very peaceful.

He sent me up to bed as soon as we got in and I fell asleep at once. I heard him moving about the bedroom later, and half turned – and as soon as he was under the sheets he pulled me against him, and I lay with my cheek pressed against his shoulder until I drifted into sleep again.

I woke late the next morning – there was a pale skin on the cup of tea beside my bed; I had not even heard him bring it up. Out in the closet I saw that my pad was barely stained; it often happened like that: when the pain was especially bad I would flood at first – then it would finish quickly, sooner than usual. I began to unfasten the belt, then stopped, my hands shaking, remembering Ben's voice: 'But lass, you'll tell me when you're ready, won't you?' I would be 'ready' tonight.

I went quickly back into the kitchen and put the kettle on, then while it boiled I went upstairs to make the bed. As I shook out the bottom sheet I remembered Pansy's wail of distress; I remembered Conan with the girl in the night club; I remembered Guy with the painted female on his arm, and my mother's matter-of-fact voice saying, 'Your brothers are normal, healthy young men, thank God.' Ben was a normal, healthy young man – and of course, while I was his wife, he would need to use me regularly. I felt calmer once I had accepted that. I came down and made the tea and then, reluctantly, forced myself to boil and eat the eggs Ben had insisted on.

The shelves and window ledges were already begrimed with a sooty dust; there were too many mill chimneys in Ainsclough. I found a block of hard soap and a scrubbing brush under the scullery draining board and took the pail to run off hot water from the range and began to scrub. At midday I made up the range and then went quickly down to the town to buy mutton chops and spring greens – I even remembered some ham for Ben's snap tin, and that we needed more bread.

When I got back I sat down to a cup of tea, then resumed my cleaning – my dolls' house would be as bright as a new pin. But as my hands worked I began to worry again – however would I tell Ben? And what would he expect of me? It was obvious from what he had said on the moors that he was used to experienced women – and I was thinner than ever now, would I be able to satisfy him? I straightened up as I knelt on the floor and looked doubtfully down at my small breasts – and remembered enviously the full bosoms of my mother and Alice – and Emmie Greenhalgh. And if I did not satisfy him – would he go elsewhere? He had said in the dog cart, 'I'll not lay a finger on another woman' – but he was a man and I knew men better than that. Except for Gerald – but I must not think of Gerald, not when tonight I would be . . . I thrust my brush into the pail of soapy water and shook it out and began to scrub viciously at the linoleum. But as I scrubbed I remembered Papa, and Conan and Guy – and wished that I had asked Alice's advice while she was at Hatton – I would feel so humiliated if my husband used other women so soon after our wedding.

He came in with a rush while I was still on my knees. 'Hello, lass – still scrubbing? Best stop now, I'll want me tea as soon as I've had me bath.'

I went into the scullery to peel the potatoes and he came in after me and began to fill his bath, 'Good lass – water's nice and hot.' I glanced round as he spoke and saw he was already unbuttoning his trousers – I picked

588

up the vegetables and almost ran into the kitchen. I heard him call out: 'You might come and give me back a scrub, lass – since you've been practising!' but I pretended not to hear as my face burned.

The pans were boiling and the chops browning under the grill by the time he came back into the kitchen, smelling of soap. 'Now let's say a proper how do.' He pulled me against his hard chest and kissed me quickly. Still holding me tight he asked, 'How 'ave you bin today, lass?'

'Better, Ben – I've been better.'

'Good – you look brighter.'

I took a deep breath and fixed my eyes on the window pane over his shoulder as I added, 'And, Ben – I – that is – I'm not, I've finished.' My cheeks were on fire by the time I had ended my halting explanation.

'Finished what, lass? Cleaning? Well, of course you – ah.' I felt his arm stiffen as he took his other hand away and began to run it down over my hips. My dress was of light cotton, so I knew what he was looking for; he pushed me a little away from him so he could explore my belly – and stood very still as his hand dropped lower. Then he gave a grunt of satisfaction – but his fingers were still probing, even though he must have known there was no pad there – and I was confused and broke away exclaiming, 'The chops are burning, Ben!'

He let me go and went and sat down at the table. I took down the plates and began to serve the meat, but my fingers were clumsy and I fumbled with the fish slice and dropped it. He moved very quickly and his hand brushed the back of my leg as he picked up the slice. 'I'll give it a rinse under tap – though floor's shining with all your scrubbing.' As he came back from the scullery I held out my free hand but he ignored it and came right round behind me and pulled me back against his chest for a moment as he put down the slice on the top of the stove. Then he let go and I felt clumsier than ever as I dished out under his intent gaze.

'Smells good.' He picked up his knife and fork and attacked the mutton, then frowned. 'It's a bit tough – where did you get them?' He flicked the chop over – and it was pink and raw on the other side. He began to laugh. 'Didn't you turn them over?' He watched the expression on my face and laughed louder. 'Wait till I tell old Jacky in the morning – my missus didn't know you had to grill chops both sides!' He stood up. 'Hand me that pan.'

I watched, humiliated, as he threw the whole meal back into the grill pan and thrust it under the light. The chops were still rather tough when he had finished, and my jaw ached from chewing – but I dared not leave anything in case Ben was angry with me.

He came out to help me with the washing up, but he had a very odd way of drying – he took each piece of cultery and crockery off the draining board separately, and carried it into the kitchen. And every time, as he came back, his body brushed against mine. As I took off my apron I asked, 'Are you going up to the plot today, Ben?'

'Aye – put your hat on, lass, and come with me.' I did not really want to go, but it was easier to do as he told me.

It was a fine summer evening and several doors were open to the street, and men sat out on chairs beside them in shirtsleeves and braces, smoking and reading their newspapers. They looked up as we passed. 'Evenin', Ben – evenin' Missus Holden.' Ben returned their greeting; I smiled shyly, my cheeks warm.

I sat in the sun on the little bench, watching Ben. He squatted over a tray of seedlings, re-potting them – his broad fingers handling the seedlings delicately before he pressed the new earth down around their slender green stalks. He had taken off his jacket and rolled up his shirtsleeves and the sun glinted on the downy brown thatch on his arms. As he bent forward each time to pick up the next pot his shirt stretched taut over the muscles of his broad shoulders; he moved with a steady, economical rhythm and I could not take my eyes from him. He swung round, suddenly, and caught my gaze – and his face flushed a dusky red before he turned back and bent forward for the next pot.

When he had finished he put his tools away in the small shed and came and stood in front of me. 'Come on now, lass, time to go home.' As I stood up I swayed towards him and taking my hand he drew it firmly through his arm.

Back in the parlour we sat either side of the fireplace; I tried to read the newspaper, and Ben had a book in front of him – but every time I glanced up he was looking at me. I said quickly, to break the silence, 'You don't smoke any more, Ben.'

'No, lass, I gave it up, after war – Company don't like it on footplate – besides, it's a waste of money.' He looked down at his book again; he must be a very slow reader – I had not seen him turn a page yet.

At half-past nine he jumped up and stretched. 'I fancy an early night meself, I've had a rough day – I were driving but I only had a lad with me, so I had to do both jobs.' I sat on. 'You must be tired too, lass – with all cleaning you've done – up you go now and I'll fetch your hot water.' I stood up slowly.

He left the jug outside on the landing for me, but I was still towelling myself dry when I heard him coming back up the stairs. I tipped the basin so quickly into the slop pail that it splashed onto my clean lino – but I dared not stop to mop it up. I began frantically to pull on my nightdress.

'Are you in bed yet, lass?' I spun round and leapt in just as he pushed the door open, and I lay down, facing the window, while he undressed. The bed springs creaked, then I felt his hand on my shoulder. 'Come on lass – give us a kiss.' Slowly I turned to face him, but even as his lips touched mine I could feel his other hand moving purposefully down over my hips – and I went rigid. His head drew back and his face was dark in the shadows; he was panting, 'Lass, lass,' and he began to tug at my nightdress, trying to pull it up – but it twisted round my behind and would not come and he began to swear softly, 'Bloody hell – it won't soddin' shift – here.' He threw the bedclothes back and rolled me over on to my belly so he could wrench my skirt free, then I was tossed on to my back again and I felt his hands trying to prise my trembling legs apart as he loomed over me. 'Let me get in, lass – let me get in!' He was almost shouting at me and his face was dark and alien as he finally dragged my legs apart. Then he was astride me, his hips heaving, and I closed my eyes as he swung down on me, pushed hard – and came in. He was stretching me wider and wider – I thought I would burst – until he drew back for a moment – but the next thrust came deeper and now my belly was full of him and his hot heavy body was splayed out over mine. He was groaning and grunting like an animal and I heard my own breath coming in frightened pants – I could not adjust to his frantic lunges as my body tensed in panic – and then, all of a sudden, it was over. He collapsed down on to me and only his hips jerked spasmodically on top of mine; and I heard his little snuffling gasps of pleasure as my belly accepted his seed. He pressed against me and nuzzled my neck, and I pulled my hand free and gently stroked his damp hair.

When he finally raised his face it looked like a young boy's, with the tense darkness gone from it now – and he smiled at me as he bent down and gently brushed my lips with his. Then he drew his shoulders back and propped himself up on his elbows; our bodies were still joined as I lay with his maleness deep inside me, but he was still now, and I smiled up at him in relief. He said softly, 'Tha don't know how much pleasure tha's given me tonight, Helena. I've been fit to burst for thee these last few days – I thought about pulling meself off – but it didn't seem right, not with us just being wed, so I waited – I wanted you to have all of it.' He bent and brushed my lips again. 'But lass – I know I were too quick for you – I'm sorry.'

I whispered, 'It doesn't matter, Ben.'

He smiled as he disagreed. 'Oh aye, it does matter – I want you to enjoy yourself too, sweetheart – it's only fair. Give us a kiss now.'

He put his lips firmly down on mine and I opened my mouth to him so his tongue could fill it – just as his manhood was filling my belly. And as we clung together I felt him quiver deep inside me, and then he was swelling again even as I held him – I pulled my face away, startled, and he chuckled and said, 'With you kissing me like that I reckon next time's already here. I knew it wouldn't be long, sweetheart – state you've had me in over last few days. Put your hands on me backside like you did on moors – I like feel of them there.' I did as he bid me and he grunted and began to move again, but more slowly this time. I watched his face stiffen and become intent as he used my body once more – and felt a surge of triumph that I had aroused him again so quickly.

It was easier now, and I relaxed under him until I sensed the quickening of his steady rhythm under my palms and braced myself ready for his final deep thrusts. As I felt him throbbing between my legs I turned my face and pressed my lips to his damp cheek and he groaned with pleasure, 'Oh lass, lass – hold me tighter, lass.' And I spread my hands on his buttocks and pulled him hard into me, and he groaned louder as he filled me for the second time.

When he had finished he raised his head and kissed me full on the lips, then slid out and rolled away from me and pulled the sheet and blanket back over us. I lay beside him in the darkness with my nightdress rucked up around my waist, waiting for him to fall asleep – I was too shy of him now to dare to wriggle in the bed and pull it down. But his breathing did not change, and at last he reached out a hand and took hold of mine. 'Helena?' His voice was low. 'Are you asleep yet, lass?'

'No, Ben.'

The mattress shook as his heavy body turned towards me. 'Then, lass, do you think you could take me again? Seems I've got more for you yet.'

I said simply, 'Yes, Ben,' and heard his deep sigh of satisfaction as he heaved himself on top of me again. He eased himself gently inside, 'That's lovely, sweetheart,' then there was silence as his hips swung steadily up and down. I was so slippery now with his seed that I scarcely felt him stretch me and he held his weight a little above me, so that when I knew he was ready I could lift my hips for him, and then I held him tightly as he slumped down on me. Afterwards he heaved a great sigh of contentment and kissed me. 'I reckon that's done trick, sweetheart – thanks, lass.' And this time I heard his breathing change as soon as he rolled off me; he was asleep at once. I waited a moment and then cautiously began to pull down my nightdress. I was very damp now, and as I turned on my side his seed oozed out of me, so I bunched the satin skirt of my nightdress up in my hand and pushed it between my legs to mop myself up, then I too fell asleep.

When I woke up again it was quite dark; I was still very damp, and I thought of the long trek down to the backyard and wished I had not had that last cup of tea – but it was no good, I had to go. I began to ease myself very carefully out of the bed. I was feeling for my slippers when a voice said, 'It's all right, lass – I'm not asleep,' so I stood up and found them with my toes. As I groped my way round the end of the bed he spoke again. 'Don't be long, lass, will you?'

I stopped, 'You can go first, Ben, if you want.'

There was a low chuckle in the darkness. 'Nay, sweetheart, I'm not after closet – it's thee I need – so be a good lass and don't take so long.'

I whispered, 'No, Ben,' and almost tumbled down the

stairs, my legs were shaking so much. But as I sat outside on the wooden seat I heard his words in my head: 'It's thee I need,' and there in the cold closet my body was suffused with a warm glow of pride. I could not even cook chops – and my breasts were too small and my body too thin – but this man wanted me, needed me – and was impatient to take me yet again. I smiled as I tugged at the chain and ran back into the small scullery.

As I came back into the bedroom the gas was on, and I stood in the doorway blinking – dazzled for a moment as I heard him say, 'Good girl – you've been right quick.' Then I saw that he had thrown back the bedclothes and was lying naked on the bottom sheet. I stood quite still, wanting to look away, but I could not. His voice was coaxing. 'Come to bed now, lass – I threw covers off 'cause it were getting too warm.' I began to edge slowly towards him, and as I came to the end of the bed I saw it – his manhood lying straight and swollen on his belly – rising out of the dark bushy fullness between his legs. And as I stared at it, it jumped, and jumped again. He laughed softly, 'He's saying hello to you – but don't keep him waiting, lass – he wants to get in warm where he belongs.' And suddenly I ran forward and tumbled on to the bed on my belly and hid my frightened face in my pillow – but his strong arm scooped me up and rolled me over and began to push up my nightdress – his hands were confident and unhurried now as he separated my legs. 'Bend your knees – bring 'em up – that's the ticket, sweetheart – I can get in easier like that – aah.'

Afterwards I lay beside him and knew he was not asleep; a church clock chimed and I listened to the four strokes. He stirred a little, and then reached out for me. 'Let's have a feel of you, lass – we've not had much time for cuddling tonight – turn over then.' We lay face to face in the darkness and his breath was warm on my cheek as he unbuttoned the low bodice of my nightdress. 'Let's see what's at top end, now, shall we?' He slipped his hands inside and began to stroke my breasts, steadily, rhythmically, until I felt as though I were floating. He murmured, 'You like that, don't you sweetheart? I saw that first morning after we were wed – like a little she-cat you were – almost purring with it.' And as he stroked me I saw again the picture I had seen as I came into the bedroom – but now it was not frightening – and I reached out and my fingers touched his hip. He stiffened a moment, then in the same low coaxing voice murmured, 'That's right, sweetheart – you give me a bit of a stroke too – fair's fair – I bin labouring hard over you tonight.' He chuckled softly and my hand began to stroke his hip, and then it moved round to stroke his flat firm stomach and then, of its own volition, it slid down – and found it. It was like damp silk under my fingertips, and it was already firm – but it became firmer with my touch and jumped under my hand so that I quickly pulled back – but now his large hand clamped down over mine and pressed my palm against it so that I felt the steady pulse as it swelled. He held me imprisoned there for a while, then he released my hand and drew me to him. 'Come on then, lass – I reckon I can give you what you want now.'

He moved so smoothly this time it was like a dream, and afterwards my belly felt so soft and comfortable that I drifted into sleep at once.

CHAPTER THREE

I was scarcely conscious of his kissing me goodbye, and it was much later when I awoke. Lying in bed drowsy and relaxed, I saw his jacket hanging behind the door – and the sight of it reminded me that my wedding night had come at last. My whole body blushed with the memory of it, and for a moment I convinced myself that it had all been a dream – but then I felt the stickiness of his seed, and there was a feeling deep inside me – not of pain, or even soreness – but a sensation that told me he had indeed been there. I sat up in bed and looked down at my nightdress – it was crumpled and stained so I pulled it off and threw it on the floor. Then I knelt on the mattress and gazed down at my small breasts and flat belly and narrow hips, and wondered that I had ever been able to accommodate him, but he had made sure that I did – very sure.

And suddenly I wanted to laugh aloud; I was different this morning – I had been made a wife. Not with a quick, apologetic fumble under the bedclothes – oh no – my man had nearly split me in two with his lusty strength. I shivered as I saw the bruises inside my thighs where he had prised my knees apart – and then I smiled again, because I knew he had not meant to hurt me; he had not known what he was doing in the feverish heat of his need for me. And it was I, I who had aroused him to that pitch – and then I had satisfied him. But I laughed softly as I remembered how long it had taken to satisfy him – I had had to take him inside me and receive his seed five full times before he had been spent. And I was glad, because I knew he had had to take me in marriage – I had not been his choice – but at least he had got full value from me last night.

I slid off the bed and went to the washstand and splashed myself all over with the cold water, towelled myself briskly dry until I was glowing – then dressed quickly and ran downstairs. As soon as I had drunk my tea and eaten my eggs I attacked the sweeping and dusting vigorously – I felt full of energy today. I went upstairs to make our bed and my face was burning as I pulled off the tumbled sheets. As I shook up the bolster and laid it across the head I smiled to myself at the thought of the naive Helena who had been so surprised that there was only this one bed in the house – I knew now that a dressing room would be no use to a man like mine; he needed his woman close beside him, ready to take him when he woke swollen and throbbing in the dark.

It was Friday, so I bought fish. I had just put the damp package away in the larder when the postman came with a parcel – I recognized Letty's handwriting and shied away from it – I would open it later when I had time.

That afternoon the hands of the clock crawled at first – then they began to race round and it was time for Ben to come home and I saw my face pink with embarrassment in the scullery mirror, and I bent over the sink peeling potatoes with trembling hands. I was in the kitchen when I heard him at the door and I quickly picked up my fish and was arranging it in the frying pan as he came through. I smelt the coal dust on him as he said, 'Hello lass – I'm in a mucky sweat today – I'll run me bath.' I heard his whistling in the scullery, then he came out in his fresh clothes and took the frying pan out of my hand and pushed it to the back of the stove. 'They'll keep – you won't. Come here.' He kissed me full on the mouth and slid one hand down my back and on to my behind and began to knead my buttocks. As his tongue pushed at my closed lips I pulled away. 'Ben – I – the fish – it'll be burning – ' But it was my cheeks that were burning as he laughed and let me go.

He nodded over to the dresser. 'There's a parcel come.'

'Yes – I know – it's from Letty.' Then I was aware of the sudden silence behind me; I swung round and saw he was staring at the parcel, his face immobile. He picked it up and held it out to me. 'So you're still "Lady Helena".' His voice was expressionless. Letty had addressed it clearly in her characteristic red ink: 'The Lady Helena Holden'.

I explained, 'Yes, I am – it's a courtesy title, you see.'

'So you keep it – even if you get wed?'

'No, not always – if I'd married Lord . . .' then my

voice trailed away. He waited in silence so I added, 'I keep it unless I marry a man of higher rank than Papa – then I take his title.'

He said flatly, 'Well, you certainly 'aven't done that, Lady 'Elena.' The dropped h grated on me – he had never made that mistake with my name before.

The herrings had fried quite well, but Ben did not seem to enjoy them very much. After he had pushed his plate away he suggested, 'Best open Letty's parcel, lass – see what it is.'

I slit the brown paper slowly – please God not more photographs – but it was a book, a new one. I looked at it blankly – why on earth had Letty sent me this? It was a cookery book. Ben pulled it round so he could read the spine and then gave a great shout of laughter. 'Your kid – she's a smart lass – a very smart lass, fancy her thinking of that.' I stared down at the book in my hand: *Plain Cookery for the Middle Classes*. Ben grinned and pointed to the title. 'I suppose she reckons as I'm a working man and you're a lady we average out in the middle when it comes to food.' That was exactly what Letty had written in her first sentence, so I passed it over to Ben, and he laughed again as he scanned it.

I said frigidly, 'Perhaps you should have married Letty, since you obviously share her sense of humour.'

Ben stood up and came round the table and pulled me back against him with one hand; the other fondled my breast and then slid down to pat my belly. 'No, lass, like I said, she's smart – too smart to open her legs to a mere footplateman. Nobody less than a duke'll be allowed to tumble our Letty.' He kissed my ear and went out into the scullery and through to the backyard, whistling. I glared at his retreating back, then as the closet door closed I looked down again to read the rest of Letty's letter. It was quite short and she finished with: 'Norah told Fisher you were "unwell" on the morning of your wedding, so Mother's more angry than ever.

And you never did tell me what it was like, you spoilsport
– now I'll have to find out for myself!

Your affectionate sister

Violet Clare Dorothea

P.S. I hope this is in time to prevent your poisoning
Ben – still, I suppose after Maconochie he can stand
anything!'

The cheek of Letty – she had never cooked anything
in her life! But I picked up the book and looked up 'fish'
– and discovered I should have rolled my herrings in
oatmeal.

Ben came back, dumped down the filled coal hod by
the range, then went to his working jacket, reached into
the pocket and brought a handful of money over to the
table. He began to count it out in front of me; I looked
at him, bewildered. 'Here's your housekeeping, lass. I've
kept back the eight and ninepence for the rent and set
aside what we'll need for th'ire of cooker and to pay coal
and insurance, and rest is yours.' As I began to scoop
up the money he coughed and said, 'It's custom to give
your husband back a bit for his paper and baccy and
such like – of course, I don't smoke now, but I like a
pint from time to time.'

I dropped the money again. 'Then you take what you
need, Ben.'

He said patiently, 'No, lass, as long as I gets a shilling
or two it's up to you how much – depends on what you
think we can afford.'

'Ben, I don't *know* what we can afford – how could I
possibly know that?' I was getting exasperated, and he
looked hurt.

'I thought you'd'a got it sorted by now, lass . . . Well,
you could always pop round and ask Mrs Greenhalgh,
she'd give you a word of advice – and young Emmie'd
be pleased to see you . . .' I just sat staring at him, then
I pushed a ten-shilling note in his direction. 'Take that,
Ben.'

600

He pursed his lips. 'I reckon that's too much, mebbe half of that . . .'

I picked up the crumpled note and held it between the fingers of my two hands and told him, 'Then I'll tear it in half – that should satisfy you.' It was whipped out of my fingers and stuffed into his trouser pocket. 'Don't be so daft, Helena.' He sounded quite huffy. 'I'm going up plot to do watering.'

He arrived back just as I was finishing the washing up. He came up behind me and put his arm round my waist. 'I'm back, lass.'

'I can see that, Ben – I've got the sink to clean.'

'Oh, aye.' He let me go. 'I'll be in parlour then, when you're through.'

He looked up from his paper as I went in. 'I forgot to tell you – Ivy's Joe left a note for me at shed to say Ivy's expecting us both for dinner on Sunday.' He frowned slightly. 'I dunno – with it being me day off I reckon we could have done with a bit of time together – get to know each other, like.' I remembered the previous night, and wondered what he meant – surely we already knew each other, after our bodies had been joined so fully; there could scarcely be more intimacy between us than that – and tonight . . . My cheeks burned and I could not look at him as he added, 'Still, we'll have to go – Ivy's very particular, and it'll save you having to cook a roast with all the trimmings.' I felt a rush of gratitude to the unknown Ivy.

I put my head back in the chair and closed my eyes; I felt drowsy. He said, 'You look quite tired, lass – reckon us'd better have an early night. You've bin over-doing it with all th'ousework.' I heard the chair creak as he got up, and his shadow came over my closed lids, his voice much nearer now. 'How about a nice lie down, upstairs' – there was a loud rat-a-tat-tat at the front door. 'Who th' hell's that then?' He did not sound very pleased. The door banged again, and a voice shouted, 'Come on, Ben lad – we know tha's in theer – oppen

601

up.' 'A'm coming – give us a chance.' He went through into the small lobby and pulled the door open. 'So it's you, Wally.'

A cheerful male voice answered. 'T'lads sent me to fetch thi, Ben – it's Friday, and we've not celebrated thi getting wed yet. Put your jacket on, lad.'

'But Wally, me missus . . .'

'Ben – thi only gets wed once – and lads are down theer waiting – first round's been set up.'

He still seemed to be hesitating so I called out, 'Of course you must go, Ben – don't worry about me.'

A ruddy face behind a large walrus moustache appeared round the lobby door and beamed at me. ''Ow do, Missus 'Olden – theer th'art, Ben, oo can't say fairer nor that – catch my missus being so obliging.' Ben went to fetch his jacket and cap. Wally stood waiting for him, and Ben barely brushed my cheek with his lips as he said goodbye. I smiled at him. 'Enjoy yourself, Ben.' Then, as soon as the door closed behind him I curled up in the armchair and fell asleep.

A child's voice calling outside woke me briefly, but there was no sign of Ben and I dozed off again at once. It was much later when I was woken again by the noise in the street of heavy boots clattering on the cobbles and men's voices singing. My ear distinguished the words as they came up the street – it was not difficult, since they were bawling 'She's a lassie from Lancashire', with the full force of their powerful lungs. The voices came nearer, then they suddenly skidded to a halt outside the window. ''Ere tha art Ben – this mun be thy place, in wi' thi, owd lad.' The door burst open and I froze in my seat. 'Nah then, be'ave thissen, now tha's wed!' Then there were shouts of: 'See thee, Ben – see thee Ben,' followed by a slam – and Ben lurched out of the small lobby, his face bright red and glistening with sweat. He stumbled, and reached out to hold himself up on the wall.

'Where ish she – where'sh me little lassie from – from

602

Sheshire – that'sh it, *my* lassie's from Cheshire.' His eyes swivelled round the room until they lighted on me. ''Ere she ish – waitin' up for 'er master.' His face was one enormous, foolish grin; he was obviously completely drunk. I watched as he very carefully negotiated the lino, tripped over the rug, and came to a swaying halt in front of my chair. He put his two hands down on the arms, leant forward and breathed a gust of beery breath full in my face: 'Give ush a kiss, luv.' I managed to turn my mouth away, and his lips collided with my cheek. He pulled back, looking puzzled, then smiled again. 'You look tired, lass – you should be in,' he hiccuped, then said very loudly, 'in bed! That'sh place for you and me, lass. I bin – ah bin shelebrating getting wed wi' lads – an' now I want ter teli – beli – shelibrate, wi' you!' He finished triumphantly.

I edged myself away from him. 'I think I'll stay downstairs a little longer, Ben – I'm not really tired.'

But he obviously was not listening. 'Tell you what, lass – I'll carry you upstairs, let'sh get 'old o' you.'

He swayed forward and tried to slide his hand underneath me, but it became entangled with my skirt and as I tried to wriggle away he managed to push up under my petticoat. He lost his balance and fell across me so that I was pinned into the chair and I heard his breathing quicken as his strong fingers tugged open the leg of my knickers. 'That feels real nish, 'Elena.' He began to push against me as his hand probed higher into the soft moistness between my legs. 'Oo, 'Elena, that ish nice, that ish nice.' His red face leered foolishly at me, and I tried to pull away, but his strong arm hauled me back as the hand between my legs became more insistent. He whispered, 'Come on, lass – get your drawers down – I got summat for you – you're me wife now.' And of course, I was – 'in sickness and in health' – in drunkenness and sobriety. He muttered again, 'Come on, lash – be nice to me.'

I said resignedly, 'All right, Ben – I'll be nice to

603

you; but let's go upstairs first, shall we? It'll be more comfortable.'

His hand stopped moving as his fuddled brain mulled over my suggestion, then his face broke into a beaming smile. 'What a good idea, 'Elena – what a clever little lass you are – it'sh draughty on 'earthrugs. I'll carry you upstairs.' Slowly his hand began to slide out from under my skirts, and he pushed himself upright and straightened, like a large, shambling bear. He repeated again, 'I'll carry you up, 'Elena.' His hand came down on my knee but I managed to jump up and shake it off. 'No thank you, Ben – I can manage.'

He swayed a moment, then pursed his lips in solemn agreement. 'You'm right, 'Elena.' He bent over me and said, his voice low and confidential, 'Truth t'tell – I've 'ad a little drink, tonight, an' now I need a leak, so I'd best get outside and 'ave one.'

'Yes, Ben – you do that.' I gave him a little push towards the inner door and he set off obediently. As soon as he was in the kitchen I headed for the stairs and ran up them full tilt. I banged the bedroom door behind me and glanced down – there was a key in the lock, and for a moment I thought of turning it – but suppose he tried to beat the door down? Besides, as he had said, I was his wife now. I began to take my clothes off.

I was still struggling into my nightdress when I heard his heavy footsteps on the stairs; he came in before I was in bed, and lumbered towards me, his face one big beaming smile. ''Ello, lash.'

I said quickly, 'I haven't washed yet, Ben.'

'Doeshn't matter – you're clean enough for me.' He began to tug at his braces and I climbed into bed and lay waiting for him. I did not have to wait long – he pulled his trousers and underpants off together and then tumbled on to the bed in his shirt and socks. 'Let'sh get at you, 'Elena, let's get at you.' For a moment I tried to pull away, but even drunk he was much too strong for me, and as he began to tug at my nightdress I stopped struggling and let him get on with it. 'I don't know why you bother with theshe thingsh, 'Elena – they only getsh in my way. Thatsh better.' He began to pull my legs apart – although he was drunk tonight his hands were much gentler than the evening before, and he kept stopping to pat and stroke me. And when he had positioned himself above me he asked, 'Are you ready, shweetheart – cosh I'm ready.'

I was almost smiling as I replied, 'Yes Ben – I can see that.'

He lunged his hips forward and his maleness pressed hard against my thigh; he pulled back and then swung forward again – and now it was the other thigh he was pushing unavailingly at. He drew back again and exclaimed, 'I can't find me way in, 'Elena – it's gone! 'Ave you moved it?' He looked so surprised that I began to giggle. Then I remembered last night and drew up my knees and spread my legs as wide as I could and he heaved forward again – and this time I felt him push full inside. 'Aah – thatsh better – I've got in, 'Elena, I've found me way in.' His red sweating face was inches from mine and he had obviously been eating pickled onions; I turned a little sideways and he began to pant in my ear. 'Thatsh lovely, 'Elena – thatsh really lovely. You're a shweet lash to be so good to me.'

I said tartly, 'I don't seem to have much choice, Ben,' but he was too far gone to understand me as he grunted and panted between each thrust. Then he gave a loud, satisfied groan and his full weight slumped down on top of me as he began to throb. I could scarcely get my breath for the weight of him as he filled me. He still lay sprawled across my body long after his hips had stopped jerking, and for a moment I wondered if he had fallen asleep, then he slowly raised his head. 'It's 'ot in 'ere – in your little fire 'ole.'

'Then come out, Ben!'

'Aye, thatsh an idea.' He heaved himself obediently off me; my nightdress was sodden with sweat where he had lain on it, and I began to pull it down. He gave an enormous belch as his hand came out and seized my wrist. 'It'sh not worth it, lash – I'll be ready again in a minute. 'Ere, let'sh 'ave your 'and.' He pulled it down and clamped it over his maleness, as he had done the night before. But this time there was no answering quiver – it remained limp and soft in my palm. 'It'sh not working!' He sounded incredulous.

I decided I had had enough; I wrenched my hand away and said loudly, 'You're drunk, Ben Holden,' then rolled over and turned my back on him.

As I lay there I heard him muttering to himself. 'She shays I'm drunk – she shays I'm drunk.' He gave another enormous belch then called, "Elena – '

'Yes, Ben – what is it?'

'I'm drunk.'

'Go to sleep.'

'Yesh, 'Elena – goo'night.' He gave a mighty heave and pulled all the bedclothes off me as he turned on his side and began to snore. I waited a few minutes then exerted all my strength to haul them back again – if he got cold it was his own fault. Then I pulled down my damp nightdress and dropped off to sleep to the dissonant music of my husband's drunken snores.

I woke later to hear him pushing himself out of bed and pulling open the bedside cupboard; I lay rigid until, muttering under his breath, he began the long trek down to the backyard. After he had gone the second time I started to giggle – it really did serve him right. When the mill hooters sounded in the morning, I glanced at the clock; then I realized he had forgotten to set the alarm, and leant over and shook him awake. He groaned and pushed his face into the pillow. 'Make us a cup of tea, there's a good lass.'

I went downstairs to put the kettle on and he shuffled down after me a few minutes later; he looked very shame-faced, and did not meet my eyes. He was pallid and sweating, and as he moved past me his breath stank. I asked, my voice very sweet, 'Would you like me to fry you an egg, Ben?' and watched his face go green as he mumbled a hasty refusal.

I tackled my housework quite cheerfully as soon as I had had my breakfast – and every time I remembered Ben's ghastly face that morning I wanted to laugh – really, men were such children at times. The gallant Sergeant-Major Holden – rallying his men for the counter-attack, leading them forward across No-Man's-Land to capture an enemy trench – and with a few pints of beer inside him he could not even find his way into his own wife! I heard again his puzzled: ''Elena – it's gone! 'Ave you moved it?' and dissolved into helpless giggles. But despite his drunkenness he had found his way in eventually – and then he had taken me forcefully and fully, as a man should take his wife. I shivered a little as I wondered whether he would have recovered by tonight – and felt my cheeks burn as I wielded the duster more vigorously.

After lunch I decided to black lead the range; Letty's book told you how to instruct a servant in this art. I got quite filthy and broke a nail, but finally the range gleamed soft black and I was satisfied. It was soon burning well again so I was able to run off some hot water and carry it through to the scullery to treat myself to a bath. I lay back in the warm water and explored my breasts just as he had explored them – and watched my nipples rise firm and pink, just as they had done for him. I raised myself a little and looked down at my flat belly, and the dark soft mound below – and wondered whether he would be pushing his way in there tonight – and knew that of course he would; he was a strong man, a vigorous man: he would fill me every night now until I bled again. I stood up and shook off the silver drops and began to towel myself slowly dry. It was time to cook his meal.

Ben looked very embarrassed as he came in, and still could not meet my eye. He had his bath and sat down to the food I put in front of him without speaking a word. It was only as he chased his last sausage round the plate that he broke the silence, then without looking at me muttered, 'I reckon I owe you an apology, lass – it's not often I'm worse for drink, but I were last night.'

'That's all right, Ben. I've seen men drunk before.'

He still looked down at his plate, then mumbled. 'But – well, I reckon I shouldn't have – well, you know – not when I were drunk.'

I felt quite sorry for him. 'But I am your wife, Ben.'

He looked up, and I smiled at him, and he seemed much more cheerful as he agreed, 'Aye, that's right – so you are.'

CHAPTER FOUR

After he had been up to his plot he sat yawning over his newspaper until I suggested an early night. I half expected him to fall asleep as soon as he climbed in after me, but we had only been in bed for a minute or two when I heard his breathing quicken at my back and felt his hand reach out and squeeze my behind. Then it slid down over my satin-covered thigh and began to push up under my nightdress until it could stroke the inside of my legs. I parted them a little and his stroking fingers moved higher as his other arm came round me and pulled me hard back against his chest. He whispered in my ear, 'Reckon I'd best check where I'm going first – after performance I put up last night.' I felt his hand gently open me, and lay very still as his blunt fingertip pushed fully inside and began to stroke. He kissed the back of my neck. 'By feel of that I got a lass here who needs a bit more 'an a finger to see her right. Over you come, and we'll get this nightie out of way.' Slowly I rolled over on my back, and lifted my hips so he could push my nightdress up: he came into me at once and I curled my legs round his and tried to move in time to his steady rhythm. 'That's lovely lass, that's lovely – push a bit harder now, don't be afeared – you won't push me out. That's right lass – oh, Helena, Helena . . .' and then he was groaning and panting and he did not speak again until he had finished. 'Thanks, sweetheart.' He fell asleep at once with his leg across mine and he was too heavy for me to move, so I slept under him.

Waking later I could tell by his breathing he was no longer asleep, and his maleness was pressed hard against me, swollen and throbbing. I felt a flicker of excitement as it jumped against my thigh and stirred a little. At once his voice came out of the darkness, 'Are you awake, lass?'

'Yes, Ben.'

I heard his sigh of relief. 'Come here then, sweetheart – I seem to have been lying here for hours waiting for you to wake up.' I tugged my nightdress up and raised my knees, spreading them wide. 'Good lass – you're getting th' idea now.'

As soon as he came out he fell asleep again. I lay beside him in the darkness listening to his steady breathing; he had needed me, and I had satisfied him – I could still feel deep in my belly the passage of his strong thrusts – and I tingled between the legs where his weight had pressed against me. I edged myself closer to him and his body seemed to curl round mine as he slept.

Much later I drifted into wakefulness, conscious that a firm hand was pushing between my thighs; he began to stroke them, high up, then his movements became more purposeful – his fingers were so determined now they were almost hurting me. 'Come on, sweetheart, wake up – I need you again.' But I felt so drowsy, and did not want to wake up as I muttered, 'What time is it, Ben?'

With a laugh he replied, 'Time you were opening your

legs again, lass.' But I lay still; I did not want to bother now. 'Come on, lass, come on.' Slowly I made room for him. 'You'll have to hold me properly, Helena – I'm near sliding out – you're that slippery down below.' He chuckled, 'I dunno what you been doing in there.' I thought resentfully, it's what *you've* been doing Ben Holden, and he added, as if he had heard my thoughts, 'Course, I have been presenting me compliments to you pretty regular tonight – and I suppose with you being so narrow round the hips you're not able to accommodate as much as most women.' He continued to pound up and down on my narrow, inadequate hips until he suddenly pushed hard and grunted and began to force even more of his seed into me. As he pressed against me I felt quite sore, and it was a relief when he finally came out. His hand fumbled for my nightdress. 'I'll pull this down under you, lass – sheets are all damp, they'll be stained in morning, I shouldn't wonder. Still, you'll be washing them on Monday, so it won't matter.' As he fell asleep his last remark suddenly struck me – he was expecting me to do the household washing on Monday, just like all the other wives in Royd Street – and I had not the faintest idea how to go about it. I remembered the smell of soap and steam in the laundry at Hatton, the sweet scent of freshly-washed clothes being ironed, and the bustling laundrymaids who had never been too busy to spare a smile and a word to us as children when we had peeped in on our way back from the stables. I felt a sudden pang of homesickness, and wondered however I would cope. Then I finally faced up to the fact that I needed to make the long trek to the backyard again and begun to edge myself out of bed.

I woke to the ringing of church bells. The man beside me stirred and stretched his brawny arms. 'I'll pop down and make a nice cup of tea, and bring it up to you, lass.' He heaved himself out and padded off barefoot, the tails of his nightshirt flapping. I lay in bed waiting – I needed to visit the closet again, but I did not like to go while he was in the kitchen – and it was comfortable in bed on my own.

He came back quite quickly, but he had two cups and saucers on a tray, and as soon as he had put them down he climbed back into bed beside me. He pressed his large body against mine as he leant across for his cup, and I stiffened uneasily; then he lay back against the pillows, watching me intently. I lingered over the last dregs in my cup, but had to put it down at last, and he reached out for me at once. As he held me to him, stroking my belly, I knew I should tell him that I needed to go downstairs first, but I was embarrassed and then suddenly it was too late – in one quick movement he had entered me. The force of his thrusts on my full bladder were very uncomfortable, but there was nothing I could do now except put up with them.

When he had finished he rolled off me and slid down under the bedclothes; I began to move towards the side. 'That's right, lass, you go down and fry me a couple of eggs for me breakfast – I like a nice soft yolk. I feel right comfortable now I've eased meself again – reckon I'll snooze for a few minutes. You give me a shout when they're ready.' He closed his eyes.

But I was anything but comfortable as I sat over the bowl – and as soon as I got back into the kitchen I felt as if I needed to go out to the closet yet again. My hands were clumsy, tapping the first egg with the knife over the frying pan, and the yolk broke – I would have to eat that one myself. I managed to get two more in safely but as soon as their whites were set I felt I just had to run out to the closet – though when I got there I could barely squeeze anything out – and back in the kitchen I found the yolks were already solid.

I called up the stairs to him and began to butter some bread. When he appeared he was in his shirtsleeves and braces, with the dark shadow of his overnight bristles clearly visible on his chin; he sat straight down at the table. 'Smells good.' I watched him raise his knife and bring it down with a quick slice on the yolk of his first egg, and saw his face fall. 'Yolk's hard, Helena.'

'I'm sorry, Ben.' I toyed with my own battered egg.

He sighed and began to cut his eggs into squares and put them between two slices of bread to make a sandwich. When he had swallowed his last mouthful he said, 'Emmie Greenhalgh always used to cook me Sunday breakfast at Clegg Street – she's got a real knack with a yolk, has Emmie – lovely and soft every time.' I put down my knife and fork and pushed my plate away. 'Don't you want that, Helena?'

'No thank you, Ben – I've had enough.'

'Pass it over here, lass, and I'll finish it for you.'

'I thought you didn't like hard yolks.'

He grinned. 'That's a lesson I learnt in war – you can't afford to be too fussy, you got to make use of what's available.'

As I stood up and went to fill the kettle I felt the soreness between my legs and thought bitterly, yes, and I am available – and he is certainly making use of me – even though my hips were too narrow and my womb too small to accommodate all his seed, and I could not cook.

When I came back he swung round in his chair. 'Come here, lass.' I went to him slowly and he pulled me down on his lap and began to kiss me. His bristles scratched my cheek, but his lips were warm and coaxing and after a little while I felt my bitterness ebb away and I began to respond. Then I felt his hand come down on my knee and lift my skirts; he did not waste time stroking my leg, it was obvious where he was aiming for and the blunt directness of it sickened me and I tore myself from his grasp. 'Ben – how dare you – at the breakfast table!' I was shaking with anger.

He said defensively, 'Don't be so highty-toighty, Helena – with them lace curtains at window nobody can see owt – besides, I were only having a feel.' When I did not reply he shrugged and pushed his cup towards me. 'Give us a refill then – we mun be leaving for Ivy's shortly, and I've still got to have a shave.'

At the last minute I darted back to the closet; as I came back he was standing at the front door with his watch in his hand. 'Come on, Helena – or we'll miss train.' As I came up to him he put Eddie's gold watch back into his waistcoat pocket, and my legs began to tremble. He seized my hand and rushed me out.

By the time we were on the train to Blackburn my bladder had filled once more and it was difficult to sit still. I rushed to the cloakroom as soon as we arrived and because I had to wait, we missed the connecting tram. Ben was tight-lipped as we stood at the stop waiting for the next one. I was already uncomfortable again – and I felt miserably apprehensive.

A grey-haired woman in her fifties opened the front door as we walked up the short path; her eyes were scanning me closely. Ben kissed her cheek then pulled me forward, 'Here she is, Ivy. Here's Helena.' We shook hands warily. 'And this is Fanny, me eldest niece.' The fair-haired woman behind Ivy smiled shyly, then there was the thunder of boots and three tousled heads broke out of the front room: 'Uncle Ben, Uncle Ben!' Ben laughed and tossed the smaller boy high up in the air and he shrieked with glee as his brother demanded, 'Did you like our rug, Uncle Ben? We picked colours – I did blue stripes and Edie did red.'

'It were champion, young Benjamin – you both must'a' worked real hard – and your new auntie thought it were right beautiful, didn't you, lass?'

I moved from one foot to the other and managed to smile at the beaming faces. 'Yes, yes – it was a lovely surprise – thank you so much.'

The children's jaws dropped a little, and the youngest boy's voice was piercing as he tugged at Ben's hand, 'Uncle Ben – lady talks right funny.' There was total silence for a moment, then everyone spoke at once. It was Ivy who overbore the others: 'What am I thinking of, lass – keeping you in hallway like this – come upstairs and leave your hat.' I opened my mouth to refuse – one always lunched in one's hat as a visitor, what an odd thing to suggest – then thought better of it; it would give me a chance to ask Ivy the whereabouts of her water closet. Upstairs I sensed Ivy's eyes watching me as I patted and pushed my hair tidy, but she only spoke of the weather. The house was a terrace, but larger than Royds Street, with a wide staircase and full landing, and I looked anxiously about me. Ivy said quickly, 'End door's the bathroom,' and I rushed towards it. Yet when I sat on the mahogany seat I could scarcely squeeze out a few drops – and it was no longer soreness I was experiencing, it was pain.

Fanny took the protesting children back up the street to their own lunch. 'Uncle Ben'll still be here after dinner – but I'll not let you come back unless you behave yourselves now.' Silence fell and the three of them headed for the door while Ben's jovial brother-in-law ushered us into the dining room.

There were no serving dishes on the table – instead the plates arrived already heaped high with food; I looked helplessly down at mine. I was not even hungry and there was so much – but I would have to force it down somehow. I was still struggling when everyone else had finished, and my cheeks began to burn as I chewed desperately – then Ben leant across and speared one of my roast potatoes and put it on his plate. 'For shame, Ben – stealing the poor girl's dinner!'

Ben winked at his sister. 'I never could resist your taters, Ivy – you know that.' As soon as Ivy went out to the kitchen to stir the custard he took the other one; and I managed to swallow the rest of the cabbage myself.

The tea pot came out after lunch. Ivy's Joe glanced at me, then said, 'Perhaps Helena don't drink tea at midday, Ivy.' Two pairs of eyes swivelled in my direction, then Ben said casually, 'Course she does – she was a nurse, remember? And nurses drink tea any time of

day and night.' He smiled at me and I managed to smile
back. My bladder was pressing again, and I felt so damp
that I was afraid there would be a mark left on the back
of my dress when I had to get up. The man who had
filled my womb until it overflowed went on stolidly
sipping his tea.

Ben had to nod at me twice when Ivy said she must
be off to do the washing up, then I jumped up so quickly
I almost upset my tea over the tablecloth. 'Oh, please
do let me help – after you've cooked such a lovely meal.'

She made the conventional disclaimers, but I sensed
she was pleased and she thawed slightly in the scullery,
confiding over the soap suds, 'Ada and I have been
thinking it were high time Ben got wed – we did wonder
about young Emmie Greenhalgh, but when Ben came
over and told us, he said as how he'd had his eye on you
ever since you nursed him in war.' I was grateful for
Ben's tactful lie as I smiled nervously at Ivy and reached
for another plate. The front door opened with the sound
of children's high voices, then banged shut again and
there was silence. Ivy gestured towards the passageway.
'That'll be Ben going out with the childer – he always
takes them out for a walk when he comes over – he's
got more patience with them than Fanny's Bob has.' She
turned and looked straight at me. 'Ben's looking forward
so much to having a family of his own, he were talking
about it only last week, just before the wedding. And I
can tell you, lass, you couldn't't'a' picked a better father
for your babbies.' The small scullery had become very
close and hot; I felt trapped there with Ben's sister as
she talked of his future – the future she expected me to
give him. Then she added, 'He were always good with
youngsters before he joined up – but I reckon it were
war as made him so set on idea of having his own – it's
only natural with so many of his friends not coming
back.' I turned my flushed face to the dresser but Ivy
came up behind me, and gently touched my shoulder.
'We were real sorry to hear about your brother, lass – it

don't seem fair for it to happen later like that – when you thought he'd come back safe.' My throat tightened as I fought to control my breathing – I knew I should answer, but I could not. Her plump arm came round my shaking shoulders. 'Lass, I'm sorry I spoke; you come with me now and we'll have a nice sit-down and a chat in kitchen before rest of them get back.'

We sat in the stuffy kitchen and she talked about Ben – but my tired brain seemed unable to comprehend her words; I nodded and smiled mechanically and she appeared to be satisfied. After refilling my cup she went to the mantelshelf and picked up a photograph; as she held it out to me it took me a moment to realize it was of Ben – in his sergeant-major's uniform. He was standing very straight, facing the camera, with his left arm bent at the elbow and resting on his hip so that the three stripes and the crown of his rank showed clearly – and equally clear above the peak of his hat was the emblem of the Lancashire and Cheshire Light Infantry – the emblem my brothers had worn. 'It's a good likeness, isn't it, lass? It's me favourite picture of Ben – Ada and me asked him to have it taken, and he did, just to please us. We wanted to have it by in case . . . But he came back, and now he's wed so I reckoned as how you'd like to have it.' Somehow I uttered the necessary words of thanks as I took it from her.

Ben came back with the children and we all sat down to a lavish high tea of ham and pork pie and bread and butter, with a feather-light sponge and rich dark fruit cake and spicy fruit buns washed down with strong tea and rounded off with a sherry trifle. Ben ate his way steadily through everything Ivy offered to him, then sat back with a deep sigh of satisfaction and let his belt out a couple of notches. Joe laughed. 'Reckon you've eaten enough for the week there, Ben lad.'

Ben grinned back. 'Reckon I need to, Joe – my lass's cooking is still in what you might call the rudimentary stage.' He turned and winked at me; my face froze.

As we walked down the street to the tram stop he took my arm and said, 'I hope you didn't mind me having a little joke with Joe, lass – about your cooking, I mean.'

I said coldly, 'How could I object, Ben? Since you only spoke the truth.'

'Ah – well.' He sounded uncomfortable. 'Perhaps it would have been better . . .' His voice trailed away, and we walked on in silence. There was no one else at the tram shelter and he suddenly pulled me round. 'Look, lass – you don't need to take offence – truth is, when you keep me warm and satisfied like you have been these past few nights I wouldn't care if you served me army biscuits and bully beef every day. I can't say fairer than that, can I?'

He was waiting for my reply, so at last I answered. 'No Ben, you can't say fairer than that.'

'So you just keep giving me a good time like you have been doing, and I'll not say a word against your cooking. Is that a bargain?'

'Yes Ben, that's a bargain.'

He leant forward to kiss me and the soreness between my legs flared up; but I forced myself to ignore it – I had made a bargain on the moors, and I would keep it.

At our front door Ben said, 'You go in, lass, and I'll run up to plot now. I'm due at shed at half-three tomorrow so we'll have to get to bed early. Fill me snap tin for me and then go upstairs.'

'Ben, I . . .'

He put his hand in his pocket and drew out a grease-proof paper parcel. 'And Ivy sent this – she said she found herself with too much roast beef, and she'd take it kindly if you could use it up for her. So that's all right, then.' He smiled at me, and I knew he knew I had forgotten all about his bait, but was pretending not, to save my face.

'Thank you, Ben – that's very kind . . . of Ivy.' He closed the door on me and I turned and ran out to the back. As I tried unavailingly to force out a few burning

617

drops I suddenly realized I was still clutching the roast beef in one hand. I started to smile, and then the pain caught me as I stood up and the smile turned to a grimace – my discomfort was permanent now.

I was already in bed when I heard him coming back, talking to someone. A man's voice answered, and they laughed together, then Ben called out a 'Sithee, Wally' and I heard him go through to the scullery. It was not even dark yet in the small bedroom – the summer evening light filtered through the drawn curtains – and I watched him undress below my lashes and saw he was already fully erect. I braced myself as he climbed into the bed and pulled me towards him, his hands already at work on my nightdress. 'Lass – you looked lovely today – I could hardly keep my hands off you. Come on now, and I'll show you me appreciation.'

It was an effort not to flinch back as he drove into me, but I managed to stay still – and luckily he did not take long, and I began to relax as I felt his manhood subside inside me; he would slip out more easily than he had gone in. But he did not slip out; instead, he put his mouth over mine and began to push his tongue against my lips, and with a sinking heart I realized what he was doing, and opened my mouth to him so that he would get it over with. His hips began to move as soon as he was fully swollen and I held grimly on to his buttocks as he began to press into me again – my bladder had filled and the pressure on it increased my discomfort, so that I almost cried with relief when he began to throb and I knew I would not have to endure much longer.

When he finally came out he pulled me close and nuzzled my neck. 'I enjoyed that, lass.' He settled himself more comfortably against me – he was emptied and at ease now, and he wanted to talk. 'You know, first time I come up again like that inside a woman I couldn't believe what were happening. I were that surprised I tried to pull out! But she knew better. She were a farmer's wife – her husband had been killed early on in war, she managed farm herself, very capable woman she were – but when she had British troops billeted in her barn she'd look 'em over like – see which one she fancied and I were lucky one that time – and by chance we were sent back to that village again and your brother, he said, "I'll put you back with Madame Dupont, if you want, Sergeant Holden," giving me a wink and a nod like – there weren't much got past him – though he were only a youngster. And we'd been up in front line and then in support for weeks, and I'd not seen sight nor sign of a woman, so you can imagine state I were in when Maree meets me at doorway. "Vennez issi, Benjameen," she says – and I didn't half vennez, I can tell you.' He chuckled, and moved his head so it pressed against my breast. 'And that were first time I did a double in the once, if you see what I mean. That Maree she knew a thing or two – but I'd best not talk about that to you, lass – what I were going to say were that with other women I'd only come up inside when I'd been without for a good while, and was full up with it – but with you, I can't seem to stop meself. I only had you this morning, and state I were in by dinnertime!' He kissed my bare arm, his lips very soft, before continuing. 'You get me that excited, Helena – when you sat down to table at Ivy's you just happened to flick your skirt up and I saw a bit of your lace frills.' He shivered. 'Christ, I could have thrown you on floor there and then.' He began to laugh. 'I'd'a' liked to have seen Ivy's face if I had!' And the vibration of his heavy body as he laughed brought the pressure in my bladder to a point almost past bearing.

I whispered desperately, 'Ben – I'm rather tired.'

'All right, lass, I'll stop nattering and let you get some sleep. Goodnight.' He moved up and kissed my cheek and then turned over. As I waited for him to fall asleep I felt a little tremor of pride that I could arouse him to a pitch beyond that of other women – beyond fat ugly Maree 'who knew a thing or two'. Then I wondered how many other women he had had, pushing into them with

619

his strong hips rising and falling as he told them: 'That's lovely Maree – Jeanette – Louise . . .' and I felt sick. But he was asleep at last, so I could get out and go downstairs to try to quell my insistent bladder.

Twice more I woke and had to go down, but was very cautious and managed not to wake him; the third time I stumbled against the bed and his hands were pulling up my nightdress even as I was getting in – and as soon as I was under the covers he clambered on top of me. He did not bother to ask me now – he only grunted as he used me – while I lay beneath him with gritted teeth. But when he had finished he said, 'You're running out back a lot – have you caught a chill?'

I muttered, 'I think I must be drinking too much tea, Ben.'

'Aye, happen.' He snorted and fell asleep.

I was dozing when there was a rat-tat-tat at the door and a voice calling out. I jerked up in bed. 'It's all right, lass – it's only lad sent from shed to knock me up – it's always done for a shift afore six – you'll get used to it.' He scrambled over me to get at the window, and shouted down; then he jumped quickly back into bed. 'Now, come on, lass – I haven't got much time, and I want to say goodbye properly.'

I felt his weight come over on to me, and now as he pushed in he hurt so much I had to clench my teeth to avoid crying out loud. He was still thrusting vigorously when the church clock struck three; he paused in mid stroke to listen. 'Christ, ruddy knocker-up were late! I'll have to get a move on.' The speed of his thrusts intensified until my whole belly seemed to be on fire, then he gave a last grunt and fell forward. But he began to pull out almost at once, while still throbbing, so he hung panting over my belly for a moment as his hips jerked to expel the final spurts – then he was off the bed and scrambling frantically for his clothes. He threw himself out of the door without a single glance in my direction, and I heard the clatter of his boots receding over the cobbles as he ran down the street. He had not even said goodbye.

I lay on the bed with my nightdress pushed up above my waist and my legs sprawled apart, and as the last careless smear of his seed dried stickily on my belly I remembered Guy's words on the sand dunes at Étaples: 'and let me use her like a whore'. And now I knew exactly how Pansy must have felt, because my husband too had used me as casually and thoughtlessly as he would do a whore. Except that a whore would not also have to scrub his floors and black lead his grate and cook his meals – and even, perhaps, bear his children. I shuddered as I lay there with the tears running slowly down my cheeks and his seed seeping messily out of my womb. But eventually I had to get up – my bladder insisted.

I did not go back to bed again; I sat huddled painfully over the cold range and accepted that it was my fault – he had had to marry me because I had behaved like a whore on the open moors; I could hardly blame him for using me as one now. Then I pulled myself slowly up and went into the scullery; it was Monday, wash day.

CHAPTER FIVE

I tried to light the copper, but the fire only smouldered, and then went out. So I fetched buckets of water from the range and poured them into the bath and pushed his shirts and underpants into it. I knelt on the floor and leant over the hard iron rim and tried to wash them; but the union shirt he had worn for work was grimy with coal dust and stained with his sweat and I had to scrub and scrub before the dark marks at collar and cuff were shifted. And the bending over intensified the discomfort in my belly – he had emptied himself so fully into me that now my womb felt bruised and swollen; and every few minutes I had to haul myself painfully up and go outside in the rain to the closet – although I had drunk nothing all morning.

I could not face refilling the bath so I put his white shirts in with the others – and watched despairingly as they turned grey from the filthy water. I forced all the garments through the mangle, but because of the rain I had to let down the drying rack from the kitchen ceiling and hang them over the rails, and as I pulled on the rope to raise it again pain pierced my belly and I panicked at the thought of the night ahead. But then I remembered all the times in the war when I had had to drive my tired body on in pain and discomfort; and knew I would survive – I was not a young silly girl any more, dreaming innocently of her handsome cavalry officer – and at least my dream had come true for a brief idyllic time; I would cling to that memory. And I went through into the parlour and picked up Gerald's photograph and raised it to my lips – Gerald whose hands had been so gentle on my body, whose kisses had been soft and reverent for my innocence. But the war had hardened me, had torn aside that innocence – and so I had taken into my body a very different man, and let him use me casually and without love – and tonight I would have to pay the price. I kissed the pictured face again, then reluctantly put it back and went through into the kitchen.

But thinking of Gerald seemed to have cleared my wits and now I remembered who I really was – I did not have to soak my hands until they wrinkled, or bend my back in aching toil. I stood looking at the pile of grubby towels and stained sheets and that filthy, crumpled overall, and thought: you fool, Helena – there will be laundries in Ainsclough for those who have money to pay for their services – and I had the money, thank God. But I would have to be cleverer than I had been with the gas stove – and conceal what I was doing; but that should not be difficult, as he worked long hours every day and expected me to deal with the woman's work. I bundled up all the dirty washing and took it upstairs and hid it in the back bedroom – I would arrange for the van to call tomorrow; in the meantime my dowry would supply all the clean linen that was needed. I found my umbrella and basket and set out for the town to do my daily shopping.

But before I reached the main street I had to turn aside to visit the building under the small green dome. I had to go back there again as soon as I had interviewed a suitable laundry, and then I headed for the butcher's. I had barely received my loaded basket back from the greengrocer when I knew I could not hold out any longer – and I almost ran down the street in my haste to find sanctuary. Yet when I got inside only a few drops came burning out.

As I came out of the cubicle for the third time the attendant was standing in the doorway. She turned and waddled towards me, her heavy breasts shaking under her flowered overall. 'Now you come along with me for a nice drink of tea.' When I tried to protest she simply seized me by the elbow and steered me into her lair. 'Sit down, lass – it won't take a minute – soon as I saw you come in for third time I put kettle on gas ring.'

I sank down on to the chair, wondering wildly if there was some obscure Ainsclough ritual – three visits to the convenience and you were entitled to a cup of tea. I said weakly, 'It's very kind of you – but I'm trying not to drink anything today.'

She sat down heavily opposite me. 'And that's your first mistake, lass – and your second is not sorting out that husband of yourn.'

I stared at her, before finally whispering, 'I – I think I've caught a chill.'

She laughed and laughed until all her chins wobbled, then leant forward and said, 'Th' only chill you've caught, my girl, is from Ben Holden pushing your nightie up too often.' I felt my face crimson. 'Oh, I've seen it all before, lass – they're all the same, men! When they first get wed they're like children with a new toy – they can't stop playing with it.' She heaved her bulk upright and began to attend to the tea pot. 'I'll make it nice and weak – that's thing for you at moment. Nah – men! My Henry was just the same – I were already carrying our Gladys when we got wed, but that didn't stop him. So at th'end of first week I put on me shawl and went straight back to sleep with me mam. He came round, whining, but she soon sent him packing – went down there every night for a fortnight I did, till he were ready to see sense.' Her eyes narrowed. 'Here, where does your mam live?' I thought of my mother's face were I to suddenly arrive back demanding to sleep with her to escape Ben's over-enthusiastic attentions – and for a moment I wanted to laugh; then the desire evaporated, and I simply shook my head. 'Oh well, then you'll just have to speak to him yourself, lass – tell him to tie a knot in it for a few days till you're right again. Now, drink this up – it'll ease you.'

I gulped down the weak tea gratefully – I was very thirsty by now. But I knew I would never dare to 'speak to' Ben. My hostess pursed her lips, 'By way, lass – have you got blood in your water?'

'No – no, I don't think so.'

'You'll soon be all right then – looks as if we caught it in time. It can get right nasty once a lass is passing blood. Now on the way home you pop into Sammy Whittle's and fetch some barley – cook a nice big jug of barley water and keep drinking it down – your water-works is like these closets here' – she waved an expansive arm – 'it needs plenty of flushing to keep it sweet.'

I stood up. 'Thank you, Mrs Fairbarn – you've been very kind. But I must go now – my husband will be home soon and I have to cook his lunch. Thank you again.'

She smiled. 'You're welcome, lass. I get a lot of brides

in here, you know – with same trouble – you're not th'only one, not by a long chalk. In fact,' – her small eyes twinkled – 'soon as I hear there's a wedding, I has a little bet with meself: "What price that lass'll be running in and out in a day or two, Edna me girl?" I'm not often wrong. When I heard Ben Holden were getting wed I knew I'd be seeing his missus in here – you can tell by look in their eye.' Her fat elbow nudged my ribs. 'Tell you truth, I were expecting you earlier!' Her chins wobbled again as she laughed. I had given up blushing by now. She lumbered out of the doorway of her cubby-hole. 'Now you be sure to give him a good ticking off soon as he walks in – he'll argue a bit but he'll behave hisself in end – he's been spoilt, has Ben, but he's not a bad lad at heart. You be sure and sort him out, now.'

I shook my head. 'I'm grateful for your advice, Mrs Fairbarn, but I really couldn't . . .'

'Don't be mardy, lass – if you lets 'em get away with owt now you'll never be boss in your own home.'

I dropped my eyes, then promised, 'I'll be sure to make the barley water – and now – I'll just . . .' I began to fumble in my purse.

She swept forward, brandishing her brass key. 'No lass – this one's on me.' As soon as she had the door open I ran into the small cubicle.

When I called in at the corner shop for the barley, on an impulse I bought some flour and lard as well – I had noticed a recipe for a pie in Letty's book – I would follow it and cook him a pleasant lunch. I felt much calmer in my mind now after listening to Edna Fairbarn – I was still very sore and uncomfortable but now I knew that there was nothing seriously wrong with me: I could cope with it. I smiled a little at her choice of words as I walked up Royds Street. It was no use blaming Ben for my state – he was a man, so of course he would use me as often as he wanted. And I was his wife, so I would just have to put up with it.

The pastry would not stick together at first, but I

managed to line the enamel pie dish eventually, and the gravy smelt good as I tipped the beef and onion mixture into it. I carefully draped the rest of my pastry over it and sat down in the rocker, waiting for Ben to come in – I wanted to watch the expression on his face when he sniffed the appetizing aroma.

I heard his boots thundering through the front, then the kitchen door was slammed back and his presence seemed to fill the small room. 'How could you, Helena, how could you?' He was bellowing and his face was contorted with rage. 'Complaining about me – tittle-tattling the secrets of our marriage bed – to Edna Fairbarn of all people.' His voice seemed to bounce against the walls and I shrank back into my chair. 'Edna Fairbarn, who's got a tongue as long as me arm! I were walking up street, after a hard shift's work to earn money to keep you' – he glared at me – 'and Edna Fairbarn comes creeping out, like a fat white slug from under her lettuce leaf, and says, as loud as you like: "You want to lay off your little missus, Ben Holden – you're making her ill keep jumping on her all night like that." Christ, the whole street could hear her.' His face was scarlet with fury.

In desperation I pointed to the stove. 'I've made your lunch, Ben.'

'I don't want no bloody lunch!' He exploded again: 'You can throw it in back of fire for all I care.' He took a deep angry breath and came a step nearer – I flinched away from him; then suddenly he swung round and headed for the door. As he put his hand on the latch he threw over his shoulder. 'I'm sick of bloody women – I'm going to pub.'

The slamming of the front door brought the weak tears of relief to my eyes. But then I saw his belt, hanging behind the kitchen door – and remembered how he had threatened me in the dog cart at Hatton. I had not gone with another man, but he had been wild with rage – if he was still angry when he came back, what might he do? And I remembered the dozen dead Germans and felt sick with fear.

The pie was obviously burning; but there seemed no point in rescuing it now. I crouched in the chair with the tears trickling down my face, too frightened to move.

Then I heard the front door slam again – he had come back – he had been gone only ten minutes, and already he was back – I was very scared. As I heard him push open the door I closed my eyes and cowered into my chair with my hands raised to ward off the blows.

'Oh God – Helena, Helena – I'm sorry, I'm sorry.' I crouched on in my chair; I heard him approaching but I still could not look at him. 'Helena, please.' His voice was muffled, and slowly I opened my eyes, and saw him kneeling beside my chair with his head in his hands, his shoulders shaking. At last I reached out to him, uncertainly, and touched his wrist; at once he caught hold of my hand and pressed it against his cheek – it was damp, and with a shock I realized that he was crying. He raised a tormented face to mine. 'Helena, I'm sorry, I'm sorry. I never touched me pint – just as I were picking it up I thought: she'd never have done that, and even if she did, well, it were my fault for pestering her too much. I knew this morning you didn't want it, but I couldn't help meself, lying there beside you – but I won't do it again, I promise. From now on I won't lay a finger on you unless you're willing.'

I explained, hesitantly, 'I didn't tell her, Ben – she guessed, because I had to keep going in there.'

He asked urgently, 'Look, lass – is there blood in it?' His face was anxious.

I felt a spurt of anger against the fat woman. 'No, Ben – and she knew that, she'd already asked me – she shouldn't have told you that.'

He sighed. 'She didn't say it were so, exactly – I think she were trying to frighten me. But at first I were so angry – then when I came back and saw you with your hands up like that, as if you were expecting me to hit you . . .' The hand holding mine tightened.

I felt so tired, 'It's all right, Ben – I understand.'

He stood up very slowly, still holding my hand. 'I've got a bit of a temper, and I fly off the handle sometimes – but I'd never hurt you, lass, never.' Then he sniffed the air. 'And you made a nice dinner for me too – when you weren't feeling so good . . .'

I climbed stiffly out of my chair. 'I'm not ill, Ben – it's just that I need to . . .' I pulled away my hand and edged towards the scullery door – and then ran out into the yard.

When I got back he was chipping the burnt bits off my pie. 'It'll be all right lass, it weren't too far gone. You sit down and I'll see to the veg.'

He praised my pie extravagantly, though the gravy had almost dried up. I had to leave the table twice during the meal to visit the closet – I had drunk warm water and it was a little less painful, but the angry scene with Ben seemed to have lessened my control and I was terrified of wetting my drawers whenever I stood up. His eyes watched me anxiously each time I came in from the back and I had difficulty keeping back the tears of weakness. As soon as I had finished my cup of tea he ordered, 'You go upstairs and have a nice rest on your own – I won't disturb you.' Wearily I headed for the backyard again.

As I was pulling myself upstairs he came behind me and called, 'Another thing – you've got to start using chamber in bedroom – you can't keep running up and down stairs the way you are now.' I knew he was right, but I could not reply.

I did sleep at last, I was so tired. On awakening I crept down the stairs and peered into the kitchen – it was empty so I hurried back to fetch the chamber and empty it; there was no sign of blood in it. When I came down again he was stretching in the parlour doorway. 'I've had a bit of a nap meself, seeing as I were on

628

so early.' He followed me into the kitchen and asked, diffidently, 'How are you, lass?'

I whispered, 'Better,' and set off for the closet again. Walking back down the yard I saw his dark shape behind the net curtains in the kitchen window, watching me. But he was sitting down with the paper by the time I had washed my hands. I stood, uncertain, by the table. 'Lass' – he kept his eyes on the newspaper – 'I just noticed – you're walking a bit – difficult.' He raised his head and looked at me. 'Did I hurt you, as well?'

'I – I –' I did not know how to reply, but at last managed to get out, 'I'm just a bit sore, Ben.'

'So I did.' His voice was flat.

'Only last night – and –' I saw from his face I had made it worse.

He said softly, 'Christ – and I took you four times last night alone. You should have told me, Helena.'

I whispered, 'You're my husband, Ben.'

'That don't give me right to behave like an animal.' Then he went on, his voice awkward, 'I'm wondering now if I'm, well, too big for you down there. When I'm . . . that is . . . you're so tight. All the women I been with before, they never had trouble like you're 'aving – but they were wider round th'ips than you are, so happen they were built different inside, as well.'

He sat waiting for me to answer. At last I muttered, 'I – remember, I'm not – not very used to being with a man yet.' I finished in a rush.

I heard his sigh of relief. 'Aye, that's true. Me other women, they weren't whores – I kept meself clean like – but, well, they'd done it regular – so I suppose that's why they were more accommodating.'

He picked up his paper and I dragged my useless, unaccommodating body up the stairs and began to put on the clean sheets. I cried while making the bed up, then I stopped – what was the point? His gold band tightened round my finger: 'for better for worse, for richer for poorer, in sickness and in health . . .'

He went for some cheese while I cut the bread and butter and made the tea. Afterwards I did the washing up while he went up to the plot, then we both sat in the front parlour in silence. He read steadily and I listlessly turned over the pages of Letty's book.

He sent me up to bed early and it was longer than usual before he followed me. I was still awake when his heavy body climbed in beside me – but he kept well over on his side. I lay thinking of those generous-hipped women who were 'happen built different inside' and felt miserably guilty. 'I'm sorry, Ben.'

He sighed. 'Don't fret, lass – I've seen to meself already downstairs. But if I cuddle up to you like, then I'll come up again, so it's best I keep to me own side. Goodnight, Helena.'

'Goodnight, Ben.' I knew I would not sleep until I had tried to satisfy my bladder again so I began to edge my way out. When I got to the door he suddenly called out, 'Where are you going, lass?'

'Just to the closet.'

He moved very quickly; before I had stepped off the landing my arm was held tight. 'Look, my lass, you mun use chamber.'

'I can't Ben – not with you here.'

He said heavily, 'Lass, I'm your *husband* – if I hadn't been behaving like one you wouldn't be in this state now.'

I could not argue with his logic, but I could not use the chamber in his presence either. We stood there until I began to shift uneasily from foot to foot – then he let me break away.

When I came back he had the gas lit. 'Helena, I've put the chamber in the other room – if you won't use it in here than you mun do it in there – do you understand me?' I nodded. 'Lass, I don't want no insubordination, I want a promise.'

'I promise.'

'Good – now mebbe we can both get some sleep – I've got to be up afore three.'

But while I was sleeping I must have turned towards him, for I woke to feel his strong hands pushing me away. I was confused. 'Ben?'

'Christ, lass – 'aven't you got more sense than to wrap yourself round me like that? It were difficult enough first few days we were wed – but at least I'd not got th'abit o' you – now when I've been used to having me fill of you . . .'

He was panting heavily. I crouched away from him, then whispered, 'Perhaps, just once . . .'

He reared up in the bed. 'It wouldn't be bloody once, you stupid lass!' Then he subsided a little. 'Besides, how could I do it, knowing every push were hurting you? I'm not so hard, Helena – I'd hate meself afterwards.' He sighed. 'I'll have to go downstairs again and sort meself out.'

I lay on my own, consumed with guilt. He came back quite quickly, and got back into bed; he was calmer now. 'I'm sorry for shouting at you, lass – only a woman don't understand how it is for a man.' He put out his hand and squeezed mine briefly. 'Go to sleep now, and stop fretting.'

I dozed fitfully – I was frightened of touching his body and arousing him again, and he was restless too. We were both already awake when the knocker-up came banging on the door. Ben shouted 'A'reet' through the window, then groaned. 'At least he's in good time this morning – I had a few sharp words to say to young Tommy Bradshaw yesterday, catching me on th'op like that without even time for a goodbye kiss. Come here, lass, let's have a quick cuddle afore I leave you.' As he pulled me towards him I slipped my arms round his neck and he stroked my back and nuzzled my cheek. Then he raised his face to mine and whispered, 'Let's have a proper kiss, Helena – that'll not harm you.' So I opened my mouth to his and his tongue came in and licked mine – and he pulled me closer to him and suddenly he was groaning and panting and pushing his hard swollen maleness against my belly. I stiffened and he pulled away and threw himself back and jumped off the bed. 'Bloody hell! That were a mistake – I'd best wave from door in future.' He tugged on his clothes and flung himself out. 'Sithee, lass.'

As I heard his boots clattering down the street, I lay trembling in the bed where he had left me: I had been so naively proud of the power I had to arouse him, but now that I was no longer able to satisfy his needs I was frightened by the very strength of them. My mind began to picture him taking those other women with their full, womanly bodies who 'never had no trouble' – and I began to cry. Then I remembered that at least I was free of him for his eight-hour shift, so I used the chamber again, went back to bed and fell gratefully asleep in its emptiness.

I got up with the mill hooters and dragged myself through my housework, but the small house oppressed me today – it was no longer a doll's house to be played in – its demands weighed me down. And although he was out at work there were signs of him everywhere: his best boots under the draining board in the scullery; his weekday jacket hanging behind the kitchen door; his paper thrown carelessly down beside his armchair in the parlour. And I had to cope with the wearisome routine of shopping and cooking for him.

I was nervous of going down to the town, but by concentrating hard on what I had to do I succeeded in ignoring the demands of my bladder – and realized with relief that they were already becoming less urgent. Edna Fairbarn had been right – I had not caught a chill at all – my symptoms had been entirely due to Ben's over-use of me.

On my return I opened Letty's book and began to follow the instructions for making a stew – at least this was one of a wife's duties which I could try to carry out.

I had just finished peeling the potatoes, ready for when he came in, when there was a knock at the door: it was a boy in an over-large cap. He raised it politely and asked, 'Are you Ben Holden's missus?'

'Yes, yes I am.'

'Then 'e give me tuppence to tell you 'e'd be late 'ome today.' He skidded off down the street.

The stew was almost cooked – I lifted the saucepan and peered in, wondering how late Ben would be – and why was he late? He must have completed his eight-hour shift by now. I turned off the gas and stood hesitating, then found my polishing rags and went through to the parlour – the sideboard and piano were looking rather dull and I wanted to occupy my hands while I waited; I wondered again where he had gone. When the sideboard was shining I moved rather reluctantly across the room – handling the piano made my throat tighten. My voice had been my constant companion all my life – and now it had deserted me; it had grown up with me, just as my brothers had done . . . I forced my mind to blank out those memories that lurked always in the shadows – threatening to destroy me. My hands worked mechanically, until only the top remained to be done. I began to pick up my photos: Guy and Pansy at their wedding – and I heard again Pansy's small sad voice as she told me: 'He may not come in later – he often doesn't come back at all,' just as my husband had not come back. The thought lingered in my mind as I picked up the photo of my sisters – with Conan. I remembered my cousin's voice as he had exclaimed: 'Christ, Hellie, over the years you've cost me a fortune in whores!' My cousin whom I had also aroused – who had controlled himself with me – and had gone to obtain relief with other women. Ben had had to share a bed with me the whole night through, and my female presence had excited him past bearing – but he had controlled himself – so where was he now? My hand was trembling as I picked up Mother and Papa and Maud – so elegant in their silver frame – Papa was

633

devoted to Maud: but his affection for her had not stopped him in Munich. Whereas Ben Holden, who had felt obliged to marry me, would use me when I was available – but I had not been available to him last night, and he had needed a woman this morning.

I remembered how he had talked of 'Maree' – in France, in the war – and obviously there had been other Frenchwomen who had known my husband intimately. But a man like Ben would not have remained celibate since his return – there must be women in Ainsclough he had used, women who would be ready to receive him again when the need arose – and the need had arisen today. Probably he was even now in the next street, casually coupling with one of those women – one with wide hips who could accommodate him easily and give him the satisfaction that I could not – and so he would be late home. I supposed I should be grateful that he had at least sent the boy to warn me – like a considerate husband. I heard Guy's voice as we had stood looking out over the sand dunes together: 'So after that I only used the reputable establishments – and thought I was being a considerate husband!' I was lucky – I too had a considerate husband! I began to laugh, and heard the hysteria in it. I must stop being silly and take a hold of myself – clearly there was no point cooking the vegetables yet because a man like Ben would need to stay with this woman and take her several times so as to make sure he was fully emptied before he came home to spend the night with me. I would have to wait until he had finished. After all, I was a woman of the world, understanding men and their needs – I remembered Letty's startling blondness in her cradle, and Papa and Maud returning tanned from their trip abroad together. There had been Sir Ernest, creeping stealthily out of my mother's bedroom – and Papa with a pretty German whore on his arm. Oh yes, I had been lucky, I had learnt early that marriage vows were merely empty mouthings; now the knowledge stood me in good stead – I did not need to be shocked. I shrugged and put the photographs back and went to sit down in the armchair. I picked up yesterday's newspaper and began to read – and my hands scarcely trembled as I held it.

It was more than four hours later that he came in – still in his work clothes of course – I was glad that he had not bothered to wash for her. He looked quite drained. 'Hello, lass.'

I replied politely, 'Good afternoon, Ben.'

'I'm sorry I'm so late, but I . . .'

I broke in very quickly, 'Don't bother to explain Ben – I quite understand.' I tried to keep my voice even.

'Look lass – I know you're annoyed, but it's part of me job. Being a passed fireman, see, I get me turn altered when a driver's needed. I know it's a bind, but at least I don't often get lumbered with nights in this link. Any road, today I had to take a special to Blackpool, so I've only just got back.'

I said stupidly, 'You've been *working* – you've been working all afternoon?'

He stared at me. 'Course I have – what else did you think I'd been doing?'

'I thought you'd been with . . .' as my voice trailed away I glanced involuntarily at the photographs of my family, and his eyes followed my gaze, then turned to take in my crimson cheeks.

He stood looking at me, and I knew he had read my mind when he spoke. 'Christ, Helena – they brought you up right well, didn't they? You must'a' learnt a thing or two at your mother's knee afore I could tell lads from lasses.' He drew a deep breath and said heavily, 'I'm so bloody furious with you I can't trust meself to speak. I'll go and have me bath.' I heard him cursing in the kitchen as he realized I had let the range go out.

We ate our meal in silence. When he had finished he put down his knife and fork and said, 'I told you when we were courting, I told you then that I'd play fair with you, and I meant it. So I don't want to come in and see

that look on your face ever again. I'm going up plot.'
He stood up and reached for his jacket, then turned back
to me. 'And if I say I'm going up plot then that's where
I'm going. And if I call at pub on me way back then
that's where I'll be, not lifting some tart's skirts because
me own wife can't give me what I want for time being.
And I 'aven't forgotten *that* were me own fault.' Then
he added bitterly, 'I suppose if you'd married your
precious "my lord" he'd have been spending hisself wi'
th'ousemaid, and wouldn't have needed to wear you out.'

I was screaming, 'Get out! Get out!' He left, very
quickly. I subsided, crying and shaking, into my chair
– Gerald, oh Gerald – my love, my only true lover.

It was very late before he came in and climbed heavily
into bed beside me, but I was still awake. 'I didn't go
to pub – I've been for a long walk on tops. I reckon,
well I reckon we both need to be a bit patient with each
other. It's not easy, getting wed so sudden – and being
as far apart as we are. I'm sorry for what I said at t'last,
lass – but it did upset me, you thinking I'd go with
another woman, when we'd only been wed a week.'

I said at last, 'Then I apologize too, Ben – I didn't
think you'd mind so much. But – Gerald, Lord Staveley
– I loved him and I always will, and I know – I know
he would never have been untrue to me. So I don't want
you to speak of him ever again.'

'All right, lass – I'm sorry.' He sounded very tired.

I slept right through the night, barely hearing the
knocker-up when he came to rouse Ben, and when I
woke up I was alone in the bed. The ugly scene with
Ben lingered in my mind, but I pushed it from me: he
was a working man, his ways were cruder than those I
was used to – but I supposed I could put up with them
for a while. I got up and dressed and went down to
perform my household chores.

That evening he said he would take me out to the
pictures; I did not want to go but knowing it was meant
as a peace offering I went up for my hat and coat. It was

dark and stuffy in the small picture house and I could not keep my eyes open. The banging of the seats at the end roused me, and Ben gently eased my head off his shoulder and took me home.

He made a mug of cocoa and brought it up to me to drink in the bedroom. Then, standing looking down at me, he said, 'You look right washed out, lass – I think you'd best stay in bed tomorrow, leastways till I come home.'

'But I can't, Ben – your lunch . . .'

'I'll go down to pie shop and fetch it – they bake a nice light crust there. Mind you do as I say, now.'

I did as he told me, and when he got home he called up the stairs for me to stay where I was and came up soon after with my lunch on a tray. I ate some of the pie – the pastry was much lighter than mine – then lay down and went straight back to sleep again. Scarcely aware of his coming to bed, I was still asleep when he left on Friday morning.

When I eventually did wake up I felt so much better that I got out Letty's cookery book and made a fish pie, stewed some rhubarb to follow and stirred the custard as briskly as I could – it was easier than making a linseed poultice – and had everything ready for when he came in.

Ben praised the meal warmly and I felt much happier as I went out to do the washing up. He came out to clean his boots in the scullery and as he passed by he put his arm round me and held me close for a moment. He had scarcely touched me since Tuesday morning and now he felt very warm and strong as I leant back against him. He brushed my hair with his lips before he let me go. And as he began to rub in the blacking – whistling softly to himself as he did so – I realized that I had not visited the closet for hours – and the soreness between my legs had quite vanished.

CHAPTER SIX

When he came up to bed that night I moved towards him and whispered, 'Ben – I'm quite well again now, if you want . . .'

He grunted in the darkness. 'You should have told me sooner, lass – I've just seen to meself.' And as he spoke I was almost disappointed. Then his arm came round me. 'Just give us a cuddle, sweetheart – and I'll soon be ready to do you justice.' I tensed as I felt his free hand slide up under my nightdress, but his slow, rhythmical strokes on my belly soothed me, and my whole body relaxed in the shelter of his arms. Then his hand moved lower, down between my legs, and the gentle stroking became more insistent as his breathing quickened; but I was not frightened. And when I felt his fingers part me I realized that I was already slippery to his touch. 'I won't hurt you now, lass – you're ready for me – I'll slip in so easy you'll hardly know I'm there.' He hoisted himself above me as he asked, 'Can I come in now, sweetheart?'

'Yes, Ben.' I lay trustingly beneath him as he gently inserted himself, and smiled a little in the darkness at the feel of him there, then raised my hands to hold his strong buttocks. He moved so slowly, stroking the soft inside of my belly now – and I felt warm and welcoming. I closed my eyes.

His voice was anxious: 'How does that feel, sweetheart?'

And I opened my eyes and smiled up into his concerned face as I told him, 'That feels nice, Ben,' and he laughed in relief and bent down to brush my lips with his. When his movements quickened I held him more tightly and then he was throbbing between my legs giving little grunts of delight as I hugged him to me, smiling at his pleasure in my body. But then I remembered what he had said and began to worry – were my narrow hips still too tight for him?

He rolled off me, then gathered me to his chest. 'That were lovely, sweetheart, real lovely.'

And in the warm darkness I dared to ask, 'But, Ben – was I still too tight for you?'

'Too tight? You're not fretting about that, are you?' He kissed me before going on, 'It's better for me, sweetheart, you being so snug – I were only worried about you.' My body relaxed against him in relief as his hand gently stroked my back, then he whispered, his voice almost shy, 'When I'm with you, Helena, you're like a silk glove to me – you fit so beautiful and warm. There, is that what you wanted to know?' I put my cheek against his neck and felt his chuckle, and he was silent for a minute or two before he began to speak again. 'Helena, I done a lot of thinking these past few days – after I found out what you were thinking of me on Tuesday – gave me a nasty shock, that did. Then I reckoned mebbe it were partly my fault, behaving with you the way I had been. I said to myself: There you are, Ben Holden, with a lovely little lass that you broached yourself – so you knew you were only man she'd ever taken inside her' – his fingers touched me, intimately, caressingly – 'and then all you can think of is your own pleasure, keep taking her like that when it were obvious she weren't ready for it yet, with you being her first man.' His fingers caressed me again.

I murmured, 'I didn't mind, Ben.'

'Aye, you were a game little lass you were – opening your legs to me every-time I wanted – but it weren't good for you in long run, were it? I were more 'an you could take – I can see that now – you need treating gentle, with a bit of stroking and fondling to get you ready.' He stopped, then said with a sigh, 'I'm right ashamed of meself lass – I am that.'

I was sorry for him, 'But, Ben – you did stroke me.'

'Aye, mebbe – but it were afterwards, not afore – leastways, it often were afore next time, but that weren't what I should have been doing, with an inexperienced lass – I see that now. But, well, like I told you on tops, I'd never had a virgin before – all women I'd been with were either married, or widows, like Maree.' I stiffened and he said quickly, 'Anyroad, them's all past – it's only you now, so I reckon I'd better make sure as I use you careful.'

As he kissed me once more I felt his maleness throb against my belly and drew back a little, but his voice was firm. 'It's all right lass, I've talked myself into a better frame of mind and we're going to take it slow next few weeks. You cuddle up against me nice and close and him down there'll just have to learn he can't always have what he wants.'

So I curled myself against him, warm and content, until I dozed off.

As soon as he came home the next day he kissed me, before going for his bath – and again when he came out. I pressed myself against him, and he gently stroked the back of my neck.

When I had finished the washing up that evening he was sitting in the armchair in the kitchen. 'Come here, lass.' I went to him and he pulled me down on his lap; I turned and nestled against him, until I could feel the steady beat of his heart. His hands moved to the buttons of my blouse, unfastening them one by one, and then they slid inside – his fingers were rough on my silk petticoat, but they were very warm on the skin of my breasts as he began to knead them gently. 'How about an early night, love?' I pressed my head into his neck in answer. 'I were thinking, if I saw to meself first, like last night – '

I said quickly, 'No, don't.'

He tipped my chin up and studied my face. 'Are you sure, lass? It'd be easier for you.'

'I'm sure, Ben.'

He smiled. 'You're a funny lass, sometimes – come on, then.' I climbed slowly off his lap; I felt languid and heavy.

I washed drowsily, then lay watching him undress in the half light through the curtains – the very size of him told me he had not 'seen to himself', and my belly stirred in response. He stroked me again before pushing in; he was bigger and firmer tonight but I opened myself to him, and he did not hurt me. As I felt his movements quicken my legs tightened over his and my hands caught hard at his buttocks – ripples of excitement washed through me – and then he was filling me as I lay beneath him, panting with relief. His breath tickled my ear as he murmured his thanks – then he began to pull out. But I would not let him go – I wanted him to stay, locked into me, and with all my strength I held him there. 'Lass, I'll be coming up again, if you keep me inside.' I did not answer – only my hands continued to hold him until he said, 'Give us a kiss, then, if that's what you want.'

We lay with our mouths opened to each other, until I felt him stir and swell inside me; and as he did my belly seemed to swell in reply and fill with the remembered sweetness. When he began to move again his every touch was an exquisite pleasure and I was moving with him, lifting myself, opening myself – pulling him deeper and deeper and moaning aloud at the blissful torment of it. I heard him laugh and with his laughter the pressure mounted and I was pushing, pulling – frantic with the ecstatic agony of it – then he drove deeply in and I exploded.

I scarcely knew when he had finished, but I saw his face above me and heard his chuckle – 'No wonder you wanted all of it' – then fell suddenly asleep still holding him inside me.

When I woke again his warm arm was lying across my breasts, and as I lay in the dark beside him I knew that I wanted him. I turned and reached out and began to stroke his chest, and then my fingers slid down to his flat stomach. He stirred and groaned as he woke. 'No lass – not again tonight; it'll be too much for you.' He turned so his back was to me, but the sweetness was filling my belly and I needed him so much. I pressed myself against him murmuring, 'Please, Ben, please.'

I heard the smile in his voice as he replied, 'All right, lass – I never say no to a lady. Let's be having you.' He rolled over and came into me at once and I panted and clung to him and now the sweetness flooded through me in waves until I was overwhelmed by it.

When I awoke in the morning I found myself alone in the bed, then I heard his footsteps on the stairs and the hot blood rose in my cheeks as he came in with my cup of tea. I held out my hand for it without looking at him, but he put it down out of my reach and said, 'I'll say me good mornings first.' Sitting on the edge of the bed he slipped his arm round my shoulders and pressed his lips on mine – I lay against him as his tongue roved slowly around the soft inside of my mouth. When he finally pulled back I saw the look of confidence on his face; he had control of me now, because I needed him. I blushed and he laughed aloud, slid his hand under the bedclothes and up into the moistness between my legs. Watching my face he stroked and pressed, and my belly began to contract – I tried to control myself but could not, and he held me against him as I writhed and squirmed – then he pushed his finger in hard and I exploded on to it. As I lay panting against him I felt the laughter vibrate in his chest. 'That were a free one, sweetheart, to make up for last week.'

I whispered, 'Ben, if you want . . .'

I felt him tense, then he said, 'No, there's not time, we mun get to Ada's, besides you're a bit swollen down there and I don't want you running complaining to Edna

642

Fairbarn. I'll see you right this evening, sweetheart.' He was laughing as he ran down the stairs.

I could scarcely look at him over breakfast; every time I moved the dampness in my drawers reminded me of how I had held him inside me – frantic in my need for him. And as my cheeks flamed he looked at me and laughed.

He was waiting at the front door when I came down in my hat and costume, but instead of opening it he pulled me casually to him in the small lobby and reached down to put his hand under my skirt. 'Ben, we'll be late!'

'It's all right lass – I won't set you off again. I just want to handle you a bit – so you know who you belong to.' As his finger tugged at my knicker legs he said, 'You'd best get out them French things you had on tops – I can hardly move in here for elastic – aah.' He gave a soft grunt of satisfaction and his fingers fondled me gently for a moment or two as I clung to him. Then he slowly withdrew his hand and held it out to me. 'Take the handkerchief out of me jacket pocket and give us a wipe – looks like I over-filled you last night.' My hands were shaking as I obeyed him. Then, thrusting the handkerchief back into his pocket, he smacked me gently on the behind and reached for the latch. 'Come on, sweetheart – let's be off.'

I was acutely aware of his strong body beside me on the train to Bolton; I stole small glances at him and he smiled back, triumphant, watching my blushes rise. There was nobody else in the tram shelter so he put his arm round me and pressed my hip against his. 'Ben – people are looking!' He laughed and kissed me full on the lips and I was clinging to him for a moment before I pulled away, and his warm hand still clasped mine.

Ada was some years younger than Ivy, and she still had a child at home: a boy of ten or so who wanted Ben to mend his model engine. As they both crouched on the floor over it Ada turned to me and smiled, 'Our Ben's

643

right good with the youngsters – he's looking forward to having a family of 'is own.' And for a moment I stirred uneasily on the sofa, seeing how close the two brown heads were – the boy leaning trustingly against his uncle's shoulder as they peered into the mechanism of the toy together.

We ate lamb instead of beef and spooned out mint sauce instead of horseradish; afterwards I sat watching Ben's broad shoulders and strong hands as he drank his tea; he looked up and smiled at me and I blushed and shifted a little on my seat and hoped there would be no damp patch on my skirt when I stood up to help Ada with the washing up. Ben followed us into the scullery, and Ada flapped her dish cloth at him. 'Get out from under our feet, lad – kitchen's no place for men.' Laughing, he dodged round her and pulled me casually against him to kiss my cheek. 'See you later, love.' He winked at me as he left.

Ada smiled at my scarlet cheeks. 'Well, you'd best make most of it – once the babbies come along there's not much time for cuddling – 'cept to make more babbies!' She laughed as she bent over the sink and I felt that shadow of unease touch me again. We left soon after tea; Ada was smiling as Ben carefully eased my jacket over my shoulders – and I flushed yet again.

As soon as we were inside the front door at Royds Street Ben said simply, 'I'm sorry, lass – I can't wait. I'll 'ave to take you upstairs now, afore I go to plot' I looked at him, uncertain, then ducked my head and ran to the stairs. He followed close on my heels, already loosening his tie, and his jacket was flung to the floor as soon as he came into the bedroom. His waistcoat dropped on to a chair, then he dragged off his trousers and underpants all together, caught hold of me and swung me up on to the bed. I scarcely had time to take off my hat before he began to tug at my skirt – but he could not get the fastening undone quickly enough so he simply pushed it up above my hips, pulled down my drawers and came into me at once.

I was very uncomfortable; it was so hot in my Sunday costume with his weight on top of me and he was thrusting far too hard – but I could not move my legs to accommodate him more easily because my drawers were tangled round my knees. So I simply lay still and accepted the urgency of his need – he had satisfied me during the previous night, now it was his turn, and I did not really mind the discomfort.

He grunted and fell heavily forward on to me, and I held him until he was spent. At last he raised his damp face and looked down at me. 'You're a good girl, aren't you? There's many a one who'd have said no, and sent me packing up plot – but you came straight upstairs and let me mess up your nice costume and all and never complained.' He took a deep breath and said, 'Oh Helena, I do love you – I love you so much.'

I looked up into his grey-blue eyes and went very cold. It seemed a long time before I was able to reply. 'But – I – I thought, up on the moors, it was – just because I made you.'

He bent his head and nuzzled my ear, then rested his cheek on the pillow beside me; I stared up at the ceiling, unable to look at him as he said, 'A woman can't make a man who doesn't want to. No, sweetheart, I've loved you from moment I opened my eyes and saw you bending over me in th'ospital – or mebbe it were even afore that, when I felt your breasts under me cheek and heard that beautiful voice of yours coaxing me to drink. That were biggest moment of me life, Helena, I'll never forget that as long as I live. I were in hell, and I'd given up – I'd had too much to bear and I could feel me life draining out of me – and I didn't care, I were glad to go. And then you called me back.' His voice thickened. 'And when I opened me eyes and saw your lovely face there above me – why, if th'entire Prussian Guard had marched into ward that night – I reckon I'd'a' got off

645

me bed and had a go at them! That's effect you have on me, sweetheart.' He moved so as to settle his heavy body more comfortably across mine: he was heavy and hot and I felt as if I would suffocate under the weight of him. 'After that I knew you were only woman for me -- leastways, I got to be honest, Helena – I were a soldier, so I'd ease meself from time to time if a lass were willing and we'd had a good time together – but it didn't mean nothing to me, it were only me body taking its pleasure, and afterwards I'd lie there beside her thinking of you.' Of me, of me! My very soul shrank from him. 'I knew it wouldn't be easy, you being who you were. But in hospital you'd always treated me a bit special – t'other lads noticed – so it gave me hope.' I thought impatiently, of course I did – you'd carried in Eddie, you had been Robbie's sergeant-major! But you fool – how could you think I would have looked in any other way at a common soldier? And the common soldier shifted himself a little, so that his hips crushed me further into the bed as I lay with my skirt creased up around my waist and my drawers pushed down to my knees – and my traitorous belly bare and sticky to his touch. And now he moved a fraction further so he could touch it as he said, 'But I got me chance,' and his stubby fingers moved down to handle me, and push possessively into the most private parts of my body as he laughed. 'I learnt to act fast in war – so I acted fast on tops, and took me chance, and took you too, my lass. And I knew there wouldn't be a second opportunity, so I made a thorough job of it! But then, sweetheart, you like thorough jobs, don't you? He'd be no use to you, a man who couldn't properly fill your belly with himself – even first week we were wed when you were still a bit nervous like, there you were, pulling me in, when I were ready to come off – like a little she-cat you were, desperate to be served. And then, last night' – he breathed in, complacently – 'I reckon I gave you all the pleasure that a man can give a woman – and today, when you kept looking at me, then blushing

646

– and hanging round and pressing yourself against me – I knew I could do anything with you today. So I thought, now's time to tell her, it won't upset her now – because I knew at first I'd penned you into a corner, and you were a bit frightened of me – wary like – but way you've been last couple of days, well, you're not exactly indifferent to me, are you, Helena?'

No, I was not indifferent to him – I hated him! I hated him for what he had done to me, for trapping me here on this bed, in this room, in this house, in this town – in this life. Oh God, save me! But there was no God, only a man's rough, ill-educated voice saying, 'Well, I suppose it's all been a bit of a shock to you, lass, so I'll not expect an answer yet awhile – and I know lasses can be shy. But you mun never think again that you trapped me into wedding you; when I made them vows in that church with you beside me I meant them, every word of them – and I'll keep them, all the days of me life.' And his mouth came down and imprisoned mine, just as his ring had imprisoned my body.

He lifted himself off me and sat up, brisk now. 'You mun be all hot and sweaty in them clothes, with me jumping up and down on you – even your drawers look worse for wear. Come on, sweetheart, we'll get you changed into something nice and cool – it's a fine evening.' He got up and went to the chest and opened *my* drawers and began to rummage familiarly through them. 'Where's young Letty's flim-flams, then?'

I replied, quickly, lyingly, 'I threw them away.'

His face dropped for a moment, then he shrugged. 'Let's see what else I can find – you have some lovely underthings, Helena – all them silks and satins – I'll admit to you now that once or twice these last couple of weeks I've come up here when you've been busy in scullery and run me hands through 'em – just for pleasure of feel of them.' How dared he, how dared he!

I watched as he pulled out a pair of wide-legged pink satin knickers, and held them up in his big red hand.

'You can put these on for starters, lass – so's I can get a feel of you anytime I want.' He tossed them on to the bed then drew out a pale-blue silk chemise. 'There, that'll do.' He went over to the alcove and pulled back the curtain and found a jade-green muslin dress. 'Just the ticket – now, let's see you get changed.'

He threw himself down full length on the bed, and lay there in his crumpled shirt and socks. I picked up his choice of clothing as if it would burn my fingers and began to edge round the bed. 'I'll go next door.'

'Oh no you don't, my lass.' His voice was quite good-humoured, but totally inflexible. 'I've never seen you naked. You take your clothes off in here, where I can watch you.' Turning my back on him I began to pull off my skirt with shaking fingers, then reached for the pink satin drawers to pull them on under the shelter of my creased petticoat – but he snatched them away from me, laughing. 'Take everything off first.'

It seemed a long time before I was naked. 'Turn round, I want to see your front.' Slowly I turned round, holding my two hands protectively over my breasts and my belly. 'Come on lass, drop your hands – I'm your husband, remember.' So now I was quite unprotected before him, standing with his seed damp between my legs and smeared on my thighs. His eyes roamed over me, and I seemed to stand in front of him for ever. Then he heaved a great sigh. 'Oh, Helena, you're beautiful – I never seen anything so beautiful.'

I whispered, 'May I get dressed now?'

'Come over here, lass, and I'll put them on you meself.' I moved forward very slowly until I stood before him, where he sat on the edge of the bed. He caught hold of my cold hands and pulled my body down over him, and kissed each of my nipples in turn; then bent his head lower and kissed my belly; then, lower still, I felt his lips press against the dark fan of hair between my legs. He stood up and ordered, 'Raise your arms, Helena.' He pulled the silk chemise over my head and smoothed it down over my hips. 'Put your hand on me shoulder, lass, and lift your foot – now the other.' His fingers slid up over my thighs as he drew on the satin knickers. He pushed down under the elastic and fondled my belly, then the green muslin was put on me. I reached for my suspender belt but his hand on my wrist held me back. 'No, no stockings tonight, sweetheart, wait for me, just like this.' He turned and tugged on his own discarded clothing, caught me to him for a moment – then left. As I heard the front door slam I collapsed shaking on to the bed – cold as ice in that warm room.

Oh God, what ever had I done? The small bedroom was a prison, and I was trapped in it, like a linnet in a cage. For the first time since I had driven the needle into Robbie's arm I had regained my right mind; oh my brother, my brother – what have you made me do? In my pain and guilt I came to this man, and now he has locked me in his cage in this alien town. The years ahead stretched before me like a dark tunnel as I thought of his rough accent, his dropped hs, the dark line that never seemed to leave his fingernails – fingernails that were short and broken, because he spent eight hours of every day shovelling coal – and this man held me captive.

I knew then, in an agony of self-reproach, that I had made my marriage vows carelessly, unbelievingly – in the back of my mind I had seen a way out. Mother would have arranged it, divorce was not so difficult when you had money to pay lawyers. I had been so sure that he was merely doing his duty, discharging a debt incurred years ago in the war when I had refused to allow him to die – and that when the time came he would let me go. But he would never let me go now – for he loved me. He dared to love me – I whom Gerald had honoured with his hand, Gerald my hero, my love, my only true lover. The idea seemed so absurd that I began to laugh – until my laughter turned to deep, racking sobs as I saw again the look on his face as he lay on the bed – and made me stand naked before him. I sat

649

wearing the ridiculous outfit his hands had dressed me in and wept as I remembered how this man had invaded my body and filled my womb – so that even now his seed was oozing stickily out from between my legs.

At last I stood up and pulled on a jacket over my frozen arms. I had been mad and now I was sane; I must pay with the rest of my life for those weeks of insanity. But the soft sheen of gold caught my eyes, where Eddie's watch lay on the chest and I knew then, with a total, deadly certainty, that if it had not been for this man I would have had no life to pay with. He had saved me as surely as I had saved him; his debt was cancelled now, but mine was still owing, and I would pay it here, in this small ugly town, among uncouth harsh-voiced strangers, every day of my life.

I stood up and went through to the back bedroom and began to search for the operatic score. When I found it I shook out the photograph of the three laughing youngsters: two boys and a girl, carefree and unaware. I kissed the pictured faces and put them in a frame, then I took them downstairs and added them to the rest of my past – frozen in time on the top of the polished piano.

CHAPTER SEVEN

I lived now like a puppet. I cooked and cleaned, and shopped and scrubbed: I washed his clothes and made his bed. I replied when he spoke to me, and gave answers when he questioned me on my small daily doings – but I told him nothing.

Only my body was alive now; my mind, my heart, my soul were dead. But my body – that remained alive. It ate and drank and carried me back and forth between the terrace and the town. And at night, up in the small bedroom, it wanted him. At first when he had come to bed I had turned my back, pretending to be asleep – I knew he would not force himself upon me now. But it was no use, my body would not be denied and I would wake in the night with a terrible insistent fullness in my belly and turn to him urgently – and he would fill me and give me rest – for a little while. So then I began to put out my arms to him blindly as soon as I felt him heaving his heavy body on to the bed; he never failed me.

Once he had to go out on a night shift – to work a goods train over into Yorkshire, he told me. I listened apathetically, but that night my body cried out for him in the empty bed. As soon as he came in in the morning I ran to him and he looked at me, with surprise in his red-rimmed eyes; then he shook his head. 'It's no use, Helena – I'm worn out.'

All morning I went mechanically about my daily tasks, aware that he was there, in the bed above me. At lunch-time I crept up the stairs and into the room; he was fast asleep. I took all my clothes off and slid into the bed beside him, twining my bare arms and legs around his sleeping body, pressing my belly against his. He began to stir, as I had known he would, and at last he came heavily over on top of me and began to thrust, as I had known he would. He was already asleep again by the time I pushed him off me and crawled out of the bed.

That evening as he sat over his meal he said, 'I had a funny dream today – almost like real it were . . .' He watched me, his eyes wary. I felt the blood rise in my cheeks, and he added, heavily, 'Aye – I reckoned mebbe it weren't a dream. You can't go a day without, can you?' I stood up and took the used plates out to the scullery.

But outside of the bedroom door there was nothing. Whenever he entered or left the house he put his lips to mine and held them there; I did not move. Once, early

on, he came back from the plot while I was in the parlour
– he put his arm round me and bent to lift my skirt and
I felt his warm hand fumbling between my legs, seeking
to get inside my drawers. For a moment my legs opened,
but then I turned my eyes and fixed them on Gerald's
photograph and I was able to hold my body rigid until
the man dropped his hand and backed away, shame-
faced, mumbling some words – of pleading, of apology
– I did not know because I did not listen. When he had
stumbled to a halt I told him, 'The bedroom is the place
for that – can you not wait another hour?'

'Aye, aye lass – of course – I didn't mean . . .'

I smiled at him, without looking into his eyes, and my
voice was honeyed as I promised, 'You may have your
fill of me in the bedroom, Ben Holden, just as you always
do – have I ever denied you there?'

'No, no, lass – you been a good wife.'

He slunk through into the kitchen and I smiled at
Gerald's face, whispering, 'Thank you, my darling,
thank you.'

And now I let my mind dwell often on Gerald; I would
linger before his photograph, remembering – remembering the first time I had seen him, riding in his shining
breastplate and plumed helmet at the head of his troop.
I remembered his tall slim figure and smiling eyes as he
had greeted me in the pension at Munich, that first
Christmas, and I remembered – oh how I remembered
– his strong hands propelling me across the ice of the
Englischer Garten as I reclined in the carved wooden
swan – skimming like a bird over the frozen meadows
at his touch. I rode with him again in the shires, and
sang to him again before the German Ambassador, and
worshipped him as my lost voice soared up to the
shadowy beams of the small church at Hammersmith –
and then I was happy for a little while. But when *he*
came in, smelling of coal dust and sweat, with his rough
awkward voice – then my dreams were broken, and I
hated him for what he had done to me.

I often saw him looking at me strangely, and in the evening he would try to make conversation; I would answer him politely – I was always polite – but he seemed uncertain, dissatisfied. But that night I would close my eyes and reach out for him, and sometimes cry out and writhe and moan and explode under him. Then he would kiss me and say, 'I love you, Helena, I love you!' I would turn my face away and shut my ears – but in the morning he would be more cheerful.

Once the fat woman under the green dome spoke to me. 'How are you these days, lass? You don't look quite right, somehow.' Her big round face was concerned, kindly – and for a moment my eyes filled with tears – but I blinked them away, smiled politely and left. I did not visit the green dome again, though it was difficult, because my body was changing.

The first weeks I had still fostered a faint hope in the corner of my mind – I searched my underwear as I came near my time. Perhaps God would relent, perhaps I might still escape. But each day my drawers showed only the white stains of his seed; the red blood did not appear. And my breasts, which had always been so small, became fuller and heavier, my nipples grew and darkened, and I felt my womb pressing on my bladder – so I knew God had not relented, and hope died.

So now I needed Gerald more and more; he became my refuge, my hiding place. It was not enough simply to remember him – especially not down in the parlour where he was a stern soldier. Upstairs I took out my other picture of him, smiling at me, in his morning suit – not Major Lord Staveley now, but Gerald, my lover. But I did not want *him* to see this picture of the intimate, private Gerald, so I took my treasure into the back bedroom, where *he* never came. Opening a trunk, I took out a thick soft blanket and a pillow, then pulled the boxes into a square to make a small shelter, where I could be safe and unobserved, building a little nest for myself in which I could dream. Because memories were not enough now – my memories only led to the war, and the terrible blankness it had brought. So I followed my memories just to the moment when he put his ring on my finger, and then I transmuted them into dreams. And in my dreams there was no war: Franz Ferdinand and his duchess were safely buried and forgotten; the Kaiser continued to strut before his parading soldiers – but only in Berlin; and the Belgians went contentedly about their daily business in the picturesque little town of Ypres; the world was at peace.

And so my wedding day came, as planned – my real wedding day, to Gerald. I stood before the altar beside his tall, handsome figure – and for once I was beautiful, because he loved me. We journeyed to Munich and stayed in the Regina Palace Hotel on Maximilian Platz – with its sixty bathrooms and its palm house – and visited Frau Reinmar and Franzl – Franzl still with two hands and the smile of friendship on his face. We went to Elsa Gehring's studio – and Gerald praised her for my singing – then we visited the opera every night – and perhaps, one afternoon, if the weather was kind, we skated again on the frozen meadows beyond the Englischer Garten. And then we came back, to Bessingdon – to our home.

I had never seen Bessingdon, and now I was glad because I could imagine it exactly as I wanted it to be, golden and glowing in the afternoon sun as it welcomed us home. The tenants cheering us from the station, the indoor staff lined up in the hall – all were there; so too was Moira Staveley, but she was a shadowy figure in the background, for I was mistress now.

I pictured my bedchamber, with silver brocade hangings, and walls of the palest blue – a cool, gracious room. And there, at one side, was the door which led to Gerald's dressing room, with his bedroom beyond. I would glance at it shyly, my heart fluttering at the thought of him there, asleep. Sometimes there would be a gentle tap on that door, and I would call out to come

654

in, my breathing quickening, and he would enter and walk towards me, elegant in his silk dressing gown. He would bend over me as I lay waiting in the wide bed, his low voice asking. 'Are you asleep, Helena?' And I would whisper back, 'No, Gerald, not yet.' Still he would stand beside me, until I felt the gentle touch of his fingertips on my cheek. 'Then, Helena, may I join you for a little while?' 'Yes Gerald – please do.' And my face would be suffused with blushes in the darkness as he slipped gracefully under the covers beside me.

But try as I might I could imagine no further – for my experience in this house overshadowed that dream. Gerald would never have roughly thrust up my night-dress and prised my thighs apart – and I, I would never have turned to him with that terrible driving insistence in my belly – no, because I loved Gerald, so it would have been quite different. But I knew that afterwards he would have kissed me very gently, then whispered goodnight and left me there to dream. And in my dreams I was always cool and clean and fresh-smelling – my belly was never damp with his sweat nor my thighs sticky with his seed – Gerald, my pure true lover.

But sometimes my dreams were dangerous. There was a day when a boy came to tell me Ben Holden would be late – so I knew I had hours for myself. I turned off the gas and ran up the stairs, as excited as a girl going to her lover – I *was* a girl going to her lover. I curled up in my nest and gave myself to my dreams – but I dreamt too long, and one night Gerald's face changed, and his hands became harder, and he loomed over the bed and there was no gentle touch on my cheek, instead he seized me and used me, violently – and then left me without a word; and I lay sobbing and broken. I was still trembling when I heard the latch of the door downstairs. I stumbled to my feet and ran down, and my husband was there in the kitchen, hanging up his working jacket. 'Have you been having a lie down? Good girl.' Then he turned and

saw my face. 'Lass, you look as if you seen a ghost –
happen you've had a nightmare.'

'Yes – yes – a nightmare!'

'Poor little lass.' His large dirty hand reached out to
stroke my cheek, and this time I did not flinch away;
his voice dropped. 'Never mind, sweetheart, I'm home
now.'

'Yes – yes, you're home.'

'You sit down in a chair, I'll not be a minute in bath,
then I'll give you a hand dishing up tea.'

After that I learnt to ration my dreams as I walked on
the terrace at Bessingdon, with Gerald, and sang in the
drawing room after dinner, to Gerald; and rode in the
park, beside Gerald. But then, one day, I knew I ought
not to be going on horseback any longer, and when he
asked, smiling, 'Will you ride with me this morning,
Helena?' I shook my head and blushed: 'No, Gerald – I
shall not be riding now, for a while.' And I saw the joy
in his face as he came to me and his lips brushed my
cheek. 'Helena, my dear – you have made me so happy,
so very, very happy.' And that evening he would come
to my room, still in his evening suit. 'I've come to say
goodnight, my dear – because now . . .' I would smile
back in understanding and gratitude. 'Thank you, my
dearest – goodnight, Gerald.' And I would lie in the cool
darkness, with his child below my heart.

When I uncurled my cramped limbs I was weeping;
but I had to go downstairs and peel the potatoes and
shell the peas and prepare the fish – for my husband.

June had ended, July came, and now the peas that I
cooked were from his plot – from those plants whose
tiny tendrils I had watched him train up the sticks so
long ago. Each day he brought in more of his growing,
and I cooked them for him, hot and sweating as I bent
over the stove in the stuffy kitchen.

At the end of August he began to talk of taking a
week's holiday in the autumn; he wrote to a farm in
Yorkshire, I was not sure where because I did not listen.

But I would go with him, because I needed him more now – my womb was becoming more urgent as it filled. Yet he had become hesitant – sometimes he asked, 'Do you think, lass . . . ?' But the scent of his strong body next to me was past bearing and I beat at his shoulders with my balled fists and pressed my belly desperately against him, until he responded and took me – and then I was satisfied, for a while.

One day he called me upstairs, and I saw he was in the back bedroom – I hurried up in a panic, but he was nowhere near my sanctuary. He waved his hand at the piled-up boxes. 'Look, lass – I'd best get some of this clutter cleared out – we'll need space soon, with child coming.'

I stared at him like a small animal at bay. 'How did you guess?'

He touched my hand diffidently. 'Lass, you've come to me every night, so I know you've not bled since day we were wed.' The silly rhyme rang through me: 'not bled since the day we were wed, not bled since the day we were wed.' I held myself very still. 'I reckon you must have fallen that evening when we come back from Ada's first time – you been different since – looking inward all time.' He straightened his back from the trunk he was inspecting and told me, 'You mun go to doctor's soon.' Vehemently I shook my head. Not yet, not yet – he might tell me it was true.

I followed him listlessly downstairs, stumbling on the last step; he swung quickly round and reached up to steady me. 'And another thing, lass – you shouldn't be wearing them shoes – you might catch your heel and fall, it's that steep round here. I'll buy you some more.' I took no notice of his words: they were *my* shoes; I ate the food he earned and slept in the bed he had bought – but I would not wear shoes he had paid for.

So I cooked and cleaned and washed and shopped – and each day I retreated into the solace of my dreams, and each night I used his strong body in the bed upstairs, while my breasts became fuller and my body swelled – and by now, September was half over. It was a Tuesday when I heard the brisk rat-tat at the door – so I thought it was the rent man. I picked up the money left ready under the clock and walked slowly through the parlour and opened the front door – and there, on the step, was Conan.

CHAPTER EIGHT

'Hello, Hellie – can I come in?' I stepped back and he walked through the lobby and into the parlour, elegant and handsome in an immaculately tailored suit fashioned from the finest grey cloth. He balanced his cane across one of the bentwood chairs, peeled off his gloves and slipped them inside his hat. 'No, Hellie – it's not a ghost; it really is me. China's a big place, you know – a very big place; messages take a long time arriving – but I came as soon as I could.'

I said dully, 'You're too late.'

'Poor old Hellie.' He came over and took me in his arms, and I wept hopelessly on his fine grey shoulder. He smelt of cigars and expensive shaving soap.

After a while, when my sobs had slowed, he put me away from him a little. 'Let's have a look at you.' I stood before him as his blue eyes slowly travelled over my tear-stained cheeks, then he leant forward and kissed me lightly on the lips before leading me to the armchair. He pulled the other chair up close to me and sat down in it himself.

I held out my left hand and repeated, 'You're too late.'

'Yes, I know, Aunt Ria told me. But it's not too late – I've got a motor outside, we could scarper in it now – your mother wouldn't give us away.'

As I looked at him, longing overwhelmed me; then I felt the new heaviness in my breasts and shook my head. 'I'm – I'm carrying his child.'

Conan raised his eyebrows and smiled. 'Then you'd better bring the child along too.' I wanted so much to go – oh, how I longed to go. He sat watching me. 'It's up to you, Hellie – I'm offering you a way out. I'm not bothered about the child, I've fathered enough bastards on other men in my time – I can hardly object if your Ben Holden does the same to me.'

I wished he had not used that word; my child was not a bastard – Ben Holden was my legal husband. My cousin stood up and went to look at the photographs on the piano; he picked one up and brought it back to me. 'Is this him – who are those nippers?'

'His nephews and his niece – that is, his great-nephews and his great-niece.' I looked at the picture as Conan held it out to me: Ben was smiling as he held the toddler on his lap – and the other two children leant against him so confidingly; I remembered them all running to greet him at Ivy's. Conan put it back, then picked up the other photo of Ben, in his sergeant-major's uniform.

He studied it for a while, then said, 'He looks a decent enough chap.'

'He is a decent enough chap.'

'Then what's wrong, Hellie?' I shrugged my shoulders. As he returned Ben's photo I saw him pause in front of the piano, and his eyes narrowed. Then he came back to the empty hearth, propped one elbow up on the mantleshelf and said casually, 'You're not still mooning over Gerald, are you?'

My whole body went rigid. My eyes dropped to the shining black toecap next to the fender; I could not answer.

'Hellie – it's five *years* now, more than five years!'

I threw my head back and cried, 'He told me, he told me there would never be another woman – and now, look at me now.' I put my hand to my belly, despairingly. 'I've betrayed him.'

'For God's sake, Hellie, be reasonable – I could have had you myself half a dozen times since then.'

I put my head in my hands. 'But you didn't.'

'No – well, I'm inclined to think I was a bloody fool – the only time I've ever behaved with decency and restraint, and then some other so-and-so jumped in instead. Still, that's life. Are you coming with me now, or not?'

I wanted to, how I wanted to – but Ben Holden's face smiled out of the frame on the piano, holding a child on his lap – just as I held his child in my womb. His child.

I stood at the crossroads and looked at Conan: my cousin, my almost brother, companion of my childhood – whom I loved, whom I had always loved. Then my eyes turned against their will to the pictured face of Ben Holden: whom I did not love, but who loved me, and who was my legal husband – and who had told his sister, just before our wedding, how much he was looking forward to having a family of his own. I wrestled with myself for a long time, but I knew I could not take his child away from him – he deserved better of me than that. And his child was lodged in my body, so my body would have to stay here, in Ainsclough.

My head was so heavy that I could barely move it, but I managed to shake it at last.

'Well, it's your decision, Hellie.'

'Yes, it's my decision.'

He took out a cigarette and lit it. 'Poor old Robbie – it was hard lines for him, after coming back at the end.'

'Yes, it was.'

'Letty told me how he never got over that wound – so the bloody Germans killed him after all.'

I said, 'No, I killed him.'

Conan's jaw dropped; he took the cigarette out of his mouth and stared at me. 'The wound infected his lungs – they were rotting, he was dying – but it was I who killed him. He knew it would be very painful, a[nd] had suffered so much already, so he asked the docto[r] but the doctor didn't get there in time, so I injected hi[m] with a lethal dose of morphia – it was I who killed him.'

'Good God, Hellie – I – I didn't know.' His face was appalled.

'Nobody knows, except the doctor – and Ben, of course.'

'And Ben, of course,' he echoed me. 'Why Ben, of course?'

It was a relief to talk, I had not talked for so long. 'After – after it happened, I was going to kill myself – it seemed the only thing to do. But Robbie had asked me to give Eddie's watch to Ben – Ben was the sergeant who . . .'

Conan nodded. 'Yes, I know – Letty told me.'

'So I came here first – and I said something – referring to what had happened when we were in the hospital together – there was a boy, then – so he guessed, and he stopped me.'

Conan was still looking at me as if he had never seen me before. 'And how did he stop you?'

'He made me drunk.'

Conan's blue eyes sharpened. 'Is that when . . . ?'

I understood and butted in quickly, 'No, Ben would never have done that. That was – he was trying to help me and – it was my fault.'

Conan stared at me for a long time. 'So you gave Robbie an overdose – Robbie, your own brother.'

'Yes – I killed Robbie. There was no one else to do it, you see.'

Conan sat down, and kept looking at me. Then at last he said softly, 'Poor old Hellie, poor little Hellie.'

I stood up stiffly, my legs were cramped. 'I'll put the kettle on and make you a cup of tea.'

When I came back Conan was prowling round the small room, looking very tall and slim. 'Look here, Hellie – when does your Ben come home?'

he clock. 'In an hour or so. That is, if
＿＿＿ out for a longer turn – he's a passed
＿＿＿ ee.'

＿＿onan said, 'Oh,' then raised his cup. When he put
＿ down again he told me, 'I'll wait and meet him – I'm
on my way up to Scotland for a few days, then I was
thinking of heading for Norway, to join Sam Killearn's
fishing party – but there's no rush, I can stay overnight
on the way.'

'You don't have to wait for him.'

'Hellie, I'm not leaving here until I've seen the kind
of man you're married to. Aunt Ria hates him, Letty
likes him: I want to make up my own mind.' He drained
his cup and then said, his voice light, 'Have you heard
– Juno's running a chicken farm in Cornwall, together
with that fluffy-haired blonde female, Ogden's youngest
daughter. Letty appears to have the gravest suspicions –
she's very precocious, your sister – I don't know what
on earth she reads.'

I exclaimed, 'Oh, but Juno wouldn't . . .' Then my
voice tailed off.

Conan caught my eye and laughed. 'Exactly! And I
tried to kiss that Ogden girl once in the conservatory –
just to keep in practice – and she jumped back like a
startled rabbit – it's not a reaction I usually encounter.'

I smiled a little. 'No, it wouldn't be.'

Then he began to tell me about my family. My parents
were leaving Hatton at the end of the week and going
to the Eames' shooting lodge in Yorkshire; Mother was
annoyed because Letty had announced she intended
going up to Cambridge early instead of accompanying
them. He told me Alice was in Mentone – she was
reported to be very bored with her Fred, and had been
knocking around with Jimmy Danesford again. He
retailed more gossip and I listened gratefully – I had
never realized before what a beautiful voice my cousin
had.

Ben's heavy boots pounded on the cobbles outside,

then he came in in his baggy, grimy overall and collarless striped shirt. Conan jumped to his feet in one quick, lithe movement. 'Holden, old man, I'm so glad to meet you. I'm Hellie's cousin, Conan Finlay.' He held out his hand.

Ben shook it firmly. 'How do.' He glanced at me. 'How 'ave you been today, lass?' I did not reply.

Conan continued smoothly, 'Hellie and I have just been having a good old gossip – I hope you don't mind my dropping in like this without any warning?'

'No – no, I'm right pleased to see you – she's been a bit peaky lately – she'll have been glad of company. Helena, lass – have you invited your cousin to tea?'

Tea! Conan only drank tea at teatime – he ate dinner. But I did not want him to go. 'Yes, do stay – we'll be eating soon, we eat early in Ainsclough.'

'Thanks, I will.'

Ben said, 'I'll go and have me bath then.' I began to haul myself to my feet. 'No, lass, you stay here and enjoy your chat – I'll see to veg. 'Sides, your ankles are a bit swollen – you'd best look after yourself.' He picked up the round leather pouffe and set it before me, then he knelt and raised my feet, one after the other, and placed them both on it. 'These shoes are too tight for you now, lass – I keep telling you. I fetched some flat ones for you – why don't you wear them?' I did not answer and after a moment he got heavily to his feet and clumped out into the kitchen.

Conan said pleasantly, 'Did you ever think of keeping a dog, Hellie?'

I stared at him. 'A dog – whyever should I?'

He shrugged. 'No, I suppose a dog wouldn't be so much use – besides, it might even expect a pat from time to time.' I looked at him angrily, but said nothing, and he began to talk lightly of mutual acquaintances.

Ben had prepared extra vegetables, and served himself with less meat. I toyed with mine, until he said quietly, 'Eat it up, Helena.'

'It's too tough.'

He pulled my plate over in front of him and meticulously cut up the meat into tiny pieces, then he pushed it back to me and waited. Slowly, grudgingly, I began to force it down, while Conan and my husband reminisced about the war.

When I had finished Conan lit a cigarette and told me, 'I'm going up to Argyllshire, Hellie – quite near the twins' estate. You'll know the area, of course.' I nodded; yes, I remembered that last carefree autumn of peace. 'Uncle Victor said Kintonish is in very good heart; during the war Eddie and Robbie used some of the money from their London properties to bring it up to tip-top condition.' He sighed. 'God, it's so unfair – how they would have been enjoying themselves now, if they'd only been lucky.' He gave a long pull on his cigarette and I glanced away from his drawn face, so like my brothers', and yet so unlike – and saw that Ben's eyes were fixed on me speculatively.

Conan swung round. 'Ben, old man – I'd like to see a bit more of you before I move on. Perhaps we could have a drink together this evening?'

Ben's gaze swivelled from me. 'Aye, I'd like that. I'll get changed into me best.'

Conan jumped to his feet. 'Where's the nearest telephone? I'd better warn my hosts I'll be late – I'll stay over in Carlisle tonight.'

Ben took him to the front door and gave him directions; I winced as I heard his accent deepen. But he did not go straight upstairs; instead he came back and sat down in the kitchen opposite me. 'So your brothers had property, did they? And who did they leave it to, lass?'

At last I said, 'Eddie left everything to Robbie, of course.'

'And who did Robbie leave "everything" to?' I sat there, my cheeks reddening, until he said heavily, 'You don't need to tell me – I know. I don't want your money, lass, I made that clear from start – but, well, you might

664

have trusted me.' He got to his feet and stumped slowly up the stairs.

Conan was already back by the time Ben came down. As they left Ben began to lean towards me; I kept my eyes fixed on the empty hearth. He straightened his back again, saying, 'Don't bother with washing up, lass – I'll see to it. You need a rest. Put your feet up on buffet, I've put it ready for you.' He lumbered out.

I was lying back in the armchair when they finally returned; I felt heavy and languid. Ben was staring at me intently as he came out of the lobby, but my eyes looked beyond him – to Conan, so tall and slim. My cousin came forward. 'Well, Hellie – it's time I was on my way.' He leant down, put his arm round my shoulder and bent to kiss my cheek – but I turned my face so that my lips met his and pressed my body against him; my womb was swollen and ready, and I wanted him. I sensed him trying to draw back, but I clung to him, longing for him – until a heavy hand on my shoulder jerked me roughly aside, while Conan's fingers caught at my wrists and held them stiffly away from him. My cousin stood for a moment, staring at me his hands gripping my wrists like a vice until I twisted sharply and he suddenly let them go and backed away. Ben still held me fast, and his face was a dusky red as he looked down at me – then his fingers slowly unclamped themselves from my shoulder and the two men moved towards the door. I could hear Conan's low voice, 'I'm so sorry, old man – I wouldn't have touched her if I'd thought . . .' He was apologizing – how dared he apologize? He was my cousin – surely I had the right to kiss my cousin?

When Ben came back his face was set. 'I'm going up plot – but before I go I'd best give you what you want – else happen you'll be out on streets looking for it.' He began to unbutton his trousers. 'Get your drawers down, lass, and we'll use hearthrug. It won't take me long and I'll not bother to get undressed – it won't make any difference to you.'

I looked at him, and saw he was swollen and ready for me, so I slid down on to the hearthrug and opened my legs. 'Take your drawers off, I told you.' I pulled them off and threw them aside; I hated him – but my body was already opening for him as he knelt and lifted my hips. Even as he thrust into me I was writhing and moaning, but he held me fast until he had finished. Then he got up, rebuttoned his trousers and said, 'That should satisfy you for an hour or two,' and slamming the door hard behind him, he left.

CHAPTER NINE

I lay there on the hearthrug with my skirts crumpled up around my hips; dark shapes passed in the street behind the thick lace curtains, and clogs clattered on the cobbles as children played. At last I heaved myself heavily to my feet and went upstairs to bed; at least I would not need him again today.

But it was no use. When he came in and I heard him moving about my womb began to swell, and I knew I could not lie beside him all night without demanding his body once more. Turning, I pushed my belly against him, and he grunted, 'Aye, I reckoned you'd be ready again, soon as you heard bed springs creaking. All right, lass – I can give you what you want.'

Afterwards I felt him touch my hair and I went very still. Then his face was above me in the gloom – he was going to kiss me! I flung myself round, burying my mouth in the pillow. He said roughly, 'I wonder if you'd have been using your precious "my lord" like this – after less 'an four months o' marriage.'

Anger surged up inside me and I raised my head. 'Don't you dare speak of him to me – don't you dare!'

'I reckon I'll say what I want in me own house, to me own wife. He may have had a handle to his name – but he weren't all he were cracked up to be, your precious Lord Staveley – not by a long chalk he weren't.'

I was screaming at him now. 'Don't speak of him – don't soil his name with your tongue – you, you're not fit to black his boots!'

He breathed heavily as he said, 'But I'm fit to shag his girl – which is more 'an he ever did.'

I reached out and brought my hand across his face as hard as I could. 'Because he was a gentleman!'

'Because he were a gentleman as preferred schoolboys and handsome young soldiers, more like.'

My body went rigid and my flesh turned to ice. But he was still speaking. 'No, he would have been no use to a lass like you – what needs it regular.'

I hissed, 'Get out – get out of this bed, and take your filthy lying tongue with you.'

'I'm not lying, lass – you ask your cousin – you ask Conan. He knows the truth.'

'You fool! Conan never even met Gerald.'

'No, but he had it all from your brother-in-law – he knew him all right.'

I put my hands over my ears and buried my face in the pillow – how dared he, how dared he! But my hands were wrenched away and he flung me round on to my back and held me trapped there. I struggled, but it was useless. 'I've had enough of you treating me like dirt, and never listening to a word I say because you can't tear your eyes away from that bloody photo – for once I'm going to make you listen. Lie still.' He loomed over me, his heavy leg pinning me across the thighs, his iron hands gripping my wrists so that I could not block my ears. Then he began, 'I wanted to get it right, lass, so I asked him careful – exactly what he knew. And he wanted to tell me – he said he were going to set you right hisself once, but he couldn't face it – but now he reckoned you ought to know, for your own good. It were like this, see. Your brother-in-law's brother – Charles he said he were called, Charles Knowles – he were at Sandhurst with him, with your "my lord", and there were a scandal there – it were hushed up, but they all knew about it. Then, just afore he went to South Africa, it happened again – but when war broke out it got forgotten like. When he came back he were more careful, but they all knew what he were up to, only they kept quiet about it – no washing dirty linen in public. Conan told me your Hugh said his brother wouldn't likely have told him, if it weren't that this Gerald came to stay with them – and he took a fancy to your brother-in-law, who were only a youngster at time – so his elder brother told him, to put him on his guard, like.'

No, no! As he hung above me in the darkness my numbed brain began to reason. 'It can't be true – he asked me to marry him. No man like the one you talk of would have done that.'

He answered flatly, 'He would have done if there were land and titles at stake. And well – I reckon he could have forced himself once or twice, to put a child inside you – it wouldn't have taken much with a woman like you, look how quick you fell to me.'

'No, no!'

'I'm telling truth, lass. Your brother-in-law were right worried when he heard you were engaged to him – Hugh seems to have been a decent bloke from what Conan said – he didn't know what to do – he seems to have known, even then, that – that you were a girl as needed more.' He broke off, then said, 'I didn't ask Conan how he knew that – I could see your cousin weren't going to tell. But I reckon officers' messes aren't only ones who know how to hush things up – to keep them in family.' He added quickly, 'But I'm not complaining, lass – I know you came to me unbroken, and I'm grateful for that.'

I felt as if I were slowly drowning; but still he held me prisoner, and his harsh voice would not stop. 'So

Hugh, Hugh spoke to my lord and put it to him straight, and he swore he'd play fair by you, once you was married. But then war came, and I suppose he couldn't help hisself – he'd had a steady bloke, Conan said, they were like David and Jonathan, always together, so when war came, well, that was that. So it's time you stopped mooning over him my girl, because he weren't worth it, and he were ready to play you a dirty trick.' He shifted his leg and released my wrists; I did not move. 'Best try and sleep now, lass, you've got babby to think of.'

I lay quite still – it was a great effort but I knew I had to wait until my jailor slept. When at last he did I eased myself out of the bed and crept very quietly down the stairs. And then the full horror of what he had told me flooded over me – I tried to tell myself it was not true, but, God help me, I knew in my bones that it was.

Standing in the dark parlour I stared at his photograph – I did not need a lamp to see it, the handsome features depicted there were engraved on my soul – and now I used my trained singer's memory to recall every word Gerald had said, every gesture he had made – those gestures which I had treasured and kept safe in my heart for so long. Now the images were replayed as I stood there, and I saw, as if in a cinema, one flickering episode following another as reel after reel unwound in the darkness. I saw myself on the steps at Hatton, waving goodbye to him as he left me so soon after our betrothal. I saw his small neat handwriting telling me that his return would be delayed – because he was spending the weekend in Leicestershire – with a friend. I saw Hugh's anxious face, while Alice was exclaiming in delight over my news, and I saw Hugh and Gerald coming late from the dining room that evening – Hugh's nod in my direction, and the determination on Gerald's face as he strode towards me – because he was going to force himself to kiss me, for the first time. I shut my inner eyes; I would not look any longer, but now the words began to take shape and assault my ears in the darkness – the words which would have told me, if only I had listened. His grief after Stavey's death: 'And so he became my son – the son I had never had, and never looked to have.' 'I, who was always known to be a confirmed bachelor.' And finally, his words when I had offered him the son he longed for, offered him myself, to take as he chose: 'No, Helena – no.' And the flat: 'Nature is not always so obliging.'

And the pictures began to force themselves under my lids again: Gerald, usually so cool and calm – talking animatedly – because he was talking to Edward Summerhays; Edward, who had so automatically accompanied him to hear me sing in the *Messiah* – but poor Stavey had still been alive, then – so there had been no land and titles to consider. And I saw Edward as I had last seen him in the war, leaning on Gerald's arm, the fair head bent over him so protectively. I saw them getting into the cab together and driving off; and I saw myself, waiting all day for Gerald – who did not come; because Gerald was with Edward, his lover. My heart had been wiser than my brain, and had racked me with jealousy. But I, brought up with my brothers, with Conan – seeing Papa with Lady Maud, Mother with Sir Ernest and his rivals – I had thought only of a woman – silly, foolish Helena. And yet, he had told me himself, he had spoken truly; I fought against the memory, I pressed my fingers into my ears – but it was no use, I heard them, the words I had treasured, had worshipped: 'There is not, and never has been, any woman but you. And there never will be.' And in my inner ear he spoke those words again and again, until finally they were revealed in all their jeering cruelty; for he had deceived me with the truth. My own true lover – how he must have laughed up his sleeve at my silly, childish credulity. And I began to laugh too – there in the small parlour I laughed aloud – silly, stupid Helena! Then I heard the floorboards creak in the room above me so I stifled my laughter, for my husband must not hear it; and when there was quiet again I collapsed into the armchair, giggling softly until I fell asleep.

When I woke I was stiff from sitting in the chair – but not cold because a blanket had been wrapped around me. I did not know at first what I was doing in this small strange room, but then I saw Gerald's photograph – he was looking straight at me, smiling a little – so I knew it was all right; he would come for me soon. I remembered now – I had been made a prisoner in this house in a strange dirty town – but I only had to be patient and wait – for he would come and save me.

I uncurled my cramped limbs and shook off the blanket; it had been folded so carefully round me – perhaps Gerald had come in the night and tended me? Was it like the fairy tale of the princess who was imprisoned, and her prince could only come to her after darkness fell? Yes, that must be it, for it was light now – and he had gone away – I was sure he was not in the house; but he would come back, and care for me – I knew that now. I held the coarse grey blanket to my cheek for a moment, because it had been wrapped around me in love; then I folded it neatly to put away, for it was daytime now, so I must be patient.

His eyes smiled at me from the top of the piano; I moved towards it, humming a little tune – it must be time to do my singing practice – but no, something hard and sharp caught at my memory . . . But I muffled the shining blade and turned it aside before it could touch me: I would be happy while I waited for him.

I seemed to know my way around the small house: I went straight out to the backyard – so I must have been held here in my prison for some time. In the small closet I noticed spots of blood on my drawers – and for a moment I was disturbed. Perhaps Gerald would not like me if I bled; but of course, I was not bleeding now, because I was with child – his child – it must be his child since I loved no other man. I smiled and pulled up my drawers and went back inside again.

I climbed up the stairs to dress – there was a bed, a rumpled bed, – and my eyes seemed to shy away from it – I could not bear to look at that bed, so I bundled up my clothes and took them downstairs and got dressed before the warm range. My hands knew what to do: I cleaned and tidied and swept – until I found a jacket hanging behind the door – a badly-made jacket, misshapen with wear. I touched it, puzzled for a moment – then remembered my jailor. A dark shape formed in my mind – it must be his. And of course, I must shop and cook for him – I must not let him suspect, or he would seize me and take me away again, and then Gerald would never find me. So I put on my hat and coat and picked up the basket I found and went out into the small town – the people spoke very oddly, but I seemed to understand them and know what to do.

By the time I came back up the hill I felt very tired; my body was too heavy for my legs, which dragged awkwardly. But I made myself keep moving, and cook what I had bought – everything must be ready, then perhaps Gerald would come for me today – after dark. When I had finished I went through to the small parlour to fetch his picture; I sat holding it on my lap, gazing at it, trustingly – he would come for me, when darkness had fallen.

But the sun had not even set when I heard a hand at the door – I stood up, confused – then I thought it must be him, and I ran through to the front. But the dark shape outlined in the doorway was shorter, and broader and heavier – and I gasped in fear and shrank away; it was my jailor. Turning, I stumbled back into the kitchen on shaking legs and hid my picture away.

'How are you, lass?' A hand touched my shoulder; flinching away, I turned my back and my jailor sighed. I hurried through to the scullery, thinking of my picture of Gerald – trying to remember that he was coming tonight. But it was more difficult now – the jailor had disturbed my dreams. But after he had bathed he went out, and left me in peace with my memories.

He came back again and laid the table and told me to eat my tea. I did as he bid me because otherwise he might suspect, and lock me away where Gerald could never find me – my heart trembled with fear at the thought – and in my anxiety to propitiate him I made myself smile at my jailor. It seemed to please him. 'That's better, lass – I know you were upset, but, well – we mun live together.'

Yes – of course – until Gerald came for me.

But he was speaking again. 'It's hard for you to have to accept – but in long run it's best you know truth. Anyroad, put it out of your mind now – after all, your Gerald's been dead a long time. I'll just pop out back, then we'll have an early night – I'm on first thing in morning.'

He had said Gerald was dead! No, no – he couldn't be – he was coming for me – he must – I drew the tattered shreds of my fantasy about me, and huddled beneath their fragile protection.

When my jailor came back he sent me upstairs, and brought me hot water – so I undressed and washed quickly with hands that trembled – then I climbed into the bed and hid my head under the blankets. The man got in beside me, and touched my shoulder – but I stayed quite still until I heard him sigh again and roll away.

I slept and dreamt and woke – and did not know whether I was dreaming or waking. I saw Gerald, with Edward Summerhays beside him – he was smiling down at Edward in the church at Hammersmith. And I saw Gerald again, leaning over Edward as they came down the steps of the hospital together – looking at him as a man looks at his beloved – and they climbed into a cab and drove away, leaving me desolate.

When I awoke at last I knew that I was no longer dreaming; and I knew that Gerald was dead – and that, living, he had never loved me.

I pulled myself up out of the bed; I was alone. I felt very sick and ill because I was carrying another man's child in my womb. I dragged myself downstairs and found the picture of Gerald in its hiding place. I swayed as I looked down at it for the last time, then raised my arm and threw it with all my strength at the hard iron range. The glass shattered and splintered in its silver frame and I felt wild anger flare up and consume me as I screamed again and again: 'I hate you, I hate you, I hate you!'

Then the flame died down, and went out – and there were only dead ashes in my heart. I had lost my love more than five years ago – but always I had carried his dream in my heart; now my dream was dead too. I knelt down on the coarse rag hearthrug and began to pick up the tiny slivers of glass, one by one.

Chapter Ten

That day I performed my morning tasks, just as I always did; I had a house to clean and a husband to be fed – and I was carrying his child; that was why I felt so ill. But every so often I would come to myself, my hands motionless in the sink or on the broom handle, and realize that I had been waiting for Gerald – still sure he would come. And as I was shaking the mat I thought, I must tell the twins about that – and only afterwards did I remember that they were both dead. My heartbeat quickened with fear, for I knew now that all yesterday I had lived in a dream – my mind had escaped to wander in a world of its own – I had become accustomed to sending it there deliberately, and now it kept slipping away from me as I forgot where I was and what I was doing.

I made myself a cup of tea and sat down and drank it very hot – it seemed to help me. But later, while I was dusting the piano, I began to talk to Robbie – I was laughing with him, I knew he was there beside me – but when I turned he had vanished. Now I was very frightened, and although I felt so heavy and ill I stumbled through to the kitchen and found my basket, and dragged myself upstairs for my coat and hat – I would walk down to the town, to the market – with people around me surely I would be able to grasp what was real and hold on to it?

But I found myself standing by the fish stall with a clammy parcel in my hand – and did not know how it had got there. I whispered, 'Did I – have I paid?'

The fishmonger looked up in surprise. 'Aye, missus – but tha can pay again if tha wishes.' His teeth gleamed a moment as his swift knife filleted another herring. I turned quickly away and my ankle gave under me and I stumbled – I felt sick and shaken. And when I got back there was blood again in my drawers and the sight of it confused me – but it was only spots; perhaps my eyes were deceiving me, like my brain.

It was lunchtime when he came back; his boots sounded heavy on the parlour floor and he came into the kitchen, solid and smelling of sweat – so I knew he, at least, was real. 'Are you feeling better today, lass?' My tongue would not work, but I managed to nod in reply. 'Good, good.'

Listening to him splashing in the scullery steadied me a little. I watched him go out to the closet, real and substantial – and as he came back he paused and reached up to the wall – there was a cat perched there – a ginger cat. It arched its back as he stroked it, and seeing them together reminded me – I remembered the kitchen at Étaples: this was the man who had brought me the cat, because I was so frightened of rats. He was a kind man – quick to anger, but kind. He would help me. I stood there, waiting, and as he came in, my eyes sought his and he looked back at me, anxious and pleading. I wanted so much to speak, to bridge the gulf between us and so ease my desolation – but the words stuck in my throat and I was dumb. As I turned away to pick up the plates I saw the disappointment in his face. But I was dumb.

After we had eaten he followed me into the small scullery and began to help me wash up – but he was too big, he got in my way and I became tense and impatient. Putting down the glass cloth he went to the doorway and said, 'I'll not bother you any longer – I'll go up plot. You sit down and have a rest.' I heard the bang of the front door – and I was alone again.

He came back at teatime. I laid the table, then we sat facing each other, eating and drinking, and nothing was said until he got up at the end. 'Come and sit down in parlour – I'll see to pots meself, later.' I followed him into the small front room and we sat down opposite each other, either side of the empty hearth. He cleared his throat several times before he began to speak. 'Lass, I'm sorry about way I told you t'other night – I shouldn't have used language I did. But I lose me temper when I get jealous, and seeing you throw yourself at Conan way you did – I were that angry.' I looked down at my hands; I still could not speak. He went on heavily, 'After all, you're me wife, you're carrying my child – you didn't ought to touch other men – I've got right to keep you from them.'

Yes, he was still my jailor, and there was no one to rescue me now. Gerald was dead, and my brothers were dead, both of them. Although it was too early I stood up and went upstairs; I took off my clothes and washed, then climbed into bed. As I lay there Gerald's face danced under my closed lids – behind him was the blue sky at Eton and he smiled at me and teased me and spoke kindly to me; I was a girl again and I loved him – Lord Gerald, my handsome hero. But as I smiled back at him his expression changed, his mouth twisted and he was jeering at me from a face grown distorted and ugly. I felt the tears damp on my cheeks as I whispered aloud, 'Oh God, you took him from me in life – was that not bereavement enough? Why did you have to take him from me in death as well?'

And as I lay there my brothers came to me and comforted me with their dark eyes so loving and loyal – and I knew that they, at least, would never betray me. Then Eddie faded – but Robbie was still with me – Robbie who loved me and smiled at me so warmly. But as I looked up into his beloved face my hand rose, and it held a syringe – and I seized his arm and held him tight so he could not escape and pointed the needle and drove it hard into him and pushed down the plunger as far as it would go. And all the time his eyes smiled at me in love – until the syringe was empty and then, very slowly, his jaw sagged and his eyes closed – and I was alone. I knew now why God had punished me so.

An eye for an eye, a tooth for a tooth, a life for a life – a death for a death. But I had been a coward and not paid that final price. The man who was moving about in the house below, whose heavy footsteps were even now on the stairs – he had stopped me. As he came into the room I flung myself forward and cried, 'You should not have stopped me – you were wrong to stop me!'

His face was angry. 'Of course I stopped you – you're me wife – am I supposed to watch you with another man and stand by and do nothing – and you carrying my child in your belly?'

He did not understand and I fell back and closed my eyes. But as his heavy body climbed in beside me I realized he had given me the answer: I was paying the price – not with death but with life. I had given death, but in a few months I would give life – that was why I had gone running to this man, so that he would put a child into my body and let me pay the price that way. And as he had done, so he would do again, and year after year I would pay my debt, here in this small alien town. I closed my eyes and lay still beside him until he slept.

By the time I awoke in the morning he had gone; and I was calmer. I felt very tired and ill, but that was to be my restitution; I had killed Robbie, but if God would let me pay my debt in this way, then it was only right and proper that I should suffer. When I stood up, my womb tugged at my belly and dragged me down; my back seemed to be breaking in two. But I pulled myself up straight – as straight as I had been when I had worn the back harness in the schoolroom at Hatton, long ago. I had a debt to pay, a punishment to be endured – I would not show weakness.

But on the last step, when my ankle gave way under me and my foot twisted and threw me forwards, so that I had to cling shaking to the rail, then I was frightened – and remembered the neglected flat shoes upstairs; but I still could not bring myself to wear them. I shared his bed and carried his child, but I would not wear his shoes, though I moved so clumsily about the small rooms as I swept and dusted and cleaned and tidied. Then I put on my hat and coat and picked up my basket and went out to do my shopping. My ankle hurt, but I put my foot down firmly; I would not limp. Instead I would walk with my back straight and my chin held high – just as once I had walked towards my king in his palace, the three ostrich feathers bobbing on my head and my long train heavy behind me.

But as I began to climb up the steep slope of Royds Street a child ran out of a doorway and collided with me so that I stumbled. And as my whole weight came down on that foot my ankle twisted again – I threw myself back but it was no use, my balance had gone – I swayed and then went flying forward until I hit the hard grey flags – full on my belly.

I lay dazed on the ground with two women bending over me. They helped me gently to my feet. 'Are you all right, lass – are you all right?'

As they dusted me down and retrieved my spilled groceries I whispered, 'Yes – yes – I'm quite all right.' But I was not. The fall had jarred every bone in my body – I felt so sick and ill and shaken. They brought out a chair and offered me a drink of tea but I refused both – I wanted to get back, back to my refuge, and despite my weak ankle and trembling legs I almost ran up the street.

When I reached my own front door I fumbled with the key – I could barely turn it – the latch was almost too heavy for me to lift. My hands struggled to unfasten my coat and back in the warm kitchen I slumped down into the rocking chair, shivering. I made myself take deep slow breaths, trying to be calm – telling myself I was only shaken – I would soon be over it; but then I felt the warm blood begin to seep out of my body and trickle down my legs – and now I was very frightened.

I eased myself very slowly to my feet, and moved like an old woman to the linen cupboard. I took out one of the towels and wrapped it round my belly and between my legs and told myself that if I sat very still, then it would stop. But it did not. And soon the cramps began – I was gasping with pain and fear – they were worse than I had ever known; they seized my belly like a giant hand and squeezed it relentlessly until I had to drive my nails into the palms of my hands to stop myself screaming aloud. They came and took my body over and wrung it until the blood gushed from between my legs and the towel became sodden and heavy. I crouched in my chair while they squeezed my womb dry, and then I knew I was with child no longer.

I could not move; I sat huddled in that chair as the clock ticked on and the high-pitched voices of children called to each other in the yard next door. But at last the door opened and he said, 'Sorry I'm late, lass – I had a driving turn.' He was shrugging off his jacket and rooting in his pockets as he turned and saw me. 'Having a rest, lass – that's right.' Then his face changed. 'Helena

– what's happened?' I looked up at him, I still could not speak; then he fell on his knees in front of me and touched my bloody skirt. 'Oh Christ! What happened – Helena – you must tell me.'

At last I replied, very slowly, 'I fell, I fell in the street.'

'I mun fetch doctor.'

'No – no!'

'Helena, I must.' I stared down at my sodden skirt – how could I let a strange man see me like this? Then he understood. 'I'll get Mrs Ingham t'come in, and clean you up.'

I shrank back – Mrs Ingham – whose children were even now calling to her in the yard outside. 'No – no!' It was all I could say.

He looked at me steadily. 'All right, lass. I'll put kettle on – top up water from range.' I wondered what he meant – then I saw that he was filling the bowl himself, fetching the soap, the flannel – and a clean towel. Now I could not even say no as he knelt down before me and lifted my skirt. And as he had put the child inside me, so now he was taking it out. I closed my eyes as his hands moved, unwinding the towel. 'I'll put this to soak in pail – but – I remember our Ada once – ' He was fumbling with china, I heard the chink of it. Then his hands were on me again as he mopped and wiped and cleansed.

When he had finished he went upstairs and found my belt and eased it on me, and fastened a clean dry pad between my legs. He muttered, 'That might not be enough – you're still bleeding badly,' and I felt him raise my hips and wrap a warm towel around me. Then he lifted me out of the chair and carried me up the stairs. In the small bedroom he took off the rest of my clothes, dressed me in a clean nightgown and laid me down on the bed. Tucking me firmly in, he said, 'I'm going for doctor now.'

The doctor was grey-haired, with tired, red-veined eyes; I cringed from his probing hands. When he had finished he sat down on the bed and said, 'I think it's all come away, missus – your husband showed me downstairs. Now, lass, I know women get upset at a time like this, but there's only one cure. You must start thinking about the next child – don't leave it too long. I've told your man – as soon as the bleeding stops. Then you'll have something to look forward to again.' I turned my face away and his voice was tinged with impatience as he told me, 'It happens often enough, there's nothing unusual about it.' He repeated, 'It happens – especially when a woman's carrying two.'

And now I heard him. 'Two – you mean, twins? I was carrying twins?'

'Aye, that's right.'

He picked up his bag and turned to go. I had to ask him, I had to know – but of course, I knew already – oh yes, I knew what I had done. 'What were they? What were they?'

He paused in the doorway and looked at me a moment, then said, 'Boys, both boys.' And clumped off down the stairs.

So I knew just what I had done. In my foolish pride I had worn my fine heeled shoes and made myself walk upright – and I had stumbled and fallen and killed my babies before they were even born. I had not paid my debt – no, instead I had killed my brothers again.

Ben Holden's head peered round the door. 'He's gone lass – he said as how – well, I reckon he told you same as me.'

'Where are they?'

He looked at me, puzzled. 'Where are what?'

'My twins, my twin babies.'

'I've cleaned up – then I threw it all on range.'

I screamed at him, 'You burnt them, you burnt them! You could at least have given them burial – you know where the grave is, you know!' He came towards me, his face a mask of horror – I thought he would touch me, so I stopped my scream, I stopped it, and lay still

681

and closed my eyes against him. When I felt his hand on my shoulder I struck it away, crying, 'Get out, get out!' over and over again, until he went.

CHAPTER ELEVEN

I lay unmoving on the bed as the blood trickled out of my empty womb; God had not accepted my payment. He was a jealous God; he would allow no restitution – no giving of life in return for death. Only a death for a death. I had failed to pay with my own life and so now I had killed again – my two dead babies. He had exacted vengeance because I had been a coward; I must be a coward no longer.

But I heard a heavy tread on the stairs, and Ben Holden came into the room, carrying a tray. As he set it down beside the bed I turned my head away. 'No, lass, you mun eat.' I did not move. 'I'm staying here, and if you won't eat it yourself, then I'll feed you. But you will eat, I'll make sure of that.' So I pulled myself up and let him put the tray on my lap; then I picked up the spoon and began to swallow the broth. 'It's Mrs Ingham's making – I've bin to have a chat with her and she's willing to come and oblige while you're laid up. Mebbe you'll be better with a woman about at a time like this.' Reaching out his hand he rested it on my hair a moment; I shrank away from him.

I ate while he was watching me – I had no choice – but as soon as I had finished I pushed the tray from me and closed my eyes – to make him go away. But once the door closed behind him I began to shift restlessly on my pillow because I knew I could not die while I was with this man; he would stop me now just as he had stopped me before. I must wait.

For three days I lay on my bed, waiting. The woman came in with food and spoke to me; I answered her, but I saw she was ill at ease, nervous of my manner and way of speaking, so when I dismissed her she went, and did not stay to make me eat. As soon as I heard the front door close behind her I crept downstairs on my shaking legs and threw the food on the range. But when he came back he made me eat, so I knew I could not die here. Besides, he was a strong man, a vigorous man; when he thought the time was right he would come to me again and put another child inside me, so that I could not die. I had to go soon.

On the fourth day I sent the woman away, and got up while he was still at work. I dressed myself in my best clothes and took the money I had kept safe in my dressing case – Robbie's money, my brother's last gift to me – then I climbed slowly down the stairs already wearing my hat and coat. But I knew I had to be careful and cunning – he was a determined man, if he guessed the truth he would come after me – I must prevent that. So I took a piece of paper from my writing case and wrote on it: 'I have gone away with Conan.' I looked at it, hesitating, but I had to be sure, so I added, in large clear letters: 'I love him.' And I put my message on the table, where he would see it as soon as he came in.

Then I left the small house, walked down the cobbled street and through the grimy town until I came to the station; there I sat down and waited for the train to Manchester.

Mr Shepherd came out of his office at Hareford. 'My lady, were you expected? The family are all away and no one has come to meet you. Shall I telephone the Hall?'

'Thank you – please tell them to send a groom with the governess cart – that will do.'

It was a young groom; I did not know him. I climbed very slowly into the governess cart, Mr Shepherd's hand below my elbow. As the boy picked up the reins I told him, 'To Lostherne first, to the church.'

He drew up in front of the lych gate and helped me out. I walked on my unsteady legs up between the graves until I came to the one I knew so well. I stood before the white stone with the two beloved names carved on it and told them, 'Not long now, my brothers – I will come to you soon.' I had delayed too long already. And the breeze on the hillside ruffled my hair and caressed my cheek as I smiled at the stone and whispered, 'I will not keep you waiting.' Then I walked back to the governess cart and was driven home, to Hatton.

Cooper met me at the door. I said, 'I have been ill, I need to rest. I will take all my meals in my room, thank you.' He stepped aside and I walked with my back held straight up the wide staircase; I would not walk down it again.

They brought me my meals, and as soon as the maid had gone I crept along to the housemaid's pantry and flushed them all away. I would defeat my body at last. But on the second day I was careless – the girl came in as I was finishing – I walked past her without speaking, my face averted, but I was frightened. It was Mrs Hill herself who came up with my dinner tray; she said Cook had prepared a special soup for me but she was not sure if it was well-enough seasoned – would I try a little now? I knew I must not betray myself so I picked up the spoon and swallowed the soup and she stood there, watching me, until I had drunk most of the bowlful, then at last she went away. I waited while her footsteps receded, then stole out to my pantry. When I came back the tray by my bedside seemed to have moved a little – I was nervous – but then I decided it was only a trick of the light and climbed once more into my bed.

As I dozed through the next morning I heard the door opening, and Mrs Hill came in again – with Letty. My sister came to my bed and looked down at me. 'Hello, Hellie – how are you?' I did not reply and after a moment she turned to the housekeeper and said, 'Yes, Mrs Hill – you and Mr Cooper were quite right to phone me. You may go now.' Letty moved closer and spoke again: 'What are you doing here, Helena, at Hatton?' When I did not answer she asked again, 'What are you doing here?' Her steady gaze held mine.

At last I answered, 'I'm resting.'

'Why? Have you been ill?' I turned my face away but she persisted. 'You do look ill, Helena – I wonder what's wrong with you?' It was not long before she inquired, 'Are you expecting a child?' I could not keep my face expressionless and when she asked again, 'Are you expecting a child, Helena?' I felt the tears of weakness on my cheeks.

'Not any longer, not any longer,' and I closed my eyes.

'I'm sorry.' But still she would not leave me in peace. 'Did Ben send you here?' When I did not reply she answered herself. 'But no, he would have brought you himself, and Cooper told me you came alone.' I looked up and saw that she was reasoning, she was thinking – my clever, logical sister. She drew up a chair and sat down in it, making herself comfortable, like one who intends to stay – I hated her. 'And Ben has not been to see you, not even written – that's strange, Helena, very strange, because he loves you. So I wonder why not?'

I closed my eyes against her, but she was merciless. 'I'm sure he would not have stayed away – unless ' – her fingers seized my wrist – 'What did you write in your note, Helena? The note you must have left for him.' I pressed my lips tightly together but her nails bit into my flesh and her voice was tireless, inexorable. 'Tell me, Helena – what did you write? Tell me.' She asked over and over again until at last I told her.

Then she stood up and said, 'Conan's in Norway, he went last week. But I don't think you came here to find Conan.' She left me shaking in my bed, and when she came back in the afternoon she had Ben with her. When

I saw him I turned and buried my face in the pillow; my whole body jerked with shudders. I heard his voice: 'Lass, lass – what have I done to you, what have I done to you?'

Letty's reply rang clear and firm. 'Nobody has done anything to her, Ben, what she has done she has done herself. They should be here by teatime – I telegraphed this morning.' She left, but I knew he was still there, sitting in the room, watching me – but I shut my mind against him; I had a duty to perform.

Then it was my mother's voice that spoke. 'Helena, wake up!' I dared not disobey. 'Why will you not eat, Helena?' Her dark eyes were hard, demanding the truth – and at last I told it.

'Because I killed my babies.'

'Don't be silly, Helena – you miscarried. They were not even formed yet, it was too early.'

She did not understand. My babies were formed, they were beautiful. They had lain on Nanny's lap, wrapped in fleecy white, and I had seen their small round faces – two in one and one in two – and Ena had lifted me up so I could lean over and kiss them. Mine, all mine. And now I had killed them. Twice I had killed them.

But she would not let me be; she repeated over and over again, 'Why will you not eat, Helena? Why will you not eat?' until I could bear her anger no longer and cried aloud in my despair, 'Because I must die!'

There was silence in the room – my eyes lighted on each figure in turn. Ben sat in his chair, his face in his hands, his shoulders shaking – I knew I had nothing to fear from him. My father stood beside him, his face ashen and shocked – he could not meet my eye; Papa had always been a coward – good. My eyes moved on – and checked; it was the women, the women I had to fear. They stood tall and strong at the foot of my bed and looked straight back at me – their level gaze did not drop. I turned desperately from pale blue to dark brown and back again – neither pair of eyes wavered; and now I was frightened. It was I who looked away.

'A nursing home – they will know how to make her eat.' Mother's voice was inflexible.

Letty nodded in agreement. 'Yes, they will.'

Mother began to move towards the door. 'There's a place in Surrey – I will phone at once.'

'No, Mother, not Surrey.' My mother drew breath sharply. Letty's hand gestured towards Ben's huddled shape. 'She has a husband – it must be Manchester.'

'Surrey.'

'Manchester.'

The two pairs of eyes locked; it was the brown which gave way. 'Manchester.'

Two men came, wearing white coats. They lifted me up and rolled me on to a stretcher; as I had so often done to others. Then I was carried down the wide staircase and out into the darkness. A nurse sat in the back of the ambulance with me, her cap white and starched as mine had once been.

It was not a long journey. They carried me out again and up another flight of stairs and into a high white room. Another nurse came forward and helped to lift me from the stretcher; as I had done in my turn. My mother spoke, their starched caps dipped in assent, then they turned and looked at me: compassionate but passionless. One said, 'She will eat.' And her eyes were the eyes of Sister Foldus and all the sisters I had known – sisters who would not willingly let their patients die – sisters who would fight, and win, and defeat me.

The slow tears oozed from under my lids as they washed me and dried me and combed my hair and plaited it. Then one came to me with the feeding cup and said: 'Drink.' I turned my face away. She spoke quite quietly: 'If you do not drink doctor will sedate you, and we will pass a tube through your nose and pour food into your stomach. Then we will empty your bowels and insert nutrient enemas, too – so you see, you have no choice.' And I, whose hands had passed those tubes, whose fingers had put food into the bowels of others, I knew she spoke the truth – so I drank.

The next day my mother came. 'Why, Helena, why?' Her eyes bored into mine.

'Because I killed my babies.'

'Why do you keep saying that, Helena? Of course it is nonsense – women often lose children in the womb – it has happened to many of us.'

'I killed my twins, my brothers. I killed my brothers.'

Her eyes narrowed as she raised the long ebony cigarette holder to her lips. She drew in the smoke, then repeated, 'You killed your brothers? But that too is nonsense, Helena. Victor and I were both there with you when Eddie died – we were there, beside you.' I stared up at her. 'And Robbie – they told us afterwards, Robbie had been dying for months – that at the end he was lucky to go so quickly.' She looked down at me for a long time, her cigarette forgotten in her hand, then said, 'But it wasn't luck, was it Helena?' And read the answer in my face.

And then, at last, I understood; I had been wrong – God was far-off and remote – it was not to God that I owed my debt; it was to this woman. 'Man that is born of a woman hath but a short time to live, and is full of misery. He cometh up and is cut down, like a flower.' Born of a woman – and I had cut him down. This woman, who stood so straight and terrible before me: she had carried Robbie for nine long months in her womb, and had laboured to give him birth. So it was she who had the right of judgement over me – and she who would exact vengeance.

I looked up into her stern dark eyes and made my confession. 'No, Mother – it was not luck. I killed him. I killed your son.' And then I lay silent, waiting for my sentence.

She moved away from me, and I heard her address me from near the high narrow window: her voice was very clear. 'Helena, I always thought you were weak – too timid, too yielding, to be my daughter – but now I see how wrong I was, how terribly, foolishly wrong.' She turned from the window and came and stood at the foot of my bed; her eyes found mine and held them, so that I could not look away as she pronounced her judgement. 'Helena, he was my son – I gave him life.' I lay waiting, far beyond hope. Her voice was strong and unflinching: 'And if he had come to me in his agony and begged for death – than I would have given him that also.' I saw her face soften with compassion, and she leant over the bed and took my cold hands in hers. 'But he did not come to me, it was you he came to in his pain and suffering – and you gave him the gift he craved. I thank you, my daughter, I thank you.' I felt her hand rest on my cheek for a moment – then, with a soft rustle of skirts, she was gone.

As I lay in my high white bed I heard again her words of absolution. Then I turned my cheek into the pillow and whispered aloud, 'And I thank you, my mother – I thank you.' Then I fell asleep.

The next day she came again. 'I am sending to you a man who will help you, Helena. You must do as he says.'

'Yes, Mother.'

He was tall and thin and stooping, with a long pale face and sparse grey hair. He sat by my bedside and said, 'Tell me about the war, Lady Helena – tell me what you did in the war. I want to know all of it.' His clear light eyes fixed on mine, and his voice was low and even – so my lips moved and I began to tell him what I had done in the war. The stench of the East London in autumn, the staring frightened eyes – the pus, the blood and the fear. The days when Gerald came home and betrayed me in my innocence. The pathetic bobbing stumps I had held, the wounds I had probed as men lay sweating under my hurting hands. The bodies I had laid out. Eddie, babbling in his delirium as he lay dying –

but there was no time to grieve. The Somme days – the reek of the battlefield as convoy after convoy brought in its burden of torn bodies and mutilated limbs. The men without feet, the men without hands, the men without faces, and the men with raw holes between their legs where their genitals had been blown away. And I had nursed them all – and learnt to smile at them, every one.

The blackened frostbitten feet of the men in Rouen; the gasping, choking sound of men drowning in their own lungs. Conan, weeping on my lap in the small hotel. Then those slimy green legs I had clutched to my chest as the surgeon's saw crunched through the bone while stretcher after bloodstained stretcher was carried into the small theatre hut at Étaples. My feet, slipping and sliding in the pus and blood as I moved from table to table in an endless desperate fight against death.

More men, tired and mudstained, soiled with their own excrement, men weary and weeping, men at the end of their tether and far, far beyond. Their pitiful, frightened faces as the bombs dropped – my own body rigid with fear as it huddled in the slit trenches while the enemy flew above. I heard my voice in the gas marquee again – singing, singing – as I pulled apart the seared eyelids and dropped liquid on to sightless, staring eyeballs. The war ended, but mine did not; the men still died, blue faces vomiting up their own lungs as the flu destroyed the survivors. And last of all, my brother, my own brother, choking and crying in my arms – until at last I reached for the syringe and plunged in the needle, and rubbed his arm with my palm and whispered, 'It's all right, Robbie – not much longer now, little brother.'

Then the man stood up and leant over me and touched my face as he said, 'But there is time now, my child – now there is time to grieve.' And I knew he spoke the truth and I began to weep. I cried and slept and woke to cry again. I wept as they cleansed my body, I wept as they fed me, I wept as they washed my hair and laid it out on the pillow to dry – and I wept as they held me over the bed pan. Ben Holden came – I saw him through eyes blurred with tears, and still I wept on.

Then, one day, the man came again, and his pale eyes held mine as he told me, 'You have wept enough – now sleep.' So I closed my swollen lids and slept. I slept as they washed me and made my bed. They woke me to eat and I swallowed in a daze; they held me over the bed pan and I was asleep by the time they lifted me off. I woke for a moment and saw Ben Holden, through sleep-blurred eyes, and heard him murmur, 'Sleep, my Helena – sleep, sweetheart,' and I closed my eyes and slept again.

PART VII

DECEMBER 1920
to
JANUARY 1922

CHAPTER ONE

But one day I woke up.

The wall was white and empty in front of my eyes, so I turned my head a little and looked through the high window at the pale-blue sky outside. Grey wisps of cloud chased each other, like children playing tag – it must be windy today. The nurses sat me up to eat my breakfast and it was good to be sitting up and looking around me. The brass fender glinted in the light from the fire, and I smiled at the flames leaping and dancing behind it as I rested against the pillows, waiting. That morning Ben came.

He wore his best serge suit and his round black toecaps shone with polishing. His shirt was white and crisp, but his brown hair had ruffled a little where he had pulled off his cap too quickly, and he was panting slightly. He pulled up a chair and sat down at the foot of the bed. 'How are you today, lass?'

Smiling I said, 'Better, Ben – I'm feeling better today.'

He smiled back at me. 'Aye, I can see that – you've woken up.'

I nodded, slowly, because I had not long left my dreams. Then I asked, 'What will you be doing today, Ben?'

'I'm on at one, lass – that's why I came so early. I'll likely be doing a shunting turn at Sykes today. I won't complain if I am – I had a rough shift yesterday, driving the banker up to Haslam. Boiler were overdue for a wash-out, so we had to keep opening draincocks and shutting regulator – just when we needed steam to get up bank.'

'Did you get up the bank?'

'Oh aye – we got her up at finish – with a bit of cursing and swearing!'

We sat and looked at each other, then I asked, 'How long have I been here, Ben?'

'More'n two months now, lass – it'll be Christmas 'afore very long.'

'Christmas – I wonder if it will snow?' I smiled. 'I do hope it snows, just once.'

'Aye, happen it will.'

We sat in silence for a while; he held his cap between his knees and his blue-grey eyes never left my face. Then he stood up slowly. 'I mun be going now, lass – take care of yourself. I'll come again tomorrow.' He moved to the doorway, pausing to look back at me again. 'I love you, Helena.' Then he was gone.

I snuggled down in the warm bed and thought of this man whom I had abused and misused, humiliated and lied to – yet who still loved me.

That afternoon the nurse came in smiling. 'You have another visitor my lady – your cousin, Mr Finlay.'

Conan strolled in, tall and lithe; drawing up a chair to the foot of my bed he placed his cane and his hat and his gloves beside it on the carpet and sat down saying, 'How are you, Hellie?'

'Better, Conan – I'm feeling better today.'

Crossing one elegant grey-trousered knee over the other he drew out his gold cigarette case. 'Good – but I knew you must be, because they wouldn't let me past your door when I called before.' His bright blue eyes watched me as he lit his cigarette. 'You've had a rough time, Hellie.' He inhaled and blew out a circle of smoke and watched as it rose to the ceiling. Then he looked back at me and said quietly, 'Hellie, there's something I must tell you. I've never told anyone else except Aunt Ria, but now I must tell you.' I waited while be blew another perfect ring – but this one wavered and vanished almost at once. He shrugged his shoulders and leant

696

back in the chair. 'Hellie, do you remember the spring of '17 – when I came to see you in Rouen?'

'Yes – just before you were shot down.'

'No, Hellie – I wasn't shot down. They shot at me – even did some damage – but they didn't shoot me down. I came down of my own accord, on the wrong side of the line. I daresay I could have got back – the machine was still handling – but I didn't even try. So I landed on the Boche side. I destroyed my papers, set fire to my plane, then I sat on a log in a corner of the field, waiting for their cavalry to come and find me. And only when I heard the jingle of their spurs and saw that cluster of field-grey uniforms did I move – and then it was towards them.' He fell silent, his eyes looking past me, staring at the blank wall.

I whispered, 'I'm glad you did, Conan – I'm glad you did.'

He gave a sudden snort of laughter and turned to me, his mouth curving. 'So am I Hellie, so am I – I've never regretted it, not for one minute. But it was the act of a coward, for all that. I was at the end of my tether, so I gave up.'

'You weren't alone – lots of men were ready to give up. Why, even Ben – when they brought him into the hospital after Cambrai – he was ready to give up too.'

Conan looked at me. 'But he didn't, did he? He went back.'

'He had no choice – they sent him back.'

'Maybe – but he didn't have to go back and fight like a ruddy hero – that was his choice, Hellie.'

His choice – and I knew now exactly when he had made it; in the crowded YMCA hut at Étaples, sitting at the table with Juno and myself, assuring me: 'Don't you worry, Sister, we'll keep you safe – we'll hold them back somehow – you'll see.' And he had. Conan was speaking again: 'And you went on to the end, Hellie, too. No one made you, you were a volunteer, but you

697

went on to the end, and beyond. You were braver than I was.'

'But – it wasn't the same – I was a nurse – in any case, it doesn't matter now.'

I could hardly hear his reply. 'I think it does, Hellie – I think it does.' I saw him bracing himself, then he told me, 'Hellie, if I had been with you that night when Robbie – when Robbie asked to die – I could not have helped you – I could not have done what you did.' And as I gazed into his serious blue eyes I knew that he spoke the truth.

He turned away from me, and his hands shook as he lit another cigarette. When it was drawing he looked up again, then said abruptly, 'Robbie knew.'

I repeated, bewildered, 'Robbie knew? What did Robbie know?'

'He knew how Ben Holden felt about you – Ben told me himself. I've seen your husband while you've been in here, Hellie – we had a drink together one evening. It was then he told me Robbie had known how he felt – Robbie challenged him point blank.'

My heart was thudding. 'Conan, please tell me – what did Robbie say?'

Conan stood up and began to pace the room, waving his cigarette. 'Once, when Ben came to see Robbie at Hatton, you were out – and Ben, well he must have asked after you – so Robbie just looked at him and said: "You think a lot of my sister, don't you, Holden?" And Ben replied, like the perfect sergeant-major he was: "Yes sir – I worship every square inch of the soil she walks on." '

'And what did Robbie say then?'

'Apparently he said he couldn't hold out much hope for him – but that he was glad Ben felt as he did. Well, he would, wouldn't he? What else could he have said?'

But I remembered Ben's last visit to Robbie – when Robbie had known he was dying. My brother had sent me with Ben, to walk part of the way to the station with him; he had sent me out with a man he knew cared for me deeply – a man whom Robbie had learnt to trust completely in France; a man who would help me. And again, I remembered my brother's voice as he held out Eddie's watch: 'You take it, Hellie, and see it gets delivered.' Delivered to Ben, so he would know – and come to me in my need. My brother, my little brother. And you knew that Ben loved me – and told him you were glad.

Conan spoke sharply. 'You're not going to sleep again, are you, Hellie?'

'No – no, I was just thinking. But, Conan, why did Robbie ever ask that question of Ben in the first place? How could he have guessed anything so – so – unlikely?'

Conan smiled. 'Why should it be so unlikely that a man should love you, Hellie? After all, you're very lovable.' Then he came to the bed and bent over me, and his blue eyes held mine as he said, 'I love you, Helena.' But as I watched his face his eyes became bleak and empty and he quickly kissed me on the cheek and left. His kiss had been a cousin's kiss – but his voice as he had said, 'I love you' had not been the voice of a cousin.

After he had gone I lay in the twilight and wept. Now I was awake again the memories came flooding back – and all the nerves in my body were raw and sensitive. The war had taken my brothers, as it had taken Lance and Hugh and so many, many men; and it had mutilated so many others – even those like Conan and Guy who were physically unmarked, were scarred inside themselves, as I was too. And the wound that Gerald had inflicted was still fresh and gaping – he had been my hero, my ideal – I had loved him with all my being. When I had lost him, I had lived with that loss for the sake of the love which had been – but now I knew there had been no love, only a mocking sham. And that knowledge had scourged my heart once more, causing new injuries that would never heal – I would not love again; my life stretched before me, bleak and hopeless. So I lay in the twilight and wept.

The nurse rustled in. 'Dear me, crying again? We won't let Mr Finlay in, in future, if this is the effect he has on you – and you were so nice and cheery after your husband had been. Come along now, it's time for your tea. And if you're a good girl and stop this crying, doctor will let you sit out in the armchair tomorrow – won't that be nice?'

When I woke in the morning I felt empty and sad – I did not really want to get up and sit in the armchair but I was too weak to protest, so I let them help me up. When I sat down my legs were trembling with the effort of it – yet I felt a small tremor of satisfaction – I had been in my bed for so long, and now I was out of it at last.

As Ben came through the door his face lit up, seeing me sitting there in my armchair – and for a moment his open pleasure warmed me, so I held out my hand to him and he came forward and took it – cradling it gently in both of his, touching my skin as though it were made of the most delicate porcelain. His hands were warm and strong so I curled my fingers round his broad ones and smiled up at him – and suddenly he fell down on his knees in front of me and buried his face in my lap. I gently stroked his hair, remembering how I had done the same in the long grey ward at Étaples. I was his wife now and he loved me – but my heart was empty, I would never love again. Poor Ben.

At last he sat back on his heels, and taking his handkerchief out of his pocket he dried his damp cheeks; then he pulled up a chair and sat down beside me, asking, 'How are you today, lass?'

'Better, Ben – better.' And I saw there were still tears in his eyes so I inquired, 'What will you be doing this afternoon, Ben?'

He took a deep breath, but his voice was steady as he

told me, 'Foreman said yesterday as how he'd likely put me on Pilley Bob.'

'With Pilley Bob – who's Pilley Bob?'

He smiled, 'Nay lass – on it – it's rail motor to Pilley. They like a passed fireman to fire rail motor, so's driver can leave him to it when he drives from t'other end. It's a nice simple job – report at station half an hour afore it's due to leave, go on shed to get coal, then relieved at end to the minute. You know where you are and when you're finishing, when you're on rail motor. But I wouldn't fancy it all time – I'd get bored.'

I liked to hear him speak – people had spoken to me softly and gently for so long, because I had been an invalid; now it was good to hear a strong loud voice in that high white room. I looked at him – he was the world outside, and for a moment I wanted to reach out and touch it – but then I was frightened and let my eyelids droop once more. He stood up. 'I'm tiring you lass – I'd best go.' I felt his hand touch my hair and then heard the door close firmly behind him. The nurses came in soon after. 'It's time you were back in bed, my lady.' I swayed against them as they helped me back under the white covers. The world outside the windows was dark and threatening.

They got me up regularly now, and one day I walked between them to the bathroom; I was growing stronger. As the days passed, the high bare room began to seem empty and cold. The nurses smiled as they helped me up and made me walk, but theirs were the smiles of professionals; I was their patient so they cared for me, but my body was healing and soon I would not need them – where then could I go?

My mother came, beautifully groomed as always, her skirts shorter than I had ever seen them; fashions were changing, and she must always be in fashion. Alice was with her and they smoked together, using elegant ebony cigarette holders, talking of house parties and shooting, and of men and women I did not know and did not wish to meet.

Letty arrived with Papa, having finished her first term at Cambridge – a different Cambridge from that of my brothers: a Cambridge of labs and experiments, lectures and tutorials. She was formidable in her intelligence; my father sat beside her, as always a little bewildered by this cuckoo in his nest. I asked him about Maud and he brightened. 'She's a wonderful woman, Helena – a wonderful woman – still riding to hounds like a trooper, you should have seen her last week.' It was difficult to believe that once I too had been galloping on horseback beside them.

As they left Letty turned back and came to my chair. 'Go back to Ainsclough, Helena. There is nothing for you at Hatton now.' She bent and kissed my cheek and waved as she slipped through the door. A cuckoo, but not an unkind one.

The nurse came in with her bright smile to escort me along the corridor to the water closet; when we got back she said cheerfully, 'Why, you're so much stronger now, my lady, that doctor says you'll be home for Christmas.' Her starched skirts rustled as she bustled out. But where was my home? Soon I must leave this empty white world – but where could I go?

Ben came in the evening and I asked him what he had been doing; I always did now, and he always told me the story of his day. He looked tired, but said he had had an easy shift. 'We had no booked job, but we had a run out all t'same. We fetched a pug from Horwich Works, brought it back over Withnell and had it screwed down at gasworks by teatime – they're borrowing ours while theirs gets repaired. Then we caught a lift from gasworks on pick-up and when we got back to shed there were so many spare hands there were nowt to do but send us home.' I did not understand everything he talked of, but his words and turns of phrase were becoming more familiar now; when he had gone I would try to build a little picture in my mind of him doing the jobs he had told me about; it helped me to get through the long hours in the empty room. This evening, when he had finished his story he rolled up his cap and began to knead it between his big hands, then he said, without looking at me, 'Your sister – she's been to see me twice – she's giving me earache – said I been wrong over – over your money.'

'Robbie and Eddie's money.'

'Aye – that's what she called it too. And she said if you' – he swallowed and then continued in a desperate rush – 'she said if you ever came back to Ainsclough it mun be used to give you help in th'ouse – seeing as you'd be weak a while yet.' He watched my face, then gave a wry smile. 'Besides, I see now as I were foolish – you can't make a sow's ear out of a silk purse.' I still did not answer so he said, 'She's been telling me I ought to swallow me pride, for your sake – and I been thinking it over, and I reckon – well, I reckon mebbe she's right.'

We sat in silence for a long time; then at last I asked, 'Is there – is there someone in Ainsclough who could come in every day?'

His head shot up and as I saw the longing blaze out in his eyes I looked away. 'Aye, I made a few inquiries – there's Jim Grimshaw's missus. Jim lost both his legs at Givenchy – he can't work and they've got four young 'uns – it's not easy to manage on pension. And Mary Grimshaw, she used to be in good service afore she were married, round Bolton way.'

I stared at the blank bare wall in front of me and whispered, 'Then – if you think – '

He jumped to his feet; suddenly he was very big and strong above me. 'I'll see her tonight – soon as I get back – I know she'll be glad to start any time. We'll pay her a decent wage – a bit above the odds, I reckon her and Jim have earnt it.'

'Yes – Robbie would have wanted that. He used to help men from the regiment who were in difficulties –

and he remembered some of them in his will.' My voice dropped a little on that last word, but as least I could talk of my brother now – to Ben, who had known him so well.

Ben glanced at me, then looked away. 'Aye – reckon he would have done – he were a generous officer, your brother – generous with his time as well as his money. When you've got yourself sorted out, lass, we'll have to see if we can carry on same – since I been lucky and kept me health and strength, and can earn a living wage. Which is what we'll be living on lass, as far as we can. I don't mind telling you it goes against grain with me that fees of this place are being paid by your dad – I have offered, several times, but he wouldn't hear of it. And he put it very tactful, I'll say that for him. Anyroad, what we're interested in now is getting you out; I'll speak to Matron tonight and I know Doctor's in tomorrow – with a bit of luck you'll be home by weekend.'

He came towards me, and bent to kiss my mouth – but I turned my face away a little and his lips touched my cheek instead. I sensed his hesitation, then he said gently, 'Aye – you've had a bad time, lass – I know that. Don't be feared I'll press you.' Then he strode out of the door. I lay back in my chair; the decision had been made – it was out of my hands now.

The doctor was blunt. 'You'll need to rest for a long time yet; I've questioned your husband and he seems to have made adequate provision – but there's something else to be considered. I've told him you're barely able to carry yourself yet – you're certainly not fit to carry a child. He said he understood and that he'd buy another bed and sleep in a separate room – but if you've the slightest doubt, if you think he can't be trusted . . .' He looked at me keenly.

I felt the blood rise into my cheeks, then I murmured, 'No – I think he can be trusted.'

The doctor seemed satisfied. 'Then you can go on Saturday.'

My mother came the next day. 'Are you sure you want to go back, Helena?' Her dark eyes bored into mine.

'It's all arranged – I'm going on Saturday.'

She looked at me for a long time. 'I'll order the Delaunay-Belleville to take you – it'll be more comfortable.'

'Thank you, Mother.' She lit a cigarette and began to talk of Alice. As she got up to go she said, 'Still, at least there's still one of my daughters who shows no signs of embroiling herself in some crazy matrimonial escapade – I suppose I should be grateful to Cambridge. Goodbye, Helena.' She swept out.

When Ben came after work on Saturday it was already dark. The nurses dressed me and wrapped me warmly in rugs and helped me out to the car. It was strange to be driving through a town: to see people moving about in front of lighted shop windows, streets bustling and busy because it would soon be Christmas. But beyond Bolton we came on to the open moors – darkness surrounded us and pressed us in and we saw only the beam of the electric lamps on the road ahead. It seemed a long time before we came down the long hill into Ainsclough, through the town centre and up again, to Royds Street. I had left in the warmth of autumn – now it was almost Christmas.

Barnes opened the door and helped me out; I stood swaying, on ankles whose strength had seeped away during the long weeks in bed. Ben's arms came round my waist. 'Lean on me, lass. Shall I carry you in? I'll take you straight upstairs.'

'Please, Ben.' I was so tired.

He swung me up and carried me through the small parlour, up the steep stairs and into the bedroom – the back bedroom. He said gruffly, 'It's the same size as front and I thought it 'ud be quieter in here for you – and in any case, there's knocker-up. Fire's ready lit – it should be warm enough for you.'

I whispered, 'Thank you, Ben,' and he laid me gently down on the bed.

He was back very quickly with a cup of tea. 'You get that inside you, sweetheart. I'll have to pop down to see the choffer – can't send a man back on a night like this without a bit of summat to stay him.'

I lay on the bed and heard the chink of china below; their voices rumbled in turn and I wondered what they were talking about – the battle of Arras, perhaps. Then I heard the muffled revving purr of the motor and the front door closing; the Delaunay-Belleville had gone, back to Hatton.

Ben came up at once with a tray. 'Try and take a little of this broth, lass – Mary Grimshaw made it fresh today – it's right tasty.' As I swallowed obediently he told me, proudly, 'Them's me own taters and carrots in that – from plot.'

'Thank you, Ben – they're delicious.' His plain face glowed.

When I had finished he bit his lip and asked, 'Lass – can you undress yourself?'

I said quickly, 'Yes Ben – I think so.'

'Then I'll go outside – but I'll only be on landing, in case you need me.'

I pulled off my coat – it weighed like lead, and my arms ached as I raised them to my hat. I fumbled with the buttons of my frock, but I could not get it over my head, so I had to call him. I lay with my eyes closed while he took off my dress and my petticoat and my bodice. 'Raise your arms, sweetheart, and we'll get your nightie on afore you catch cold.' Only when my night-gown was well pulled down did he reach under it and tug off my drawers, and I was grateful for his thoughtfulness. His hands were gentle on my legs as he slid down my stockings and removed my suspender belt. 'Up you come now, lass – so's I can put you between sheets.' I sat up and looked down – to see the betraying bulge in his trousers. My head jerked up and his face reddened. 'It's all right, lass – doctor spoke to me – I know I can't – But, mebbe you'd give me just the one kiss?'

I held up my lips and his warm mouth pressed mine; but I felt – nothing.

I said helplessly, 'I'm sorry, Ben, I'm sorry.'

He touched my shoulder briefly. 'It's all right, lass – I understand. After all, it's been a long time. Goodnight, sweetheart.' He swung round and quickly left the room.

As I heard his boots clattering down the stairs I thought, and it's been a long time for you, too, Ben – and now I am back I can do nothing to satisfy you. I turned my face into the pillow and wept. In my madness I had coupled shamelessly and without tenderness – but at least I had given him something he needed. What could I give him now?

CHAPTER TWO

It was dark and so quiet – where was I? I lay, clutching at the edge of consciousness, slipping over it – so that I saw a world like the real one – yet not quite like – a world where the odd was normal and the door moved and the window opened itself so that the curtains flapped in at me, coming closer – I cried out.

The door flew open; Ben was standing on the threshold in his nightshirt, his hairy legs bare. My breath came in frightened pants – I could not control it. Then I felt his arm come round me, and I clung to him desperately because he was warm and breathing and alive; his hand rubbed my back, hard and heavy – and at last I knew I was awake.

'Was it a nightmare, lass?' I nodded; it was too difficult to explain that it was the almost-reality which had terrified me. 'I'll go down and put kettle on, fetch us both a cup of tea.'

I was frightened. 'No – please don't leave me!'

He grunted, and tugged a blanket off the bed and rolled me in it, then bent to swing me up. 'Your slippers – you've no slippers on.'

He smiled, 'I'll fetch them later – don't you fret now. Let's get you downstairs.'

So I sat in the kitchen where he had put me in a wooden windsor armchair and saw by the light of the gas mantle that the rocker had gone; I was thankful.

He came back in his slippers and trousers. 'Do you fancy a rasher o' bacon wi' your tea?' He did not wait for my reply but dumped the frying pan down on the gas ring. The bacon sizzled and spat and it smelled good – it was months since food had smelled like that. He glanced at my face and smiled. 'Best have some bread with it.' I bit eagerly into the thick sandwich and he laughed aloud. 'I reckon you'll need more'n invalid food now if you're going to build your strength up. I'll put joint in oven soon – Mary'll be popping in later to see to the veg and the gravy – she makes a capital gravy, does Mary.'

'Ben – how long have you known Mrs Grimshaw?'

'We were at school together – started same day in infants' – she sat in front of me with a lovely pair of brown plaits hanging down her back, so I tied them to straps of her pinny – when she bent her head forward they pulled and she screeched! Teacher gie me a clout across me hand with t'ruler – first day, and all! But me Mam said it served me right.'

I began to stand up. 'I'd better get dressed, before she comes.'

'No need – she'll help you.' But suddenly I wanted to be dressed and tidy and ready.

Mary Grimshaw's plaits were still brown, but wound neatly round her head now. She was efficient and polite – as Ben said, she had been in good service. I sat in the parlour and heard her chatting to him in the kitchen – but when she came through to announce lunch she ducked her head and murmured, 'My lady.'

708

Mrs Grimshaw went home to her family and I began to cut the tender roast beef – but all of a sudden I could not eat it. I put my knife and fork down. 'I'm sorry, Ben.' I tried not to cry, but I felt so ill and dreary; knowing I would never laugh again. The tears began to flow of their own accord.

'Just sit still a while, lass – I'll put your dinner warming.'

'Please, Ben – you finish yours.' And he did, while I fastened my eyes on his steadily moving knife and fork – they seemed the only reality. When he had finished he coaxed me to eat a little more, but the cutlery was weighted with lead so that I could scarcely lift it, and I felt deathly tired.

'Upstairs now, lass.'

'No – don't leave me!'

So he carried me through to the small front room, even smaller now that a sofa had replaced one of the armchairs, and I lay on it and finally slept – reassured by the rustling of his Sunday paper as he sat by the fire reading.

The next day was a little easier: Ben had to go to work early but I could hear Mary Grimshaw moving about downstairs. She brought me my morning tea on a tray with a white cloth, and offered to come back and help me dress; but I refused, and managed to get up by myself. As soon as I opened the bedroom door she came up the stairs again. 'Ben said I must stay close to you on the steps, my lady,' and I was glad of her sturdy body just below me as I staggered down – I was still so shaky.

There was a letter from Mother; she was coming to call on me – in Royds Street, Ainsclough! I stared down at the crested notepaper, rather frightened, then told Mary we must be ready to receive a visitor tomorrow.

We heard the Delaunay-Belleville draw up outside, to the excited shouts of the children playing in the street, and I hastily patted my hair tidy while Mary sprang to open the door. She ushered Mother through the tiny lobby then announced: 'Lady Pickering, my lady,' to the small, cluttered parlour.

My palms were damp with nervousness but Mother was gracious – though her arched eyebrows rose as she surveyed the room. Mrs Grimshaw appeared with the tray – carefully arranged with my best wedding tea set. I poured, a little shakily, and handed Mother her cup.

She sipped her tea before saying, 'Your maid appears quite well trained – but you really should tell her to wear an apron in the afternoons – not that overall.' Her lips tightened a little.

I drew a deep breath before telling her, 'Mary is not my maid, Mother, she was at school with Ben. Her husband was disabled in the war, so it suits her to come and help us at present.'

Mother frowned, but turned the conversation to Conan: he had taken a tumble out hunting, but luckily only suffered bruising – and been back in the saddle next day. He was flying regularly from an aerodrome near Blackpool, but she said she was sure he was more careful now – 'I think he had several close shaves in China, Helena, and they taught him a lesson.' She gave a small sigh and for a moment her beautifully made-up face looked drawn and tired.

After half an hour she stood up, saying, 'You seem no worse, Helena – and that woman is obviously a competent housekeeper – remember what I have told you, always be prepared to pay for good service, it's well worth it.'

'Yes, Mother.' Then I dared to add, 'It was Ben who arranged Mary's wages – and he quite agrees with you.'

I saw the flicker of surprise in her eyes, then she said dryly, 'I doubt whether his *motives* were in agreement with mine, however – since he proclaims himself a socialist.' And for a moment we almost smiled at each other. Then her expression changed to one of distaste as she noticed the black smut on her grey suede gloves, and she turned towards the door. My hand groped for the non-existent bell, then I remembered to call, and Mrs Grimshaw came swiftly through from the kitchen and showed my mother the three paces out to the front door.

I saw the relief on Mary Grimshaw's face as she came back out of the lobby. 'Mrs Grimshaw – please do make a fresh pot of tea and sit down and join me.' She demurred a moment, and I added awkwardly, 'I know you were at school with Ben, so . . .' Then she understood and went to do my bidding and came back and sat rather primly down on the chair my mother had vacated. She was obviously unsure of herself until in desperation I asked after her children, and at once her eyes lit up and she began to talk, her face vivid and alive.

By the time she left that day I could picture nine year-old Mab – 'Who's such a help round the house – so steady-like,' and Frank and Joe, 'very close in age and typical lads – but not an ounce of vice in them,' and Betsy, 'Born after Jim's last leave, afore the shell took his legs.' Betsy, who was spoilt by her father and who teased the cat and was so naughty she drove her mother to distraction – but Mary smiled as she spoke of Betsy.

As I sat waiting for Ben I remembered that it would soon be Christmas, and when we had eaten our meal I asked him if he would take me down to Ainsclough in a cab the next day – if he were back in time. He looked doubtful and sat stroking his chin for a while, then admitted he would probably be on the Pilley Bob next day, so it might be managed. But only if I slept well and he was sure I would not tire myself, he added hastily.

So on the following afternoon he took me, well-wrapped up, down to the toyshop, and I sat on a chair by the counter and chose presents for Mab, and Frank and Joe – and naughty Betsy. I was stumbling with weariness by the time I got back and Ben said I must go to bed at once and have my meal on a tray – but I felt a small glow of achievement. Next morning I lay and thought of my parcels – then suddenly remembered Ben; I puzzled over what to do, then decided to write a letter as soon as I got up, to Sherratt's in Manchester, and send Mary Grimshaw out to the post with it at once.

That afternoon she took a bundle of washing with her as she left. I said, 'Mrs Grimshaw – that's too much to do as well as your own – we'll send ours to the laundry.'

'Laundry'll ruin this fine linen – they can't be trusted – besides . . .' Her round face flushed. 'It's Jim as does them.'

I was astonished, 'Your husband! But, surely . . .'

'You see, my lady, afore Ben asked me to come here I used to take in washing – to try and make ends meet – and Jim, well, his arms are as strong as ever, so he'd bash away with posser, and turn mangle for me – he wanted to help, it made him feel less of a burden – I even taught him to use iron. And Ben knows that, so when he came and asked me if I'd oblige you he said if Jim wanted to do washing, for extra like, then he'd be grateful. And Jim were right pleased – it gives him a bit of his own, see. He manages champion, he can get about with crutches and he wedges himself against wash-house wall on a chair. He makes a lovely job of it, but he can't hang out, of course, so on washing day I wondered if I could just run home for a while . . .'

'Of course you can, Mrs Grimshaw. You must organize the day however you please – we're truly grateful for all you're doing.'

The day before Christmas Eve, Ben asked rather awkwardly, 'Do you mind if we manage ourselves on Christmas Day and Boxing Day? Mary's willing to come in, but she's got the four childer – and I'm off both days . . .'

'Yes Ben – of course we can manage.' But I felt a little shy – we would not have been on our own together for so long since I had come out of the nursing home.

On Christmas morning Ben brought up my early cup of tea and after I had drunk it I dressed in a fine cashmere frock and went slowly downstairs, clinging to the rail, all by myself. He swung round as I came into the kitchen. 'Lass, you should have called me!' Then he smiled. 'But I'm glad to see you down so soon – I've got summat for you.'

He held a tissue-wrapped package out to me, and stood over me as I undid it, his face quite pink and anxious. Nestling inside the tissue was a white satin blouse, embroidered with pale pink rosebuds. I stroked the soft sheen of it. 'Thank you Ben – it's beautiful – thank you so much. I'll put it on today – I'll run upstairs and change at once.'

He beamed at me. 'You're not up to running anywhere yet, lass – I'll fetch a skirt for you; you can dress down here in the warm, and save yourself the stairs.' He thundered up the stairs and came down panting, clutching a dark-blue serge skirt. 'I'll wait in front room.'

The blouse was a little too full over my breasts, but I tucked a pleat into my waistband at the back and when he came and looked at me his face shone with pride. 'You look lovely, lass – really lovely.'

As I felt my cheeks blushing I said quickly, 'Ben, there's something for you – a brown paper parcel in the bottom of the alcove in my bedroom – perhaps you could bring them down, they're a little heavy for me.' His face lit up and he rushed up the stairs again.

He unwrapped the set of gardening books I had bought for him, delicately fingering the gold embossing on the spines and then turning the pages and exclaiming over the coloured plates of fruit and vegetables. When he looked up his face was tender. 'I wasn't expecting nothing, lass, with you being so poorly like – and now I'm right thrilled, I can hardly wait to start reading 'em.' He came towards me, hesitant, until I held up my face; his warm lips gently touched my cheek. 'Thanks, lass, thanks.'

And I felt a little bubble of happiness well up – only

713

a very fragile bubble, so I scarcely dared acknowledge it – but for a moment I knew it was there.

Sitting at the table I helped to prepare the vegetables while Ben bustled over the stove – we were comfortable together, like a brother and sister. I ate every scrap on my plate and then we dozed for a while in the armchairs in front of the warm range, until it was time to do the washing up. I wanted to help – he told me not to, the scullery was cold – but I managed, holding the glass cloth carefully. But then I tried to be too clever – I picked up two plates at once and they both slipped and fell, shattering on the stone-flagged floor. I stared at the pieces, tears filling my eyes. 'Oh Ben – I'm so clumsy – I'm useless, useless.'

'Aye, lass – so you are. In fact, I'm thinking that when rag-bone man comes round next week I'll put you on cart and let him take you away – I reckon a pretty lass like you should be worth half a dozen donkey stones!' I looked at his face and saw the quiver of his lips, and swallowing my tears managed to smile back at him. He put his arms round me and hugged me tightly for a moment, then he guided me into the parlour. 'Put your feet up, sweetheart – I'll finish clearing up.'

And as my eyelids drooped I saw a tiny clear picture of myself, perched high up on the rag-bone man's cart as he rattled down Royds Street – while Ben stood at the doorway of No. 10, clutching a fistful of grey donkey stones. I smiled a little before I slept.

On Boxing Day morning Ben told me Ivy and Ada were coming to see us. 'Just the two of 'em – they've been asking how you were, and they wanted to come – only for an hour or two.' I was nervous – what would they think of me? Last summer I had ignored their friendly advances after those first two visits, had made their brother unhappy and then lied to him as I left him. How would they greet me now?

They arrived together – Ivy in sealskin, Ada in broadcloth; Ivy had her two elder grandchildren clinging to a hand apiece. 'They would come – said they hadn't seen their Uncle Ben for so long.' They threw themselves on him and he laughed. 'How about a walk then, the pair of you?'

After the bustle of their departure it was suddenly quiet in the small parlour. Ivy looked at Ada, cleared her throat and leant forward. 'Lass, we're right glad to see you up and about again – we've been so worried for you.' Their round grey-blue eyes gazed at me in concern – I had never realized before how like Ben they were.

I swallowed and murmured, 'Thank you – I'm – much better now – thank you.'

Ivy said, 'Ben came and told us – what it were like for you nurses in war – what you had to do. So it's no wonder it all got on top of you – you deserve a rest now.'

'And you're such a frail slight lass – working all hours God sent – and having to do all that lifting as well,' Ada broke in.

I smiled back at them. 'I really am much stronger than I look – much stronger.' And as I spoke I realized with a small shock of surprise that it was true. There was a pause, then I asked, 'How is Fanny? And your other children?'

They chattered on, one interrupting the other, sparring together in an easy friendly fashion until Ben came back with the rosy-cheeked boy and girl and put the kettle on.

As they left Ivy bent over me and whispered, 'Now, lass, you be firm with our Ben – no canoodling until you're right again – babbies wear you out even when you're well.' My face flushed as she turned towards the door.

Ben waved them off, then clicked the door to. I watched him as he came back into the room: a well-built man, with broad shoulders and a straight back – a man I trusted, a man I felt affection for – but my woman's body did not flicker as he stood looking down at me. His hand touched my hair for a moment, then he bent

715

down to pick up the tea tray and carry it through into the kitchen.

Those winter days I liked to lie in bed of a morning when I woke early, listening to the rattle of doors and the clatter of clogs as people dashed across their yards in the frosty air. Then I would doze off again until Mary came and I heard the sound of the fire irons as she attended to the range, followed by her footsteps on the stairs as she carried up my morning cup of tea and the jug of hot water. I washed and dressed quickly, but it was never as cold in the small bedroom as it had been in the big draughty bedchambers at Hatton – Ben would bank up the fire last thing at night if he was in, so often there was still a small red glow in the morning.

Downstairs I would sit in the warm kitchen and eat my breakfast, while Mary told me the latest news of her neighbours, and mine. I knew more about them now than I had ever done in those first months of my marriage. One morning she said, 'I ran into Edna Fairbarn yesterday afternoon – she asked after you, Lady Helena – said she hoped you were feeling brighter these days – and not to forget what she told you!' I felt my cheeks grow hot and Mary glanced at me out of the corner of her eye and laughed. 'Aye, she's an interfering old besom is Edna – but she's no fool for all that. I remember when Jim came back from hospital without his legs – I were at me wits' end; he were so irritable, not like hisself at all, and he kept saying he were no use to me anymore – it would have been better if Jerries had made a proper job of it. Well, she gave me some advice then – I'd blush to repeat it, Lady Helena, so I won't.' Her cheeks flushed as she spoke, then she smiled a little. 'But she were right – and it made all the difference to Jim, though I were watching for me monthlies real anxious like the next week or so – but I were lucky that time and Edna – well, she knows a thing or two about that too. And I'm willing to take the risk – it matters so much to a man, though I've never been that interested meself.'

She bustled out to the scullery and her words hung in the air: 'It matters so much to a man, though I've never been that interested meself.' But I had been. And later, as I lay resting on the sofa in the parlour, I remembered that day when his strong fingers had handled me in the doorway before we had gone out to Ada's; I remembered, as though I were another woman, how I had longed for his body on mine. I turned my face away from the door – the war had taken so much from me: my brothers, my voice – and now this. Then, as I blinked back the threatening tears I saw the picture of Ben on the piano – Sergeant-Major Holden, with his three stripes and his crown – the war had spared him, at least.

He was due back around eight that evening, but at six there was a rattle at the door. A grimy-faced youngster stood on the doorstep. 'Missus 'Olden – Ben says 'e'll be late tonight – 'e's gone out on the breakdown, and fog'll slow 'em up.' I looked out and down the street, and could scarcely see the light of the lamp at the next corner. The lad told me, 'It's worse in valley bottom, missus – so 'e said don't wait up for 'im – 'e'll likely be well after midnight.' He replaced his greasy cap and vanished into the mist.

But I did not want to go to bed early – I had been watching the clock, expecting Ben to be home in a couple of hours. I would have gone into the kitchen to heat up his meal, listening to the splashing of his bath water, and then we would have sat either side of the table while he ate his supper – telling each other the small doings of our day.

By half-past nine I knew I should be going to bed, but instead I wandered about restlessly, and went upstairs to peer into the front bedroom; it was very neat and tidy – Mary had turned it out today, so there was nothing for me to do. I felt uncomfortably superfluous – he was my husband, but another woman had done all that was needed. Then, on the pile of clean clothing left ready for him after his bath, I noticed the pair of socks and thought, with a little touch of excitement, that surely there must be some that needed darning – I would mend them for him.

I tugged open a drawer and began to search through the neat piles, but someone else had been busy with their needle – I felt absurdly cheated. I took one out and studied the darns – they were neat, but not as neat as mine – I would tell Mary in the morning that darning was not part of her duties. I pulled the drawer out further – perhaps she had missed one that needed attention – and found a tissue-wrapped parcel, right at the back – a sock-shaped parcel. I lifted it out and unwrapped it, and there was another pair of socks. Then my hand stilled – I recognized those darns, they were my darns: I had woven them at Clegg Street. The socks had obviously never been worn since – the darns had not matted together. Yet the tissue paper was creased with much handling – he had wrapped up the socks and hidden them at the back of the drawer to take out from time to time – to look at, even hold against his cheek. I smiled as I raised them now to my cheek, and held them there a moment. Then I carefully covered up the coarse grey wool again and concealed the parcel where I had found it – one day, perhaps, I might tell Ben that I knew they were there – but not yet.

Downstairs I went over to the piano and picked up the photograph – his level eyes gazing back at me – and I said aloud, 'I *will* wait up for you, Ben.'

I made up the fire in the parlour and attended to the range, so that his bath water would be piping hot when he came in, then carried down a blanket and put it round my shoulders and sat down to wait.

I dozed and woke and dozed again. When I next looked at the clock it was five past one. I uncurled my cramped legs and went to the window and peered out – there was nothing but a thick, muffling greyness. The

718

fog was denser than ever. I built up the fires and went back to my vigil.

When the hands of the clock crept round to three I began to worry – thinking of the great engine movingly cumbrously – unseeingly – through the fog; the tired men on the footplate straining their eyes to see the signals – suppose they did not see one? Suppose another engine was moving through the dense darkness too? I thrust the thought away and got up to see to the range again. As I closed the lid I heard his key in the door. I ran through to him, and he stood there in the doorway, his eyes red-rimmed, his face grey with smoke and dirt. 'Lass – are you all right? I seed the gas still on, so I ran up rest of street . . .'

'Of course I'm all right, Ben – I just decided to wait up for you, and keep the range in, that's all.' He swayed a moment against the darkness outside. 'Come in, Ben – I'll close the door.' I looked past him, smelling the smoke and coal dust on his jacket. 'Why the fog's lifting.'

'Aye, aye – it's lifting.'

He sounded so tired that I began to scold him. 'Don't just stand there, Ben – come through to the kitchen – and you're absolutely exhausted, so you must have a cup of tea before your bath. The kettle's already warm, it won't take a minute.'

He sat slumped in the chair in the kitchen while I bustled about making his tea, then he drank it gratefully, while I put the bucket under the tap of the range.

'I'll see to that, sweetheart, I've come round now – nothing like a nice cup of tea to put me right.'

I put his supper to warm while I listened to him splashing in the scullery then I sat with him while he ate – neither of use spoke much, but it was a companionable silence. Then he stood up and came round to my side and bent over me, smelling of soap. 'Time you were in bed now, my lass – up you go.' He kissed me quickly on the cheek then pushed me towards the stairs with a

719

light pat on my behind. As I began to climb up I heard him whistling softly as he moved about the kitchen.

Soon his own footsteps were on the stairs, and I heard his voice, calling softly, 'Goodnight, lass – and thanks for waiting up for me,' before the front bedroom door closed behind him.

CHAPTER THREE

The fog had cleared away altogether by the next morning; the sun came out for a fine bright day – and it was Sunday, so Ben would be at home. We ate our breakfast late, lingering over it in the warm kitchen; there was no need to hurry because we made our own Sunday dinner now and could have it when we pleased – Mary left everything ready and then spent the day with her family.

Pushing back his chair, Ben stretched the muscles in his arms until his joints cracked, then glanced at me and asked, ''Ow do you fancy a little walk, lass? Just to end of street and back?'

For a moment I was frightened – I had only been beyond the front door that once, before Christmas, and then he had half-carried me to the cab. I had lived safe in my warm little cocoon ever since – so now I was nervous of the world outside. But Ben would be with me – and looking at his broad shoulders I knew he would help me if need be, so I drew a deep breath and told him, 'Yes – yes Ben, I'd like to try.'

'You mun wrap up well, then. Fetch down a thick coat.'

It was strange to be putting a hat on my head after so long, and easing my fingers into gloves. When I came shyly down he looked at my feet and grunted, 'You never give up, do you? First walk out and it's got to be in heels.'

'These are my *lowest*, Ben – and I wear them round the house, all the time.'

'Aye – I suppose you do.' His gaze travelled slowly up to my face and he smiled. 'With having such a neat pair of ankles mebbe it's only natural you want to show them off.' He added, quite seriously, 'I reckon change in fashions did us all a bit of good where you're concerned – legs like yours are too fine to be hidden – now your ma, hers 'ud be better covered up, like.' I felt a small surge of triumph – Mother was beautiful, but Ben was right – her legs were shapeless. I slipped my hand through his arm and he led me to the door.

The winter sun was so bright outside that I stood blinking in the doorway, dazzled by it. Then Ben pressed my hand. 'Come on now, lass – us'll take it slowly. We'll go up first, then you've only got the downhill run when you're tired.'

As we turned to head up the street the door opposite opened, and a man came quickly across the cobbles, tugging his jacket on over his braces, his hand outstretched. "'Ow are you, Missus Holden? I'm reet pleased to see you up and about. My Lizzie says, as soon as door opened, "Sid, that's Missus Holden out for a walk – you get straight over to 'er and say good morning and wish 'er all the best" – so 'ere I am.'

As he pumped my hand vigorously I murmured, 'Thank you – thank you so much.'

Other doors opened; Mrs Ingham came out wiping her hands on her apron, a round-eyed toddler clinging to her skirts. 'How are you, Mrs Holden? First time out, is it? Now you just take it steady. I'm right glad to see you on the mend.'

We moved slowly up the street – it was like a royal progress. My hand was shaken over and over again while Ben's shoulder was vigorously thumped. I kept murmuring, 'Thank you, thank you,' the tears filling my eyes.

As we reached the top of the street a fat, balding man came rushing out with a chair and planted it on the flagged pavement. 'Here you are, Missus Holden – you just have a rest afore y' goo down again.' I collapsed on to the seat gratefully. Ben said, 'Albert here, we were in same company for a while early on.'

Albert beamed, a great gap-toothed grin. 'Aye, that's reet.' Then his face became serious. 'And I knew your brothers, lass – they were as like as two peas in a pod, and always ready with a laugh and a joke. I were sorry, reet sorry.' He added, 'An' I were sorry when I heard how bad you were – but I were in hospital at Eatapps meself, so no wonder you were worn out. How about a cup o' tea now, just to keep your strength up? Florrie's got kettle on.'

The small wiry woman in the doorway smiled, but Ben said, 'Thanks, Albert – another time we'll take your offer, but I best get lass back now, afore sun goes in.' He helped me up and I set slowly off again, clinging to Ben's arm.

He put me straight on the sofa as soon as we got home and plumped the cushions up behind me. My legs were trembling a little. 'How kind everyone was, Ben – how very kind – but' – I swallowed, then plunged on – 'but when I first came here, back in June – I mean – that is – people were always polite, but . . .'

He smiled a little. 'You were a foreigner, lass – and so different – they was scared of you, with your voice and your ways. And then, you weren't yourself, either . . .' I remembered the days I had walked in my grief and despair down this street, unseeing, uncaring. His voice was dry as he added, 'But there's nowt like illness for getting folk interested – though it's genuine interest, I'll not say it isn't – but it brings you down to same level, like – and they feel you're more one of us now, I suppose.' He stared into the leaping flames of the fire as he told me,

'We unveiled war memorial in park back in October – so we all paraded there – with t'mayor and some general, though it were Mrs Illingworth who pulled flags off – she lost all her lads over them years, so it were right for her to do it. Anyroad, I were standing beside Albert, him as lives at top house with Florrie, and he said to me: "Your missus should be here today, Ben – wearing her ribbons just like us – I reckon if anyone's got right to wear ribbons it's her."' He looked up at me for a moment and added softly, 'He were right, lass. I know from things you've let drop that you feel you've been weak over these last few months – just lying there in bed in nursing home, but you moan't think like that – you were wounded in war, like me – and you needed rest – and still do – to get properly right. So no more of this nonsense about being a burden, being useless – do you hear?'

I smiled across at him. 'Oh, Ben – and I've been hiding under the stairs every time I heard the rag-bone man calling in the street!'

He threw back his head and laughed, then slipped from his chair and knelt on the rug, putting his arms around me. I rested my head on his shoulder, feeling warm and safe. He lifted my chin gently and reached up to press his mouth on mine; I kept my lips still and let him kiss me. When he pulled back his head he was breathing deeply and I said, 'Ben – if you want to – it would be all right.'

His gaze held mine, until my eyes fell; then he shook his head. 'Nay, lass – I can tell difference – there'd be no pleasure in it for you. And you've only been up street once, hanging on me arm – you're a long way from being right yet.' He smiled and touched my cheek. ''Sides, I reckon with you being the way you are I'd only have to hang me trousers over end of bed and you'd be in family way by morning – and then what would your ma say to me?'

As he spoke I felt a little fluttering of pride – I was

thin and small-breasted, but I had quickened to this man easily. Then I glanced at his vigorous body and ventured, 'But you had something to do with it, too, Ben Holden.'

He grinned. 'Aye, happen – 'cept on moor that first time – I must have missed then.' He sounded almost ashamed of himself and I wanted to laugh – then he reached for his paper and muttered, 'But if I'd taken you in maze when I came on that visit you'd 'a' been walking up th'aisle with a full belly, my girl.' I saw him give a small smile of satisfaction to himself before he began to read the news.

Watching him I thought, and when you filled my belly it was with two babies – not just one, but two – and I waited for the trembling to start, but it did not. The two I had lost had been unformed, come too early, when neither I nor they were ready. And they had not been my brothers – my brothers had died for their country, as so many other men had done.

I lay with my eyes closed for a while, resting, then I opened them and looked across at the man reading the paper: with his straight nose, his full firm mouth, his neat, curving ears. I said suddenly, 'Ben – you've got very nice ears – they don't stick out like most men's do – they lie so beautifully flat against the side of your head.'

He looked up, his mouth twitching slightly. 'Aye – you mun thank me old mam for that. She used to pin them to side of me head with a meat skewer every night, regular.' I stared at him. ''Course, it were difficult to sleep, like – ' He burst out laughing. 'The look on your face, lass! You believed me for a minute there, didn't you?' I blushed and laughed at myself, then he jumped up. 'You stay there, sweetheart – I'll start veg.'

Next morning Mary Grimshaw arrived late; she flushed and began to apologize. 'I'm so sorry, Lady Helena – but Jim's not so well – his stumps are playing him up – he reckons he can feel his legs again, and it always upsets him – and our Betsy's in such a mood –

she keeps pestering him and he hasn't got patience when he's like this.'

She sighed as she put down my tray. I said quickly, 'Mrs Grimshaw – go and fetch Betsy – she can spend the day with us, then your husband can rest.' She hesitated, biting her lip, so I added, 'I'm sure I'll enjoy her company – I'm going to walk up the street again, and she can come with me and hold my hand.'

Her face lightened. 'If you're sure, Lady Helena – she likes to think she's helping, does Betsy – and it need only be for morning. Right, I'll do that – and thank you kindly.'

Betsy's curly fair hair was tied ruthlessly back into two stubby pigtails; her eyes were ferociously blue. As soon as she was inside the door she held out one chubby hand. 'I'll tek you up street, missus – I'll see you reet.'

'Now, Betsy – my lady's got to have her breakfast, first.' Betsy's lower lip pouted ominously.

I rushed in with, 'Perhaps you would like to share a slice of toast with me, Betsy', and watched her mouth change direction. 'Wi jam, missus? Wi' jam?' Then she saw her mother's expression and added hastily, 'Please.'

I was walking more easily this morning – I was proud of myself; Betsy clung to my hand and planted her small clogs firmly in the gutter as she 'helped' me down the curb. I thanked her when we got back and her blue eyes shone.

Later I heard her 'helping' her mother in the kitchen, and Mary's voice raised in irritation, so I went out and invited her to sit in the front room with me. But I was not used to small children and could barely follow her dialect, so I let her roam around the parlour exploring while I lay back and closed my eyes.

It was the clashing discord which jerked me upright – Mary had the child by her plait – Betsy, red-faced and defiant, was anchored to the piano leg. 'Wanter make a noise, wanter make a noise!'

Mary drew breath – she had been up in the night, her

patience was gone – I intervened quickly, 'I'll make a noise for you, Betsy – I'll show you how to do it.' I pulled out the piano stool and began to play, 'Baa, baa, black sheep, have you any wool?'

The child's eyes went rounded, her mouth fell open. 'Baa baa – baa baa.'

I laughed. 'Clever girl, Betsy – that's right. Can you sing it?'

She took a deep breath and as I slowly played began: 'Baa, baa, black sheep, 'ave you any wool? 'Ess, sir, 'ess sir' I saw her groping for the words and I picked up the tune and helped her continue: 'Three bags full.' Then together we sang on to the end: 'One for the master, and one for the dame, And one for the little boy that cries down the lane!'

Her voice rose in a shriek of delight: 'Again! Again!'

So I played it again, and when we had tired of the black sheep we sang of little Miss Muffett, frightened by the spider – Betsy screeched in a truly blood-curdling fashion at the end – then we sang for our supper with little Tommy Tucker and popped with the weasel before moving on to the horrifying tale of the three blind mice. I taught Betsy to sing 'Ring a Ring of Roses' and she flung herself to the floor at the final: 'And they all fall down' – and then it was lunchtime.

We all ate together in the kitchen and then Mary went home to see how Jim was. She took a protesting Betsy with her – 'Mrs Walsh said she'd take her after dinner.' I opened my mouth to offer but Mary silenced me: 'No, Lady Helena – you mun rest, you only went out first time yesterday – Ben'd never forgive me if you tired yourself out.'

But I did not feel so very tired, though I went back into the parlour and put my feet up obediently. My eyes kept returning to the piano – Mary would be back soon – I jumped up and ran over to it in a guilty rush. As soon as I was sitting down I began to play my scale – raising my voice and singing. But when I reached G I knew I was forcing, and on top A I cracked. I breathed in and tried again – the same thing happened. I made myself wait five full minutes by the clock, then began the scale a third time – but it was no use; I did manage top A but it was only with the greatest of effort – and it was not true.

I went back and lay down on the sofa. I, I who had soared effortlessly to high C, who with careful training and practice had learned to go easily beyond – I could no longer reach the high notes; I was only fit to sing nursery rhymes to children. I cried a little, then fell asleep.

Ben came home at teatime. Through the half-open door I heard Mary talking to him in the kitchen. 'Lady Helena's been up street – and I hope she hasn't overtired herself – I brought Betsy with me this morning and my lady were right good with her. Betsy were thrilled because my lady played pianner to her and sang with her for hours.'

I heard Ben's sharp question: '*She* sang – Helena sang?'

Mary said apologetically, 'Betsy didn't know all words of nursery rhymes, you see – but Lady Helena's been asleep most of the afternoon – so mebbe Betsy were too much for her – she is for most folks, I reckon.' She sighed.

As soon as Mary had left Ben came through to me. His voice was elaborately casual as he said, 'Mary says you've been singing with the youngster.'

There was no point in pretence. I shook my head. 'It's no use, Ben – after she'd gone I tried to sing my scales – my usual scales – and I can't reach the top notes any more. It hasn't come back.'

'But mebbe – with time . . .'

'No Ben – I know my own voice, and it's changed, I can hear it. The capacity just isn't there any more.'

He moved restlessly around the room. 'What about that singing teacher – the one you used to go to in

727

Manchester – I remember the Captain telling me when I went to see him – couldn't she help?'

'Madame Goldman can only train a voice – she can't create one that isn't there.'

'But it's half there, lass.'

'Ben – I can see line after line of music in my mind's eye – and every time the notes rise . . . I would be dumb. You can't *half* sing songs.'

'No, no – happen not.' He drew in a breath and said, 'I'm glad you went out for a walk today, lass – but don't over-do it, will you?'

The next day I asked for Betsy again, and we went a little further; her four-year-old legs and my rusty ones moved at the same pace. Neighbours stopped and spoke to us both in the streets and gradually, by listening to the child, my ears picked up the pattern and rhythm of their speech and I no longer had to strain to understand.

We ventured further afield each day, and on the Friday we came to the corner of Clegg Street. Betsy began to lead me up it – I hesitated but she tugged at my hand so I followed slowly behind her. We had just passed No. 6 when the door opened and Mrs Greenhalgh came out to stand on her snowy step. 'My lady – ' Reluctantly I pulled Betsy round; Mrs Greenhalgh advanced. 'My lady, I'm glad to see you on your feet again – we heard you'd been poorly.' Her face was stern, but not unkind.

'Thank you, Mrs Greenhalgh – thank you.' Then I plunged on, 'And Emmie – how is Emmie?'

She permitted herself the indulgence of a small smile. 'She's very well, my lady – courting steady now. A decent young lad, she met him through chapel choir – he'd not long moved to Ainsclough. He works in District Bank – a nice steady job, with prospects.'

'I am so glad – Emmie is such a sweet girl.'

Mrs Greenhalgh inclined her head. 'Other than a touch of flightiness I've not got any serious complaints about her – I will say that, my lady, though she is my own daughter. And she'll settle down once she's wed, women have to.' Her eyes held mine a moment, and I felt my cheeks go red. 'And young Alfred'll have no cause to complain of her cooking, and that's what matters most to a man, I always say. Of course, wedding'll not be for a year or two yet, they'll have to have a bit put by – but there's no harm in waiting. He comes round every Wednesday and Saturday evening regular, and we all have a bite to eat and a little chat together. I've got one o' teachers from infants' school lodging in Ben's old room now – a very nice lady, close to meself in age, and between us we keep an eye on the youngsters.'

'Please do give Emmie my very best wishes.'

'I will, my lady – I will.' As Betsy tugged impatiently at my hand Mrs Greenhalgh fired her parting salvo: 'And it's such a comfort to me that he's a regular attender at chapel – twice every Sunday without fail – and a nice clean job, too – no coming home covered with muck and leaving dirty overalls to be washed.'

And now I smiled properly. 'You're so right, Mrs Greenhalgh, so right. Come along Betsy, your mother will be wondering where we've got to. Goodbye, Mrs Greenhalgh.' I let Betsy haul me away – then I thought of poor Emmie and her Alfred, so securely chaperoned by Mrs Greenhalgh and the 'very nice lady' who taught at the infants' school, and began to giggle.

I told Ben all she had said when he came in that evening and we laughed together. 'I hope that Alfred's got a bit o' spunk in him – else he'll find he's married her mother more than Emmie – she'll run their lives for them, given half a chance – or less,' he added thoughtfully. He glanced at me. 'I'll say this for your ma, she's said some harsh things to me in her time, especially when you were ill – but she's never interfered since you came back here.'

'She hasn't the time, Ben – she's too busy leading her own life.'

He started to chuckle. 'Aye – an' it's sort o' life Mrs Greenhalgh doesn't know exists this side of hell!'

'Ben!'

'It's true, lass – painting, drinking, smoking – and running around with other men – you didn't bring your ma up right at all!' He was still chuckling as he took the plates out to the scullery.

I was getting stronger every day now, and I was able to help Mary with the odd task around the house; but I was careful never to do too much – she was so anxious to earn her wages – and I still tired easily. Ben watched me closely, and sent me to lie down if he thought I was looking pale; I told him I had always been pale, but he took no notice and shooed me off regardless – and I knew he was right.

One evening he stayed in the kitchen, and when I went to look for him he was writing a letter. He pushed the blotting paper over the sheet. 'Won't be a minute, lass – you go back in parlour.' I was a little curious but he sat waiting for me to go, so I went.

Later, as we sat either side of the fire, I asked casually, 'Were you writing a letter, Ben?'

'Aye, that's right.' He turned a page of the newspaper and shook his head. 'I'm having me doubts about Mr Lloyd George – I thought he'd be a better bet 'an a Tory prime minister, but now I'm not so sure there's anything to choose between them. What do you think, lass?'

'I think you voted Labour in the last election anyway, Ben Holden.'

He grinned at me. 'Happen I did – but you won't know, sweetheart, will you? Seeing as ballot box is secret – like post box.'

I bent my warm cheeks over the sock I was darning.

He was on early all that week; I would listen drowsily to the banging of the knocker-up and Ben's answering shout, and then fall asleep again after I had heard him creep down the stairs. As soon as he arrived home on Friday he said, 'Lass – I fancy a trip to Manchester –

are you coming with me?' Manchester! It seemed a very long way away. 'Course you're coming with me. Fetch your hat and coat and we'll leave Mary in peace.'

It was exciting to sit on a train again, but Manchester seemed so big and gloomy after Ainsclough, and I clutched Ben's arm as we headed through the traffic towards the trams.

It was only as he helped me out of the tram that I realized where he was taking me. I shrank back. 'No, Ben – '

He hauled me forward. 'No use arguing, lass – just do as you're told.' He was every inch a sergeant-major this afternoon.

Madame Goldman was alone; smilingly she took my hand. 'I am so glad to see you my dear – I heard that you had been ill. Sit down and rest a little before we begin.'

I shook my head. 'No, Madame – it's no use – I only have half a voice . . .'

'Then I shall listen to your half voice.' She smiled like a cat as she sat down at the piano.

I sang my scale, badly – and cracked on A. I sang it again, a little better, but A was difficult for me. Madame was imperturable. 'We will try another scale.' Her fingers rippled over the keys. 'This too was a scale of yours.' I sang that scale, all of it. 'Good – now once more.' I sang again, and she turned to me and smiled.

'Madame – It's no use; I am a soprano, that was not a soprano's scale.'

Ben broke in. 'What about her high notes? She keeps on about them.' He had asked what I had not dared to.

Madame Goldman pursed her lips. 'With care we might make you safe on A – even perhaps B – but not often, and not for long, I think.'

I felt my eyes fill with tears. She swung round on her stool and took both my hands in hers. 'Lady Helena, God gave you your high notes – and God has taken them away.' The bitterness of loss swept over me, but she was still speaking: 'However, Elsa Gehring gave you your low notes, and those you still have. You will sing again, my dear, but you will sing mezzo.'

'But – but I'm not . . .'

She waved me to silence. 'How wise Elsa was! I must admit at the time I thought her work on your lower register unnecessary – although I encouraged you to practise it – but I thought there had been no need to extend your range since all young girls wish to sing soprano – ' She shrugged, smiling. 'But Elsa was wiser than I. I will write to her this evening – she always inquires of you – and I shall tell her that her work has endured longer than God's, that will please her. She thinks already that she is cleverer than God – but she will like to be told it!' Madame Goldman laughed, then became brisk. 'How often can you come to Manchester each week, Lady Helena? We have a lot of work to do, you and I.'

Ben butted in. 'She can come as often as she's fit to, ma'am. We've got a good woman in to see to shopping and cleaning and suchlike. Helena's only got to catch train.'

I was still uncertain, still protesting a little on the way back, but Ben would have none of it. 'Just think of all those priv. tickets you're going to use, lass – reckon it's time we got summat back from company!' He winked at me and squeezed my hand.

We did work hard. I was using my chest notes more now, and had to strengthen them and my middle register. It seemed very odd at first – I had always sung higher – and yet, because I had trusted Elsa Gehring I had regularly practised the lower notes as well as the middle and upper. But it was a shock when Madame Goldman gave me Mendelssohn's aria from *St Paul* to prepare: 'But the Lord is mindful of his own'. 'Colour, Lady Helena, colour – darken your voice – you are still thinking like a soprano! You are not a choirboy any longer, you are a woman, so you must sing like a woman.' And slowly, gradually, more confidently, I did.

I sent for my music from Hatton and began the long task of transposing. I knew I did not need to – I had been able to transpose on sight since before I had first gone to Munich – but I wanted to make a completely fresh start. My high bell-like voice had gone – it was buried in the grave with my brothers – I did not want any reminders of it. Madame was right – I was not a choirboy any longer, I was a woman who had loved and lost and lost a second time – and who now must come to terms with her loss and live again. So Ben would carry a small table to the sofa and I would sit at it with my pen and rewrite line after line.

Ben asked once, 'Couldn't you just buy new music, like?'

I flexed my cramped fingers and looked down at the opening bars of *Frauen Liebe und Leben*, then smiled up at him. 'Most of my songs are by German composers, Ben – they might not be so easy to buy in England today. Besides, I must make a fresh start.'

He bent back over his book and I took up my pen once more. I had accepted my new voice now; the light high notes had been like those of a young boy – they had drawn Gerald to me against his instincts – just as my body had been a boy's body, slim and spare of flesh. I had lost my babies but my breasts remained a little fuller, my bottom was rounder – I put my hand up and touched the swelling curve of my bosom – than glanced up to see Ben's eyes fixed on me. I felt my face crimson and blurted out, without thinking, 'I'm getting fat, Ben.'

He threw back his head and laughed. 'No – you'll never be that. But you have fleshed out like, since we were wed.' His eyes narrowed a little. 'I seen it afore in lasses – being with a man seems to – well, develop them like. I noticed it in you, even after a week or two.'

His face was redder now; he was watching me intently.

'Ben.' I held out my hand, uncertainly, nervously; he began to move out of his chair.

Then he sank back again. 'Nay, lass – you're not ready for it yet, so I'd best not touch you at present. Talking like that, and looking at you – it's got me a bit excited.' Then he smiled gently. 'I'll settle down in a minute if I just sit quietly with me book. Then I'll give you a good-night kiss.'

He found his place again and I picked up my pen. There had been no answering call in my belly – and yet – I had liked to see his eyes on my breasts and to know that they had pleased him.

CHAPTER FOUR

The parlour became my music room now, my work room. I played the piano for hours every day while Ben was at work, and my fingers gradually regained their suppleness.

Madame Goldman set me several simple English songs to learn with my new voice. I studied them carefully before beginning to practise them, phrase by phrase. One morning Ben was still at home – he was on the late shift that day – and he slipped in and sat listening to me. When I had sung the whole song through and closed the piano he said, 'Lass – I never understood before – I always thought you just sang natural like – that you opened your mouth and out it came. But seeing you over these last few weeks it seems to me it's a job of work to you same way firing and driving is to me. You pore over notes and practise them and keep worrying away at it until it's exactly right – you must've spent years and years learning your music, way you handle that piano – but you're still not satisfied until it's just how you think it should be. And you've been so much happier since you've been doing it – I reckon you need to do it – it's part of you.' And as he spoke I knew he was right: since I had lost my voice there had been a void in my life and only now was that void being filled. Dearest Elsa – I would write to her tonight. But still there was that sense of loss and I said to Ben, 'But I'll never sing as I once did, never.'

He came and stood close to me. 'Lass, don't regret them high notes – they were beautiful and I'm glad I heard you sing them – but your voice these days' – he paused, groping for the right words – 'it's warmer and fuller – it's like your body is now.' Then he added, in a rush, 'It's more womanly – and when you sing I see you sometimes as you used to look in th'ospital, bending over Young Lennie or one of t'others who were in pain – with your face all soft and gentle' – he turned away from me – 'like you did to me, too. I mun be going.' He kissed me quickly and left hastily, his face brick-red.

I ran to the window and lifted the corner of the curtain, watching him stride across the street. When he was out of sight I returned to the piano and opening it again began to sing: 'Du bist die Ruh, Der Friede mild' – you are rest, and gentle peace. And I did not know whether I sang of my music – or of him.

Ben began to work on his plot again; sometimes I went up there and sat watching him dig. He was behind with his preparations, because he had had no time for digging in the autumn, but he never reproached me. One Sunday, Fanny's three children came to see us on their own: their father put them on the train at Blackburn and then Ben and I went down to meet them at Ainsclough; young Benjamin chivvied his charges out of the compartment: 'Edie – help me lift Baby' – he was very much the older brother – then he saw Ben and his face lit up in a beaming smile. 'I brought them, Uncle Ben – all way fra' Blackburn!'

'Well done, me lad – all present and correct.' Ben

took out his handkerchief and wiped the toddler's nose, then swung him up squealing into his arms. 'Now you hang on to your Auntie Helena, Edie.' The little girl shyly took my proferred hand – I was almost as shy as she was, being used to Betsy Grimshaw who chattered all the time; I missed her now she was at school. But I did not need to worry, the three males talked non-stop; Edie and I were able to relax as we walked sedately beside them.

Then it was March. A year ago I had sat beside my brother, watching him gasp desperately for breath. Ben did not say anything, but I knew that he was remembering too; he was very gentle with me and he exchanged a shift the day before that night, so that he would be home early.

I sat over my music, forcing myself to concentrate on the score. I could not sing. At last he said, 'You'd best go to bed, sweetheart. I'll be up meself soon, and I'll come and see if there's owt you want.'

I lay in bed with the gas turned low; he tapped and crept in, and I felt his hand on my hair. 'Lass, if you want me beside you tonight I'll come – you needn't fear owt.'

I replied at last, 'I don't know, Ben – I don't know.'

'Then I'll leave doors ajar – I'll come if you call.'

I lay and slept and woke, and slept again, uneasily. Finally I heard the church clock strike four – and knew that a year ago it had been all over. I slid out of bed and went quietly downstairs to put the kettle on.

Ben came down as I sat crouched over the table. He sat with me, not speaking, drinking his tea. When he had finished he sighed heavily. 'He were a good officer – not one of them who'd jump on top of parapet and do daft things, but he cared about his men – he wouldn't let them down. And he knew all their names and always had a word for them; they could talk to him, and he'd do his best to help where there was trouble at home, or suchlike. I remember once, Dan Ogden – a little fat lad

he were, from Bolton – he got a letter from his girl –
he'd got her into trouble on last leave. I don't reckon
she were all that bright – he showed me letter, she could
hardly string two words together, poor lass, and it were
all blotched where she'd been crying over it. Her family
were strict chapel and they'd thrown her out. He came
to me, he were really worried about her – and guilty too.
So we went to your brother and told him all about it
and he spent the whole of one of his rest days going back
to HQ and pulling every string he could to get young
Dan special leave – and he weren't feeling too good then,
the Captain weren't, had a touch of flu – but he went,
all t'same. In end Dan got forty-eight hours and we sent
him off with a bottle of vino in his pack for wedding.
After he'd gone I remembered licence – but your brother
had thought of that too and given him money for it.
When Dan got back he said her mam had taken her in
again, soon as ring were on her finger – but the old
besom wouldn't let them have even half an hour alone
together. We told him he could make up for it after war,
but then they sent us back to Wipers, so he never got
his wedding night. Still, at least youngster wouldn't be
brought up a bastard. If it were a boy she were going to
call it "Robert", Dan said – after the Captain. I don't
know whether she did or not.'

My brother, my dearest brother. I put my hand over
Ben's and we sat waiting for the dawn.

On the Monday, Mary Grimshaw said, rather diffidently, that their minister had spoken in the chapel of its
fiftieth anniversary celebrations: 'At end of August, –
it'll be a big do, and they're planning to put on *Messiah*.
He were saying we'd have to be thinking about soloists,
so after service I told him you sang lovely – and 'e
wondered mebbe if . . . ?' She looked at me hopefully.

I shook my head. 'I'm sorry, Mrs Grimshaw – I did
sing in a performance of *Messiah* once – but my voice
has changed now, I couldn't.' After she had gone back

into the kitchen I remembered the church at Hammersmith, and the tears filled my eyes.

I had a lesson with Madame Goldman later that morning, and just as I was finishing Wally Jenkins came in. I had not seen her for well over a year and we talked eagerly together; she told me she had been touring in opera, but had come back to Manchester now. 'My mam's not so good so I'm only taking local engagements at present.' Her face was tired, then she laughed. 'Fancy you going to live in Ainsclough of all places – where Miss Nellie Girvan made her only public appearance! Do you remember us singing the *Barcarolle* together? You'll be able to pop down the Co-op Hall for an engagement any time now!'

I smiled at her. 'As it happens, an engagement in Ainsclough *was* offered to me – only this morning – an anniversary *Messiah* at the local chapel.'

Madame broke in. 'When is this anniversary?'

'In August, but – '

'Good, then we have time to prepare.'

'But Madame, – I can't sing "The Redeemer" now – I might crack on the G.'

Madame shook her head. 'You would not, Lady Helena, you are still capable – but I agree, it is best not to – you must think of yourself as a mezzo now, so this is for you.' She signalled the accompanist away from the piano, sat down herself and began playing; I heard the first bars of, 'He was despised and rejected of men; a man of sorrow and acquainted with grief.' She stopped, her fat fingers splayed on the keys. 'You have been acquainted with grief, Lady Helena – you will sing this well. We will start practising tomorrow.'

I began to protest but Madame waved me to the door. 'Go home and find your score, my dear – eleven o'clock tomorrow.'

As I picked up my gloves Wally said, 'Madame's right, Lady Helena – they'll find a local soprano easily enough, but we altos are thin on the ground.'

738

I mentioned what they had said to Ben that evening, thinking he might object, but instead his face lit up. 'You do it, lass – and I'll move heaven and earth to get right shift so I can come and hear you.'

So next day I said to Mary, 'If they can't find anyone else, perhaps – '

The minister came that same evening. I sang for him, 'But the Lord is mindful of his own', and he beamed at me. It was as Wally had predicted: there was a young soprano in the congregation who could cope. 'But for the alto part we often have to bring in an outsider – I am so very grateful, Mrs Holden – '

He stopped, flustered, and Ben broke in, 'She'll answer to "Lady Helena", Mr Whitworth – though she's sung under another name in Ainsclough.' He winked at me.

As he was leaving the minister said, while shaking hands with Ben, 'I haven't seen you in chapel yourself for a long time, Ben.'

Ben flushed. 'Aye, not since afore the war.'

After the door closed Ben looked at me, explaining. 'I used to be in choir, but – when I came back – there didn't seem much point – ' He shrugged his shoulders.

'I know, Ben – it was the same with me.' He sat down and picked up his paper.

At my next lesson I told Madame Goldman that I was not sure I should sing the *Messiah* in a chapel: 'Since the war – I'm not sure I believe any longer – I have had so many doubts – '

Madame silenced me. 'Who does not have doubts? We can only sing in hope, we can do no more.'

At my next lesson Madame greeted me warmly. 'Ah, good – you look well, Lady Helena – you will be able to sing at Accrington tomorrow evening.'

'Accrington – sing at Accrington?'

'Yes – it is not far for you, luckily. Poor Wally will be so relieved – her mother has taken a turn for the worse, but she doesn't like to let people down, so she suggested you might take her place. You are free?'

I stammered. 'Yes – but – Madame – '

'Good, I will telegraph. The programme is all in your repertoire, except for the third item – I suggest Parry's "O Mistress Mine", instead. We will run over them now.'

'But Madame – Wally is a deep contralto – '

She waved my objections aside. 'No matter – I know the soprano, she is very high – a little "reedy" ' – her lips turned down a moment – 'so you will be a sufficient contrast. We will start with "The Oak and the Ash" – they are a little old-fashioned in Accrington.' She gestured to her pianist and I stopped protesting and began to sing:

> 'A north country maid up to London had strayed,
> Although with her nature it did not agree;
> She wept, and she sighed, and she bitterly cried,
> "I wish once again in the north I could be . . . " '

Ben was on a late turn that week so I stayed up to tell him my news, rather apprehensive about his reaction. His face fell. 'I wish you'd given me more notice, lass – I might have been able to do a swap, even though it is Saturday night – then I could have come to hear you.'

'I didn't know myself until today – but, are you sure you don't mind?'

He grinned at me. 'I'll mind if you don't get up them stairs sharpish now, and I'll mind if you don't spend tomorrow resting on sofa – but if you promise to do both them two things then I'll let you go to Accrington.' He put out his hand and placed it firmly on my behind; it was warm and I hung back a minute, then he pressed harder until I moved towards the stairs. 'Bed now.' He kissed me quickly on the lips and I ran obediently up.

After we had eaten an early lunch the next day he settled me on the sofa in the parlour. 'You should be able to catch 10.20 this evening – it's nowt but a step from th'all – and, then mind you take a cab back up here.'

'Yes, Ben.'

He leant over to kiss me. 'I'd best be going now.' I put my arms round his neck and clung to him for a moment. When he lifted his head he was breathing harder; he whispered, 'I love you, sweetheart, and I wish I could come and hear you tonight – you'll have to give me a little concert later, all on me own.' Smiling, I watched him stride across the room.

But I missed the 10.20. The organizers had prepared refreshments for us after the performance and they invited us to stay a little while. I was happy to do so – from the moment of walking out on to the platform I had been exhilarated – I had sung, and sung well. The audience had applauded enthusiastically, the chairman was pressing me to come again; I glowed with pleasure.

They were kindly, hospitable people and two of the committee insisted on escorting us to the station, where the other soloists headed for the Burnley platform while I went to wait for the last train, that would take me home – to Ainsclough. I was too restless to sit down, so I walked along the curving platform and watched the Burnley train slide smoothly in opposite. I glimpsed the dark head of the engine driver outlined for a moment against the station lights and remembered with a little jolt that Ben was somewhere out in the night – in charge of just such another huge panting monster. I smiled to myself at my fanciful picture – to Ben it was merely his job.

The Ainsclough train rumbled in with a scrape and squeal of brakes – a monster, but a tamed monster, obediently slowing for its stop. I looked up at the white blur of the face of the man who had tamed it – and something about the set of his shoulders alerted me; I was already running along the platform as it came to a halt.

I called out, 'Ben, Ben!' His dark shoulders appeared above me and I saw the white flash of his teeth.

'I thought it were you, lass – and I told you to catch th'early!' But I heard the laughter in his voice and clinging to the shining steel rail I laughed back up at him. 'Keep an eye out, Frank – I'm dropping down.' As soon as he was on the platform beside me I put up my face for his kiss. 'I'm all over mucky, lass' – but he kissed me all the same.

I looked up into the cab and saw the gleam of brass wheels, and steel levers glinting in the glare from the fire – it was mysterious and exciting, a man's world, my husband's world – and I wanted to see more of it. I did not want to travel tamely back to Ainsclough in a dull compartment when Ben was there in front of me, driving the monster. I swung back to him. 'Ben – let me come on the footplate with you – take me with you.'

'Lass, there's nowhere to sit – and what about your nice coat?'

'Ben, please – I'll stand, it's not far. I'm not tired, and I've got lots of other clothes.' I put my hand on the sleeve of his jacket. 'Please, Ben.'

Suddenly he laughed. 'Come on, then – but you'll have to do as you're told.' He glanced quickly round. 'Now, while no one's looking – lucky platform curves or guard'd be on me tail. Take a hold.' Clasping the shining steel rail I put my foot on the first step, his hands lifted my hips and then we were both on board. He held me firmly round the waist. 'Now don't move unless I tell you – there's not much room and I don't want you falling out o'side o' cab. This is young Frank, by the way – me missus, Frank.'

A hand moved up to a cap and a man's voice said, 'Pleased to meet you, Missus Holden – Ben, guard'll be flashing porter any minute.'

'Aye, you go on Frank's side, lass.' He moved me bodily across. 'Stand in corner by tank and hang on to this handle – we'll not be using hand brake until we get

742

back to shed. Keep your gloves on – then your hand won't show up. There's whistle.'

I stood stock still in my corner, watching him lean out of the cab. Then he ducked his head back in and his left hand reached for a handle. Beside me Frank whispered, 'He's taking brakes off.' I watched Ben's strong knuckles grip, push up and forward, then ease back; the monster gave a long gusty sigh. Ben's right hand flashed out in the shadows and pushed one heavy lever away from him – then we began to move. The monster gave several short sharp barks, and as it did so I saw the chinks of light from the fire wink in sympathy. The barks quickened into a rhythmical growl and Ben's left hand was on the wheel now, turning it slowly until the monster's heartbeat steadied and became quieter.

It was very dark on the footplate now, the only light coming from that bright curving line round the fire door and the faint glimmer of the oil lamp hanging between the glass gauges. The cold night air rushed past as we gathered speed and I dared to raise one hand to my hat and pull it more securely down over my ears. Ben stood opposite me, leaning casually against the side of the cab, with the confidence of a man who knew his job and had done it a thousand times before. He glanced across at me and his teeth flashed in a white grin. 'When they sent me out on this driving turn tonight I thought about you – but I reckoned you'd be safe home by now. What we got, Frank?'

Frank was leaning out of the gap behind me as the track curved. Now he shouted back, 'One off.' Then his voice close to my ear explained, 'Signals, missus – dusta see?' But I was looking at Ben, watching his right hand go up and pull the heavy lever effortlessly towards him. I heard the engine note change as we slowed, then Frank called again: 'Two off,' and Ben pushed the heavy lever back up and we gathered speed once more as the dimly lit signal box flashed past.

'Soon be in Church. Excuse me, missus.' Frank stretched his arm round me and began to manipulate his own small circular handle. But it was Ben who was in command, Ben who was touching the brake handle again, rocking it backwards and forwards until the monster sighed and slowed and ran down into the small station with a final protesting squeal.

'Keep forward, sweetheart, and hang on tight.'

As the compartment doors began to slam Frank whispered in my ear, 'I thought for a moment he were talking to me!' Then he pushed past and went to lean out of the cab on the platform side, his broad shoulders close to Ben's, hiding me from view.

As we set off again Frank said, 'I reckon she needs a shovel or two, Ben.'

'I'll bring lass over my side, then, Frank.' Ben came towards me in the gloom. 'Give me your hand, sweetheart.' He drew me across the swaying footplate to the driver's corner. 'Take hold of the wheel.' I did as he bid me and felt his strong arm come round my waist. 'I'll hold you steady, lass – you keep close to me.'

Frank leant forward; there was a roar and I saw the door swing open, exposing the fierce whiteness of the fire. We pounded through the night and Ben held me safe while Frank flicked coal into the nearest corners, hefting the heavy shovel as though it were a child's toy – just as Ben must have done for years – and still did. The wooden floor jolted beneath me and the heat of the monster's heart fanned my legs; then the door swung back and only a faint glowing curve showed where it had devoured its food.

'I'll take you back over t'other side, sweetheart.' I edged back, clutching his hand. 'Good lass – stay out of sight as we run into Rishton.' Frank crouched down at my feet, and I heard the whisper of a brush as he swept the floor clean. When the station lights appeared I fixed my gaze on Ben and watched his strong hands moving: turning, pulling – and I felt the excitement rise in the pit of my belly. I was mesmerized by the strength and command of him – I wanted to reach out to touch those shoulders, stroke those arms – but I knew I could not – yet.

The engine began to clatter downhill. Ben called over to me, 'We're running into tunnel – hang on tight,' and suddenly steam swirled into the cab and I smelt oil and smoke and soot; and my ears were deafened by the roar until we shot out again into the fresh night air. Ben's hand rested easily on the wheel; we were running faster and faster now, down into Blackburn. There were lines joining us, signal boxes, lights in the streets – and then another tunnel; we rattled through, safe with my man in charge. I saw his hand on the brakes as he said, 'Greasy as ever in here, Frank – I'll give her some sand.' The wheels slowed as they gripped, then Ben's voice came again, loud above the tumult of the tunnel. 'Soon as we're out of this you'll have to lean well forward, lass, so you're hidden by front of cab.' I ducked my head in acknowledgement, breathing in the steam and the smoke. I bent forward as we ran out of the tunnel, as Ben had told me to. 'Don't touch boiler lass, it'll scorch you. Frank, give her your injector wheel to hold, you can use mine. That's right lass, just there – good girl.'

I stood like an obedient statue as the sickly yellow lights of Blackburn station flared out either side of us. Then two pairs of broad shoulders blocked the light again, shielding me, until the guard's whistle blew, and Ben reached for his levers and we were off again. The curving line of the fire was white now from the heat inside as we ran over the town and out towards Ainsclough – towards home.

We heard the porter shouting, 'Ainsclough! Ainsclough! All change 'ere.' Ben grunted, 'That's Ernie by sound of it – he'll not give us away – still, with a bit of luck he won't even notice.' He clamped on the brake then swung out of the cab and down on to the platform. 'Come on, lass.' I was down into his arms, his warm mouth was on mine and we clung together for a moment

– then he released me quickly. 'Off you go – I'll be home in half an hour.'

'Goodbye, Ben,' I called softly back as I headed for the barrier – and as soon as I reached it I turned and waved – the engine whistle pooped in answer, then the guard's green lamp swung out, his shrill whistle blew and the monster began to move away from me. I felt quite bereft – but Ben would be coming home to me soon. I fumbled for my ticket, then walked swiftly down the ramp and out of the station.

CHAPTER FIVE

As I pushed open the front door I was quivering with excitement, but when I looked at the clock of course it was too early – he would not be home yet. I almost ran through to the kitchen and attacked the range; it glowed and flared up and I stood gazing at the flames, mesmerized – for a moment I was back on the swaying footplate, feeling the heat from the white-hot heart of the monster. But the monster was just a game – the man who had controlled it was not; and he would be home soon with his broad shoulders and strong hands; I shivered as excitement surged through me.

Back in the parlour I sat down on the sofa – but I could not sit still. Jumping up I pulled off my hat and tossed it on to the top of the piano; as I shook my hair back I felt it freeing itself from its pins – but I did not care. It was warm in the small room so I shrugged off my coat and dropped it over the armchair. The blue sheen of my satin frock rippled as I moved; I ran my hands over the softness that clung to my hips and slid them round over my belly – it was sweet and full and as I stroked it I felt the pressure rise. I bent my head and murmured his name – he must come soon, my body was hungry for him.

And then I heard him – his footsteps rang on the cobbles – he was half-running up the street and the pressure in my belly mounted as the pounding of his boots came nearer. He thrust the door open and stood in the lobby: a broad-shouldered man in faded blue overalls with a dirt-smeared face glistening with sweat. I ran to him. He laughed and caught my hands and held me away. 'Lass, I'm mucky all over – I mun have me bath.'

I was frantic, twisting and turning in his grasp, crying: 'Let me go, let me go!' His face stiffened, at once his hands released me – then I flung myself against him and buried my mouth in his neck, pressing my belly against him. In a moment I felt his arms hugging me tight as he whispered again, 'Lass, I mun have me bath.' But I pulled his mouth down to mine and found his lips and opened myself for him.

When he drew away he laughed aloud and putting his hands under my behind swung me up off the floor while I twined my hands around his neck. He shouldered the door shut behind us. 'Come on then, since you can't wait let's be having you.'

He carried me over to the hearthrug and we collapsed in a heap together, then I was pulling at the buttons of his bib while his hands were already far up between my thighs, working at the fastenings of my suspenders inside the silk of my knickers. I squirmed at the touch of him as my own fingers fought with the strong material of his overalls, then I was crying his name as he swung me down – I opened my legs and slid under his heavy body, lifting myself for him: 'Ben, Ben!' And even as he entered me I lost control – I was crying and shuddering, raising my hips under him – I needed him deeper and deeper inside – my legs wound round his buttocks and I was thrusting as vigorously as he was now – and with each thrust our bodies locked into each other. All sense, all reason, had gone – I wanted him, how I wanted him. As he quickened I cried out: 'Now, Ben – now!' And heard his voice from far away shout triumphantly, 'Now!' as with a last great swoop he drove far inside me until my whole body seemed to be filled with his. And as he flowed into me the surging pressure in my belly rose and rose – but it would not explode and I was frantic with it – I sank my teeth into his bare neck and thrust myself against him again and again until at last, beyond all hope, I burst on to him and was lost.

It was a long time before I opened my eyes; his were very close above me. I gazed up, bewildered and adrift, and he whispered, 'Helena, lass – are you all right?' I had no voice, I could only move my lips a little. He gathered me to his damp chest and stroked my hair, cradling me in his arms. He sat up, but I still lay quiescent against him, limp as a rag doll. Vaguely I saw the red teeth marks low down on his neck, and slowly began to remember. I reached out and touched where I had bitten him. 'I'm sorry, Ben – I hurt you.'

I felt the laughter vibrate in his chest. 'I don't reckon you did it on purpose, lass. You were in such a state, I've never seen owt like it. And then – well, it was as if you couldn't take any more and you just passed out. It must have bin from th'excitement, but you had me afeared for a moment, I can tell you – I thought I'd been too rough with you. Give us a kiss lass, now you've woken up – there weren't hardly time for it afore!'

I raised my face and opened my mouth under his. Our tongues twined lazily together, then more urgently – I clung to him. When he drew back he was panting. He said, his voice thick, 'Reckon I'd best get me bath – now you be a good lass and lay still for a moment.' He unfastened my arms and put me back down on the rug. He stroked my bare behind for a moment, then left me. I did not move.

I heard him filling pails in the kitchen, then he came back through to the parlour. I lay watching him walk towards me; he was completely naked and I could see the dark line of coal dust round his hips and the grimy V where his shirt opened. He knelt down and began to undress me.

When I was as naked as him he picked me up and carried me through to the scullery, our damp skins clinging together. He sat me on the edge of the bath and kept one arm round my shoulder, holding me up while he clambered in. Then he pulled me suddenly in after him and I landed with a splash to the sound of his laughter. Sliding his arms round my waist he pulled me back close against his chest; his large legs were either side of me, gripping my hips. 'Now you mun wash me and I'll wash you.' He handed me the soap and I began to slowly rub his legs – and as I did so I felt his own warm wet hands caressing my breasts. I wriggled away and reached down to tickle his feet – he began to squirm behind me. 'Eh – lass – stop it!' Then his fingers were in my armpits and I was squirming too, giggling and trying to dodge away, but there was no room and at last he held me pinned tightly against him and we laughed together like two children playing – until I felt the pressure of his maleness on my back and my belly flared up in reply – and we were not children any longer, but man and woman.

'Come on, sweetheart – let's have you out.' I stood still for him as he towelled me dry, then he rubbed himself rapidly down, swung me quickly up in his arms and carried me up to the front bedroom.

This time he moved slowly inside me; each gentle thrust caressed me and I smiled with pleasure and held him tight until he was ready, feeling the warm satisfaction well up as he emptied himself into me.

I was drifting into sleep when I felt him begin to chuckle – then he threw back his head and shook with laughter. When he had stopped he kissed me, saying, 'I've seen for weeks now you were almost ready, but I didn't know what to do to bring you up to it, like – I

749

thought of all sorts, some daft ideas I had – but one as never crossed me mind was taking you for a ride on footplate of a radial tank – and that's what did trick!' He laughed again, then his hand slid down to rest comfortably between my legs as his lips brushed mine. 'Go to sleep, sweetheart.' I turned a little so that I was sprawling across his warm hard body – and fell asleep.

But when I awoke I was suddenly frightened; I was lying naked beside this man – this man who was no longer a friend, a brother – but a husband again. And a husband who would make demands of me: expect loyalty, obedience – and love. And that above all I could not give him – my heart had died with my dreams of Gerald; I would never love again.

He stirred beside me, his hand slid up between my thighs and I was already slippery to his touch – because my body was opening to him; as it had done last summer, over and over again – when I had hated him even as I coupled with him. And now I whispered, 'No, Ben, no – ' but he grunted and heaved himself on top of me. 'Don't be daft, lass – you're as ready as I am,' and even as I whispered 'No,' my legs were twining themselves round his and my hips were lifting for him and I cried out and caught at him and moaned until we were both spent.

Then he tried to pull me to him, but I thrust him away: 'Leave me alone, leave me alone!' I flung myself out of bed, stumbled across to the back bedroom and slammed the door; then I began to pull on my clothes, weeping. I heard his hand on the latch: 'Go away!' When he had gone back into the other bedroom I crept downstairs to sit huddled over the kitchen table, the tears still on my face. How could I live like this with a man I did not love – taking his body into mine night after night, as I had done last summer – taking him casually, carelessly, as a man does a whore – as I had done last summer?

I heard his footsteps on the stairs and he came in in

750

his shirtsleeves and braces, with his chin unshaven – I backed away. 'It's all right, lass – I won't touch you.' He dropped heavily down on to the chair opposite me. 'Sit down again, Helena – it's time we had a talk, you and me.' I sank back into the chair. He cleared his throat, his eyes were fixed on mine. 'Helena, when you were lying there in hospital – and no one knowing if you'd ever come alive again – ever want to be alive again – then I made a promise.' He swallowed: his voice was thick. 'I promised that if, if you got well again – then I'd offer you your freedom.'

'But – I'm your wife, Ben.'

'Aye – but there's ways round that – your mother made that very clear to me while you were ill. You see, I forced you to marry me, Helena – I trapped you like a butterfly in a net; you never had no choice. So now I'm offering you choice: do you want to stay – or go?'

I thought of Hatton, and the life I had been born to; I was well now, I could go back. Then I looked at the man in front of me, in his heavy braces and union shirt – and saw how the sweat stood out on his forehead as he waited for my answer. At last I said, 'But Ben – you've been so kind to me . . .'

'Helena, I weren't kind to you on the moors that day – I were a bastard, a selfish bastard. I didn't mean it to be like that, I swear it; I meant to court you proper. It didn't seem too impossible in war – we were up to our eyes in muck together, comrades, like. But afterwards . . . I went to Hareford, you know, when I come back – I thought I might happen to see you, in town. But when I asked on station they said Family was away – might not be back till Christmas – and that made me realize – there's only one Family round there, and that was yours. I went a bit wild after that – I suppose it were because of war, too – seeing all me mates killed in front of me – I did some stupid things then. But every week I used to go down library and look through *Times* – to see if you were going to be wed. I'd walk in with

751

me heart in me mouth – and come out like a man with a reprieve. And then I saw you in Manchester, and you introduced me to your sister and invited me to your home – and I thought, there's still a chance. And your brother, the Captain, I told him how I felt – '

'Yes, I know.'

'Well, I'm not saying he were in favour – but he weren't against, Helena. We'd been through a lot together, him and me – we trusted each other. I knew he'd do what he could. But next time I came I saw he were dying. I knew what it'd do to you, losing him – and when it happened it were worse than I ever dreamt. I didn't know what to do to help you – and no one else seemed to care. When I invited you on tops, I didn't mean it to happen way it did – I swear that, Helena. But soon as you got off train that day – you were all soft and loving, almost as if you were my girl.' Your mill girl, Ben – your mill girl. 'So suddenly I thought there was hope. And I carried you over stream as if you were most precious thing in world – you were the most precious thing in the world, Helena – and always will be, whatever you decide today. But then, you changed – put me at a distance; and yet, I knew you still wanted a man; I could smell it on you.' Like a bitch on heat. 'I suppose it were only natural – you'd seen a death, now you wanted the other. I knew by then it weren't me – any man would have done.' Like Rory Foster in the fern house. 'But, I were tempted, and – But I still don't know if – It were that crack you made about me making a good footman, Helena, that were what made me mind up, I thought: That's it, my lass, I'm going to have you before th'afternoon's out – and I did. I felt bad afterwards, especially when I saw bloodstains – but I knew I'd have done same again, if I'd had the chance. Because I wanted you, Helena – I wanted you so much. But I never asked whether you wanted me.' He looked at me, his face set. 'But I'm asking now, Helena – I'm giving you choice.' He paused, then added hesitantly, 'Could you – do you think, mebbe – you could come to feel something for me?'

And I saw the love and longing in his face, and my heart was pierced with pity – because I did not know how to reply. I moved restlessly in my chair, and as I did so I felt the stickiness on my thighs, where his seed had slipped out of my womb. 'Ben – last night – this morning – I may be with child.'

I saw the hope blaze up in his eyes, and knew that would be my answer. I could not decide – but my body would. 'Shall we wait and see, Ben?'

'You'd stay then, would you lass – for the child's sake?'

'Yes, Ben – I'd stay then.' I stood up. 'Go and have your shave, while I cook the breakfast.'

We did not talk about it again; I lived only in the present. But as the time of my monthly bleeding loomed I became nervous and uncertain; when he came in from work I would run to him and kiss him – then pull abruptly away and rush into the kitchen. And he was on edge too: I saw him watching closely as I dressed in the morning – and whenever I came back from the yard he would glance up at me, then look quickly away.

As we sat in the parlour one evening he suddenly said, 'You're late.'

I snapped, 'I've been late before.' I heard him sigh as he went back to his paper. We were awkward and ill at ease with each other.

Now when he took me at night he was very gentle; I did not explode under him any more, and as his arms pulled me to him I was not sure if I wanted him inside me at all – but once he was there I did not want him to go, and clung to him long after he had finished, until our bodies became hot and sticky with sweat. One night when he finally slipped out of me I began to cry, and he hugged me to him until I could hardly breathe, whispering, 'Helena lass, oh Helena lass – I wish you'd been born in Clegg Street.'

Next day in the kitchen I broke a cup and the tears filled my eyes and I began to sob. He lifted me on to his lap saying, 'Helena, sweetheart – don't fret, there's a good lass.' But I was fretting and so was he; I did not want to have to decide; I wanted my body to take this decision for me.

The next morning I woke feeling wretched and ill; I pushed my hand fearfully down between my legs, then brought it up – but there was no blood on my fingers. He was still sleeping beside me and I slid my hand cautiously on to my belly; it was not cramping but it was not comfortable either. I turned slightly and suddenly my stomach lurched and my throat closed and I was throwing myself out of the bed and over to the washstand. I was only just in time – with a great heave I vomited into the basin, then stood swaying and coughing, the vile taste of it in my mouth and nose. He came up beside me and wiped my lips with the damp flannel. 'I'll fetch you a glass of water.' When he came back I rinsed out my mouth and blew my nose – I felt weak and feeble, but more comfortable. He helped me back into bed and lay holding me close to his warm body. 'Better now, lass?'

'Yes, Ben – better.'

'You'll have to keep slop pail by bed – you only just made it today. And I'll bring up jug of fresh water each night, so you can swill your mouth out – it could be a few weeks yet.'

'Weeks, Ben?'

'Afore you get over the sickness – I remember Ada saying she were four months gone last time, but mebbe you'll be luckier.' He laughed softly, and at last my numbed brain understood. I would never leave Ainsclough now.

CHAPTER SIX

As his arms still held me, pictures flickered through my mind: the green parkland at Hatton; the great house glowing golden in the sun; brightly clad, elegant figures strolling on the terrace. I heard the sharp crack of the croquet mallet, the thud of tennis ball on racket, and the clip-clop of horses' hooves on the stable cobbles in the early morning. All this was taken from me now, and I felt the pang of its loss.

The man holding me shifted slightly; one of his hands broke free and slid down on to my belly. He pressed it there a moment, gently, reverently, before heaving a great sigh of contentment. 'This'll be best Christmas present I've ever had, lass.' He laughed almost shyly as he whispered. 'Thank you, sweetheart, thank you.' His mouth nuzzled my hair and I did not know whether he was thanking me for the child – or for staying: perhaps it was both. I still saw Hatton in its green parkland, but now I heard the voices of the gaily-clad guests: high, confident voices – witty and sharp-tongued – with myself gauche and awkward among them. They would not miss my presence, but this man had longed for me to stay with him. I had seen his face light up at the sight of me when he came home from work, and he had turned to me eagerly, anxious to tell me the news of his day, and to hear of mine. Besides, I was his wife, and I was carrying his child.

I moved a little so I could slip my arms around his neck, and press my womb against his flat belly; he stroked my back and kissed my hair until I fell asleep.

When I woke up later I was ravenously hungry; Mary cooked breakfast for us and as I reached for yet another piece of toast she smiled at me, a woman's smile of complicity – and I blushed as I remembered Ben emptying the basin earlier.

Before he left for work Ben said, 'I'll take you to Blackburn Saturday. My turns come earlier each day this week, so we can go in afternoon and I'll buy you some sensible shoes.' I held up my face and he kissed me goodbye.

He was late that evening and I was already in bed and asleep when he came in. But as I heard his heavy body sliding in beside me I turned and opened myself to him; he moved slowly and gently inside me and when he eased himself off me I fell deeply asleep. I opened myself to him each evening that week, as soon as he climbed into bed, but on the Friday I was tired and heavy from the child so I did not move towards him. But when he pulled me close I felt the swollen tenseness of him, so I parted my legs for him and lay still and let him use my body. When at last he lay limp and relaxed in my arms, he kissed my mouth and whispered, 'Thanks, lass – I needed you badly tonight.' The child would take from me what it needed, and so would he; only I could satisfy them both. He rolled off me and gathered me to him; I put my head against his neck and heard his contented breathing – the breathing of a man comfortable and at ease now, because I had given him what he wanted. I drifted into sleep.

The next day we went for my shoes. Although I was only a couple of weeks overdue my breasts were already swelling, and I was being sick every morning now. Clinging to Ben's arm as we walked through the soot-blackened streets I sensed the swagger in his walk; he had planted his seed in me and it had taken root, at once.

When we got home he made me lie down on the sofa, and fussed around me with cushions for my head and cushions for my feet. I smiled at him. 'I feel quite well, Ben – don't be silly.'

'You rest, lass – we don't want to take any chances. I'll go and make tea.' And while he was in the kitchen I began to worry a little myself, as I remembered last summer.

As soon as he came back with the tray I said, 'Ben – but suppose, suppose I fall down in the street again?'

'You're not going to, lass – not in your new shoes. Besides, last year were different: you weren't in no state to carry then, I know that now. And you would keep scrubbing th'ouse out from top to bottom – now we've got Mary.' He smiled at me. 'No, lass – you're as fit as a flea this time, except for mornings – and that don't last long. I've seen them breakfasts you're eating – talk about eating for two – I reckon you're stoking up for next half dozen!' I blushed. 'And look at you now, you're blooming like a rose – you look lovelier than ever – in fact, I can hardly keep me hands off you!'

I raised my arms to him; I felt warm and loving. 'You don't have to keep your hands off me, Ben.'

He kissed my cheek before shaking his head. 'No, lass – I been expecting too much on you; it's time I rationed meself – every other night from now on.'

I lay and watched him drinking his tea; a strong broad-shouldered man. I went out to the kitchen to help him prepare our meal – and brushed past him several times; his back stiffened whenever I touched him. On my way back from the yard I undid the top button of my blouse, then went to sit opposite him in the parlour and opened the mending basket. I held the sock I was darning high up, and kept my shoulders well back – so that my full breasts strained against the thin lawn of my blouse; every time I looked up from my needle I saw his eyes riveted on them. I shifted in the chair so as to pull my skirt up a little, and then crossed one leg over the other. His intent gaze travelled down. I waited a moment and then leant right over the arm of the chair and pretended to search in my basket; as I was doing so my skirt rode up to my knees – and the lace edging of my petticoat showed. I

757

heard him suck through his teeth. 'Are you all right, Ben? Not too cold?'

'No – no. In fact, I'm a bit hot, to tell you truth.' He ran his finger round the inside of his collar; sweat was beading his forehead. I smiled at him and then exclaimed as I dropped my needle; I bent down, leaning right over the hearthrug and my breasts fell forward and pressed against the fabric of my blouse. I could see the needle glinting on the rug, but pretended to search for it for a long time. When eventually I did pick it up and sat back again I took a deep breath and stretched – and the next button of my blouse burst open. His breathing was quickening.

Looking down at my leg I cried, 'Oh, Ben – I must have laddered my stocking! I wonder if it's gone right up to the top.' He watched, mesmerized, as I slowly drew my skirt up to the fastening of my suspenders – then his face went brick-red and he burst out, 'You little monkey – you're doing it on purpose! All that bending and stretching and, "Oh Ben – me stockings got a ladder".' He mimicked my voice.

Widening my eyes, I gazed at him: 'But Ben – it *has* got a ladder – look, I'll show you.' I stood up and stepped across the hearthrug and sat down on his lap. 'Look, Ben – ' then his mouth was covering mine and I felt his hands on my breasts and I knew I had won.

Afterwards we lay very close on the rug and he told me, 'Tomorrow night you'll have to do without.'

I murmured meekly, 'Yes, Ben,' and kissed his neck.

But the sickness lasted longer the next day; I still felt queasy at lunchtime, and my head ached. I had to go out to the backyard more often too, and Ben began to look worried. I only toyed with my meal and he made me go and lie down in the parlour afterwards while he washed up. When he had finished he muttered, 'I'm just going up street,' and when he came back Albert's wife was with him.

758

He drew up a chair for her and she sat herself down and beamed at me. 'How are you, lass?'

Ben mumbled the words 'tea' and slipped away. I smiled at Mrs Henshaw. 'I'm quite well, really – just a little sick, only – '

She leant forward and patted my hand. 'But you're afeard of losing again.'

'Yes – yes I am.'

'Are you spotting blood? Or feeling any cramps?'

'No – nothing like that.'

She sat back, satisfied. 'That's all right, then. Now, you listen to me, lass. Me old mam were local midwife, and she always reckoned lasses who were sick early on weren't likely to lose – there's some were upset when she told them that!'

I said quickly, 'I wasn't sick last time.'

'There you are, then – me old mam weren't often wrong. What with them who wanted and couldn't and them who could and didn't want she 'eard all the stories!'

Ben pushed the door open, carrying a tray. 'How is she, Mrs Henshaw?'

'Well naturally she's not feeling on top of the world, but that's the way it is, innit? You men have all the pleasure and then the woman pays the price – but don't get upset, lad, she's all right. You pour us a nice cup of tea now, you've got to look after 'er.'

When she had finished her tea she stood up and came over to me, and took my hand. 'Stop fretting now, lass, and let him wait on you for a change – make 'em pay for their pleasures with a bit of cosseting.'

After he had shown her to the door Ben sat down heavily, looking relieved. 'She knows a thing or two does Florrie Henshaw, and she's had eight on her own, so you just do as she says.' Then he glanced at me with a grin. 'Though I dunno about men getting all the pleasure – it seemed to me you weren't exactly uninterested in idea at time, either.' I blushed as he came over and knelt beside me. 'All the same, it 'ud best be rationed now.'

He kissed me full on the lips, then hoisted up the tray and took it out to the kitchen, whistling.

I was sick again the next day but half an hour later I felt so well I sang all morning – I was brimming with life. I stood looking in the mirror, admiring my new figure; I had always envied the ripe fullness of Alice and my mother, and now it was becoming mine too. I walked down to the town with Ben in the late afternoon, and saw men's eyes resting on me – one youngster in a smart black bowler came out of the bank and tripped over the step, so intently was he looking at me. Ben said grimly, 'It's time we bowt you some new clothes, you're bursting out of that frock at top.' Laughing, I swung round and brushed his arm with my full breasts – and watched his face turn a dark red. I pressed myself against him as we came back up the street and as soon as we were inside the parlour he pulled me into his arms. 'Helena, Helena!' He buried his face in my neck and began to fumble with the buttons of my frock – and I laughed because I knew men wanted me and that this man was going to take me.

But later that evening I suddenly felt sick; my head was heavy, and I huddled miserably on the sofa. Ben glanced over at me. 'Just as well you had your fun earlier, you don't look up to it now. Best get to bed, I'll come up later.' I stood up and my hand flew to my mouth: I was gagging. He leapt to his feet. 'Hang on, lass, while I fetch bowl!' After I had finished retching he carried me up to bed.

That became the pattern for me now: some days I would wake feeling totally wretched, and then an hour later the sun would come out and I would feel ready to dance and sing – not even remembering that I had ever felt ill; other days I would be glowing with health one minute, then running for the scullery sink the next. But I continued travelling to Manchester for my singing lessons, and Madame Goldman praised my voice for its new depth and fullness. In the evenings I often played and sang for Ben: he would turn over my music and ask me the meaning of the German, rarely forgetting a word once he had heard it explained. One day he found *Frauen Liebe und Leben*, and sat puzzling over it; he pointed to the fourth stanza:

> 'Du Ring an meinem Finger
> Mein goldenes Ringelein.'

'So it's about a woman getting wed, then.'

'Yes – it's called *A Woman's Life and Love*.' I waited apprehensively for him to ask me to sing it to him – but he did not.

One day at the beginning of the third month Ben finished at twelve, so I suggested that he come into Manchester after my lesson. I went to Victoria to meet him; I was too early and had to wait, a little excited because he had left that morning without waking me, so I had not even kissed him goodbye.

He came striding through the barrier in his best suit, rather shiny at the elbows. 'How are you, lass? Not that I need to ask, you're looking beautiful.'

I glowed as I raised my face for his kiss. 'Ben, you can help me choose some new clothes, just at Kendal's . . .'

His mouth tightened. '*Just* at Kendal's – '

'I've opened an account there.'

'With the Captain's money.'

'Yes – with Robbie's money.' I cried out. 'He was my *brother*, Ben.'

He stood still, biting his lip, then at last said, 'I mun pay the rent, Helena – I mun do that.'

'Yes, Ben.' I was submissive now.

His ideas about my clothes were very definite; the saleswomen looked astonished. As soon as the choices for me had been made I said casually, 'Now we'll get you measured for a suit, Ben – I've opened an account at the tailor's too.'

He gave in eventually. I wanted to see him in a well-cut suit. Since he was broader than most of the men of

761

my family, and more muscular, he needed to be properly fitted to show his figure to its best advantage. I moved closer to him.

As we were leaving the tailor's he told me, 'There's summat I want to fetch from Sherratt's – I'll take you to tea shop first, so you can sit down while I'm gone.'

He came back with a brown paper parcel, and put it down on one of the chairs without meeting my eye; he looked rather flushed.

He did not unwrap his parcel until after our meal that evening; I craned forward to peer at the title – it was *Tweedy's Practical Obstetrics*. I began to laugh. 'Ben – whatever are you doing with that?'

He looked up, his face very red. 'I'm reading it – I want to know what's happening inside you, and how it'll be for you. I always like to find out as much as I can – about everything.'

'You shouldn't read that, Ben – medical textbooks always make things seem worse than they are.' He stuck out his chin and reached for the dictionary.

When I looked up from my score later I saw that he was staring at me fixedly, his face white. He swallowed and said, 'Oh, lass – I wish we hadn't done it now. I didn't realize it were going to be like that.'

I laughed. 'I told you not to read it, Ben – those kind of books always go on about the complications. I'm sure I shall have a normal birth.'

He was almost shouting. 'It's normal birth I'm reading about! I haven't got to rest yet.' His face looked so horrified that I started giggling. He put the book down and came and stood over me. 'Lass, I never realized what I were going to make you go through.'

I stifled my giggles. 'Well, it's too late now, Ben. What's been put in will have to come out.'

He still looked down at me with the same expression on his face; I began to laugh again. He said, 'You're not bothered, are you? You're not even worried about it.'

'Not really, no – there's no point, is there? After all, women do it all the time.'

He said bluntly, 'It'll hurt.'

'I know that, Ben – but lots of things hurt, don't they?' I said flatly, 'After all those years in the war hospitals I think I should be able to stand this.' Then I added, 'No, that's not quite true – I *want* to stand this, because there's a purpose in the pain – it's natural, it's right – not like all the other.'

'And you'll have a babby at th'end on it.'

'Yes.'

But he still stood shamefaced so at last I smiled up at him and said gently, 'My mother had six with no trouble, and Emmie Greenhalgh told me once that your mother didn't even know you were coming until you arrived – so why should I worry?'

He went back to his chair and sat down, opening his book again. I nearly stopped him, then remembered what Florrie Henshaw had said to him: 'You men have all the pleasure and then the woman pays the price.' I would let Ben pay a little of the price tonight.

He was still reading when I went up to wash and get ready for bed. He brought the book up with him as I was climbing under the covers; his face was excited. 'Lass, just take your nightie off, will you?'

I said teasing, 'But Ben – we did last night, and you said – '

'No – I only want to look at you.'

I pulled my nightdress over my head and he drew back the sheets. 'It's a warm night, you won't catch cold.' He sat down on the edge of the mattress with the book in his hand. 'Let's have a look at your breasts.'

As his hands began to move over my right breast he muttered to himself. 'Aye, it is darker, and bigger.' I lay back, soothed, as he stroked the area around my nipple. He glanced at his book again. 'Now lass, I won't hurt you – I'm just going to squeeze a bit.' He took my full breast in his hands and gently squeezed it; my belly began to soften. He exclaimed, 'There lass – you got it already! Look at that.' He held up his hand; there was a drop of clear liquid on his finger. 'It says here that in primigravida – that's a lass on her first, like you – it's sometimes found at th'end of second month, but more often at th'end o' third. You're nowhere near th'end of third, but you're doing it already!' He seemed so pleased with me that I felt as though I had passed a difficult exam and come out top. 'Let's do t'other one.' He squeezed again and my belly became still softer – I shifted a little against him, but he was intent on my left nipple now. 'Clever lass – you done it in both! It says it's a very constant sign in primigravida, so it looks as if you're definitely expecting.'

I exclaimed. 'Ben – we knew that already!'

He ignored me. 'Now let's have a look at your belly.' His hands left my breasts and moved lower down.

'But I thought you'd already diagnosed, Dr Holden!'

He gave a small, laughing grunt. 'I'm interested, lass, right interested.'

As his hands began to touch my belly more firmly I thought: And I'm interested too, Ben – but not in your textbook. I could feel the soft moistness between my legs.

'Now let's have a look at your thighs.' He pulled them apart. 'Hm – little veins, that's right.' He coughed, 'Lass, the next signs are a bit intimate like – do you mind if I . . . ?'

I smiled up at his reddening face. 'No, Ben, that's quite all right – you go ahead.'

His fingers began to open me. 'Mm – "faint violet colour", that's right – so that's what they're called . . .' He pushed his finger inside me – it was too much; I started to writhe and moan. He looked up, startled. 'What's matter, lass – am I hurting you?' He began to pull his hand away so I reached down frantically and pressed it hard against me until I burst on it – and lay back limp and relieved upon the pillow.

His eyes stared at me out of a brick-red face. 'Helena – I were doing an *examination*' – his voice was reproachful – 'how can I concentrate when you go and do that? You've got me all excited now – and I've lost me place.'

I started to laugh; I laughed and laughed, and I was still laughing by the time he had got his clothes off and was pushing into me. I managed to stop long enough to whisper, 'That's not your hand you're using, Dr Holden,' then I began to laugh again until I came quivering down on him a second time – just as he filled me.

When he rolled off he said, 'You're not taking this seriously at all, are you? And it were wrong night.'

I protested. 'Ben – what did you expect, handling me like that? And you must have been able to tell I was ready.'

He shouted, 'I never realized!' Then he reached for his discarded book, and began leafing through it; he found the page he was looking for and held it under my nose: 'Look, lass – it says, here, under "Signs of Pregnancy", that one sign is that you're moist and soft and pulsating down below.' I giggled again, then realizing I was very tired, I turned over on my back, pushed the sheets down and parted my legs. 'Ben, I'm going to sleep now – you have a good look and tell me all about it in the morning.' I closed my eyes and fell instantly asleep.

As we sat in the parlour the following evening Ben cleared his throat and announced, 'It's time you thought about going to see doctor.'

I widened my eyes. 'But Ben – you've got your book – '

'Don't be daft, lass – I'm serious. What I thought was – well, I've been making some inquiries and there's a good doctor down end of Bolton Road – a lady doctor.'

My whole body went rigid. 'Ben Holden – what are you implying?' His face reddened; I jumped to my feet and ran at him. 'How dare you, how dare you!'

'Lass – I – ' He dodged behind the armchair; I felt

fury sweep over me and raised my hand to strike – but he caught hold of me and held me away from him. 'Look, lass – I'm sorry – I should have explained – it's not that I think you – I mean, I know it 'ud be different with a doctor . . . It's me, see – reading that book, thinking about another man . . .'

'A doctor, Ben!'

'I don't care – I don't want any man handling you like that – 'cept me.'

My anger drained away as I remembered last summer, and my miscarriage. 'It's too late, Ben – I was examined before, when I, when I fell.' I shuddered.

He was watching me. 'And you didn't like it much, either – did you?'

'No, no I didn't.' I drew a deep breath then surrendered. 'All right, Ben – I'll go to your lady doctor. I think I'd prefer to.'

He sat down, rather shamefaced. 'I know I'm like one of those Arab sheiks, with his harem . . .'

I smiled a little. 'Don't you dare bring home a harem, Ben Holden.'

He threw back his head and laughed. 'I wouldn't have energy for it, lass – it takes me all me time to keep you served.' My face was on fire as I picked up my score again.

I went to the woman doctor; her waiting room walls were hung with photographs of women in khaki uniform and high riding boots, of others in nurses' veils, and men lying in bed outside tents.

Dr Hartley was tall and middle-aged, with pepper-and-salt hair drawn severely back into a bun, and a strong pleasant face. She shook my hand briskly. 'Now what can I do for you, my dear?'

I told her, 'I'm pregnant.'

She crossed to the sink and began to wash her hands, smiling at me over her shoulder. 'You seem very sure.'

I smiled back; I liked her. 'I am – my husband has

bought a midwifery textbook – he's checked for all the symptoms.'

She laughed outright. 'But he doesn't feel quite up to handling the delivery, is that it?'

'That's right.' We laughed together.

She dried her hands. 'Pop next door and empty your bladder, then get undressed – the couch is behind the screen.' She questioned me as her confident fingers carried out their examination. When she had finished she smiled. 'Mm – your husband's right – not much doubt there. Your first, I take it?'

'I miscarried last year – twins – I wasn't very well – and I fell in the street.'

'You seem in very good shape this time – just be sensible and make sure you get enough rest if you feel tired. Up you get, then.'

When I came and sat down by her desk she asked, 'What's brought you to Ainsclough?'

'I live here.'

She smiled. 'But you haven't always, have you?' Then, without waiting for an answer she picked up her pen. 'Now let me have your name.'

'Lady Helena Holden.'

She glanced up, intent. 'I heard about you – it was in the paper: "Local war hero weds earl's daughter" – just a paragraph.' I had not known. She continued, 'It said you met your husband while you were nursing – where were you nursing, Lady Helena?'

I told her, and she listened, her face alight with interest. 'We must have a good chat, you and I – compare notes. You see I was in Serbia myself, with Dr Inglis' team. The War Office wouldn't touch women doctors, of course – not at the start – they were glad enough later, but most of us had found something more exciting to do by then. I didn't do much obstetrics out there, of course – only the occasional peasant woman, and I sorted out a goat, once! But I did plenty before I went and I do it now, so I'll book you in, if you want.'

767

'Yes, please do.'

'About the second week in January, I think. There's quite a good nursing home – '

'No – no, I want to be delivered at home, in our own bed.'

I flushed as I finished, and she said, shrewdly and bluntly, 'Take it out where it went in, eh?'

I smiled. 'Yes.'

'Well, it's the tradition of your class. Come and see me every month, then – or sooner if you're worried about anything. I work with a midwife, so I'll send her round to see you nearer the confinement.'

Ben was pleased when he heard my report. 'And she were in the Serbian campaign. I wonder if she were in Retreat? I'll have to ask her – different sort of fighting it were out there – it'll be interesting to have a chat.'

CHAPTER SEVEN

I was glad I had been to see Dr Hartley; I trusted her: she would deliver my son safely when the time came. Ben teased me when I talked of the child as a 'he'. 'It might be a girl, lass – then what'll you do, send it back?'

I laughed and shook my head. 'It's a boy, Ben – I know it is.'

Then he had a long chat with Florrie Henshaw and came back to tell me he thought it would be a boy, too. 'Florrie says women who put it all on front are generally carrying lads, and there's no doubt where you're putting it, sweetheart – from back no one could tell you're expecting. Mind, your belly only really shows when you're undressed – but those little breasts o' yours . . .' He smiled and pulled me on to his lap.

The next day was Sunday; we sat drowsily in the

parlour after lunch pretending to read as we dozed a little. Then Ben stood up and shook himself. 'Time I made a pot of tea to wake us up.'

While he was out in the kitchen there was a rat-tat-tat at the door. 'I'll go, Ben.' I pulled myself up.

Outside on the step stood Barnes, resplendent in uniform. 'Are you at home my lady? Lady Pickering and Mr Finlay have driven over.'

'Yes – yes, of course I am, Barnes.'

He sprang back to the Delaunay-Belleville and swung the door open, and my mother stepped gracefully out. Conan emerged quickly from the other side. 'Hello, Hellie – we thought we'd have a run out and see if you were in.'

Ben came through from the back, struggling into his jacket. Mother extended two gloved fingertips; he seized her whole hand and shook it vigorously – her eyes narrowed. Conan slapped Ben on the shoulder. 'Good to see you, old man – and how's little Hellie?' He swung round to me – and his face stilled. Then he said, in a voice that was not quite steady, 'You're blooming, Helena, aren't you? Blooming.' It was one of my good times. I saw his gaze flick down to my swelling breasts, and on to my full hips – my belly was barely curved yet, my waist still slim, but the rest of my body was ripening. He leant forward and took my hand. 'I must give you a cousinly kiss.' He pressed his lips to my cheek, but as he drew back they brushed my mouth – and I could scarcely stop myself from moving towards him. Conan's blue eyes rested on mine as he said, 'She's just like a luscious ripe peach, eh, Aunt Ria? Ainsclough seems to suit her.'

My mother selected the best armchair and arranged herself elegantly on it before asking, 'Are you with child, Helena?'

'Yes, Mother.'

Her glance swung up to Ben, standing beside me; it swept over his broad shoulders and down to his hips –

appraising him. Ben said quickly, 'I were just putting kettle on – I'll get back to it.' He went out to the kitchen.

Conan began to chat, easily, casually – but his gaze never left me. He broke off from what he was saying and turned to Mother. 'I can't get over it – I haven't seen her since she was in the nursing home, and now she seems so well. She's looks beautiful, doesn't she, Aunt Ria?'

My mother nodded grudgingly. 'Some women are suited to pregnancy – like cows.'

As my face flushed Conan gave a great shout of laughter and slapped my mother's hand – however did he dare? She only smiled at him indulgently.

Ben came back with the tray and set it in front of me; I poured while Conan and Ben talked together. I saw my mother studying Ben – she began to unbend slightly, to address the odd remark directly to him. I glanced sideways at my husband and saw what my mother saw: a man who had behaved in a most inconvenient and annoying fashion, but who had broad shoulders and a strong, virile body – for that, much could be forgiven him. Besides, Mother was a pragmatist; I was in Ainsclough and it was clear I was going to stay here.

She began to speak of Letty: 'Immured in that nunnery of a women's college – her fingers quite stained with chemicals – seeming to spend all her time in laboratories or libraries – I don't understand her at all, she doesn't seem like a daughter of mine.' She sighed and glanced at Ben, and I thought, oh yes – she understands me though, I am a daughter of hers. The others were talking so I picked up the tea pot and went to refill it in the kitchen. As I put down the kettle I heard the latch click behind me; Conan slipped in and closed the door softly after him. We stood looking at each other. His blue eyes passed slowly over me, up and down – then up again to my swelling breasts; my body tingled. He gave a slightly unsteady laugh. 'That blouse is too small for you, Helena.'

'I know,' and as I took a deep breath I felt the fine silk strain.

He moved towards me a step. 'God, Helena – you look lovely – I've never seen you so beautiful – you've always had something about you, but now it's . . .' He moved another step forward and I felt myself sway towards him – then the door swung suddenly open and Ben loomed dark behind us.

'Do you need any help, Helena?'

Conan said hastily, 'I don't think so, old man – I came out to offer myself. I'll leave you to it.'

Ben came forward and took the full tea pot from me. 'Button up your jacket, Helena.'

'But it's too hot – '

'Do as I say.' I buttoned my jacket, though it was too tight and hurt my breasts.

Back in the parlour Conan and Ben continued to chat together, my mother throwing in the odd word – but I sat silent, feeling the familiar sickness rise in my belly, and my head began to throb. I was glad when Mother stood up to leave – I felt quite ill now.

Ben came back in as the motor purred off down the street. 'Not feeling too good, lass?'

'No – I feel rather queasy.'

His heavy hand came down on my shoulder; his fingers tightened. 'Conan couldn't take his eyes off you.'

I dared not look up at his face. 'Conan – Conan likes women.'

'Aye – and he likes you more'an all the others. But you're my wife, Helena – remember that.' His fingers were biting so deeply into my shoulder now, they were hurting me.

My voice was no more than a whisper. 'Yes, Ben. But – I – ' I tore myself away from his grasp and lurched as quickly as I could out into the scullery – just in time to heave my lunch into the sink. He did not come near me, though he pushed a chair forward for me to collapse on to when I had finished.

He stood watching me as I wiped my mouth, still gagging a little, then he said, 'Aye, likely you won't forget I'm your husband, way things are with you now – but remember, Helena, I'm a jealous man. I were looking at your ma this afternoon and I thought that if I'd been your pa I'd have put my lady across my knee and tanned the backside off her. She wouldn't have played tricks with me again.' He swung round and slammed the door behind him.

Alone in the scullery I began to giggle weakly at the thought of my mother's expression if she had heard what Ben had said. But back in the front room I defended her. 'Remember, Ben, that it's six of one and half a dozen of the other. Papa – '

He put down his paper and his eyes were steady, holding mine. 'Lass, I've played fair with you, and I always will – will you promise to do the same with me?'

'Yes, Ben – I will.' My stomach lurched again.

He smiled a little. ' "In sickness and in health" – and, poor lass, it looks as if you're one with sickness at present. I'll go and fetch pail.'

But as I lay beside my sleeping husband in bed that night I remembered the way Conan's blue eyes had looked at me in the kitchen; I supposed I was glad I was not married to him, but for a moment I wished – oh, how I wished – that they had left us together in the maze that evening when we were young and innocent and carefree. Then I turned over on my side and felt the tenderness of my swollen breasts – and thought that perhaps it was as well they had not.

Guy's letter came as usual, from Canada. He had written to me faithfully every month since he had left, although I had often failed to answer, especially last year. This time he wrote that he and Pansy were coming home, for a long leave, in the autumn.

I ran to Ben as soon as he came in from work. 'Guy – Guy's coming home, in October!'

He looked at my excited face, before asking, 'Do you want to go and stay for a bit, while he's here?'

I hesitated. 'I don't want to leave you, Ben – not for long.'

'I'll manage, with Mary coming in.'

I dropped my eyes. 'It's not just that, Ben – I'll miss you.'

'Aye – and I'll miss you, too – but you want to see your brother. Look, I'm due for me week's holiday in September; I were thinking about two of us going to Yorkshire, to stay at a farm – but I daresay someone'll swap with me, then we could go to Hatton together – if you want me there, that is.'

'Yes, yes, I do, Ben.'

'Then that's settled – as long as your ma says yes.'

I laughed. 'She will – Papa does put his foot down occasionally.'

Ben grinned. 'You could have fooled me – I'll get me bath.'

Ben came with me the next time I went to see Dr Hartley, as he had said he would. They got on well, and she invited us both to supper one evening the following week. As we sat over our meal we talked of Germany – she had studied in Berlin before the war, and she knew Munich, too. After the maid had cleared the table its polished top was spread with maps as she and Ben thrashed out the Serbian campaigns. She brought out her box of photographs and we matched them to place and time. Several of them were of a sweet-faced Serbian officer – an older man with badges of rank on his uniform. He smiled so trustingly at the camera that I exclaimed, 'he looks too gentle to be a soldier.'

Dr Hartley took the photo from me and held it very delicately in her large, capable hands, gazing at the pictured face. Then she said, 'yes – he was. But he did his duty and died for it.' As she looked up at me I flinched from the naked loss in her eyes; then she put the photograph down, saying, 'But it's not such a bad life, delivering other women's babies.' She turned back to the maps.

I dropped suddenly asleep in my chair, awakening to hear her and Ben discussing pregnancy fatigue. Ben reached out and touched my hand. 'Why don't you sing to the doctor, Helena – mebbe some of your German songs?' So I sang German Lieder to an English doctor who had loved a Serbian officer and lost him to the Bulgarian guns – in that greatest of all wars. Thank God we would never have to fight such a war again.

The performance of the *Messiah* was coming nearer and I was still having to run very frequently out to the closet; I was rather worried but Ben told me there would be no problem, since during the fourth month my womb would rise up into my abdomen and so stop pressing on my bladder. He also insisted that my morning sickness would shortly disappear, and when it did I felt slightly piqued – after all, I was the one who was carrying the child. But I was relieved – I did so want to sing in Ainsclough again.

Madame Goldman had coached me thoroughly, so now I went along to the Methodist church to practise with the organist and choir. The choirmaster asked me if I would give some advice to the soprano soloist; her voice was a little weak for the high-galleried chapel. She came forward nervously to sing for me; she was a pretty nineteen-year-old. Her voice was pleasant but occasionally flat, and she needed help with her breathing, so I suggested she come up to Royds Street in the evenings after work. I practised with her at the piano and she was admiring and grateful; I began to feel like an elder sister.

If he was at home Ben would sit listening to us, and after she had gone one day I said, 'Olive's a very pretty girl, isn't she, Ben?'

He looked at me and smiled. 'Aye, I suppose she is – but when you're in room I've not got eyes for any other woman.'

I blushed and looked down at my thickening waistline. 'But I'm getting fat, Ben.'

'Aye, you are – with my child. I like looking at that too,' he added simply.

A week before the *Messiah* I was lifting a steak pie out of the oven when I felt a fluttering in my belly; I stilled, crouched before the open oven door. Ben jumped up. 'What's matter, lass?'

As he took the dish from my hands and helped me up I whispered, 'He's moving – I felt him moving!' and began to cry. Ben pulled me to him and kissed my wet cheeks, murmuring words of love.

In the front room later he got out his book. 'You're right on target for quickening, lass – but it don't say anything about crying when it happens.' He grinned at me and I hauled myself off the sofa and went to climb on his lap. Dropping the book, he put his arms round me and hugged me tight. 'Reckon I'll concentrate on practical side for a while.' He unbuttoned my blouse and began to unfasten my bodice. I leant against him as his warm hands explored my body, and when he put his lips to mine I opened my mouth for him. He drew back a moment. 'You'll tell me when you don't want it any more, won't you, lass?' In answer I began to undo his shirt buttons.

Afterwards he said, 'We'll soon have to think of another way of doing it – so I don't press down on you.' I pulled his face to mine and kissed him; his hand gently stroked my belly and I felt the fluttering again.

My womb was rising now and I had to have a dress altered for the performance. Ben walked down to the church with me and I leant on his arm, excited and rather nervous – but Olive was in the vestry, white-faced and wringing her hands, and by the time I had calmed her down I had forgotten my own fears.

As we walked out into the crowded church she whispered, 'I'm glad you sing before I do, Lady Helena – it'll help me to settle.'

We seated ourselves on the rostrum; the choir was already ranged behind us and the choirmaster took up his position in front, a sheen of perspiration on his face. The church was full; when I raised my eyes to the gallery the massed ranks of Ainsclough looked back, resplendent in their Sunday best. I dropped my gaze again, to look at Ben; he was in the front row with Dr Hartley beside him. Mary Grimshaw and Jim were behind, with their three elder children – I knew Betsy had wanted to come, but Mary had said it was too late – 'She can't be trusted to behave herself in chapel yet, that's truth of it, but I daren't tell her that!' A little further back were the Inghams, while a row of well-scrubbed Henshaw faces filled an entire side pew, under the watchful eye of Florrie. I felt the warmth coming from that congregation of friends and neighbours, and relaxed in my upright chair. Olive glanced over at me, nervous again; as I smiled back the organist began to play the overture.

The tenor rose first: 'Comfort ye, comfort ye My people, saith your God . . .' He sang his opening air, then the chorus swelled out: 'And the glory of God shall be revealed . . .' It was the turn of the bass – the chorus again – and then I was standing on the platform, my own body heavy with child as I lifted up my voice and sang: 'Behold! A Virgin shall conceive and bear a Son . . .'

Olive went white again during the Pastoral Symphony – I smiled across at her and gave a slight downward nod – she fixed her eyes on her score and her colour slowly returned. She stood up during the closing bars, waiting – then took that imperceptible breath as I had taught her and began: 'There were shepherds abiding in the field . . .' Her voice wavered a little, then steadied. I relaxed: she was singing well.

As 'Rejoice' ended I rose to my feet. 'Then shall the eyes of the blind be opened, and the ears of the deaf unstopped; then shall the lame man leap as a hart, and the tongue of the dumb shall sing.' And for a fleeting moment I remembered the pain of my dumbness – and now I was singing again: I thanked God for it.

I launched into the beautiful air: 'He shall feed his flock like a shepherd', and sang on until I came to that loving conclusion: 'And gently lead those that are with young'. And as I repeated the phrase I rejoiced in the fullness of my own body – for I too was with young.

Olive picked up the melody, 'Come unto Him, all ye that labour . . .' and inwardly I smiled; for I would have to labour to bring forth my child, when the time had come. As she sang I looked down to the front pew, to Ben. He gazed up at me, steadfast and true. I held his eyes with mine and his mouth curved in answer – and the child in my womb fluttered in reply. He saw me give the tiny jerk I always did when it happened, and smiled more broadly.

We came to the Second Part. The chorus opened: 'Behold the Lamb of God that taketh away the sin of the world.' Then I rose to sing: 'He was despised and rejected of men; a man of sorrows and acquainted with grief.' With grief. I remembered my brothers, Lance, Hugh – and Gerald; my heart was bitter no longer. They had all suffered and died in those four terrible years – so that I might sing in freedom in this peaceful church in an unconquered land. And Ben, he too had suffered – but he had lived, lived to beget the child in my womb. I felt peace steal over me.

After I had sat down again I realized how tired I was – I was glad I had little more to sing. It was as well that I was not singing the soprano part – it would have been too much for me; I was heavy with child and I needed to rest.

Then it was the Third part. Olive stood young and slim and sparkling as she sang: 'I know that my Redeemer liveth . . .' Her execution was not faultless, but she sang it with verve and conviction. I no longer had that conviction – and yet . . . It was with a deep

777

thankfulness that I realized that the faith of my child-hood had not wholly deserted me.

Later I rose with the tenor and our challenge rang out: 'O death, where is thy sting? O grave, where is thy victory?' The sting would never go, but my beloved brother had gone to his grave undefeated, and I would never again regret what I had done.

Olive's voice rang out triumphantly: 'If God be for us, who can be against us?' And as the child alive in my womb moved again I knew that God had relented.

In the vestry I hugged Olive. 'You sang beautifully, my dear – beautifully.'

She whispered, 'And so did you, Lady Helena – and thank you, thank you so much.'

Ben thrust his way through the crowd of choristers. 'Come on, lass – I can see you're tired out. Doctor came to hear you and she's got car outside – she said she'd run you home.'

I sat back on the leather seat. 'Thank you, Dr Hartley – my legs do feel rather tired. Didn't Olive sing well? And she's so young and had so little training.'

Ben's voice behind me said, 'Aye, she did – but she'll never sing as well as you do, lass. You've got summat special.'

I laughed. 'You're prejudiced, Ben.'

'Aye, happen I am – but there's others saying it beside me. They were all congratulating me while you were in vestry and there were a lot of folk said they were in tears during "Man of Sorrows".'

Dr Hartley spoke briskly. 'He's right, my dear – but you're not performing again before January.'

Ben half-carried me out of the car, and did carry me upstairs. He helped me undress and lifted me into bed. 'You can wash in morning, sweetheart. There's only me as'll notice, and I'm not telling.' He bent over me and the last words I heard as I drifted into sleep were, 'I love you, Helena, I love you.'

CHAPTER EIGHT

It was the middle of September and I was moving more slowly now my womb had risen. Ben knelt on the bed with his ear low down on my belly, listening for the child's heartbeat. I stroked his hair and laughed at the excitement on his face. He reached for his book. 'Best guinea I ever spent – let's see if I can hear this blowing sound at side.' He put his head down again. 'I think I can, but I'm not sure – I'll have to ask doctor.'

He sat up and took hold of the olive oil; tipping the bottle over his fingertips he began to gently massage my swollen belly. At the feel of his hands I began to move a little. He smiled. 'You'll have to wait lass, till I've done your nipples.' His oiled fingers caressed my breasts.

I whispered, 'Ben,' and he put the stopper back in the neck of the bottle and set it down before turning back to me. As he lay down I slid my legs over his strong thighs and felt him curl underneath, and the gentle pressure as he entered me. I pulled his head down and kissed his mouth as he began to push. My body flowed around him.

Later, as he held me close to his side he told me, 'Book says, on no account in t'last month. So you'll 'ave to behave yourself then.'

Murmuring, 'Yes, Ben,' I fell asleep on his shoulder.

The arrangements had been made for our visit to Hatton: I was to go first, then Ben would follow me four days later when his holiday began. Guy and Pansy were arriving with their family the week before, Alice was coming on the same day as myself and Conan soon after – I was longing to see them all.

So during the first week in October Ben took me down

to the station to put me on the train. As I clung to him on the platform he said, 'People are looking, lass.' But I did not care; I kissed him again and again. He hugged me, laughing. 'Lass, I'm not going back to France – only to shed! Come on, behave yourself.' He was still smiling as he bundled me on to the train.

As the stocky figure on the platform finally vanished from sight I sank back on to the seat. Four days, four whole days without seeing Ben; I felt the tears fill my eyes. Already I was remembering the small incidents of the previous day which I had not had time to tell him this morning – I would write, as soon as I got to Hatton. The child moved and I jumped a little, then the tears dried; I had left Ben behind, but I carried his child with me. My thoughts turned to Guy and to Pansy who had carried my brother's sons through the long years of war – and had been always loyal and loving to Guy – to Guy who had, in his despair, used and humiliated her. Just as Ben had steadfastly loved me, even though I had used and humiliated him. Guy and I had both been luckier than we deserved: much, much luckier.

Guy was waiting for me on the platform at Hareford. He stepped forward, arms outstretched, and I threw myself awkwardly into them. He hugged me tightly, yet carefully – like a man who was used to holding a woman heavy with child. We drew back and looked at each other – my brother, my brother. My only brother now. My eyes filled with tears and he said, 'Poor old Robbie – what rotten luck. And after going right through like that – to have it happen afterwards.' Then he added, 'Still, Mother told me that at least it was pretty quick at the end, thank God. And you were with him.'

I put my head on his shoulder and echoed, 'Yes, I was with him – thank God.' I would never distress Guy by telling him the truth.

We drove up the long road from the Hareford gate, through the green rolling parkland – and I remembered how I had seen Ben's lonely figure, tramping up the empty slope as I galloped towards him. Poor, overawed Ben – ready to turn and flee, so he had told me – but he had not. I smiled a little and eased my back against the seat; I would not be going to meet him on horseback this time.

Guy told me, 'Pansy's expecting again – it's early days, but she seems pretty certain.'

I smiled at him. 'She should know.'

He laughed. 'Yes – I suppose she should. You've not seen our Helena, have you? Our little Canadian? This will be number six – I'm not sure it's good for Pansy, but I can't seem to stop her.'

'Oh, Guy!'

'Well, you know how it is, Hellie – I tell her she should say "no" sometimes, but she never does – and then the damn sheep's gut slipped and that was that. She's so pretty, my daughter – just like her mother.'

But when Pansy came out to greet me in the hall I saw that she was no longer pretty; her hair was dull and lifeless and there were small red veins on her cheeks – but as she turned from welcoming me her blue eyes smiled adoringly up at my brother, and as she clung to his arm Guy bent and kissed her on the cheek. I felt a sharp pang of longing for Ben.

Before lunch Pansy took me up to the nursery. Nanny swam forward out of a sea of small dark heads. 'My chick, my darling – how are you keeping?'

I hugged her familiar carbolic-soap-scented body – dearest Nanny. She drew back from me and looked me over, then shook her head regretfully. 'I shan't be able to come to you, my chick, when you need me.' She glanced complacently at Pansy. 'My lady here keeps me busy – but the eldest nursemaid, Clara, I've trained her well' – nodding towards a smart, pink-cheeked brunette potting the small girl – 'I'll send her –'

I broke in quickly, 'Thank you Nanny – but we won't have a separate nursery at Ainsclough – there's no room.'

Nanny's jaw dropped. 'No room! but – my lady –'

'The woman who comes in each day, she'll give me a hand, but otherwise I shall be caring for my child myself.'

'Well – I never did! Well I never!' Nanny sank down into a chair, looking at me as if I'd suddenly sprouted two heads. 'All my mothers have nursed their babies themselves, as long as they were able – even with the twins, Lady Pickering was in no hurry to wean – but – my lady – ' She bent forward, her face grave, and hissed. 'Napkins! Dirty napkins!'

I patted her round plump shoulder. 'We'll manage, Nanny, we'll manage.' I had a sudden sharp vision of myself at Étaples, taking handfuls of tow and wiping clean the whimpering, incontinent Lennie; Ben by my side, helping me. I said simply, 'My husband will expect me to care for my own children.' We had never discussed it, but I knew it was true.

As we went back down the stairs Pansy said wistfully, 'You are lucky, Helena – fancy being able to have your babies with you all day. Guy's very good with them when they come down after tea – and he often pops into the nursery in the morning – not many fathers would do that' – her voice was proud – 'but, well – once the first dressing bell rings they're packed off upstairs, and by the time I go to say goodnight they're already asleep. But Nanny's quite right – I couldn't change a dirty nappy – I just couldn't.' She shuddered.

As we both stepped carefully down the wide staircase I knew that I certainly could – so I had gained something from the war. Then, with a little jolt, I remembered that if it had not been for the war, Nanny would have been presiding over my nursery, at Bessingdon. Gerald's sleek blond head swam before my eyes, and I tightened my grip on the bannister.

Alice arrived just in time for luncheon. Afterwards Pansy went upstairs to rest, and the others disappeared to their own pursuits – I had forgotten how very impersonal Hatton could be – people appeared and disappeared as if in a hotel; not like at home, where I always knew exactly where Ben was and what he was doing. So now I sat in the small drawing room with Alice as she smoked a cigarette. She glanced at me, then said abruptly, 'Has Mother told you I'm divorcing Fred?'

'No – no she hasn't.'

She blew a smoke ring before telling me, 'It was all too sordid, Helena – he was going to divorce me! Apparently he'd hired a private detective to watch me.' Her eyes hardened. 'And he was going to cite John Thornton as one of the co-respondents – John! We've known each other for years.'

'But surely, if you hadn't actually – '

'Oh, be your age, Helena – of course we had. I told you, we're old friends, but think of poor Dora – how embarrassing it would have been for her. Anyway, he grudgingly said he'd drop that one and just name Jimmy Danesford – luckily Iris divorced him last year, so there was no problem there – but I was still furious – you can imagine. I should never have married Fred, he just doesn't understand the rules. Anyway, I could see I'd get no further with him, so I went to Mother, and she was marvellous. She put me on to this lawyer, terribly discreet, and he said: "Stall for a month, Lady Alice, and meanwhile we'll see what we can come up with." And what they came up with was a little love nest in Fulham – Fulham of all places! Fred had installed this shop-girl there, and she was actually enceinte! I can't think how she managed it, I had to get the doctor to him on our honeymoon – nervous prostration he said – I tell you, I was the one with nervous prostration, I've never been so bored in my whole life. So of course I confronted him with this, and it was checkmate. But I soon realized I had him over a barrel, because, believe it or not, he wants to marry this female – Gladys she's called, I ask you – whereas I'm not particularly bothered about getting my freedom; so finally he had to agree to do the decent thing and go off to a hotel in Brighton with one of these women you can hire for the purpose. Of course, he's got to keep away from Fulham in the meantime, or we'll both have the King's Proctor on our tail.' She smiled rather smugly. 'Mother's invited Jimmy down next week – the King's Proctor won't get past her. But Fred's had Fulham for the time being.' Her voice was edged with malice, then she said, 'I still can't get over it, you know, he was so . . . In fact, I'd always assumed that basically he must be one of those who preferred other men – like your Gerald.' I felt myself stiffen. Alice glanced at me from under her long dark lashes. 'Conan told me he'd spilled the beans. Does it still rankle, Hellie?'

I whispered, 'I don't know.'

'There's no point your losing any sleep over it, after all this time – though it certainly cost poor old Hugh some worry.'

'Then why didn't he – say something – stop me?'

'Oh, Hugh wanted to – he was going to speak to Papa – but I persuaded him not to.'

I asked baldly, 'Why, Alice?'

She shrugged. 'I have my faults as a sister, Hellie – but I was never jealous of you. I didn't see why you shouldn't have it all: the ironstone quarries, the Irish estate, that lovely house – you never saw it, did you? A perfect Palladian mansion – a title . . .'

I added bitterly, 'And a husband who preferred choirboys.'

Alice's mouth curved. 'Well, you can't have everything in this world, Helena.' Then she bent forward and stubbed out her cigarette. 'No, damn it – it wasn't that – or not just that – it was you. You were in love, Hellie, you were radiant with it, you were glowing like a candle whenever he was near you – your eyes followed him everywhere. Your whole body seemed to be swaying towards him, you looked like a girl who'd been given the Crown Jewels, the Koh-i-Noor diamond and the Taj Mahal, all in one. How could I let Hugh take that from you? It doesn't last long, whoever you marry – I'd felt like that about Hugh, but as soon as the morning sickness started the scales fell from my eyes.'

I said, my throat tight, 'Hugh was a good husband – and he loved you.'

She was impatient. 'I know that, Hellie – and God knows I missed him, even if I wasn't always faithful to him. But I'm talking about something else, something that's nothing to do with marriage or babies, something that only happens once in a lifetime. And it had happened to my little sister, so I wasn't going to see it trodden underfoot and covered with filth. Besides, Hugh had had a long talk with Gerald – Gerald was a good man, Helena, and he was very fond of you – I think he even loved you, in his fashion. He couldn't help the way he was, but he intended to play fair by you. He'd been to Edward Summerhays and said goodbye the weekend after he'd proposed to you – it cost him dear, but he'd done it, and he promised Hugh that he'd stick by it. And Hugh asked him outright if he would be able to act as a husband to you – he'd never had a woman, you see, he was quite honest about that – but he said he was sure he could.'

Remembering, I said, 'I had the figure of a boy then, Alice.'

Alice nodded. 'I suppose it would have helped. And he wanted children, he wanted them desperately – it could have worked – he would have played fair by you and you need never have known.'

I looked down at my swelling breasts and full hips, and touched my curving belly. 'And when he had got me with child, Alice – what then? Would he have come to me as a husband, the way I am now?'

Alice looked at me for a long time, then slowly shook her head; her voice was sad. 'No. I was wrong, Hellie, wasn't I? He would have made some excuse about not harming the child and it would have sounded reasonable – but pregnant women aren't reasonable are they? I remember when I was carrying my two – when I wasn't being sick I was hot for Hugh, all the time. And dear Hugh, he never failed me.'

She watched my face. Ben had said I must be rationed; 'Not tomorrow' he said each night – but when tomorrow became today . . . occasionally we had not come together, through my sickness or his shifts, but otherwise – no, he had never failed me, either.

'Sorry, Hellie. I still saw you as my little sister, and that thought didn't cross my mind. You'd have had to find somebody else.'

'And once I did that – how long would it have been before Gerald cast his eye on a good-looking footman . . . ?'

Alice finished for me, 'Or went back to Edward, as he did, of course.'

'I know – I saw them together the last day of his leave.' Poor Gerald, spending each morning at the hospital, then having to tear himself away from his lover to come to me – a jealous, demanding girl. 'What happened to him, to Edward?'

'He went back and was killed that summer in an attack near Festubert. Hugh said the story was that he behaved quite recklessly, as if he wanted to die – Gerald had been everything to him.'

Poor Edward. I said softly, 'Then I'm glad that at least they had that one last day together.'

I stood up and walked out into the garden by the small door, and went round to the orangery, where the trees were heavy with fruit. I slipped in and sat down on the bench I had sat on while Gerald knelt before me and offered me his hand; Gerald, who had loved me as far as he was able. And now I let him go in peace.

Then I got up and walked out, across the green velvet lawn. As I looked down over the park the child in my womb moved restlessly; I put my hand to my belly and murmured, 'Patience, little one – your father will be here soon.' And he quietened.

CHAPTER NINE

Soon Mother's guests began to arrive. Conan came, and shortly after him Eileen Enscombe – who had been Eileen Fox on that long-ago day at Eton, and had been engaged to Guy and thrown him over. I wondered why Mother had invited her – not that Guy seemed to bear her any ill will – but then I noticed the look of satisfaction on Conan's face as his eyes rested on her mass of glossy dark hair, and Alice, seeing the direction of my gaze, whispered, 'It's been going on for months – quite a record for Conan!'

I overheard Eileen's finely-modulated voice expressing her sorrow at her husband's absence – 'But the gas still affects his lungs, Lady Pickering – so I had to insist he stayed quietly at home.'

'Such a shame, my dear' – my mother allowed her eyes to stray for just that fraction of a second too long to where Conan lounged on the settee, then she murmured to her guest, 'So sad for you.'

Eileen's lovely complexion did not even change colour as she echoed, 'Yes, Lady Pickering – so sad.' Lucky Guy.

The drawing room was crowded that night, and Conan and I scarcely exchanged more than a few words, but the following morning he suggested a stroll in the garden before lunch. We walked slowly over the lawn, arm in arm – not saying much but happy in each other's company; then I realized that he was leading me down to the maze. As we came up to the entrance I hung back – and he turned to me, smiling. 'They should have let us be, that evening – shouldn't they, Helena?'

He was waiting for my answer, but I hesitated, before

finally saying, 'But – I might have fallen with a child – and we were very young.'

'Then we'd have had a son of – what would it be – eleven, by now! Just imagine that, Helena.'

I shifted a little, uneasily – before remembering what he had once told me, 'But you must have a child of that age, Conan – the housemaid, who had to be married off to the groom . . .'

'Good lord – so I must – I never thought of that. But I'd rather it had been *your* son, Helena.'

I pulled his arm round; I was tired, I wanted to go back to the house. *My* son was in my womb now – and his father would be here tomorrow.

Conan allowed me to lead him back up through the garden, without protest, but when we drew level with the magnolia tree he drew me under its boughs, and lifting my face to his, gently kissed me on the lips. 'Goodbye, Hellie.'

I was startled. 'But – I thought you were staying all week – are you going so soon?'

His smile was rueful. 'I'm not going anywhere, Hellie – but you've already gone.' Then he laughed. 'I had some mad idea of one last romp in the maze – but you wouldn't have come, would you?'

'No, Conan – I wouldn't.'

His hand slipped down, clasped mine and squeezed it. 'Besides, any tricks of that sort and that over-muscled husband of yours would rend me limb from limb and strew the pieces all over the Japanese garden! And I'm a coward, sweet Coz, you know that.' He laughed again and this time I laughed with him; then we went back into the house.

I went up to my room before the dressing bell that evening, and lay on my bed, resting. I dozed off and, half-waking up, reached out – only to realize that I was alone. I wondered where he was and what he was doing; I missed him. But he would come in the morning.

I had to refuse most of the heavy meal – the child was

788

pressing on my stomach. After dinner I sat in the brightly lit drawing room while clever, handsome people chattered and laughed and smoked all around me. I listened idly: 'Harry said . . .' 'Horace and Betty . . .' 'No – not really – how too dreadful!' It was not my world any longer but it was pleasant to sit on the fine brocade sofa, smelling the scents of the garden wafting in through the open window behind me, holding the fragile porcelain coffee cup in my hand.

Cooper threw open the door. 'Mr Holden, my lady.' I jerked forward and the coffee cup bounced back on to its saucer – then I dumped them down anyhow and began to struggle to my feet. Ben – Ben was walking through the doorway – now I was standing – his face lit up as he saw me – I began to run down the length of the gilded room – straight into his arms.

He held me tight, too tight – but I did not mind. 'Ben – oh Ben – you came early!'

His cheek was on mine, his arms hugging me. 'Aye, lass – I swapped shifts with Jethro Yates, and I reckoned if I had everything ready and ran like hell in Manchester I should be able to do it. So here I am.' He kissed me, and I clung to him, then he drew back, smiling. 'Come on lass, we'd best sit down – we're in road.'

As he released me I glanced round – the babble of conversation was silenced, and the eyes of that whole smartly-clad throng were fixed on the two of us. My mother's face was a mask; then she turned and picked up her conversation with Lady Maud and the room came alive again.

Ben led me to a seat, settled a cushion behind my back and said, 'I'd best say hello to the dragon, lass – and your pa.'

Mother took his proferred hand, but her face was frigid; then her eyes flicked over his figure – he was wearing one of his new suits which fitted him well – and her expression softened a fraction. She beckoned to the waiting Cooper. 'Tell Mrs Hill to have the bed made up in Lady Helena's dressing room.'

But Ben interrupted her. 'That won't be necessary, my lady – if her bed's not big enough I'll sleep on floor beside her.'

Eileen Fox's titter was distinctly audible. My mother's eyebrows arched as she looked at Ben, then she asked him, 'Have you eaten?'

'No, my lady – there weren't time.'

She turned to Cooper. 'Mrs Hill need not bother with the dressing room, but ask her to send up some refreshments for my son-in-law.'

When Cooper came back Ben held out his hand to me. I went with him to the morning room and sat down beside him at the big oval table; as soon as the butler had left us Ben said, 'You're not near enough, sweetheart,' and pulled my chair closer to his. I leant on his shoulder and he put his arm round my waist and hugged me to him. 'Reckon I can drink soup one-handed.' The chicken soup smelt delicious; I could feel my nostrils quivering. Ben laughed. 'Open your mouth.' I did as he bid me and he tipped in a spoonful of the savoury liquid.

He fed me alternate spoonfuls, and I sat with my lips parted ready, like a fledgeling. The door opened just as Ben was feeding me, and I swallowed quickly, embarrassed – but it was only Alice. 'Don't get up, Ben' – she glided forward – 'I just came to tell you that Letty's arrived, she'll be joining you in a minute – she had a breakdown at Derby and was delayed.'

Letty came bouncing in shortly after. 'Hello, Ben – how are you, Helena? Gosh, I'm starving – I was late starting as it was, and then that wretched motor of mine . . . The engine was misfiring – I thought it was just water in the petrol at first, but it was getting worse, so I had to stop and clean the pick-ups on the magneto – thank goodness that did the trick.'

'I didn't know you had a car, Letty?'

'Oh yes – a nice little Morris Oxford, a late birthday

present from Uncle Arnold, since he was abroad in the summer.' She winked at me. 'I'm not officially allowed to keep it while I'm in college, but I've made an arrangement.' Yes, Letty would. Leaning against Ben's shoulder, I listened while she chatted to him.

Ben nudged me. 'You're almost asleep, sweetheart – time you were in bed. I'll just go and say me goodnights and tell your ma I'm taking you straight upstairs.' I imagined Eileen Fox's titter when he delivered that message, but I did not care.

As he left us Letty buttered another roll and asked, 'Is Maud here?'

'Yes, of course.'

'So they've made it up, then.'

'Made it up?' I was puzzled.

'There was an awful row in the summer – Maud caught Papa creeping out of Mother's bedroom one morning – he'd been there all night!'

I stared at her. 'Not – Mother and Papa?'

'Apparently – it does seem indecent, doesn't it? Poor old Maud was in quite a state – she didn't blame Papa, she said men were like that – but she was so hurt about Mother, they've always been such good friends, you see. I'm glad they've made it up. To tell you the truth I think Mother was quite upset by it too – she never thought she'd get found out. I guessed she was up to something at Easter – she had that smug she-cat look on her face – but I couldn't think who it was – and she obviously thought she'd been covering her tracks. Still, even the cleverest operator makes mistakes occasionally, I should know that – I really am thrilled with this car!'

Ben came back. 'I've done the rounds and been polite to everybody.' He was pleased with himself. 'Up you get now.'

In bed I nestled up against him. 'Go to sleep now, lass.'

'Ben . . .'

'No, you're tired out.'

I slid my hand down. 'But you want me, Ben.'

''Course I do, after three days – but that don't mean I got to have you.'

I was very sleepy but I had missed him; I wanted to feel him inside me, so I stroked him gently, 'Please, Ben.'

His arms tightened, then he whispered, 'All right, sweetheart – come across me legs, then.' He lifted me over his thighs and curled himself under my behind; I clasped him in my arms.

Next morning he said accusingly, 'You were asleep afore I'd finished.'

I laughed and kissed his neck. 'But I had nice dreams, Ben!'

'I've got no control over you, my girl – no control at all. I'm ashamed to admit I were once a sergeant-major. Now, let's see how youngster's getting on.'

Ben still had his ear pressed to my belly when the maid came in with the jug of hot water and the tea tray; she stared astounded at the enormous lump in the bed. Ben poked his head out, saw her and dived frantically back under the bedclothes again. 'It's eight-thirty, my lady – shall I draw the curtains?'

'Thank you.'

I shook with suppressed laughter as Ben choked against my belly. When the door clicked shut he emerged, red-faced and spluttering. 'You might've told me she were coming – at least I'd have put me nightshirt on.' Giggling, I put my arms around him. 'You think you can kiss me and I'll forgive you owt.' When he took his mouth away he added, 'Well, you're right. Lass, I have missed you.'

I put up my hand and gently stroked his face: his strong curved eyebrows, his neat straight nose. With the tip of my finger I traced the shape of his mouth; his blue-grey eyes held mine. The skin of his chin was rough to my touch as I brushed my cheek against him. I felt warm and soft and loving. His hand slipped inside my nightdress and began to caress my breasts. I whispered, 'I missed you, too, Ben.'

We were last down to breakfast; my mother looked up at us, her eyes narrowed. Ben beamed at her as he said his good mornings, then glanced at me with the ghost of a wink before leading me to a seat. 'I'll fetch you summat – you take it easy now.'

Beside me Alice murmured, 'Did the maid forget to wake you, Helena?'

'Yes – I mean – no, she did bring the tea.' I was blushing as Alice's mouth curved into a smile, while her eyes rested on Ben's broad shoulders, leaning over the hot-plate. I called to him, 'Some devilled kidneys, please, Ben.'

He grunted as he continued his exploration under the silver lids, but when he came back there was only scrambled egg and a crisp rasher of bacon on my plate. 'Ben, I wanted . . .'

'Aye, I heard you, sweetheart, but them's too rich for you at present – you'll only get indigestion. You eat what I've given you.' I started to get up – he was right, but I did enjoy devilled kidneys – and felt a large hand come down on my shoulder. 'No, lass.' I sank back into the chair. Opposite me Eileen Fox looked astounded.

I told him, 'You're a bully, Ben Holden.'

'Aye, happen I am – and happen you need a bit of bullying sometimes.' I felt his fingers move from my shoulder and begin to stroke the nape of my neck; turning my head I pressed my cheek against his warm hand – then I picked up my knife and fork and began to eat the scrambled eggs. He carefully carved two wafer-thin slices of kidney from those on his own plate and transferred them to mine. Slowly I ate his gift, savouring the strong, spicy flavour. As I reached for my cup I saw Eileen Fox watching me, her mouth pinched; then, turning to my cousin, she began to flirt with him, in her carefully tuned voice. Conan answered her politely, but his mind was obviously elsewhere.

I remembered how once, long ago, I had envied Eileen's quick wit and vivid presence; now she was pale under her rouge – poor Eileen, with a husband to be hoodwinked and a lover to be placated – I did not envy her any more. I felt Ben's warm thigh press mine under the table, while his son kicked me hard so that I jumped a little in my chair – and my husband smiled at me in quick understanding.

Papa wiped his mouth with his napkin and tossed it down beside his plate. 'Do you fancy coming out to the butts this morning, Holden – try your hand at the partridges? I can fix you up with a gun.'

Ben looked pleased. 'Yes, I'd like that my lord – thanks.'

I said quickly, 'Didn't you have enough shooting in the war?'

'This is different – birds don't shoot back!' He winked at Conan and they both laughed. 'Don't you fret, sweetheart, I'll not stay out all day. You put your feet up this morning and have a rest then I'll be back at midday to share a bite with you – and you can play me some songs this afternoon.'

Soon after, he kissed me goodbye and left with the men; I wandered through to the music room and began to leaf through my old music. Alice came in while I was sitting with a couple of scores in front of the crackling fire and I smiled up at her. She drew up a chair opposite me, lit a cigarette and inhaled deeply, watching me in silence for a few minutes; then she asked. 'What are you looking for, Helena – love songs?' I glanced at her in surprise as she continued, 'I was wrong, wasn't I? It wasn't once in a lifetime for you, it's happened a second time – you're in love again.'

I stared at her: whatever was she implying? Then I guessed what she meant and retorted defensively, 'Conan and I are just cousins!'

Her eyebrows arched in amazement, then she burst out laughing. 'Oh Helena, you are priceless – of course you're not in love with Conan, you never have been. It's Ben Holden you've fallen in love with – your own husband!'

'But – but I had to marry him – because . . .' My voice trailed away, I was totally confused – Ben was just – Ben.

'Silly little Helena! You should have seen your face yesterday, when you ran to him like that – the whole room was stunned into silence. I've never seen anything like it – and in your condition, too! You may have glowed like a candle with Gerald but with him you blaze up like one of those naphtha flares. You look as if you'd scorch anyone who came near you – except Ben of course – with him it's all big soft eyes and lying on his shoulder.' She stubbed out her cigarette, almost angrily. 'You've been lucky, Helena – bloody lucky.' She sprang to her feet and walked out. I sat on by the fire, shaking. I remembered Ben telling me so many times: 'I love you, Helena, I love you'. But I had never said it to him, and suddenly it was very important that I should do so – I must go to him, say it to him – now.

I hurried out of the music room, spurring my clumsy body into a trot, and headed for the family entrance. The butts were too far – I could not walk there fast enough, so I turned towards the stables. The groom offered to take me in the governess cart, but I asked him just to harness the lawn-mower pony for me – I had driven him since childhood. I climbed awkwardly up to take the reins and at my signal the pony plodded obediently off.

The sharp crack of the shotguns told me I was nearing my goal, and swinging round the corner I saw Letty, barrel aimed high. Beside her was Ben. His body was slightly crouched, because he was used to firing from a trench, from a hole in the ground.

I drove closer and he turned and saw me; at once he thrust his gun into the hands of my sister's loader and came striding forward. 'What the hell do you think you're doing driving that thing – in your condition!' He was angry. 'You get down this minute.' Climbing quickly in, he seized hold of me and half-lifted me out; the lawn-mower pony bent his head and began placidly cropping the grass. 'Now, what do you think you're up to?'

'I wanted to tell you something, Ben.'

'Well, it'ud better be worthwhile, after you risking your neck like that.'

'Ben, I was absolutely safe – why, I could still ride if I wanted – in a side-saddle.'

'Ride! You ride like you are now – just you try, my lass – just you try!' His face was purple with fury. 'Now, what do you want to tell me, then I can get back to me gun – and then you'll have to wait out here until dinner time.'

I looked at him, and my lips would not form the words. I had been rehearsing then all the way down in the governess cart – and now I was here he was impatient – he wanted to get back and shoot partridges. 'It doesn't matter now, Ben – you go and shoot.' I turned and began to stumble away, trying to hide my tears.

He came after me. 'Obviously it does matter – what is it, lass?' His arm came round me, and pulled me against him. I buried my face in his jacket. 'You're not starting, are you?' Now his voice was urgent.

'No – no, nothing like that.'

'Just stay here a minute.' He propped me against the back of the game cart and I sagged there, still fighting my tears.

When he came back Letty was with him. 'It's all right, Helena – I'll drive you.' She jumped lithely up and took the reins. Ben helped me in after her – then climbed in himself and latched the door. 'Where do you want to go?'

'Somewhere quiet, Letty lass – but not too far from th'ouse.'

She pursed her lips a moment before deciding, then

shook her hands – the cart started with a jolt. I was a much better driver than Letty – it was not fair.

Ben lifted me down on the slope below the ha-ha, and led me up to one of the horse chestnut trees just beyond the end of the garden. He had brought a rug with him from the shoot, and now he spread it out on the sheltered side of the trunk. 'There you are – sit yourself down on that.' He called. 'Ta, Letty.' My sister raised her hand before the cart jerked off.

He dropped down beside me, his voice more gentle now. 'What is it you want to tell me, lass – that's so important?' I could not answer – I felt painfully, desperately shy. 'Come on now – out with it.'

I could not look at him. My fingers plaited the fringe of the rug. 'It was – it was something Alice said to me – this morning.'

'Oh, ah – and what did Alice say, then?'

I stared down at the plait, then plunged on: 'She said – she said I was in love with you, Ben.'

I heard him laugh softly. 'Aye – I reckon you are.'

I looked up at him; his blue-grey eyes were warm. 'But – how did you know?'

'If I'd not known afore I reckon I'd 'a' known last night – when you come to me in a room full o' smart folk – waddling like a duck you were, but you kept going – with your eyes as round as saucers!' He laughed. 'But I knew afore that, from the way you've bin with me these past weeks.'

I felt rather flat. 'So I didn't need to come and tell you.'

'Oh yes you did, lass – oh yes you did. Knowing it's one thing, but hearing it said, that's quite another. And you haven't said it yet – only what Alice said. I want to hear you say it now.'

He put his hands out and clasped mine. I looked back into his eyes, took a deep breath and said, 'I love you, Ben – I love you,' and threw myself forward into his arms.

We lay together on the rug with the autumn leaves rustling above our heads while he stroked my hair and whispered words of love. Then he pulled me even closer to say, 'It's a funny thing, Helena – I'm lying beside you feeling on top of world – and for first time I'm not standing to attention down below. I love you so much it's gone beyond that.' He kissed my cheek. 'But you needn't worry, lass – I reckon it'll come back later!' I felt the familiar vibration of the laughter in his chest – and laughed with him.

CHAPTER TEN

I sang to him, my German love songs. He puzzled over the translations, fitting the English words to the German; so he understood when I sang of his gold ring on my finger, and of the joyful day when his image would smile up from the cradle beside my bed. When I had finished he said, '*Our* bed, Helena, you'll have to alter that.'

Teasing, I sang 'Der Schmied' – the 'Song of the Blacksmith' was the best I could do, since Brahms had written no tunes celebrating footplatemen.

> 'Am schwarzen Kamin,
> Da sitzet mein Lieber,'

At the black furnace, there sits my lover.

> 'Doch geh ich vorüber,
> Die Bälge dann sausen,
> Die, Flammen aufbrausen
> Und lodern um ihn.'

But if I pass by the bellows then whistle, the flames flare up – and blaze all about him.

798

He laughed aloud. 'You got it wrong – it were Frank who worked blower that evening on radial tank – and I reckon it were your flames as were blazing up – when I got home that night you fair scorched pants off me!' My face burnt with blushes.

I sang Strauss' song: 'Glückes genug' – abundant happiness – the abundant happiness of holding him in my arms as he slept, and of lying against his heart in the night. As he read it he said, 'Way it's written it should be a man singing it – still, if we both feel like that, it can't be bad, can it Helena?'

'No Ben – it can't be bad.'

Then it was Beethoven:

'Ich liebe dich, so wie du mich,
Am Abend und am Morgen,'

I love you as you love me, at evening and at morning.

He held me as I sat on his lap afterwards, a little breathless, and reflected, 'You know, life's real odd sometimes – to think of me sitting here in a house like this – hearing you sing me love songs – and in German, of all tongues. Still, I suppose if it hadn't been for Germans we'd never have come together – so there's justice in it somewhere.'

Ben held his own at Hatton; speaking carefully, moderating his accent; and he had something to say. He was a trade unionist, a Labour voter, and he defended his beliefs vigorously: putting forward the point of view of his class but always arguing on equal terms. And of course, all the younger men had served in the war; it was a common bond between them, regardless of rank or social status. Ben, like them, had wielded authority and taken decisions – decisions which had meant life and death to those men they had been responsible for.

One night, I wept in Ben's arms, remembering my brothers, and the next day I made my pilgrimage. As soon as breakfast was over we walked together down the avenue to the Lostherne gate and out into the lane. I stood beside my husband in the windswept graveyard gazing at the white stone:

> 'They were lovely and pleasant in
> their lives, and in their death
> they were not divided: they were
> swifter than eagles, they were
> stronger than lions.'

Beside me Ben said gently, 'They were only youngsters, lass – but at least they had a good time afore they went – growing up here and with everything young lads could wish for ready and waiting for them. And they had each other for first twenty years, at least; and the Captain had you with him right to th'end.'

So we left the green churchyard where my brothers lay together – in the peace they had fought to achieve for all of us, and for their unborn nephew, still in my womb. I would tell him of them one day, and he would be grateful.

The first time I took Ben up to meet Nanny in the nursery he dropped down to the floor where Guy's sons were playing with our old fort. He joined in with the game, taking it as seriously as the children did. But when Lance and Ted squabbled for possession of a guardsman and began to push at each other, Ben's voice rang out, 'Now then – that's enough of that,' and they stopped at once and agreed to his suggestion to toss for the toy.

After that Ben took me up to the nursery every day and I sat with Pansy and Nanny while the children competed for his attention. One day, when Pansy had gone downstairs before us, he turned to me outside the nursery door saying. 'They seem happy enough – and I know you think the word of your old Nan – but, well, it seems funny to me – keeping them shut up there like they were wild animals.'

I laughed. 'They *are* wild animals, sometimes.'

'Mebbe – but you're going to look after our youngsters yourself, Helena – with a bit of help if you need it.' He glanced at me watchfully.

I squeezed his hand. 'I know, Ben. I've already told Nanny – she was terribly shocked!'

'I can see now, since I been staying here, that Ainsclough must have been quite a shock to you, lass – more 'an I ever realized at first. You been a good lass – never complaining.'

But I thought of the other women in Royds Street, who did not have Mary Grimshaw's smiling face bringing them a cup of tea every morning, and said, 'We've had Robbie's and Eddie's money, Ben – it makes a big difference.'

'Aye – and I reckon I'm coming round to thinking it's as well we have. You'd've coped because you'd have made yourself cope – but it would have been hard on you, Helena. I never thought clear enough afore.'

'We neither of us thought – before.'

'No. But – mebbe.' He stopped, and reflected a while, before he went on, 'Mebbe our bodies knew better 'an our heads. Because, for all them differences between us, Helena, we're two of a kind, you and I. We fit together.' I looked at him as we stood there in the draughty nursery corridor at Hatton and knew that, incredibly, he was right. Then he laughed. 'Just as well we do, seeing as I've already put my youngster in your belly – so we're tied together, whether we like it or not.'

'Oh, but I do like it, Ben – I do.'

He pressed my hand against his warm thigh. 'So do I, lass – so do I.'

The little house in Royds Street seemed very small when we got home. In the kitchen Ben put the kettle on then sat down with a sigh. 'I enjoyed me week – it weren't like anything I'd ever done afore, or expected to do – but it's nice to get home and be on our own together. And I'm even looking forward to going back to shed tomorrow!' He laughed. 'Life with the aristocracy is all right for a change – but I couldn't live like that all the time. Happen you have to be born to it.'

As I had been. But the war had come and had changed me as it had changed all of us – and now my home was in this small smoky valley, with my husband. I had much to be thankful for – and the child kicked in my womb.

November 1921, Armistice Day. As the church bells tolled their signal the whole country came to a standstill; in those two long minutes of silence we stood motionless, remembering our Dead. The following Sunday the service was held to unveil the war memorial panels in our Methodist church. The names of all the men of the congregation who had served were written in gold, with a star beside each one who had died.

We walked down to the church together; Ben's medals were pinned on his breast, my service ribbons were fastened to my black coat, buttoned tight across my full belly.

We raised our voices in Kipling's hymn:

'God of our Fathers, known of old,
Lord of our far-flung battle line . . .'

The minister proclaimed: 'I am the Resurrection and the Life, saith the Lord.'

We rose to sing again the age-old words of trust and comfort:

'The Lord is my shepherd; I shall not want . . .'

And then the panels were unveiled: 'Let us remember with thanksgiving, and with all honour before God and men, those who have died, giving their lives in the service of their country.'

The roll of the starred names was read. Ben's face was taut beside me as he listened to them – the names of the boys he had played with, the men he had worked with – and the soldiers he had fought with. We listened silently, grieving for their unlived lives.

As the echo of the last name died away my eyes rested on the name which was not starred:

C. S. M. Holden, Benjamin, DCM, MM, L & CLI. He had come back, back to love me.

The minister's voice rang out in the dedication: 'To the glory of God and in grateful memory of those who gave their lives, and of all those who served their King and country in the Great War.'

The Great War – the final war – the war which had ended all other wars. We bent our heads and prayed together, and then the sobbing lament of the Last Post pierced our hearts – to be followed by the hope of the Reveille. Ben's hand touched mine; for a moment we were back in France, serving our King and country.

We sang and prayed and sang again. We listened to the lesson, the address – and then rose for the closing hymn:

> 'O God, our help in ages past,
> Our hope for years to come,
> Our shelter from the stormy blast,
> And our eternal home.'

'The grace of our Lord Jesus Christ, and the love of God, and the fellowship of the Holy Ghost, be with us all evermore. Amen.'

At home that evening, the child was restless. I lay on the sofa, my hand on my belly, while he kicked vigorously. I whispered, 'Be calm, little one – there will be no battles for you. Your father and your uncles went to fight for us, and they gave all that they had so that there would be no more war. Because of their sacrifice, you may sleep in peace.'

But the child kicked on.

CHAPTER ELEVEN

The last month. Outside, the streets of Ainsclough shone grey and black in the rain and the days became shorter and shorter; up in the bedroom I lay close to Ben's warm body, but that was all, now. He had been firm and I was glad – I needed all my energy for the child. My womb had dropped and the baby's head pressed down into me; every night now Ben had to help me out of the bed and hold me on the chamber.

I still walked out each day but when I came back my legs ached and by the evening my ankles were swollen – as Ben put them up on the pouffe his face creased with concern, though Dr Hartley said there was no cause for anxiety. She told me, upstairs one day when Ben was at work, that the child might come sooner than expected: 'The head's well down, my dear – I don't think you'll go much beyond the beginning of January.'

'Please, don't tell Ben – he'll only worry more – let him think it's further off.' She smiled her agreement.

We spent Christmas quietly together. At the chapel service I thought of my own son, so soon to be born, and happiness flooded through me. Ben's sisters came on Boxing Day; Ada brought clothes she had knitted for the child, Ivy a large woollen shawl for me. 'Best thing in world when you're nursing a babby – keeps you both wrapped up so snug and warm together.' I thanked them gratefully, and they shooed Ben away and settled down to give me the benefit of their experience; I liked to talk about babies and births now, but it only distressed Ben, and I had taken the textbook away from him – it was upsetting him. But I read it myself when he was out of the house; I wanted to know exactly what was going on inside me, so that when the time came the child and I could work together. Now that my womb had dropped I could breathe easily again, and when he was restless I sang lullabies to him. Safe in my womb he listened to me, and his movements would slow and settle. 'Not much longer, little one – not much longer.'

On the last day of December I woke early – alert and full of energy, although I moved clumsily. Mary found me scrubbing the bath when she came; she said as she took the brush from me, 'You won't be long now – I remember whitewashing th'entire scullery day afore Mab arrived – Jim couldn't stop me!' She smiled. 'Lucky Ben's on early shift – he'd be scolding you for this. Poor lad looks right haggard these days – it takes men different. But they do say as where the man suffers the woman gets it easier – so that should do you a bit of good.' She laughed as she flapped the cleaning cloth at me. 'Into the kitchen with you and put your feet up.' But I still prowled restlessly around.

That night the bells rang out to welcome the new year: 1922. Ben stirred in his sleep and kissed me before dropping off again, but I lay awake listening to them; a new year – and under my heart I carried a new life.

New Year's Day was a Sunday, and Ben was home with me. I walked a little way, leaning on his arm, in the morning – but I could not settle when we got back, and that afternoon I kept visiting the closet. After the third time, when I came back warmly wrapped in Ivy's shawl, Ben looked up anxiously. 'Are you all right, lass?'

I smiled at him. 'I'm fine, Ben – just something I must have eaten.' I sat down and eased my aching back.

We started getting ready for bed before eight – the knocker-up would be coming to rouse Ben at four the next morning. As I stood up to make my final visit out to the back I felt an odd slipperiness between my legs; I moved as quickly as I could out into the yard. In the dim light of the lantern hanging close to the lagged pipe I saw the soft mass on my drawers – like reddish-purple jelly – it was my show. I crouched in the small cold closet and felt the excitement course through me; pressing my hand to my swollen belly, I whispered, 'Not long now, little one – not long now.' But back in the warm bright kitchen I saw my husband's face turn to me, drawn with anxiety – so I smiled my reassurance and said nothing.

Upstairs Ben had lit a fire in the grate so I undressed completely and washed myself all over, very thoroughly, then pulled the flannel nightdress over my ungainly body. Hearing Ben's step on the stairs I whispered to the child, 'We must say nothing, my son, for your father will worry.'

When Ben slid into the bed I held my arms out to him, as I always did, and he held me as close as he could, just as he always did. We kissed, then he murmured, 'Sleep well, sweet Helena,' and turned and slept; and I slept too, while there was yet time. I would need all my strength tomorrow.

But my son was impatient, he would not wait. I woke to feel the first cramp beginning – but it was slight yet, so I lay still and breathed slowly until it finished. Then I heaved myself over against Ben's warm body and began to drift into sleep again – as the church clock struck once. I dozed and woke again as my womb tightened, then dropped off once more. By the time I heard the clock strike three the pains were coming closer – but not very close yet. I breathed carefully and evenly, as Elsa Gehring had taught me to do, so many years go – I was not singing now, but it helped. I was very moist between the legs where my body was making itself slippery to help the child out – but I worried a little: had my waters broken so soon? I eased myself off the mattress and sat over the chamber, and found to my relief that I was only damp, not dripping. Ben stirred and spoke, 'Art thi all right, Helena?'

'Yes Ben, I'm fine – I'm not due till next week, remember.'

'Aye – that's true.' He helped me back into the bed

again and turned over. I hoped the knocker-up would be early this morning – I wanted to move around now.

The bang at the door came before the clock struck again, and Ben eased himself out and opened the window softly to wave down to the lad below – trying not to disturb me. I whispered, 'It's all right, Ben – I'm awake.' He came back and leant over me and kissed my cheek – but I turned my lips to find his mouth, and then told him, 'I love you, Ben – I love you.'

He paused. 'Are you sure you're all right, lass?' His voice was a little suspicious.

'Of course I am, Ben – I feel fine. Go on, or you'll be late.'

When he was dressed he kissed me again. 'I love you, Helena.' Then I heard him plodding down the stairs. I breathed more heavily, waiting impatiently for the front door to close. As soon as his boots clattered off along the street I hauled myself out of bed and began to dress; it was cold in the room now. I climbed carefully down-stairs, clinging to the bannister.

The kindling was ready beside the range, so I riddled the ashes and laid the fire, then set match to the paper at once – we would be needing plenty of hot water today. As I leant back from the grate the pain caught me, hard – my womb was beginning to open. I began to walk slowly round the small kitchen and then through into the parlour, backwards and forwards – helping my body with its work. Several times I pulled Ivy's shawl more tightly about me and trekked out into the back yard; my bladder was pressing now.

Soon after six there was a tap at the door; on the step was the be-shawled figure of Mrs Ingham. 'I saw your gas on, lass – have you started?' I nodded. 'I'll rouse our Sammy and send him for midwife, then make us both a cup of tea.'

I held the door wider. 'Not yet, thank you – let her have her breakfast first – but I'd like some tea.'

When it was made I paced backwards and forwards

with my cup while Mrs Ingham gossiped placidly; I was glad of her company, as the pains were coming closer together now. As I put the second cup down I clutched at my belly. Mrs Ingham glanced at the clock and stood up. 'You'd best let me send our Sammy, then I'll pop upstairs and light fire in front bedroom.'

When she came down she filled the saucepans and set them on the range ready, then there was a rat-tat at the door; the midwife had come. 'Morning, Mrs Ingham.'

'Morning, Nurse Fletcher – she's in kitchen.'

She came through, her face red and glowing from the cold, and set her bag down square on the table. 'Still on your feet, lass? Good, keep moving. Have you had a show?'

'Yes, yesterday evening – then the pains started in the night.'

'How often are they coming now?'

Mrs Ingham told her, 'Every three minutes by the clock.'

'Any sign of the waters?'

I shook my head, gasping as the next pain caught me. The midwife went out to the scullery, and as she washed her hands she called, 'You get upstairs now, lass, and into your nightie, so's I can see where you're at.'

I lay on the bed with my knees apart while she washed me thoroughly, then waited for the next pain to conduct her examination; her fingers were deft and sure. 'You've a while to go, you're only dilated half-a-crown yet – plenty of time for an enema – over on your side, then.' As she unpacked her bag she told me, 'We've got a nice presentation there, head well down – Doctor'll be pleased. I'll just shout Mrs Ingham to send her Sammy to phone, then we'll get your bowels emptied.' I lay still while the syringe was inserted – it was uncomfortable lying down, but she was quick and confident, and I had soon been cleansed again and set free. 'There, you'll feel easier now – up you get. Soon as I've emptied this I'll get room ready.'

I roamed restlessly up and down in front of the hearth while she drew the sheets off the bed, unrolled the long length of mackintosh and spread out the thick squares of cotton wool. The bedside rugs were rolled up and taken away and paper put down instead. Blankets were folded ready and towels set to warm by the fire. 'Have you a good thick shawl, lass?'

I gestured to Ivy's gift, hanging behind the door. 'But I'm quite warm enough.'

She smiled. 'Aye, there's nowt like work of labour for warming you up – but you'll need it when you've finished.'

As the next pain started I slipped my hand up inside my nightdress, and put it over my bare skin – I felt my womb harden and rise up and panted faster and faster until it began to soften and sink back to rest in my belly again. I rested with it, waiting.

The front door opened and there was a cheerful call of welcome; it was Dr Hartley. I heard her bounding up the stairs, then she came into the small bedroom, bag in hand. 'How are you, Helena – bearing up?' I gasped and panted my greeting and she laughed. 'Bearing down, more like!'

The midwife shook her head. 'Not yet, Doctor – she's still in first stage – but not for much longer, I reckon.'

They spoke quietly to each other, then Dr Hartley swung round to me. 'You're doing very nicely, Helena – when exactly did the pains start?'

'At one – I heard the clock strike one.'

'Good. Now you'd best have another cup of tea while there's time – Mabel, pop down and ask Mrs Ingham if she'll brew up for us.'

Mrs Ingham came back with the tray almost at once – she had obviously been ready and waiting. As we sipped our tea Dr Hartley said, 'Where's Ben, Helena? Already at work?'

'Yes – he's on early, so he went at four.'

She smiled sympathetically. 'He's best out of the way – but the poor man won't have any peace today.'

I gasped and panted, then told her, as my womb relaxed again, 'He doesn't know – I didn't tell him.'

We smiled at each other, all women together. Mrs Ingham said firmly, 'He's best out of road,' and picked up the tray to take it back downstairs. Soon after I heard Mary Grimshaw's voice; it must be nine o'clock already.

The tea made me queasy, and as the bile rose in my throat I reached for the basin and retched over it, until it all came up again. 'We only just got that down you in time,' I heard the midwife saying as she wiped my forehead, 'You don't want to have to do that on an empty stomach.'

Dr Hartley's voice, clear and sympathetic, explained, 'The first stage is nearly over, Helena, the sickness is a sure sign – don't worry, it'll soon pass.'

She was right – and as the nausea receded I felt a warm gushing between my legs – my waters had broken.

I staggered back to the fire while the midwife picked up the sopping paper and replaced it with fresh – and then the pain caught me harder than ever. And this time I felt him – he was pushing his way out. He drove me down to squat on the hearthrug, to push with him. Beside me Dr Hartley ordered, '*Ease* him down, Helena, ease him down – there's no hurry, you're both doing very well.'

That pain passed, I squatted on – waiting for the next. It came, and with it the doctor's voice: 'Pant now, pant like a dog.' I panted and pushed, and felt him pushing with me – he was sturdy and vigorous and eager to come – and as the pain passed and I rested, I laughed aloud with excitement and longing.

The doctor bent over me. 'You'd best get up on the bed now, my girl – I don't want to deliver the baby on the hearthrug.'

Looking up into her smiling face I gasped, 'Why not?